Samuel Davies, William B. Sprague

Sermons by the Rev. Samuel Davies, A. M., President of the College of New Jersey

Vol. 3

Samuel Davies, William B. Sprague

Sermons by the Rev. Samuel Davies, A. M., President of the College of New Jersey
Vol. 3

Reprint of the original, first published in 1864.

1st Edition 2022 | ISBN: 978-3-75259-138-5

Verlag (Publisher): Salzwasser Verlag GmbH, Zeilweg 44, 60439 Frankfurt, Deutschland
Vertretungsberechtigt (Authorized to represent): E. Roepke, Zeilweg 44, 60439 Frankfurt, Deutschland
Druck (Print): Books on Demand GmbH, In de Tarpen 42, 22848 Norderstedt, Deutschland

SERMONS,

BY THE

REV. SAMUEL DAVIES, A. M.,

PRESIDENT OF THE COLLEGE OF NEW JERSEY.

WITH A
FUNERAL SERMON BY THE REV. SAMUEL FINLEY, D. D.,
HIS SUCCESSOR IN THAT OFFICE,
AND SOME ACCOUNT OF PRESIDENT DAVIES, BY THE REV. THOMAS GIBBONS, D. D., OF LONDON, AND THE REV. DAVID BOSTWICK, M. A., OF NEW YORK.

CONTAINING ALSO
AN INTRODUCTORY MEMOIR OF PRESIDENT DAVIES,
BY THE
REV. WILLIAM B. SPRAGUE, D. D.

IN THREE VOLUMES.

VOL. III.

PHILADELPHIA

CONTENTS

OF

VOLUME III.

SERMON LVII.
THE SUCCESS OF THE MINISTRY OF THE GOSPEL OWING TO A DIVINE INFLUENCE.

1 COR. III. 7.—So then neither is he that planteth anything, neither he that watereth; but God that giveth the increase. 9

SERMON LVIII.
THE REJECTION OF GOSPEL LIGHT THE CONDEMNATION OF MEN.

JOHN III. 19.—And this is the condemnation, that light is come into the world, and men loved darkness rather than light, because (or, for,) their deeds were evil. 35

SERMON LIX.
A NEW-YEAR'S GIFT.

ROM. XIII. 11.—And that, knowing the time, that now it is high time to awake out of sleep; for now is our salvation nearer than when we believed. 52

SERMON LX.
ON THE DEATH OF HIS LATE MAJESTY KING GEORGE II.

2 SAM. I. 19.—How are the mighty fallen! 73

SERMON LXI.
RELIGION AND PATRIOTISM THE CONSTITUENTS OF A GOOD SOLDIER.

2 SAM. X. 12.—Be of good courage, and let us play the men for our people, and for the cities of our God. And the LORD do that which seemeth him good. 94

CONTENTS.

SERMON LXII.
THE CRISIS; OR, THE UNCERTAIN DOOM OF KINGDOMS AT PARTICULAR TIMES.

JONAH III. 9.—Who can tell if God will turn and repent, and turn away from his fierce anger, that we perish not. 120

SERMON LXIII.
THE CURSE OF COWARDICE.

JER. XLVIII. 10.—Cursed be he that doeth the work of the LORD deceitfully; and cursed be he that keepeth back his sword from blood. . 147

SERMON LXIV.
THE SIGNS OF THE TIMES.

LUKE XXI.10, 11–25, 26.—Then said he unto them, Nation shall rise up against nation, and kingdom against kingdom; and great earthquakes shall be in divers places, and famines, and pestilences, and fearful sights: and great signs shall there be from heaven.—And there shall be signs in the sun, and in the moon, and in the stars; and upon the earth distress of nations with perplexity: the sea, and the waves roaring; men's hearts failing them for fear, and for looking after those things which are coming on the earth. 167

SERMON LXV.
THE HAPPY EFFECTS OF THE POURING OUT OF THE SPIRIT.

ISAIAH XXXII. 13–19.—Upon the land of my people shall come up thorns and briers; yea, upon all the houses of joy in the joyous city: because the palaces shall be forsaken, the multitude of the city shall be left, the forts and towers shall be for dens for ever, a joy of wild asses, a pasture of flocks: *until the Spirit be poured out upon us from on high*, and the wilderness be a fruitful field, and the fruitful field be counted for a forest. Then judgment shall dwell in the wilderness, and righteousness remain in the fruitful field. And the work of righteousness shall be peace; and the effect of righteousness, quietness and assurance for ever. And my people shall dwell in a peaceable habitation, and in sure dwellings, and in quiet resting places, when it shall hail, coming down on the forest. . . 202

SERMON LXVI.
A TIME OF UNUSUAL SICKNESS AND MORTALITY IMPROVED.

JEREMIAH V. 3.—O LORD, are not thine eyes upon the truth? Thou hast stricken them, but they have not grieved: Thou hast consumed them, but they refused to receive correction: they have made their faces harder than a rock; they have refused to return. 229

CONTENTS.

SERMON LXVII.
THE RELIGIOUS IMPROVEMENT OF THE LATE EARTHQUAKE.
ISAIAH XXIV. 18-20.—The foundations of the earth do shake. The earth is utterly broken down; the earth is clean dissolved; the earth is moved exceedingly; the earth shall reel to and fro like a drunkard, and shall be removed like a cottage; and the transgression thereof shall lie heavy upon it; and it shall fall, and not rise again. 260

SERMON LXVIII.
SERIOUS REFLECTIONS ON WAR.
JAMES IV. 1.—From whence come wars and fightings among you? Come they not hence, even of your lusts, that war in your members? . 280

SERMON LXIX.
ON THE DEFEAT OF GENERAL BRADDOCK GOING TO FORT DE QUESNE.
ISAIAH XXII. 12-14.—And in that day did the LORD God of hosts call to weeping, and to mourning, and to baldness, and to girding with sackcloth; and behold, joy and gladness, slaying oxen, and killing sheep, eating flesh, and drinking wine; let us eat and drink, for to-morrow we shall die. And it was revealed in mine ears by the LORD of hosts, Surely this iniquity shall not be purged from you till ye die, saith the Lord GOD of hosts. 307

SERMON LXX.
GOD THE SOVEREIGN OF ALL KINGDOMS.
DANIEL IV. 25.—The Most High ruleth in the kingdom of men, and giveth it to whomsoever he will. 329

SERMON LXXI.
A THANKSGIVING SERMON FOR NATIONAL BLESSINGS.
EZEKIEL XX. 43, 44.—And there shall ye remember your ways, and all your doings wherein ye have been defiled, and ye shall loath yourselves in your own sight, for all your evils that ye have committed. And ye shall know that I am the LORD, when I have wrought with you for my name's sake, not according to your wicked ways, nor according to your corrupt doings, O ye house of Israel, saith the Lord GOD   355

SERMON LXXII.
PRACTICAL ATHEISM, IN DENYING THE AGENCY OF DIVINE PROVIDENCE, EXPOSED.
ZEPHANIAH I. 12.—And it shall come to pass at that time, that I will search Jerusalem with candles, and punish the men that are settled on their lees; that say in their heart, the LORD will not do good, neither will he do evil. 379

SERMON LXXIII.

THE PRIMITIVE AND PRESENT STATE OF MAN COMPARED.

ROMANS V. 17.—For if by one man's offence, death reigned by one, much more they which receive [the] abundance of grace, and of the gift of righteousness, shall reign in life by one, Jesus Christ. 407

SERMON LXXIV.

THE CERTAINTY OF DEATH.—A FUNERAL SERMON.

EZEKIEL XXXIII. 8.—O wicked man, thou shalt surely die. . . 434

SERMON LXXV.

EVIDENCES OF THE WANT OF LOVE TO GOD.

JOHN V. 42.—But I know you, that ye have not the love of God in you. 457

SERMON LXXVI.

THE OBJECTS, GROUNDS, AND EVIDENCES OF THE HOPE OF THE RIGHTEOUS.

PROVERBS XIV. 82.—The wicked is driven away in his wickedness: but the righteous hath hope in his death. 474

SERMON LXXVII.

THE LOVE OF SOULS A NECESSARY QUALIFICATION FOR THE MINISTERIAL OFFICE.

1 THESS. II. 8.—So, being affectionately desirous of you, we were willing to have imparted unto you, not the gospel of God only, but also our own souls, because ye were dear unto us. 500

SERMON LXXVIII.

THE OFFICE OF BISHOP A GOOD WORK.

1 TIMOTHY III. 1.—This is a true saying, if a man desire the office of a bishop, he desireth a good work. 529

SERMON LXXIX.

A CHRISTMAS-DAY SERMON.

LUKE II. 13, 14.—And suddenly there was with the angel a multitude of the heavenly host, praising God, and saying, Glory to God in the highest, and on earth peace, good-will toward men. 562

CONTENTS.

SERMON LXXX.

CHRISTIANS SOLEMNLY REMINDED OF THEIR OBLIGATIONS.

JOSHUA XXIV. 22.—And Joshua said unto the people, Ye are witnesses against yourselves that ye have chosen you the LORD, to serve him. And they said, We are witnesses. 587

SERMON LXXXI.

THE GUILT AND DOOM OF IMPENITENT HEARERS.

MATTHEW XIII. 14.—By hearing ye shall hear, and shall not understand; and seeing ye shall see, and shall not perceive. 617

SERMON LXXXII.

THE APOSTOLIC VALEDICTION CONSIDERED AND APPLIED.

2 COR. XIII. 11.—Finally, brethren, farewell. Be perfect, be of good comfort, be of one mind, live in peace; and the God of love and peace shall be with you. 637

SERMONS

ON

IMPORTANT SUBJECTS.

SERMON LVII.

THE SUCCESS OF THE MINISTRY OF THE GOSPEL, OWING TO A DIVINE INFLUENCE.*

1 Cor. iii. 7.—*So then neither is he that planteth anything, neither he that watereth; but God that giveth the increase.*

The design of God in all his works of creation, providence, and grace, is to advance and secure the glory of his own name; and, therefore, though he makes use of secondary causes as the instruments of his operations, yet their efficacy depends upon his superintending influence. It is his hand that sustains the great chain of causes and effects, and his agency pervades and animates the worlds of nature and of grace.

In the natural world, he makes use of the instrumentality of the husbandman to till the ground, to sow the seed, and water it. But it is he that commands the clouds to drop down fatness upon it, and the sun to diffuse its

---

* Dated Hanover, November 19, 1757.

vital influence. It is he that continues to the earth, and the other principles of vegetation, their respective virtues; and without this influence of his the husbandman's planting and watering would be in vain; and after all his labour, he must acknowledge, that *it is God that giveth the increase.*

So, in the world of grace, God uses a variety of suitable means to form degenerate sinners into his image, and fit them for a happy eternity. All the institutions of the gospel are intended for this purpose, and particularly the ministry of it. Ministers are sowers sent out into the wild field of the world, with the precious seed of the word. It is the grand business of their life to cultivate this barren soil, to plant trees of righteousness, and water them that they may bring forth the fruits of holiness. It is by the use of painful industry, that they can expect to improve this wilderness into a fruitful field; and the Lord is pleased to pour out his Spirit from on high, at times, to render their labours successful; so that they who *went forth bearing precious seed* with sorrow and tears, return, *bringing their sheaves with joy.* But alas, they meet with disappointments enough to convince them that all their labours will be in vain, if a sovereign God deny the influence of his grace. The agency of his holy Spirit is as necessary to fructify the word, and make it the seed of conversion, as the influences of heaven are to fructify the earth and promote vegetation. A zealous Paul may plant the word, and an eloquent Apollos may water it; one may attempt to convert sinners to Christianity, and the other to build them up in faith, but they are both nothing, as to the success of their labours, unless God gives the increase: that is, unless he affords the influence of his grace to render their attempts successful in begetting and cherishing living religion in the hearts of men. This is the great truth contained in my text: "Neither is he that planteth anything, nor he that watereth; but God that giveth the increase."

The Corinthians had been blest with the labours of several ministers, particularly of the Apostle Paul, who had been the happy instrument of turning them from their native heathenism, and planting the gospel among them, and of Apollos, who succeeded him, and watered the good seed he had planted among them. But the Corinthians, instead of peaceably and thankfully improving the different gifts of different ministers for their spiritual and everlasting benefit, fell into factions, through a partial admiration of the one, in opposition to the other. Some of them were for Paul, as an universal scholar, and a strong reasoner; others were all for Apollos, as an accomplished orator. And thus they considered these ministers of Christ, rather as the ringleaders of factions than as unanimous promoters of the same catholic Christianity. To suppress this party spirit, the apostle asks them, "Who, then, is Paul, or who is Apollos?" "What mighty beings would you make us in your idolatrous attachment to us? Alas! what are we more than feeble ministers of Christ, by whom ye believed? We were not the authors of your faith, but the humble instruments of it in the divine hand; and the success that either of us has had has not been from our own power, but just as God hath been pleased to give to every man, (verse 5.) I first planted the gospel among you; Apollos afterwards watered it: this was all we could do: but we could not make it bear the fruits of holiness in one soul. It was God alone that gave the increase, and made our respective labours successful, (verse 6.) Therefore turn your regard to him alone:—*Cease ye from man, whose breath is in his nostrils ; for wherein is he to be accounted of?* Isai. ii. 22. Do not idolatrously share the honour of your conversion between God the efficient, and us, the humble instruments of it; but ascribe it to him alone: for *neither is he that planteth anything, nor he that watereth; but God that gave the increase;* he is all in all."

When we see a people enjoy the frequent cultivations of the gospel, and the means of spiritual fruitfulness, and yet few new trees of righteousness planted, and those that have been planted seemingly withering and unfruitful, we cannot but conclude that something is wanting: without which all the means they enjoy will be of no service. We should naturally turn our thoughts to an inquiry, what was wanting, had we tilled our lands from year to year without a crop. And since we find at present, that notwithstanding all the labours bestowed upon us, we lie in a deep sleep, and hardly know what it is of late to be animated with the news of some careless sinner here and there awakened to serious concern about his eternal state, it is high time to inquire what is wanting? There is certainly something wanting, which is of greater consequence than anything we have. Here are the gospel, and its ordinances, which at times have done great things, and sinners have yielded to their resistless energy; here is a minister, who, however weak, has sometimes been the happy instrument of giving a sinner an alarm, and speaking a word in season to those that were weary; here are hearers that crowd our sanctuary, hearers of the same kind with those whom we have seen ere now fall under the power of the word. And what, then, is wanting? Why God, that alone can give the increase, is not here by the influences of his grace: and in his absence, "neither he that planteth is anything, nor he that watereth:" they are all nothing together; and may labour till dooms-day, and never convert one soul. "Where is the Lord God of Elijah?" Where is he that can do more execution with one feeble sentence, than we can with a thousand of our most powerful sermons? Why, he hath hid his face; and hence there is none that calleth upon his name, and stirreth up himself to take hold of him. Isai. lxiv. 7. And till the Spirit be poured upon us from on high, nothing but briers and thorns will come up among us. Chap. xxxii. 13, 15.

Let your thoughts, therefore, with eager attention now pursue me, while I am proving, illustrating, and making remarks pertinent to our case, from this affecting truth contained in the text: that the success of the ministry of the gospel with respect to saints and sinners, entirely depends upon the concurring influences of divine grace; or, that without the divine agency to render the gospel successful, all the labours of its ministers will be in vain.

This truth can give us no surprise as a new discovery, if we have any acquaintance with the present degeneracy of human nature—with the declarations and promises of the word of God—with the accounts of the different success of the means of grace in various periods of the church—or with matters that might have come within the compass of our own experience and observation.

I. Such is the present degeneracy of human nature, that all the ministrations of the gospel cannot remedy it, without the concurring efficacy of divine grace.

So barren is the soil, that the seed of the word falls upon it and dies, and never grows up; as though it had never been sown there, till it be fructified by divine grace. It is a soil fruitful of briers and thorns, which grow up, and choke the word; so that it becometh unfruitful till divine grace root them up. Or it may be represented by a rocky or stony soil, where the word of God can take no deep root, and therefore withers, till it be modified by influences from heaven. Thus our Lord represents the matter in the famous parable of the sowers. Matt. xiii. 3, &c., 18, &c.

The metaphors used in sacred Scripture to illustrate this case, sufficiently prove the degeneracy of mankind, and their entire opposition to the gospel. They are represented as spiritually dead, Eph. ii. 1; John v. 25; that is, though they are still capable of the exercises of reason and animal actions, yet they are really destitute of a super natural principle of spiritual life, and incapable of suitable exercises towards God. And can a Paul or an Apollos quicken the dead with convictive arguments, with strong persuasions, or tender and passionate expostulations? No; none but he can do it whose Almighty voice bade Lazarus come forth. Sinners are also represented as blind. 2. Cor. iv. 4. Now what can feeble mortals do to such? We can exhibit divine things before them; we can expose the horrid deformity of sin, and its tremendous consequences; we can display the glories of God, the the beauty of holiness, and the allurements of redeeming love: but, alas! all this is but like exposing colours to the blind. We cannot open their eyes; we cannot communicate such views of things to their minds as are in any measure adequate to the things themselves. What can tender arguments avail to break hearts of stone? What signifies reasoning to govern headstrong obstinacy, which regards it no more than a whirlwind? What can persuasions do to extirpate inveterate, implacable enmity? Rom. viii. 7. What can the charms of eloquence do to charm deaf adders that stop their ears? Psalm lviii. 4. The Israelites might as well pretend to overthrow the walls of Jericho with the sound of rams' horns, as we with our feeble breath to overthrow the strongholds of Satan in the hearts of sinners! It is the divine agency alone that gives the success in both cases. Clay cannot open the eyes of the blind, except in his Almighty hands, who could form a world out of nothing, and who can work without or against means as easily as with them.

The Scripture representations of the degeneracy of mankind are confirmed by universal experience. If we form any observations of ourselves or others, we find that the whole bent of our souls by nature is contrary to the gospel. The gospel is designed to reclaim men from sin; but they are obstinately set upon it; it is designed to make sin bitter to them, and to dissolve their hearts into tender sorrows for it; but we naturally delight in sin, and our hearts are hard as the nether millstone; it is intended to bring apostate rebels back to God, and the universal practice of holiness; but we love estrangement from him, and have no inclination to return. We abhor the ways of strict holiness, and choose to walk in the imaginations of our own hearts. The gospel is calculated to advance the divine glory, and abash the pride of all flesh, in the scheme of salvation it reveals; but this is directly contrary to the disposition of the sinner, who is all for his own glory. This requires no tedious arguments to prove it. Look in upon your own hearts; look back on your own conduct; look round you on the world; and there the evidences of it will glare upon you.

Now, since the innate dispositions of men are thus averse to the gospel, it is evident that nothing but divine power can make it effectual for their sanctification. Instructions may furnish the head with notions and correct speculative mistakes, but they have no power to sway the will and sweetly allure it to holiness. Persuasions may bring men to practise what they had omitted through mistake, carelessness, or a transient dislike: but they will have no effect where the heart is full of innate enmity against the things recommended. In this case, he that planteth, and he that watereth, are nothing; it is God alone that can give the increase; as is more than intimated by,

II. The promises and declarations of the word, which appropriate all the success of the gospel to God alone.

Jehovah is not fond of ostentation and parade, nor wasteful in throwing away his blessings where they are not needed; and therefore if the means of grace were sufficient of themselves to convert sinners and edify believers, he would not make such magnificent promises of the supernatural aids of his grace, nor claim the efficacy of them as his own. He would not assert the insufficiency of them without his influence, nor assign the withdrawment of his grace as one cause of their unsuccessfulness. But all this he does in his word.

Notwithstanding all the miraculous as well as ordinary means of grace which the Israelites enjoyed, there was need of this divine promise. "The LORD thy God will circumcise thy heart, and the heart of thy seed, to love the LORD thy God, with all thy heart, and with all thy soul." Deut. xxx. 6. And this promise was not peculiar to the Mosaic dispensation of the covenant of grace, which was less clear and efficacious; but we find that one superior excellency of the gospel dispensation is, that it is more abundant in such promises. It is to the gospel church that this promise is more particularly made; "Behold the days come, saith the LORD, that I will make a new covenant with the house of Israel, &c., not according to the covenant which I made with their fathers, in the day that I took them by the hand, to bring them out of the land of Egypt, &c.,—but this shall be the covenant that I will make with them; I will put my law in their inward parts, and write it in their hearts." Jer. xxxi. 31, 33; Heb. viii. 8, &c.

This is a promise of so much importance, that it is frequently repeated with some circumstantial alteration, as the very life of the New Testament church. "I will give them one heart and one way, that they may fear me for ever; and I will put my fear in their hearts, that they shall not depart from me." Jer. xxxii. 39, 40. Ezekiel echoes back the same language by the inspiration of the same Spirit, "I will give them one heart; and I will put a new spirit within you; and I will take the stony heart out of their flesh; and I will give them a heart of flesh; and they shall walk in my statutes, and keep mine ordinances, and do them." Ezek. xi. 19, 20. See also chap. xxxvi. 26, 27.

What was the success of St. Peter's sermon (Acts ii.) in the conversion of 3000 but the accomplishment of those promises in Joel and Zechariah? "I will pour out my Spirit upon all flesh." (Joel ii. 28, 29.) "I will pour out upon the house of David, and upon the inhabitants of Jerusalem, the Spirit of grace and of supplications, and they shall look," &c. Zech. xii. 10. These promises were substantially renewed by Christ, to encourage the drooping apostles, John xvi. 8, 9, 10. "I will send the Spirit; and when he is come, he will convince the world," &c. All their miraculous powers were not sufficient for the conviction of mankind, without the agency of the divine Spirit; but by this, that promise of the Father to his Son was accomplished: "Thy people shall be willing in the day of thy power." Psalm cx. 3.

I might subjoin many other promises of the same kind; but these are sufficient to show the absolute necessity of divine influence, or the utter insufficiency of the best means without it. And what further time might be allotted to this particular, I shall lay out upon this pertinent and useful remark, which, if rightly attended to, would rectify mistakes, and remove many scruples and controversies upon this point. The remark is this, That the promises of God to bestow blessings upon us, do not render needless our most vigorous endeavours to obtain them; and, on the other hand, that our most vigorous endeavours do not supersede the influences of the Spirit to work in us the dispositions we are labouring after: or, that *that* may be consistently enjoined upon us as a duty, which is promised by God's free favour; and *vice versâ*. This may be illustrated by various instances. God commands us as strictly to circumcise the foreskins of our hearts, to make ourselves new hearts and new spirits, (Jer. iv. 4,) and to cleanse ourselves from moral pollution, (Isa. i. 16,) as if this were wholly our work, and he had no efficiency in it. In the meantime, he promises as absolutely to circumcise our hearts to love him, to give us new hearts, and to purge us from all our filthiness, and from all our abominations, as though he performed all the work without our using means. Now we are sure these things are consistent; for the sacred oracles are not a heap of contradictions. And how does their consistency appear? Why, thus: it is our duty to use the most vigorous endeavours to obtain those graces promised, because it is only in the use of vigorous endeavours that we have reason to expect divine influences. And yet these endeavours of ours do not in the least work those graces in us, and therefore there is certainly as much need of the promised agency of divine grace to effect the work, as if we should do nothing at all. Our utmost endeavours fall entirely short of it, and do not entitle us to divine assistance; and this we must have an humble sense of, before we can receive the accomplishments of such promises as the effect of free grace alone. But we should continue in these endeavours, because we have no reason to hope for the accomplishment of the promises in a course of sloth and negligence.

This point may be illustrated by the consistency of the use of the means and the agency of providence in the natural world. God has peremptorily promised, "that while earth remaineth, seed-time and harvest shall not cease," Gen. viii. 22. But this promise does not render it needless for us to cultivate the earth; nor does all our cultivation render this promise needless: for all our labour would be in vain without the influence of divine providence: and this influence is to be expected only in the use of labour. Thus, in the moral world, the efficacy belongs to God, as much as if we made no use of means at all; and the most vigorous endeavours are as much our duty, as if we could effect the work ourselves, and he had no special hand in it. Were this remark attended to, it would guard us against the pernicious extremes of turning the grace of God into wantonness, and pleading it as an excuse for our idleness: and of self-righteousness, and depending upon our own endeavours. In this guarded manner does St. Paul handle this point: "Work out your own salvation with fear and tremblimg; for it is God which worketh in you both to will and to do of his good pleasure." Phil. ii. 12, 13. But to return: As we may infer the necessity of divine influences from the promises of God, so

We may infer the same thing from the many passages of sacred Writ ascribing the success of the gospel upon sinners, and even upon believers, to the agency of divine grace. If even a well-disposed Lydia gives a believing attention to the things spoken by St. Paul, it is *because the Lord hath opened her heart.* Acts xvi. 14. Thus the Philippians believed, because, says the apostle, to you it is given on the behalf of Christ, to believe, Phil. i. 29. Thus the Ephesians were spiritually alive, because, says he, "you hath he quickened, who were dead in trespasses and sins." Eph. ii. 1. Faith is not of ourselves; but is expressly said to be the gift of God, Eph. ii. 8. Nay the implantation of faith is represented as an exploit of Omnipotence, like that of the resurrection of Christ. Hence the apostle prays, Eph. i. 19, 20, that the Ephesians might be made deeply sensible of the "exceeding greatness of his power to us-ward that believe, according to the working of his mighty power, which he wrought in Christ when he raised him from the dead." Repentance is also the gift of God: Christ is exalted to bestow it. Acts v. 31. When the Jewish Christians heard of the success of the gospel among the Gentiles, they unanimously ascribed it to God: "then hath God also to the Gentiles granted repentance unto life," Acts xi. 18; and it is upon this encouragement that St. Paul recommends the use of the proper means to reclaim the obstinate: "if God, peradventure, will give them repentance to the acknowledging of the truth," 2 Tim. ii. 25. Regeneration also, in which faith and repentance, and other graces are implanted, is always ascribed to God. If all things are made new, *all these things are of God*. 2 Cor. v. 17, 18. If, while others reject Christ, some receive him, and so are honoured with the privilege of becoming the sons of God, it is not owing to themselves, but to him. "They are born, not of blood, nor of the will of man, nor of the will of the flesh, but of God." John i. 11, 12, 13. He begets such of his own sovereign will by the word of truth, James i. 18; and every good and perfect gift with which they are endowed is not from themselves, but from above, and cometh down from the Father of lights, who is the great origin of all moral excellency, as the sun is of light, ver. 17. Hence this change is expressed by such terms as denote the divine agency, and exclude that of the creature; as a new birth, John iii. 3; *a new creation*, 2 Cor. v. 17;

Col. iii. 10; the workmanship of God *created in Christ Jesus*, Eph. ii. 10; a resurrection from the dead, John v. 25; Eph. ii. 1; Col. iii. 1. Now it is the greatest absurdity to speak of a man's begetting or creating himself, or raising himself from the dead. Thus we find that the first implantation of grace in the heart of a sinner is entirely the work of God; and, lest we should suppose that, when it is once implanted, it can flourish and grow without the influence of heaven, we find that the progress of sanctification in believers is ascribed to God, as well as their first conversion. David was sensible after all his attainments, that he could not run the way of God's commandments unless God should enlarge his heart. Ps. cxix. 32. All the hopes of Paul concerning his promising converts at Philippi depended upon his persuasion, that "he that had begun a good work in them, would perform it until the day of Christ." Phil. i. 6. Nay, it was upon this he placed his own entire dependence. "We are not sufficient of ourselves," says he, "to think anything as of ourselves, but our sufficiency is of God." 2 Cor. iii. 5. If I am faithful, it is "because I have obtained mercy of the Lord to make me so." 1 Cor. vii. 25. "By the grace of God I am what I am; and if I have laboured more abundantly than others, it is not I, but the grace of God that was with me." 1 Cor. xv. 10. "I can do all things through Christ that strengtheneth me." Phil. iv. 13. He was relieved under his despondencies by this answer, "My grace is sufficient for thee, and my strength is made perfect in weakness." 2 Cor. xii. 9. This is more than intimated in his prayers for himself and others: for example, "The God of peace make you perfect in every good work, to do his will; working in you that which is well-pleasing in his sight, through Jesus Christ!" Heb. xiii. 21. And indeed all the prayers of the saints for the aids of divine grace, imply the necessity of them; for they would not pray for superfluities, or for what they already have in a sufficient measure. It is the Spirit that helps our infirmities in prayer, and other exercises of devotion, Rom. viii. 24, and all our preparation for the heavenly state and aspirations after it, are of God. "He that hath wrought us for the self-same thing is God." 2 Cor. v. 5. In a word, "it is God that worketh all our works in us," Isa. xxvi. 12; "it is he that worketh in us both to will and to do, of his own good pleasure." Phil. ii. 13. Now the actual communication of divine influence, implies their necessity. Accordingly we find

The necessity of divine influences is stated in the plainest terms in Scripture. *No man, says Christ, can come unto me, except the Father draw him*, John vi. 44. *He that hath heard and learned of the Father, and he only, will come to him*, ver. 45; and this influence is not purchased by our endeavours, but it is the free gift of grace. Hence Christ varies his former declarations into this form; *no man can come unto me, except it be given unto him of my Father*, ver. 65; and the agency of divine grace is necessary, not only to draw sinners to Christ at first, but also to make them fruitful afterwards. Hence Christ represents even the apostles as dependent upon him as the branch upon the vine; and tells them plainly, that "without him they can do nothing." John xv. 4, 5. Through all the stages of the Christian life, we depend entirely upon him; and without his influences, we should wither and die like a blasted flower, however blooming and fruitful we were before. Hence says God to his people, *in me is thy fruit found*, Hos. xiv. 8. Since then this is the case, it will follow that when God is pleased to withhold his influences, all the means of grace will be unsuccessful. Accordingly we find,

The unsuccessfulness of the gospel is often resolved into

the withholding or withdrawing of the influences of grace, as one cause of it. Thus Moses resolves the obstinacy of the Israelites under all the profusion of wonders that had attended them, into this, as one cause of it: "The Lord hath not given you a heart to perceive, and eyes to see, and ears to hear, unto this day." Deut. xxix. 2, 3, 4. If none believe the report of the gospel, it is because the arm of the Lord is not revealed, Isa. liii. 1. If the mysteries of the kingdom of heaven are hidden from the wise and prudent, while they are revealed to babes; it is because God in his righteous judgment and sovereign pleasure, hides them from the one, and reveals them to the other. Matt. xi. 25, 26. Nay, the evangelist speaks in yet more forcible terms, when speaking of the unbelief of the Jews, who were witnesses of Christ's convictive miracles and discourses; "therefore they could not believe, because that Esaias said he hath blinded their eyes, and hardened their hearts," John xii. 39, 40; and in the same strain St. Paul speaks: "he hath mercy on whom he will have mercy, and whom he will he hardeneth. So then it is not of him that willeth, nor of him that runneth, but of God that showeth mercy." Rom. ix. 16, &c. These passages are so opposite to the prevailing divinity of the age, that they are dangerous weapons to meddle with; and it is well they are the very words of Scripture, otherwise we should be charged with blasphemy for mentioning the truth contained in them. We must indeed be cautious that we do not infer from the Scriptures any such horrid doctrine as this, that men are compelled to sin, and pushed on to ruin, by a necessitating decree, or the resistless impulse of Providence; or that, though they were disposed to turn to God, they are judicially kept back and hindered by the divine hand. This would be contrary to the whole current of Scripture, which charges the sin and ruin of sinners upon themselves; but these passages mean, that God denies to obstinate sinners those influences of his grace which are necessary to convert them, and which, if communicated, would have subdued their utmost obstinacy; and that in consequence of this denial, they will rush on in sin and irreclaimable impenitence, and perish; but yet that God, in denying them his grace, does not act merely as an arbitrary sovereign, but as a just judge, punishing them for their sin in abusing the blessings he has bestowed upon them, by judicially withdrawing the aids of his grace, and withholding farther influences. And surely he may punish obstinate sinners with privative as well as positive punishment; he may as justly withhold or withdraw forfeited blessings, as inflict positive misery. This we all own he may do with respect to temporal blessings, he may justly deny them to such as have forfeited them; and why he may not exercise the same sovereignty and justice with regard to spiritual blessings, is hard to say. His hardening the heart, blinding the eyes, &c., of sinners, signify his withdrawing the influences of grace which they have abused, his withholding those additional influences which might irresistibly subdue their obstinacy, and his suffering them to fall into circumstances of temptation. These passages do but strongly and emphatically express thus much: thus much they may mean, without casting any injurious reflections upon God; and less than this they cannot mean, unless we would explain away their meaning.

From the whole, then, we find that the doctrine of the reality and necessity of divine influences to render the administrations of the gospel effectual for saving purposes, is a doctrine familiar to the sacred oracles. This will receive additional confirmation if we find it agreeable to matter of fact; which leads me to observe,

III. That the different success of the same means of

grace in different periods of the church, sufficiently shows the necessity of gracious assistances to render them efficacious. The various states of the church in various ages are but comments upon the sacred pages, and accomplishments of Scripture.

Now we find that religion has flourished or declined, not so much according to external means, as according to the degree of divine influence. Alas! what could Noah, that zealous preacher of righteousness, do, during the one hundred and twenty years of his ministry? He might warn, he might persuade, he might weep over a secure world in vain; they would rush upon destruction before his eyes; and he could only persuade his own family; and even among them there was a cursed Ham. How little could Moses, the favourite messenger and intimate of God, prevail to make his people dutiful? Alas! after all the astonishing wonders he wrought before their eyes, they continued obstinate and rebellious; *for the Lord had not given them a heart to understand,* &c., Deut xxix. 4. This Moses mentions, as what was beyond his power, and could be effected by Omnipotence only. What inconsiderable success had that zealous prophet Elijah, the eloquent Isaiah, or that tender-hearted, mourning, weeping prophet Jeremiah! Surely, many feeble servants of Christ, in all respects inferior to them, have been crowned with more extensive success! Nay, when the Son of God descended from heaven, a teacher to the world, who spake as never man spake, who carried omnipotence along with him to attest his doctrine by the most astonishing miracles, how few, during his life, were brought seriously to regard his doctrine? He was pleased to defer the remarkable effusion of his Spirit till his return to his native heaven. And when it was poured out, what a glorious alteration followed! then Peter, a poor fisherman, is the happy instrument of converting three thousand with one short sermon; which is more, perhaps, than his divine Master had done by a hundred. Then, in spite of the united opposition of earth and hell, the humble doctrines of the cross triumphed over the nations, and subdued millions to the obedience of faith. Then the doctrines of Jesus, who was crucified at Jerusalem like an infamous malefactor, between two thieves, became the mighty, all-conquering weapons, through God, to demolish the strongholds of Satan. 2 Cor. ii. 4. And whence this strange alteration? It was from the more abundant effusion of the Spirit upon the minds of men; upon their minds, I say, for, as to the external evidences from miracles, prophecies, &c., they were sufficiently clear before this happy season. But there was not the same degree of internal illumination by the Spirit. It is often intimated by Christ, in his last discourses with his disciples, that the Holy Spirit was not yet given; and hence it was that he and they laboured so much in vain. But upon his ascension, he performed the promise he had so often repeated, and sent the Spirit both upon them and their hearers; and then the aspect of affairs was happily altered; then the word had free course, and was glorified. Then the world was *convinced of sin, of righteousness, and of judgment.*

This point might be illustrated farther, by a history of the various periods of the church, from the apostolic age to the present time; but it would be too tedious; and what has been offered is sufficient to convince us that it is not by power, nor by might, but by the Spirit of the Lord of Hosts, that the interests of religion are carried on. Zech. iv. 6. Especially if we add,

IV. Our own experience and observation, which furnish us with many instances in which this great truth has been exemplified.

Our observation furnishes us with such instances as these: Sometimes a minister, who is a universal scholar, a masterly reasoner, and an accomplished orator, and withal, sincerely engaged for the conversion of sinners, labours in vain, and all his excellent discourses seem to have no effect; while another of much inferior accomplishments, is the successful instrument of turning many to righteousness. This cannot be accounted for without ascribing the distinction to the peculiar concurrence of divine grace; for if it depended upon the instruments, it would be quite the reverse. Sometimes a clear, convictive, and withal, solemn and warm discourse, has no effect; while, at another time, the same doctrines, delivered in a weak, incoherent manner, have strange efficacy and reach the heart. Sometimes the reading of a sermon has been the means of awakening careless sinners, when, at other times, the most solemn and argumentative preaching has been in vain. Sometimes we have seen a number of sinners thoroughly awakened, and brought to seek the Lord in earnest; while another number, under the very same sermon, and who seemed as open to conviction as the former, or perhaps more so, have remained secure and thoughtless, as usual. And whence could this difference arise but from special grace? We have seen persons struck to the heart with those doctrines which they had heard an hundred times without any effect. And indeed there is something in the manner of persons being affected with the word, which shows that the impression is not made by the word itself, or by any other power than divine. The truths that make such deep impressions upon their hearts, are no new discoveries; they are the old common repeated truths of the gospel, which they had heard before a thousand times; and the manner in which they are represented by the minister, may not be clearer than usual. But, to their surprise, these familiar doctrines flash upon them as new discoveries; they appear to them in a quite different light, as though they had never heard them before; and they reach the conscience, and pierce the heart with such amazing energy, that the sinner is cast into a consternation at his own stupidity, that he never had such apprehensions of things before. He was wont to regard the word as a speculation, or a pleasing song, but now he finds it living and powerful, &c.; the secrets of his heart are laid open by it, and he is obliged to own that God is with it of a truth. Thus a believer also discerns the doctrines of the gospel in a quite different light at one time than at another: he sees new glories in them. Hence one sermon leaves him cold and hard-hearted, while another, no better in itself, sets him all on fire. Hence also, one receives advantage from a discourse, which had no effect upon another: and from this proceeds the difference in judgment about the excellency of sermons, which we may observe among Christians. Every one forms a judgment according to his own sensations, and not according to the discourse in itself. And indeed when we hear an exercised Christian expatiate in praise of a discourse, it is a happy sign that it was made of special service to him.

Many such instances as these familiarly occur in the sphere of our observation; which prove, by matters of fact, that the success of the gospel depends upon the influence of divine grace. But we need not look about us to observe others. Turn your eyes inward upon what has passed in your own minds, and you shall find, that

Your own experience proves the same thing. Have you not found that the very same things have very different effects upon you at different times? Those truths, which at one time leave you dull and sleepy, at other times quicken all your powers to the most vigorous exercise? Sinners, do you not return from the house of God in very different frames, though the service there has been substantially the same? At one time you sweat and agonize under a sense of guilt, and make many resolutions to change your course of life; and at another time, there is a stupid calm within, and you matter not all the concerns of eternity. Some indeed have lain so long under the rays of the Sun of Righteousness, that they are hardened like clay, and hardly susceptive of any deep impressions at any time, after they have murdered their conscience, and silenced all its first remonstrances. These may go on serene and placid, till the flames of hell give them sensation; and this is most likely to be their doom; though it is not impossible but that this gospel, this stale, neglected gospel, which now makes no impression on their stony hearts, may yet be endowed with almighty power to break them into the tenderest contrition: and I pray God this may be the happy event. I pray God, oh sinner, that thou mayest yet fall under the resistless energy of those important things which now appear but trifles to thee. But till persons are thus become proof against the gospel, they generally feel a variety of dispositions under the ministry of it: and this variety is to be principally ascribed to the various degrees of divine influence upon them at different seasons. And you, saints, you also experience a like vicissitude. Sometimes, oh how divinely sweet, oh how nourishing is the sincere milk of the word! How does the word enlighten, quicken, and comfort you! How exactly it suits your very case! At other times it is tasteless; it is a dead letter, and has no effect upon you. At times a sentence seems almighty, and carries all before it: and you feel it to be the word of God; at other times you perceive only your feeble fellow-mortal speaking to you, and all his words are but feeble breath; as different from the former as chaff from wheat. See Jer. xxiii. 28, 29. Your own memories can supply my deficiency under this head, by recollecting such instances as these perhaps during your whole life; and the time urges me to make some remarks upon what has been said. These are so numerous and copious, that though I had them principally in view, and chose this subject for the sake of them, yet I can but superficially touch upon them.

Hence we learn,

1. How essential and important the doctrine of divine influence is to the church of God. The very life, and the whole success of the gospel depend upon it. And since this necessarily supposes the utter depravity and spiritual impotence of human nature in its fallen state, that doctrine also must be frequently and plainly inculcated.

Alas! the great defect of the system of divinity too fashionable in our days, and one great cause of the languishing state of religion in our age, and of the prevalence of vice and impiety! Since it has been the mode to compliment mankind as able to do something very considerable in religion, religion has died away. Since it has been the fashion to press a reformation of men's lives, without inculcating the absolute necessity of divine grace to renew their nature, there is hardly such a thing as a thorough reformation to be seen; but mankind are evidently growing worse and worse. Since men think they can do something, and scorn to be wholly dependent on divine grace, the Lord, as it were, looks on and suffers them to make the experiment; and, alas! it is likely to be a costly experiment to multitudes. God withholds his influence in just displeasure, and lets them try what mighty things the boasted powers of degenerate nature can do without it; and hence, alas! they lie all secure and asleep in sin together. Sermons are preached; the house of God is frequented; the ordinances of the gospel administered; yet vice is triumphant; carnal security almost universal; and so few are earnestly seeking after religion, that one would hardly suspect from the success, that these are intended as means to bring them to this. Thus, alas! it is around us if we believe our senses: and thus it will continue to be, till ministers and people are brought to the dust before God, to acknowledge their own weakness and entire dependence upon him. Therefore, hence we learn

2. That when we enjoy the ministrations of the gospel in the greatest purity and plenty, we should not place our trust upon them, but wholly depend on the influence of divine grace for the success. We are apt to think, if we had but such a minister among us, how much good would be done! It is true, that faithful and accomplished ministers are singular blessings to the places where they labour, because it is by their instrumentality that the Lord is wont to work: but still let us remember, that even a Paul or an Apollos is nothing, unless the Lord give the increase. One text of Scripture, one sentence, will do more execution, when enforced by divine energy, than all the labours of the ablest ministers upon earth without it. For this divine energy therefore let us look; for this let us cry, *cursed be the man that trusteth in man, &c.* When we depend upon the instruments, we provoke the Spirit of God to leave us. If we are fond of taking ministers in his stead, we shall make the trial, till they and we wither away for want of divine influences. This provokes the blessed Spirit to blast the gifts of his ministers, to suffer them to fall, or to remove them out of the way, when they

are set up as his rivals, that their idolaters may see they are but men. This provokes him to leave the hearers fruitless under the best cultivations, till experience sadly convinces them that they can do nothing without him. Therefore let not ministers trust in their own abilities, nor people in their labours; but all in the Lord.

That we should ascribe all the success of the gospel to God alone, and not sacrilegiously divide the honour of it between him and the instruments of it, or between him and ourselves, the ministers of Christ are ready to answer you, in the language of Peter, If we be examined of the good deed done to impotent sinners, by what means they are made whole; be it known unto you, that by the name of Jesus do they stand whole before you. Acts iv. 9, 10. Why do ye look so earnestly upon us, as if by our own power or holiness we have done this? chap. iii. 12. It is a very shocking compliment to them to be accounted the authors of your faith. Good ministers love to be humble, to lie in their proper sphere, and would have God to have all the glory, as the great efficient; and when we ascribe the work of God to the instrument, we provoke him to withdraw his influence, that we may be convinced of the mistake. Let us also take care that we do not assume the honour of the work to ourselves. Alas! we had no hand in it, but opposed it with all our might; and, therefore, *not unto us*, &c., Ps. cxv. 1. The Lord hath done great things for us in this place, for which we are glad. One can name one, and another another, as his spiritual father, or the helper of his faith; but still remember, these only planted or watered; but it was God that gave the increase; and therefore to him alone ascribe his own work.

3. Hence also we may learn, whither we should look for grace to render the gospel successful among us. Let

us look up to God. Saints, apply to him for his influences to quicken your graces, and animate you in your Christian course. Sinners, cry to him for his grace to renew your nature and sanctify you. Not all the men, nor all the means upon earth, can be of any service to you without him. Carefully attend upon the gospel, and all its institutions; but still be sensible, that these alone will not do; more is necessary; even the supernatural agency of divine grace.

How dangerous a thing it is to grieve the Spirit, and cause him to withdraw! In that cursed moment when a sinner has quenched the Spirit, all the means of grace become useless to him. Our salvation depends entirely upon the divine agency; and therefore to forfeit this, is to cut ourselves off from all hope. Let us then indulge every good motion, entertain every solemn thought, cherish every pious resolution, and so, as it were, invite the blessed agent to accomplish his work, instead of provoking him to leave us. Alas! how natural is it for mankind to resist him! how averse are they to indulge his motions, and submit to his operations! And are not some of you guilty in this respect?

4. We observe that whatever excellent outward means and privileges a church enjoys, it is in a most miserable condition, if the Lord has withdrawn his influences from it; and whether this be not too much our own condition, I leave you to judge. Some of you, I doubt not, are even now, when others are withering around you, flourishing in the courts of the Lord, and feel the dews of heaven upon you; such I heartily congratulate. But in general, it is evident that a contagious lukewarmness and carnal security have spread themselves among us. Matters would not be thus still and quiet, if there was any considerable number of sinners among us anxiously seek-

ing after salvation. The violence of their concern would constrain them to unbosom themselves to their minister, and to Christians around them. Our public assemblies would not wear so stupid and unconcerned an aspect, were they generally pricked to the heart. And what is the cause of this declension? Why, the Lord denies the increase; the Lord withholds his influence. This complaint is become fashionable among us, and often upon our lips; but, pray consider what you say when you utter this complaint. And is the Lord indeed withdrawn from us? Then all is gone; then saints may languish, and sinners may perish; and there is no remedy. We may indeed have preaching, sacraments, societies, &c., but, alas! what will all these avail, if God deny the increase? they will not save one soul; nay they will but aggravate our condemnation. Let sinners take the alarm, and consider how sad their case is, who have outlived the season of remarkable divine influences! The harvest is past, the summer is ended, and you are not saved; and what do you think will become of you? How poor a chance, if I may so speak, have you for life, when the Spirit is thus restrained! You hardly know one careless sinner, in the compass of your knowledge, that has been made seriously religious, within these two or three years. If men were pressing into the kingdom of heaven, you might be helped forward, as it were, in the crowd; but now all lies as a dead weight against you, and is it not time for you to cry mightily to God that he would pour out his Spirit upon you?

SERMON LVIII.

THE REJECTION OF GOSPEL-LIGHT THE CONDEMNATION OF MEN.

JOHN III. 19.—*And this is the condemnation, that light is come into the world, and men loved darkness rather than light, because* [or *for*] *their deeds were evil.*

WHAT a strange, alarming declaration is this! *Light is come into the world :* the Sun of Righteousness is risen upon this region of darkness; therefore it is enlightened; therefore it is bright intellectual day with all its rational inhabitants: therefore they will no longer grope and stumble in darkness, but all find their way into the world of eternal light and glory. These would be natural inferences: this event we would be apt to expect from the entrance of light into the world. But hear and tremble, ye inhabitants of the enlightened parts of the earth! hear and tremble, ye sons of Nassau Hall, and inhabitants of Princeton! The benevolent Jesus, the Friend of human nature, the Saviour of men, whose lips never dropped an over-severe word, or gave a false alarm: Jesus himself proclaims, " This is the condemnation, that light is come into the world," &c.

This is the condemnation ; that is, this is the great occasion of more aggravated condemnation at the final judgment, and of more severe and terrible punishments in the eternal world; or, this is the cause of men's condemning themselves even now at the bar of their own consciences.

That light is come into the world—Jesus, the Sun of the moral world, is risen, and darts his beams around him in the gospel. And this furnishes guilty minds with materials for self-condemnation; and their obstinate resistance of the light enhances their guilt, and will render their condemnation the more aggravated; and the reason is, that

Men love darkness rather than light. They choose ignorance rather than knowledge! The Sun of Righteousness is not agreeable to them, but shines as a baleful, ill-boding luminary. If they did but love the light, its entrance into the world would be their salvation; but now it is their condemnation. But why do they hate the light? Truly, light is sweet, and it is a pleasant thing to the eyes to see the sun: and no light so sweet as this from heaven: no sun so bright and reviving as the Sun of Righteousness; and why then do they not love it? Alas! there is no reason for it but this wretched one,

Because their deeds are evil. And evil deeds always excite uneasiness in the light, and afford the conscience matter of self-accusation, therefore they wrap themselves up in darkness, and avoid the painful discoveries of the light.

The text directs us to the following inquiries:

What is that light which is come into the world? What is the darkness that is opposed to it? What are the evidences of men's loving darkness rather than light? What is the reason of it? And in what respects the light's coming into the world, and men's loving darkness rather than light, is their condemnation?

1. What is that light which is come into the world?

The answer to this and the other questions I shall endeavour to accommodate to our own times and circumstances, that we may the more readily apply it to ourselves.

The light of reason entered our world as soon as the soul of man was created; and, though it is greatly obscured by the grand apostacy, yet some sparks of it still remain.

To supply its defects, the light of revelation soon darted its beams through the clouds of ignorance, which involved the human mind, on its flying off to so great a distance from the Father of lights. This heavenly day began feebly to dawn upon the first pair of sinners, in that early promise concerning *the seed of the woman:* and it grew brighter and brighter in the successive revelations made to the patriarchs, to Moses, and the prophets, till at length the Messiah appeared, as an illustrious sun after a gradual, tedious twilight of the opening dawn.

The light of human literature has also come into the world, and shines with unusual splendours upon our age and nation; and lo! it illuminates this little village, and extends its beams through the land.

But it is not light in any of these senses that our Lord principally intends, but himself and his blessed gospel; a more clear and divine light than any of the former.

He often represents himself under the strong and agreeable metaphor of light. "I am the light of the world," says he: "he that followeth me shall not walk in darkness," John viii. 12. "I am come a light into the world, that whosoever believeth on me, should not abide in darkness." John xii. 46. Light is a strong and beautiful metaphor for knowledge, prosperity, comfort, and happiness; and these are the rays which the blessed Jesus diffuses around him:—but wherever he does not shine, all is sullen and dismal darkness. Hell is *the blackness of darkness for ever,* because he does not extend to it the light of his countenance. That country where he does not shine is *the land of darkness and the shadow of death;* and that heart which is not illuminated with *the light of the knowledge of his glory,* is the gloomy dungeon of infernal spirits; but wherever he shines, there is intellectual day, the bright meridian of glory and blessedness.

His gospel also is frequently represented as a great light; and no metaphor was ever used with more emphasis and propriety. It is the medium through which we discover the glory of the Deity, the beauties of holiness, the evil of sin, and the reality and infinite importance of eternal, invisible things. This is the light that reveals the secrets of the heart, and discovers ourselves to ourselves. It is this that gives us a just and full view of our duty to God and man, which is but imperfectly or falsely represented in every other system of religion and morality in the world. It is this that discovers and ascertains a method in which rebels may be reconciled to their offended Sovereign, and exhibits a Saviour in full view to perishing sinners. Hail! sacred, heaven-born light! welcome to our eyes, thou brightest and fairest effulgence of the divine perfections! May *this day-spring from on high* visit all the regions of this benighted world, and overwhelm it as with a deluge of celestial light! Blessed be God, its vital rays have reached to us in these ends of the earth; and if any of us remain ignorant of the important discoveries it makes, it is *because we love darkness rather than light!* Which leads me to inquire,

II. What is that darkness that is opposed to this heavenly light?

Darkness is a word of gloomy import; and there is hardly anything dismal or destructive, but what is expressed by it in sacred language. But the precise sense of the word in my text is, a state of ignorance, and the absence of the means of conviction. *Men love darkness rather than light;* that is, they choose to be ignorant, rather than well-informed; ignorant particularly of such things as will give them uneasiness to know; as their sin, and the danger to which it exposes them. They are wilfully ignorant: and hence they hate the means that would alarm them with the mortifying discovery. They would rather be flattered than told the honest truth, and know their own character and condition; and hence they shut their eyes against the light of the gospel, that would flash the painful conviction upon them. Though the light of the gospel shines round you, yet are not some of you involved in this darkness? This you may know by the next inquiry.

III. What are the evidences of men's loving darkness rather than light?

The general evidence which comprehends all the rest, is their avoiding the means of conviction, and using all the artifices in their power to render them ineffectual.

It is not impossible to characterize such of you as *love darkness rather than light*, though you may be so much upon your guard against the discovery, as not to perceive your own character.

Though you may have a turn for speculation, and perhaps delight in every other branch of knowledge, yet the knowledge of yourselves, the knowledge of disagreeable duties, the discovery of your sin and danger, of your miserable condition as under the condemnation of the divine law, this kind of self-knowledge you carefully shun; and, when it irresistibly flashes upon you, you endeavour to shut up all the avenues of your mind, through which it might break upon you, and you avoid those means of conviction from which it proceeds.

You set yourselves upon an attempt very preposterous and absurd in a rational being, and that is, Not to think.

When the ill-boding surmise rises within, "All is not well: I am not prepared for the eternal world: if I should die in this condition, I am undone for ever:" I say, when conscience thus whispers your doom, it may make you sad and pensive for a minute or two, but you soon forget it: you designedly labour to cast it out of your thoughts, and to recover your former negligent serenity. The light of conviction is a painful glare to a guilty eye: and you wrap yourselves up in darkness, lest it should break in upon you.

When your thoughts are like to fix upon this ungrateful subject, do you not labour to divert them into another channel? You immerse yourselves in business, you mingle in company, you indulge and cherish a thoughtless levity of mind, you break out of retirement into the wide world, that theatre of folly, trifling, and dissipation; and all this to scatter the gloom of conviction that hangs over your ill-boding minds, and silence the clamours of an exasperated conscience! You laugh, or talk, or work, or study away these fits of seriousness! You endeavour to prejudice yourselves against them, by giving them ill names; as melancholy, spleen, and I know not what; whereas they are indeed the honest struggles of an oppressed conscience to obtain a fair hearing, and give you faithful warning of approaching ruin: they are the benevolent efforts of the Spirit of grace to save a lost soul. And oh! it would be happy for you if you had yielded to them, and cherished the serious hour!

For the same reason, also, you love a soft representation of Christianity, as an easy, indolent, inactive thing; requiring no vigorous exertion, and attended with no dubious conflict, but encouraging your hopes of heaven in a course of sloth, carelessness, and indulgence. Those are the favourite sermons and favourite books which flatter you with smooth things, putting the most favourable construction upon your wickedness, and representing the way to heaven as smooth and easy.

Or if you have an unaccountable fondness for faithful and alarming preaching, as it must be owned some self-flatterers have, it is not with a view to apply it to yourselves, but to others. If you love the light, it is not that you may see yourselves, but other objects: and whenever it forces upon you a glance of yourselves, you immediately turn from it and hate it.

Hatred of the light, perhaps, is the reason why so many among us are so impatient of public worship; so fond of their own homes on the sacred hours consecrated to divine service: and so reluctant, so late, or so inconstant in their attendance. It is darkness, perhaps, at home; but the house of God is filled with light, which they do not love.

This also is one reason why the conversation of zealous communicative Christians, who are not ashamed to talk of what lies nearest their hearts, I mean their religion, their Saviour, and their God, and to express an abhorrence of what they so sincerely hate, I mean the vices of mankind, and every appearance of evil; I say, this is one reason why their conversation is such a heavy burden, such a painful restraint to many. Such men reflect the beams of the Sun of Righteousness and the beauties of holiness all around them; they carry light with them whithersoever they go, and strike conviction to the guilty. The strictness, the warm devotion and spirituality of their lives, pass a sentence of condemnation upon sinners; a sentence which they cannot but feel, and which, therefore, renders them uneasy. Hence it is that such lively and circumspect Christians are not at all popular in the world; but the favourites of the world are your pliable, temporizing, complaisant Christians, that never carry their religion with them into polite company, but conform themselves to the taste of those they converse with. These give no man's conscience uneasiness, they reflect no heavenly light, but thicken the darkness of every company in which they appear; therefore, they are acceptable to the lovers of darkness.

Another expedient that has often been used, and which some of you perhaps have attempted, to avoid the light, is, to endeavour to work up yourselves to a disbelief of the Christian revelation. If you could banish that heavenly light out of the world, or substitute darkness in its place, then you might perpetrate the works of darkness with more confidence and licentiousness. Therefore you eagerly listen to the laughs, the jeers, the railleries, and sophisms of loose wits against it; and you are afraid to give a fair hearing to the many satisfactory evidences in its favour. Thus you cherish that hideous monster, Infidelity; your own offspring, not Satan's, though the father of lies; for he *believes and trembles.* James ii. 19.

These artifices and the like, are the effects, and consequently the evidences and indications of men's loving darkness rather than light. And instead of a larger illustration, I shall conclude this head with a plain, honest appeal to my hearers.

As in the presence of the heart-searching God, I solemnly appeal to your consciences, whether you do not deal partially with yourselves, and refuse pursuing those hints of your dangerous condition, till you make a full discovery? Do not your hearts smite you, because you have suppressed evidence, when it was against you, and shut your eyes against conviction? When the glass of the divine law has been held up before you, and shown you your own hideous image, have you not gone away, and soon *forgot what manner of men you were?* Do you not know in your consciences, that the hopes you entertain of future happiness are not the result of severe, repeated trial, but on the other hand, owe their strength and even their being to a superficial examination, or none at all, to blind self-flattery and excessive self-love, which tempt you to believe things as you would have them? Is it censoriousness, or is it evidence and faithfulness, that constrains me to cry out, Oh! how rare are well-grounded, well-attested hopes among us? Hopes that have not been slightly entertained, nor retained without good evidence, after impartial, repeated trials; hopes that have risen and fallen, gathered strength or languished, been embraced or abandoned, perhaps a thousand times, according to the various degrees of evidence; and after a series of such vicissitudes, attended with a variety of correspondent passions, of joys and fears, of discouraging anxieties and transporting prospects, have at length arrived at a settled, confirmed state, supported by that only sufficient proof, conspicuous holiness of heart and life. For the decision of this important doubt, I appeal from my own judgment, from the judgment of a censorious spirit and a blind charity, from every judgment but that of your own hearts: at that tribunal I lodge the appeal; and there I insist the matter should be tried. And remember this, *if your hearts condemn you*, much more does God, the Supreme Judge: for *he is greater than your hearts, and knoweth all things;* knoweth many causes of condemnation and perhaps unsuspected by you. But, brethren, if your hearts condemn you not, then you have confidence towards God. 1 John iii. 20, 21. I proceed to inquire,

IV. What is the reason of this absurd preference, that *men love darkness rather than light?*

The melancholy reason of this is easily discovered, and has been partly anticipated; and it is this, that men love ease and security of mind, rather than fear and anxiety. They are really obnoxious sinners, under the terrible displeasure of almighty God, and on the slippery brink of everlasting destruction. Now to have a full conviction of this would alarm their fears, imbitter their pleasures, damp their eager pursuits, and cast their minds into a ferment of anxiety and terror. But to be blind to all these miserable prospects, to be elated with sanguine expectations of the contrary, to have all serene and calm within, to be charmed with all the fine chimeras of a flattering imagination; to be fearless of danger, and pleased with themselves; this is a state they naturally delight in: in this state they will lull themselves asleep at all adventures, regardless of the consequence; and as darkness is the most proper attendant of sleep, therefore they choose it. But the light of the gospel let into the conscience would give them quite another view of things, would overturn all their towering hopes, and set the terrors of the Lord in array against them; would open such shocking prospects in the ways of sin, that they could no longer dare to walk in them; would constrain them to indulge the sorrows of a broken heart, and to long, and pant, and look, and cry for a Saviour. This would be a very painful exercise to them; and therefore they hate and shun the light, which would force the unwelcome conviction upon them.

This is the reason which Christ himself assigns for some men's loving darkness rather than light. "He that doeth truth cometh unto the light, that his deeds may be made manifest, that they are wrought in God." Such a one is willing to be searched: the presumption is in his favour, and the trial will turn out to his honour. "But every one that doeth evil hateth the light, neither cometh to the light, lest his evil deeds should be reproved." John iii. 20, 21. It is the fear of this reproof that makes him afraid of the light; for he cannot but be conscious that his evil deeds deserve it: and to be thus reproved will yield him pain.

"But since they have such favourable thoughts of themselves, and entertain such high hopes, why are they afraid of the light? Must they not rather presume its discoveries will be in their favour? And if so, why do they hate it?" I answer, that notwithstanding all their high sentiments of themselves, they have often a secret suspicion they are not well grounded, and that the light would make some terrible discoveries concerning them; and hence they will not venture to trust themselves in the light, lest their secret suspicion should be confirmed, and rise into a full conviction. It is really so evident that they are guilty, unholy creatures, unfit for heaven, and their consciences sometimes give them such hints of this alarming secret, that they cannot keep themselves altogether ignorant of it. They, therefore, try to evade the trial, lest the sentence should go against them. I appeal to your own breasts, my brethren, whether this be not the true reason why you are so unwilling to examine yourselves, and submit to the severe scrutiny of the light of revelation? why you are averse to self-knowledge, and the means that would obtrude it upon you? Is it not because you cannot but pre-judge the matter even against yourselves, in spite of all the arts of self-flattery? And if there are such strong presumptions against you, that even yourselves cannot but dread a trial at the tribunal of your consciences, is it not evident, that chosen darkness is your only guard against conviction, and that your case is really bad? And if so, how sorry a relief is it to avoid the discovery, since all your preposterous care to avoid it will but aggravate your condemnation. Which naturally introduces the last inquiry:

V. In what respects the light's coming into the world,

and men's loving darkness rather than light, is their condemnation.

Here I have only to illustrate two particulars already hinted; that this furnishes them with matter for self-condemnation now, and will be the occasion of their more aggravated condemnation in the eternal world.

I. This furnishes them with matter of self-condemnation in the present state. It is hard, perhaps impossible, for sinners under the meridian light of the gospel, to avoid all conviction of their guilt and danger. That light is very penetrating, and will dart its rays through the thickest glooms of ignorance: it is vital and powerful, sharper than a two-edged sword; piercing and dividing asunder the soul and spirit, the joints and marrow; and is a discerner of the thoughts and intents of the heart. Heb. iv. 12. Such of you, my brethren, as are resolved to shun the mortification of self-knowledge, live in a situation very unfavourable to your design. You have had "burning and shining lights" among you;* who, I doubt not, *shine as the sun, and as the stars in the firmament for ever and ever ;* but, when they are translated to a higher sphere, the gospel has not left you, but still shines around you; and you will find it very difficult, I hope impossible, to wrap up yourselves in Egyptian darkness in such a Goshen, such a land of vision. In Tartary or Japan, or some savage region of darkness, you might have lived in contented ignorance, and avoided those unacceptable glares of light which will now break in upon you, in spite of all your vigilance; for under the faithful and solemn preaching of the gospel, your consciences will often be disturbed, and you will find yourselves unable to go on in sin bold and intrepid. And though in the thoughtless gaiety of health, and the hurry

---

* Mr. Burr and Mr. Edwards, Presidents of the College at Nassau Hall before Mr. Davies.

and din of business, you may drown the clamours of conscience, yet in a retired hour, upon a sick-bed, and in the near views of death and eternity, conscience will speak, and constrain you to hear: and thus you will live unhappy, self-condemned creatures in this world, till you are condemned by the righteous sentence of God in the world to come. Therefore consider,

II. Your loving darkness rather than light, will occasion your more aggravated condemnation in the eternal world. It was in your power to receive warning, and discover your danger in time; nay, it cost you some pains to avoid the discovery, and make light of the warning. And what a fruitful source of self-tormenting reflections will this be! How will you fret, and vex, and accuse, and condemn yourselves, for acting so foolish a part! How will you exhaust and spend yourselves in eager, fruitless wishes, that you had admitted conviction while the danger was avoidable! But, oh! it will then be too late. Hell is a region of darkness too, but not of that soothing, peaceful darkness of ignorance, which you now prefer to the light of the gospel, but a lowering, tremendous, tormenting darkness, that will for ever hide every bright and pleasing prospect from your eyes, and yet be the proper medium for discovering sights of wo and terror: a thick darkness, occasioned by the everlasting eclipse of the Sun of Righteousness and the light of God's countenance, who will never dart one ray of comfort or of hope through the sullen gloom. In this blackness of darkness you must dwell for ever, who now love darkness rather than light. And oh! how will your consciences haunt and terrify you, in that cheerless and stormy night! Your guilt will also appear great in the sight of God, as well as to your own consciences, and therefore he will inflict the greater punishment upon you. You have despised the richest blessings that even infinite goodness could bestow upon the children of men; I mean, his gospel and his Son: you have made light of his authority in the most open and audacious manner. He knows you were even afraid to discover your duty towards him; he knows you would not regard your own consciences when they were his advocates, and that you were unwilling to admit so much conviction as would render you sorry for your offences against him. Nay, he knows that your being convinced that this or that was an offence against Him, was no restraint to you from the commission of it. In short, he knows you spent your lives either in sinning against knowledge, or in avoiding that knowledge which would have prevented your sinning. And while he views you in this light, what obstinate, wilful, daring offenders must you appear in his eyes? And what aggravated punishment must he judge your due! He also knows you reluctated and struggled against your own salvation, and hated that light which would have shown you the way to everlasting life. And must he not think you worthy of that destruction you have voluntarily chosen, and refuse you admittance to that happiness which you wilfully refused?

This is the representation which the Scriptures uniformly give us of such as love darkness rather than light. *If I had not come and spoken to them,* says the blessed Jesus, *they had not had sin : but now they have no cloak for their sin.* John xv. 22. *It shall be more tolerable in the day of judgment for Sodom and Gomorrah, for Tyre and Sidon,* though most notorious for all manner of wickedness and debauchery, *than for Chorazin, Bethsaida, and Capernaum,* in which Christ's mighty works were done, and the light of his gospel shone so bright, Matt. xi. 21, 24. And this is agreeable to the eternal rules of righteousness, that much should be required where much has been given;

and that the degree of guilt should be estimated by the degrees of obligation and advantages for obedience.

And now, my dear hearers, upon a review of this subject, you see your own circumstances; the light is come among you; it shines all around you; and, I doubt not, but at times it finds some openings through which it forces its way even into unwilling minds. You have light to distinguish between truth and error; between sin and duty; between the way to heaven, and the way to hell; you are warned, admonished, and instructed; you have the strongest inducements to a life of religion, and the strongest dissuasives from a course of sin. I leave you, therefore to determine what your guilt and punishment must be if you choose darkness rather than light; light so clear, so reviving, so salutary, so divine! This alarming subject is very pertinent to us all, and we shonld all apply it to ourselves; but it is so peculiarly adapted to the residents of this house, that I cannot but direct my address particularly to you, my dear pupils, who are the children of the light in more respects than one.

There is not one in a thousand of the sons of men that enjoys your advantages. Light, human and divine, natural and supernatural, ancient and modern; that is, knowledge of every kind shines upon you, and you are every day basking under its rays. You have nothing to do but to polish your minds, and, as it were, render them luminous. But let me put you in mind, that unless you admit the light of the glorious gospel of Christ to shine in your hearts, you will still be the children of darkness, and confined in the blackness of darkness for ever. This is intolerably shocking, even in supposition. Suppose any of you should be surrounded with more light than others, for no other purpose but that you may have a stronger conflict with conviction, and that your consciences may with greater force raise tumults and insurrections within you; suppose your sins should be the sins of men of learning and knowledge, the most daring and gigantic sins on this side hell; suppose you should turn out sinners of great parts, fine geniuses, like the fallen angels, those vast intellects; wise but wicked; wise to do evil, but without knowledge to do good; suppose it should be your highest character that you can harangue well, that you know a few dead languages, that you have passed through a course of philosophy; but as to that knowledge which sanctifies all the rest, and renders them useful to yourselves or others; that knowledge which alone can make you wise to salvation, and guide you to avoid the paths of destruction, you shun it, you hate it, and choose to remain contentedly ignorant in this important respect; suppose your parents, who have been at the expense of your education; your friends, who have entertained such high and pleasing expectations concerning you; church and state, that look to you for help, and depend upon you to fill stations of importance in the world, and your careful instructers, who observe your growing improvements with proportional pleasure;—suppose that, after all this generous labour, and all these pleasing prospects, they should see you at last doomed to everlasting darkness, for your voluntary abuse of the light you now enjoy;—suppose these things, and ——but the consequences of these suppositions are so terrible, that I am not hardy enough to mention them. And oh! shall they ever become matters of fact?

Therefore, my dear youth, admit the light, love it, and pursue it, though at first it should make such discoveries as may be painful to you; for the pain will prove medicinal. By discovering your danger in time, you may be able to escape it; but never expect to remove it by the silly expedient of shutting your eyes. Be impartial inquirers after truth as to yourselves, as well as other things, and no longer attempt to put a cheat upon yourselves. Alas! how childish and foolish, as well as wicked and ruinous, would such an imposture be! The gospel, in this particular, only requires you to be honest men; and surely this is a most moderate and reasonable demand. Therefore, be ye *children of the light and of the day*, and walk as such, and then it will be a blessing to the world and to yourselves, that ever you were born.

Finally, let us all remember the terror of this friendly warning, *That this is the condemnation, that light is come into the world, and men love darkness rather than light, because their deeds are evil.*

SERMON LIX.

A ·NEW YEAR'S GIFT.

ROM. XIII. 11.—*And that, knowing the time, that now it is high time to awake out of sleep; for now is our salvation nearer than when we believed.**

TIME, like an ever-running stream, is perpetually gliding on, and hurrying us and all the sons of men into the boundless ocean of eternity. We are now entering upon one of those imaginary lines of division, which men have drawn to measure out time for their own conveniency; and, while we stand upon the threshold of a new year, it becomes us to make a solemn contemplative pause; though time can make no pause, but rushes on with its usual velocity. Let us take some suitable reviews and prospects of time past and future, and indulge such reflections as our transition from year to year naturally tends to suggest.

The grand and leading reflection is that in the text, with which I present you as a New-Year's Gift: *Knowing the time, that it is now high time to awake out of sleep.*

The connection of our text is this:—The apostle, having enjoined sundry duties of religion and morality, subjoins this consideration, namely, that the time remarkably required them, as if he should say, Be subject to magistrates, and love one another, and that the rather, knowing the time, that it is now high time, or the proper hour,† to

---

* This Sermon is dated, Nassau Hall, Jan. 1, 1760. † Hora,

awake out of sleep. A sleepy negligence as to these things is peculiarly unreasonable at such a time as this.

The Romans, to whom this epistle was written, were Christians indeed, in the judgment of charity; they were such, whose salvation the apostle could point at as near approaching: *Now*, says he, *is your salvation nearer than when you believed:* and yet he calls even upon such to awake out of sleep. Even sincere Christians are too often apt to fall into negligence and security; they contract an indolent, dull, lazy temper, as to the duties of religion and divine things: sometimes their love languishes, their zeal cools, and they become remiss or formal in their devotions. Now such a state of dullness and inactivity is often represented by the metaphor Sleep; because as sleep disables us from natural actions, and blunts our animal senses, so this spiritual sleep indisposes the soul for the service of God and spiritual sensations.

Hence it follows, that to *awake out of sleep*, signifies to rouse out of carnal security, to shake off spiritual sloth, and to engage in the concerns of religion with vigour and full exertion, like men awake.

And as even Christians are too often liable to fall into some degrees of spiritual sleep, as they often nod and slumber over the great concerns of religion, which demand the utmost exertion of all their powers, notwithstanding the principle of divine life implanted in them, there is great need to call even upon them to awake. Thus the apostle rouses the Roman Christians, including himself among them, as standing in need of the same excitation. *It is high time* for us, says he, that is, for you and me, *to awake out of sleep.*

This is a duty proper at all times. There is not one moment of time in which a Christian may lawfully and safely be secure and negligent. Yet the apostle intimates, that some particular times call for particular vigilance and activity; and that to sleep at such times is a sin peculiarly aggravated. *Now*, says he, *it is high time* for us, *to awake out of sleep :* this is not a time for us to sleep: this time calls upon us to rouse and exert ourselves: this is the hour for action: we have slept too long already: now let us rouse and rise.

The apostle also intimates, that the serious consideration and right knowledge of time, is a strong excitement to awake out of sleep. "Knowing the time," says he, "that now it is high time to awake out of sleep;" that is, your knowing and seriously considering the importance, the uncertainty, and the shortness of time in general, and the peculiar circumstances of the present time in particular, may be sufficient to rouse you. Natural sleep should be in its season: "They that sleep, sleep in the night." But, says he, "we are all the children of the light, and the children of the day. We are brought out of darkness into the glorious light of the gospel;" therefore let not us sleep, as do others. Consider the time, that is it day-light with you; and you cannot but be sensible, that it is now high time for us to awake out of sleep: this is the hour to rise. Therefore let us awake to righteousness.

The reason the apostle urges upon the Roman Christians to awake at that time is very strong and moving: it is this: "Now is our salvation nearer than when we believed." Salvation is hastening quick towards us upon the wings of time. As many years as are past since we first believed in Christ, by so many years nearer is our salvation: Or, as he expresses it in the next verse, "The night is far spent, the day is at hand." The gloomy, turbulent night of the present state is near over; the dawn of eternal day is just ready to open upon us; and can we sleep at such a time? What! sleep on the very threshold of heaven! sleep, when salvation is just ready to embrace us! sleep, when the dawn of celestial day is just about shining around us! Is it possible we should sleep at such a time? Must not the prospect of everlasting salvation so near us, the thought that in a very little time we shall be in heaven, rouse us, and fix us in a posture of eager expectation and constant watchfulness?

The text implies, that Christians should always be growing in grace; and that the nearer their salvation is, the more lively and zealous should they be; and since it is nearer this year than the last, they ought to be more holy this year than the last. The nearer they are to heaven, the more heavenly they should be. The approach of salvation is a strong motive to holiness; and the stronger by how much the nearer it is.

My chief design, at present, is, to lead you to know the time, and to make such reflections upon it, as its nature and circumstances require, and as are suited to our respective conditions.

The first thing I would set you upon as a necessary introduction to all the rest, is the important but neglected duty of self-examination. Methinks it may shock a man to enter upon a new year, without knowing whether he shall be in heaven or hell before the end of it: and that man can give but a very poor account of the last year, and perhaps twenty or thirty years before it, that cannot yet give any satisfactory answer to this grand question. Time is given us to determine this interesting point, and to use proper means to determine it in our favour. Let us therefore resolve, this day, that we will not live another year strangers to ourselves, and utterly uncertain what will become of us through an endless duration. This day let us put this question to our hearts: "What am I? Am I an humble, dutiful servant of God? Or am I a disobedient, impenitent sinner? Am I a disciple of Christ in reality? Or do I only wear his name, and make an empty profession of his religion? Whither am I bound? For heaven or for hell? Which am I most fit for in temper? For the region of perfect holiness, or for that of sin and impurity? Is it not time this inquiry should be determined? Shall I stupidly delay the determination, till it be passed by the irrevocable sentence of the Supreme Judge, before whom I may stand before this year is at a close? Alas, if it should then be against me my doom will be remediless. But if I should now discover my case to be bad, blessed be God, it is not too late to alter it. I may yet obtain a good hope, through grace, though my present hope should be found to be that of the hypocrite."

If I should push home this inquiry, it will probably discover two sorts of persons among us, to whom my text leads me particularly to address myself; the one, entirely destitute of true religion, and consequently altogether unprepared for a happy eternity, and yet careless and secure in that dangerous situation; the other, Christians indeed, and consequently habitually prepared for their latter end; but criminally remiss or formal in the concerns of religion, and in the duties they owe to God and man. The one, sunk in a deep sleep in sin; the other, nodding and slumbering, though upon the slippery brink of eternity. Now, as to both these sorts of persons, it is high time for them to awake out of sleep. And this exhortation I would press upon them, first, by some general considerations common to both; and then, by some particular considerations proper to each respectively.

The general considerations are such as these:

I. Consider the uncertainty of time as to you. You may die the next year, the next month, the next week, the next hour, or the next moment. And I once knew a minister* who, while he was making this observation, was made a striking example of it, and instantly dropped down dead in the pulpit. When you look forward through the year now begun, you see what may never be your own. No, you cannot call one day of it your own. Before that day comes, you may have done with time, and be entered upon eternity. Men presume upon time, as if it was entailed upon them for so many years; and this is the delusion that ruins multitudes. How many are now in eternity, who begun the last year with as little expectation of death, and as sanguine hopes of long life, as you have at the beginning of the present? And this may be your doom. Should a prophet, instructed in the secret, open to you the book of the divine decrees, as Jeremiah did to Hananiah, some of you would no doubt see it written there, *This year thou shalt die.* Jer. xxviii. 16. Some unexpected moment in this year will put an end to all the labours and enjoyments of the present state, and all the duties and opportunities peculiar to it.

Therefore, if sinners would repent and believe; if they would obtain the favour of God and preparation for the heavenly state; and if saints would make high improvements in religion; if they would make their calling and election sure, that they may not stumble over doubts and fears into the presence of their Judge; if they would do anything for the honour of God, and the interests of the Redeemer's kingdom in the world; if they would be of service to their families, their friends, their country, and mankind in general; now is the time for them to awake out of sleep, and set about their respective work. Now is the time, because this is the only time they are certain of. Sinners, you may be in hell before this year finishes its round, if you delay the great business of religion any

---

* The Rev. Mr. Conn, of Bladensburg, in Maryland.

longer. And saints, if you neglect to improve the present time, you may be compelled to shoot the gulf of eternity, and launch away to unknown coasts, full of fears and perplexities; you may be cut off from all opportunities of doing service to God and mankind, of endeavouring to instil the principles of religious knowledge and practice into the minds of your dear children, and those under your care, unless you catch the present hour. For remember, time is uncertain. Youth, health, strength, business, riches, power, wisdom, and whatever this world contains, cannot insure it. No, the thread of life is held by the divine hand alone; and God can snap it asunder, without warning, in whatever moment he pleases.

II. Consider the shortness of time as to you. Time in its utmost extent, including what is past from the creation, and what is future to the conflagration, is nothing to eternity. But the time of your life is vastly shorter. That part of time which is parcelled out to you, is not only uncertain, but extremely short: it is uncertain when it will end, but it is absolutely certain it will end very soon. You cannot hope to surpass the common standard of long lives: and that is but seventy or eighty years. Nay, you have but very little reason to hope you shall arrive to this. There are at least ten that die on this side of seventy or eighty, for one that lives to that period: it is therefore far more likely that you will never spend seventy or eighty years upon earth. A shorter space than that will probably convey you from this world to heaven or hell. And is it not high time then for you to awake out of sleep? Your work is great; your time is short: none to spare; none to trifle away; it is all little enough for the work you have to do.

III. Consider how much of your time has been lost and misspent already.

Some of you that are now the sincere servants of God may recollect how late in life you engaged in his service; how long you stood idle in his vineyard, when his work was before you, and his wages in your offer. How many guilty days and years have you spent in the drudgery of sin, and in a base neglect of God and your immortal souls! Others of you, who have the noble pleasure of reflecting that you devoted yourselves to God early, in comparison of others, are yet sensible how many days and years were lost before you made so wise a choice, lost in the sins and follies of childhood and youth. And the best of you have reason to lament how much of precious time you have misspent, even since you heartily engaged in the service of God; how many opportunities, both of doing good to others and receiving good yourselves, you have lost by your own carelessness. How many seasons for devotion have you neglected or misimproved! Oh! how little of your time has been devoted to God and the service of your souls! How much of it has been wasted upon trifles, or in an over-eager pursuit of this vain world? Does not the loss, upon the whole, amount to many days, and even years? And a day is no small loss to a creature, who has so few days at most to prepare for eternity.

And to many of you, is it not sadly evident you have lost all the days and years that have rolled over your heads? You have perhaps managed time well, as to the purposes of the present life; but that is but the lowest and most insignificant use of it. Time is given as a space for repentance and preparation for eternity; but have you not entirely lost it, as to this grand use of it? Nay, are not your hearts more hard, and you less prepared for eternity now, than you were some years ago? Have you not been heaping up the mountain of sin higher and higher every day, and estranging yourselves from God more and more? To heighten the loss, you should consider it as irrecoverable. Nothing is more impossible than to recall past time. It is gone! it is gone for ever! yesterday can no more return, than the years before the flood. Power, wisdom, tears, entreaties, all the united efforts of the whole universe of creatures, can never cause it to return.

And is there so much of your time lost? Lost beyond all possibility of recovery? And is it not high time to awake out of sleep? Have you any more precious time to throw away? Shall the time to come be abused and lost, like the past? Or will you not endeavour to redeem the time you have lost, in the only way in which it can be redeemed; that is, by doubling your industry in time to come? Much must now be done in a little time, since you have now but little left. You have indeed had ten, twenty, thirty, or forty precious years; but, alas! they are irrecoverably lost. And may not this thought startle you, and cause you to awake out of sleep? the loss of the same number of kingdoms would not be half so great. To a candidate for eternity, whose everlasting state depends upon the improvement of time, a year is of infinitely greater importance than a kingdom can be to any of the sons of men.

IV. Consider, the great purposes of the present life can be answered only in time; for there are certain important duties peculiar to this world, which, if unperformed here, must remain so for ever, because eternity is not the season for them.

Both worlds have their proper business allotted them; and the proper business of the one cannot be done in the other. Eternity and time are intended for quite different purposes. The one is seed-time; the other, harvest: the one is the season for working; the other, for receiving the wages: and if we would invert the unchangeable order of things, and defer the business of life till after death, we shall find ourselves miserably mistaken. Therefore, if saints would make progress in the religion of sinners, I mean that religion which becomes our present sinful state; that religion which is a course of discipline to prepare and educate us for heaven; which is a painful process for our refinement, to qualify us for that pure region; if they would cherish a noble ambition, and not only ensure happiness, but high degrees of it; if they would be of service to mankind, as members of civil or religious society; and particularly, if they would be instrumental to form others for a blessed immortality, and save souls from death, by converting sinners from the errors of their way: if they would do these things, the present life is the only time. In heaven they will have more noble employ. These things must now be done, or never. And oh! what pious heart can bear the thought of leaving the world while these are undone? Would you not desire to enter into heaven ripe for it? To be completely formed by your education, before you enter upon a state of maturity? Oh! does not your heart burn to do something for that gracious God and Saviour, that has done and suffered so much for you? To be an instrument of some service to the world, while you are passing through it? If this be your desire, now is the time. When once death has laid his cold hand upon you, you are for ever disabled from such services as these. Then farewell to all opportunities of usefulness, in the manner of the present life. Then, even your children and dearest friends may run on in sin, and perish, while it is not in your power so much as to speak one word to dissuade them. Therefore, enter upon this new year with hearty resolutions to be more zealous and laborious in these respects than you have ever yet been.

Again, if sinners, who are now in a state of condemnation, would escape out of it; if they who are at present slaves to sin, would become sincere converts to righteousness; if they would use the means of grace for that purpose, now is the time. There is none of this work in hell: they no sooner enter into the eternal world, than their state will be unchangeably and eternally fixed. The present life is the only state of trial; and if we do not turn out well in this trial, we shall never have another. All are ripe for eternity, before they are removed into it; the good ripe for heaven, and the wicked ripe for hell; the one, vessels of mercy afore-prepared for glory; and the other, vessels of wrath fitted for destruction, and for nothing else: and therefore they must remain for ever in their respective mansions. In hell indeed sinners repent; but their repentance is their punishment, and has no tendency to amend or save them. They mourn and weep; but their tears are but oil to increase the flame. They cry, and perhaps pray; but the hour of audience and acceptance is past—past for ever! The means of grace are all gone: the sanctifying influences of the Spirit are all withdrawn for ever. And hence they will corrupt and putrefy into mere masses of pure unmingled wickedness and misery. Sinners, realize this thought, and sure it must rouse you out of sleep. Trifle on a little longer, and it is over with you: spend a few days more as you have spent your time past, and you will be ingulfed in as hopeless misery as any devil in hell. Another year now meets you, and invites you to improve it to prepare for eternity; and if you waste it like the past, you may be undone for ever. Therefore take Solomon's warning, *Whatsoever thy hand findeth to do, do it with thy might; for there is no work, nor device, nor knowledge, nor wisdom in the grave whither thou goest.* Eccl. ix. 10.

These considerations, methinks, must have some weight, both upon slumbering Christians and impenitent sinners, to persuade them to awake out of sleep. I now proceed to a few considerations peculiar to each.

Upon slumbering saints I would again try the force of the apostolic consideration in my text: "awake, for now is your salvation nearer than when you believed." Heaven may be only at the distance of a year or an hour from you: it is, however, certainly nearer to-day than ever it was before. As many days as are past, so much the less time have you to groan away in the present life. And shall you indeed, in so short a time, be imparadised in the bosom of your God? Shall you so soon have done with all the sins and sorrows that now oppress you? Are your days of warfare with temptation so near a close? Shall you so soon be advanced to all the glory and blessedness of the heavenly state, and be as happy as your nature can bear? Is this indeed the case? And must not the prospect rouse you, and fire your hearts? Is not salvation the thing you have been longing and labouring for? And now, can you slumber when it is so near? Can you sleep when the night of life is so far spent, and the dawn of eternal day is ready to shine around you? Can you sleep on the brink of eternity, on the threshold of heaven?

The apostle here intimates, that the approach of salvation is great cause of joy to believers—cause of joy though death lies between, and salvation cannot reach us till we pass through the gloomy vale. Therefore, believers, I may wish you joy, in prospect that you shall soon die. This wretched world shall not be your residence always. Your worst enemies upon earth or in hell will not be able to confine you here the length of Methuselah's age, much less for ever. You may rejoice in the prospect of your speedy dissolution, because death is not nearer to you than your salvation. Before your cooling clay is shrouded, your enlarged souls will be in heaven. You will be striking instances of the truth of Solomon's remark, that "the day of one's death is better than the day of his birth." Eccl. vii. 1. Your death will be your birth-day, which will introduce you into a better world. Mortals in their language will pronounce you dead; but angels will shout an immortal born: born to an everlasting life! born to a crown! born to "an inheritance incorruptible, and that fadeth not away." And must not the prospect of this glorious day so near rouse you out of sleep? Can you not watch one hour, or one year? Shall salvation surprise you asleep?

Some of you perhaps are now thinking, "Oh! if I were certain my salvation is so near, it would even transport me, and inspire me with flaming zeal and unwearied activity. But alas! I am afraid of a disappointment. It is true, I cannot but entertain some humble hope, which the severest trial cannot overthrow. But oh! what if I should be mistaken? This jealousy makes me tremble, and shrink back from the prospect."

This may be the case of many an honest soul. But can this be pleaded as a reason or excuse for security? Alas! can you sleep in such a dreadful suspense? sleep, while you are uncertain what shall become of you through an endless duration? If you have not the sure prospect of salvation to awaken you, methinks the fear of damnation must effectually do it; for it is certain, one or the other is near you: therefore endeavour by severe self-examination, to push the matter to some certain issue. Resolve that you will not spend another day, much less another year, in a state of such dangerous, alarming uncertainty. If this point is not yet determined, it is certainly *high time for you to awake out of sleep.*

Consider farther how far your religious improvements have come short of your own resolutions and expectations, as well as your obligations. Ye happy souls, who now enjoy a good hope through grace, recollect the time when you were in a very different and more melancholy condition; the time when your spirits bled with a thousand wounds; when the terrors of the Lord set themselves in array against you, and the thunders of Sinai rung the most alarming peals in your astonished ears; when the arrows of God stuck fast in you, and the poison of them drank up your spirits; when guilt lay heavy upon your consciences, and sunk you down into the depth of despondency; when you were haunted with alarming apprehensions of divine vengeance night and day; when you went about crying for a Saviour—"Oh for a Saviour!"—but your cries seem to be in vain: oh! what were then your vows and resolutions, if it should please God to deliver you! Did you then expect you would fall asleep so soon after your deliverance? Recollect also the happy hour, when the face of a reconciled God first smiled upon you, when Jesus appeared to your minds in all the attractive glories of a Saviour, an all-sufficient Saviour in a desperate case; when he "delivered your soul from death, your feet from falling, and your eyes from tears;" when he inspired your desponding hearts with hope, and revived you with the heavenly cordials of his love: oh! what then were your thoughts and resolutions? How strongly were you bent to make him returns of gratitude! how firmly did you bind yourselves to be his servants for ever! But how soon, alas! did you begin to slumber! How far short have you fallen of your vows and promises! Recollect also what were your expectations at that memorable time. Oh! would you then have believed it, that in the space of ten or twenty years, you would have made such small progress in your heavenly course, as you have in fact done? Had you not better hope? But, alas! how are you disappointed! what sorry servants have you been to so good a master, in comparison of what you expected! And can you bear the thought of slumbering on still? Oh! shall this year pass by like the former? Sure you cannot bear the thought. Therefore awake out of sleep; rise and work for your God.

Let me conclude my address to you, with this advice: Begin this new year by dedicating yourselves afresh to God, and solemnly renewing your covenant with him. Take some hour of retirement, this evening, or as soon as you can redeem time. Call yourselves to account for the year past, and all your life. Recollect your various infirmities, mourn over them, and resolve, in the strength of divine grace, you will guard against them for the time to come. Examine yourselves both as to the reality of your religion, and as to your proficiency in it. Conclude the whole by casting yourselves anew upon Jesus Christ, and devoting yourselves for this new year entirely to him; resolved to live more to him than you have hitherto done, and depending upon him to conduct you safe through whatever this year may bring forth, whether prosperity or adversity, whether life or death. This is the true and only means whereby we can attain that happiness we ought all to be in pursuit of: that pleasure which will never end.

Let me now address a few considerations to impenitent sinners, peculiarly adapted to them.

Consider what a dreadful risk you run by neglecting the present time. The longer you indulge yourselves in sin, the harder it will be to break off from it; and do you not then run the risk of cementing an eternal union with that deadly evil? The longer you cherish a wicked temper, the stronger the habits of sin will grow. And are you not in danger of becoming eternal slaves to it? The longer you continue impenitent, the harder your hearts will grow; the oftener you do violence to your consciences, the more insensible they will become. And are you not taking direct ways to confirm yourselves in impenetrable hardness of heart, and contracting a reprobate mind? The more you sin against God, and grieve his Spirit, the more you provoke him to withhold the influences of his grace, and in righteous judgment to give you up. And dare you run so dreadful a risk as this? The more time you waste, the greater is your work, and the less your time to perform it. By how much the longer you waste your time, by so much the shorter you make your day of grace. Alas! the day of your visitation may be drawing fast towards evening, when the things that belong to your peace will be eternally hid from your eyes. Is it not then high time for you to awake out of sleep? Will you rather run such a dreadful risk than rouse out of your stupid security? Oh! what will be the end of such a course?

Let me deal plainly and without reserve with you, on a point too dangerous to allow of flattery. If you do not now awake, and turn your attention to the concerns of your souls, it is but too probable you will still go on in carnal security, and at last perish for ever. Blessed be God, this is not certain, and therefore you have no reason to despair; but it is really too probable, and therefore you have great reason to fear. This alarming probability, methinks, must force its evidence upon your own minds, upon principles you cannot reasonably dispute. You have lived twenty, thirty, or forty years, or more in the world. In this time you have enjoyed the same means of grace which you can expect in time to come. You had done less to provoke the great God to cast you off; your sinful habits were not so strong, nor your hearts so much hardened through the deceitfulness of sin; you were not so much inured to the gospel, nor were your consciences so stunned by repeated violences, as you may expect in time to come; and the longer you live in this condition, the more and more discouraging it will grow. I will by no means limit a sovereign God in the exercise of his free grace. But this is evident, that in human view, and according to appearances, it was much more likely you would have been converted in time past, than that you will be converted in time to come. The most hopeful part of life is over with you; and yet even in that, you were not brought to repentance. How much less likely is it, then, that you will be converted in time to come?

Suffer me to tell you plainly (for it is benevolence that makes the declaration) that I cannot but tremble for some of you. I am really afraid some of you will perish for ever; and the ground of my fear is this: The most generous charity cannot but conclude, that some of you are impenitent sinners; your temper and conduct proclaim it aloud; and it is very unlikely, all things considered, that you will be ever otherwise. Since you have not repented in the most promising season of life, it is much to be feared you will not repent in the less promising part of it. And since no impenitent, unholy sinner can enter into the kingdom of heaven, it is much to be feared you will perish for ever; not because the mercy of God, or the merit of Christ, is insufficient to save you, if you apply to him for it, according to the terms of the gospel; not because your case is in itself hopeless, if you would awake out of sleep, and seek the Lord in earnest; nor because you have not sufficient encouragement for laborious endeavours; but because it is too likely you will go on careless and secure, as you have done, and persist in it, till all your time is gone, and then your case will be desperate. I honestly warn you of your danger, which is too great to be concealed. And yet I give you sufficient encouragement to fly from it, while I assure you, that if you now lay your condition to heart, and earnestly use all proper means for your conversion, you have the utmost reason to hope for success; as much reason as the saints now in heaven once had, when in your condition; and in your condition they once were.

Therefore, now, sinners, awake out of sleep. Instead of entering upon this new year with carousals and extravagances, consecrate it to the great purpose for which it is given you, by engaging in earnest in the great work of your salvation. What meanest thou, O sleeper? Arise, call upon thy God, if so be he will think upon thee, that thou perish not. Jonah i. 6. "Awake, thou that sleepest, and arise from the dead, and Christ shall give thee light." Eph. v. 14.

Consider, this year may lay you low in the dust of death. How many are now in the grave, who saw the last new year's day! And though I cannot point out the persons, yet, without a spirit of prophecy, I may venture to foretell, that some of us will be in heaven or hell before this year performs its round; some gray head or some sprightly youth; perhaps you, or perhaps I. And since none of us know who it shall be, none of us are exempted from the necessity of immediate preparation. Oh! that we may all be so wise, as to consider our latter end!

I beg leave of my promiscuous auditory to employ a few minutes in addressing myself to my important family, whom my paternal affection would always single out from the rest, even when I am speaking in general terms to a mixed crowd. Therefore, my dear charge, my pupils, my children, and every tender and endearing name! ye young immortals, ye embryo-angels or infant-fiends, ye blooming, lovely, fading flowers of human nature, the hope of your parents and friends, of church and state, the hope, joy and glory of your teachers! hear one that loves you; one that has nothing to do in the world but to promote your best interest; one that would account this the greatest blessing he could enjoy in his pilgrimage, and whose nights and days are sometimes made almost equally restless by his affectionate anxieties for you; hear him upon a subject in which you are most intimately interested; a subject the most important that even an apostle or an angel could address you upon; and that is, the right improvement of time, the present time, and preparation for eternity. It is necessary that you in particular, you above all others, should know the time, that it is now high time for you to awake out of sleep. I make no doubt but you all look upon religion as an object worthy of your notice. You all as certainly believe there is a God, as that there is a creature, or that yourselves exist: you all believe heaven and hell are not majestic chimeras, or fairy lands, but the most important realities; and that you must in a little time be the residents of the one or the other. It cannot, therefore, be a question with any of you, whether you shall mind religion at all! On that you are all determined. But the question is, what is the most proper time for it? whether the present, or some uncertain hereafter? And in what order you should attend to it, whether in the first place, and above all, even in your early days? or whether you should not rather indulge yourselves in the pleasures of youth for some time, and then make religion the dull business of old age. If any of you hesitate upon this point, it may be easily solved. This is the most convenient, promising season for this purpose that you are likely to see; never will you live more free from care, or more remote from temptation. When you launch out into the noise, and bustle, and hurry, and company, and business, and vice of the world, you will soon find the scene changed for the worse. He must be a tempter to himself, who can find a temptation, while immured under this roof, and immersed in books. Never will you see the time, in your natural state, when your sins will be so conquerable, and your hearts so tender, and susceptive of good impressions; though even now, if you know yourselves, you find your sins are invincibly strong to you, and your hearts impenetrably hard. Therefore now, my dear youth, now is the inviting season, awake out of sleep; awake to righteousness and sin not. I beg you would not now commit sin with a design to repent of it afterwards; for can you be so foolish as knowingly and deliberately to do that which you explicitly intend to repent of? that is, to do that which you intend to wish undone, and to lament with broken hearts that ever you did it. Can Bedlam itself parallel the folly of this? Oh take warning from the fate of your wretched predecessors in this course. Could you ask the crowds of lost ghosts who are now suffering the punishment of their sin, whether they intended to persist impenitent in it, and perish? they would all answer, that they either vainly flattered themselves they had repented already, or intended to repent before they died; but death seized them unawares, and put an end to all their sanguine hopes. Young sinners among them imagined they should not die till old age; and old age itself thought it might hold out a few days longer, and that it was time enough to repent. But oh! they have now discovered their error, when it is too late to correct it. Therefore do not harbour one thought of putting off repentance to a sick-bed, or to old age; that is the most inconvenient and desperate season in your whole life; and if you fix upon this, one would think you had viewed your whole life on purpose to find the most unfit and discouraging period of it for the most necessary, difficult, and important work in the world. Come, then, now devote yourselves to God, and away with all excuses and delays. Remember, that upon the principles I have laid down, principles that must gain your assent by the force of their own evidence; I say, remember, that upon these principles it is extremely likely you will always persist impenitent in sin, and perish for ever, if you waste away the present season of youth, destitute of vital religion. You may every day have less and less hope of yourselves; and can you bear the thought of perishing for ever? Are your hearts so soon arrived to such a pitch of hardness, as to be proof against the terrors of the prospect? It cannot be; for "who among us can dwell with the devouring fire? Who among us can dwell with everlasting burnings?" Isa. xxxiii. 14. As for such of you as have not the great work to begin, I have only this to say, " BE steadfast, unmoveable, always abounding in the work of the Lord, forasmuch as ye know that your labour is not in vain in the Lord." 1 Cor. xv. 58.

SERMON LX.

ON THE DEATH OF HIS LATE MAJESTY, KING GEORGE II.*

2 Sam. i. 19.—*How are the mighty fallen!*

GEORGE is no more! George, the mighty, the just, the gentle, and the wise; George, the father of Britain and her Colonies, the guardian of laws and liberty, the protector of the oppressed, the arbiter of Europe, the terror of tyrants and France; George, the friend of man, the benefactor of millions, is no more!—millions tremble at the alarm. Britain expresses her sorrow in national groans. Europe re-echoes to the melancholy sound. The melancholy sound circulates far and wide. This remote American continent shares in the loyal sympathy. The wide intermediate Atlantic rolls the tide of grief to these distant shores; and even the recluse sons of Nassau Hall feel the immense bereavement, with all the sensibility of a filial heart; and must mourn with their country, with Britain, with Europe, with the world—George was our Father too. In his reign, a reign so auspicious to literature, and all the improvements of human nature, was this foundation laid; and the College of New Jersey received its existence. And though, like the sun, he shone in a distant sphere, we felt, most sensibly felt, his benign influences cherishing Science and her votaries in this her new-built temple.

In doing this humble honour to the memory of our late

* Delivered in Nassau Hall, Jan. 14, 1761.

sovereign, we cannot incur the suspicion of mercenary mourners, paying homage to the rising sun. But we indulge and give vent to the spontaneous, disinterested sorrows of sincere loyalty and gratitude, and drop our honest tears over his sacred dust, who can be our benefactor no more; too distant, too obscure and undeserving, to hope for the favourable notice of his illustrious successor. Let ambition put on the face of mourning, and all the parade of affected grief, within the reach of the royal eye; and make her court to a living prince, with all the ceremonial forms of lamentation for the deceased; but let our tears flow down unnoticed into our own bosoms. Let our grief, which is always fond of retirement, cherish and vent itself without ostentation, and free from the restraint of the public eye. It will at least afford us the generous pleasure of reflecting, that we voluntarily discharge our duty unbribed and disinterested; and it will give relief to our bursting hearts, impatient of the suppression of our sorrows.

How is the mighty fallen!—fallen under the superior power of death! Death, the king of terrors, the conqueror of conquerors; whom riches cannot bribe, nor power resist; whom goodness cannot soften, nor dignity and loyalty deter, or awe to a reverential distance. Death intrudes into palaces as well as cottages; and arrests the monarch as well as the slave. The robes of majesty and the rags of beggary are equal preludes to the shroud; and a throne is only a precipice, from whence to fall with greater noise and more extensive ruin into the grave. Since death has climbed the British throne, and thence precipitated George the Mighty, who can hope to escape? If temperance, that best preservative of health and life; if extensive utility to half the world; if the united prayers of nations; if the collected virtues of the man and the king, could secure an earthly immortality—never, O lamented George, never should thy fall have added fresh honours to the trophies of death. But since this king of Britain is no more, let the inhabitants of courts look out for mansions in the dust. Let those gods on earth prepare to die like men; and sink down to a level with beggars, worms, and clay. Let subjects *be wise and consider their latter end,* when the alarm of mortality is sounded from the throne; and he who lived for their benefit, dies for their benefit too;—dies to remind them, that they also must die.

But how astonishing and lamentable is the stupidity of mankind! Can the natural or the moral world exhibit another phenomenon so shocking and unaccountable? Death sweeps off thousands of our fellow-subjects every year. Our neighbours, like leaves in autumn, drop into the grave, in a thick succession; and our attendance upon funerals is almost as frequent and formal as our visits of friendship or complaisance. Nay, sometimes death enters in at our windows, and ravages our families before our eyes. The air, the ocean, the earth, and all the elements are armed with the powers of death; and have their pestilential vapours and inclemencies, their tempests and inundations, their eruptions and volcanoes, to destroy the life of man. A thousand dangers lie in ambush for us. Nay, the principles of mortality lurk in our own constitutions: and sickness, the herald of the last enemy, often warns us to prepare. Yet how few realize the thought, that they must die! How few familiarize to their minds that all-important hour, pregnant with consequences of great, of incomparable, of infinite moment! How many forget they must die, till they feel it; and stand fearless, unapprehensive, and insolent, upon the slippery brink of eternity, till they unexpectedly fall, and are ingulfed for ever in the boundless ocean! The sons of Adam the sinner, those fleeting phantoms of a day, put on the air of immortality upon earth; and make no provision for their subsistence in the proper regions of immortals beyond the grave. Pilgrims and strangers imagine themselves everlasting residents; and make this transitory life their all, as if earth was to be their eternal home; as if eternity was but a fairy land, and heaven and hell but majestic chimeras. But shall not this loud alarm, that spreads over half the globe, awaken us out of our vain dream of an earthly immortality? When *the mighty is fallen,* shall not the feeble tremble? If the father of a people must cease to live, shall not the people expect to die? If vulgar deaths are so frequent or insignificant, that they have lost their monitory force, and are viewed with as much indifference as the setting of the sun, or the fading of a flower, shall not the death of a king, the death of the king of Britain, constrain his subjects to realize the prospect of their own mortality, and diffuse that universal seriousness among them which that prospect inspires? If thus improved, this public loss would be a public blessing; and the reformation of a kingdom would be a greater happiness than the life of the best of princes. Thus improved, how easy and how glorious would the death of George the Second render the reign of George the Third, who now sways the sceptre, and in whom the hopes of kingdoms centre! To govern subjects on earth, who are prepared for the hierarchy of heaven, would be a province worthy of an angel.

Since the mighty is fallen, since George is no more, how vain are all things beneath the sun! *Vanity of vanities ; all is vanity !* How unworthy the hopes, how inferior to the desires, how unequal to the duration of human nature! Can the riches of Britain, or the honours of a crown; can the extent of dominion, or the laurels of victory, now afford the least pleasure to the royal corpse that lies senseless in the dust; or to the royal spirit which has winged its flight to its own region, to the world of kindred spirits! No; all these are now as insignificant as mere nothings to him, as the conquests of Alexander, or the riches and honours of the Henries and Edwards, who filled the same throne centuries ago.

"Who then art thou who settest thine affections on things below? Art thou greater than the deceased? Dost thou value thyself on thy birth? The most highly descended is no more! Dost thou value thyself on thy riches? The king of Britain is no more! Dost thou value thyself on thy power? The master of the seas, the arbiter of Europe, is no more! Dost thou glory in thy constancy, humanity, affection to thy friend; justice, veracity, popularity, universal love?" But I forbear. Human vanity cannot swell so high as to presume upon the comparison.

"How lately were the eyes of all Europe," and America, "thrown upon this great man? For man let me call him now, nor contradict the declaration which his mortality has made. They that find him now, must seek for him, and seek for him in the dust! What on earth but must tell us this world is vain, if thrones declare it? if kings, if British kings, are demonstrations of it?

———Oh, how wretched
Is that poor man that hangs on princes' favours!

"A throne is the shutting period, the golden termination of the worldly man's prospect. His passions affect, his understanding conceives, nothing beyond it, or the favours it can bestow. The sun, the expanse of heaven, or what lies higher, have no lustre in his sight; no room in his pre-engaged imagination: it is all a superfluous waste. When, therefore, his monarch dies, he is left in darkness: his sun is set: it is the night of ambition with him; which naturally damps him into reflection; and fills that reflection with awful thoughts.

"With reverence then be it spoken, what can God, in his ordinary means, do more to turn his affections into their right channel, and send them forward to their proper end? Providence, by his king's decease, takes away the very ground on which his delusion rose: it sinks before him: his error is supplanted, nor has his folly whereon to stand, but must return, like the dove in the deluge, to his own bosom again. By this he is convinced that his ultimate point of view is not only vain in its nature, but vain in fact: it not only may, but has actually failed him. What then is he under the necessity of doing, this boundary of his sight being removed? Either he must look forward, (and what is beyond it but God?) or he must close his eyes in darkness, and still repose his trust in things which he has experienced to be vain. Such accidents, therefore, however fatal to his secular, are the mercy of God to his eternal interest; and say, with the sacred text, 'Set your affections on things above, and not on things on the earth.'"*

If even kings cannot extract perfect happiness from things below; if the gross, unsubstantial, and fleeting enjoyments of life are in their own nature incapable of affording pure, solid, and lasting felicity, must we not all despair of it? Yet such a happiness we desire; such we need; nay, such we must have; or our very existence will become our curse, and all our powers of enjoyment

* Dr. Young's True Estimate of Human Life, pp. 59, 60.

but capacities of pain. And where shall we seek for it? where, but in the supreme Good? Let us "lay up for ourselves treasures in heaven and be rich towards God;" and then we shall live in state affluence and consummate felicity, when crowns, and thrones, and kings, nay, when stars, and suns, and worlds, are sunk into promiscuous ruin.

But though crowns, and thrones, and kings, though stars, and suns, and worlds, sink into promiscuous ruin, there is one gift of heaven to mankind which shall survive; which shall flourish and reign for ever; a gift little esteemed or solicited, and which makes no brilliant figure in mortal eyes; I mean religion. Religion! Thou brightest ornament of human nature! Thou fairest image of the divine! Thou sacred spark of celestial fire, which now glimmers with but a feeble lustre, but will shine bright in the night of affliction; will irradiate the thick gloom of death, and blaze out into immortality in its native element! This will be an unfailing source of happiness, through the revolutions of eternal ages. May I be the man to whom Heaven shall bestow this most precious gift of divine bounty! and let crowns and kingdoms be scattered with an undistinguishing hand to the worthless and the brave, to the wise man and the fool; I will not murmur, envy, nor despond. These majestic trifles are not the tests of real worth, nor the badges of heaven's favourites; it is religion that marks out the happy man; that distinguishes the heir of an unfading crown; who, when the dubious conflict of life is over, *shall inherit all things*, and sit in triumph for ever with the King of kings, and Lord of lords.

If majesty has any charms to a mind truly noble; if dominion has any attractive influence upon a benevolent spirit; it must be as it affords a more extensive sphere of beneficence, and yields the generous, disinterested, godlike pleasure of making multitudes happy. This may reconcile a mind intrinsically great to the self-denial of a court, to the cares of government, and render the burden of a crown tolerable. And in this respect, how happy and illustrious was our late king! It was an honour which could fall to the lot of but few of his subjects, to have such intimate access to the royal presence, as to furnish materials for a panegyric upon his personal and private virtues! but his public and regal virtues diffused their beams to every territory of his vast dominions, and shone with efficacious though gentle force, even upon us, in these remote ends of the earth. His public virtues as a king, thousands attest and celebrate in every region of the world. These we know, of these we have had a long and delightful experience of four-and-thirty years. These, therefore, we can justly celebrate; and to these I shall confine myself; though I am not altogether uninformed of some amiable anecdotes of his majesty's personal virtues and private life.

Can the British annals, in the compass of seventeen hundred years, produce a period more favourable to liberty, peace, prosperity, commerce, and religion? In this happy reign, the prerogative meditated no invasions upon the rights of the people; nor attempted to exalt itself above the law. George, the great, but unambitious, consulted the rights of the people as well as of the crown; and claimed no powers but such as were granted to him by the constitution; and what is the constitution but the voluntary compact of sovereign and subject? and is not this the foundation of their mutual obligations? The commons who, from their situation in the various parts of the kingdom, are presumed to be best acquainted with its state, always found his majesty condescending to leave the interests of the country to their deliberations; and ready to assent to all their salutary proposals. The times when parliaments were a troublesome restraint are forgotten, or remembered with patriotic indignation. The monarch himself frowned upon the principles of arbitrary power; and was an advocate for the liberties of the people. His parliament were his faithful counsellors; to whom he communicated his measures, with all the frankness and confidence natural to conscious integrity. In an aristocracy the House of Lords could hardly enjoy more authority and independence, nor the House of Commons in a democracy more freedom of speech and determination, but far less dignity and unanimity than under the monarchy of George the Second. In his were united the advantages of all forms of government; free from the inconveniences peculiar to each in a state of separation. Happy! thrice happy, to live under a reign so gentle and auspicious! How different would have been our situation under the baleful influence of the ill-boding name of Stuart.

Fond of peace, and tender of the life and blood of man, our late most gracious sovereign never engaged in war, but with compassionate reluctance, and with the unanimous approbation of his people. He drew the sword, not to gratify his own ambition or avarice, or to revenge a personal injury; but to defend the rights of his subjects, to relieve the oppressed, and to restrain and chastise the disturbers and tyrants of the world. He always aimed the thunder of Britain against the guilty head: but innocence had nothing to fear from the terrors of his hands. French perfidy and Austrian ingratitude roused his generous sentiment: but the merit of Frederic, the Prussian hero, the second champion of liberty and the protestant religion, when oppressed by confederate kingdoms and empires, erased the memory of past differences, and made him his friend and ally.

What a vigilant, fatherly care did he extend to the infant colonies of Britain, exposed in this savage wilderness! Hence the safety our once defenceless frontiers now enjoy. Hence the reduction of that mongrel race of French and Indian savages, who would have been the eternal enemies of humanity, peace, religion, and Britons. And hence the the glory of Amherst and Wolfe; and the addition of Canada to the British empire in America. Surely the name of George the Second must be dear in these rescued provinces, and particularly in Nassau Hall, while peace and safety are esteemed blessings, while the terrors of a barbarous war are shocking to humanity, and while gratitude lives in an American breast. And George the Third will be dearer to us, as he bears the ever-memorable name of our great deliverer.

He never usurped the prerogative of Heaven, by assuming the sovereignty of conscience, or the conduct of the human understanding, in matters of faith and religious speculation. He had deeply imbibed the principles of liberty; and could well distinguish between the civil rights of society and the sacred rights of religion. He knew the nature of man and of Christianity too well, to imagine that the determination of human authority, or the sanctions of penal laws, could convince the mind of one divine truth or duty; or that the imposition of uniformity in minute points of faith, or in the forms of worship and ecclesiastical government, was consistent with free inquiry and the rights of private judgment; without which genuine Christianity cannot, though the external grandeur of the church may, flourish. In his reign the state was not the dupe of aspiring churchmen, but the guardian of Christians in general; nor was the secular arm the engine of ecclesiastical vengeance, but the defence of the Dissenter as well as the Conformist; of the toleration, as well as the establishment. His reign was not stained with blood, shed by the ferocious hand of blind bigotry: but the thoughts, the tongue, and the pen were free; and truth was armed only with her own gentle and harmless weapons; those weapons with which she has always spread her conquests, in opposition to fires and racks, to the tortures of death, and to the powers of earth and hell. Long may Britons continue free in a world of slaves! And long may George adorn the throne, and guard the sacred rights of conscience.

Was ever king more beloved by his people? Was ever government more deeply founded in the hearts of his subjects? Whatever factions have embroiled the nation; whatever clamours have been raised against the ministry; whatever popular suspicions of the abilities or integrity of his servants; still the king was the favourite of all; he was the centre in which all parties were united.

Rebellion indeed, (to the horror and surprise of posterity let it be known!) the most unnatural, unprovoked rebellion, presumed to lift up its head even under his gracious reign, and attempted to transfer to a despicable pretender the crown conferred upon him by a free people. But how gently, and yet how effectually, was the monster quelled! And how happy have been the consequences to thousands; particularly to the brave, misguided Highlanders, who, by the munificence of that very king they risked their lives to depose, now taste the sweets of liberty and property; and need no farther argument in favour of the illustrious house of Hanover.*

* The dissolution of the Highland Clans, those petty tyranies, upon terms not disadvantageous to the chiefs themselves, and highly agreeable to their vassals; the opening a communication into those once inaccessible regions by public roads; the establishment of protestant missionaries and English schools; and the introduction of manufactories, supported by the royal bounty, and particularly by the income of the estates confiscated in the last

The evening of his life was the meridian of his glory; and death seized him on the summit of human greatness. What illustrious victories have attended his arms in every quarter of the globe! Asia and Africa, as well as Europe and America, have trembled at his name; and felt the force of British revenge, executed by his righteous hand. What a shining figure will the three last years, the era of British glory, make in the history of the world! And how will they at once eternize and endear the name of George the Second!

How bloody and extensive has been the present war! And how important the interests at stake! It has spread over both the old and new continent, like an all-devouring conflagration. Nations have bled in a thousand veins; and the precious blood of man has streamed by sea and land, shed by the savage hand of man. The balance of power, the liberty, the peace, and religion of Europe, as well as the independency, the freedom, the commerce, and the territories of Britain and her colonies, have been the prize in dispute; a prize equal to the whole world to us. And how gloomy and ill-boding was the aspect of our affairs in the first years of this war! The people factious, clamorous, and exasperated! The ministry divided, improvident, and dilatory! Commanders imprudently brave and foolhardy, or weak and dastardly! What abortive schemes and blasted expeditions! What sanguine hopes and mortifying disappointments! What pompous undertakings and inglorious results! What British, un-British gasconade and cowardice, boasting and timidity! And what Gallic bravery and success! (*Proh curia! inversique mores!*)

rebellion;—these have been the gentle but effectual expedients to extirpate popery and rebellion, under the administration of George the Second. These were agreeable to so mild a reign; and these have already done infinitely more to accomplish this patriotic and Christian design, than all the severe, preposterous measures of former ages.

What depredations and barbarities, what desertion and consternation, upon our frontiers, through a length of above a thousand miles! What downcast airs on every countenance! What trembling expectations in every heart! But in that anxious, dubious crisis, George was alive! (Let both sides the Atlantic resound with praises, let every British heart glow with gratitude to the Sovereign of the universe, who prolonged the royal life, and preserved his capacities unimpaired in the decline of nature!—George was alive!) And with a steady, skilful hand, managed the helm in the threatening storm, and conducted the sinking state, in which our all was embarked, within sight of the harbour of peace, safety, and glory, before he resigned the charge. His gracious ear was open to the voice of the people, when he received the illustrious Pitt to so great a share of the administration. And what a happy and glorious revolution have we since seen in the schemes of policy and the events of war! Had heaven punished a guilty nation, by removing their guardian in that period of discord, languor, dejection, and mortification, while the heir of the crown was in his minority, how dismal might have been the consequences! Indeed, we could have sincerely paid to so good a king that eastern compliment, *O king, live for ever!* for never, O lamented George! never could thy subjects be weary of thee. But since the mighty must fall, as well as the feeble; since George, the august and well-beloved, must die, how great the mercy, that the melancholy period was so long delayed! It would be ingratitude, it would be impiety, it would be atheism, not to acknowledge the agency of Providence in so important an event.

George, our father, is no more! No more, I mean the ornament of the British throne; no more the benefactor of mortals: no more the inhabitant of earth. His precious dust is ere now deposited with his royal predecessors, where majesty lies in ruins :* and we doubt not but the last honours have been performed to his venerable remains, agreeable to the gratitude and generosity of the nation, and the munificent prince who inherits his crown and kingdom.

And is this senseless dust all that is left of the greatest of kings? Has he suffered a total extinction of being? Is he entirely dead to himself, to the universe, and to God? No, he lives! He greatly lives the life of immortals! He lives in the immense region of spirits, where monarchs and kings are private men: where all the superficial distinctions of birth, riches, power, and majesty, are lost for ever: and all the distinction that remains, arises from virtue and vice—from our having acted our part well or ill in the station where we are fixed; whether on the throne of majesty, in the chains of slavery, or in the intermediate classes of life: there royalty appears disrobed and uncrowned before him, *who regardeth not the rich more than the poor:* there triumphant tyranny, that bade defiance to human power, is blasted and degraded by the frown of Omnipotence: and there, those rulers of men, who were the servants of God, are advanced to a higher sphere of dominion and beneficence; and the badges of earthly majesty are superfluous to their dignity, and would but conceal their real worth. There they are clothed with *the robes of salvation, and the garments of praise,* and wear

---

* In Westminster Abbey.

"That ancient, sacred, and illustrious dome,
  Where, soon or late, fair Albion's heroes come,
  From camps and courts, tho' great, and wise, and just,
  To feed the worm, and moulder into dust;
  That solemn mansion of the royal dead,
  Where passing slaves o'er sleeping monarchs tread."

Young's Last Day.

crowns of unfading glory, infinitely brighter than those which the gold, and gems, and glittering trifles of earth can compose. There our charity would place our departed sovereign in a station as much superior to that of king of Great Britain, as an angel to a man. But it is not for mortals to pry into the inviolable secrets of the invisible world.

When we view him in this light, the medium in which persons and things appear in eternity, we no longer revere the king. The crown, the sceptre, and all the regalia of earthly majesty, vanish. But we behold something more venerable, more majestic, more divine—the immortal! The great spirit stripped of all the empty parade and pageantry of outward show, and clothed with all the Godlike regalia of its own nature? Illustrious in its own intrinsic dignity! This view of kings and emperors does not diminish, but heighten and brighten their majesty. This is the most venerable and striking attitude in which kings and emperors themselves can appear; though in this view peasants and slaves claim an equality with them. All equally immortal! And what renders the nature of man, or even of angels, so important, so noble, so divine, as immortality? This makes the man infinitely superior to the monarch; and advances the offspring of the dust to a kind of equality with the natives of heaven.

But though George still lives to himself, to the universe, and to God, (for all live to him) yet to his once-loved kingdoms he is no more. Here, again, I must retract the melancholy thought—he still lives, he still adorns the throne, he still blesses the world, in the person of his royal descendant and successor. And if the early appearance of genius, humanity, condescension, the spirit of liberty and love of his people; if British birth, education, and connections; if the favourable prepossessions and high expectations of the nation; if the present glory and terror of the British arms; if the wishes and prayers of every lover of his country, signify any thing, or have any efficacy, George the Third will reign like George the Second.

What, then, remains, but that we transfer to him the loyalty, duty, and affection, we were wont to pay to his amiable predecessor? He ascends the throne in the prime of life and vigour, at a juncture more honourable and glorious, than Britain, perhaps, or America, has ever seen. He had early the example of the best of kings before his eyes, as a finished model of government, upon principles truly British. And this has received a powerful sanction from the example and instructions of his royal mother, the honour of her sex; who has made so shining and amiable a figure in the British court, ever since her first appearance. He has able generals in the field; able admirals in the navy; a navy perhaps equal to the united fleets of the universe; and able counsellors in the cabinet. His subjects numerous, rich, free, brave, loyal, and affectionate: his enemies defeated, dispirited, exhausted, disappointed in their last efforts, and baffled in their forlorn hope: the commerce of Britain, as extensive as the globe, and collecting the riches of the world from every soil and climate. In this promising situation of affairs, what a long, happy, and glorious reign have we in prospect! How may we congratulate the contemporaries of our young king, who enter into life as he ascends the throne, and are likely to share in the honours and felicities of his administration! And with what ardent gratitude and devotion should we bow the knee to him, *by whom kings reign and princes decree justice*, who opens so bright and glorious a prospect! If the agency of the Most High, *who ruleth the kingdoms of men, and giveth them to whomsoever he pleaseth*, be ungratefully overlooked, our loyalty is no longer a virtue:

it loses its worth, and degenerates into a mere compliment to the creature, at the expense of the Creator's honour. It is acknowledging the deputy, but rejecting the constituent.*

But notwithstanding this favourable and promising posture of affairs, methinks we cannot make a transition from reign to reign without some suspense. We are passing into a new state of political existence; entering upon a strange, untried period; and it is natural to be a little damped at our first entrance. The changes of life are so

---

* Thus agreeable and encouraging did the dawn of the present reign appear to me, before any public act had confirmed those favourable anticipations. But since I have found that one of the very first acts of government was "A proclamation for the encouragement of piety and virtue, and for preventing of vice, profaneness, and immorality," the transport of my mind would almost constrain me to put on the airs of a prophet; and, without my usual diffidence as to futurities, to foretell the increasing glories and felicities of the beginning administration. Hail! desponding religion! Lift up thy drooping head, and triumph! Virtue, thou heaven-born exile, return to court. Young George invites thee: George declares himself thy early friend and patron, "and promises to distinguish persons of piety and virtue, on all occasions, by marks of royal favour." Vice, thou triumphant monster! with all thy infernal train, retire, abscond, and fly to thy native hell! Young George forbids thee to appear at court, in the army, in the navy, or any of thy usual haunts, and rouses the powers of his kingdoms against thee. Sure this cannot be an empty flourish, at first appearance on the stage. Certainly this must be the honest declaration of a heart long a secret friend to religion and virtue:.and now impatient of silence. And if so, what happy days are before us, when religion and George shall reign!

   Aspice, venturo lætentur ut omnia sæclo!
  Jam redit et Virgo, redeunt Saturnia regna:
  Jam nova progenies cælo demittitur alto——
  Te Duce, si qua manent sceleris vestigia nostri,
  Irrita perpetua solvent formidine terras——
  Pacatumque reges patriis virtutibus orbem
           Virg. Eclog. iv.

It is impossible to be calm under such a presage. Such a presage renders the blessings we shall receive under the reign of George the Third almost as sure as those we have received under that of George the Second; and I am ready to retract all I have said above in the language of diffidence and uncertainty.

frequent and unexpected, and the course of human affairs so seldom runs on in a steady, uniform tenor for a length of years, that we can be certain of almost nothing but what is past. The most promising posture of affairs may put on another form; and all the honours and acquisitions of a well conducted and successful war, may be ingloriously lost by the intrigues of negotiation and a dishonourable peace. The best of kings (with all due deference to majesty be it spoken) may have evil counsellors, and evil counsellors may have the most mischievous influence, notwithstanding the wisdom and goodness of the sovereign.

But may not even this anxious contingency be productive of good, by exciting us more powerfully to the duty of Christians and good subjects?

Are the kingdoms of men forlorn, outcast orphans, discarded by their heavenly Father; or independent, self-sufficient sovereignties, capable of managing themselves by their own power and policy? Or, are they not rather little provinces or districts of Jehovah's immense empire, in which he presides, and manages all their affairs? Are kings absolute and self-supported? Or are they not sustained by him who is the support of archangels? Does *the prayer of a righteous man avail much?* Or is it but empty breath of no efficacy? A light much more obscure than that of Christianity has enabled heathens to answer such questions as these. Since, "then, the Most High ruleth in the kingdoms of men;" and since prayer is invested with (shall I dare assert it?) a kind of almighty importunity, shall we not often appear in the posture of petitioners at the throne of grace for our young king? In praying for this one great personage, we intercede not only for him, but for ourselves, and millions on both sides the Atlantic; not only for individuals, but for nations, for Europe and America, for the world! And may petitions of such immense import never languish into spiritless, complimental formalities! May they exhaust all the vigour of our souls, and be always animated with the united ardours of devotion, patriotism, and loyalty!

As good subjects, whatever our present or future stations may be in society, or in whatever territory of his majesty's dominions we may act our part on the stage of life, let the principles of loyalty and liberty, let cheerful obedience to our king, and a disinterested love to our country, let that generous virtue, public spirit, inspire our hearts, and appear in all our conduct. Let us *be subject, not for wrath, but for conscience' sake.* Let our obedience be, not a servile artifice to escape punishment; not the mercenary cringing of ambition or avarice; not the fulsome, affected complaisance of flattery; but the voluntary offering of an honest and sincere heart. Let this always be an essential part of our virtue, our religion, and whatever we esteem most sacred.

To you, my dear pupils, the hope, the joy, and the ornament of your country; who, if the wishes and expectations of your parents, your friends, your tutors, and the public, be accomplished, will yet make an important figure in life; to you I must particularly address myself on this melancholy occasion, with all the affectionate solicitude and earnestness of a father's heart; and while only my voice sounds in your ears, imagine you hear the voice of your other tutors, of the trustees of this institution, of your country and your God, inculcating upon you the same exhortation.

While I invite you to drop your filial tears over the sacred dust of our common father, who has hitherto cherished your tender years, I cannot but congratulate you once more upon your being coevals with George the Third; and that you will date your entrance upon public life so near the time of his accession to the royal seats of his ancestors. The happy subjects of George the Second will soon give place to you, and visit their beloved king in the mansions of the dead. But long may your king and you live, and many happy days may you see together.

You have a king, who has already taught you how to live, and recommended piety and virtue to you from the throne. Let this, therefore, be your first care. This will qualify you for both worlds, and render you at once good subjects to your earthly sovereign, and to his Master and yours in heaven. The Christian cannot but be a patriot. He, who loves all mankind, even his enemies, must certainly love his country. The Christian cannot but be a good subject. He who loves his neighbour as himself, must certainly love his sovereign: and he who *fears God*, will not fail to *honour the king*.

Let every soul be subject to the higher powers. This, my dear youth, this is the great precept of Christianity, which this day demands your attention. From this day cherish a public spirit, and dedicate yourselves to the service of your king and country. Whatever character you may hereafter sustain, you will not be so insignificant as to be incapable of any service to your sovereign and fellow-subjects. Whether the health, the liberty and property, or spiritual interests of mankind, be the object of your future profession; whether you choose the peaceful vale of retirement, or the busy scenes of active life, remember, you will still have connections with the throne. You are parts of that great community over which his majesty presides; and the good of the whole, as well as the ease, honour, and prosperity of his government, will, in some measure, depend upon your performing your parts well. Civil society is so complicated a system, and concludes so many remote, as well as intimate connections, references, and mutual dependencies, that the least irregularity or defect in the minutest spring, may disorder and weaken the whole machine. Therefore, it becomes you to know your own importance to your king and country, that you may exert your influences in your respective spheres, to execute all his patriot designs. Let your literary acquisitions, your fortunes, and even your lives, be sacred to him, when his royal pleasure demands them for the service of your country. This you must do, or turn rebels against your own hearts and consciences. I well know you cannot be disaffected, or even useless subjects from principle. Your education, both at home and in Nassau Hall, has invincibly pre-engaged your inclination, your reason, and your conscience in favour of our incomparable constitution, and the succession in the Hanover family: of liberty, the Protestant religion, and George the Third, which are inseparably united. Therefore act up to your principles, practise according to your political creed, and then my most benevolent wishes, nay, the highest wishes of your king and fellow-subjects, will be amply accomplished in you. Then you will give the world an honourable and just specimen of the morals and politics inculcated in the College of New Jersey; and convince them that it is a seminary of loyalty, as well as learning and piety; a nursery for the state, as well as the church. Such may it always continue! You all concur in your cordial Amen.

SERMON LXI.

RELIGION AND PATRIOTISM THE CONSTITUENTS OF GOOD SOLDIERS.*

2 SAM. x. 12.—*Be of good courage, and let us play the men for our people, and for the cities of our God: and the* LORD *do that which seemeth him good.*

A HUNDRED years of peace and liberty in such a world as this, is a very unusual thing; and yet our country has been the happy spot that has been distinguished with such a long series of blessings, with little or no interruption. Our situation in the middle of the British Colonies, and our separation from the French, those eternal enemies of liberty and Britons, on the one side by the vast Atlantic, and on the other by a long ridge of mountains, and a wide extended wilderness, have for many years been a barrier to us; and while other nations have been involved in war, we have not been alarmed with the sound of the trumpet, nor seen garments rolled in blood.

But now the scene is changed: now we begin to experience in our turn the fate of the nations of the earth. Our territories are invaded by the power and perfidy of France; our frontiers ravaged by merciless savages, and our fellow-subjects there murdered with all the horrid arts of Indian and Popish torture. Our general, unfortunately

---

* Preached to Captain Overton's independent company of volunteers, raised in Hanover county, Virginia, August 17, 1755.

brave, is fallen; an army of thirteen hundred choice men routed, our fine train of artillery taken, and all this, (O mortifying thought!) all this by four or five hundred dastardly, insidious barbarians!

These calamities have not come upon us without warning. We were long ago apprised of the ambitious schemes of our enemies, and their motions to carry them into execution: and had we taken timely measures, they might have been crushed before they could have arrived at such a formidable height. But how have we generally behaved in such a critical time? Alas! our country has been sunk in a deep sleep: a stupid security has unmanned the inhabitants; they could not realize a danger at the distance of two or three hundred miles: they would not be persuaded that even French Papists could seriously design us an injury: and hence little or nothing has been done for the defence of our country, in time, except by the compulsion of authority. And now, when the cloud thickens over our heads, and alarms every thoughtful mind with its near approach, multitudes, I am afraid, are still dissolved in careless security, or enervated with an effeminate, cowardly spirit.

When the melancholy news first reached us, concerning the fate of our army, then we saw how natural it is for the presumptuous to fall into the opposite extreme of unmanly despondence and consternation; and how little men could do, in such a panic, for their own defence. We have also suffered our poor fellow-subjects, in the frontier counties, to fall a helpless prey to blood-thirsty savages, without affording them proper assistance, which, as members of the same body politic, they had a right to expect. They might as well have continued in a state of nature, as be united in a society, if, in such an article of extreme danger, they are left to shift for themselves. The bloody barbarians have exercised on some of them the most unnatural and leisurely tortures; and others they have butchered in their beds, or in some unguarded hour. Can human nature bear the horror of the sight? See yonder! the hairy scalps clotted with gore! the mangled limbs! Women ripped up! the heart and bowels still palpitating with life, and smoking on the ground! See the savages swilling their blood, and imbibing a more outrageous fury with the inhuman draught! Sure these are not men: they are not beasts of prey; they are something worse; they must be infernal furies in human shape. And have we tamely looked on, and suffered them to exercise these hellish barbarities upon our fellow-men, our fellow-subjects, our brethren? Alas! with what horror must we look upon ourselves, as being little better than accessaries to their blood!

And shall these ravages go unchecked? Shall Virginia incur the guilt, and the everlasting shame, of tamely exchanging her liberty, her religion, and her all, for arbitrary Gallic power, and for Popish slavery, tyranny, and massacre? Alas! are there none of her children, that enjoyed all the blessings of her peace, that will espouse her cause, and befriend her now in the time of her danger? Are Britons utterly degenerated by so short a remove from the mother country? Is the spirit of patriotism entirely extinguished among us? And must I give thee up for lost, O my country! and all that is included in that important word? Must I look upon thee as a conquered, enslaved province of France, and the range of Indian savages? My heart breaks at the thought. And must ye, our unhappy brethren on our frontiers, must ye stand the single barriers of a ravaged country, unassisted, unbefriended, unpitied? Alas! must I draw these shocking conclusions?

No; I am agreeably checked by the happy, encouraging prospect now before me. Is it a pleasing dream? Or do I really see a number of brave men, without the compulsion of authority, without the prospect of gain, voluntarily associated in a company, to march over trackless mountains, the haunts of wild beasts, or fiercer savages, into a hideous wilderness, to succour their helpless fellow-subjects, and guard their country? Yes, gentlemen, I see you here upon this design; and were you all united to my heart by the most endearing ties of nature or friendship, I could not wish to see you engaged in a nobler cause; and whatever the fondness of passion might carry me to, I am sure my judgment would never suffer me to persuade you to desert it. You all generously put your lives in your hands: and sundry of you have nobly disengaged yourselves from the strong and tender ties that twine about the heart of a father, or a husband, to confine you at home in inglorious ease, and sneaking retirement from danger, when your country calls for your assistance. While I have you before me, I have high thoughts of a Virginian; and I entertain the pleasing hope that my country will yet emerge out of her distress, and flourish with her usual blessings. I am gratefully sensible of the honour you have done me, in making choice of me to address you upon so singular and important an occasion: and I am sure I bring with me a heart ardent to serve you and my country, though I am afraid my inability, and the hurry of my preparations, may give you reason to repent your choice. I cannot begin my address to you with more proper words than those of a great general, which I have read to you: "Be of good courage, and play the men for *your* people, and for the cities of *your* God: and the Lord do what seemeth him good."

My present design is, to illustrate and improve the sundry parts of my text, as they lie in order; which you will find rich in sundry important instructions, adapted to this occasion.

The words were spoken just before a very threatening engagement by Joab, who had long served under that pious hero, King David, as the general of his forces, and had shown himself an officer of true courage, conducted with prudence. The Ammonites, a neighbouring nation who had frequent hostilities with the Jews, had ungratefully offered indignities to some of David's courtiers whom he had sent to condole their king upon the death of his father, and congratulate his accession to the crown. Our holy religion teaches us to bear personal injuries without private revenge: but national insults and indignities ought to excite the public resentment. Accordingly, King David, when he heard that the Ammonites, with their allies, were preparing to invade his territories, and carry their injuries still farther, sent Joab his general, with his army, to repel them, and revenge the affronts they had offered his subjects. It seems the army of the enemy were much more numerous than David's: their mercenaries from other nations were no less than thirty-one thousand men; and no doubt the Ammonites themselves were a still greater number. These numerous forces were disposed in the most advantageous manner, and surrounded Joab's men, that they might attack them both in flank and front at once, and cut them all off, leaving no way for them to escape. Prudence is of the utmost importance in the conduct of an army: and Joab, in this critical situation, gives a proof of how much he was a master of it, and discovers the steady composure of his mind while thus surrounded with danger. He divides his army and gives one party to his brother Abishai, who commanded next to him, and the other he kept the command of himself, and resolves to attack the Syrian mercenaries, who seemed the most formidable; he gives orders to his brother in the meantime to fall upon the Ammonites; and he animates him with this noble advice: *Be of good courage, and let us play the men for our people and the cities of our God*, which are now at stake: *and the Lord do what seemeth him good.*

"Be of good courage, and let us play the men." Courage is an essential character of a good soldier—not a savage, ferocious violence; not a fool-hardy insensibility of danger, or headstrong rashness to rush into it; not the fury of inflamed passions, broke loose from the government of reason; but calm, deliberate, rational courage; a steady, judicious, thoughtful fortitude; the courage of a man, and not of a tiger; such a temper as Addison ascribes with so much justice to the famous Marlborough and Eugene:—

> Whose courage dwelt not in a troubled flood
> Of mounting spirits and fermenting blood;—But
> Lodged in the soul, with virtue over-ruled,
> Inflamed by reason, and by reason cooled. THE CAMPAIGN.

This is true courage, and such as we ought all to cherish in the present dangerous conjuncture. This will render men vigilant and cautious against surprise, prudent and deliberate in concerting their measures, and steady and resolute in executing them. But without this they will fall into unsuspected dangers, which will strike them with wild consternation; they will meanly shun dangers that are surmountable, or precipitantly rush into those that are causeless, or evidently fatal, and throw away their lives in vain.

There are some men who naturally have this heroic turn of mind. The wise Creator has adapted the natural genius of mankind with a surprising and beautiful variety to the state in which they are placed in this world. To some he has given a turn for intellectual improvement, and the liberal arts and sciences; to others a genius for trade; to others a dexterity in mechanics, and the ruder arts, necessary for the support of human life: the generality of mankind may be capable of tolerable improvements in any of these; but it is only they whom the God of nature has formed for them, that will shine in them; every man in his own province. And as God well knew what a world of degenerate, ambitious, and revengeful creatures this is; as he knew that innocence could not be protected, property and liberty secured, nor the lives of mankind preserved from the lawless hands of ambition, avarice, and tyranny, without the use of the sword; as he knew this would be the only method to preserve mankind from universal slavery; he has formed some men for this dreadful work, and fired them with a martial spirit, and a glorious love of danger. Such a spirit, though most pernicious when ungoverned by the rules of justice and benevolence to mankind, is a public blessing when rightly directed: such a spirit, under God, has often mortified the insolence of tyrants, checked the encroachments of arbitrary power, and delivered enslaved and ruined nations: it is as necessary in its place for our subsistence in such a world as this, as any of the gentler geniuses among mankind; and it is derived from the same divine original. He that winged the imagination of a Homer or a Milton; he that gave penetration to the mind of Newton; he that made Tubal-Cain an instructor of artificers in brass and iron,* and gave skill to Bezaleel and Aholiab in curious works;† nay, he that sent out Paul and his brethren to conquer the nations with the gentler weapons of plain truth, miracles,

* Gen. iv. 22. † Exod xxxv. 30,31, &c.

and the love of a crucified Saviour; he, even that same gracious power, has formed and raised up an Alexander, a Julius Cæsar, a William,* and a Marlborough, and inspired them with this enterprising, intrepid spirit; the two first to scourge a guilty world, and the two last to save nations on the brink of ruin. There is something glorious and inviting in danger to such noble minds; and their breasts beat with a generous ardour when it appears.

Our continent is like to become the seat of war; and we, for the future, (till the sundry European nations that have planted colonies in it, have fixed their boundaries by the sword,) have no other way left to defend our rights and privileges. And has God been pleased to diffuse some sparks of this martial fire through our country? I hope he has; and though it has been almost extinguished by so long a peace, and a deluge of luxury and pleasure, now I hope it begins to kindle; and may I not produce you, my brethren, who are engaged in this expedition, as instances of it?† Well, cherish it as a sacred heaven-born fire; and let the injuries done to your country administer fuel to it; and kindle it in those breasts where it has been hitherto smothered or inactive.

Though nature be the true origin of military courage, and it can never be kindled to a high degree where there is but a feeble spark of it innate; yet there are sundry things that may improve it even in minds full of natural bravery, and animate those who are naturally of an effeminate spirit to behave with a tolerable degree of resolution and fortitude in the defence of their country, I need not tell you that it is of great importance for this end that

* King William the Third, the deliverer of Britain from Popery and slavery, and the scourge of France and her haughty Grand Monarque.

† As a remarkable instance of this, I may point out to the public, that heroic youth, Col. Washington, whom I cannot but hope Providence has hitherto preserved in so signal a manner, for some important service to his country.

you should be at peace with God and your own conscience, and prepared for your future state. Guilt is naturally timorous, and often struck into a panic even with imaginary dangers; and an infidel courage, proceeding from a want of thought, or a stupid carelessness about our welfare through an immortal duration beyond the grave, is very unbecoming a man, or a Christian. The most important periods of our existence, my brethren, lie beyond the grave; and it is a matter of much more concern to us what will be our doom in the world to come, than what becomes of us in this. We are obliged to defend our country; and that is a sneaking, sordid soul indeed that can desert it at such a time as this; but this is not all; we are also obliged to take care of an immortal soul; a soul that must exist, and be happy or miserable through all the revolutions of eternal ages. This should be our first care; and when this is secured, death in its most shocking form, is but a release from a world of sin and sorrows, and an introduction into everlasting life and glory. But how can this be secured? Not by a course of impenitent sinning; not by a course of stupid carelessness and inaction; but by a vigorous and resolute striving; by serious and affectionate thoughtfulness about our condition, and by a conscientious and earnest attendance upon the means that God has graciously appointed for our recovery. But "we are sinners, heinous sinners against a God of infinite purity, and inexorable justice." Yes, we are so; and does not the posture of penitents then become us? Is not repentance, deep, broken-hearted repentance, a duty suitable to persons of our character? Undoubtedly it is; and therefore, O my countrymen, and particularly you brave men that are the occasion of this meeting, repent; fall down upon your knees before the provoked sovereign of heaven and earth, against whom you have rebelled.

Dissolve and melt in penitential sorrow at his feet; and he will tell you, *Arise, be of good cheer, your sins are forgiven you.* "But will repentance make atonement for our sins? Will our tears wash away their guilt? Will our sorrows merit forgiveness? No, my brethren, after you have done all, you are but unprofitable servants; after all your sorrows, and prayers, and tears, you deserve to be punished as obnoxious criminals; that would be a sorry government indeed, where repentance, perhaps extorted by the servile fear of punishment, would make atonement for every offence. But "I bring you glad tidings of great joy; to you is born a Saviour," a Saviour of no mean character; he is Christ the Lord. And have you never heard that he has "made reconciliation for iniquity, and brought in everlasting righteousness; that he suffered, the just for the unjust; that God is well-pleased for his righteousness sake," and declares himself willing to be reconciled to all that believe in him, and cheerfully accept him as their Saviour and Lord? Have you never heard these joyful tidings, oh guilty, self-condemned sinners? Sure you have. Then away to Jesus, away to Jesus, ye whose consciences are loaded with guilt; ye whose hearts fail within you at the thoughts of death, and the tribunal of divine justice; ye who are destitute of all personal righteousness to procure you a pardon, and recommend you to the divine favour; fly to Jesus on the wings of faith, all of you, of every age and character; for you all stand in the most absolute need of him; and without him you must perish, every soul of you. But alas! we find ourselves utterly unable to repent and fly to Jesus; our hearts are hard and unbelieving; and if the work depend upon us, it will for ever remain undone. True, my brethren, so the case is: but do you not know that this guilty earth is under the distillings of divine grace, and Jesus is entrusted with the influences of the Spirit, which can *work in you both to will and to do;* and that he is willing to *give his Holy Spirit to them that ask him ?* If you know this, you know where to go for strength; therefore, cry mightily to God for it. This I earnestly recommend to all my hearers, and especially to you, gentlemen, and others, that are now about generously to risk your lives for your country. Account this the best preparative to encounter danger and death; the best incentive to true, rational courage. What can do you a lasting injury while you have a reconciled God smiling upon you from on high, a peaceful conscience animating you from within, and a happy immortality just before you? Sure you may bid defiance to dangers and death in their most shocking forms. You have answered the end of this life already by preparing for another; and how can you depart off this mortal stage more honourably, than in the cause of liberty, of religion, and your country? But if any of you are perplexed with gloomy fears about this important affair, or conscious you are entirely unprepared for eternity, what must you do? Must you seek to prolong your life, and your time for preparation, by mean or unlawful ways, by a cowardly desertion of the cause of your country, and shifting for your little selves, as though you had no connection with society? Alas! this would but aggravate your guilt, and render your condition still more perplexed and discouraging. Follow the path of duty wherever it leads you, for it will be always the safest in the issue. Diligently improve the time you have to make your calling and election sure, and you have reason to hope for mercy, and grace to help in such a time of need. You will forgive me, if I have enlarged upon this point, even to a digression; for I thought it of great consequence to you all. I shall now proceed with more haste.

It is also of great importance to excite and keep up your courage in such an expedition, that we should be fully satisfied we engage in a righteous cause—and in a cause of great moment; for we cannot prosecute a suspected, or a wicked scheme which our own minds condemn, but with hesitation and timorous apprehensions; and we cannot engage with spirit and resolution in a trifling scheme, from which we can expect no consequences worth our vigorous pursuit. This Joab might have in view in his heroic advice to his brother: "Be of good courage," says he, "and let us play the men for our people, and for the cities of our God." *q. d.* We are engaged in a righteous cause; we are not urged on by an unbounded lust of power or riches, to encroach upon the rights and properties of others, and disturb our quiet neighbours; we act entirely upon the defensive, repel unjust violence, and avenge national injuries; we are fighting "for our people and for the cities of our God." We are also engaged in a cause of the utmost importance. We fight for our people; and what endearments are included in that significant word! our liberty, our estates, our lives! our king, our fellow-subjects, our venerable fathers, our tender children, the wives of our bosom, our friends, the sharers of our souls, our posterity to the latest ages! and who would not use his sword with an exerted arm when these lie at stake? But even these are not all; we fight *for the cities of our God*. God has distinguished us with a religion from heaven; and hitherto we have enjoyed the quiet and unrestrained exercise of it; he has condescended to be a God to our nation, and to honour our cities with his gracious presence, and the institutions of his worship, the means to make us wise, good, and happy; but now these most invaluable blessings lie at stake; these are the prizes for which we contend; and must it not excite all our active powers to the highest pitch of exertion? *Shall we tamely submit to idolatry and religious tyranny?* No, God forbid; *let us play the men, since we take up arms for our people, and the cities of our God.*

I need not tell you how applicable this advice, thus paraphrased, is to the design of the present associated company. The equity of our cause is most evident. The Indian savages have certainly no right to murder our fellow-subjects, living quiet and inoffensive in their habitations; nor have the French any power to hound them out upon us, nor to invade the territories belonging to the British crown, and secured to it by the faith of treaties. This is a clear case: and it is equally clear that you are engaged in a cause of the utmost importance. To protect your brethren from the most bloody barbarities—to defend the territories of the best of kings against the oppression and tyranny of arbitrary power—to secure the inestimable blessings of liberty, British liberty, from the chains of French slavery—to preserve your estates, for which you have sweat and toiled, from falling a prey to greedy vultures, Indians, priests, friars, and hungry Gallic slaves, or not more devouring flames—to guard your religion, the pure religion of Jesus, streaming uncorrupted from the sacred fountain of the Scriptures; the most excellent, rational, and divine religion that ever was made known to the sons of men; guard so dear, so precious a religion, (my heart grows warm while I mention it,) against ignorance, superstition, idolatry, tyranny over conscience, massacre, and fire, and sword, and all the mischiefs beyond expression, with which Popery is pregnant—to keep from the cruel hands of barbarians and Papists your wives, your children, your parents, your friends—to secure the liberties conveyed to you by your brave forefathers, and bought with their blood, that you may transmit them uncurtailed to your posterity. These are the blessings you contend for; all these will be torn from your eager grasp, if this colony should become a province of France. And Virginians! Britons! Christians! Protestants! if these names have any import or energy, will you not strike home in such a cause? Yes, this view of the matter must fire you into men; methinks the cowardly soul must tremble, lest the imprecation of the prophet fall upon him, "Cursed be the man that keepeth back his sword from blood." To this shocking, but necessary work, the Lord now calls you, and "cursed is he that doeth the work of the Lord deceitfully"—that will not put his hand to it when it is in his power, or that will not perform it with all his might.] Jer. xlviii. 10. The people of Meroz lay at home in ease, while their brethren were in the field, delivering their country from slavery. And what was their doom? "Curse ye Meroz, said the angel of the LORD, curse ye bitterly the inhabitants thereof, because they came not to the help of the Lord, to the help of the Lord against the mighty." Judges v. 23. I count myself happy that I see so many of you generously engaged in such a cause; but when I view it in this light, I cannot but be concerned that there are so few to join you. Are there but fifty or sixty persons in this large and populous country that can be spared from home for a few weeks upon so necessary a design, or that are able to bear the fatigues of it? Where are the friends of human nature? where the lovers of liberty and religion? Now is the time for you to come forth and show yourselves. Nay, where is the miser? let him arise and defend his Mammon, or he may soon have reason to cry out with Micah, "They have taken away my gods, and what have I more?" Where is the tender soul, on whom the passions of a husband, a father, or a son, have a peculiar energy? Arise, and march away; you had better be absent from those you love for a little while, than see them butchered before your eyes, or doomed to eternal poverty and slavery. The association now forming is not yet complete; and if it were, it would be a glorious thing to form another. Therefore, as an advocate for your king, your fellow-subjects, your country, your relatives, your earthly all, I do invite and entreat all of you, who have not some very sufficient reason against it, voluntarily to enlist, and go out with those brave souls, who have set you so noble an example. It will be more advantageous to you to go out in time, and more honourable to go out as volunteers, than be compelled to it by authority, when perhaps it may be too late.

The consideration of the justice and importance of the cause may also encourage you to hope that the Lord of Hosts will espouse it, and render its guardians successful, and return them in safety to the arms of their longing friends. The event, however, is in his hands; and it is much better there than if it were in yours. This thought is suggested with beautiful simplicity in the remaining part of my text: "The Lord do that which seemeth him good." This may be looked upon in various views; as,

1. It may be understood as the language of uncertainty and modesty; *q. d.*, Let us do all we can; but after all, the issue is uncertain; we know not, as yet, to what side God will incline the victory. Such language as this, my brethren, becomes us in all our undertakings; it sounds creature-like, and God approves of such self-diffident humility. But to indulge sanguine and confident expectations of victory, to boast when we put on our armour, as though we were putting it off, and to derive our high hopes from our own power and good management, without

any regard to the providence of God, this is too lordly and assuming for such feeble mortals; such insolence is generally mortified; and such a haughty spirit is the forerunner of a fall. Therefore, though I do not apprehend your lives will be in any great danger in your present expedition to range the frontiers, and clear them of the skulking Indians; yet I would not flatter you, my brethren, with too high hopes either of victory or safety. I cannot but entertain the pleasing prospect of congratulating you, with many of your friends, upon your successful expedition and safe return: and yet it is very possible our next interview may be in that strange, untried world beyond the grave. You are, however, in the hands of God, and he will deal with you *as it seemeth him good:* and I am persuaded you would not wish it were otherwise; you would not now practically retract the petition you have so often offered up, "thy will be done on earth as it is in heaven."

2. This language, *the Lord do as seemeth him good*, may be looked upon as expressive of a firm persuasion that the event of war entirely depends upon the providence of God; *q. d.*, Let us do our best; but after all, let us be sensible, that the success does not depend on us; that it is entirely in the hands of an all-ruling God. That God governs the world is a fundamental article of natural as well as revealed religion: it is no great exploit of faith to believe this: it is but a small advance beyond atheism and downright infidelity. I know no country upon earth where I should be put to the expense of argument to prove this. The heathens gave striking proofs of their belief of it, by their prayers, their sacrifices, their consulting oracles, before they engaged in war; and by their costly offerings and solemn thanksgivings after victory. And shall such a plain principle as this be disputed in a

Christian land? No; we all speculatively believe it; but that is not enough; let our spirits be deeply impressed with it, and our lives influenced by it: let us live in the world as in a territory of Jehovah's empire. Carry this impression upon your hearts into the wilderness, whither you are going. Often let such thoughts as these recur to your minds: I am the feeble creature of God; and blessed be his name, I am not cast off his hand as a disregarded orphan to shift for myself. My life is under his care; the success of this expedition is at his disposal. Therefore, O thou all-ruling God, I implore thy protection; I confide in thy care; I cheerfully resign myself, and the event of this undertaking, to thee. Which leads me to observe,

3. That these words, *the Lord do what seemeth him good,* may express an humble submission to the disposal of Providence, let the event turn out as it would; *q. d.,* We have not the disposal of the event, nor do we know what it will be: but Jehovah knows, and that is enough: we are sure he will do what is best, upon the whole; and it becomes us to acquiesce. Thus, my friends, do you resign and submit yourselves to the Ruler of the world in the present enterprise: he will order matters as he pleases; oh! let him do so by your cheerful consent. Let success or disappointment, let life or death, be the issue, still say, "Good is the will of the Lord, let him do what seemeth him good:" or if nature biasses your wishes and desires to the favourable side, as no doubt it will, still keep them within bounds, and restrain them in time, saying, after the example of Christ, *not my will, but thine be done.* You may wish, you may pray, you may strive, you may hope, for a happy issue; but you must submit; *be still, and know that he is God,* and will not be prescribed to, or suffer a rival in the government of the world he has made. Such

a temper will be of unspeakable service to you, and you may hope God will honour it with a remarkable blessing: for submission to his will is the readiest way to the accomplishment of our own.

4. These words, in their connection, may intimate, that let the event be what it will, it will afford us satisfaction to think that we have done the best we could. *q. d.*, We cannot command success; but let us do all in our power to obtain it, and we have reason to hope that in this way we shall not be disappointed: but if it should please God to render all our endeavours vain, still we shall have the generous pleasure to reflect, that we have not been accessary to the ruin of our country, but have done all we could for its deliverance.

So you, my brethren, have generously engaged in a disinterested scheme for your king and country: God does generally crown such noble undertakings with success, and you have encouragement to hope for it: but the cause you have espoused is the cause of a sinful, impenitent country; and if God, in righteous displeasure, should, on this account, blast your attempt, still you will have the pleasure of reflecting upon your generous views and vigorous endeavours, and that you have done your part conscientiously.

Having thus made some cursory remarks upon the sundry parts of the text, I shall now conclude with an address, first, to you all in general, and then to you, gentlemen, and others, who have been pleased to invite me to this service. I hope you will forgive my prolixity; my heart is full, the text is copious, and the occasion singular and important. I cannot, therefore, dismiss you with a short, hurrying discourse.

It concerns you all seriously to reflect upon your own sins, and the sins of your land, which have brought all these calamities upon us. If you believe that God governs the world, if you do not abjure him from being the Ruler of your country, you must acknowledge that all the calamities of war, and the threatening appearances of famine, are ordered by his Providence: there is no evil in a city or country but the Lord hath done it. And if you believe that he is a just and righteous Ruler, you must also believe that he would not thus punish a righteous or a penitent people.

We and our countrymen are sinners, aggravated sinners: God proclaims that we are such by his judgments now upon us, by withering fields and scanty harvests, by the sound of the trumpet and the alarm of war. Our consciences must also bear witness to the same melancholy truth. And if my heart were properly affected, I would concur with these undoubted witnesses; I would cry aloud and not spare; I would lift up my voice like a trumpet, to show you your transgressions and your sins. O my country, is not thy wickedness great, and thine iniquities infinite? Where is there a more sinful spot to be found upon our guilty globe? Pass over the land, take a survey of the inhabitants, inspect into their conduct, and what do you see? What do you hear? You see the gigantic forms of vice braving the skies, and bidding defiance to heaven and earth, while religion and virtue are obliged to retire, to avoid public contempt and insult: you see herds of drunkards swilling down their cups, and drowning all the man within them: you hear the swearer venting his fury against God and man, trifling with that name which prostrate angels adore, and imprecating that damnation, under which the hardiest devil in hell trembles and groans: you see Avarice hoarding up her useless treasures, dishonest Craft planning her schemes of unlawful gain, and Oppression unmercifully grinding the face of the poor.

you see Prodigality squandering her stores, Luxury spreading her table, and unmanning her guests; Vanity laughing aloud and dissolving in empty, unthinking mirth, regardless of God and our country, of time and eternity; Sensuality wallowing in brutal pleasures, and aspiring, with inverted ambition, to sink as low as her four-footed brethren to the stall: you see cards more in use than the Bible, the backgammon table more frequented than the table of the Lord, plays and romances more read than the history of the blessed Jesus. You see trifling and even criminal diversions become a serious business; the issue of a horse-race or a cock-fight more anxiously attended to than the fate of our country; or where these grosser forms of vice do not shock your senses, even there you often meet with the appearances of more refined impiety, which is equally dangerous; you hear the conversation of reasonable creatures, of candidates for eternity, engrossed by trifles, or vainly wasted on the affairs of time: these are the eternal subjects of conversation, even at the threshold of the house of God, and on the sacred hours devoted to his service: you see swarms of prayerless families all over our land; ignorant, vicious children, unrestrained and untaught by those to whom God and nature have entrusted their souls: you see thousands of poor slaves in a Christian country, the property of Christian masters, as they will be called, almost as ignorant of Christianity as when they left the wilds of Africa: you see the best religion in all the world abused, neglected, disobeyed, and dishonored by its professors; and you hear Infidelity scattering her ambiguous hints and suspicions, or openly attacking the Christian cause with pretended argument, with insult and ridicule: you see crowds of professed believers, that are practical Atheists; nominal Christians, that are real heathens; many abandoned slaves of sin, that yet pretended to be the servants of the holy Jesus: you see the ordinances of the gospel neglected by some, profaned by others, and attended upon by the generality with a trifling irreverence, and studied unconcernedness. Alas! who would think that those thoughtless assemblies we often see in our places of worship are met for such solemn purposes as to implore the pardon of their sins from an injured God, and to prepare for an all-important eternity? Alas! is that religion, for the propagation of which the Son of God laboured, and bled, and died; for which his apostles and thousands of martyrs have spent their strength, and shed their blood, and on which our eternal life depends—is that religion become such a trifle in our days, that men are hardly serious and in earnest when they attend upon its most solemn institutions? What multitudes lie in a deep sleep in sin all around us! You see them eager in the pursuits of the vanities of time, but stupidly unconcerned about the important realities of the eternal world just before them: few solicitous what shall become of them when all their connectious with earth and flesh must be broken, and they must take their flight into strange, unknown regions: few lamenting their sins: few crying for mercy and a new heart: few flying to Jesus, or justly sensible of the importance of a Mediator in a religion for sinners.

You may indeed see some degree of civility and benevolence towards men, and more than enough of cringing complaisance of worms to worms, of clay to clay, of guilt to guilt: but oh! how little sincere homage, how little affectionate veneration for the great Lord of heaven and earth! You may see something of duty to parents, of gratitude to benefactors, and obedience to superiors: but if God be a Father, where is his honour? If he be a Master, where is his fear? If he be our Benefactor, where is our gratitude to him? You may see here and there some instances of proud, self-righteous virtue, some appearances of morality: but oh! how rare is vital, evangelical religion, and true Christian morality, animated with the love of God, proceeding from a new heart, and a regard to the divine authority, full of Jesus, full of regard to him as a Mediator, on whose account alone our duties can find acceptance! O blessed Redeemer! what little necessity, what little use do the sinners of our country find for thee in their religion! How many discourses are delivered, how many prayers offered, how many good works are performed, in which there is scarce anything of Christ! And this defect renders them all but shining sins, glittering crimes. How few pant and languish for thee, blessed Jesus! and can never be contented with their reformation, with their morality, with their good works, till they obtain an interest in thy righteousness, to sanctify all, to render all acceptable! You may see children sensible of their dependence on their parents for their subsistence; you see multitudes sensible of their dependence on clouds, and sun, and earth, for provision for man and beast: but how few sensible of their dependence upon God, as the great Original, the *primum mobile* of natural causes, and the various wheels of the universe? You see even the dull ox knows his owner, and the stupid ass his master's crib; you see the workings of gratitude even in your dog, which welcomes you home with a thousand fondling motions; but how is Jehovah's government and agency practically denied in his own territories! How few receive the blessings of life as from his hand, and make him proper returns of gratitude! You see a withered, ravaged country around you, languishing under the frowns of an angry God; but how few earnest prayers, how few penitential groans do you hear! Pass over the land, and bring me intelligence, is not this the general character of our country? I know there are some happy exceptions; and I hope sundry such might be produced from among you: but is not this the prevailing character of a great majority? Does not one part or other of it belong to the generality? The most generous charity cannot hope the contrary, if under any scriptural or rational limitations. May it not be said of the men of Virginia, as well as those of Sodom, *they are wicked, and sinners before the Lord exceedingly?* And thus, alas! it has been for a long time: our country has sinned on securely for above one hundred and fifty years; and one age has improved upon the vices of another. And can a land always bear up under such a load of accumulated wickedness? Can God always suffer such a race of sinners to go unpunished from generation to generation? May we not fear that our iniquities are now just full, and that he is about to thunder out his awful mandate to the executioners of his vengeance, "Put ye in the sickle; for the harvest is ripe; come, get ye down, for the press is full, the vats overflow; for their wickedness is great."

And is there no relief for a sinking country? Or is it too late to administer it? Is our wound incurable that refuseth to be healed? No, blessed be God; if you now turn every one of you from your evil ways, if you mourn over your sins, and turn to the Lord with your whole hearts, then your country will yet recover. God will appear for us, and give a prosperous turn to our affairs; he has assured us of this in his own word, "At what instant," says he, "I shall speak concerning a nation, and concerning a kingdom, to pluck up, and to pull down, and to destroy it; if that nation, against whom I have pronounced, turn from their evil, I will repent of the evil that I thought to do unto them." Jer. xviii. 7, 8. Therefore, my brethren, as we have all rebelled, let us all join in unanimous repentance and a thorough reformation. Not only your eternal salvation requires it, but also the preservation of your country, that is now bleeding with the wounds you have given it by your sins. The safety of these our friends, who are now engaged in so generous a design, requires it: for an army of saints, or of heroes, cannot defend a guilty, impenitent people, ripe for the judgments of God. If you would be everlastingly happy, and escape the vengeance of eternal fire, or (to mention what may perhaps have more weight with some of you,) if you would preserve yourselves, your families, your posterity, from poverty, from slavery, ignorance, idolatry, torture, and death; if you would save yourselves and them from all the infernal horrors of popery, and the savage tyranny of a mongrel race of French and Indian conquerors: in short, if you would avoid all that is terrible, and enjoy every thing that is dear and valuable, repent and turn to the Lord. This is the only cure for our wounded country; and if you refuse to administer it in time, prepare to perish in its ruins. If you go on impenitent in sin, you may expect not only to be damned for ever, but (what is more terrible to some of you) to fall into the most extreme outward distress. You will have reason to fear not only the loss of heaven, which some of you perhaps think little of, but the loss of your estates, that lie so near your hearts. And will you not repent when you are pressed to it from so many quarters at once?

And now, my brethren, in the last place, I have a few parting words to offer to you who are more particularly concerned on this occasion; and I am sure I shall address you with as much affectionate benevolence as you could wish.

My first and leading advice to you is, Labour to conduct this expedition in a religious manner. Methinks this should not seem strange counsel to creatures entirely dependent upon God, and at his disposal. As you are an independent company of volunteers, under officers of your own choosing, you may manage your affairs more according to your own inclination than if you had enlisted upon the ordinary footing: and I hope you will improve this advantage for the purposes of religion. Let prayer to the God of your life be your daily exercise. When retirement is safe, pour out your hearts to him in secret; and when it is practicable, join in prayer together morning and evening in your camp. How acceptable to Heaven must such an unusual offering be, from that desert wilderness! Maintain a sense of divine Providence upon your hearts, and resign yourselves and all your affairs into the hands of God. You are engaged in a good cause, the cause of your people, and the cities of your God; and therefore you may the more boldly commit it to him, and pray and hope for his blessing. I would fain hope there is no necessity to take precautions against vice among such a select company: but lest there should, I would humbly recommend it to you to make this one of the articles of your association, before you set out: That every form of vice shall be severely discountenanced; and if you think proper, expose the offender to some pecuniary or corporeal punishment. It would be shocking indeed, and I cannot bear the thought, that a company, formed upon such generous principles, should commit or tolerate open wickedness among them: and I hope this caution is needless to you all, as I am sure it is to sundry of you.

And now, my dear friends, and the friends of your neglected country, *In the name of the Lord lift up your banners; be of good courage, and play the men for the people, and the cities of your God: and the Lord do what seemeth him good.* Should I now give vent to the passions of my heart, and become a speaker for my country, methinks I should even overwhelm you with a torrent of good wishes, and prayers from the hearts of thousands. May the Lord of Hosts, the God of the armies of Israel, go forth along with you! *May he teach your hands to war, and gird you with strength to battle!* May he bless you with a safe return, and long life, or a glorious death in the bed of honour, and a happy immortality! May he guard and support your anxious families and friends at home, and return you victorious to their longing arms! May all the blessings your hearts can wish attend you wherever you go! These are wishes and prayers of my heart, and thousands concur in them: and we cannot but cheerfully hope they will be granted, through Jesus Christ. Amen.

SERMON LXII.

THE CRISIS, OR THE UNCERTAIN DOOM OF KINGDOMS AT PARTICULAR TIMES.*

JONAH III. 9.—*Who can tell if God will turn and repent, and turn away from his fierce anger that we perish not?*

A STATE of uncertainty, a suspense between hope and fear, about a matter of importance, is a very painful and anxious state. And by how much the more important and interesting the matter, by so much the more distressing is the uncertainty. Now what can be more important, what more interesting, than our country? Our country is a word of the highest and most endearing import: it includes our friends and relatives, our liberty, our property, our religion; in short, it includes our earthly all. And when the fate of our country, and all that it includes, is dreadfully doubtful; when we are tossed and agitated between the alternate waves of hope and fear; when, upon taking a view of the present posture of our affairs, we can only ask with painful solicitude, *what will be the end of these things?* and when even the consideration of the divine mercy upon our repentance cannot give us any assurance of deliverance in a political capacity, but only a per-

---

* Preached at Hanover, Virginia, October 28th, 1756, being the day appointed by the Synod of New York, to be observed as a general fast on accouut of the present war with France.

adventure, *who can tell but God will turn and repent!* when this, I say, is our situation, every mind that has the least thought, must be agitated with many eager, dubious expectations. This is the present situation of our country; and this was the state of that populous and magnificent city of Nineveh, when the words of my text were first spoken.

Nineveh was the metropolis of the Assyrian empire: and how prodigiously populous it was, you may calculate from hence, that it contained more than six score thousand children, that were so young that they could not distinguish the right hand from the left: and the number of adults, in proportion to these, must be vast indeed. Its extent was no less than three days' journey. Profane authors tell us, it was forty-seven miles in circumference; and that, notwithstanding its vast extent, it was surrounded with lofty walls and towers: the walls two hundred feet high, and so very wide, that three chariots might drive on them abreast: and the towers two hundred feet in height, and fifteen hundred in number. But what became of this mighty Nineveh at last? Alas! it was turned into a heap of rubbish. Divine patience was at length wearied out; and though the vengeance denounced by Jonah was suspended, yet that foretold by Nahum was dreadfully executed.

And what was the cause of this execution, and that denunciation? The cause of both was sin; national, epidemical sin, against an unknown God, the God of Israel; I say, against an unknown God; for Nineveh was a heathen city, not favoured with the knowledge of the true God by supernatural revelation; much less with the gospel, that most perfect dispensation of divine grace towards the sons of men. The Ninevites could not sin with such horrid aggravations as we: and yet even they could sin to such a degree, as to become utterly intolerable. They sinned against the light of nature, and that sufficed to bring down remediless destruction upon them. This is mentioned as the cause of the divine displeasure in Jonah's commission. *Arise, go to Nineveh, that great city, and cry against it: for their wickedness is come up before me.* Jonah i. 2. Their wickedness has reached to heaven; and can no longer be endured. But before the fatal blow falls, let them have one warning more—Oh! how astonishing are the grace and patience of God towards a guilty people! Even when their wickedness has scaled the heavens, and come up before him, he condescends to give them another warning, and suspends the blow for at least forty days longer, to see if they will at length repent.

Jonah, having tried in vain to disengage himself from the message, is at length constrained to undertake it; and with the solemn and awful gait of a prophet, he walks from street to street, making this alarming proclamation: *Yet forty days, and Nineveh shall be overthrown.* Jonah iii. 4. This was the substance of his sermon: but no doubt he spoke much more than is here recorded. No doubt, he produced his credentials from the God of Israel, and gave them the history of his reluctance to accept the commission; of the storm that pursued him, while attempting to make his escape; of his miraculous preservation in the belly of a fish, and his deliverance thence. No doubt, he also let them know what was the cause of the divine displeasure against them, viz.; their national vices and irreligion; and he perhaps intimated, that repentance was the only possible method of escaping the threatened destruction. It is plain, however, they understood him in this sense; for they actually did repent; but whether it was from the light of nature, or from

Jonah's preaching, they received this direction, does not appear.*

And now, while the prophet is delivering his message, their consciences tell them how ripe they are for this dreadful doom; and the Spirit of God no doubt concurs, and impresses the conviction upon their hearts. Now, methinks, I see eager, gazing crowds following the prophet from street to street; paleness in every countenance, and horror in every heart. Now the man of business remits his eager pursuits: the man of pleasure is struck with a damp in his thoughtless career: pride and grandeur lower their haughty airs; and a general horror spreads from the cottage to the throne. The people agree upon a public fast: and when the emperor hears of the awful message, he issues forth his royal edict, requiring an universal abstinence from food, and a deep repentance and reformation. He enjoins all to put on sackcloth, the habit of mourners and penitents in those ages and countries; and laying aside his royal robes, and descending from his throne, he puts on the mortifying dress himself, and lies in the dust. That the humiliation might be the more moving and affecting, he orders, according to the custom of the time upon such occasions, that even the beasts, the flocks, and herds, should be restrained from

* Upon second thoughts, it seems to me that God thought it most proper to be upon the reserve upon this point; and that he did not reveal to Jonah his gracious design to pardon them upon their repentance; nor Jonah to the Ninevites. That God did not reveal it to Jonah, seems probable from hence, that he had some expectation the city would be destroyed, though he saw their repentance; and hence he waited for the event, and was greatly chagrined when disappointed. He seemed indeed to have presumed what the event would be, from the known mercy and patience of God, (ch. iv. 2,) but this implies that he had no express revelation for it. That Jonah did not reveal this to the Ninevites appears from my text, where they speak of the event as dreadfully uncertain, even though they should repent.

food, and compelled to join, as it were, with more guilty men, in the general humiliation, and in deprecating that vengeance which was about to fall upon man and beast.

We have now a very moving sight before us; a gay magnificent city in mourning; thousands mourning in every street: king and subjects, high and low, old and young, all covered in sackcloth and rolling in ashes. And their repentance does not wholly consist in these ceremonies: the royal proclamation further requires them to *cry mightily unto God; and turn every one from his evil way.* They are sensible of the propriety and necessity of prayer, earnest prayer to God, and a reformation of life, as well as of afflicting themselves with fasting. The light of nature directed them to this as the only method of deliverance, if deliverance was possible. The case of such a people looks hopeful. That so many thousands should be brought to repentance by one warning, the first and only warning they had ever received from a prophet of the true God; a prophet that was a contemptible stranger from the despised nation of the Jews; this certainly appears promising.

Alas! brethren, our countrymen are not so easily brought to repentance: no, this is not an easy thing among us. Ten thousand warnings, not only from conscience, from divine providence, from this very Jonah, and the other prophets of the Old Testament, but also from the gospel, that clear and perfect revelation; I say, ten thousand warnings, thus peculiarly enforced, have not so much effect upon our country, this Christian, this Protestant country, as one short warning from the mouth of Jonah had upon a city of heathens and idolators. All along as I have been considering this case, I could not cast out of my mind that dreadful declaration of Christ, "The men of Nineveh shall rise in judgment against this generation, and shall condemn it; because they repented at the preaching of Jonas; and behold a greater than Jonas is here." Matt. xii. 41. Nineveh never had such loud calls to repentance, and such a rich plenty of all the means of grace, as Virginia. The meanest in the kingdom of heaven, *i. e.*, the meanest Christian under the full revelation of the gospel, is greater in spiritual knowledge, not only than Jonah, but than John the Baptist, the greatest prophet that ever was born of a woman. And therefore, I may accommodate these words to us, *Behold, a greater than Jonas is here.* Here are clearer discoveries of the will of God, and stronger motives and encouragements to repentance, than ever Jonah could afford the men of Nineveh. But alas! where is our repentance! Where are our humiliation and reformation! Shall the light of nature, and one warning from a prophet, bring the heathens to the knee before God; and shall not the gospel, and all its loud calls, have that effect upon a Christian land! Shall Nineveh repent in sackcloth and ashes; and shall Virginia sin on still, impenitent, thoughtless, luxurious and gay? Alas! what will be the end of this?

The case of the Ninevites, who were brought to repentance so readily, and so generally, looks hopeful, and seems to promise them an exemption from the threatened vengeance. And yet, so sensible was the king of Nineveh of their demerit, and the insufficiency of their repentance to make atonement for their sins, that he is doubtful, after all, what would be the consequence. *Who can tell*, says he; who knoweth, *if God will turn and repent, and turn away from the fierceness of his anger, that we perish not!* *q. d.*, Let us humble ourselves ever so low, we are not assured we shall escape; vengeance may, after all, seize us; and we may be made monuments to all the world of the justice of the King of kings, and the dreadful consequences of national impiety and vice. His uncertainty in this matter might proceed from the just sense he had of the intolerable height to which the national wickedness had arrived, and of the strictness of the divine justice. He knew, that even in his own government, it would have very bad consequences, if all crimes should be forgiven, or pass unpunished, upon the repentance of the offender; and he forms the same judgment concerning the divine government. Indeed, it is natural to a penitent, while he has a full view of his sins, in all their aggravations, and of the justice of God, to question whether such sins can be forgiven by so holy a God. He is apt even to fall into an extreme in this respect. It does not now appear so easy a thing to him to obtain a pardon, as it once did, when he had no just views of his guilt. Now it appears a great thing indeed; so great, that he can hardly think it possible. Or the uncertainty of the king of Nineveh, in this point, might proceed from Jonah's being so reserved upon it. He might have had no commission from God to promise them deliverance upon their repentance; but he was to warn them, and then leave them in the hands of a gracious and righteous God, to deal with them according to his pleasure. This tended to make them more sensible that they lay at mercy, and that he might justly do what he pleased with them. The event indeed showed there was a condition implied in the threatening; and that God did secretly intend to spare them, upon their repentance. But this was wisely concealed, and it was sufficient that the event should make it known. It is certain that national as well as personal repentance, may sometimes come too late; and that sometimes the punishment may fall by way of chastisement, even when the repentance is sincere, and the sin is forgiven, so that it shall not bring on the destruction of the sinner in the eternal world.

But we may well suppose a heathen monarch, who probably had no instruction but from Jonah's short warning, would be much at a loss about these things. From this uncertainty of his about the fate of his empire, we may infer this truth which I intend to illustrate with regard to ourselves, viz.:

That sometimes a nation may be in such a situation, that no man can tell what will be the issue; or whether it shall be delivered from the threatened vengeance, or destroyed.

But though the king of Ninevah was uncertain about this; yet, there was one thing that he was very certain of, viz., That if there was any possibility of escape, it was to be hoped for only in the way of earnest prayer to God, general humiliation and reformation. This is evident from the connection of the context. "Let man and beast," says he, "be covered with sackcloth, and cry mightily to God, yea, let them turn every one from his evil way; who can tell if God will turn and repent, and turn away from his fierce anger, that we perish not!" *i. e.*, Who can tell but he may turn away from his fierce anger, in case we turn from our evil ways, and humble ourselves before him? If we do not reform and humble ourselves, the case is dreadfully plain; any one can tell that we cannot escape; there is not so much as a peradventure for it; unavoidable destruction will be our doom, beyond all question. But if we repent, who knows what that may do? "Who knows but God may repent, and turn from the fierceness of his wrath!" If there be any hope at all, it is in this way. This he learned from the light of nature, if not from Jonah's preaching. And this suggests another seasonable truth, which, if my time will allow, I shall also illustrate, viz.:

That when a nation is in such a state, that no man can certainly determine what will be its doom, if there be any possible hope, it is only in the way of general humiliation, earnest prayer, and public reformation.

To prevent mistakes I have one thing more to observe upon the text; and that is, that when God is said to repent, it only signifies that the visible conduct of divine Providence has some resemblance to the conduct of men when they repent; and not that he is capable of repentance in a proper sense, or of that changeableness, imperfect knowledge, sorrow, and self-accusation, which repentance among men implies. When men repent that they have made a thing, they destroy it; and therefore, when God destroyed man by a deluge, he is said to repent that he made him; and when he deposed Saul, it is said, he repented that he had made him king. When men do not execute their threatenings, it is supposed they repent of them; and hence, when God does not inflict the threatened evil, he is supposed to repent of the evil; *i. e.*, he acts as men do when they repent of their purposes; though when he made the denunciation, he well knew the event, and determined not to execute it, upon the repentance of the offenders. So with regard to Nineveh, there was no proper repentance in God, but an uniform, consistent purpose. He purposed to denounce his vengeance against that city; and he did so: he purposed and foresaw their repentance; and it accordingly came to pass: he purposed to spare them upon their repentance; and he did so. All this is very consistent, and implies no proper repentance in God; for in this sense, "God is not a man that he should repent," Numb. xxiii. 19; but "he is in one mind, and who can turn him? and what his soul desireth, even that he doeth." Job xxiii. 13.

I now enter upon the illustration of the first reference upon the text, viz.:

I. That sometimes a nation may be in such a situation,

that no man can tell what will be their doom; whether the threatened vengeance will fall upon them, or whether they shall escape.

This, we have seen, was the situation of Nineveh, though now lying in deep repentance, and not in danger, as far as appears from any visible cause. Thousands were now mourning, praying, and reforming; and we have no account of an enemy preparing to invade them. And if Nineveh, in this situation, which seems so promising, was, notwithstanding, in such danger that no man could determine what would be their doom, alas! what shall we say of Virginia and the kingdoms to which we belong, when they are neither penitent before God, nor safe from the arms of a powerful and victorious enemy? If the repentance of the Ninevites gave them no assurance of escape, but only a peradventure, *Who can tell if God will turn from his fierce anger?* Certainly our doom must, at best, be equally uncertain, when, instead of repentance, reformation, and mighty crying to God, we see the generality impenitent, unreformed, and prayerless still. I would not damp you with unmanly fears, but I cannot help saying that our doom is dismally uncertain. I know not what a provoked God intends to do with us and our nation. I have my hopes indeed; but they are balanced, and sometimes over-balanced, with fearful and gloomy apprehensions. But,

1. The issue of the present war will appear dreadfully uncertain, if we consider the present posture of affairs.

We are engaged in war with a powerful, exasperated enemy: and blood is streaming by sea and land. Some decisive blow will probably be struck ere long: but on what party it will fall, and what will be the issue of this struggle and commotion among the nations, is an anxious uncertainty. It seems but too likely, though it strikes me with horror to admit the thought, that a provoked God intends to scourge us with the rod of France, and therefore gives surprising success to her arms. Who can tell, but the king of France may have the same commission given him by that God whom we and our mother country have so grievously offended, as was given to the Assyrian monarch, in Isaiah's time, when God speaks of him as his rod, to chastise his own people, and as acting by a commission from him, though he neither knew or designed it, but only intended to gratify his own ambition? "O Assyrian, the rod of mine anger, and the staff in their hand is mine indignation. I will send him against a hypocritical nation; and against the people of my wrath will I give him a charge to take the spoil, and to take the prey, and to tread them down like the mire of the streets. Howbeit, he meaneth not so; neither doth his heart think so: but it is in his heart to destroy, and cut off nations not a few." But at the same time it is foretold, that "When the LORD hath performed his whole work upon Mount Zion, and on Jerusalem, I will punish the fruit of the stout heart of the king of Assyria, and the glory of his high looks." Isa. x. 5, 6, 7, 12. And if the same commission be given to the king of France, I doubt not but his end will be the same. When God has finished his work of correction with this rod, he will break it, or burn it in the fire. The like commission was given to Nebuchadnezzar, king of Babylon; and when he, and his son, and his son's son, had served as the executioners of God's wrath upon his people, and the neighbouring nations, they and the Babylonian empire were destroyed together. "Thus, saith the LORD of hosts, because ye have not heard my words, behold I will send and take all the families of the north, saith the LORD, and Nebuchadnezzar, the king of Babylon, my servant, (*my servant*, to execute this my work of correction and of vengeance,) and I will bring them against this land and against the inhabitants thereof, and against all these nations round about, and I will utterly destroy them, and make them an astonishment, and a hissing, and perpetual desolations. But it shall come to pass, when seventy years are accomplished, (the space of time allotted for his power, and the correction of God's people,) that I will punish the king of Babylon, and that nation, saith the Lord, for their iniquity, and the land of the Chaldeans, and will make it perpetual desolations." Jer. xxv. 8, 12, 14. Thus you see it is no uncommon thing for God, when transgressions are come to the full, to raise up some power to perform his work of chastisement and vengeance, and render it victorious and irresistible, till that work is done, and then to crush it in its turn. And whether divine Providence is now about to employ the power of France for this purpose, is a dreadful uncertainty. We hope, indeed, matters will take a more favourable turn; but the present posture of affairs, and particularly the rapid conquests of that power, which is now become so formidable even in America, give us reason to fear this may be the event, and that matters are now ripening fast for this terrible result.

I may add, that we have reason to fear from this disposition and conduct of many among ourselves, some in high places have been suspected of treachery or cowardice, or at least bad conduct. A spirit of security, sloth, and cowardice, evidently prevails; nothing great is so much as attempted, much less executed. We have also many black foreigners among ourselves, as may justly alarm our fears. Now if the French should invade our frontiers; if the Indians that are now neuter, or in the British interests, should join with them, and with those tribes that are already so active upon their side; and if their united forces should pour down upon us, and meet with welcome reception and assistance from so powerful an enemy among themselves; I say, should this be the case, I need not tell you what unexampled scenes of blood, cruelty, and devastation would open in our country. This may not be the event; and I hope and pray it may not: but it is not so improbable as we could wish; much less is it impossible. Who knows but this may actually be the consequence!

And if the natural allies of France should form a confederacy against our mother country, and attack her with their united strength, how terrible would be the consequence probably be, both to her and to us, especially if the protestant powers should not vigorously concur with us against them! This event may not happen; and I hope and pray it may not: but it is not so unlikely as one could wish. But,

2. The event of the present war will appear dismally doubtful, if we consider some Scripture prophecies, particularly in Daniel and the Revelation.

I cannot pretend to enter deeply into this subject at present; a subject that has filled so many volumes, and employed the thoughts and pens of so many great men. It will be sufficient to my present purpose to observe,

(1.) That the idolatrous persecuting power of Popery, seated at Rome, is undoubtedly meant by the little horn in Daniel, (Dan. vii. 8,) that rose up out of the Roman empire, when it was divided into ten kingdoms by the barbarous nations that broke in upon it: a horn which had a mouth, speaking great things; which made war with the saints, and prevailed against them; a horn which speaks great things against the Most High, and wears out the saints of the Most High; and thinks to change times and laws; *i. e.*, to alter and corrupt the ordinances of God, ver. 24, 25. The same idolatrous, persecuting power, is also intended in Revelation (Rev. xiii.) by the beast with seven heads and ten horns, that had a mouth given him, speaking great things and blasphemies; and he opened his mouth in blasphemy against God, &c., and it was given unto him to make war with the saints, and to overcome them; and power was given him over all kindreds, and tongues, and nations; and all that dwell on the earth shall worship him, whose names are not written in the Lamb's book of life. The same idolatrous and persecuting power is intended likewise by the woman (Rev. xvii.) sitting upon a scarlet-coloured beast, having seven heads and ten horns; full of names of blasphemy, and drunk with the blood of the saints, and with the blood of the martyrs of Jesus. Protestant commentators generally agree in this application of these prophecies to the Papal power; but I cannot take time to lay before you the full evidence upon which they proceed. However, I cannot but just observe, that the angel-interpreter expressly tells St. John, that this woman was that great city which then reigned over the kings of the earth, (ver. 18,) which undoubtedly means the city of Rome, that was then the seat of universal empire. But,

(2.) The time of the reign of this idolatrous and persecuting power is determined in prophetic numbers, both in Daniel and the Revelation. In Daniel, it is said, the saints shall be given into the hand of the horns until a time, times, and the dividing of time, Dan. vii. 25; and that he shall scatter the power of the holy people for a time, times, and half a time. Dan. xii. 7. In the Revelation, we are told that the church of Christ, represented by a woman, shall continue in the wilderness, *i. e.*, in a state of oppression and persecution, under the Popish power, for a time, times, and half a time; Rev.

xii. 14; *that the outer court of the temple and the holy city,* another emblem of the true church of Christ, *shall be given to the Gentiles, i. e.*, subjected to a power no better than heathen, *and by them trodden under foot forty-two months;* that the church should be fed in the wilderness for *twelve hundred and sixty days,* Rev. xii. 6; and *that the two witnesses, i. e.*, the small remnant of the faithful who shall retain the purity of the gospel, and witness against the corruptions of the church of Rome, *shall prophesy twelve hundred and sixty days in sackcloth.* These are but different representations of the same period: and in order to understand them, you are to observe, that, in this calculation, a day signifies a year; and therefore twelve hundred and sixty days are twelve hundred and sixty years. A month consists of thirty such days, *i. e.*, thirty years; for the months among the ancients were invariably made up of but thirty days, as their year consisted only of three hundred and sixty days. Now forty-two months, multiplied by thirty, just make twelve hundred and sixty years. So time signifies one year, times two years, and half a time, or the dividing of time, half a year: now one year and two years, making three years, and the half year added to them, make three years and a half. These three years and a half contain thrice three hundred and sixty years, and the half of three hundred and sixty, (viz., one hundred and eighty,) which make exactly twelve hundred and sixty years. So that all these calculations amount to the same thing, viz., twelve hundred and sixty years. This is undoubtedly the duration of the Popish tyranny, and of the oppression of the saints, and the cause of truth. Now, if we could find out when it begun, whether when the Pope usurped and exercised the substance of ecclesiastical authority, as universal bishop, which was in the fifth century; or when he was formally invested with that authority by the Emperor Phocas, A. D. 606; or when he was made a secular prince, and had a civil authority added to his ecclesiastical, by Pipin, king of France, A. D. 756; I say, if we could find out when this space of twelve hundred and sixty years began, we could easily find out when it will end: and this would help us to determine what will be the event of the present war, whether the oppression of the Protestant cause, or the downfall of the bloody power of Popery, that has undoubtedly held the world in ignorance, idolatry, and slavery, for above a thousand years. But after all the searches I can make, I am not able to form a certain determination upon the point; and commentators differ so widely among themselves, that I have received but little light from them. I must therefore leave you in that uncertainty in which I am myself; and consequently destitute of light from these predictions concerning the event of the present war. But,

(3.) Though this period of twelve hundred and sixty years is to be, all through, a series of tyranny and persecution; and the cause of truth and its advocates are continually under oppression; yet there is a short space in this period, I suppose, from the calculation in the Revelation, (Rev. xi. 9,) about three years and a half, in which the cause of truth shall seem entirely suppressed, and its friends utterly extinct; so that there will be no human probability of their revival, any more than of a human body that has lain dead three days and a half. And upon this the Popish powers shall exult and triumph, as if they had obtained an entire and lasting victory. This is probably the time referred to in Daniel, (chap. xii. 1,) as "a time of trouble, such as never was since there was a nation, even to that same time." During the rest of the twelve hundred and sixty days, the witnesses prophesied in sackcloth, in a state of mourning and persecution: but in this period they are killed; and their dead bodies lie unburied and insulted, in the street of the great city, *i. e.*, in the Roman territories: "and they that dwell upon the earth shall rejoice over them, and make merry, and shall send gifts one to another." Rev. xi. 7–10. This is a melancholy time indeed for the few servants of Jesus Christ. And who can tell whether it be past, or whether it be future, and the issue of the present war? I could easily lay before you the opinions of good and great men on this point; but they are so various, that they could not bring you to any certain conclusion upon it. Some suppose it past; and that it was either a little before the reformation, when the Albigenses and Waldenses, who had been witnesses for a long time against the corruptions of Popery, were, in appearance, utterly extirpated by a series of bloody persecutions, at the Pope's instigation: and if this was the period, then the resurrection of the witnesses, and their being caught up into heaven, must signify the revival of their cause at the Reformation, and the raising up of Luther, Calvin, and other reformers, in the same spirit. Or, as others suppose, this melancholy time was about the year 1550, when the persecution raged in England, under Queen Mary, and the civil wars in France, Germany, and the Low Countries, on account of religion, seemed to threaten the utter extinction of the Protestant cause. Those that suppose this time is past, have sundry arguments, that are at least plausible, to support their opinion; and if I have any opinion at all, in so doubtful a matter, I incline to this.

There are others of no small judgment in such matters, that apprehend this melancholy period is yet to come; and they too have their reasons which I cannot now mention.

And if this be the case, who can tell but the melancholy time is now at hand, and that the present commotions in Europe are working up to it? This is certain, it will be introduced by war; for we are expressly told, that when the two witnesses have finished their testimony, "the beast shall make war against them, and shall overcome them and kill them," Rev. xi. 7; and that just before the pouring out of the seventh vial, which shall utterly destroy the popish powers, and introduce the kingdom of Christ, the kings of the earth, by popish instigation, shall gather themselves together to the battle of the great day of God almighty, in a place called Armageddon, (Rev. xvi. 13, 14, 16,) or Megiddo, where good Josiah, the great reformer of the Jewish religion, was slain. "I saw the beast," says St. John, "and the kings of the earth and their armies, gathered together to make war against him that sat on the horse," *i. e.*, against Jesus Christ and his army. Rev. xix. 19. Popery will die hard, and its last struggles will be very violent. It will collect all its forces, and make a bold push to recover its lost authority; and this will undoubtedly be attended with much slaughter. But whether it will be victorious in the first attack, and at this time slay the witnesses, or whether the Lamb and his army shall immediately prevail, as he certainly will at last,* this seems uncertain. Now who can tell, but the present war is the commencement of this grand decisive conflict between the Lamb and the beast, *i. e.*, between the Protestant and the Popish powers? The Pope first received his principality and secular authority from Pipin, one of the kings of France; and there seems to be something congruous in it, that France should also take the lead, and be, as it were, the general of his forces in this last decisive conflict

---

* See the final issue of this grand decisive conflict, described in most lively terms, Rev. xix. from ver. 11. *ad fin.*

for the support of that authority. This is also remarkable, and almost peculiar to the present war, viz., That Protestants and papists are not blended together in it by promiscuous alliances; but France and her allies are all Papists; and Britain and her allies are all Protestants; and consequently whatever party fall, the religion of that party is like to fall too. If France and her allies should prove victorious, then we may conclude the period for slaying the witnesses is just coming. But if Britain and her allies should be victorious, then we may conclude that time is past, and the time is just come, when it shall be proclaimed, *Babylon is fallen! is fallen!* but all this is uncertain, at least to me, till the event make it plain; and for that we must wait with anxious suspense.

But here I cannot help mentioning one thing to mitigate your anxieties; and that is, that however bloody and desolating this last conflict may be, it will bring about the most glorious and happy revolution that ever was in the world. It will change the face of things, introduce "a new heaven and a new earth, wherein righteousness shall dwell;" and it will new-model the kingdoms of the world, "and they shall become the kingdoms of our Lord and of his Christ; and he shall reign for ever," Rev. xi. 15; then Satan shall be bound and Christ shall reign in the hearts of men, a thousand years. How remarkable upon this head are the prophecies of Daniel, above two thousand years ago! "I beheld," says he, "and the same horn made war with the saints, and prevailed against them until the Ancient of days came;" *i. e.*, came to give dominion, and glory, and a kingdom to the Son of man; Dan. vii. 21, 22: and then judgment was given to the saints of the Most High; and the time came that the saints possessed the kingdom, ver. 13, 14. They shall be uppermost in their turn, and be finally triumphant. All the other empires and kingdoms of the world have been subject to revolutions, passed from hand to hand, and at length fallen to pieces; but this, says Daniel, is a kingdom which shall never be destroyed; a kingdom that shall not be left to other people; but it shall break in pieces and consume all the kingdoms that were before it, and it shall stand for ever. Dan. ii. 44. Hail, happy period! how long wilt thou delay? Lord Jesus, let thy kingdom come; let it come, though to make way for it, many thrones must totter that are now the supporters of Antichrist: let it come, though many kingdoms should be overturned, and many countries stream with blood; though we and millions more should be crushed in the grand revolution. See, brethren, the happy result of all the commotions that are or have been on this restless globe: see to what a glorious end they all tend! And who would not willingly live a while longer in this world of sin and sorrow, and share in calamities of war, and all the plagues reserved for the latter times, if he may but see this blessed period? But if we should not be so happy as to see it with mortal eyes, such of us as *die in the Lord* shall receive the welcome intelligence of it in heaven, and rejoice in it as much as its proper subjects on earth. You will forgive me if I have dwelt too long upon this new and curious subject. I shall now proceed with more haste. Therefore,

3. The event of the present war, and the doom of our country and nation, will appear dreadfully uncertain if we consider our national guilt and impenitence.

Let Atheists and Epicureans say what they please, it is an eternal truth, which all the world will be made to know at last, that Jehovah is the Ruler of the universe; that the fate of kingdoms is in his hands; that he is the sovereign Arbiter of war, and determines victory as he pleases. It is also certain that rewards and punishments are as essential to his government, as they are to all other governments. In the world to come he will reward or punish individuals, according to their personal works; and in the present world he will reward or punish nations, according to their national work; in the present world I say, because it is only in the present world they subsist in a national capacity, and are capable of national rewards and punishments. Now there is a time, *when the transgressors are come to the full,* Dan. viii. 23; when the measure of a people's iniquity is filled up, and they are ripe for vengeance. And then the executioners of divine vengeance, the sword, famine, pestilential diseases, earthquakes and the like, are turned loose among them; then the dread commission is issued out, "Put ye in the sickle, for the harvest is ripe; come, get ye down; for the press is full; the fats overflow; for their wickedness is great." Joel iii. 13. Then all the undertakings of such a people are blasted; and even the worst of the heathen (Ezek. vii. 24) succeed against them. That nation is thrown off from the hinge on which empire turns, and therefore must fall. The Lord of armies is against them; and by a secret but irresistible hand, brings on their destruction.

Now whether that fatal period be arrived, with respect to us and our nation, I will not determine, nor indeed am I capable: but I am sure it is not evident that it is not come; I am sure our land is full of sin against the Holy One of Israel. On this subject I have often enlarged; and now I am afraid it is a trite, disregarded tale. The sins of our land lie heavy upon it; the sins of all ranks and denominations: the sins of past and present generations: sins against the law and against the gospel; sins against mercies and against judgments; sins in heart, in language, in practice; sins of all kinds and degrees, and against all sorts of obligations: Oh! what a huge heap, what an intolerable burden do all these sins make! The sins of many millions on both sides the Atlantic! Our body politic is a huge mass of corruption! the whole head is sick; and the whole heart faint; from the sole of the foot unto the head there is no soundness in it, but all full of wounds, and bruises, and putrefying sores. Isa. i. 6. And does not this leave our doom in a dreadful suspense? Who can tell what will be the fate of so guilty a people? Can we indulge high hopes with such a load of guilt upon us? Sin lies like a dead weight upon our counsels, our designs, and expeditions; and crushes all of them. What though our enemies be as wicked as ourselves, with only this exception, that they have not our advantages, and therefore cannot sin with our aggravations? But what if they were in all respects as bad? It has been no unusual thing for God to employ one guilty nation to execute his vengeance upon another; and when that drudgery is done, (which, by the by, is more properly devolved upon a hated nation than upon his people; he has more beneficent and agreeable work for them,) I say when that drudgery is done, he executes the executioner: just as one among a number of criminals may be appointed to execute the rest; and then he is executed himself by some other hand. Thus God employed the Assyrians and Babylonians to punish his people, the Jews; and when they had, though undesignedly, done him that service, he punishes them in a yet severer manner. And thus he threatens the Jews by Ezekiel, that he would bring the worst of the Heathen against them: they were good enough to be executioners. So he employs devils, the worst of beings, to execute his vengeance upon sinners in hell. And so in human governments, the refuse of mankind are appointed hangmen.

But though our land be so full of sin, yet there would be some ground to hope, could we see any appearances of a general repentance and reformation. But alas! where shall we find it? I have not been a heedless observer of the effects of the corrective and vindictive providences of God towards our land, the sword, a threatened famine, and a deadly, raging distemper.* But I have been really shocked to observe the issue. I am afraid that even the people of God are not so effectually roused by these warnings as they should be. One would think they would be all life and vigour at such a time as this: but, alas! I am afraid it is otherwise. I am especially afraid that impenitent sinners, instead of being melted into repentance, are hardening more and more like clay in the sun. Alas! I see and hear no more of serious concern about eternal things among us, than if we lived in a healthy neighbourhood, and a peaceful, unmolested country. I am afraid the case of some bears a dismal resemblance to that described in Rev. xvi. 10, 11. "They gnawed their tongues for pain, and blasphemed the God of heaven, because of their pains and their sores, and repented not of their deeds;" no, they are sullenly obstinate to wickedness still.

Brethren, what are we doing? Are we asleep at such a time as this, when the judgments of heaven are around us, and the fate of our country is so terribly doubtful? for God's sake, for our souls sake, for our country's sake, let us rouse ourselves from our security; and let us humble ourselves before God, "and cry mightily to him; and who can tell but he may turn away from his fierce anger?" Which leaves me to the second inference from my text, viz.,

II. That when a nation is in such a doubtful situation that

---

* At this time a flux raged in the congregation and elsewhere, which baffled all the powers of medicine, and swept off some whole families almost entirely.

no man can know its doom, if there be any hope, it is only in the way of repentance, reformation, and earnest prayer.

This appears the only way of hope on two accounts:

1. National sin has a direct tendency, in its own nature, to weaken and destroy a nation. It is the deadly disease of a body politic which will destroy it, without the hand of an executioner. It spreads corruption, injustice, treachery, discord, confusion, cowardice, through a nation; and it destroys public spirit, the love of our country, unanimity, courage, and all the social and heroic virtues which naturally tend to strengthen, defend, and advance a people. Now, repentance, reformation, and prayer, is the proper cure for this disease; it purges out these internal principles of death, and implants and cherishes the opposite principles of virtue and life. But this is not all; for,

2. Repentance, reformation, and prayer, is the only method to *turn away the displeasure of God*, and obtain his favour and protection. Sin brings on a people the curse of a provoked God; and under this they fade and wither away, like a blasted flower, or a tree struck by lightning from heaven. But if it be possible to remove it, and obtain the divine favour, it is only by deep humiliation before him, by a thorough reformation from those sins that provoke him, and by earnest cries for mercy. The light of nature taught the men of Nineveh that this was the only way of hope; and revelation assures us of the very same thing. It is only to the penitent that the promises of deliverance are made; and without repentance, we have no possible claim to them. Deliverances are generally answers to prayer; and therefore without earnest prayer we cannot expect them. National judgments are inflicted for national sins, and therefore reformation from national sins is the only hopeful way to escape them.

Therefore, my brethren, let us betake ourselves to this only method of hope. Let us deeply humble ourselves before God; "let us cry mightily to him—and let us turn every one from our evil ways;" and then, "who can tell but God will turn and repent, and turn away from his fierce anger, that we perish not?"

But in all my exhortations of this kind, I remember that repentance and reformation is the duty of fallen creatures; of creatures so depraved and feeble, that they are not able, of themselves, so much as to apply the remedy. If you attempt this work with the pride of imaginary self-sufficiency, you may be sure disappointment will be the consequence. Therefore remember, that it is the Holy Spirit of God alone that is the author of a thorough repentance and effectual reformation. It is he alone that can effectually convince the world of sin. If he be absent, legislators may make laws against vice, philosophers may reason, ministers may preach, nay, conscience may remonstrate, the divine law may prescribe and threaten, the gospel may invite and allure; but all will be in vain; all will not produce one true penitent. The strongest arguments, the most melting entreaties, the most alarming denunciations, from God and man, enforced by the highest authority, or by the most compassionate tears, all will have no effect; all will not effectually reclaim one sinner, nor gain one sincere proselyte to righteousness; Paul, Apollos, and Cephas, with all their apostolical abilities, can do nothing to the purpose without the Spirit. Paul may plant, and Apollos water; but God alone can give the increase. So then neither is he that planteth anything, nor he that watereth; they are both nothing together; but God who giveth the increase (1 Cor. iii. 7) is all in all. Till the Spirit be poured forth from on high, says Isaiah, briers and thorns shall come up upon the land of my people; *i. e.*, that their country shall be laid waste, and be made a mere wilderness of briers and thorns, by the ravages of war; or the people themselves shall be like briers and thorns, fruitless, noxious, and troublesome. In this language the prophet Micah describes the same people; the best of them is as a brier; the most upright is sharper than a thorn-hedge. (Micah vii. 4.) Such shall they continue, until the Holy Spirit be poured forth upon them from on high. But when the happy time comes, "then the wilderness shall be a fruitful field; then judgment shall dwell in the wilderness, and righteousness shall remain in the fruitful field." This effusion of the Spirit shall put an end to the desolation of war, and establish them in the possession of lasting and extensive peace; for, as it is there added, the work of righteousness shall be peace, and the native effect of righteousness shall be quietness and assurance for ever; and my people shall dwell in a peaceable habitation, and in sure dwellings, and in quiet resting-places. (Isaiah xxxii. 13, 18.) You see, my brethren, of how much importance and necessity the Spirit is to produce a reformation, and that blessed peace and security, both personal and national, both within and without, which is the effect of it!

And how are we to expect his sacred influences? Or in what way may we hope to attain them? The answer is, Pray for them: pray frequently, pray fervently. "Lord, thy Spirit! Oh give thy Spirit! that is the blessing I want; the blessing which families, and nations, and the whole human race want." Pray in your retirements; pray in your families; pray in societies appointed for that purpose; pray in warm ejaculations; pray without ceasing, for this grand fundamental blessing. Hear what encouragement Christ has given to prayer in this particular, "Ask, and it shall be given you; seek, and ye shall find;

knock, and it shall be opened unto you. If ye being evil, know how to give good gifts unto your children, how much more shall your heavenly Father give his Holy Spirit to them that ask him!" Luke xi. 9–13. Endeavour to repent in this humble, self-diffident manner, and you may hope it will at least avail to your eternal salvation; and who knows but it may avail also to turn away the fierce anger of God from your country and nation?

SERMON LXIII.

THE CURSE OF COWARDICE.*

JER. XLVIII. 10.—*Cursed be he that doeth the work of the* LORD *deceitfully ; and cursed be he that keepeth back his sword from blood.*

NOTHING can be more agreeable to the God of Peace, than to see universal harmony and benevolence prevail among his creatures, and he has laid them under the strongest obligations to cultivate a pacific temper towards one another, both as individuals and as nations. *Follow peace with all men,* is one of the principal precepts of our holy religion. And the great Prince of Peace has solemnly pronounced, *Blessed are the peacemakers.*

But when, in this corrupt, disordered state of things, where the lusts of men are perpetually embroiling the world with wars and fightings, throwing all into confusion; when ambition and avarice would rob us of our

---

* Preached to the militia of Hanover county, in Virginia, at a general muster, May 8, 1758, with a view to raise a company for Captain Samuel Meredith.

At the close of this discourse the quota for the company was immediately filled up, and the Captain was obliged to refuse the names of many more persons who offered to enlist. From the muster ground Mr. Davies went to the tavern to get his horse, when the whole regiment, following, pressed around him to catch every word he uttered. Seeing their desire, he stood on the tavern porch and again addressed them until he was exhausted.

[EDITOR OF THE BOARD OF PUBLICATION.]

property, for which we have toiled, and on which we subsist; when they would enslave the free-born mind, and compel us meanly to cringe to usurpation and arbitrary power; when they would tear from our eager grasp the most valuable blessing of heaven, I mean our religion; when they invade our country, formerly the region of tranquility, ravage our frontiers, butcher our fellow-subjects, or confine them in a barbarous captivity in the dens of savages; when our earthly all is ready to be seized by rapacious hands, and even our eternal all is in danger by the loss of our religion: when this is the case, what is, then, the will of God? Must peace then be maintained, maintained with our perfidious and cruel invaders? maintained at the expense of property, liberty, life, and every thing dear and valuable? maintained, when it is in our power to vindicate our right, and do ourselves justice? Is the work of peace then our only business? No: in such a time, even the God of Peace proclaims by his providence, "To arms!" Then the sword is, as it were, consecrated to God; and the art of war becomes a part of our religion. Then happy is he that shall reward our enemies as they have served us. Psalm cxxxvii. 8. Blessed is the brave soldier: blessed is the defender of his country, and the destroyer of its enemies. Blessed are they who offer themselves willingly in this service, and who faithfully discharge it. But on the other hand, "Cursed is he that doth the work of the Lord deceitfully; and cursed is he that keepeth back his sword from blood."

As to the original reference and meaning of these words, it is sufficient to my purpose to observe, that the Moabites, against whom this prophecy was immediately denounced, were a troublesome and restless nation in the neighbourhood of the Jews, who, though often subdued by them, yet upon every occasion struggled to recover their power, and renewed their hostilities. By this, and various other steps, they were arrived to the highest pitch of national guilt, and ripe for execution. The Babylonians were commissioned for this work of vengeance : and they were bound to execute the commission faithfully, under penalty of a curse. To them this denunciation was immediately directed, *Cursed be he that doeth the work of the* LORD *deceitfully*, or negligently;* *and cursed be he that keepeth back his sword from blood*. This is expressly in the form of an imprecation, or an authoritative denunciation of a curse: and in this form it might be used consistently with benevolence, by a prophet speaking as the mouth of God. But this is not a pattern for our imitation, who are peculiarly obliged, under the gospel, to *bless, and curse not*, and to *pray for all men*. However, it may be pronounced even by our lips as a declaration of the righteous curse of God against a dastardly refusal to engage in war, when it is our duty; or a deceitful, negligent discharge of that duty, after we have engaged in it. These are the crimes that seem intended in my text; and against each of these the tremendous curse of Jehovah is still in full force in all ages, even under the mild and gentle dispensation of the gospel. Cowardice and treachery are now as execrable as ever.

Cursed be he that keepeth back his sword from blood. This denunciation, like the artillery of heaven, is levelled against the coward, who, when God, in the course of his providence, calls him to arms, refuses to obey, and consults his own ease and safety more than his duty to God and his country.

Cursed be he that doeth the work of the LORD *deceitfully*. This seems to be levelled against another species of cowards; sly, hypocritical cowards, who undertake the work

* Ἀμελῶς. Septuag.

of the Lord; that is, take up arms; but they do the work of the Lord deceitfully; that is, they do not faithfully use their arms for the purposes they were taken up. They commence soldiers, not that they may serve their country, and do their duty to God, but that they may live in ease, idleness, and pleasure, and enrich themselves at the public expense. *Cursed is he that doeth the work of the* LORD *deceitfully*, and serves himself under pretence of serving his country.

You, gentlemen, and others, whom I this day behold with peculiar pleasure engaged in the cause of your neglected country, and who have done me the honour of inviting me to this service; a service which I am sure I should perform to your satisfaction if my preparations and abilities were proportioned to my benevolence for you, and my concern for your success: you are peculiarly interested in the remarks I have made upon the text. And that I may contribute all in my power both to increase your number, and direct you to a proper conduct in the honourable character you sustain, I shall lay before you a brief view of the present circumstances of our country: from which it will appear, that the war in which we are engaged, is a duty, or the work of the Lord; and consequently, that we are all obliged, according to our respective characters, to carry it on with vigour, under penalty of falling under the curse of God. And then I shall show you what is the deceitful performance of the Lord's work, or unseasonably keeping back of the sword from blood, which exposes to the curse.

I. I am to lay before you a brief view of the present circumstances of our country, which render the war in which we are engaged the work of the Lord, which consecrate swords as instruments of righteousness, and call us to the dreadful but important duty of shedding human blood, upon penalty of falling under the tremendous curse of God.

Need I inform you what barbarities and depredations a mongrel race of Indian savages and French Papists have perpetrated upon our frontiers? How many deserted or demolished houses and plantations? How wide an extent of country abandoned? How many poor families obliged to fly in consternation, and leave their all behind them? What breaches and separations between the nearest relations? What painful ruptures of heart from heart? What shocking dispersions of those once united by the strongest and most endearing ties? Some lie dead, mangled with savage wounds, consumed to ashes with outrageous flames, or torn and devoured by the beasts of the wilderness, while their bones lie whitening in the sun, and serve as tragical memorials of the fatal spot where they fell. Others have been dragged away captives, and made the slaves of imperious and cruel savages; others have made their escape, and live to lament their butchered or captivated friends and relations. In short, our frontiers have been drenched with the blood of our fellow-subjects, through the length of a thousand miles; and new wounds are still opening. We, in these inland parts of the country, are as yet unmolested, through the unmerited mercy of Heaven. But let us only glance a thought to the western extremities of our body politic; and what melancholy scenes open to our view! Now, perhaps, while I am speaking; now, while you are secure and unmolested, our fellow-subjects there may be feeling the calamities I am describing. Now, perhaps, the savage shouts and whoops of Indians, and the screams and groans of some butchered family, may be mingling their horrors, and circulating their tremendous echoes through the wilderness of rocks and mountains! Now, perhaps, some tender, delicate creature may be suffering an involuntary prostitution to savage lust; and perhaps debauched and murdered by the same hand! Now, perhaps, some miserable Briton or Virginian may be passing through a tedious process of experiments in the infernal art of torture! Now, some helpless children may be torn from the arms of their murdered parents, and dragged away, weeping, and wringing their hands, to receive their education among barbarians, and to be formed upon the model of a ferocious Indian soul!

And will these violences cease without a vigorous and timely resistance from us? Can Indian revenge and thirst for blood be glutted? or can French ambition and avarice be satisfied? No, we have no method left, but to repel force with force, and to give them blood to drink in their turn, who have drank ours. If we sit still and do nothing, or content ourselves, as, alas! we have hitherto, with feeble, dilatory efforts, we may expect these barbarities will not only continue, but that the Indians, headed by the French, will carry their inroads still farther into the country, and reach even unto us. By the desertion of our remote settlements, the frontiers are approaching every day nearer and nearer to us; and if we cannot stand our ground now, when we have above a hundred miles of a thick-settled country between us and the enemy, much less shall we be able, when our strength is weakened by so vast a loss of men, arms, and riches, and we lie exposed to their immediate incursions. Some cry, "Let the enemy come down to us, and then we will fight them." But this is the trifling excuse of cowardice or security, and not the language of prudence and fortitude. Those who make this plea, if the enemy should take them at their word, and make them so near a visit, would be as forward in flight as they are now backward to take up arms.

Such, my brethren, such, alas! is the present state of our country; it bleeds in a thousand veins; and without timely remedy, the wound will prove mortal. And in such circumstances is it not our duty in the sight of God; is it not a work to which the Lord loudly calls us, to take up arms for the defence of our country? Certainly it is; and *cursed is he* who, having no ties sufficiently strong to confine him at home, *keepeth his sword from blood*. The man that can desert the cause of his country in such an exigency; his country, in the blessings of which he shared while in peace and prosperity; and which is therefore entitled to his sympathy and assistance in the day of its distress; that cowardly, ungrateful man sins against God and his country, and deserves the curse of both. Such a conduct in such a conjuncture, is a moral evil, a gross wickedness; and exposes the wretch to the heavy curse of God both in this and the eternal world.

And here I cannot but observe, that among the various and numberless sins under which the country groans, and which must be looked upon as the cause of our public calamities, by every one that believes a divine Providence: a doctrine so comfortable, and so essential both in natural and revealed religion; an article in the creed of heathens and Mahometans, (as well as Jews and Christians;) I say, among these various sins, cowardice and security are none of the least. He that hath determined the bounds of our habitations, hath planted us in a land of liberty and plenty; a land, till lately, unalarmed with the terrors of war, and unstained with human blood; indeed, all things considered, there are but few such happy spots on our globe. And must it not highly provoke our divine Benefactor, to see a people, thus distinguished with blessings, so insensible of their worth, so ungrateful for them, and so unacquainted with their own unworthiness to receive them? What can be more evidential of their undue apprehensions of the worth of these blessings, than their being so little concerned to secure and recover them? The generality among us have acted as if their interests at stake were so trifling, that it would not be worth while to take pains, or encounter dangers, to preserve them. What greater evidence can be given of ingratitude than a supine neglect of these blessings, and such a stupidly tame and irresisting resignation of them into bloody and rapacious hands? And what can be more evidential of a proud insensibility of our unworthiness of such blessings, than our being so inapprehensive of losing them, even in the most threatening and dangerous circumstances? Our countrymen in general have acted, as if beings of their importance and merit might certainly rest in the quiet, unmolested possession of their liberty and property, without any one daring to disturb them, and without their doing anything for their own defence; or as if neither God nor man could strip them of their enjoyments. What vain, self-confident presumption, what intolerable insolence is this, in a sinful nation, a people laden with iniquity, who have forfeited every blessing, even the ground they tread upon, and the air they breathe in; and who live merely by the immerited grace and bounty of God! Is not cowardice and security, or an unwillingness to engage with all our might in defence of our country, in such a situation, an enormous wickedness in the sight of God, and worthy of his curse, as well as a scandalous meanness in the sight of men, and worthy of public shame and indignation? Is it not fit that those who so contemptuously depreciate the rich and undeserved bounties of Heaven, and who swell so insolently with a vain conceit of their own importance and worth, should be punished with the loss of these blessings! What discipline can be more seasonable or congruous? May we not suppose, that divine Providence has permitted our body politic to suffer wound after wound, and baffled all our languid efforts, in order to give it sensibility, and rouse us to exert our strength in more vigorous efforts? Has not the curse of God lain heavy upon our country, because we have "done the work of the LORD deceitfully, and kept back our swords from blood?"

And shall this guilt increase from year to year, till we are entirely crushed with the enormous load? Shall neither the fear of Jehovah's curse, nor the love of our country, nor even the love of ourselves, and our own personal interest, constrain us at length to relieve our ravaged country, and defend the blessings which God has entrusted to our custody, as well as lent us to enjoy? Blessed be God, and thanks to you, brave soldiers, for what I now see. I see you engaged in this good cause: and may the effectual blessing of Heaven be upon you, instead of the curse entailed upon cowardice and treachery! But are there no more to join with you? What! none more in this crowd? None more in Hanover? which I think should show itself worthy of precedence, and exhibit a brave example to other counties: this is what may reasonably be expected, from the number of our militia, the high price of our staple commodity, the frequency and variety of our religious instructions; and, I may add, from our own former good conduct in such an emergency. Hanover had the honour of sending out the first company of volunteers that were raised in the colony.* And are we degenerated so soon? Or is our danger less now than immediately after Braddock's defeat? Or are we now inured and hardened to bad news, so that the calamities of our frontiers, which have been growing every year, have now ceased to be objects of our compassion?

* Under Captain Averton, immediately after General Braddock's defeat.

I am sorry to tell you, that the company now forming is not yet completed, though under officers from among yourselves, from whom you may expect good usage; and the encouragement is so unusually great, and the time of service is so short.* May I not reasonably insist upon it, that the company be made up this very day before we leave this place? Methinks your king, your country, nay, your own interests, command me: and therefore I must insist upon it. Oh! for the all-prevailing force of Demosthenes' oratory—but I recall my wish that I may correct it. Oh! for the influence of the Lord of armies, the God of battles, the Author of true courage, and every heroic virtue, to fire you into patriots and soldiers this moment! Ye young and hardy men, whose very faces seem to speak that God and nature formed you for soldiers, who are free from the incumbrance of families depending upon you for subsistence, and who perhaps are of but little service to society while at home, may I not speak for you and declare as your mouth, "Here we are, all ready to abandon our ease, and rush into the glorious dangers of the field, in defence of our country?" Ye that love your country, enlist; for honour will follow you in life or death in such a cause. You that love your religion, enlist; for your religion is in danger. Can Protestant Christianity expect quarters from heathen savages and French papists? Sure, in such an alliance, the powers of hell make a third party. Ye that love your friends and relations, enlist; lest ye see them enslaved or butchered before your eyes. Ye that would catch at money, here is a proper bait for you: ten pounds for a few month's service, besides the usual pay of soldiers. I seriously make the proposal to you, not only as a subject of the best of kings, and a friend to your country, but as *a servant of*

* Only till the first of December next.

the Most High God: for I am fully persuaded, what I am recommending is his will; and disobedience to it may expose you to his curse.

This proposal is not liable to the objections that have been urged against former measures for raising men. You cannot any longer object, "that you are dragged away like slaves against your wills, while others are without reason exempted:" for now it is left to your own honour, and you may act as free men. Nor can you object "that you are arbitrarily thrust under the command of foreign, unknown, or disagreeable officers:" for the gentleman that has the immediate command of this company, and his suborbinate officers, are of yourselves, your neighbours, children, and perhaps your old companions. And I hope I may add, you need not object, that you shall be badly used: for, Gentlemen-Officers, may I not promise for you, that not one man in your company shall be treated with cruelty or injustice as far as your authority or influence can prevent? May I not be your security, that none but the guilty shall be punished, and they only according to the nature of the offence? Perhaps some may object, that should they enter the army, their morals would be in danger of infection, and their virtue would be perpetually shocked with horrid scenes of vice. This may also be a discouragement to parents to consent to their children's engaging in so good a cause. I am glad to hear this objection, when it is sincere, and not an empty excuse: and I wish I could remove it, by giving you an universal assurance that the army is a school of religion; and that soldiers, as they are more exposed to death than other men, are proportionably better prepared for it than others. But alas! the reverse of this is too true; and the contagion of vice and irreligion is perhaps nowhere stronger than in the army; where one would think the supreme tribunal should be always in view, and it should be their chief care to prepare for eternity, on the slippery brink of which they stand every moment. But, Gentlemen-Officers, I must again appeal to you, that as for this company, you will not willingly allow any form of vice to be practised in it with impunity: but will always endeavour to recommend and enforce religion and good morals by your example and authority, and to suppress the contrary. May I not give the public the satisfaction of such an assurance concerning you, that whatever others do, as for you and your company you will serve the Lord? Do you not own yourselves bound to this in honour and duty? Such a conduct, I can assure you, will render you popular among the wise and good; though perhaps it may expose you to the senseless contempt of fools, who make a mock at sin, and who esteem it bravery to insult that God, "in whose hand their breath is, and whose are all their ways." Such a conduct will afford you pleasure in the review, when the terrors of the bloody field are spread around you, and death starts up before you in a thousand shocking forms. Such a conduct will be a source of true courage, and render you nobly indifferent about life or death in a good cause. And let me honestly warn you, that if you do not maintain such a conduct, you will bitterly repent it, either in time or eternity.

But I return to invite others to join with you in this important expedition. What a crowd of important arguments press you on every hand! What can our legislature do more than they have done to engage you? If such an unusual encouragement does not prevail upon you to enlist as volunteers, what remains but that you must be forced to it by authority? For <u>our country must be defended</u>: and if nothing but force can constrain you to take up arms in its defence, then force must be used: persons of such a sordid, unmanly spirit, are not to expect the usage of freemen. Think what the paternal care of our sovereign has done for us: and how many millions of money, and thousands of men, our mother country has furnished for our defence. And shall we do nothing for ourselves? Great Britain, I own, is interested in our protection: but can she be as much interested as ourselves? Consider what the brave New England men have done, after so many mortifications and disappointments, and their treasury so much exhausted. By the best accounts I have had, the little colony of Massachusetts Bay has raised no less than seven thousand men, though not larger perhaps than fifteen or twenty of those fifty-three counties contained in Virginia. And since we have the same interests at stake, shall we not cheerfully furnish our quota for the public service? We all admire the bravery and success of the King of Prussia: but his success must be greatly owing to the bravery of his subjects, as well as his own: he has almost as many soldiers as subjects. And while he has almost miraculously stood his ground against such superior numbers, shall we, with the advantage of numbers on our side, be perpetually flying before a pitiful enemy, and tamely give up our country to their ravages? Let us strenuously exert that superior force which a gracious Providence has put into our hands: and we may soon expect, through the concurrence of Heaven, that we shall again enjoy the blessings of peace. Whatever intelligence our artful enemies may send, or the cowardly among ourselves may believe, there is no reason to conclude that the French regulars upon this continent are half so many as ours: and as to the *coloni*, or country-militia, we are certainly twenty, perhaps forty, to one. Let us, then, in the name of the Lord of Hosts, the God of the armies of Israel, let us collect our whole strength, and give one decisive blow; and we may humbly hope victory will be ours.

Every one can complain of the bad management of our public undertakings, and lament the general security and inactivity that prevails: every one can wish that something were effectually done, and that this and that person would enlist: every one can tell what great achievements he would perform, were it not for this or that, a hundred obstructions in his way. But all this idle complaining, wishing, lamenting, and boasting, will answer no end. Something must be done! must be done by you! Therefore, instead of assuming the state of patriots and heroes at home—to arms! away to the field, and prove your pretensions sincere. Let the thunder of this imprecation rouse you out of your ease and security, "Cursed be he that doth the work of the LORD deceitfully; and cursed be he that keepeth back his sword from blood." God sent an angel from heaven to curse the dastardly inhabitants of Meroz, who refused to take up arms for defence of their country. (Judges v. 23.) "Curse ye Meroz, said the angel of the LORD, curse ye bitterly the inhabitants thereof: because they came not to the help of the LORD, to the help of the LORD against the mighty." And shall this curse fall upon Virginia? No, fly from it by venturing your lives for your country: for this curse is far more terrible than any thing that can befall you in the field of battle. But it is not enough for you to undertake this work: you are also obliged faithfully to perform it, as the work of the Lord. And this leads me,

II. To show you what is that deceitful performance of the Lord's work, or unseasonably keeping back the sword from blood, which exposes to his curse.

If soldiers, instead of abandoning their ease and pleasure, and risking their lives in defence of their country, should unman themselves with sensual pleasures and debauchery; if, instead of searching out the enemy, they keep out of their way, lest they should search out and find them; if they lie sleeping or rioting in forts and places of safety, while their country is ravaged, perhaps in their very neighbourhood: when they waste their courage in broils and duels among themselves, or in tyrannizing over those that are under their command: when they lay themselves open to false alarms, by being credulous to every account that magnifies the force of the enemy: when they are tedious or divided in their consultations, and slow and faint in the execution: when they consult rather what may be most safe for themselves than most beneficial for their country: when they keep skirmishing at a distance, instead of making a bold push, and bringing the war to a speedy issue by a decisive stroke: when they are fond of prolonging the war, that they may live and riot the longer at the public expense: when they sell themselves and their country to the enemy for a bribe: in short, when they do not conscientiously exert all their power to repel the enemy, and protect the state that employs them, but only seek to serve themselves, then they do the work of the Lord deceitfully; and his curse lights upon them as their heavy doom. I leave others to judge, whether the original of this ugly picture is to be found anywhere in the universe. But as for you of this company, may I not presume that you will behave in a nobler manner? Shall not sobriety, public spirit, courage, fidelity, and good discipline, be maintained among you? This I humbly recommend to you; and may God enable you to act accordingly!

Thus far have I addressed you as soldiers, or at least as persons concerned in your stations to do all in your power to save your country. But we must not part thus. It is possible we may never meet more, till we mingle with the assembled universe before the supreme tribunal: therefore, before I dismiss you, I must address myself to you as sinners, and as candidates for eternity. You are concerned to save your souls, as well as your country: and should you save or gain a kingdom, or even the whole world, and lose your souls, your loss will be irreparable.

None of you, I hope, will reply, "I am now a soldier, and have nothing more to do with religion." What! has a soldier nothing to do with religion? Is a soldier under no obligations to the God that made him, and that furnishes him with every blessing? Is not a soldier as much exposed to death as other men? May not a soldier be damned for sin as well as other sinners? And will he be able to dwell with devouring fire and everlasting burnings? Are these things so? Can any of you be so stupid as to think them so? If not, you must own that even a soldier has as much concern with religion as another. Therefore, hear me seriously upon this head.

You are about entering into the school of vice: for such the army has generally been. And are any of you already initiated into any of the mysteries of iniquity there practised? Must I so much as suppose that some of you, who have bravely espoused the cause of your country, are addicted to drunkenness, swearing, whoredom, or any gross vice? I cannot now take time to reason with you for your conviction: it may suffice to appeal to your own reason and conscience, Do you act well in indulging these vices? Will you approve of it in the honest hour of death? Will this conduct prove a source of courage to you when the arrows of death are flying thick around you, and scores are falling on every side? No, you are self-condemned; and may I not reasonably hope you will endeavour to reform what you cannot but condemn? Soldiers, indeed, are too commonly addicted to such immoralities; but are they the better soldiers on that account? Can an oath or a debauch inspire them with a rational fortitude against the fears of death? Would not prayer and a life of holiness better answer this purpose? Their courage, if they have any, must be the effect, not of thought, but of the want of thought; it must be a brutal stupidity, or ferocity; but not the rational courage of a man or a Christian.

Some of you, I doubt not, are happily free from these gross vices: and long may you continue so! But I must tell you, this *negative* goodness is not enough to prepare you for death, or to constitute you true Christians. The temper of your minds must be changed by the power of divine grace: and you must be turned from the love and practice of all sin, to the love and practice of universal holiness. You must become humble, broken-hearted penitents and true believers in Jesus Christ. You must be enabled to live righteously, soberly, and godly, in this present evil world. This is religion: this is religion that will keep you uncorrupted in the midst of vice and debauchery: this is religion, that will befriend you when cannons roar, and swords gleam around you, and you are every moment expecting the deadly wound: this is religion that will support you in the agonies of death, and assure you of a happy immortality.

But are not some of you conscious that you are destitute of such a religion as this? Then it is high time for you to think on your condition in sober sadness. Pray to that powerful and gracious Being, who can form your hearts and lives after this sacred model. Oh! pray earnestly, pray frequently, for this blessing: and use all the means of grace in that manner which your circumstances will permit. Remember, also, that if you try to prolong your life by a dastardly conduct, your life will lie under the curse of heaven: and you have little reason to hope you will ever improve it as a space for repentance. Remember also to put your confidence in God; who keeps the thread of your life, and the event of war, in his own hand. Devoutly acknowledge his providence in all your ways, and be sensible of your dependence upon it.

And now, to conclude my address to you, as the mouth of this multitude, and of you, countrymen in general, I heartily bid you farewell. Farewell, my dear friends, my brave fellow-subjects, the guardians of your ravaged country. God grant you may return in safety and honour, and that we may yet welcome you home, crowned with laurels of victory! Or if any of you should lose your lives in so good a cause, may you enjoy a glorious and blessed immortality in the region of everlasting peace and tranquility! Methinks I may take upon me to promise you the prayers and good wishes of thousands. Thousands, whom you leave behind, will think of you with affectionate anxiety, will wish you success, and congratulate your return, or lament your death. Once more I pour out all my heart in another affectionate farewell. May the Lord preserve your going out, and your coming in, from this time forth, and even for evermore. Amen.

Here I thought to have concluded. But I must take up a few minutes more to ask this crowd, Is there nothing to be done by us who stay at home, towards the defence of our country, and to promote the success of the expedition now in hand? Shall we sin on still impenitent and incorrigible? Shall we live as if we and our country were self-dependent, and had nothing to do with the Supreme Ruler of the universe? Can an army of saints or of heroes defend an obnoxious people, ripe for destruction, from the righteous judgment of God? The cause in which these brave men, and our army in general, are engaged, is not so much their own as ours: divine Providence considers them not so much in their private personal character, as in their public character, as the representatives and guardians of their country; and therefore they will stand or fall, not so much according to their own personal character, as according to the public character of the people, whose cause they have undertaken. Be it known to you, then, their success depends upon us, even more than upon themselves. Therefore let us all turn every one from his evil ways. *Let the wicked forsake his way,* &c. Let us humble ourselves under the mighty hand of God, which is lifted up over our guilty heads, that we may be exalted in due time. I could venture the reputation of my judgment and veracity, that it will never be well with our country till there be more of the fear and love of God in it, and till the name of Jesus be of more importance among us. I could prescribe a method for our deliverance, which is at once infallible, and also cheap and safe, and so far from endangering the life of any, that it would secure the everlasting life of all that comply with it. Ye that complain of the burden of our public taxes; ye that love ease, and shrink from the dangers of war; ye that wish to see peace restored once more; ye that would be happy beyond the grave, and live for ever, attend to my proposal: it is this, a thorough, national reformation. This will do what millions of money, and thousands of men, with guns and swords, and all the dreadful artillery of death, could not do; it will procure us peace again; a lasting, well-established peace. We have tried other expedients without this long enough: let us now try this new expedient, the success of which I dare to warrant. And do not object that such a general reformation is beyond your power; for a general reformation must begin with individuals: therefore do you, through the grace of God, act your part; begin at home, and endeavour to reform yourselves, and those under your influence.

It is a natural inference from what has been said, that if the defence of our country, in which we can stay but a few years at most, and from which we must ere long take our flight, be so important a duty, then how much more are we obliged to seek a better country, *i. e.*, a " heavenly ;" and to carry on a vigorous war against our spiritual enemies, that would rob us of our heavenly inheritance! therefore, in the name of Jesus, the Captain of our salvation, I invite you all to enlist in the spiritual warfare. Now proclaim eternal war against all sin. Now " take to you the whole armour of God; quit you like men, be strong:" and, for your encouragement, remember, " He that overcometh shall inherit all things;" he shall enter into a kingdom that cannot be shaken—cannot be shaken with those storms of public calamities which toss and agitate this restless ocean of a world. In that blessed harbour may we all rest at last!

SERMON LXIV.*

THE SIGNS OF THE TIMES.

LUKE XXI. 10, 11–25, 26.—*Then he said unto them, Nation shall rise up against nation, and kingdom against kingdom; and great earthquakes shall be in divers places, and famines, and pestilences, and fearful sights: and great signs shall there be from heaven.—And there shall be signs in the sun, and in the moon, and in the stars; and upon the earth distress of nations with perplexity; the sea and the waves roaring; men's hearts failing them for fear, and for looking after those things which are coming on the earth.*

ALL the works of God are worthy of our admiring notice; and to overlook or disregard them, is at once an instance of stupidity and wickedness. It was a heavy

---

* The preceding sermons were published in the earlier editions issued in this country and abroad. This, and the remaining ones, were first published in London, A. D., 1806, in a separate volume, and with the following advertisement:—

WE have scarcely ever felt more highly gratified, than in the opportunity we now embrace of presenting to the religious public, one more volume of the interesting sermons of that most excellent man, the late Rev. PRESIDENT DAVIES, of America—Sermons, admirably calculated to promote the grand interests of vital evangelical godliness; or increase the knowledge and influence of real religion in the hearts and lives of men.

That they are the genuine productions of the masterly pen to which they are ascribed, no other evidence need be adduced than an appeal to the discourses themselves. Let them be compared with those already abroad in the world, and they will be clearly seen to carry their own witness along with them. The instant they meet our eye, with but a common degree of

charge against the ancient Jews, that they were sunk in luxury and pleasure, while the signals of divine vengeance should have cast them into the posture of anxious expectation. "The harp and the viol, and the tabret, and the pipe, and wine, are in their feasts; but they regard not the work of the Lord, neither consider the operation of his hands." Isaiah v. 12. And if all the works of God, even those that are ordinary and according to the known course of nature, are worthy of observation and wonder; certainly much more so are those which are extraordinary —those which are done by the *immediate* hand of God, above the course of nature; or which are accomplished according to such laws of nature as are *unusual*, and in-

---

discernment, we cannot but be struck with the coincidence with respect to method and order—to a free and masculine diction—a rich vein of evangelical doctrine—an impartial regard to the cases of all his hearers, and an animated and pathetic application, between this and the preceding volumes "The sun," it has been remarked on a similar occasion, " discovers himself to be the sun, by the beams with which he irradiates and enlivens mankind, and is easily distinguished from the other heavenly bodies by his surpassing lustre."

It is not for a moment to be doubted, but that these composures, had they passed under the revision of their worthy author, would have received considerable embellishment. That they were not so favoured, is a circumstance not a little to be regretted. But we need not inform the intelligent reader, that this is a too frequent disadvantage attached to posthumous publications. It is, however, pleasing to reflect, that the several former volumes—the manly compositions of the same capacious, soaring genius, were not, on this account, perused with less cordiality by a discerning public.

As it is more than probable this will be the last volume of the admired author that will ever be introduced to public notice; we do most affectionately accompany it with our warmest wishes—that a portion of the mantle fallen from our Elijah may become the perquisite of every reader of these discourses; in which "the various excellences of learning, judgment, eloquence, piety, and seraphic zeal, mingled in one uncommon glory—not unlike the beams of the sun, collected by a burning-glass, that at once shine with the most resplendent brightness, and set fire, wherever the blaze was directed, to every object susceptive of their celestial influence."

> What happy prophet shall his mantle find,
> Heir to a double portion of his mind ?   WATTS.

tended to be carried into execution only in extraordinary periods, and for purposes of uncommon importance. To disregard these, is the more stupid and inexcusable, as they have a natural and direct tendency to engage and fix our attention by their *new* and *strange* appearances: for things common and familiar to us, cease to be objects of our admiration and wonder, however great and surprising in themselves: whereas, things new and strange, attract the gaze of mankind, though not more astonishing or important than the former. And if these unusual works of God are also *prognosticative;* if these extraordinary appearances in the natural world are *signals* and *premonitions* of some important revolutions in the moral world, for which our duty and our interest require us to prepare; I say, if this be the case, then, to disregard them is still more stupid, and aggravatedly wicked; it is highly ungrateful to God, who is kindly pleased to give us warning of the impending events, that we may put ourselves into a proper posture to meet with them: and it may be highly injurious to ourselves, who may feel, to our cost, the unhappy want of that preparation, which we might have obtained by timely notice of these monitory signs.

Now my present intention is to inquire, Whether unusual phenomena, or appearances, in the *natural* world, may not be really intended, by the great Ruler of nature, as *prognostics* or *fore-tokens* of some grand events in the *kingdoms* of the earth, and in the *church*, for which it becomes us to prepare; and to prepare us for which, these monitory passages may be given us?

I own it has been with hesitation, that I have ventured to devote an hour of your sacred time to so unusual an inquiry. But after much thought, that which determined my fluctuating mind, was this consideration: That if these unusual commotions and appearances are *intended* by divine Providence to be *premonitions* and *signs* of some grand and interesting revolutions among mankind, they would *miss* their end entirely upon us, unless we should regard them in that view; and we should be guilty of hardening ourselves against warnings kindly given us from heaven. But if we should be mistaken in looking upon these things in this *prognosticative* view, still it would be a harmless, and even a *profitable* mistake, if it might render us more thoughtful and serious, and set us upon preparing for all events, whether presignified or not.

That which has turned my mind to this inquiry has been the late unusual and strange commotions and appearances in heaven and earth, which have been felt and seen in various parts of the world, particularly in Europe and America. An earthquake of prodigious extent and violence has shaken half the globe, buried cities in ruins, split the earth into hideous chasms, which have swallowed many thousands of mankind in Europe and Africa, and tossed the ocean into an unusual ferment for thousands of miles. Great Britain has trembled from shore to shore, and some parts of America seemed to *sympathize* with it. "Solid rocks have split to pieces, and huge unwieldy mountainous fragments have been hurled to some distance, while the ground a little way off was not affected; particularly a well-known ledge of rocks, called *Whiston Cliffs*, in Yorkshire, in England, where a horrid rumbling noise was heard for some days; and at length, sundry large pieces of rock were torn off and hurled through the air into a valley, one of which was about thirty yards high, and between sixty and seventy broad; and there did not appear to be any cavities in the rock, where air might be imprisoned to cause the rupture. But (says one that saw it*) one part

---

* Mr. John Wesley.—See his Thoughts on the Earthquake at Lisbon, an excellent and seasonable performance.

of the solid stone is cleft from the rest in a perpendicular line, and smooth as if cut with instruments." Near this, two pieces of ground, thirty or forty yards in diameter, have been removed entire, without cracks, with all their load of rocks; "some of which (says the same relater) are as large as the hull of a small ship, and a tree growing out of one of them." In various parts of Europe a strange and unaccountable motion has been observed in the waters, not only that of the sea and the rivers communicating therewith, but even that in canals, ponds, cisterns, and all other large or smaller collections of water; and that without the least motion of the earth around, or of the vessels which contained the water. Strange meteors and appearances have also been seen in the aerial regions; a fiery, bloody-coloured sky—the modern phenomenon of the Aurora Borealis, or a midnight brightness in the north—three unusual circles, intersecting the sun and each other, which some of us have seen not many years ago—unusual rains, hail, thunder, and lightning, in England, in the winter season—a severe drought last summer in our country, that threatened many parts of it with famine—irregular tides, and inundations of seas and rivers,* by which much loss has been sustained, and many lives perished. Besides these strange phenomena, which have already appeared, if we regard the calculation of that great philosopher, Doctor Halley, and of some others, we are to expect a visit from that portentous stranger, a *comet*, in about two years hence; a huge globe, heated, according to Sir Isaac Newton's calculation, two thousand times hotter than red-hot iron. And doctor Halley observes, that the last time it revolved, it moved in the same line in which the earth performs her annual course round the sun; but then the

---

* Particularly of the Rhone, in France, some months ago; and of the sea at Charleston, in South Carolina, about two or three years ago.

earth was on the other side of her orbit; whereas, in this revolution, it will move not only in the same line, but in the very same part of that line in which the earth moves. And will not this, upon the principles of philosophy, occasion a collision of those two bodies, or such a near approach as would prove fatal to our earth? For such an enormous body of solid fire would burn it to a coal, and cause an universal conflagration; and we have no reason, that I know of, to hope the contrary but from revelation, in which we find many prophecies not yet fulfilled. But upon the principles of infidel-philosophy, this dreadful consequence seems unavoidable.

These are certainly very uncommon things: it is not in every year, nor in every century, that they appear. Some of them, particularly earthquakes, inundations, et cetera, are evidently the judgments of a righteous God upon our guilty globe: and in this view they undoubtedly demand a serious regard; but is this the *only* view we should have of them? May we not look upon these and the other harmless phenomena as *signs* and *forerunners* of some revolutions in the world of *mankind*, as strange and extraordinary as these are in the material world? May not the convulsions of the globe be an omen of the agitations and confusions of the kingdoms of men that are to follow? May not a fiery, bloody-coloured sky be a signal to the world below to prepare for scenes of blood and slaughter? And as to comets, may we not use the words of a good philosopher, as well as a divine poet?

> " Lord of the armies of the sky;
> He marshals all the stars;
> Red *comets* lift his banners high,
> And wide proclaim his wars!"—*Watts.*

Are there not some strange events in the womb of

Providence? And are not these the struggles and pangs of nature labouring with the prodigious birth? I will not be peremptory in determining this point. Nor am I about to assume the airs of a prophet, or the low character of a fortune-teller: but I shall humbly offer my opinion with the reasons of it, and then allow you to judge for yourselves. Nor shall I inquire into the *philosophy* of these things. Perhaps they are *all* the effects of *natural* causes, as *some* of them undoubtedly are. We are not on the one hand to feign needless miracles;* and, on the other hand, I see no reason why we should be so scrupulous, as some seem to be, of supposing the immediate agency of the Divine hand in some unusual appearances above or contrary to the laws of nature. By forming servants to do his work, the Lord of nature has not rendered himself dependent upon them, so that he *cannot* work without them; and he has nowhere informed us that he has so tied himself down to them, that he will *never* work without them; or that, because miracles were more *frequent* in those ages in which the true religion was introduced and confirmed, therefore they shall not be wrought in other ages *at all*. Such immediate interpositions of the Divine hand can afford the Almighty no trouble; for it is as easy for him to manage the universe without instruments as with them. Upon the whole, I can see no sufficient reason to suppose that he never works but by secondary causes, and according to the established laws of nature, even in the ordinary ages of the world. Even in such ages there may be some events to be accomplished which it may be most proper for him to take into his own hands, and order his servants to suspend their agency—to stand still and see the works of God: but to determine this point is by no means neces-

* Nec Deus intersit, nisi dignus vindice nodus inciderit.—*Hor.*

sary to my present design. These commotions and appearances in nature may be *ominous* or *prognosticative*, and yet be the effects of the *established* laws of nature; for, besides the *usual* laws established at the creation for the regulation of the world in *ordinary* times, and which are *every* day carried into execution, and obvious to *common* observation; besides these, I say, why may there not be, as I hinted, other laws equally fixed and regular, but not carried into execution, except in *extraordinary* seasons, and as *signals* and premonitions of some important events, of which it is proper mankind should have some previous intimations, that they may prepare for them? May not the wise Contriver of the machine of nature have placed in it certain *hidden* springs, which, like the stroke of a clock at the hour, will move and operate at the appointed period, and rouse the attention and admiration of a stupid world? Besides the causes of the *daily familiar* phenomena of nature, may there not be causes *in reserve* for some grand purposes to produce some strange, unusual phenomena, adapted to the exigencies of some extraordinary periods? All the exigencies of such periods were known to the omniscient Creator when he first formed this vast machine, when he wound it up and put all its wheels in motion; and there he could easily adjust those *latent* springs in such a manner, as that they should operate exactly in the *appointed* period, when it should be fit, that for extraordinary reasons, extraordinary appearances should be produced, whether at the distance of twenty, a hundred, or a thousand years: there he might place certain powers, for this end, to give an alarm to the world when he should be about to accomplish some important revolution. Thus, you see, it is not necessary to the present inquiry to determine whether these unusual appearances are *miraculous* or agreeable to the *stated course of nature;* for whether you suppose them the one or the other, they may be *portentous,* and forebode some great revolutions.

This is certain, that such strange appearances *have been* prognosticative in times *past,* particularly in that period to which my text primarily refers; namely, the destruction of Jerusalem and the church and state of the Jews. It is to that dreadful, unparalleled calamity, the predictions in this chapter primarily refer; though, it must be owned, it is described in such language, and under such majestic images, as naturally carry our minds forward to the still more dreadful destruction of this guilty globe at the final judgment. And indeed, it is a very usual thing for the prophets to have two events in view in the same description, the one more *immediately,* and the other more *remotely:* and that part of the description which is not fully accomplished in one, has its final and complete accomplishment in the other; particularly, it is common for them to make the judgments of God inflicted upon guilty nations in this world, and the overthrow of cities and empires, a representation of his still more glorious and terrible appearance in the character of universal Judge at the last day, to inflict everlasting punishments, of a more terrible kind, upon the world of the ungodly; and of the universal overthrow and conflagration of the earth and all that it contains. This is certainly a wise method of instruction, as it makes the events of this life so many hints and *mementos* of the more important scenes before us at the end of this world, and in that awful eternity which is to follow. Thus, the ruins of cities, the fall of kingdoms, and unusual commotions in the natural and moral world, are made warnings to us to flee from the wrath to come, and provide for our safety in the wrecks of dissolving worlds. In this *double* view, we should consider the chapter where my text lies; though the most, if not all, the strange signs and prodigies here foretold, did actually appear before the destruction of Jerusalem.

Then the kingdoms of the earth were in a ferment and perturbation, and rumours of wars spread their terrors from country to country. "Nation rose up against nation, and kingdom against kingdom." This may have a particular reference to the insurrection of the Jews, at that time, in various places, particularly at Jerusalem, upon the Roman emperor's ordering his image to be set up in the temple:[*] and at Alexandria, and about Babylon, where they flew to arms, and many of them were slain.[†] As the revolutions and destruction of kingdoms are generally brought about by the force of arms; rumours of wars, and insurrections of nations against nations, are the usual forerunners of such melancholy events; and to look upon these as a presage, is but to infer *the effect from the cause.* I need not tell you that this is the present posture of affairs in those parts of the world in which we are most concerned. Armies marching, arms brightening, magazines filling, forts and castles besieged, countries ravaged and deserted, blood streaming by sea and land, and the world of spirits peopling fast: and this ferment is not likely to subside till some important revolution be brought about. Some decisive blow is likely to be given, that may be fatal to one or other of the contending parties, and on whom the blow will fall is as yet an anxious uncertainty, and

---

[*] Jussi a Caio Cæsare effigiem ejus in Templo locare, arma potius sumsere; quem motum Cæsaris mors diremit. Tacit. Hist. v.

Præbuerunt Judæi speciem motus ortæ seditione. Id. An. xii.

[†] Vid. Josephus Αρχαιολογιας xviii. et Philo adv. Flac. To these we might add the tumults and slaughter of the Jews at Cæsarea, Scythopolis, Ptolemais, Tyre, Gadaris, and Damascus; and the wars of the Jews of Perea against the Philadelphians, of the Jews and Galileans against the Samaritans, &c.

holds our minds in a painful suspense. May heaven determine it in favour of religion, liberty, and justice!

The convulsions of the *earth* were also an omen of the destruction of the Jews. "There shall be earthquakes in divers places," says our divine prophet. Accordingly, history informs us, that in the reigns of Claudius and Nero, there were frequent earthquakes in Crete, Smyrna, Miletus, Samos, Laodicea, and other places; in all which the Jews were settled, and consequently had their share in the common calamity.* Now, if, as Grotius judges,† earthquakes are not only severe judgments in themselves, but also *signs* of divine vengeance, which either causes them, or does not hinder them by restraining their natural causes; if, I say, they *forbode* future calamities and revolutions, as well as *produce* present, certainly our age may stand in the posture of eager expectation, "looking after those things that are coming upon the earth;" for perhaps there never was a more terrible and extensive earthquake than that which happened about ten months ago, since the universal one which broke upon the fountains of the great deep at the deluge.

The word rendered *earthquakes*,‡ in my text, properly signifies shakings or concussions, without determining in what element; and therefore may be taken in a larger latitude, to signify unusual tremours and motions, not only in the earth, but in the sea and air. And accordingly the Jewish historian, Josephus, informs us, that at that time there were prodigious storms of the sea, tempestuous winds,

---

* Josephus gives an account of an earthquake, about this time, in Judea also, in which no less than thirty thousand men were swallowed up. De Bell. Jud. c. xix.

† Terræmotus autem, præterquam quod *signa* sunt iræ divinæ, eos aut procurantis, aut impedire nolentis, graves etiam clades sæpe urbibus adferunt. Grot. in Matt. xxiv.

‡ Σεισμοί.

vehement rains, terrible lightnings, and roarings of the trembling earth. And if these wonders have a prognosticative signification, we and our mother country may forebode unusual things; for there they have all been perceived.

Another presage of the destruction of Jerusalem, here foretold, was a *famine*. This was the famine foretold also by Agabus, Acts xi. 28, which gave occasion for that collection for the poor saints in Judea, which St. Paul so often and so warmly recommends to the Gentile churches: Josephus also mentions the same famine. This calamity, which is at once a severe *judgment* and an *omen*, we have not yet felt in all its extremity; but we have been terribly threatened with it, both in Great Britain and Virginia: there, by the deadly plague that has raged so long among the cattle,* and here, by the severe drought of the last season, which actually reduced many poor families to great straits.

As to the *pestilence*, another presage of the destruction of the Jews, and which raged with such unexampled violence during the siege of their metropolis; through the kindness of Providence, Europe and America have not been lately visited with it: but how soon the deadly contagion may break out among us is unknown. This is obvious in the history of the world, that earthquakes, famines, and pestilences,† have generally been companions, or followed close upon one another. And our cold climate,

---

* In the year 1750.

† λιμος et λοιμος, famine and pestilence, are generally used together in Greek authors, as Grotius (in loc.) observes: and the reason may be, not only that which he assigns, viz., their resemblance in sound; but also, because they generally happen together, or closely follow upon each other, in the world. Old Hesiod has λιμὸν ὁμοῦ καὶ λοιμόν. Hes. Op. 241.

Seneca also observes, "Solere post magnos terrarum motus pestilentiam fiori." (De nat. q. l. vi. ch. 27.) And he assigns this reason for it, that the air and water are corrupted by the effluvia from the bowels of the earth, vented through the chasms.

and pure air are no security against the infection: for, two or three years before the first English settlers arrived in New England, there had been a plague among the Indian natives which had swept off some tribes entirely, and diminished others so much, that the English found the wilderness in some places covered with sculls and bones; for in some tribes none survived to bury the dead.* Thus were the heathen cast out to make room for these pious puritans, as the Canaanites were before the children of Israel. Now, what was justly inflicted upon the savages, who could not sin with our aggravations, we certainly cannot claim exemption from upon the footing of innocence, nor, I am afraid, of superior goodness; and we see we cannot promise ourselves exemption from our climate.

The remaining signs of this desolation I shall mention together. Fearful sights, and great signs from heaven—signs in the sun, and in the moon, and in the stars—the sea and waves roaring. The mere simple relations of these portentous appearances strike us with horror: and Josephus, who has left us a full history of these times, informs us that they all actually happened at that tragical period. When he enters upon the subject, he uses some of the very words of this chapter, proposing to speak of the *signs* and *prodigies*† which pre-signified the approaching desolation; and mentions the following horrendous prognostications: A star, in the shape of a sword, or a comet, pointing down upon the city, was seen to hang over it for a whole year. There were other strange and unaccountable meteors seen in the aerial regions: armies in battle-array, and chariots surrounding the country and

* See Prince's Chron. of New England, vol. 1. p. 99.
† Evenerunt prodigia, visæ per cœlum concurrere acies, rutilantia arma, et subito nubium igne collucere templum, expassæ repentè delubri fores et audita major humanâ vox excedere Deos, simul ingens motus excedentium. Hist. 1. v.

investing their cities; and this before sunset. The great gate of the temple, which twenty men could scarcely shut, and which was made fast with bolts and bars, opened of its own accord to *let in their enemies:* "for so," says Josephus, "our wise men understood the omen. At the ninth hour of the night a great light shone upon the temple and the altar, as if it had been noon-day; and at the feast of Pentecost, when the Priests went at midnight into the temple to attend their service, they first heard a kind of noise as of persons removing from a place, and then a voice, "LET US AWAY FROM HENCE."

Tacitus, a Roman historian of the same age, confirms this, by relating the same things;* and as he had no connections with the Jews, his testimony is liable to no suspicion. Josephus further adds, what he counts more terrible than all this, that a certain person began, at the feast of Tabernacles, to cry, "A voice against Jerusalem and the temple! A voice against all the people! Wo, wo to them!" And that he continued crying, "Wo! wo!" incessantly for seven years, notwithstanding all the barbarities the Jews exercised upon him to silence him; of which he seemed entirely regardless. Josephus also mentions, as I observed, uncommon perturbations and inundations of the sea; hurricanes, thunder and lightning, and subterranean rumblings and bellowings of the trembling globe. Thus exactly does history agree with this prophecy, and prove it true and divine.

I need not tell you that some of these, or the like horrendous portents, have appeared in *our* age; and we shall presently see, whether they do not probably forebode some grand event to *us* also, as they did to the Jews.

It is evident, that, at least, some of the Jews and other

* σηµιια καί τίρατα. Lib. vii. c. 81.

nations did then consider them as tokens of some dreadful approaching judgments; for we are told in the text, that, as the effects of these appearances, "Men's hearts should fail them for fear, and for looking after those things that are coming upon the earth." The posture of eager, anxious expectation seemed natural, at such a time, when heaven and earth were struggling and travailing, to bring forth some astonishing revolution. And may not the late extraordinary phenomena of nature cast us into the same posture, and set us upon preparation for some new astonishing scenes? Certainly they may, and ought, if these phenomena are indeed prefigurative, or portend something future. And that they *are* really so; that they are *intended* for that purpose by the supreme Manager of the world, and *ought* to be looked upon in that view by us, will, I think, appear at least probable from the following considerations:

1. There seems to be a correspondence and propriety in it, that there should be a kind of *sympathy* between the *natural* and *moral* world; that when the kingdoms of the earth are tossed and agitated, the earth itself should totter and tremble under them;—that when the light of the rational world, the splendour of courts and kingdoms, is about to be extinguished or obscured, the sun and moon, and other lights of the material world, should abate their glory too, and, as it were, appear in mourning; that when some grand event is hastening to the birth, that terribly illustrious stranger, a *comet*, should make us a visit, as its harbinger, and shake its horrendous tail over the astonished world: that when peace is broke among the nations, the harmony of the elements should likewise be broken, and they should fall into transient animosities and conflicts, like the restless beings, for whose use they were formed. There is an apparent congruity and propriety in these

things; and therefore the argument is at least plausible; but as it is drawn only from analogy, which does not *universally* hold, I shall not lay much stress upon it. And yet, on the other hand, as there is an obvious analogy, which does unquestionably hold in *many instances*, between the natural and moral world,* the argument is not to be utterly disregarded.

2. These unusual appearances are peculiarly *adapted* to raise the attention of mankind, and prepare them for important revolutions.

There is a propriety and advantage, if not a necessity, especially with regard to that part of mankind, (and there are always many such upon earth) whose benefit is intended by these extraordinary events and revolutions, that they be prepared for them. And they cannot prepare for them without some general expectation of them; and they can have no expectation of them without some warning or premonition of them. Now the *ordinary* appearances in nature cannot answer this end, *because* they are ordinary, and therefore not adapted to rouse and fix the attention; and because they really have no such premonitory signification. And as to the word of God, it may have no direct perceivable reference to such extraordinary periods; and, therefore, can give us no previous warning of their approach.

But these unusual phenomena are peculiarly adapted to this end: their novelty and terror catch the attention of the gazing world.† They stare and shudder, and pause

---

* See that masterly performance, Bishop Butler's Analogy, in which this is incomparably illustrated.

† Seneca has a remarkable passage to this purpose: Nemo usque eò tardus, et hebes et demissus in terram est, ut ad DIVINA non erigatur, ac toto mente consurgat; utique ubi novum aliquid è cœlo miraculum fulsit. Nam quamdiu solita decurrunt, magnitudinem rerum consuetudo subducit. Ita enim compositi sumus, ut nos quotidiana, etiamsi admiratione digna sunt, tran-

and think, and naturally bode something important impending. They tremble at the power which hangs out these tremendous ensigns of his wrath. They reflect upon their guilt, which makes them timorous, and fear the worst. They view the frame of nature with horror, sensible of its frailty and liableness to disorder, and that they may be buried in its ruins. They begin to reflect upon the necessity of preparation for all events in this fluctuating state of things, and seek the favour and protection of the great Ruler of the universe. These prodigies have this natural *tendency:* and upon some, who were unaffected and unreformed by all the ordinary works of God and means of grace, they have actually had this happy *effect*. Thus some are prepared for the events which these things forebode; and others have had timely warning, and therefore are inexcusable. Now, if these things have *naturally* a tendency to promote this benevolent end, is it not a strong presumption, that they are *intended* for this end by a wise and gracious Providence; that is, that they are *intended* to answer an end, which they have a natural *fitness* and tendency to answer? This seems, at least, highly probable. Our stupid and senseless world, which is proof against the energy of the *usual* means of reformation, seems to need such extraordinary, alarming monitors. And as it is a maxim of the divine government to consult the advantage of his dutiful subjects, to reform those that are corrigible, and at once to punish and leave inexcusable those that continue obstinate; and, as he acts upon this

---

scant: contra, minimarum rerum, si insolitæ prodierunt, spectaculum dulce fiat. Hic itaque cœtus astrorum, quibus immensi corporis pulchritudo distinguitur, populum non convocat. At cum aliquid ex more mutatum est, omnium vultus in cœlo est. Sol spectatorem, nisi cum deficit, non habet. Nemo observat lunam, nisi laborantem. Si quid turbatum est, aut præter consuetudinem emicuit, spectamus, interrogamus, ostendimus. Nat. Q. 1, vii. c. 1.

maxim in all the judgments he inflicts upon the earth, it seems agreeable to the goodness and justice of God, to give such previous warnings when the dreadful period is at hand, in order to alarm a secure world, and set them upon preparation. This, I say, is agreeable to his perfections; and, therefore, there is some apparent reason to expect it. He may hang out a comet, like a blazing ensign over the nations, to rouse them out of their slumbers. He may cause half the globe to tremble under the inhabitants, in order to strike terror to their impenitent hearts. He may preach to them by the voice of thunder, and roaring oceans, that they may hear who were deaf to the gentle voice of his gospel. Such premonitions would be striking illustrations of the goodness and equity of his administration, who does not usually let the blow fall without previous warning, and they would contribute to the right improvement of such dispensations. This, therefore, I think, we may look upon, at least, as a probable argument; especially if we add, that, as these unusual appearances are, in their own nature, fit to be premonitions, so,

3. It seems *natural* to mankind to view them in that light; and they have been universally looked upon in that light in all ages and countries. As to the Jews, the matter is clear; for Josephus tells us, that their wise men actually put this construction upon those alarming appearances, which preceded the destruction of Jerusalem.* And as they had been accustomed to miracles for the confirmation of their religion, they were even extravagant in their demands of this sort of evidence upon every occasion;

* This, as I observed, is also evident from the text; where Christ foretells that these disastrous prodigies should actually cast the nations into distress and perplexity; and that men's hearts, at these premonitions, should fail for fear, and for looking after those things which should come upon the earth.

as we find in the history of the Evangelists. As to the Gentiles, this was the general sentiment of all ranks among them, not only of the vulgar, but of their poets and philosophers. This I could prove from their best authors: but I can now only select a few testimonies. That accurate naturalist, Pliny, says, "An earthquake is not a simple evil; it is at once a present calamity, and a *foretoken* of an equal or greater calamity to come." And he gives this instance of it: "The city of Rome (says he) was never yet shaken with an earthquake but it portended some future event."* Cicero, the greatest philosopher, perhaps, as well as the greatest orator, among the Romans, repeatedly speaks of these things as portentous. "The world has been so formed from the beginning," says he, "that certain signs do precede certain events; some in the lightning, some in strange appearances, some in the stars," &c.† "How often," says he in another place, "has the senate ordered the prophetic books of the Sybils to be consulted, when two suns or three moons have appeared; when blazing meteors have been seen in the night; when a strange noise has been heard in the air? When the earth in the Privernian fields sunk to a prodigious depth, and Apulia was shaken with most violent earthquakes; which things," says he, "were portentous, and foreboded terrible wars and pernicious seditions to the people of Rome.‡ In another place,§ he mentions as

---

* Non simplex malum, aut in ipso motu tantum periculum est: sed par aut majus *ostentum*. Nunquam urbs Romana tremuit, ut non futuri eventus alicujus id prænuntium esset. Vide Grotius, in Matt. xxiv. 7.

† A principio incohoatum esse mundum, ut certis rebus certa signa præcurrerent, &c. De divin. l. 1.

‡ Quibus portentis magna populo Romano bella, perniciosæque seditiones denuntiabantur. Ibid.

§ De Nat. Deor. 1, 2. See so also a poem recited by Cicero, de div. l. 1, (mihi) p. 258.

striking evidences of a Supreme Being, and as omens of some grand futurities, unusual "thunders, hurricanes, storms, snows, hail, devastation, pestilence, the quakings and roarings, and sudden clefts or openings of the earth and rocks; blazing meteors in the heavens, and comets; which lately," says he, "in the wars of Octavianus, were predictions of dreadful calamities; and a double sun foreboded the extinction of that other sun, Publius Africanus."

To these testimonies I might add those of Tacitus, Suetonius, Plutarch, Homer, Virgil, Horace, and many others of the best authors of the heathen world. But my time will not allow me; and besides, it is needless to descend to particulars; for any one that has the least acquaintance with these authors, cannot but know that they are full of omens, prodigies, prognostics, &c. And they hardly relate any important event, without mentioning some strange thing or other that foreboded it; and this is sufficient to show that this was the common sentiment of mankind in the heathen world.* Indeed, they carried it

---

* To this common opinion Milton alludes, when he says, a comet
"————————————from its horrid hair
Shakes pestilence and war."
And that the sun
"————from behind the moon,
In dim eclipse, disastrous twilight sheds
On half the nations, and with fear of change
Perplexes monarchs."————

To this also the still more sublime psalmist may refer : "They that dwell in the uttermost parts of the earth, (*i. e.*, the remotest and most barbarous heathen nations) are afraid at thy tokens." (Psalm lxv. 8.) Remote as they are, these illustrious terrors can reach them; and, barbarous as they are, they can understand their portentous language.

"Behold, his ensigns sweep the sky!
New comets blaze and lightnings fly :
The heathen lands with wild surprise,
From the bright horrors turn their eyes!"—WATTS.

to an extravagant degree of superstition, and made an omen of almost every thing they met with. Even the flight of birds, the feeding of chickens, the entrails of beasts, and a thousand such things, were, with them, significant tokens of some important events. But though this shows their superstition, yet it also seems to show that it is *natural* to mankind to *look* upon some things as ominous, and that some extraordinary things are *really* so. From mankind's generally looking for miracles to prove a religion divine, and from impostors pretending to them, we justly infer that God has so formed our nature, that it is natural to us to expect and regard this sort of evidence in this case; and that God does adapt himself to this innate tendency, and has actually wrought true miracles to attest the true religion; and we may with equal reason, infer from the superstitions of mankind, with regard to omens and prodigies, that God has given a natural bent to our minds to look for them; and that in extraordinary periods he really does give such previous signs of future events. The consent of mankind is always counted a strong argument, and therefore ought to have its weight in this case.*

---

* I am much confirmed in my opinion by the following passage in the great Mr. Howe, whom none can justly suspect of superstition or enthusiasm: "It is (says he) not only innocent, but commendable, to endeavour the making a due improvement of *moral* prognostics; the like may be said of such unusual phenomena as fall out within the sphere, but beside the common course of *nature*, as comets, or whatever else is wont to be reckoned portentous. The total neglect of which things, I conceive, neither agrees with the religious reverence which we owe to the Ruler of the world, nor with common reason and prudence. That they should *cause* what they are thought to *signify*, I understand not; nor am I solicitous how they are themselves caused. Let that be as *naturally* as can be supposed—that hinders not their being *signs to us*, more than the natural causation of the bow in the clouds; though that being an appropriate sign for a determinate purpose, its signification cannot but be more certain; and if we should err in supposing them to signify anything of future events to us all, and that error only lead us into more seriousness, and a more prepared temper of mind for

We ought to guard against superstition in such things; but we should not extravagantly affect the philosopher, so as to look upon every thing as unmeaning, and a thing of course; and differ from the rest of mankind without any good reason for it.

4. History informs us, that such unusual commotions and appearances in the natural world, have, with a surprising regularity, generally preceded unusual commotions and revolutions in the moral world, or among the nations of the earth.

When an hypothesis is supported by experiments and matters of fact, it ought to be received as true. And this argument will appear decisive, if we find, *in fact*, that such commotions and revolutions in the world have been uniformly preceded by some prodigies: for such an uniformity of such extraordinary periods, cannot be the effect of chance, or of blind natural causes, unadjusted and undirected by an intelligent superior power; but it must be the effect of design, a wise and good design, to alarm the world, and put them in a proper posture to meet these grand occurrences. Such prodigies seem by the time, manner, and other circumstances of their appearance, to be particularly adapted to be sig-

such trouble as may be upon the earth, it will surely be a less dangerous error, than that, on the other hand, would be, if we should err in thinking them to signify nothing; and be thereby made the more supine and secure, and more liable to be surprised by the calamities that shall ensue: besides that, we shall be less excusable in departing from the *judgment of all former times and ages*, upon no certainty of being more in the right. And why should we think such things should serve us for no other purpose than only to gratify our curiosity, or furnish us with matter of wonder, or invite us to gaze and admire? It is not fit, indeed, we should be very particular or confident in our interpretations and expectations upon such occasions: but, I conceive, it is very safe to suppose, that some very considerable thing, either in a way of judgment or mercy, may ensue, according as the cry of persevering wickedness or of penitential prayer is more or less loud at that time." Howe's works, vol. ii. pp. 129, 130.

nificant and monitory; and we can give no plausible account of their appearing in such periods, in such circumstances, and with so much regularity, but upon this supposition.

Now, I could make it abundantly evident from the history of the world, that such strange commotions and phenomena have been the usual *forerunners*, and consequently the *prognostications* and tokens, of great changes and revolutions in the kingdoms of the world; and that not only in the age of miracles, and in the country of Judea, which was under an immediate providence, but (which deserves special notice) in *all* ages, and in all countries, as far as we can receive intelligence. Of this I shall give a few instances:

Not to mention the dreadful premonitions of the destruction of Jerusalem, and the preternatural darkness, the tremour of the earth, the rending of the rocks, &c., at the death of Christ;[*] the assassination of Julius Cæsar,

[*] Mr. Whiston supposes that the preternatural darkness of the sun, at that time, was a *cometary* eclipse; for it could not proceed from the usual cause, viz., the interposition of the moon, because it was at the full; whereas an eclipse of the sun can never happen but at the change of the moon. He supposes that the comet which then appeared was not only the natural cause of the eclipse, but also of the uncommon phenomena at that time; related, some of them, by the evangelists, and others, in the testament of Levi, and the recognitions of Clement, viz., the rocks rending; the sun looking fiery, and seeming for some time to be extinguished, and to tremble; the tides of the ocean and large seas swelling to an unusual height; commotions in the waters to an uncommon depth and in an uncommon degree; the waters of some lakes running down into the clefts newly opened in the earth, and so dried up. (See Whiston's Six Dissertations, p. 164, &c.) It is easy to see how many of these things have happened in our age. And if they were occasioned by the approach of a comet at that time, it seems to confirm Mr. Wesley's opinion, that the approach of the comet which is to appear in the year 1758, may be the cause of the like strange things now. It very much surprised me to find instances so nearly parallel; and yet Mr. Whiston ascribed the former to a comet, though he wrote about twenty years ago, and knew nothing of the similar phenomena of this year, before the approach of a comet.

the first Roman Emperor, in the senate-house, was an event of the utmost importance, and produced the most terrible consequences to the world. It divided the vast Roman empire into two grand factions, which carried on a most bloody civil war for some years, in which many of the greatest men of Rome, and many thousands of others, lost their lives. Now, almost all authors that write of these times, agree that this event was portended by the most terrible prodigies: such as a preternatural darkness of the sun for a year, tremours and openings of the earth, unusual ferments of the sea, inundations of the Tiber, the river that ran by Rome, and the great river Eridanus; unusual thunderings, and eruptions of Mount Etna; quakings of the Alpine mountains, the clash of arms in the air, strange meteors, and lightnings, and blazing comets.*

* These are the prodigies which Virgil and Horace so beautifully describe :—

"Sol tibi signa dabit: solem quis dicere falsum
Audeat! Ille etiam cæcos instare tumultus
Sæpe monet, fraudemque et operta tumescere bella.
Ille etiam extincto miseratus Cæsare Romam,
Cum caput obscura nitidum ferrugine texit,
Impiaque æternam timuerunt sæcula noctem.
Tempore quanquam illo tellus quoque et æquora ponti,
Obscenæque canes, importunæque volucres
Signa dabant. Quotiens Cyclopum effervere in agros
Vidimus undantem ruptis fornacibus Ætnam,
Flammarumque globos liquefactaque volvere saxa!
Armorum sonitum toto Germania cœlo
Audiit: insolitis tremuerunt motibus Alpes.
Vox quoque per lucos vulgo exaudita silentes,
Ingens, et simulacra modis pallentia miris
Visa sub obscurum noctis; pecudesque locutæ,
Infandum! sistunt amnes, terræque dehiscunt;
Et mæstum illacrymat templis ebur, æraque sudant.
Proluit insano, contorquens vortice silvas
Fluviorum rex Eridanus, camposque per omnes
Cum stabulis armenta tulit. Nec tempore eodem
Tristibus aut extis fibræ apparere minaces,
Aut puteis manare cruor cessavit; et alte
Per noctem resonare, lupis ululantibus, urbes.

The subversion and destruction of the vast Roman empire by the Goths, Vandals, and other savage nations, after it had ruled the world so long, was a revolution of the most awful importance to the nations of the earth; and this, we find in history, was preceded and prognosticated by strange commotions and disorders in the natural world, by frequent and extensive earthquakes, felt for many days successively, in most provinces of the empire: the sky appearing all in a flame over the city of Constantinople, the then seat of the empire, which so terrified the inhabitants, and the Emperor himself, that they abandoned the city, and fled into the fields; terrible overflowings of the

> Non alias cælo ceciderunt plura sereno
> Fulgura; nec diri totiens arsere cometæ.
> Ergo inter sese paribus concurrere telis
> Romanas acies iterum videre Philippi," &c.
> Virg. Georg. i. l. 468–490
> Jam satis terris nivis, atque diræ
> Grandinis misit Pater, et rubente
> Dextera sacras jaculatus arces,
>   Terruit urbem—
> Vidimus flavum Tiberim retortis
> Littore Etrusco violenter undis,
> Ire dejectum monumenta regis,
>   Templaque Vestæ, &c.—*Hor.*

Pliny also says, Prodigiosus solis defectus, occiso Dictatore Cæsare, totius pene anni pallore continuo. L. ii. c. 80.

Seneca intimates that the destruction of Troy was foreboded by such terrible omens, when he introduces Talthybius, saying—

> Vidi, ipse vidi———
> Cum subito cæco terra mugitu fremens
> Concussa, cæcos traxit, ex imo sinus.
> Movere silvæ capita, et excelsum nemus
> Fragore vasto tonuit, et lucus sacer:
> Idæa ruptis saxa ceciderunt jugis.
> Nec sola tellus tremuit: et pontus suum
> Adesse Achillem sensit, ac stravit vada.
> Tunc scissa tellus aperit immensos specus:
> Et hiatus Erebri pervium ad superos iter
> Tellure fractra præbet, ac tumulum levat,
> Sen. Trag. Troas, Act 2.

sea, which laid whole countries under water; unusual rains, thunder, and lightning, and many other prodigies.* Thus the conflicts and dying struggles of this dissolving empire, struck all nature, as it were, into sympathetic emotions and agonies.

There is nothing more natural, nothing which astronomers can compute with more exactness, than eclipses of the sun and moon; and yet these have so regularly and uniformly preceded the first grand breaches, and the total overthrow of kingdoms and nations, that we cannot but think they were intended to signify such revolutions; and thus mankind generally interpreted them. A total eclipse of the sun happened before the captivity of the ten tribes by the Assyrians;† before the captivity of the Jews in Babylon; at the death of Christ, about thirty-seven years and a half before the last destruction of Jerusalem; and about the same number of years before the slaughter of six hundred thousand Jews under Adrian; before the conquest of the Babylonians by the Medes;‡ and before the fall of the Medo-Persian, Grecian, and Roman empires. Mr. Whiston supposes a total eclipse of the sun to precede the first grand breach upon these empires; and a total eclipse of the moon to precede their total overthrow; and that upon a mean, they precede these revolutions about thirty-eight years. Thus, a total eclipse of the sun happened before the first grand breach upon the Assyrian empire, by the miraculous destruction of one hundred and eighty-five thousand Assyrians, in the days of Hezekiah; before the second grand breach in the destruction of Nineveh: and a total eclipse of the moon before the total over-

---

* See Univ. Hist., vol. xvi. pp. 445, 469, 476, 515.

† This, Mr. Whiston supposes, was foretold by Amos, ch. viii. 7-10; and Zech xiv. 5. And was attended with an earthquake. Amos i. 1.

‡ Mr. Whiston apprehends, that this was predicted by Isaiah, ch. xiii. 1-17; xiv. 9-18.

throw of the Assyrian empire removed to Babylon, by Cyrus: a total eclipse of the sun before the first grand breach upon the Persian empire, by the defeat of Xerxes in Greece; a total eclipse of the moon before its final overthrow by Alexander the Great; a total eclipse of the sun before the first grand breach upon the Grecian empire; a total eclipse of the moon the night before its total overthrow by the Romans: a total eclipse of the sun, visible from Scotland to the Euphrates, before the destruction of the Roman empire, under Augustulus, &c., as Mr. Whiston relates.* On all which, that learned writer makes this remark: " That such a regular correspondence of eclipses, total eclipses of the sun, just before the grand breaches upon every one of the four monarchies, and those all visible through those monarchies; as also that such a regular correspondence of eclipses, total eclipses of the moon, just before the *ends* of every one of the same four monarchies, and those all visible through those monarchies; should be all by chance, and without design, is plainly incredible: and if that be incredible, this correspondence can be no other than directly supernatural and providential. Known unto God are all his works from the beginning."†

These instances may suffice as a specimen of the evidence from facts which history affords us in this case. And I must remind you, that these portentous facts are not confined to the age and country of *miracles :* but are found in various ages, and in various parts of the world, which were not the seats of miraculous operations; and hence, it is probable, these prognostications are intended to be *common* warnings to mankind in *general*, in *all* ages and countries, whensoever some important and extraor-

---
*See his Six Dissert. from p. 188, to p. 258.   † Id. p. 262.

dinary period is approaching; and they appear, just when these grand exigencies render it expedient.*

Upon the whole, I think we may, without superstition or enthusiasm, reflect with awe upon the late strange appearances in nature, as forerunners of some grand events which may nearly affect *us* in common with the kingdoms of the earth. There is, at least, a great probability for it; and probability is our guide in most of our actions, and may safely be followed in this case.

But what those grand events, what those important revolutions are; whether the works of vengeance or of mercy; whether the blow will fall upon this nation or that; these things I will not pretend to determine, nor hardly venture to conjecture. This is certain, we are now come' to a very dark time; a day of trouble, and rebuke, and blasphemy, 2 Kings xix. 3; and every day seems to grow darker and darker. Our expeditions hitherto have been surprisingly unsuccessful. Our country has been ravaged with impunity. We tremble for the fate of the important island of Minorca, and for the event of the naval engagement in the Mediterranean, which, at best, has not been much in our favour.† Oswego, the most important fort on the frontiers of British America, is now in the

* I might add another argument of considerable weight, that in the language of the prophets, the trembling of the earth, the turning of the sun into darkness, and the moon into blood, the falling of stars, the removal of mountains, blood, fire, and pillars of smoke, &c., do signify the revolutions and subversion of kingdoms and nations. Of this, numberless instances might be given. These, indeed, may be understood as bold poetical images: but if we suppose such things do generally precede and forbode such events, the figures are much more natural and easy: being a familiar metonymy of the signs for the things signified. And I cannot well see the propriety of the images, if there be no sympathy between the material and moral world; or if such commotions in the kingdoms of mankind are not usually attended with correspondent commotions in nature.

† We have since received certain intelligence that Minorca surrendered to the French Marshal, Duke de Richelieu, on the 29th of June last, after a brave defence by General Blackeney, that Admiral Byng, in a most cow-

hands of our enemies; and the slow motions of our northern army afford us but little reason to hope for reprisals. The power of France, especially by land, is formidable; and the more so, because thoroughly exasperated. In short, we are alarmed from the highest authority among us,* that the dispute between the two crowns grows near to a crisis, whether these colonies are still to remain under the happy constitution of Great Britain, or become subject to the arbitrary power of a despotic prince. Our religion, our liberty, our property, our lives, and everything dear and valuable are at stake; and the die spins dreadfully doubtful: and, which is still more discouraging, the holy Spirit of God is withdrawn from us. We frequent the house of God time after time, and yet see but little appearances of his being at work among us. The work of conversion and reformation goes on but slowly, if at all. Both the inflicted and threatened chastisements of the divine hand, have little or no effect upon the generality; they are hardy enough to sin on still, in the midst of a sickly neighbourhood and a bleeding country. The horrid sound of war ringing in their ears cannot rouse them from their sinful security. And are not these *moral* prognostics very alarming, as well as the former natural ones? May not our hearts fail for looking after those things that are coming upon the earth?

What if God be now about to arise and punish the inhabitants of the world for their iniquities; and particularly us, whose sins have been attended with peculiar aggravations, by reason of our peculiar advantages. What if the measure of our iniquity, and that of our mother country, be just full? It has been filling fast for a long season.

ardly and scandalous manner, refused to attack the French fleet vigorously; and by that means the garrison in Fort St. Philip received no supplies, and were obliged to surrender.

* The Governor's Speech to the Assembly, Sept. 20, 1756.

We have for a long time sinned on with impunity: but can we expect the reins will always be laid upon our necks, without any check? Is there indeed a God that governs the world, and is he displeased with our sin; and will he not let us know it? The British isle has long been the favourite of Providence: and it is really astonishing to read in history how remarkably Providence has appeared in its favour when on the very brink of ruin; but it has been an ungrateful, guilty spot, of this guilty globe: it has forgot its God in its prosperity; abused his mercies, and despised his threatenings: and what if the rod that has been so long held over it be now about to smite? What if the commission be now issued forth to the executioners of divine vengeance, "Put ye in the sickle, for the harvest is ripe; come, get ye down, for the press is full; the fats overflow; for their wickedness is great?" Joel iii. 13. What if the liberty and plenty we have ungratefully abused, be about to be taken from us? What if the holy religion which we have at once professed and profaned, be about to be exchanged for popish tyranny and superstition? What if the last and most violent struggle of antichrist, or the powers of popery, be yet to come, and now beginning? What if, before the glorious victory which shall at length be obtained over him by the followers of the Lamb, power be given him to make war with the saints and overcome; to wear out the saints of the Most High, and scatter the power of the holy people, according to the prophecies of Daniel and Revelation? Dan. vii. 25, xii. 2; Rev. xiii. 7. What if God visit the Protestant churches, which are an huge mass of corruption, with a few grains of salt in it, notwithstanding their peculiar advantages, with severe judgments, to purify them, before the happy period of the entire downfull of popery, and the universal conversion of Jews and Gentiles? What if the time be come when judgments must begin at the house of God, his Protestant churches; 1 Pet. iv. 17; and the executioners of his vengeance must begin to slay at the *sanctuary* of the Lord? Ezek. ix. 6. "The signs of the times" look threatening and gloomy; and who knows but such dread events may be at hand?

And if so, what will become of those crowds of sinners among us, who have sinned away the days of liberty, plenty, and gospel light? With what horror must they enter upon those dark tremendous scenes? Alas! they are unprepared for dismal days; unprepared for death; unprepared for eternity! In the midst of terror and desolation, conscience follows them with its horrid, portentous alarms: God frowns upon them from above; and all nature musters up its terrors against them around.

Is it not, therefore, the highest wisdom to prepare in time for such dreadful days? Now, sinners, now be reconciled to God; fly to the arms of his grace, which are expanded wide to embrace you: fly to Jesus the only Saviour, who can protect you in all the disorders of this fluctuating world, and in all the terrors of the final judgment. Make your own conscience your friend, that it may smile upon you within, though the face of nature should frown upon you without. Now become sincere Christians; and you are safe. And now is the most proper time for it. Therefore, "Seek the Lord while he may be found: call upon him while he is near." Isaiah lv. 6. "Give glory to the LORD your God, before he cause darkness, and before your feet stumble upon the dark mountains; and while ye look for light, he turn it into the shadow of death, and make it gross darkness. But if ye will not hear it, my soul shall weep in secret places for your pride, and mine eye shall weep sore, and run down with tears, because the Lord's flock is carried away captive. Jer. xiii. 16, 17.

But, on the other hand, what if the great God be now about to take to him his great power, and reign? What if the kingdoms of the earth are now about to become the kingdoms of our Lord and of his Christ, Rev. xi. 15, and the long-expected period of the conversion of the Jews, and the fulness of the Gentiles, be just come? This would be a grand revolution indeed: and we cannot expect it will be brought about without much blood and desolation. Many thrones must totter and fall; many kingdoms must be overturned, which are now the supports of Popery, Mahometanism, and heathenism. In this sense, the gentle Saviour came not to send peace upon earth, but a sword. And who knows but the ferment that is now begun, may work up this grand revolution? Who knows but the mystery of God is about to be finished, in the days of the voice of the seventh angel; and that the sixth vial is running, and the seventh about to be poured out upon the persecuting powers of Rome? What if great Babylon is come into remembrance before God; and we shall ere long hear the proclamation, "Babylon is fallen! is fallen!" Isa. xxi. 9. If so, "rejoice over her, ye heavens, and ye holy apostles and prophets, for God hath avenged you on her." What if the signal be now given for the grand decisive conflict between the followers of the Lamb and the followers of the beast? It may be sharp and bloody; and you and I and millions more, may fall in it. But victory shall soon be determined in favour of the oppressed servants of Jesus. What if he who is called Faithful and True, and who maketh war in righteousness, be about to ascend the white horse of victory and triumph, followed by the armies of heaven, that is, by his faithful servants? And what if, according to the vision of St. John, the beast and the kings of the earth, and their armies, were about to gather together to make war with

Him that sits on the horse, and his army? Rev. xix. 19. The issue of the battle is represented in the same vision: "The beast and the false prophet were taken; and the remnant were slain with the sword of him that sat on the horse. And an angel standing in the sun," says St. John, "cried with a loud voice, saying to all the fowls that fly in the midst of heaven, Come, and gather yourselves together unto the supper of the great God; that ye may eat the flesh of kings, and the flesh of captains, and the flesh of mighty men, and the flesh of horses, and of them that sit on them, and the flesh of all men, both free and bond, both small and great." Rev. xix. 17, 18. Accordingly they were all sated with a dreadful meal. This period, we have reason to expect, though we may not exactly calculate the time of its commencement. The time indeed is determined in prophetic computation, both in Daniel and the Revelation. This grand conflict is to be in the close of three years and a half; time, times, and a half a time; forty-two months, or twelve hundred and sixty days: all which computations exactly amount to the same sum, viz., twelve hundred and sixty years.* But at what time this period commenced is not fully agreed upon; and, consequently, it is uncertain when it will end. However, it is generally agreed, that we are not far from the end of it; and, consequently, matters must

---

* The ancient year consisted of three hundred and sixty days; and a month of thirty days. A prophetic day is a year; a week, is a week of years, viz., seven years; a month is a month of years, viz., thirty years. Therefore, twelve hundred and sixty days, in the prophetical arithmetic, are twelve hundred and sixty years: forty-two months multiplied by thirty (the number of years in a prophetical month) amount to the same number, twelve hundred and sixty years; three years and a half, i. e., three times three hundred and sixty, and the half of three hundred and sixty, viz., one hundred and eighty, amount also to the same number, twelve hundred and sixty years. *Time* is one year; *times* two years; and *half a time* is half a year; which is but another way of expressing three years and a half, and makes the same number, twelve hundred and sixty.

be ripening fast for that grand result. If this glorious day be so near, let us bless God and rejoice, though we should be overwhelmed in those commotions that may introduce it. And let it be the matter of our daily prayer that it may be hastened.

Upon the whole, let us endeavour to put ourselves in a posture of readiness to meet with all events that may be approaching. Though I know not these futurities, yet I *know* it shall be well with them that fear God: but it will not be well with the wicked: neither shall he prolong his days, which are as a shadow; because he feareth not before God. Eccl. viii. 12, 13. It shall, however, be *well* with the righteous. Isa. iii. 10, 11. Their heaven is sure; and while they have a place to go to there, it is little matter to them what becomes of this earth, and all their mortal interests. The Ruler of the universe is their patron, their tutelary Deity; and under his protection they are safe, come what will. Therefore put on courage, and show the world you have a God to go to, in the greatest difficulty; and that you can confidently trust him. But at all adventures, I must say on the other hand, "Wo unto the wicked, it shall be *ill* with him; for the reward of his hands shall be given him." Isa. iii. 10, 11. Suppose these uncommon appearances in nature were wholly insignificant; suppose there were no such thing as war in the world, and you were in no danger of being involved in the ruins of your country: yet, you have death, the king of terrors; you have an angry conscience, and, which is worse, an angry God, to encounter with; you have the terrors of a dissolving world, and of a final judgment, to pass through: you have the pains of hell to endure. And are you hardy enough to encounter these without horror? Oh! that you would be so wise as to be reconciled to God, and make him your friend, whose protection you so much need.

Finally, I would recommend it to you all, to make this a praying time among you; often appear in the posture of petitioners at the throne of grace, in secret, in your families, and in those societies* which I desired you to set up for this end. Pray for the continuance of your religion and liberty: pray for the establishment of the British throne, and the preservation of the royal life, which is of so much importance at this critical juncture. Pray for the success of our arms by sea and land, and the restraint and confusion of our enemies. Pray that you and others may be prepared for all occurrences. But, above all, pray that the Holy Spirit of God may be poured out upon us, to work a general reformation. Though all these natural prodigies should be unmeaning, alas! we have moral prognostics enough to make our hearts meditate terror, and forebode some impending judgments; I mean, the general wickedness and impiety that prevail in our country. Alas! I am afraid the voice of this prodigy, though more terrible and more certainly ominous than earthquakes or blazing stars, will not be heard till it be too late. But I must repeat the declaration I have often made in your hearing, that it will never be well with our country, till there be more of the fear and love of God, more sincere practical religion, among us: and that all our military forces will not save us in the issue, without a general repentance and reformation. Could I once convince my countrymen that there is something in this proposal, I should begin to entertain some hopes of a speedy deliverance. But, alas! while it is disregarded as a chimerical project, my heart cannot but forebode some fearful things coming upon us; which may God, of his infinite mercy, prevent, for his name's sake. Amen.

* Societies for prayer, intended to be continued during the present alarming situation of our public affairs.

SERMON LXV.

THE HAPPY EFFECTS OF THE POURING OUT OF THE SPIRIT.*

ISAIAH XXXII. 13–19.—*Upon the land of my people shall come up thorns and briers; yea, upon all the houses of joy in the joyous city; because the palaces shall be forsaken, the multitude of the city shall be left, the forts and towers shall be for dens for ever, a joy of wild asses, a pasture of flocks:* until the Spirit be poured upon us from on high, *and the wilderness be a fruitful field, and the fruitful field be counted for a forest. Then judgment shall dwell in the wilderness, and righteousness remain in the fruitful field. And the work of righteousness shall be peace; and the effect of righteousness, quietness and assurance for ever. And my people shall dwell in a peaceable habitation, and in sure dwellings, and in quiet resting-places, when it shall hail, coming down upon the forest.*

IT is our lot to be born in an age of blood and slaughter; an age, in which mankind remarkably exemplify the character given of them long ago by an inspired pen, "Hateful, and hating one another;" an age, which has seen a strange revolution in that Britain that about three hundred years ago had crushed the power of France, and had the crown of that kingdom made over to her by treaty —now everywhere defeated by that very power; an age,

* This Sermon is dated, Hanover, October 16, 1757,

in which the cause of liberty and the Protestant religion is in the most alarming danger, from the formidable confederacy of Popish tyrants and their vassals; an age, in which our liberty, our property, our lives, and our religion, which should be dearer to us than all, are no longer insured to us with the usual firmness of the British constitution, but disputed with a powerful invader; and the issue of the contest is dreadfully uncertain. And in such an age can there be so stupid a soul among us, as to be thoughtless and unconcerned? Sure, if we have anything of the *man*, the *patriot*, the *Christian*, within us, we must be deeply solicitous about these important interests, and anxious for a remedy to our bleeding country and nation.

I need not detain you with a particular account of the present mortifying and alarming situation of our public affairs. I need not tell you of slaughtered families, mangled corpses, men, women, and children, held in barbarous captivity in the dens of savages; routed garrisons, demolished fortifications, deserted, desolated settlements, upon our frontiers. I need not remind you of defeated armies, blasted expeditions, and abortive schemes—of divided, dilatory counsels on both sides the ocean—a jangling, unsettled ministry, and an uneasy, murmuring, clamorous people. I need not tell you that our enemies have pushed their conquests with surprising rapidity, and executed all their schemes; while all our attempts to stop their progress have issued in disappointment and mortification; and that they are now become formidable, even in America, where, a few years ago, they were so contemptible. I need not tell you that our hopes are lowered as to our brave ally, the king of Prussia, who has lately been routed, and obliged to break up the siege of Prague; and who has almost the half of the powers of Europe for his enemies. He stands the single champion of the Protestant cause upon the continent; and should he be crushed, that important cause would probably fall with him, especially in Germany. I need not tell you how gloomy and discouraging the prospect is before us, from the growing power of the French—from their great influence with the Indian savages—from the naked and defenceless state of our country—from the dastardly, secure spirit that prevails among the generality, and from many causes that I need not name. These things are too public and notorious for me to enlarge upon them. Alas! who is ignorant of them? though but few lay them properly to heart.

The great inquiry I would now employ your time and thoughts about, is, What is the best remedy in this melancholy case? This, I think, we may clearly discover in the verses I have read to you.

At the time to which this prophecy seems principally to refer, namely, at the destruction of the Jews by the Babylonians, their iniquities were come to the full. It was inconsistent with the maxims of the divine government to delay their punishment any longer. Therefore the Babylonians were commissioned as the executioners of divine vengeance to ravage their land, destroy their city and temple, and carry away the inhabitants by three successive captivities, till the land was left uninhabited, untilled, and desolate for seventy years. In this time was fulfilled the prophecy in my text: "Upon the land of my people shall come up thorns and briers; yea, in all the houses of joy in the joyous city."* The epithet *joyous* is added with design to aggravate the calamity. "The houses of *joy*"

---

* Or, as some render the word, "*Burning* upon all the houses of joy," &c. *ב* is rendered *burning* in Isa. iii. 24; and it may bear the same version here. In this sense it was literally accomplished in the destruction of Jerusalem by the Babylonians, when the city and all the houses of state and luxury within it were burnt to ashes.

are turned into heaps of rubbish. "The *joyous* city" is made a melancholy waste, overrun with briers and thorns. The men of sensuality and luxury, who were wont to riot in these houses of joy, and to spend their time in pleasure, are now stripped of all their possessions, and feel the reverse of their usual delights in a servile, dismal captivity; and to such, the calamities of war, poverty, and thraldom, are peculiarly painful and mortifying. These effeminate souls were never inured to hardships and self-denial, and therefore must sink the lower under their weight. I leave you, my brethren, to judge, whether the calamities we fear, should they fall upon us, would not fall the heavier upon multitudes of our countrymen on this account, who have been accustomed to live in luxury and pleasure, and are by these means enervated and unmanned. The epithet *joyous* may also intimate, that the extravagant luxury and love of pleasure that prevailed among the Jews, was one cause of the destruction of their country and nation. Their houses are laid in ruins, because they have been *houses* of guilty *joy*. Their city is made desolate, because it had been unseasonably and excessively a *joyous* city. So the words may be rendered; "Upon the land of my people shall come up briers and thorns, *because** of the houses of joy in the joyous city." These houses of joy brought destruction upon the inhabitants. Their luxury and pleasure had a natural tendency to destroy them, according to the course of things. They produced thoughtless security and presumption. They turned the attention of the court and ministry from the concerns of their country, to sensual gratifications and amusements. They softened and unmanned the populace, and rendered them

---

* כי על־בל־בתי משושקריה עליזת :
 ׳כ is generally rendered *because*. So it is rendered in the very next verse, and it may be so translated here, with the same propriety.

impatient of the generous dangers and hardships of soldiers in the field. They tempted them to lay out that substance in diversions and extravagant pleasures which should have been expended in the defence of their country; and luxury and pleasure provoked the God of heaven, who holds the scale of empire in his hand, and lets it rise or fall according to his pleasure. The unseasonable joy of this people at a time when the tokens of the Almighty's anger were upon them; their taste for mirth and pleasure, when he called them to repentance, brought his heavy vengeance upon them, and he determined to destroy a people that would not be amended by chastisement. Here also I leave you to judge, whether we and our nation be not in danger from the same quarter. Has not a deluge of luxury and pleasure almost overwhelmed all ranks, from the highest to the lowest? To eat and drink delicately and freely: to feast, and dance, and riot; to pamper cocks or horses; to observe the anxious, important, interesting event—which of two horses can run fastest; or which of two cocks can flutter and spur most dexterously:—these are the grand affairs that almost engross the attention of some of our great men. And little, low-lived sinners imitate them to the utmost of their power. The low-born sinner can leave a needy family to starve at home, and add one to the rabble at a horse-race or a cock-fight. He can get drunk and turn himself into a beast with the lowest, as well as his betters with more delicate liquors. On this account, I am afraid this fruitful year, with which a gracious God has blessed our guilty country, will prove a curse to many, who add to their guilt by ungratefully abusing the additional mercies of God towards them. How unseasonable is this taste for pleasure and diversions, at such a time as this! A time, when "the Lord of Hosts calls to weeping, and to mourning, and to baldness, and to girding with sackclock;" *i. e.*, to all the solemn and public evidences of repentance. Now, if ever, these things are seasonable; they are a kind of *decencies* in our present circumstances. But, alas! instead of these, "Behold, joy and gladness, slaying oxen, and killing sheep, eating flesh, and drinking wine;" that is, all the furniture of luxury and festivity, as if they acted upon the *epicurean* maxim, "Let us eat and drink, for to-morrow we die." And I wish the secret revealed to the prophet with regard to such, may not be equally applicable to our age and country: "It was revealed in mine ears by the LORD of Hosts, surely this iniquity shall not be purged from you, till ye die, saith the Lord GOD of Hosts." Isaiah xxii. 12–14.

The prophet goes on to describe the desolation of Judea and Jerusalem, and to assign the reason why the land should be overrun with briers and thorns during the captivity; namely, "Because the palaces shall be forsaken, the multitude* of the city shall be left, and the noise of it shall cease; the forts of the towers shall be for dens for ever:" that is, for a long time, which is sometimes all the meaning of this word. These places of strength and beauty shall be "a joy of wild asses, a pasture for flocks;" where they shall graze to the full, and lie down unmolested.

When the prophet has thus described the utter desolation of the Holy Land, he fixes the time of its continuance, or informs the Jews how long it should last; and that is, "UNTIL THE SPIRIT BE POURED UPON US FROM ON HIGH." The Holy Spirit of God is represented in the Scriptures as the original fountain of all the real goodness and virtue which is to be found in our degenerate world; the only author of reformation, conversion, sanctification, and every

---

* המון here translated m*ultitude*, signifies also the *noise* or *tumult* of the multitude—the stir and hurry of a crowded city.

grace included in the character of a saint, or a good man. The POURING* out of the Spirit is a Scripture phrase, which signifies a plentiful communication of his influence to effect a thorough reformation. It is not a *distilling*, or falling in gentle drops, like the dew; but a copious effusion, or pouring out, like a mighty shower, or torrent that carries all before it. Now, as the communication of the Spirit is necessary to produce a reformation, so a *large* communication, or *outpouring* of the Spirit, is necessary to produce a *public, general* reformation; such as may save a country on the brink of ruin, or recover one already laid desolate. Without this remedy, all other applications will be ineffectual; and the distempered body politic will languish more and more, till it is at length dissolved. UNTIL this outpouring of the Spirit, says the prophet, "briers and thorns shall come upon the land; and the houses of joy, the palaces, and towers, shall be heaps of ruins, dens for wild beasts, and pastures for flocks." UNTIL that blessed time come, no means can effectually repair a broken state, or repeople a desolate country.

But when that blessed time comes, then what a glorious revolution—what a happy alteration follows! Then says the prophet, " The wilderness shall be a fruitful field, and the fruitful field be counted for a forest. Then judgment shall dwell in the wilderness, and righteousness remain in the fruitful field: and the work of righteousness shall be peace, and the effect of righteousness, quietness and assurance for ever; and my people shall dwell in a peaceable habitation, and in sure dwellings, and in quiet resting-

---

* The word here rendered *poured* (ערה) generally signifies *to be made naked*, *i. e.* to be *revealed* in full power. This may be illustrated by that expression in Isaiah lii. 10: The Lord hath *made bare* his holy arm in the eyes of all the nations;" that is, hath given an illustrious display of his Power. The sense is the same, however we render it; namely, a full exertion of the power of the Spirit to produce a reformation.

places, when it shall hail, coming down upon the forest." These are the blessed pacific effects of the outpouring of the Spirit; and these effectually cure all the ravages of war, and ensure a lasting peace, with all its blessings.

"The wilderness shall be a fruitful field;" that is, the country that had been reduced into a mere wilderness by the ravages of war, and the captivity of the inhabitants, shall again be tilled and improved, and become as a fruitful field, or a Carmel.*

"And the fruitful field shall be counted for a forest;" that is, upon this happy turn of affairs, the country of the enemy, which had been a fruitful field, a mere Carmel, shall be laid waste in its turn, and made a mere forest, a wild uninhabited wood: it shall suffer itself what it had inflicted, and be made a wilderness, as it had made other countries so. This was remarkably accomplished upon Babylon, which had spread desolation through the country of the Jews, according to the prediction of Jeremiah: "When seventy years are accomplished, (in the captivity of the Jews) I will punish the king of Babylon, and that nation, saith the LORD, for their iniquity, and the land of the Chaldeans, and will make it perpetual desolations."† And this is the usual procedure of Providence, to make use of one guilty nation to execute his judgments upon another, and then to execute the executioner. From hence we may prognosticate the future fall of France, though she should now be used as a rod in the Divine hand to chastise rebellious Britons.

"Then judgment shall dwell in the wilderness, and

---

* כרמל Carmel, was the proper name of a very fertile mountain in Judea; and hence it is here used appellatively, to signify a country fruitful like the proper Carmel: As if it had been said, "The whole country of Canaan shall be one entire Carmel." So the Septuagint renders it: "εσαι ερημος ὁ Χερμελ."

† Jer. xxv. 12. See also Isa. xxxiv. 11-15, and xiv. 22, 23.

righteousness remain in the fruitful field." *Judgment* sometimes signifies punishment from the hand of God, and sometimes the same with justice or righteousness. If we take it to signify *punishment* from the Divine hand, then the meaning is "The heavy judgments of God shall dwell (that is, long remain) upon the country of the enemy, which, though once a fruitful Carmel, is now turned into a wilderness." In this sense, the prophecy has been literally accomplished upon Babylon, which remains a wilderness unto this day. If by *judgment* we understand *righteousness*, then the meaning is, "Righteousness shall dwell in the land of Judea, which was once made a wilderness, but is now improved into a fruitful field, since the pouring out of the Spirit." And so it *designs* the same with the following sentence: "Righteousness shall remain in the fruitful field." That is, "Righteousness, which in the Scripture sense often signifies all goodness, or the whole of true religion, or a proper temper and conduct towards God and man; righteousness, in this extensive sense, shall remain in the fruitful field—it shall possess the hearts and govern the practices of the inhabitants; and this shall turn their country into a Carmel, a paradise, a fruitful field."

"And the work of righteousness shall be peace, and the effect of righteousness, quietness, and assurance for ever." When righteousness thus becomes the universal principle and rule of action, it will produce peace, quietness, and assurance, or security from danger." And in consequence of this, "my people shall dwell in a peaceable habitation," &c. They shall remain undisturbed in their possessions, and enjoy the blessings of peace, free from factions at home, and invasions from abroad. In this unmolested and happy situation shall they continue, even "when it shall hail, coming down upon the forest;" or when storms of public calamities break upon other countries, and lay them waste.

You may now have a full view of the regular gradation from truth to truth in my text. Desolation overspreads the country, UNTIL the Spirit is poured out; the Spirit poured out produces righteousness, or true religion; righteousness produces peace, quietness, and assurance; and under its influence the inhabitants live in a peaceable habitation, and in sure dwellings, and in quiet resting-places, even when storms and tempest toss and desolate other nations.

Thus, you see, the outpouring of the Holy Spirit is the great and only remedy for a ruined country; the only effectual preventive of national calamities and desolations, and the only sure cause of a lasting and well-established peace. This is the truth I now intend chiefly to illustrate.

And this is the more necessary to be illustrated and inculcated as it is but very little regarded. We all complain that our country cannot be defended, nor an advantageous peace obtained without better regulations; without timely and vigorous measures, unanimity, courage, and public spirit among all ranks. There are some also who complain, that our country cannot be safe or prosperous without a general reformation; that it cannot be expected the undertakings of a guilty, impenitent people, ripe for the judgments of God, can succeed, till their repentance be in some measure as signal and public as their sin. Thus far we look: but, unless we look farther, we do not go to the bottom of things. As all our measures are not likely to be successful without a reformation; so we may despair of ever seeing a thorough, general reformation, *unless the Spirit be poured upon us from on high.* I may illustrate this by the piece of history to which my text refers, and in which it had its accomplishment. The Jews were a numerous and powerful people: their cities were all fortified, especially Jerusalem, their capital; and yet their impenitent sinning, without reformation, rendered them an easy prey to their enemies. But why did they continue impenitent? Why were they not reformed? Was it because they did not enjoy proper means? No: they had the law of Moses; they had the ministry of the prophets, who loudly called them to repentance through a succession of ages, and in the most explicit manner denounced the judgments of God against them, if they should continue impenitent; they enjoyed all the advantages of an extraordinary immediate providence; in short, they had better helps and excitements for reformation than all mankind beside, except such as we, who have the happiness of living under the more complete and glorious dispensation of the gospel. And yet they sinned on still, impenitent and unreformed: no general reformation was carried on by all these means; and even under the hardships of captivity, they still continued the same incorrigible sinners. Hence God complains of them, "When they entered unto the heathen, whither they went, they profaned my holy name," as they had done before in their own land. Ezek. xxxvi. 20. And what was wanting all this time for their effectual reformation? Why, the Spirit was not yet poured upon them from on high; and while he was absent, they continued unreformed, and their country desolate. But when the time for their restoration came, then the Spirit was poured out. Thus their restoration and the effusion of the Spirit are connected in the divine promise: "I will take you from among the heathen, and gather you out of all countries, and will bring you into your own land; THEN will I sprinkle clean water upon you, (the usual emblem of Divine influences, John

vii. 38, 39,) and ye shall be clean; and I will put my SPIRIT within you." Ezek. xxxvi. 24–27. And when this promise was fulfilled, what was the consequence? Why a glorious public reformation followed, of which you see an account in the books of Ezra and Nehemiah. They returned to their own land as weeping penitents, according to Jeremiah's prediction, which seems to have had its primary accomplishment in this event. "The children of Israel shall come, they and the children of Judah together, going and weeping: (this is a description of the march of the captives in their return to their own country,) they shall go and seek the LORD their God: they shall ask the way to Zion, (Zion, the place where the house of God once stood, which they are eager to rebuild) with their faces thitherward, saying, Come, let us join ourselves to the LORD in a perpetual covenant that shall not be forgotten." Jer. 1. 4, 5. And when they were thus brought to repentance, what a happy revolution followed! The scattered captives were collected; they restored their ruined church and state, and again became a free and flourishing people. And what happened to them will also happen to us, and all nations of the earth in all ages, in like circumstances.

In illustrating the subject I have principally in view, I intend only to offer a few arguments to prove the absolute necessity of a general outpouring of the Spirit, to effect a general reformation.

The arguments for this truth, with which the holy Scriptures furnish us, are so many, that I can only select a few; and they shall be chiefly such as refer to nations, or bodies politic, and not to individuals, or private persons; asserting the Holy Spirit to be the only author of public national reformation, as well as of the conversion of particular persons.

The temporal prosperity of the Jews, who were under a Theocracy, or an immediate Providence, depended in a special manner upon their continued obedience: and their restoration upon their return to obedience, or their reformation. Hence, among the many promises of prosperity and restoration which Moses makes them in the name of God, this is one: "The LORD thy God will circumcise thy heart, and the heart of thy seed, to love the LORD thy God with all thy heart, and with all thy soul, that thou mayest live;" that is, that thou mayest be a prosperous people. "And the LORD will put all these curses upon thine enemies; and he will make thee plenteous in every work of thy hand, in the fruit of thy body, and in the fruit of thy cattle, and in the fruit of thy land for good." Deut. xxx. 6–9. In Jeremiah xxxi. you have many promises made to the Jews, both of temporal and spiritual prosperity, upon their conversion to God: and as the life of all, this is inserted, "I will put my law in their inward parts, and write it in their hearts." Deut. xxx. 31–33. This is substantially repeated, with an express reference to national deliverance, in the next chapter. "Behold, I will gather them out of all countries whither I have driven them in mine anger, and in my fury, and in great wrath; and I will bring them again unto this place, and I will cause them to dwell safely; and *I will give them one heart and one way,* that they may fear me for ever, for the good of them and their children after them," Deut. xxx. 37–41, &c. Ezekiel speaks in the same strain with regard to the same event: "Thus saith the Lord GOD, I will even gather you from the people, and assemble you out of the countries where ye have been scattered, and I will give you the land of Israel. And they shall come thither, and they shall take away all the detestable things, and all the abominations thereof from thence;" that is, they shall promote a general reformation in their country: and from whence shall this proceed? You find the cause of it in the following promise: "I will give them one heart, and I will put a new spirit within you; and I will take the stony heart out of their flesh, and will give them a heart of flesh—that they may walk in my statutes, and keep mine ordinances, and do them."* Zerubbabel was the great restorer of the Jewish church and state, after the Babylonish captivity: and Zechariah informs us that this was the word of the Lord unto Zerubbabel, for his encouragement, "Not by power, nor by might, but by my Spirit, saith the LORD of Hosts." The reformation of the Jews, and their consequent restoration to a flourishing state, is not effected by any human power or means, but by my Spirit alone. Zech. iv. 6. And this will hold equally true in every age, especially under the gospel, which is peculiarly the dispensation of the Spirit. Love, joy, peace, long-suffering, gentleness, goodness, faith, meekness, temperance, are virtues which have the most happy influence upon human society; and were they universally prevalent, they would effectually prevent all the calamities of war, and ensure all the blessings of peace: and these, St. Paul tells us, are the fruits, or effects, of the Spirit. Gal. v. 22, 23. And, therefore, "till the Spirit be poured out from on high," they will never grow and flourish. Faith, repentance, and every grace are the free gift of God, wrought by the Holy Spirit. Eph. ii. 8; Phil. i. 29; Acts v. 31, and xi. 18; 2 Tim. ii. 25; 2 Cor. v. 17, 18. In short, not one soul, much less a whole nation, can be effectually reformed without the power of God. If even a well-disposed Lydia gave a believing attention to the things spoken by Paul, it was because the Lord opened

* Ezek. xi. 17–20. See also to the same purpose, Ezek. xxxvi. 16–25. od. fin.; and xxxix. 25–29.

her heart. Acts xvi. 14. "No man can come unto Christ, except the Father draw him." John vi. 44. The Holy Spirit is uniformly represented, through the whole Scriptures, as the spring of all the goodness that is in the world —the sacred fire, from whence proceeds every spark of true religion that is to be found in the breasts of any of the sons of men.

And the doctrine of the Scriptures, in this respect, is confirmed by history, and matters of fact, in all ages. When the Spirit is withdrawn, it has been found a truth, that nations and particular persons have degenerated; vice and luxury have gained ground, and religion has declined, and died away; and that, too, in the midst of the most proper means to promote reformation, and to strengthen the things that remain. Then the most solemn preaching, and the most alarming providences have no effect; but men continue blind and stupid under the clearest instructions, and the loudest warnings; and grow harder and harder, instead of being refined in the furnace of affliction. But on the other hand, when the Spirit is poured out from on high, then the cause of religion and virtue is promoted, almost without means; then sinners are awakened by a word: religion catches and circulates from heart to heart, and bears down all opposition before it. Peter had preached many a sermon before that which we find recorded in Acts the second, and his Lord and master had preached many a one; but with very little success. But now by one short discourse, no fewer than three thousand are converted in a few minutes among a promiscuous, prejudiced multitude, some of whom had been accessary to the death of Jesus Christ but a few days before. And whence this happy turn? St. Peter himself will tell you, it was because then was fulfilled the ancient prophecy of Joel, " I will pour out my Spirit upon all flesh." Acts ii. 16, 17;

Joel ii. 8. Then, too, was fulfilled the promise of the blessed Jesus to his disciples; "I will send the Spirit unto you; and when he is come, he will reprove the world of sin, of righteousness, and of judgment." John xvi. 7, 8. It was this that rendered the progress of the gospel so rapid and irresistable through the world, in spite of the most powerful opposition from all quarters in that age; which, in times seemingly more favourable, has languished and lost ground.

It is my happiness to be able to furnish you with an instance of the like nature, in the review of my own short life. About sixteen years ago, in the northern colonies, when all religious concern was much out of fashion, and the generality lay in a dead sleep in sin, having at best but the form of godliness, but nothing of the power; when the country was in peace and prosperity, free from the calamities of war, and epidemical sickness; when, in short, there were no extraordinary calls to repentance; suddenly, a deep, general concern about eternal things spread through the country; sinners started out of their slumbers, broke off from their vices, began to cry out, What shall I do to be saved? and made it the great business of their life to prepare for the world to come. Then the gospel seemed almighty, and carried all before it. It pierced the very hearts of men with an irresistible power. I have seen thousands at once melted down under it; all eager to hear as for life, and hardly a dry eye to be seen among them. Many have since backslidden, and all their religion is come to nothing, or dwindled away into mere formality. But, blessed be God, thousands still remain shining monuments of the power of divine grace in that glorious day. That harvest did not continue very long: and now, in the very same places, and under the same ministry, or a better, there are hardly any appearances of it; though Providence has given them so many alarms of late, and such loud calls to repentance. And what can be the reason of such a surprising difference but this, that formerly the Spirit was poured out from on high, but now he is withdrawn; and hence the gospel and the means of grace, which were once so powerful, have now lost their general efficacy, and have either no effect or a terrible one, that is, to harden men more and more.

Now if this be so indeed, that is, if the Holy Spirit be the sole author of that reformation, which is necessary to preserve or restore public tranquility and happiness; then we may be enabled by this to form some estimate of the present situation of our country and nation. By feeling this pulse, we may learn the state of our political body.

On the one hand, we may discover that God has not as yet abandoned guilty Britons, nor entirely withrawn his Spirit from this world of sinners. If the Spirit has not been *poured* out in a copious shower of late, he has at least distilled like the dew, and caused some spots of the wilderness here and there to flourish. I have very agreeable accounts from my English correspondents, that many of the clergy there have been roused out of their long sleep; have abandoned the modish, new-fangled divinity of the age, gone back to the forsaken truths of their own articles and the reformation, and preach Christ crucified, and the unfashionable doctrines of grace, with indefatigable zeal and extensive success. This is the more unexpected, and the more promising as it has appeared in a church where religion has been declining for some time, and the things that remained were ready to die. We, I hope, have catholicism enough to rejoice in her recovery, though under another name. Some drops of divine influences have also fallen upon certain spots in America of late. I have, some time ago, given you an account of the promising religious impressions among the students in the college of New Jersey: and my worthy correspondent, Mr. Bellamy, informs me, "As at New Jersey College, so in several places in New England, there have been awakenings, and some hopeful conversions of late: but whether these are to be looked upon as bees flying to the hive before a storm, or as some drops of mercy before a general shower, I cannot tell, but fear the former: for our land, in general, is in profound security, and the cry of our sins has reached to heaven." I have several accounts of the same agreeable import from other hands. And I hope even Virginia is not left a mere barren wilderness, without one fruitful spot in it. Here and there a poor, thoughtless sinner has been alarmed, and turned to the Lord; and even some of Africa's gloomy sons have become, we hope, the Lord's freemen, and the genuine children of Abraham by faith. These things bear a promising aspect; and we would fain hope, that the Lord has reserved such a remnant among us, that we shall not be made like unto Sodom, and desolate like unto Gomorrah: nor have we reason to complain, with desponding Elijah, that *we only* are left to serve the Lord.

But, on the other hand, it is lamentably evident, there has not been of late any such general outpouring of the Spirit, as is necessary to produce a public national reformation: which is the only cure for a body politic so far gone as ours. We have lost ground indeed before our enemies, and been almost everywhere worsted: but I am afraid vice has stood its ground against the artillery of the gospel; or if it has lost in one place, it has gained in another. By all accounts from Great Britain, and the neighbouring colonies, and by our own observations in this, it appears that the generality lie in a deep sleep, presumptuous and prayerless, even when the bloody sword is unsheathed and brandished over them, and their country bleeds by a thousand wounds. They hardly ever reflect upon their sins as the cause of these public calamities; nor humble themselves under these judgments, as indications of the righteous displeasure of God. Nay, some are arrived to such a daring height of infidelity, as virtually to abjure the divine government, and to avow that they do not think the God of heaven has any thing to do with such affairs; but the potsherds of the earth dash themselves together of themselves, and the arm of flesh fights it out. Our country and nation have had the trial of the gospel a long time—the gospel, which is the most effectual expedient to reform the world, which has subdued so many obstinate sinners, and which has peopled heaven with so large a colony from our guilty globe. We have also of late had the trial of the calamities of war—a bloody and savage war with a powerful, exasperated enemy, and their barbarous allies. But, alas! it appears, upon trial, that these means will not do. After all the trial that has been made, alas! it appears that infidelity, irreligion, immorality, and luxury, still stand their ground. Yes, by all accounts, they stand their ground even among the soldiery, and among the inhabitants of our frontiers, whose lives are in danger every hour. In short, a spirit of deep sleep seems to be poured out, instead of a spirit of reformation.

I wish it were evident, that we, in this congregation, have escaped this heavy judgment. And I cannot but hope, some drops of divine influence are distilling here and there among us. But, alas! my brethren, I greatly fear, that even we have reason to lament and cry after the departed Spirit of God. I am greatly afraid *we* may be named ICHABOD, *because the glory is departed.* 1 Sam. iv. 21, 22. For what has now become of that inquiry,

"What shall I do to be saved?" Where, now, are the tears, the sighs, and groans of broken-hearted sinners? Where their eager searches and cryings for Jesus? When do we now see attentive crowds in the house of God, hearing as for their lives, with all the natural signs of raised passions in their countenances? Alas! these are rare things now-a-days. In some, vice appears impudent and barefaced, without a veil. Others indulge themselves in a stupid carelessness about religion, and think it enough if they observe some of its fashionable outward forms, while they know nothing of the vigorous, heart-exercises of genuine Christians. In short, if we make our observations upon high and low, and all ranks, on both sides of the Atlantic, alas! we find they go on still in the same old way, as in the time of peace and prosperity. The danger of their country and their own, is no reason with them, why they should repent.

Now this is a sufficient evidence, that the Spirit has not been poured upon us from on high, in a plentiful shower. And this gives us reason to fear, that the furnace which God has kindled among us is not intended to refine, but to consume: or, in other words, that the calamities which we have felt, or which we fear, are rather intended to destroy, than to reform. For you must observe such dispensations, and the means of grace in general, are intended for two very different ends; sometimes to reform and save, and sometimes to harden and destroy. Even Jesus Christ the Saviour came into our world for judgment, as well as for mercy; and is set for the fall as well as rise, of many in Israel. The ministry of the gospel is a *savour of death unto death*, as well as of life unto life. Isaiah was sent as a prophet to the Jews, when their sins were ripening fast, and their national desolation was approaching. And what was he sent for? not to reform them; that was hopeless:

but you may read his commission. Isa. vi. 9–11. "Go, and tell this people, Hear ye indeed, but understand not; and see ye indeed, but perceive not;" that is, you shall enjoy all proper means of instruction, but receive no advantage from them. "Then, said I, Lord, how long?" Isaiah inquired how long the means of grace should be unprofitable to them, and tend to harden them: the answer is, "Until the cities be wasted without inhabitant, and the houses without man, and the land be utterly desolate." I have some better hopes concerning our country: and yet I must say, I have my fears that this awful passage may be fulfilled even upon it. I have my fears that briers and thorns will grow up in our land, or, which is much the same, that it may become the range of French and Indian savages. "UNTIL the Spirit be poured upon us from on high." And when that period will arrive, whether sooner or later, is among the secrets of the divine counsels.

From what has been said, you may see what we principally want. We want arms, and artillery, and fortifications; we want more unanimity, judgment, despatch, and frugality in projecting and executing our undertakings: we want more public spirit, courage, and resolution among the populace. But, oh! these are not our only nor our principal wants: *we want an outpouring of the Holy Spirit* upon all ranks; and till this want be supplied, nothing is like to go on well with us. We want a general public reformation: and we shall always want it, "until the Spirit be poured upon us from on high." Alas! this want is little thought of; but it is by so much the more dangerous and lamentable. Never will our country and nation be safe, never will Britain or Virginia be out of the reach of some executioner of divine vengeance, till there be a public general reformation: and never will there be such a reformation, "until the Spirit be poured upon us from on high."

Here I must not forget a consideration of still greater weight; unless the Spirit be poured out upon us, thousands of Britons, thousands of Virginians, must perish for ever; perish not in their own country, but in hell; not by the sword of the French, or Indian instruments of destruction, but by the sword of divine justice, and the horrid instruments and torture in the infernal regions. This is a much more melancholy consideration than the ruin of our country. The ruin of souls, immortal souls, for ever!—without any hope of deliverance!—from among the means of salvation!—oh! what horrid ruin is this! Yet this will be the doom of thousands, unless the Spirit be poured out, to turn and sanctify them. Thousands declare by their conduct whither they are going; they proclaim aloud they are bound for hell; and nothing but the Almighty Spirit can stop them in their mad career. Some of these unhappy mortals may be our friends and relatives; at least they share with us in the same human nature, and therefore should be dear to us. Nay, are not some of ourselves of that number? Even the suspicion of this may strike us aghast, and put us upon thoughtful inquiries into the matter.

Hence it appears, the Spirit of God is the most important blessing, both to our country and our souls, both with regard to time and eternity; and without it, both our country and our souls will be lost in the issue.

Hence, therefore, you may be directed what to make the principal matter of your prayers to God. Pray for our king, for the ministry, for the parliament, for our governors, councillors, and all our officers, civil and military: pray for the Protestant churches, for our allies, and especially for the king of Prussia;* pray for our army and navy, and for our poor exposed fellow-subjects on the

* See the beginning of this discourse.

frontiers: pray for good regulations among ourselves, for the weakening of our enemies, and for the speedy return of a well-established peace: pray for our own reformation, and for the conversion even of our enemies, whether French papists, or heathen savages: but above all, pray for an *outpouring of the Spirit*. This is the grand, radical, all-comprehensive blessing: and if this be granted, everything else will go well with us.

To conclude, let me recommend a prudential to you, which you generally observe in temporal affairs; and that is, *to prepare for the worst*. Perhaps our religion may not be that cheap thing to us in time to come, which it has been hitherto: perhaps it may yet cost us our blood and lives. This we may expect will be our doom, if we should fall under a Popish government. And where is the glorious company of martyrs to be found among us? Who of you is willing to embrace a stake, and ascend to heaven in flames, for the sake of Jesus? Jesus, who died for *you*, will expect that some in this place will die for *him*, if they should ever be brought to the trial. And who of you is prepared to give this painful, this last evidence of your love and fidelity to him? Now you have time to deliberate upon it, and put yourselves in readiness: and it is prudence, as well as duty, to improve your time for this end, lest you be surprised unprepared.

Alas! what shall impenitent sinners do, if matters should come to this pass? If they part with Christ, rather than with their lives, they are undone, unless they retract the ruinous choice. And if they should die martyrs in his cause, even this would not save them. An unholy soul cannot ascend to heaven, even from a stake. "If I should give my body to be burnt," saith St. Paul, "and have not charity," love, he means, "it profiteth me nothing."

1 Cor. xiii. 3. What then remains, oh sinners, but that while you enjoy a few days of peace and liberty, you lay them out in earnest endeavours to obtain sincere religion—a religion that will stand the severest test! and then you are safe, come what will.

I will not take upon me to determine, what will be the issue of this war. But I am afraid, it will issue much to the disadvantage and mortification of Great Britain and her colonies. From the rapid conquests of France, and our own disappointments and defeats, we have reason to fear, either that a desperate war will be continued, till we are undone; till Britain is stripped of some or all her colonies, and perhaps herself become a conquered province of France: or that she will be obliged humbly to petition for peace; which we may be sure will not be granted, but on terms very disadvantageous; and which will therefore tend to weaken her more and more, and allow her enemies time to increase their strength, and enable them to finish with greater ease the conquests they have begun. The Protestant religion is also in very threatening danger; for wherever the arms of France or Austria prevail, there, we may be sure, it will be oppressed. The Popish powers threaten that small part of Europe and America that is free, with the yoke of civil and religious tyranny; while Sweden, Denmark, the seven United Provinces, and other Protestant states, lie asleep, and do not exert themselves to ward off the blow. Perhaps we are born to see such tragical revolutions as these: and if so, what awaits us but poverty and slavery, and the loss of all that is dear to us: and are we prepared for such trials as these? or are we so stupid, as not to be alarmed, and excited to prepare, even by the *peradventure* of such things coming upon us? Nothing but real vital religion, which will stand the trial of fire and fagot, and the tortures of the inquisition, will be an effectual preparative for such a time. Let us, therefore, examine whether our religion be such. If it be, we may bravely bid defiance to all the powers of earth and hell, to work our final ruin, and be secure and triumphant in Him that loved us, who will make us more than conquerors. But if not, alas! we have no room for one hour's ease and security; but should be anxiously labouring to flee from the wrath to come, whether in this world, or the next. Let us now "seek the Lord, while he may be found; and call upon him while he is near," Isa. lv. 6; and in this way we may yet escape into the chambers of divine protection, before the gloomy storm breaks upon us.

In the midst of these gloomy views, methinks a ray of dubious hope darts through the threatening cloud, and bids us take a little courage, and mingle some cheerful expectations with our fears. Who knows but the Lord will yet turn, and repent, and leave a blessing behind him? Who knows but he may yet surprise us with an effusion of his Spirit, to purify us, instead of pouring upon us the vials of his displeasure, which we deserve? His ways are unsearchable; the turns of his providence often surprising and unaccountable; and his mercy above all our thoughts. Perhaps he may suffer the power of France to rise to such a formidable height, and us to be broken and reduced to a helpless extremity, that his hand may be the more manifest in her overthrow, and in our deliverance. Perhaps the extremity of calamity may bring us to the knee, as humble penitents before our offended Sovereign, and turn us to him: and then he may appear as our deliverer, when we are sensible of our dependence upon him, and that the help of man is in vain. I am encouraged to hope for deliverance in such an extremity, from a remarkable passage in Deuteronomy, the thirty-second chapter, "The Lord shall judge his people, and repent himself for his servants, *when he sees their strength is gone*, and there is none shut up or left." Our strength is not yet gone: we have still a powerful army and navy: and therefore are full of self-confidence. But when this atheistical confidence is mortified, and we are brought to acknowledge our need of the alliance of Heaven, then God may rise for our deliverance.

There is need of preparation for deliverance, as well as for trials and calamities; and to deliver us before we are prepared for it, would not prove a blessing in the issue. To deliver a thoughtless, presumptuous, impenitent people, while they continue such, would be to encourage their presumption and impenitence, and to make them more daring in sin, and in the neglect of God and religion. To this purpose St. Peter exhorts us, to "humble ourselves under the mighty hand of God, that we may be exalted IN DUE TIME." 1 Pet. v. 6. There is a due time for exaltation or deliverance; and if we should be exalted before the time, we should only be exalted upon a precipice, where we should soon turn giddy, and fall again with greater violence. Let us therefore long and pray not only for deliverance, but that we may be prepared for it, so that it may be a real blessing to us in the issue—such a deliverance may God grant us in due time through Jesus Christ. Amen.

A HYMN.

While in a thousand open'd veins
Contending nations bleed;
While briers and thorns in blooming plains
And fruitful fields succeed:

While desolation rages round,
  Like an o'erwhelming flood,
Where can a remedy be found
  To stop the streams of blood?

Eternal Spirit! Source of good!
  The Author of all peace!
Pour down thine influence, like a flood,
  On this wide wilderness.

Oh grant us one reviving show'r,
  And let it spread afar,
Thine influence alone can cure
  The bleeding wounds of war.

Come, Thou, and then the wilderness
  Shall bloom a paradise:
And heav'nly plants of righteousness
  O'er this wide waste shall rise!

Then peace shall in large rivers flow,
  Where streams of blood have run:
Then universal love shall glow,
  And melt the world in one.

Then num'rous colonies shall rise
  From this wide world of sin
To people regions in the skies,
  And with bright angels shine.

SERMON LXVI.

A TIME OF UNUSUAL SICKNESS AND MORTALITY IMPROVED.

JEREMIAH v. 3.—*O* LORD, *are not thine eyes upon the truth? Thou hast stricken them, but they have not grieved: thou hast consumed them, but they have refused to receive correction: They have made their faces harder than a rock: they have refused to return.*

MY fellow-*mortals!* So I call you, because mortality is the certain doom of us all. This is a truth at all times evident; but now, methinks, it is more striking than usual, when death has made such ravages among us; when it has made breaches upon sundry of our families, and swept off some of them almost entirely: and when we who survive are in daily expectation of a visit from this tremendous conqueror. Therefore, my dear fellow-mortals! under this character would I address you this day—as a mortal, whose breath may be stopped the next day, or the next hour; I would speak with more seriousness than, alas! is usual to me, to you, mortals, about the great concerns of immortality!* If I would do anything to save myself and them that hear me, I see I must do it quickly. I have for some time been languishing and indisposed myself, and the contagious disease made its en-

---

* Mr. Baxter was wont to say:
 "I preach as if I ne'er should preach again,
  And as a dying man to dying men."
And oh, that I may imbibe the same spirit, and enter the pulpit always under its influence!

trance into my family; but through the amazing and distinguishing kindness of God, which I desire publicly to celebrate, and, I hope, in answer to prayer, its progress has been stopped. And what better return can I make to my gracious Deliverer, than to devote that life, which he has spared, to his glory, and the service of your souls, with increasing zeal and industry? The blind and secure world has accused me of making too great ado about religion: and when my mind is impressed with realizing views of death and the supreme tribunal, I cannot but accuse myself: but, oh! it is upon a very different account. I never feel one uneasy thought from the excess of my zeal, or from the review of those few solemn hours, when I have delivered the messages of God to you with such pathos and earnestness that the world may have thought me mad. But I accuse myself, and would lament my many infirmities, particularly my frequent langour and coldness in the care of your souls. Indeed, I have been made sensible of my defects in this respect: and oh! that I may be enabled to be more faithful and laborious for the future. I am more sensible than usual that I must work while the day of life lasts: for oh! it is short and uncertain; and the night of death is coming, when I cannot work. I have but little time to labour for my divine Master—but little time to warn, instruct, and edify my dear hearers. Therefore, now, while my mouth is not silent in the dust, I would address you with the utmost earnestness and solemnity.

But this is not the only reason for improving the present time. As I am mortal myself, so are my dear people: they are dying fast around me, and dropping into the grave from between my hands. Above twenty that were wont to mingle with us in this assembly, and to hear the word from my lips, have been hurried into the eternal world in a few days. They have now passed the grand decisive trial: their state of probation is over, and an irrevocable sentence has fixed their eternal state in the mansions of glory or misery! These I have done with for ever. No more can I labour to warn and convince them—no more can I comfort and edify them—no more can I denounce the terrors of the Lord against their sin, nor offer the blessings of the gospel to their acceptance! The most ignorant of them are now wiser than their teacher, and know more of the great realities of the eternal world than the wisest man upon earth. Farewell, then, to these our friends and neighbours—farewell, till we all meet in one vast assembly before the supreme tribunal!

But, blessed be God, all my dear people are not yet swept off from the land of the living! Here is still a goodly number, as yet in a state of trial for that strange world, whither our brethren have taken their flight. Here is a goodly number who can still hear the gospel of peace, and who are still interested to hear it; and who, unless they hear it in time, must soon be miserable for ever! And why, then, should you not all hear it with the most solemn attention and seriousness? Why, brethren, should you not all hear it so that your souls may live! Alas! is it possible there should be one vain, trifling, thoughtless mind, in a religious assembly in such circumstances! Methinks horror must set him a-trembling, and mark out the monster to the whole congregation, as a magor-missabib—a terror to himself and all around him!

Certainly, if ever there was a time for serious thoughtfulness, this is such a time. Our nation, our country, our neighbourhood, and some of our families, are in very alarming circumstances. Our nation is in danger from the victorious power of France, and the formidable conspiracy of her allies,* that seem zealous to erase the name of Britons from the face of the earth. Our country has been ravaged, and bled in a thousand veins; and the posture of our affairs threatens still more gloomy times. Our neighbourhood has been turned into a graveyard, and some of us are the remains of families that have been thinned by death; and we are escaped, like brands plucked out of the burning. And what improvement should we make of these calamities? What is the will and pleasure of God in this case? Suppose you knew what the will of your Maker and Lord is, what he desires, commands, and expects you should do, in such circumstances —suppose you knew this certainly and infallibly, must I not have so much charity for you all as to presume you would pay a serious regard to it? Is it possible you should be capable of such daring wickedness, as to contemn his royal pleasure, when you knew it beyond all doubt? Well, brethren, I am just going to put this matter to a trial; for I can assure you as certainly as if you heard it proclaimed with an immediate voice from heaven, what the will of God is in this case. It is this: that you should repent, reform, and turn to the Lord, under these threatenings and chastisements. This is undoubtedly the pleasure and the command of God; and the issue will show how much weight it will have with you.

Some of you, I doubt not, have been roused by these calamities to more earnestness and zeal in the great work of your salvation. You have re-examined your past experiences, to see if you can venture upom them into eternity. You have renewed your hold of Jesus Christ, that he may be your sure support, when nature is sinking in death. You have been trimming your lamps, and putting

* This sermon is dated Hanover, November 14, 1756.

yourselves in a proper habit to meet the bridegroom of your souls. You have been setting things in order for your last remove: and though you may have been tossed between the alternate billows of hope and fear, yet you cannot but conclude, upon the whole, that you have not delayed the grand work of life to such a time as this; but have been so wise as to make it your main business in the time of health and prosperity. Well, my dear brethren, go on in this course, and you shall be safe, come what will; and these threatening and afflictive dispensations of Providence will, in the issue, prove most blessed and beneficial dispensations to you. Yes: all things, even the heaviest calamities, shall work together for your greatest good.

May I not also allow myself the pleasure of hoping that some of you, who have formerly lived thoughtless about the concerns of eternity, have been awakened by these alarming providences to some proper sense of your danger, and to work out your salvation with fear and trembling? You begin to see that your former course will never do: that you are unprepared for eternity, and in the utmost need of a Saviour; and you are now determined to seek him with all your might. Well, my brethren, hold on in this course, and you have reason to hope it will issue well: only I must caution you against the danger of apostacy. Alas, you have reason to fear, lest, when the fright is over, all your religion come to nothing! And if so, your last state is worse than the first.

This, sirs, is a very proper time for repentance and reformation, and I am unusually desirous that it may be improved for that purpose. The calamities we have felt, and those we feel, have a direct tendency to drive us to it. This is an effectual method to make up our loss, and turn our afflictions into blessings, and our bereavements into enjoyments; and this will be the best preparative for days of distress, and the best support in them. God has also frequently set in by his Spirit at such a time, and carried on an extensive work of grace; and it is a dismal symptom, indeed, if he withdraw his Spirit from a people in such circumstances, and leave them to groan and perish under unsanctified afflictions; or deliver their bodies from the outward calamity, without delivering their souls from the slavery of sin.

This is a melancholy case indeed; and yet I am afraid this is the case of many, perhaps of most, in this congregation. You may, perhaps, be a little damped while living, as it were, among so many graves; you may have been struck into a panic, and in a serious fit poured out a few prayers. But, alas! this is but a small part of the work to be done! And unless it be carried farther, you must perish for ever. You may flatter yourselves, and make fair pretensions to others. But, "Lord, are not thine eyes upon the truth?" And dost not thou, who seest through all their designs, and knowest the reality of their case—dost not thou see that though "thou hast stricken them, they have not grieved" with deep, ingenuous sorrows, and the kindly relentings of true repentance? "Thou hast consumed them, but they refuse to receive correction;" they are not made sensible of their sin, and reduced to their duty, by all thy chastisements, though various and heavy; they are stiff and unyielding under thy rod, and will not be made wise by it; instead of being dissolved into repentance, and purified, they grow harder and harder in the furnace of affliction. "They have made their faces harder than a rock;" they can no more blush at their base conduct towards thee, than a senseless stone; they can no more wet their faces with penitential tears than a flinty rock. "They refuse to return." Not that they refuse in words—not that they expressly say in so many syllables, "We will not return;" but they refuse it practically. They refuse to return by not actually returning; for not to return, in fact, is to refuse to return. They refuse to return, by not using the means necessary for their return, and by continuing their career in their old course. They refuse to return by the habitual temper of their hearts, which reluctate, struggle, and draw back, and will not return. This was the character of the Jews, under all their calamities, in Jeremiah's time. And is not this, brethren, the character of sundry of you? Are there not blind minds, hard hearts, and profane lips, among us still? Are there not prayerless persons and prayerless families among us? Are there not some that neglect the plainest duties to God and man? Some thoughtless, careless creatures, that feel no deep impressions from eternal things? Some worldly-minded, grovelling creatures, perpetually digging in the earth for riches? Some vain, light, trifling sinners, who go on frolicking and carousing, even when the Lord of Hosts calls to "weeping, and mourning, and girding with sackcloth?" Isa. xxii. 12. Some that have never experienced a thorough conversion, and know not what it is to repent and believe? Some obstinate, incorrigible sinners, that bid defiance to all the judgments of God? Or, if they are afraid of his judgments, they are not afraid of sin, the cause of them. In a dastardly and, perhaps, unnatural manner, they keep off or fly from the contagious disorder; and helpless families may die around them, unassisted, for them; but they are not so shy of the more fatal contagion of sin, nor so solicitous to keep out of the way of temptation. If they can but live, it is enough for them; but they care not whether they live to God or not. Alas! are there not many such among us? Does not conscience witness that this is the real character of some of you? Chastisement is thrown away upon you; you are made no better by it. You will receive no correction or warning from the death of a neighbour, or even of a parent or a child.

This, indeed, is not a singular case, which renders it still the more melancholy. It seems the general curse of the present generation, that the chastisements of the divine hand do not work kindly upon them, nor bring them to repentance. Thus it generally is in England, Scotland, and the northern colonies, though in such an alarming situation. Mr. Bellamy, of New England, whom some of you know and highly esteem for his excellent writings, has these words, in a letter I lately received from him: "A dark cloud seems to be gathering over a sinful land. We have had a day of great grace: that is past and gone, and a day of great wrath seems to be at hand! Our northern army is sickly and likely to do nothing; our treasury is exhausted; people's spirits low; great *murmurings*, but no *reformation*. For all these things we feel and fear we do not return unto the Lord." Thus discouraging is the prospect in New England, where religion has so long flourished. Mr. Blair, of Pennsylvania, with whose excellent character most of you are perfectly acquainted, and whose congregation has been the scene of the Indian ravages and murders, complains in these moving terms: "Alas! I have not enjoyed the sweet supports of success in my ministry. Under all this heavy scene of judgment, our people are manifestly more and more hardened; and that, notwithstanding a gracious God has stooped to assist me remarkably in preaching, frequently this summer. A dreadful omen this!" says he. My British correspondents send me the same accounts. Mr. Erskine, a worthy minister in Scotland, writes, "I hear of no such thing as a revival of religion in Scotland: a spirit of deep slumber seems to have seized us." Mr. Adams, the excellent minister of Falkirk, writes in the same strain: "What is wanting," says he, "to encourage our hopes, is a spirit of repentance and reformation, in this age of distinguished inattention to the works, the word, and ways of God. Is it not the general case, 'Lord, when thy hand is lifted up, they will not see?' How loud are the alarms which awful Providence is sounding in our dull and heavy ears! The Lord's judgments are visibly in the earth; but where does it appear that the inhabitants are learning righteousness? In this country, infidelity and immorality of all kinds make the most provoking progress. The cup of our iniquity appears to be brim-full, and the cup of God's wrath now ready to be poured out upon the despisers of the riches of his goodness and long-suffering?" You hear a great deal of bad news, my brethren, of the political and war-like kind; but here is bad news of a still more alarming kind. This not only endangers our country, but threatens the everlasting ruin of immortal souls: and this deprives us of that good which we might extract out of those evils, and make them pure, unmingled evils to us. But shall not this congregation be an exception from this general complaint? The Lord's voice crieth unto Hanover; and will ye not hear the rod, and him that hath appointed it? Micah vi. 9. To promote this design, in my little sphere, is the great end I now have in view; and, for that purpose,

I shall endeavour to show you what good effects afflictions have upon us, especially on impenitent sinners. This my text naturally leads me to: for though, in express terms, it only contains a complaint of the misimprovement of afflictions, or incorrigibleness under them, yet this very plainly points out the right improvement of them. When it is said, "Lord, thou hast stricken them, but they were not grieved;" this implies that they should have been grieved; grieved for their undutiful conduct towards God, which has exposed them to the scourges of his rod; grieved with a godly sorrow, with kindly, generous relentings for sin, as against God, and not merely as tending to ruin themselves. When the prophet complains, "Thou hast consumed them, but they refused to receive correction," it is implied that they should have received correction, that they should have submitted to the rod, as to the chastisement of a provoked, and yet indulgent father, without sullen murmuring against it, or fainting under it; that they should be made sensible of their sin, and reduced to their duty. When the prophet complains, "They have made their faces harder than a rock," it implies that their faces should have been flushed with ingenuous shame and blushing, and washed with streams of penitential tears. And when he complains, "They have refused to return," it implies that they ought immediately to have returned to him that smote them. And hence it follows that ingenuous sorrow, shame, and repentance; a submissive, corrigible temper, and a sincere conversion to God, are the effects which afflictions should have upon us, according to my text. Indeed I know no more convictive method of showing what it is to misimprove afflictions, and be incorrigible under them, than to show positively what it is to make a right use of them, or what are their proper effects when sanctified: for if you find they have not had such effects upon you, you may be sure you have refused to receive correction.

To bring sinners to repentance, God has instituted the gospel and its ordinances, and for this end they are dispensed among you; for this end also he rouses your consciences within you, and communicates his Holy Spirit to work upon your hearts. Now afflictions are so many auxiliaries to assist these forces, to reduce you into captivity to the obedience of Christ. When the persuasions of his word are disregarded; when the warnings of your own consciences are slighted, and the motions of the Holy Spirit resisted, then our heavenly Father takes his rod, and either shakes it over your heads, to see if the threatening will answer the end, without the infliction; or he actually scourges you to make you sensible of your duty. The great design of all this, as I told you, is to bring you to repentance, or to turn you to him. This is the sum, the result of sanctified afflictions. Let us, then, inquire what this is. And that I may be the more concise, and use a uniform language on this subject, I shall include all that I have to say concerning the right improvement of afflictions under this one inquiry: What is it to turn to the Lord? to which the other expression contained in my text may be reduced.

First, turning to God presupposes a deep conviction that you have gone astray, both from the way of duty and the way of safety. You never will leave your present course, till you plainly see that it leads you down to the chambers of death. You never will turn to the Lord, till you are certain you are under the most pressing, absolute necessity to do so, both from duty and interest.

Oh, sirs, if it should please God to open the eyes of unconverted sinners among you this day, what strange, unsuspected, and astonishing views would open to you, concerning your past and present course and condition! Then, to your surprise, you would see that you have lived so many years in the world, without so much as earnestly attempting that work, which is the great business of your life. You would see that your hopes of heaven, in your present condition, are but a delusive dream; and that you are in every moment in the utmost danger of sinking into the depth of misery, under the heavy wrath of Almighty God. You would see what plain, reasonable, and important duties you have carelessly neglected, both towards God and man; and what a long train of known, wilful sin, you have obstinately persisted in. You would see how criminally deficient you have been, even in those duties which, as to the matter of them, you have performed; that even your good actions have not proceeded from good principles and ends; the love of God, a regard to his authority, and a view to his glory; but from some low, mercenary, selfish principles and views; and that the reason why you abstained from any act of sin, was not your love to God, and regard to his will, but because you had no temptation to it, or because you apprehended it might injure your character or temporal interests, or perhaps render you eternally miserable. You would see that you have not such good hearts as you once flattered yourselves you had; but that they are deceitfully and desperately wicked. You would see that they are and have always been destitute of the reality of all the Christian graces, and have imposed upon you hitherto with counterfeits and deceitful appearances; destitute of true repentance, faith, and love towards God and Jesus Christ; and full of pride, hypocrisy, ignorance, hardness of heart, disaffection to God and his government, unbelief, earthly-mindedness, sensuality, sordid and wicked lusts and passions, and an endless variety of evils too numerous to be mentioned. In short, you would see yourselves a mere mass of corruption; and you would wonder you have not sunk into hell long ago, as rotten fruits fall to the ground. This would, no doubt, be a surprising, unexpected discovery to some of you: you have no such thoughts of yourselves, but quite the contrary. But the reason why you do not see this to be your case, in fact, is because the god of this world has blinded your minds, and because your treacherous hearts flatter you. This is, indeed, the truth of your case, while unconverted, if you believe the plainest declarations of the word of God, or the unanimous testimony of all, in all ages, who have had their eyes open to see themselves, and have been taught that important and useful, though mortifying science, of self-knowledge: and if ever God enlighten your blind minds, you would yourselves see that this is really your case. But oh! the astonishing ignorance and self-flattery of the heart of man! Here, alas! lies the difficulty in dealing with unconverted sinners. We cannot open their eyes to see their guilt and danger. Could we do this, a grand point would be gained, and the work would be well begun. But alas! they will not believe they are so guilty, so vile and corrupt; and hence the gospel, which is a religion for self-condemned, broken-hearted sinners, is but an idle tale, or a vain speculation to them: and to invite them to come to Christ, is but to invite the whole to a physician.

Farther, if it should please God to bring you out of darkness this day, into his marvellous light, then you would see the exceeding sinfulness of sin. You would see, it is not that harmless, innocent thing, or that slight, excusable foible, you once took it to be: but that it is indeed the most abominable thing, the most terrible, base, and malignant evil, upon earth, or in hell. Then, instead of wondering that such a thing should be punished with everlasting destruction by a gracious God, the parent of mankind; and instead of disputing yourselves into doubts about it, or cavilling at it, as cruel and unjust; instead of this, I say, you would rather wonder that so dreadful an evil could be pardoned at all, upon any consideration whatsoever; and you would be "more apt to question the possibility of forgiveness, than the justice of your punishment."

As the foundation of these discoveries, you would see the majesty, the excellency, the holiness, justice, and goodness of God; the purity and strictness of his law, and the equity and terror of its penalty. You would see your obligations to him; your numerous, strong, endearing, and sacred obligations to him, as your Creator, Preserver, and Redeemer; and the aggravated baseness, ingratitude, rebellion, and impiety of having lived all your days in the wilful breach of such obligations. These things, and the like, you would see as in a new medium, and with other eyes than you were wont to look upon them. And you would see them with such glaring light and evidence, that you would be utterly astonished at your own sottish ignorance, that had never discovered them before. They would now appear as plain, as ever they were dark and doubtful. In consequence of this, you would be struck with wonder and horror at your former security and stupor, in so dangerous a condition. I really want words to express the views and apprehensions you would then have of things. Oh that experience may be your teacher! Blessed be God, I have seen and conversed with many a sinner formerly, upon their first receiving this conviction: formerly, I say; for, alas! now-a-days I hardly meet with one to converse with me upon this subject: No; the generality have no such alarming views of themselves: like the Laodiceans, they are rich in their own conceit; and know not that they are wretched, and miserable, and poor, and blind, and naked. Rev. iii. 17. But formerly it has been my happy employ to instruct such convinced sinners; and I can still remember, it was a very affecting conversation. Their language still seems to sound in my ears; and methinks I hear them complaining in a flood of tears, "Oh what shall I do to be saved? I see I am upon the very brink of destruction: I see I have been all my life a poor, deceived, self-flattering sinner. Oh! I never thought I was such a monster of wickedness, and upon the slippery brink of eternal ruin: but now I see it; now it is so evident to me, that I am amazed I never discovered it before. Oh! is there any possibility of escape, for such a wretch as I? Let me but know what is necessary, and I will attempt any thing; I will deny myself in any thing, if I may but get my perishing soul for a prey." Jer. xxi. 9. These are the affecting strains of awakened sinners. This must be your language, sinners, or at least the thoughts of your heart, before you can turn to the Lord. But oh! when shall we hear it from you? To teach you this lesson, God has sent the sword to ravage your country and a deadly disease to spread desolation in your neighbourhood. To teach you this, your neighbours, or perhaps your parent, your children, or some of your relatives have died: and shall they die in vain? Oh! hear them as it were crying to you from the dust. Some of you have lost pious friends, who during their life laboured to awaken you out of your security. And when you view their grave, methinks you may recollect the epitaph which a minister* wrote for his own tomb-stone:

"If all my life I tried in vain to save,
Hear me, oh! hear me crying from the grave."

But, alas! I know that even this alarming voice will not awaken impenitent sinners, unless God bear it home to their hearts by his almighty power. And oh! that that divine Agent would begin to work among us! Then, sinners, you would soon see, that the account I have been

* This, I was informed by Mr. Gibbons, of London, from whom I had the story, was the famous Dr. Trapp, the translator of Virgil, &c.

giving you of your guilt and danger is not at all aggravated. But,

Secondly, Turning to God supposes a full conviction of the necessity of turning to him immediately, without delay. Brethren, if God should begin this work upon your hearts this day, you would no longer stand hesitating and loitering. We should no more hear from you that there is no need of so much ado, or that it is time enough as yet. You would have such clear views of your own vileness, and the disaffection of your souls to God, and holiness, that nothing could be more evident to you than that you are utterly unfit for heaven, in your present condition, and that you are fitted for destruction, and for nothing else. You would not stand disputing, and hoping, and flattering yourselves in the matter, but you would come to this peremptory conclusion, "If I continue in my present condition, I am as certainly lost for ever, as ever I was born: I shall as surely be in hell in a little time, as I am now upon earth. The matter will admit of no debate. It is as plain as that a beast cannot enjoy the pleasures of reason; or a sick man the pleasures of a feast." This, sirs, is a very alarming conclusion; and you may be very unwilling to admit it: but terrible as it is, you will be forced to believe it, if ever you be converted. It is indeed one of the first steps towards your conversion: for can it be supposed you will turn to God, while you think it unnecessary, or while you are not convinced that you are turned from him, and going the opposite road? No, it is impossible. And therefore, such of you as have never been convinced of this, may be assured you are so far from being converted, that you have not taken the first steps towards it.

But this is not all: you will be not only convinced of the absolute necessity of turning to God in general, but of turning to him immediately without delay. You will see, that you are so far from having time to delay, that it will wound your heart to think this work was not done many years ago. You will see, that your having delayed it so long already, was the most desperate madness in the world: and that if you put it off any longer, you may be lost beyond recovery: for oh! you will see, you stand in slippery places, ready to be cast down into destruction every moment. You will apprehend yourselves held over the pit of hell, in the hand of an angry God, by the slender thread of life; just as we hold a spider, or some poisonous insect over the fire, ready to throw it in immediately. Now, while I am speaking to you, you would immediately set about this great work: you would pray and hear at once. And upon your returning home, instead of trifling and chattering about the world, you would retire to cry for mercy, and meditate upon your miserable condition—you would fly to your Bibles, and other good books for direction: and I should expect the pleasure once more of seeing you come to your poor minister, anxiously inquiring what you shall do to be saved? Oh! when will the crowds of unconverted sinners among us be brought to this? When will they give over their delays; and see they must engage in this great business immediately! I am sure the sickness and mortality among us have a tendency to bring them to this. Can you imagine, that conversion may be put off to some future time, when you see so many in health and youth around you seized with sickness, and hurried into the grave in a few days? This has been the doom of sundry vigorous youth, and even of little children among us: and my dear surviving youth and children, shall this be no warning to you? Alas! will you dare to sin on still as thoughtless as ever? Will you any more pretend that you may safely delay your conversion to a sick-bed or dying hour? But ask those that have made the trial, and what do they say? Do any of them tell you that that is the most proper time for this work? What do sinners say when the time comes? "Oh, (they cry out,) what a fool was I to put it off till now! Oh, how bitterly do I now repent that I did not attempt it sooner!". What do those say who made it their business in health and prosperity? Do they repent of it as premature? No: they all cry out, "I should be in a sad case, indeed, if it were left undone till now: now I have enough to do to struggle with my pains. But blessed be God, that work is not now to be done!" And dare any of you loiter and delay still, in opposition to the joint testimony of those who have arrived at and made trial of that period which you allot for turning to God? If the declaration of dying men have any weight of credibility, the present time is the most fit season: therefore, oh, improve it while you have it. But,

Thirdly, If afflictions should prove the happy means of turning you to God, they will rouse you to the most earnest persevering endeavours. You would immediately set about the work, and use all the means God has instituted for that purpose. You would pray without ceasing: you would pray in secret places: and if you have hitherto had prayerless families, they should be so no more: you would consecrate them to God with prayer this very evening. Nay, you would keep your souls always in a praying posture: you would waft up your desires to God while you are in business or at leisure, in solitude or in society, at home or abroad; and your prayers would not now be a dull, spiritless form: you would cry as for your life, and exert all the vigour of your souls. You would find frequent errands to the throne of grace; and you would cry there, like a condemned criminal pleading for a pardon, or a drowning man calling for help. When Paul was awakened, Christ himself remarks upon him, "Behold, he prayeth!" He had prayed many a time before; but no notice is taken of it, because there was no life in it. But now he puts life and spirit into his prayers, like one in earnest to be heard; therefore they are taken notice of in heaven. Thus, my brethren, will you also pray, if ever you turn to God. You will accustom yourselves to deep and solemn meditation. You will seriously attend to the gospel and its ordinances. Your Bibles will no longer gather dust by you; but you will find use for them—there you will eagerly search for the words of eternal life. You will also love and frequent the society of those who, you hope, have experienced that happy change you are seeking after; and you will catch all the instruction you can from their conversation. In short, you will leave no means untried; you will set yourselves in earnest about the work; with as much earnestness as ever a miser pursued the world, or a sensualist his pleasures. Oh! sirs, if such a concern to turn to the Lord should spread among us, how would it change the aspect of things? How different would be the desires, the labours, the pursuits, and conversation of mankind! Believe me, sirs, there is need for such an alteration among us: and wo, wo to many of us, if things run on as they have done—if the world continue to usurp the pre-eminence of God and eternal things—if you are still more solicitous to lay up earthly treasure, than to lay up treasure in heaven—if you abandon yourselves to business or pleasure, to the neglect of religion and the concerns of eternity; I say, wo unto you, if things still continue in this course! Believe me also that it is better worth your while to labour to turn to God, and secure a happy immortality, than to lay out your labour on any thing else. Need I tell you that you shall not live here always, to enjoy the things of this world? Go, and learn this truth at the graves of your friends and neighbours. Need you be told that the enjoyments of this life are no suitable happiness for your immortal souls? Do you not learn it from the uncertain, transitory, unsatisfying nature of these enjoyments? You can carry none of them with you to your eternal home; and what then will you have to make you happy there?

Farther: As you will zealously use all endeavours to promote your conversion, so you will carefully guard against every thing that tends to hinder it. You will immediately drop your wicked courses—you will have done for ever with drinking, swearing, and all the vices you were wont to practise—you will moderate your pursuit of the world, and endeavour to disengage yourselves from excessive hurries, which allow you neither leisure nor composure to mind the great business of your salvation—that business, which, whether you regard it or not, is of an infinitely greater importance than all the affairs of life, and for which alone it is worth your while to live—you will shun the company of the wicked, the vain, and secure, as much as possible; yes, you will shun them as much as you now do the families that are infected with the epidemical disorder, and with much better reason; for they are infected with a much more fatal disease—the disease of sin, which is so deadly, and which your souls are so apt to catch. In short, you will avoid every obstacle to your conversion, as far as you can; and till you are brought to this, it is in vain to pretend that you have any real inclination to turn to God: and such of you as have never been brought to it, may be sure you have never been converted.

Oh! when shall we see such earnest endeavours among us? When shall we see sinners thus vigorously striving to enter in at the strait gate? When will their dead sleep be over? When will the delusive dream of their false hopes vanish? When will they begin to conclude that they have sinned long enough—that they have delayed turning to God long enough—that they have been secure and careless, on the slippery brink of destruction, long enough? When will they begin to think it is high time to work out their salvation with fear and trembling? My dear people, I long to see such a time among you once more! And unless such a time come, I expect sundry of you, even as many as are unconverted, will perish for ever! Yes, unless such a rousing time come, and that speedily too, I fully expect that some of you will burn in hell for ever! Oh! the shocking thought. What shall be done to avoid so dreadful a doom? Come, Holy Spirit—come and work upon the hearts of these impenitent sinners; for thou only canst perform the work. Oh! come speedily, or they will be removed out of the sphere of thy sanctifying influences—out of the region of vitality, into the territories of eternal death! Brethren, till the Spirit be poured out upon us from on high, the work of conversion will never go on prosperously among us! We have had sufficient trial to convince us of this. We have had preaching, and all the means of grace, long enough to make us sensible that all will not do, without the Holy Spirit: therefore, let us earnestly cry for this blessing. For,

Fourthly, If afflictions are followed with so blessed an effect upon you as to turn you to God, you will be made deeply sensible of your own inability to turn to him, by the best endeavours you can use; and of the absolute necessity of the influences of the Holy Spirit, or the power of divine grace. While you are ignorant of yourselves, and have not put the matter to trial, you may flatter yourselves that you are able to turn to God when you please: but when you make the experiment in earnest, you will soon be undeceived. You can indeed abstain from outward acts of gross sin—you can attend upon the means of grace, and perform the outward duties of religion; and this is your duty: but, alas! this is far short of true conversion. All this you may do, and yet the heart be so far from being turned to God, that it may be strongly set against him. You will find, when you attempt the work in earnest, that, beside the drawbacks from the world, and the temptations of Satan, your own hearts will refuse to return; they will struggle, and draw back, as if you were rushing into flames, or upon the point of a sword. They will cling fast to sin and the world, and will not let go their hold. They are disaffected to strict holiness, and all you can do cannot bring them in love with it. They are hard as the nether mill-stone, and no human means can break them. In short, you will be sensible that you are so far gone with the disease of sin, so indisposed, weakened, and corrupted, that nothing but the power of divine grace can recover you, and inspire you with spiritual life and vigour. Therefore, you will lie moaning and groaning before the Lord, waiting for his assistance, as helpless creatures, in the greatest danger, and unable to deliver yourselves. Then you will understand the meaning of that inspired prayer, "Turn thou me, and I shall be turned, Jer. xxxi. 18. Draw me, we will run after thee." Solomon's Song i. 4. Then you will be convinced, by experience, of the truth of that declaration you had before heard from the mouth of Christ, and perhaps laboured to explain away: "No man can come unto me, except the Father which hath sent me draw him." John vi. 44.

Oh! when shall we see the vanity and self-confidence of sinners mortified? When shall we see them deeply sensible of their weakness and helplessness? It may seem strange, but it is undoubtedly true, that they will never strive in earnest till they are sensible that all their strivings are not sufficient, but that God must perform the work in them. It is the high idea they have of their own power that keeps them easy and careless. When they see that it is God alone who must work in them both to will and to do, then, and not till then, they will earnestly cry to him for his assistance, and use all means to obtain it. It is not the awakened sinner that feels himself weak and helpless, that lives in the careless neglect of the means of grace. No; it is the proud, presumptuous sinner, that thinks he can do great things in religion when he sets about it. It is indeed a strange sight to see those that complain they can do nothing without Christ, labouring hard; and those that boast they can do great things, standing idle!—to see those that renounce all dependence upon their good works, abounding in good works; and those that expect to be saved by their good works, living in the neglect of good works, and doing the works of the devil! This, I say, is a strange sight; but so it generally is found to be, in fact, in the world. And the reasons of it are, that they who feel their own weakness will earnestly seek for help from God; and God will help those that are sensible they need it. Whereas, others are not earnestly seeking that grace, the want of which they do not feel; and God lets them alone, to try what the vain fools can do; and will not throw away his assistance upon those who do not want nor ask it. But,

Fifthly, If ever you return to the Lord, you will be made deeply sensible that Christ is the only way of access to God. You will be sensible, that it is only for his sake that you can expect acceptance with God; and that all your transactions with heaven must be carried on through him, as mediator. If ever you return, you will come in as obnoxious criminals, upon the footing of grace, and not of merit; and you will see that it is only through Christ that grace can be communicated to you. You will renounce all your own righteousness. You will lie at mercy, and own that you deserve hell as justly as ever a malefactor deserved the gallows. Some of you, perhaps, will say, "I will never believe this concerning myself; I will never believe that I am such a guilty, obnoxious criminal!" But pray do not be too positive; do not say you never will believe it; for you may believe it yet. Yes, you certainly will believe it, if ever you be converted and saved; and I hope God has not given you up. If ever you return to the Lord, you will come in as a poor, broken-hearted, penitent rebel; and unless you come in upon this footing, you have nothing to do with Jesus, nor he with you; for he came to save sinners and to heal the sick; and till you feel yourselves such, you will never comply with the gospel, which is a method of salvation through a Mediator. Oh! that many sinners among us might thus be mortified, humbled, and brought down to the foot of their injured Sovereign, this day! Oh! that they may be made sensible that they lie at mercy, and that they have not the least possible ground of hope, but only through the righteousness of Christ! But,

Sixthly, If ever you are turned to God, you will experience a great change in your temper and conduct. Your hearts and lives will take a new bias; your thoughts and affections will be directed towards God and holiness; your hearts will be turned to the holy law of God, like wax to the seal, and receive the stamp of his image. They will then aspire towards heaven—thither they will tend, as naturally as a stone gravitates to the earth. You will contract an evangelical turn; that is, you will delight and acquiesce in the method of salvation revealed in the gospel. Jesus will be infinitely dear to you; and you will rejoice and glory in him, and put no confidence in the flesh. You will be turned to the ordinances of the gospel, and delight to converse with God in them. In short, your whole soul will receive a heavenly disposition—a new divine bent, or bias, towards God and divine things. Your thoughts will run in a new channel; your will and affections will fix upon new objects, and you will become new creatures; old things will pass away, and all things will become new. 2 Cor. v. 17. You will become fit for heaven by having heavenly dispositions wrought in you; and thence you may infer you shall be admitted there. Believe me, sirs, when you are turned to God, religion will not be such a dull, insipid thing to you, as it now is. The gospel will not be such an idle story; nor the law of God such a leaden rule, that you may bend it as you please to your own obliquities. Heaven and hell will not be such dreams and trifles; but you will be habitually affected with these things, as the most important realities, and your hearts will be deeply impressed with their influence.

As you will be turned *to* God and holiness, so you will be turned *from* sin and all its pleasures. Yes, brethren, that pride, hypocrisy, sensuality, worldly-mindedness, and all the various forms of sin which you now indulge, will become for ever hateful to you: you will abhor them, resist them, make war against them, and never allow them a peaceable harbour in your hearts more. You will see their intrinsic vileness and baseness, and their contrariety to the holy nature of God; and on this account you will hate them and fly from them, as well as because they may bring ruin upon yourselves. Oh! how will it then break your hearts to think that ever you should have lived as you now do! How bitter will your present pleasures and pursuits then be to you; and how will you bless God, that he opened your eyes and gave your minds a new turn, before it was too late!

Farther; when your minds thus receive a new and heavenly turn, your practices will be turned too. The practice follows the inward principle of action; and when this is set right, that will be agreeable to it. Conversion, sirs, would be an effectual restraint from those vices which you now practise, and an effectual constraint to those duties you now omit. It will cure you of your swearing, drunkenness, defrauding, contentions, and quarellings, and other vices; and it would bring you to pray, to hear, to meditate, to communicate at the Lord's table, and to endeavour to perform every duty you owe to God; and it would bring you to observe the laws of justice and charity, and all the duties you owe to man: and pray observe, that these things always go together. Conversion will teach you not only to pray, and perform the other duties of religion; but it will make you just, charitable, meek, compassionate, and conscientious in all the duties of morality. It will make you better members of society, better neighbours, better masters, better servants, better parents, better children; in short, better in every relation. Never pretend you are converted, unless it have this effect upon you—without this, all your religion is not worth a straw.

From hence you may see what a blessed thing it would be, even for this world, if we should all turn to the Lord. Then, what happy families should we have! What a happy neighbourhood—what a happy congregation—what a happy country! Then every man would fill up his place, and make conscience of the duties of his relation; and then Heaven would smile, and rain down blessings upon so dutiful a people.

Seventhly: If ever you are turned to the Lord, your minds will habitually retain that turn. I mean, your religion will not be a transient fit; a fleeting evanid thing; but it will be permanent and persevering. You will never more relapse into your former voluntary slavery to sin— never more indulge from day to day your old disaffection to God, and your habitual allowed indisposition to the exercises of religion. Then, farewell for ever to the smooth, enchanting paths of sin; and welcome for ever to the ways of holiness. From the happy moment of your return to God, to the end of your days, it will be habitually the great concern of your life to make progress in religion, and live to God; to carry on a war against all sin and temptation, and root out every evil principle from your souls. I do not mean, that you will be perfectly free from all sin, or that you will never relapse into some degree of lukewarmness, and indisposition of spirit towards God. But I mean, you never will be entirely and all-through what you once were, in your unconverted state; you never will relapse into that indulged and wilful love of sin and the world—that prevailing indifferency or disaffection towards God and his service, and that stupid, habitual carelessness about eternal things, which now has the dominion over you. No, never more will you be able to offend your God and neglect your Saviour and your souls as you now do—never more will you be able to rest secure and thoughtless, while your eternal state is awfully uncertain, and your hearts are out of temper for devotion. The bent of your minds towards God may be weakened; but you can never lose it entirely. Your aversion to sin may be lessened; but you will never give up yourselves to the love and practice of it. Something within will make you perpetually uneasy while your graces are languishing and sin gathering strength. There is a secret bias upon your souls, that inclines them heavenward; even while they are carried downward to the earth, by the remaining tendencies of your innate corruption. The seed of God which remaineth in you, will never suffer you to sin as you now do. Your new nature will be searching after God by a kind of spiritual instinct, like a child for the breast, and you can never more peaceably take the world in his stead.

This, I hope, sundry of you know by experience. Since the moment of your conversion, though you have had many sad relapses and backslidings, yet you can never heartily return to sin again; and all the world cannot make you let go your hold of God. You tend towards him with a propension which, though it be weak, yet neither earth nor hell, neither sin within, nor temptations without, can entirely overcome.

And hence such of you who once fancied you were converted, but are now habitually careless, earthly-minded, and luke-warm towards God—hence, you may see, you never did, in reality, turn to him. No: it was all a dream; for if you had once been turned to him with all your hearts, you would never again have turned entirely from him. Your conversion would have had some lasting good effects upon you; and having once turned to God, you would never again have bid him farewell, and forsaken him entirely. Such, therefore, should still rank themselves among the unconverted.

And now, my dear hearers, I have endeavoured, with the utmost plainness, to describe to you that turning to God which should be the result of your afflictions as well as of the means of grace, and which you must experience before you can enter into the kingdom of heaven. I have had something more important at heart than to embellish my style, and set myself off as a fine speaker.

I have endeavoured to speak, not to an itching ear, or a curious fancy, but to your understanding and your heart; that you may both know and feel what I say: and, indeed, if I should aim at anything else, I should be at once an egregious trifler, and a profane mocker of God.

Now I have one serious question to put to you, upon a careful review of what I have said; and that is, Do you really hope in your consciences, after you have impartially tried yourselves as in the sight of God, that you have been converted or turned to God? Here is the work: I have plainly described it. But where is the heart in which it has been wrought? Can you put your hand upon your breast and say, "Oh! if I know myself, here is the heart that has been the subject of it?" Pause and think upon this inquiry, and never be easy till you can give, at least, a probable answer.

I hope this will confirm the wavering hopes of some of you, and enable you to draw the happy conclusion: "Well, if this be conversion, I think I may venture to pronounce myself a converted soul." Then happy are ye indeed. I have not time to say many comfortable things to you at present; but go to your Bibles; there you will find precious promises enough for you. Live and feast upon them, and ere long they will be all fulfilled to you, and you shall live and feast with your Saviour in paradise.

But my main business to-day lies with the unconverted: and have not some of you discovered yourselves this day to be such? Well, what is to be done now? Can you go on careless and secure still under this tremendous conviction? I hardly think any of you are arrived to such a pitch of presumption and fool-hardiness as this. Must you despair and give up all hopes of salvation? No, unless you choose it—I mean, unless you choose to neglect the means appointed for your conversion, and harden yourselves in sin. If you are determined on this course, then you may despair indeed; there is not the least ground of hope for you. But should you now rouse out of your security, and seek the Lord in earnest, you have the same encouragement to hope which any one of the many millions of converts in heaven or upon earth had, while in your condition: therefore let me persuade you to take this course immediately.

But when I begin to persuade, I am in Jeremiah's perplexity: "To whom shall I speak and give warning, that they may hear?" Jer. vi. 10. Shall I speak to you, men of business and hurry? Alas! you have no leisure to mind such a trifle as your soul. Shall I speak to you, men of wealth and character? Alas! this is a business beneath your notice, What, a gentleman *cry* for converting grace! That would be a strange sight indeed. Shall I speak to you, old men: my venerable fathers in age? Alas! you are so hardened by a long course of sinning, that you are not likely to hear. Shall I speak to you, ye relics of those families where death has lately made such havoc? Sure you must be disposed to hear me—sure you cannot put me off so soon. I hope sickness and death have been sent among you as my assistants: that is, to enforce what I say, and be the means of your conversion. Shall I speak to you, young people? Alas! you are too merry and gay to listen to such serious things: and you, perhaps, think it is time enough as yet. Thus I am afraid you will put me off: and if you put me off, I shall hardly know where to turn; for of all the unconverted among us, I have most hopes of *you.* Old sinners are so confirmed in their estrangement from God, that there is but little hope of such veterans: but the habits of sin are not so strong in *you*, and God is wont to work upon persons of *your* age. If *you*, then, put me off, where shall I turn? Behold, I turn to the Gentiles. Poor negroes! Shall I find one among you that is willing to turn to God? Many of you are willing to be baptized: but that is not the thing. Are you willing to turn to God with all your hearts, in the manner I have explained to you? This is the grand question; and what do your hearts answer to it? If you also refuse—if you all refuse, then what remains for your poor minister to do, but to return home and make this complaint to him that sent him: "Lord, there were unconverted sinners among my hearers; and in my poor manner, I made an honest trial to turn them to thee; but, Lord, it was in vain—they refused to return; and therefore I must leave them to thee: to do what thou pleasest with them!" Oh! will you constrain me to make this complaint upon any of you to my divine Master? Oh! free me from the disagreeable necessity. Come, come all, rich and poor, young and old, bond and free: come, and let us return unto the Lord; for "he hath torn, and he will heal us; he hath smitten, and he will bind us up, and we shall live in his sight." Hosea vi. 1. *Amen.*

SERMON LXVII.

THE RELIGIOUS IMPROVEMENT OF THE LATE EARTHQUAKES.*

ISAIAH XXIV. 18, 19, 20.—*The foundations of the earth do shake. The earth is utterly broken down; the earth is clean dissolved; the earth is moved exceedingly; the earth shall reel to and fro like a drunkard, and shall be removed like a cottage; and the transgression thereof shall lie heavy upon it, and it shall fall, and not rise again.*

THE works of Creation and Providence were undoubtedly intended for the notice and contemplation of mankind, especially when God *comes out of his place*, that is, departs from the *usual* and *stated* course of his providence to punish the inhabitants of the earth for their iniquities; then it becomes us to observe the operation of his hands with fear and reverence. To this the Psalmist repeatedly calls us: "Come, behold the works of the Lord, what desolation he hath made in the earth." Ps. xlvi. 8. "Come, and see the works of God; he is terrible in his doing towards the children of men." Ps. lxvi. 5. To assist you in this, I shall cheerfully devote an hour to-day.

This world is a state of *discipline* for another; and therefore *chastisements* of various kinds and degrees are to be enumerated among the *ordinary* works of Provi-

---

* Preached in Hanover county, Virginia, June 19, 1756. Tua res agitur paries cum proximus ardet.—HOR.

dence. Pain, sickness, losses, bereavements, disappointments; these are the *usual* scourges of the divine hand, which our heavenly father uses *every* day, to chastise some or other of his undutiful children. But when these are found too weak and ineffectual for their reformation; or when, from their being so frequent and common, men begin to think them *things of course*, and not to acknowledge the divine hand in them; then the universal Ruler departs from his usual methods of chastisements, and uses such signal and *extraordinary* executioners of his vengeance, as cannot but rouse a slumbering world, and render it sensible of his agency. At such times, he throws the world into a ferment; and either controls its established laws, or carries such into execution, as were formed only for *extraordinary* occasions. These extraordinary ministers of his vengeance, are generally these four: the FAMINE, SWORD, PESTILENCE, and EARTHQUAKES. A famine in this land of plenty, would be an unusual judgment indeed; and yet sundry parts of our country have been reduced to the borders of it, by the severity of last year's drought. The *sword* has been a harmless weapon to *us*, till of late; but now it is brandished over our heads, and pierces our country in a thousand veins. The *pestilence* is a mischief that has not spread desolation among us; though there is not perhaps one year, in which it is not walking through some country or other upon our globe. As for *earthquakes*, we have had such shakes, as may convince us, we are not beyond the reach of that desolating judgment, even on this solid continent; though they have not as yet done us any injury. But perhaps there never was, since the earthquake at the deluge, that broke up the fountains of the great deep, so extensive a desolation of this kind, as has lately happened in Europe and Africa. And though, blessed be God, it did not immediately affect us; yet the very fame of so dreadful a judgment ought to be improved for our advantage. To this event I may accommodate the words of my text, "The foundations of the earth do shake; the earth is utterly broken down; the earth is clean dissolved; the earth reels to and fro like a drunkard: it is removed like a cottage," or a tent,* that was set up only for a night's lodging; and the reason of all is, "The transgression thereof *lies heavy* upon it." Such of you as have read the public papers, need not be informed of that wide-spreading earthquake, which begun on the first of November last, and has since been felt at different times, through most parts of Europe. For the sake of those that have only had some imperfect hints of it, I would give you this short history. The city of Lisbon, that in a little spot contained about as many souls as this wide-extended colony,† is now no more! Its vast riches, and by all accounts, between fifty and a hundred thousand persons, have been buried or burnt in its ruins. Sundry other towns in Portugal, Spain, and along the European coasts of the Mediterranean, have been damaged, overthrown, or sunk, like Sodom and Gomorrah. The earthquake also extended across that sea, and has ruined a great part of Africa, particularly in the empire of Morocco, where the large and populous cities of Mequinez, Fez, and the port of Sallee, have been demolished, with many thousands of the inhabitants. It has likewise been felt in sundry parts of Italy, Germany, France, Bohemia, and even in Great Britain and Ireland. Nay, the tremor has reached our continent; and has been very sensibly felt in Boston and other parts of New England. Though much mischief has not been done in those parts, yet a loud warning has been given; and oh! that it may not be given in vain. It would certainly be an instance of inexcusable stupidity,

* מלונה.   † About three hundred thousand souls.

for us to take no notice of so dreadful a dispensation. Such devastations are at once *judgments* upon the places where they happen, and *warnings* to others. For what end were the Israelites punished with so many miraculous judgments? St. Paul will tell you, it was not only for *their* sins, but " all these things happened to them for *ensamples*, and they are written for *our* admonition, upon whom the ends of the world are come." 1 Cor. x. 11. For what end were the cities of Sodom and Gormorrah turned into ashes? St. Peter will tell you: God "made them an *ensample* unto those who should after live ungodly." 2 Peter ii. 6. And shall not *we* regard such examples, even in our own age? Shall others perish for our admonition? and shall *we* receive no profit by their destruction? This would be stupid and inexcusable indeed. Therefore my present design is, to direct you to such meditations as this alarming event naturally suggests; and which may be sufficient to the right improvement of it.

But before I enter upon this design, I would once more inculcate upon you a doctrine, which I have often proved in your hearing; and that is, that this world is a little territory of Jehovah's government; under the management of his providence: and particularly, that all the blessings of life are the gifts of his bounty; and all its calamities, the chastisements or judgments of his hand. This I would have you to apply to the event now under consideration. It is the *providence* of God that has impregnated the bowels of the earth with these dreadful materials, that tear and shatter its frame. It is *his* providence that strikes the spark, which sets this dreadful train in a flame, and causes the terrible explosion. There is a set of little, conceited, smattering philosophers risen among us, who think they disprove all this, by alleging that earthquakes proceed from *natural causes;* and therefore, it is superstitious to ascribe them to the agency of Providence. But there is no more reason or philosophy in this, than if they should deny that a *man* writes, because he makes use of a *pen;* or that kings exercise government, because they employ servants under them. I grant, that natural causes concur toward the production of earthquakes: but what are these natural causes? Are they *independent, self-moved* causes? No: they were first *formed,* and are still *directed,* by the Divine hand. The shortest and plainest view I can give of the case is this: When God formed this globe, he saw what would be the conduct of its inhabitants, in all the periods of time; and particularly, he knew at what particular time a kingdom or city would be ripe for his judgments; and he adjusted matters accordingly. He set the train with so much exactness, that it will spring just in the critical moment, when every thing is ripe for it. And thus, by a preconcerted plan, he answers all the *occasional* exigencies of the world, and suits himself to particular cases, without a miracle, or controlling the laws of nature; or, perhaps, he may sometimes think it necessary to work with his own immediate hand, and to suspend or counteract the usual and stated laws of creation, that his interference may be more conspicuous. Let this truth, then, my brethren, be laid deep in your minds, as a foundation, that earthquakes are the effects of divine Providence, and produced to answer some of its important ends in the world. And hence I naturally proceed, according to promise, to direct you to such meditations as are suitable to this shocking event.

Now you may hence take occasion to reflect upon the majesty and power of God, and the dreadfulness of his anger; the sinfulness of our world; the distinguishing kindness of Providence towards us; and the destruction of this globe at the final judgment.

First, Let the majestic and terrible phenomenon of earthquakes put you in mind of *the majesty and power of God, and the dreadfulness of his displeasure.* He can toss and convulse this huge globe, and shake its foundations down to the centre. Trembling continents, burning or sinking mountains, wide-yawning gulfs in solid ground, explosions of subterranean mines sufficient to shiver a world, are but hints of his indignation. But my language does but sink this exalted subject; I shall therefore give you the inimitable descriptions of the sacred writers. "He is wise in heart," says Job, "and mighty in strength; who hath hardened himself against him, and hath prospered? Which removeth the mountains, and they know not: which overturneth them in his anger; which shaketh the earth out of her place, and the pillars thereof tremble." Job ix. 4, 5. "A fire is kindled in mine anger," says the Lord himself, in his own language, "and shall burn into the lowest hell, and shall consume the earth with her increase, and set on fire the foundations of the mountains." Deut. xxxii. 22. "The mountains saw thee," O God, "and they trembled: the overflowing of the water passed by: the deep uttered his voice, and lifted up his hands on high." Hab. iii. 10. "What ailed thee, O thou sea, that thou fleddest? Ye mountains, that ye skipped like rams, and ye little hills like lambs? Tremble, thou earth, at the presence of the Lord, at the presence of the God of Jacob." Psalm cxiv. 5–7. But the most striking and lively description, methinks, which the language of inspiration itself has given us, is in the prophecy of Nahum, "God is jealous, and the Lord revengeth: the Lord revengeth, and is furious; the Lord will take vengeance on his adversaries; and he reserveth wrath for his enemies; the Lord hath his way in the whirlwind, and in the storm, and the clouds are the dust of his feet. He rebuketh the sea, and maketh it dry, and drieth up all the rivers; the mountains quake at him, and the hills melt; and the earth is burnt at his presence; yea, the world, and they that dwell therein. Who can stand before his indignation? and who can abide in the fierceness of his anger? his fury is poured out like fire, and the rocks are thrown down by him." Naham. i. 2–7. And is this the Being that is so little thought of in our world? Is this he, whose name passes for the veriest trifle? whose word can hardly keep men awake, or engage their attention? whose authority is less regarded, and whose resentment is less feared, than that of an earthly king—whose laws are audaciously violated, and his threatenings despised? Is this he, who is complimented with empty, spiritless formalities under the name of religion? Oh! is this he, whom we are met this day to worship? What! and shall there be no more attention and solemnity among us? Can anything be more unnatural, more impious, or more shocking? Indeed, sirs, it strikes me with horror to think how contemptuously this glorious, almighty, and terrible God is treated in our world. Angels do not treat him so—nay, even devils, in the height of their malice, dare not thus trifle with him— they tremble at his very name. Oh! "Wherefore doth the wicked *contemn* God?" Psalm x. 13. See here is your antagonist: and can you make good your cause against him? Can you harden yourselves against him and prosper? Job ix. 4. This earth is as nothing in his hands. "He taketh up the isles as a very little thing." Isa. xl. 15. He that can shake this huge globe to the centre; he that can bury proud cities, with all their inhabitants, in the bowels of the earth; he that can toss the ocean into a ferment, and cause it to overwhelm the guilty land; he that can hurl the tallest mountains from their everlasting foundations into the sea, or sink them into the valleys, or pools of water; he that has stored the bowels of the earth, as with magazines of gunpowder, and can set it all in blaze, or burst it into ten thousand fragments; he that can arm the meanest creature, a gnat or a worm, to be your executioner, and has an absolute power over the most mighty and ungovernable elements: oh! what will HE make of *you*, when he takes you in hand? Can you rest easy one moment, while you have reason to fear the supreme Lord of nature is your enemy. For your wilful provocations? In his name (if his glorious and fearful name has any weight with you) I charge you to seek his favour; make him your friend, and dare to rebel against him no more. Dare you continue a rebel against him, or careless about pleasing him, while you walk on *his* ground, breathe in *his* air, feed upon *his* provisions, and live in *his* territories, and within the reach of *his* arm? Why, he can make that earth you pollute with your sins open its dreadful jaws and swallow you up alive, like Korah and his company. Numb. xvi. 32. Oh! my brethren, it may break our hearts to think there should be any of the sons of men so mad as to incur his displeasure, and be careless about his favour. But, alas! are there not some such among us? Well; they will soon find "It is a fearful thing to fall into the hands of the living God," Heb. x. 31, unless they speedily repent.

Secondly, This desolating judgment may justly lead you to reflect *upon the sinfulness of our world*. Alas! we live upon a guilty globe; and much has it suffered for the sins of its inhabitants. Once it was all drowned in an universal deluge; and many parts of it have since sunk under the load of guilt. If sin had never defiled it, it would never have been thus torn and shattered. We have seen, these judgments are at the disposal of Providence: and we are sure, a righteous Providence would never inflict them for nothing. It is *sin*, my brethren, that is the source of all the calamities that oppress our world from age to age: it is *sin* that has so often convulsed it with earthquakes. Do but observe the language of my text on this head. "The *transgression* of the earth shall *lie heavy* upon it." This, sirs, *this*, is the burden under which it totters; *this* is the evil, at which it trembles; *this* is a load, which men, which the earth itself, nay, which angels, and the whole creation, cannot bear up under. Why was the old world destroyed by a deluge? It was because all flesh had corrupted their way: because "the wickedness of man was great upon the earth, and every imagination of the thoughts of his heart was only evil, and that continually." Gen. vi. 5. Why was Sodom consumed with lightning from heaven, and sunk into a dead sea by an earthquake? It was because "The men of Sodom were wicked, and sinners before the Lord exceedingly." Gen. xiii. 13. In short, *sin* is the cause of all the calamities under which our world has groaned, from the fall of Adam to this day. Heaven has been testifying its displeasure against the sins of men by the most terrible judgments, from age to age, for near six thousand years. The destruction of one nation is intended not only for their punishment, but for a warning to others, that they may hear, and fear, and do no more so wickedly. Deut. xiii. 11. But men will still obstinately persist, unalarmed by the loudest warnings, and unreformed by the severest chastisements. Let the sword of war slay its thousands; let the pestilence walk about in all its desolating terrors; let the earth shake and tremble under its guilty inhabitants; let these judgments be repeated from generation to generation, from country to country; still they will sin on; and the chastisements of six thousand years have not been able to reform them. Oh! what a rebellious province of Jehovah's empire is this! and probably it has been seldom more so than in the present age; and therefore it is no wonder that the judgments of God are in the earth. The greatest part of it is overrun with all the idolatry and ignorance, vice and barbarity of heathenism. A great part of it worships the impostor Mahomet, instead of the Son of God, and groan under his yoke. This is the character of the empire of Morocco, and those African territories that have been ravaged by the late earthquake. They are either superstitious heathens or deluded Mahometans, and the knowledge of God is not to be found among them. The greatest part of Europe is corrupted with the idolatry, superstition, and debaucheries of the church of Rome, and groans under its tyranny. There the most foolish theatrical farces are devoutly performed under the name of religion; there the freeborn mind is enslaved, and dare not *think* for itself in matters in which it must *answer* for itself; there the homage due to the true God, and the only Mediator, is sacrilegiously given to senseless idols, and a rabble of imaginary saints; there the infernal court of the inquisition imitates the tortures of hell, and makes the man that would discover the truth a miracle of misery; there a market for indulgences and pardons is held; and men, for a little money, may buy a license to commit the most atrocious crimes, or they make atonement for them by the penance of bodily austerities. And can pure and undefiled religion, can good morals grow and flourish in such a soil? No: religion must degenerate into priestcraft and a mercenary superstition, and the most enormous vices and debaucheries must abound. Such, alas! was Lisbon, by universal character.

And though I would not repeat the censorious sins of the Jews, with regard to the Galileans, nor suppose that this city was more deeply guilty than all the cities upon the face of the earth; yet this I dare pronounce, that it was a *very guilty* spot of the globe, and that it was for this it was so severely punished. If we take a survey of Protestant countries, where religion is to be found, if anywhere at all, alas! how melancholy is the prospect! The good old doctrines of the reformation, which were adapted to advance the honours of divine grace and mortify the pride of man, have been too generally abandoned; and a more easy system, agreeable to the vanity and self-flattery of depraved hearts, has been dressed up in their stead. Nay, Christianity itself has been rejected, ridiculed, and exposed to public scorn, by the increasing club of deists; and where the Christian name and profession are retained, the life and spirit are too generally lost; and the practice, an open opposition to their professed faith. How are the ordinances of the gospel neglected or profaned? What a shocking variety of crimes are to be found everywhere, even in countries that profess to have renounced Popery for its corruptions? Drunkenness, swearing, perjury, lying, fraud, and injustice; pride, luxury, various forms of lewdness, and all manner of extravagances; and all these expressly forbidden, under the severest penalties, by that religion which themselves profess and acknowledge divine; and thus they continue, in spite of warnings and chastisements; in spite of mercies and instructions. They have sinned on, impenitent and incorrigible, for a length of years. God is but little regarded in the world, which owes its existence and all its blessings to his power and goodness. Jesus is but little regarded, even in those countries that profess his name; and is it any wonder the earth trembles, when the iniquity thereof lies so *heavy* upon it? Is it not rather a wonder that it has not burst to pieces long ago, and buried its guilty inhabitants in its ruins? Is there a supreme Ruler over the kingdoms of men, and shall he not testify his displeasure against their rebellion? Shall he always tamely submit to such contemptuous treatment? And shall he always look on, and see his government insulted, and his vengeance defied? No; at proper seasons he will come forth out of his place; he will depart from the stated course of his providence, to punish them for their iniquities. The convulsions of the earth, the inundations of the sea, and the sword of war shall at once proclaim and execute his displeasure. If our country have escaped the devastations of the earthquake, it is not owing to our innocence, but to the distinguishing mercy and patience of God. And, therefore,

Thirdly, This melancholy event may carry your minds gratefully to reflect upon the *peculiar kindness of Heaven towards our country*, in that it was not involved in the same destruction.

I need not tell you that we are a guilty, obnoxious people; you may be convinced of it by more authentic evidence. The lives of the generality proclaim it aloud; the terrors of war that now surround us proclaim it; and do not your own consciences whisper the same thing? And why have we been spared? How has even this *solid* continent borne up under the load of guilt that burdens it? It has been owing entirely to the grace and patience of that God, who is so little regarded among us. And shall we not gratefully celebrate his praises? Shall not his goodness lead us to repentance? or shall all his kindness be thrown away upon us, and will we constrain him to pour out his judgments upon *us* also, at last? Methinks

I hear him expostulating over Virginia, in that compassionate language: "How shall I give thee up, Virginia? How shall I make thee as Admah? How shall I set thee as Zeboim?" Cities that were destroyed with Sodom and Gomorrah. "My heart is turned within me; my repentings are kindled together." Hosea xi. 8. Oh! must not such moving language melt us down at his feet, in the most ingenuous repentance, and engage us to his service for the future? Without a spirit of prophecy, I may safely pronounce, it will never be well with our country till we are brought to this. But,

Fourthly, That which I would particularly suggest to your thoughts from the devastations of the late earthquake, is the *last universal destruction of our world at the final judgment*. Of this, an earthquake is both a *confirmation* to human reason and a lively *representation*.

It is a *confirmation* even to human reason, drawn from the constitution of our globe, that such a destruction is possible, and even probable, according to the course of nature. Our globe is stored with subterranean magazines of combustible materials, which need but a spark to produce a violent explosion, and rend and burst it to pieces. What huge quantities of these sulphurous and nitrous mines must there be, when one discharge can spread a tremour over half the world, bury islands and cities, and shatter wide-extended continents! What an inexhaustible store of fire and brimstone has supplied Etna, Vesuvius, and other burning mountains, that have been belching out torrents of liquid fire for some thousands of years, and now rage as furiously as ever? Let but the subterranean magazines, in every cave and cranny of the globe, be set in a blaze; let the central fire but break loose; let all the combustible materials near or upon the surface of the earth, be once enflamed—turf, coal, trees, cities, houses, and all their furniture; this would produce a general conflagration, which nothing could resist. In short, we may conjecture, from the construction of our world, that it was not intended for a perpetual existence in its present form, but to be dissolved by the dreadful element of fire. And Revelation assures us of this universal desolation, when the heavens shall be shrivelled up, like a parched scroll, and pass away with a great noise; and the elements shall melt with fervent heat; the earth, also, and the things that are therein, shall be burnt up. 2 Peter iii. 10.

An earthquake is also a lively *representation* of the universal ruins of that day, and the horror and consternation of mankind. Let imagination form a lively idea of the destruction of Lisbon—the ground trembling, and heaving, and roaring with subterranean thunders—towers, palaces, and churches tottering and falling—the flames bursting from the ruins, and setting all in a blaze—the sea roaring, and rushing over its banks with resistless impetuosity—the inhabitants running from place to place in wild consternation, in search of safety; or falling on their knees, and rending the air with their wild shrieks and cries—flying to the strongest buildings for shelter, but crushed in their ruins; or to the sea, and there swept away by the rushing waves. Walls falling upon thousands in their flight; or the earth opening her jaws, and swallowing them up. Can human imagination represent any thing more shocking? In other calamities, whatever else we lose, we have still the earth to support us: but when that is gone, we are helpless indeed, and must sink into immediate destruction.

Such, my brethren, but infinitely more dreadful, will be the terrors of that last, that universal earthquake, which we shall all see.

Stars drop, rush lawless through the air, and dash one

another to pieces. The sun is extinguished, and looks like a huge globe of solid darkness. The moon is turned into blood, and reflects a portentous, sanguinary light upon the earth. The clouds flash and blaze with sheets of lightning; and are rent with the horrid crash of thunder. This is echoed back by the subterranean thunders that murmur, rumble, and roar under ground. The earth is tossed like a ball, and bursts asunder like a mouldering clod. See, the yawning gulfs open! the flames bursting forth from the centre; and a horrid confusion of fire and smoke rolling through the arch of heaven! See the works of nature and art perishing in one promiscuous ruin! Mountains sinking and bursting out into so many volcanoes, vomiting up seas of liquid fire! Rocks dissolving, and pouring their melted mass into the channels of the rivers! Pyramids, towers, palaces, cities, woods, and plains, burning in one prodigious, undistinguishing blaze! the seas evaporating, and vanishing away, through the intenseness of the heat! a mixed, confused heap of sea and land! floods of water, and torrents of melted rocks! Now the earth is turned upside-down, inside-out, and reduced into a mere chaos.

> "See all the formidable sons of fire.
> Eruptions, earthquakes, comets, lightnings play
> Their various engines; all at once disgorge
> Their blazing magazine; and take by storm,
> This poor, terrestrial citadel of man.
>   Amazing period! when each mountain-top
> Out-burns Vesuvius, rocks eternal pour
> Their melted mass, as rivers once they pour'd:
> Stars rush; and final ruin fiercely drives
> Her ploughshare o'er creation——
> ——————I see! I feel it!
> All nature, like an earthquake, trembling round!
> All deities, like summer's swarms, on wing!——
> I see the Judge enthron'd! the flaming guard!
> The volume open'd! open'd every heart!
> A sun-beam pointing out each secret thought!

> No patron! intercessor none! now past
> The sweet, the clement, mediatorial hour!
> For guilt no plea! to pain, no pause, no bound!
> Inexorable all! and all extreme!"*

And where, ye hardy, presumptuous sinners, that can now despise the terrors of the Lord, oh! where will ye appear in this tremendous day? What shall support you when the ground on which you stood is gone? What rock or mountain shall you procure to shelter you, when rocks and mountains are sinking and disappearing, or melting away, like snow before the sun? How can you expect to escape hell, when the earth itself is turned into a lake of fire and brimstone? Oh! how can you bear the thought of rolling and weltering there? What is now become of your lands and possessions on which you once set your hearts? Nay, where is the country, where the continent, in which you once dwelt? Alas! they are all reduced into ashes, or calcinated into glass, a mere *caput mortuum*.

And is there no safety in this wreck of nature? Are all mankind involved in this general ruin? No: blessed be God, there are some who shall be safe and unhurt, while the frame of nature is dissolving around them. Those happy souls, who choose the Lord for their portion, and Jesus for their Saviour, and who in this tottering world looked for a city that has foundations, firm, unshaken foundations, they shall be safe beyond the reach of this general desolation; their happiness lies secure in a "kingdom which *cannot be moved*." Heb. xii. 28. There is a new heaven and a new earth prepared for them.

Then, my brethren, you will see the advantage of that despised, neglected thing, *religion*, and the difference between the righteous and the wicked; between him that serveth the Lord, and him that serveth him not. Mal. iii.

* Young's Night Thoughts, No. 9.

18. Then, those that are now so unfashionable as to make religion a serious business, will smile secure at a dissolving world. Then they will find the happy fruits of those hours they spent on their knees at the throne of grace; of those cries and tears they poured out after Jesus; of their honest struggles with sin and temptation; and in short, of a life devoted to God. Therefore, let such of you, (for I trust there are such among you,) rejoice in the prospect of that glorious, dreadful day; and let it be more and more your serious business to prepare for it. You shall rest for ever in a country that shall never be shaken with earthquakes, nor be subject to any of the calamities of this mortal state. Therefore, since this shall be your portion, be not much disturbed with any of the judgments that may befall this land of your pilgrimage and exile. The sooner it is destroyed, the sooner you will get home to the region of eternal rest. Borrow the language of the triumphant Psalmist, "We will not fear, though the earth be removed, and though the mountains be carried into the midst of the sea: though the waters thereof roar, and be troubled: though the mountains shake with the swelling thereof." Psalm xlvi. 2, 3.

But, oh! where shall the ungodly and sinner appear? Oh, where shall some of you, my dear people, appear in that dreadful day? I am jealous over you with a godly jealousy, and am really afraid for some of you. Do you not know in your own consciences, that you are generally thoughtless and careless about the great concerns of your eternal state? Your hearts have never been thoroughly changed by divine grace; nor do you know by experience what it is to believe, to repent, and to love God with all your hearts. You do not make conscience of every duty; I mean, you neglect the worship of God, in your families, though under the strongest obligations to perform it, perhaps from your own solemn vows and promises. You indulge yourselves in some known sin or other; and if you feel some pangs of repentance, your repentance does not issue in reformation. Alas! my brethren, is this the character of one soul within the hearing of my voice? Then I must tell you, that if you continue such, you will be fuel for the last universal fire: and must perish in the ruins of the world you have loved so well.

But who knows, that if you begin immediately, you may not yet have time enough to work out your salvation? Therefore, now begin the work. There is no safety but in Jesus Christ. Away to him therefore; let me lay the hand of friendly violence upon you, and hurry you out of your present condition, as the angel did Lot out of Sodom. "Up, get ye out of this condition; for the Lord will destroy all that continue in it—escape for thy life, look not behind thee—escape to Jesus Christ, lest thou be consumed." Gen. xix. 14–17.

I must tell you frankly, I studied this part of my discourse with an anxious heart; and I was almost discouraged from adding this exhortation to it. "For," thought I, "I have given such exhortations over and over: but they seem generally in vain. There is indeed a happy number among my hearers, who, I doubt not, have regarded the gospel preached by my lips. But, alas! as to the rest, I have been so often disappointed that I now hardly hope to succeed." These, my dear brethren, are my discouragements in my retirements, when no eye sees me but God. And oh! sinners, will your future conduct prove, that there was good reason for my fears? Alas! is the ministry of the gospel a useless institution with regard to *you?* Have such exhortations as these no weight with you? Will you resist my benevolent hand, when I would stretch it forth to pluck you out of the burning?

Well, my friends, I cannot help it. If you will perish, if you are obstinately set upon it, I have only this to say, that your poor minister will weep in secret for you, and drop his tears upon you as you are falling into ruin from between his hands.

Yes, sinners, God forbid that I should cease to pray for you and pity you. While my tongue is capable of pronouncing a word, and you think it worth your while to hear me, I will send the calls of the gospel after you; and if you perish after all, you shall drop into hell with the offers of heaven in your ears. Fain would I clear myself and say, "Your blood be upon your own heads: I am clean." Acts xviii. 6. But, alas! my heart recoils and fails. I have no doubt at all, but the gospel I have preached to you is indeed the gospel of Christ, and I cheerfully venture my own soul upon it. But in dispensing it among you, I am conscious of so much weakness, coldness, and unskilfulness, that I am at times shocked at myself, lest I should be accessary to your ruin. However, this is certain, great guilt will fall *somewhere.* I desire to take my own share of shame and guilt upon myself, and to humble myself for it before God. And I pray you do the same. Oh, humble yourselves before God, for your past conduct; and prepare, prepare to meet him, in the midst of a burning world.

Or, if you continue obstinately impenitent still, prepare to make your defence against your poor minister there, when he will be obliged to appear as a swift witness against you, and say, "Lord, I can appeal to thyself, that I warned them to prepare for this day, though with so many guilty infirmities, as nothing but thy mercies can forgive. But they would not regard my warnings, though given in thine awful Name, and sometimes enforced with my own compassionate tears." There, sirs, at the supreme tribunal, prepare to meet me; and thither I dare appeal for the truth and importance of the things I have inculcated upon you.

A HYMN.

BY THE AUTHOR OF THE PRECEDING DISCOURSE.

How great, how terrible that God,
Who shakes creation with his nod!
He frowns, and earth's foundations quake,
And all the wheels of nature break!

Crushed under guilt's oppressive weight,
This globe now totters to its fate:
Trembles beneath her guilty sons,
And for deliverance heaves and groans!

And see! the glorious, dreadful day,
That takes the enormous load away!
See skies, and stars, and earth, and seas,
Sink in one universal blaze!

Where, now—ah! where shall sinners seek
For shelter in the general wreck?
Can falling rocks conceal them now,
When rocks dissolve like melting snow?

In vain for pity now the cry:
In lakes of liquid fire they lie:
There on the burning billows tossed,
For ever, ever, ever, lost!

But saints, undaunted and serene,
Your eyes shall view the dreadful scene!
Your Saviour lives, though worlds expire,
And earth and skies dissolve in fire!

JESUS! the helpless creature's friend!
To thee my all I dare commend:
Thou canst preserve my feeble soul,
When lightnings blaze from pole to pole!

SERMON LXVIII.

SERIOUS REFLECTIONS ON WAR.

JAMES IV. 1.—*From whence come wars and fightings among you? Come they not hence, even of your lusts that war in your members?**

THE years that now roll over our heads are not likely to be passed over slightly in the annals of our country; they are big with very important events, in which our own welfare and that of our posterity is nearly interested. This happy country has been for a long time the region of peace; and our years have run on in one uniform tenor of undisturbed tranquility: but for some time past the scene has been changed. We have seen years of terror and alarm, of desolation and slaughter; and the prospect through future years is equally gloomy. We are as yet, blessed be God, a free and happy people! We enjoy peace in the midst of a ravaged, bleeding country: but how long we shall enjoy this distinguished happiness is a dreadful uncertainty! The fate of our country, and all that it contains, hangs in an anxious suspense. Whether the present year will leave us as it found us, is only known to Omniscience.

The religious improvement of such interesting events, whether prosperous or afflictive, is the best use we can

---

* Preached at Henrico, January 1, 1757; being a day appointed by the Presbytery of Hanover to be observed as a religious fast, on account of the present state of public affairs.

make of them. And now, while we stand upon the threshold of a new year, it is proper we should pause, and look back to the events which the past year has brought forth, and forward to those with which the coming year is pregnant. The review of the one furnishes us with occasion both for praise and humiliation, and with materials to sing of mercy and of judgment; and the prospect of the other calls for prayer and repentance, to avert those judgments with which we are threatened, and to obtain a favourable issue to the expeditions in which we may engage. That must be a thoughtless mind indeed, that can learn no useful lessons from the present posture of our affairs, even without a teacher. And that must be an atheistical mind indeed, that is not led, by the present appearances of things, to those exercises of devotion, which such a season so loudly calls for.

The presbytery, therefore, has thought proper to appoint this day to be observed as a religious fast, through all the congregations under their care, on account of the present state of our public affairs: that we may leave the old year and our old guilt, at once, behind us—that we may enter upon the new year as new creatures—that, as we bid adieu to the old year, we may drop a tear, and vent a groan, over the sins we committed in it—that we may not carry with us into this year the heavy load of last year's guilt, but may enter it with earnest prayers, that God would be with us through it, and afford the same safe conduct to our country and nation.

The better to answer the design of this day, I shall briefly recapitulate the affairs of the year past; and offer some conjectures, from the present appearances of things, concerning the events that may be before us in the year upon which we are now entering.

The last seasonable and plentiful summer, after a year

of drought and scarcity, ought always to be remembered as a surprising instance of divine bounty. How kind is our heavenly Father, even to the disobedient and unthankful!—how rich in mercy, even to the ungrateful abusers of that mercy! With how. much long-suffering does he endure even the vessels of wrath fitted for destruction! And oh! the stupid ingratitude of the sons of men! They sin on still, unmoved by the riches of his grace, as well as incorrigible under his rod. What return has God received for rain from heaven, and fruitful seasons, and a whole country full of blessings? Alas! not the gratitude of the dull ox to his owner, or the stupid ass to his master: for "the ox knoweth his owner, and the ass his master's crib," Isaiah i. 3; but how few among us know or consider? How few acknowledge their obligations to God for these blessings?

Last year, as well as that before it, our frontiers have streamed with British blood. There you might see flourishing plantations deserted; families scattered or butchered; some mangled and scalped; some escaped in horror and consternation, with the loss of their earthly all; some captivated by the savages, dragged through woods, and swamps, and mountains, to their towns, and there prostituted to barbarous lust, or condemned to lingering tortures, which, I believe, have hardly ever been equalled on this side hell. This has been the fate of some hundreds of families on the frontiers of Virginia and Pennsylvania; a fate so melancholy, that words cannot describe it, nor are our tenderest compassions equal to it.

Last year also saw the surprising loss of the important harbours and fortresses of Minorca and Oswego; a loss not likely to be soon repaired; a loss occasioned, not by the superior force of the enemy, but it is to be feared, by the cowardice or mismanagement of our own men; which renders it the more mortifying.

The last year was also sadly memorable for disappointed schemes and blasted expeditions. Our expedition against the Shawnese most unaccountably miscarried. The northern expedition against Crown Point, and the other French forts in those parts, which has been so expensive, and from which we entertained such sanguine expectations, has proved abortive last summer, as it did the preceding: and whether ever it can be carried into execution, is dreadfully uncertain. The scheme for increasing our little regiment, by drafting the young men in the militia, did not answer the end; and, instead of fifteen hundred men, we had hardly half that number. In short, there is no scheme that I can think of, that has been successful but the expedition of Colonel Armstrong against an Indian town. I know that in this world, which is now under an indiscriminate Providence, success is not peculiar to the pious; but victory and defeats happen promiscuously to the good and bad. And yet, I cannot but look upon it as very remarkable, that amidst so many disappointments and defeats, one of the most hazardous expeditions, conducted by one that fears God, and depended upon his strength, should be successful. Such is Colonel Armstrong; a Christian, as well as a soldier. I have known him seeking after Jesus, as a broken-hearted penitent, with cries and tears, for some years. Had we many officers thus prepared to serve their country, we might expect more service from them. Faith made heroes in ancient times; and I am persuaded religion is the best source of courage still. But alas! how few Christian heroes have we to boast!

Last year we had a treaty with the Catawba Indians, and with the more powerful nation of the Cherokees.

We have complied with our engagements, and had high hopes of powerful assistance from them; but we have been disappointed; and as to the latter, we fear they will not even observe a neutrality, but may be seduced to the French interest.

Last year has also heard the declaration of war between Great Britain and France: but what year will see the end of it, or what the issue will be, is utterly unknown. The commencement of war must always appear a very solemn period to a thoughtful mind. It is the commencement of scenes of blood and desolation as to thousands. Many will lose their lives in it, many their relations, many their estates, and many their liberty: and whether we may not be of the number, is all uncertain. Now the sword is drawn, and begins to maim and mangle our fellow-men. Now cannons begin to roar, and tear hundreds to pieces; now multitudes sink in the ocean, and multitudes welter in their blood on the field of battle. Now cities blaze, and are turned into ruinous heaps. Now the fate of empire, the cause of religion and liberty, is disputed; and who knows what will be the decision? Now death devours thousands at a meal; and multitudes of thoughtless immortals are hurried into the eternal world unprepared, without thought in the destroyed, whither they are going; or in the destroyers, whither they are sending them. These are the dire effects of war; and are not these very tragical and affecting? and must they not render the commencement of a war very solemn and terrible?

Last year has been remarkable for very grand alliances. The empress queen, who is indebted to Great Britain for the preservation of her dominions, and for the advancement of her husband to be emperor of Germany, and for whom our king bravely fought in person, has perfidiously and ungratefully deserted us, and entered into a confederacy with France. The empress of Russia has acted the same perfidious part, and acceded to that alliance, though bound by treaty to furnish us with no fewer than fifty-five thousand men, upon demand. The Dutch, intimidated by the French, have refused to fulfil their obligations to us. The brave king of Prussia has entered into an alliance with Britain; and is, indeed, the only important and active ally we have in the world. He has distinguished the last year with one illustrious victory over the Austrians. And may the same success still attend him in every good cause!

To sum up this review, the last year has been a very important period in the history of our country. Terror and devastation have stalked through the earth; and streams of human blood have been running by sea and land.*

To all which I may add, that God has visited a part of this congregation with a deadly contagious flux, which has thinned the neighbourhood, and swept off some families almost entirely. Blessed be God; it is now stopped: but, certainly, it becomes us always to remember that gloomy time, and reap instruction from the graves of our friends and neighbours, which are now so thick among us.

And now, may we not learn from this recapitulation, that we and our nation are a guilty people, and that a provoked God has, by this succession of calamitous events, loudly proclaimed his displeasure against us? Have our undertakings prospered, like those of a people in favour with Heaven? Far from it. And hence, we may also

* Though no decisive battle has been fought, yet frequent skirmishes have happened between scattered parties that have accidentally met in the woods, in which many lives have been lost; and, which renders the loss more affecting, they have been thrown away to little purpose; because these accidental skirmishes contribute, but in a small degree, to the decision of the grand controversy, and so to bring about a peace.

learn that we are now loudly called to repentance, humiliation, and prayer. Let us repent of those sins, that have brought these calamities upon us; let us "humble ourselves under the mighty hand of God, that he may exalt us in due time;" 1 Pet. v. 6; and let us cry mightily to God, that he would "turn away from his fierce anger, that we perish not," Jonah iii. 9.

Let us now look forward to the year before us. Blessed be God, we are blind to future events; and therefore incapable of anticipating the pain they might afford us, if known. But we may, at least, venture to form conjectures, from the present appearances of things. Who knows but still darker times are before us? Who knows but the measure of our iniquities is at length full, and God is about to call a guilty people to account? There may be a winnowing time at hand, to try and purge the Protestant churches. Popery may die hard; and its last struggles may throw the Christian world into confusion, in which thousands may be overwhelmed, and we among others.

The continent of Europe is likely to be the seat of war; and whether our brave ally, the king of Prussia, will be able to stand his ground against the formidable confederacy formed against him, is dismally uncertain. The preservation of the Protestant religion, and turning the scale of war in our favour, depends upon his success; and, therefore, though at this vast distance, we should earnestly pray, that a gracious Providence would still guard and prosper him.

Great Britain is in anxious expectation of an invasion from France; and what may be the consequence, is all unknown; though thus much may be very probably expected, that should it be so much as attempted, it will cost much blood and the lives of thousands.

Many captures will probably be made at sea this year, by which great numbers will be reduced to poverty; and, it is not unlikely, many naval engagements will happen, in which multitudes of human limbs and lives will be lost. We may also expect that this year, like the last, will produce frequent skirmishes between our men and the French and Indian savages; and that these will continue their desolating and bloody inroads upon our frontiers, and probably penetrate father into the country than they have hitherto done.

It is also likely, the expedition against Crown Point, and other French forts and settlements, will be again set on foot; but the issue is dreadfully uncertain.

It is likewise probable, that some grand decisive blow may be struck, in a general engagement, which may determine our fate; but what the determination will be, is not likely to be known till it happen.

Who knows but the Indian savages may generally desert us, and, in conjunction with the French, pour down upon us like a torrent? And if they should meet with assistance from some of our own slaves, how inconceivably terrible would be the consequence! What unexampled scenes of blood and slaughter, of desolation and torture, would fill our land! This, alas! is not so unlikely as we could wish.

In short, this year, like the last, is likely to be a turbulent, bloody season. The potsherds of the earth are dashing together, and thousands are broke to pieces in the conflict. Alas! what a world do we live in! What a restless, troubled ocean! What an aceldema, a field of blood! What savages are the sons of men, biting and devouring one another!

Now, in the present state of things, the question in my text is very proper; "Whence come wars and fightings among us?" What infernal cause is it that sets the world in arms? that sets reasonable creatures of the same race, upon disturbing and destroying one another? Whence is it that the art of war, that is, the art of killing one another with the greatest skill, is a necessary science? Whence is it that a great warrior, that is, a great destroyer of mankind, should be an honourable and celebrated character? Whence is it that swords and guns, and other instruments of death, are become necessary utensils in life, and a piece of furniture for kingdoms? To such questions my text gives the true answer: " Wars and fightings among you, come from hence, even from your *lusts*, which war in your members." This holds true with regard to lesser societies, and particular churches: contentions, quarrels, schisms, envying, and strife, proceed from this turbulent source. Families, neighbourhoods, and particular churches, would be circles of peace and tranquility, were it not for the ungovernable lusts of some of their members. It was probably to these lesser societies that the apostle immediately referred; but this assertion will also hold true in a more extensive sense; for wars and fightings among *nations* proceed from the same source, even from their lusts. The lust of dominion, the lust of riches, the lust of vain glory and applause, have set the world in arms from age to age; and the quarrel still continues and is never likely to be ended, while those restless lusts, from whence it springs, remain predominant in the hearts of men. One man has no right to superiority over others, except it was originally derived from their consent. What, then, but the lawless lust of power, could prompt a man to risk his own life, to embroil nations, to lay countries waste, and to destroy the lives of thousands of his fellow-men, that he may exercise dominion over the survivors? The wants of nature are few, and easily satisfied; and every country produces the necessaries for the support of its inhabitants. What, then, but the lawless lust of riches, or an insatiable avarice for the possessions of others, can cause nations to burst through their bounds, and make inroads upon the property of their neighbours? How peaceably did we live, till France began to fancy that she needed more plantations—that she needed a tobacco colony—that she needed the whole of the fur trade, and so forth? But now this unbounded coveteousness has set her in arms; has brought upon us and upon herself all the calamities of war; and who knows what will be the consequence? Man is not really a being of such mighty importance, as that he should set the present and future generations a talking about him, and admiring his exploits. Nor is the breath of popular applause such a substantial good, as to deserve the eager pursuit of a reasonable being. And yet, the lust of praise can carry a man through a life of fatigues and dangers to drench countries in blood, and throw away the lives of their inhabitants, merely to get a name—the name of a great destroyer, a public robber, and a murderer of his species: for that is generally the import of the names of heroes and great warriors—of the Alexanders and Cæsars of the world. What a blind, infatuated, and yet powerful lust is this! Matters of justice and property between nations, are not so intricate in themselves, but that they might be amicably decided, were it not for the strength of lust. But that they should immediately fly to arms, and shed each other's blood—that matters of property should not be determined. but by taking away the lives of the proprietors; how astonishing is this! how shocking an evidence of the horrid power of lust over them.

These lusts, says the apostle, which produce wars in

the world without, *war in your members*. There the war begins, and thence it circulates through the world. These mutinous and rebellious lusts raise an intestine war in the man's own breast. There they commit ravages upon his own soul, and throw all into a ferment. There they produce confusion and every evil work. They set the man at variance with himself and all about him. He and his conscience are often engaged in conflict; nay, he dares to resist even the Holy Spirit himself; the Spirit of all grace and benignity. His selfish, proud, and avaricious lusts set him at variance also with others. Hence proceed broils, animosities, and quarrels in neighbourhoods and families which turn them into a little hell. Were the fire of lust within but quenched, these flames would immediately go out. But a depraved heart, like an unruly tongue, "setteth on fire the course of nature, and is set on fire of hell." Jam. iii. 6. When these lusts inflame the hearts of public persons, of kings and their ministers, they set the world in a blaze around them; and their subjects, fired with the same passions, add fuel to augment the flame.

You see the proper original source of war, that it is the *lusts* of men; and my present design is, to make some reflections upon war as proceeding from this source, which may assist us in the business of this day, and in a profitable improvement of the present posture of our public affairs.

First, This subject naturally leads us to reflect upon the fallen, degenerate state of human nature. Cannons and trumpets, and all the horrid noise of war, proclaim aloud this melancholy truth, that we are a race of apostate creatures, that have fallen from our original rectitude, and become the slaves of imperious and savage passions.

What is this world but a field of battle? What are soldiers but destroyers of mankind by profession? What are heroes and conquerors but the most bold and successful butchers of the human race? What is the history of nations, from their first rise to the present day but a tragical story of contests, struggles for dominion, encroachments upon the possessions of others, bloody battles and sieges; ravaged countries, ruined cities, and heaps of slain? How many hundred thousand souls has the sword of war cut off, in Europe only, within these sixty years past? And thus it generally is, and has been, all the world over.* The earth is peopled with Ishmaelites; their hand against every man, and every man's hand against them. Twenty years of peace is a rare thing among the nations. The ocean of mankind has but few and short calms; and it is soon tossed into a tumult, and the outrageous waves dash, and foam, and break against one another. Human blood is streaming almost incessantly by sea and land; and now the tide is likely to swell unusually high—a spring tide of human blood! Swords and guns, the instruments of death, are become necessary utensils, like the instruments of husbandry or architecture. Men are tearing one another to pieces about the trifles of time, which a few years at

---

* A late ingenious author computes that the number of men killed in the field of battle amounts, at least, to forty thousand millions, from the beginning of the world to the year 1748; and to this, adding the havoc, calamity, and destruction attending war, namely, famine, disease, pestilence, and massacres in cold blood, he thinks he may fairly double the last total, and make the number no less than eighty thousand millions. And, as the number of men existing at a time upon the earth never exceeds five hundred millions, the number of men cut off by the sword of war, or its attendant evils, in all ages, must, at least, be equal to a hundred and sixty times the number of souls this day on the globe. What a prodigious and shocking computation is this!

See a vindication of Natural Society; being an ironical answer to Lord Bolingbroke.

most will tear from all their hands. A thousand swords are dividing this atom earth, among a thousand lords; and yet, strange! they cannot agree after all.* What burning resentment! What sullen enmity! What envenomed rancour! What barbarities, and tortures, and eager thirst of blood! What public authorized murders! *Murders*, I say; for if the man who takes away his neighbour's life unjustly be guilty of murder, certainly they who commence an unjust war, and thus take away the lives of thousands, perhaps at a blow, are still more deeply guilty of murder. This is a sketch of the history of the world. But is this the history of mankind in their paradisaical state? Would innocent creatures thus tear one another to pieces? Would innocent creatures be thus actuated with malignant passions? Did human nature first come out of the hands of its Creator thus inflamed with the passions of hell? Is it not plain, that the great fundamental law of all morality is not now deeply impressed upon the hearts of men, namely, that we should "love the Lord our God with all our hearts, and our neighbour as ourselves." Luke x. 27. The love of God, and the love of man, if they were the ruling passions of the human soul, would soon put an end to these confusions and bloodsheddings—would turn this earth into a heaven, a region of perfect peace and universal benevolence. And does not the strength, the inveteracy, and the universality of such infernal passions, prove that they are innate—that we are all born corrupt; and are, from the womb, in a state of universal degeneracy? "O fallen, fallen man! in what mournful strains shall we lament over thee! the offspring of God degenerated

---

* Earth's but an atom; greedy swords
Share it among a thousand lords;
And yet they can't agree.— *Watts.*

—the most curious and noble piece of Divine workmanship in our world, shattered, broken, and lying in ruins!" Who can repair these ruins, and raise the noble frame again? None but he who formed it at first. There is need of a new creation; and consequently of a new creating powers. This, and this only, is the effectual cure of war and all its bleeding wounds. This is the only inviolable bond of peace; the only firm cement of divided nations.

Brethren, while we are surrounded with the terrors of war, let us learn our own degeneracy, mourn over it, and cry for the exertion of that power which alone can form us anew, and repair these wastes and desolations. The present war, indeed, on our side, is just, is unavoidable; and consequently our duty. But how corrupt must this world be, when it is even our duty to weaken and destroy our fellow-men as much as we can? How corrupt must the world be, when peace itself, the sweetest of all blessings, is become an evil, and war is to be chosen before it? When it is become our duty to shed blood—when martial valour, or courage to destroy man, who was made in the image of God, is become a virtue? When it is become glorious to kill men? and when we are obliged to treat a whole nation as a gang of robbers and murderers, and bring them to punishment? This certainly shows that they are degenerated creatures; and as they share in the same natures with us, we must draw the same conclusion concerning ourselves. Let us, therefore, humble ourselves, and mourn in dust and ashes before the Lord; and let us lament the general depravity of the world. But,

Secondly, This subject may naturally lead us to reflect upon the just resentments of God against the sin of man.

War is not only the natural result of the depraved passions of mankind, but a just punishment from God for that depravity. It is at once the natural effect, and the judicial punishment of their lusts. As innocent creatures, under the influence of universal benevolence, would not injure one another, or fly to war, so God would not suffer the calamities of war to fall upon them, because they would not deserve it. But alas! mankind have revolted from God, and incurred his displeasure; and he employs them to avenge his quarrel and do the part of executioners upon one another. They are fighting his quarrel, even when they least design it. The sword of war is *his* sword; he designs by it to chastise his children; to punish his enemies: and in both, to testify his resentments against sin. It is sin that sets the Omnipotent in arms against this rebellious province of his dominions, and constrains him to let war loose among us, as the executioner of his vengeance. God is angry with the wicked every day; and hence it is that, according to that striking piece of imagery, he calls for the sword, and says, " Sword, go through the land, cut off man and beast from it." Ezek. xlv. 17. If, therefore, we expostulate and pray with Jeremiah, " Oh thou sword of the LORD, how long will it be ere thou be quiet? Put up thyself into thy scabbard; rest and be still:" we have the same answer, " How can it be quiet, seeing the Lord hath given it a charge?" a charge against his enemies; " there hath he appointed it." Jer. xlvii. 6, 7.

Now if this be the case, is it any wonder that the sword hath received a commission against our country and nation, seeing our land is full of sin against the holy One of Israel? The transgressors are come to the full among us; and almost all flesh have corrupted their way. " There is none righteous; no, not one." Rom. iii. 10. The fear and love of God are almost lost among his own creatures, in his own world. This is a subject I have often enlarged upon; but, alas! how much in vain, as to multitudes!

They will sin on still in spite of warnings and remonstrances. And all the most solemn and serious addresses to them on this head, seem but idle harangues, or the fashionable cant of the pulpit. But I must tell you once more, in serious sadness, whether you hear, or whether you forbear, that our country and nation are likely to sink under the burden of guilt, accumulated from so many quarters, and for so many ages; that without a reformation, we are likely to be an enslaved, ruined people; and that the present calamities of war are the punishments of the divine hand upon an ungrateful, rebellious nation. Indeed, sirs, we shall find it an evil thing and a bitter, that we have forsaken the Lord our God. Sin will be found in the issue to be the bane of society in this world, as well as of souls in the world to come. And unless we learn this by gentler instructions, we are likely to learn it by the painful lessons of experience. And, oh! how just and fit is it, that creatures in rebellion against God, should be left to avenge his quarrel upon one another; that a world of sin should be made a field of blood? Indeed, this unavoidably follows according to the course of nature. The love of God, and the love of our fellow-creatures, are the grand cements of the moral world, and the bonds of social union. And when these are broken, what must follow but mutual enmity and hostilities? Then the character of mankind is "hateful, and hating one another." Titus iii. 3.

Brethren, God is proclaiming by the sound of cannons and the martial trumpet, what he has often proclaimed unheard by the gentler voice of his word, namely, that he has a just controversy with our world for its rebellion. And shall not this make us solicitous to be reconciled to him? Blessed be his name, the quarrel may yet be made up. "God was in Christ reconciling the world to himself." 2 Cor. v. 19. And if we accept of reconciliation in this way, we shall again be received into favour. We shall be justified by his grace, and so "have peace with God through our Lord Jesus Christ." Rom. v. 1. Sinners, what do you think of this proposal? I seriously propose it to you; and it demands your most solemn attention. What do you think of being reconciled to God this day, through Jesus Christ; that he may no longer have any ground of controversy with you, nor with your country on your account. I honestly warn you, that if you still persist in your rebellion, "he will whet his sword: he hath bent his bow and made it ready. He hath also prepared for you the instruments of death: he hath ordained his arrows against you." Ps. vii. 12, 13. "He hath for a long time been silent, and refrained himself." But he will not always bear with you. "The Lord shall go forth as a mighty man; he shall stir up jealousy, like a man of war: he shall cry, yea, roar: he shall prevail against his enemies: he will destroy and devour at once." Isa. xlii. 13, 14. O sinners, are you able to engage the Omnipotent in battle? Will you not rather fall at his feet, and submit? Methinks the terror of such declarations as these from his own lips, may confound and overwhelm you. "If I whet my glittering sword, and mine hand take hold of judgment, I will render vengeance to mine enemies, and will reward them that hate me; I will make mine arrows drunk with blood, and my sword shall devour flesh." Deut. xxxii. 41, 42. Oh bring not this intolerable doom upon yourselves; but submit to the overtures of grace now, while you may; while God is reconcilable, and even entreats and prays you to be reconciled to him. Then this almighty Enemy will be your almighty Friend; and his protection will render you secure in all the calamities of life, and through all eternity. How happy would it be, if war among the nations might be the occasion of peace with God! I am sure it is a loud call to this; and oh! that we may listen to it and obey. But,

Thirdly, The consideration of war as proceeding from the lusts of men, may excite us to the most zealous endeavours, in our respective characters, to promote a reformation.

A thorough reformation would be the most effectual expedient for a lasting peace among mankind, and to put an end to the ravages and devastations of war. Were their tempers formed upon the model ef Christianity, that humane, gentle, benevolent religion of the harmless Lamb of God, they would then live like brethren, in the bonds of love; they would observe the rules of justice towards each other; they would naturally care for each other's welfare, and promote it, as that of another self. Therefore, if we would contribute to the peace of the world, let us labour to reform it. It is but *little*, indeed, that you and I can do, in so narrow a sphere, for a general reformation: but let not that *little* be undone: at least, let it not be *unattempted*. Let us first begin at our own hearts. Let it be our next care to reform our families; then let us extend our endeavours to our neighbourhood, and to our country, as far as our influence can reach. Small and unpromising beginnings have sometimes, under the divine blessing, ripened into a very grand and happy result. Twelve fishermen, with the power of God along with them, did more to reform and save the world, than was ever done before or since. And who knows what happy effects might follow, if even this small, contemptible company, should resolutely set themselves upon promoting a reformation in our country, with an humble dependence upon God for success, and exhibiting an example of it in our own practice. In the name of God, let us unanimously make the attempt. The attempt is glorious and

God-like; and if it should fail of success, it will not fail of its reward. Let our lives be a loud testimony against the wickedness of the times; and a living recommendation of despised religion. Let our children, our servants, and slaves, be instructed in the knowledge of Christ; and let us labour to make them sincere, practical Christians; let us exhort each other daily, lest any of us be hardened through the deceitfulness of sin, Heb. iii. 13; let us by our conversation and advices endeavour to bring our friends and neighbours in love with religion, and to be solicitous about the concerns of eternity. Let us zealously concur in every scheme that is likely to have a good influence upon our country. And oh! let us earnestly pray for our country; for we can never be sufficiently sensible, that the Holy Spirit is the only effectual reformer of the world. And, blessed be God, we are encouraged to hope that he will give his Holy Spirit to them that ask him, Luke xi. 13; which leads me to add,

Fourthly, that the consideration of war as proceeding from the lusts of men, may make us sensible of our need of an outpouring of the divine Spirit.

I must repeat it again, that the Holy Spirit is the only efficacious reformer of the world. It is he alone who can effectually "reprove the world of sin." If he be absent, legislators may make laws against vice, philosophers may reason, ministers may preach; nay, conscience may remonstrate, the divine law may prescribe and threaten, the gospel may invite and allure; but all will be in vain. The strongest arguments, the most melting entreaties, the most alarming denunciations from God and man, enforced with the highest authority, or the most compassionate tears, all will have no effect—all will not effectually reclaim one sinner, nor gain one sincere proselyte to righteousness. Paul, Apollos, and Cephas, with all their apostolical abilities, can do nothing, without the Holy Spirit. Paul may plant, and Apollos water; but God alone can give the increase. So then, neither is he that planteth anything, nor he that watereth; they are both nothing together: "but God that giveth the increase," 1 Cor. iii. 6, 7; he is all in all. "Until the Spirit be poured forth from on high," says Isaiah, "briers and thorns shall come up upon the land of my people," Isa. xxxii. 13; that is, their country shall be laid waste, and made a mere wilderness of briers and thorns, by the ravages of war: or the people themselves shall be like briers and thorns, fruitless, noxious, and troublesome. In this language the prophet Micah describes the same people: "the best of them is as a brier; the most upright is sharper than a thorn-hedge." Micah vii. 4. Such shall they continue, "until the Spirit be poured upon them from on high." But when the happy time comes, "then the wilderness shall be a fruitful field. Then judgment shall dwell in the wilderness, and righteousness remain in the fruitful field." Isa. xxxii. 13–18. This effusion of the Spirit shall put an end to the desolations of war, and extinguish those flaming passions, from which it proceeds. This shall introduce the blessing of lasting and extensive peace: for, as it is there added, "the work of righteousness shall be *peace,* and the native effect of righteousness shall be *quietness* and assurance for ever. And my people shall dwell in a *peaceable* habitation, and in *sure* dwellings, and in *quiet* resting-places."* This is the blessed effect of the outpouring of the Spirit; and never will harmony be established in this jangling world, until this divine agent take the work in hand. It is he alone, that can melt down the obstinate hearts of men into love and peace—it is he alone, that can soften their rugged and

* Ubi supra.

savage tempers, and transform them into mutual benevolence—it is he alone that can quench those lusts that set the world on fire, and implant the opposite virtues and graces. Love, joy, peace, long-suffering, gentleness, goodness, meekness, are mentioned by St. Paul, as *the fruit of the Spirit*, Gal. v. 22, because the Spirit alone is the author of them. And if these dispositions were predominant in the world, what a serene, calm, pacific region would it be, undisturbed with the hurricanes of human passions? "If ye bite and devour one another," says the apostle, "take heed that ye be not consumed one of another: this I say then," as the best preservative from this evil, "walk in the Spirit, and ye shall not fulfil the lusts of the flesh." Gal. v. 15, 16. O brethren! did we all walk in the Spirit, what peace and harmony would reign in families and in neighbourhoods! Were the Spirit of God poured out upon the nations, we should no more hear the sound of the trumpet, nor see garments rolled in blood; but peace would spring up in every country as its native growth, and allure contending kingdoms into friendship with its fragrance. Oh how much do we need the influence of this blessed Spirit to calm the tumult of the world, to restrain the ambition and avarice of princes and their ministers, and to quench the savage thirst of blood? How much do we need him for a purpose more important still; that is, to make this gospel, this neglected, inefficacious gospel, which sinners are now hardy enough to trifle with, to make it powerful to their salvation—to make the weapons of our warfare mighty to the pulling down the strong-holds of Satan, and to bring every thought into captivity to the obedience of Christ? How much do we need him to break the heart of stone, to enlighten the dark mind, and to comfort the desponding soul? This kind office, alas! we cannot perform to a dear child or friend. But oh! the joyful thought! he is able.

And how are we to expect this blessing? In what way is it to be obtained? The answer is, Pray for it. Pray frequently, pray fervently, "Lord, thy Spirit! Oh give thy Spirit! that is the blessing I need; that is the blessing families, and nations, and the whole race of man, need." Pray in your retirements, pray in your families, pray in warm ejaculations, pray without ceasing, for this great fundamental blessing. O brethren! had many among us done this, the Spirit would not be so much withdrawn; and should many now do this, he would not be long absent. Hear what encouragement Christ has given to prayer, in this particular: "Ask, and it shall be given you; seek, and ye shall find; knock, and it shall be opened unto you. If ye, being evil, know how to give good gifts unto your children, how much more shall your heavenly Father *give the Holy Spirit to them that ask him?*" Luke xi. 9–13. Therefore, brethren, let us earnestly cry to God for his Spirit. Would you beg for bread, when famishing? Would you beg for life, if condemned to die? Oh then beg for the Spirit: for this gift is of more importance to you and the world, than daily bread, or life itself. I shall only add,

Fifthly, The consideration of the present commotions and tumults among the kingdoms of the world, may carry our thoughts forward to that happy period which our religion teaches us to hope for, when the kingdom of Christ, the Prince of Peace, shall be extended over the world, and his benign, pacific religion shall be propagated among all nations.

Blessed be God, vice shall not always be triumphant in the world. The cause of truth and righteousness shall not always be kept under. Heathenism, Mahometanism, and Popery, though now supported by the powers of the earth, and seemingly invincible, shall yet fall before this gospel, and rise no more. Jews and Gentiles, whites and blacks, shall all submit to Jesus, and own him as their Saviour and Lord. Of this grand and happy revolution in the world of mankind, we have abundant evidence. The apostle tells us, "blindness is but in part happened to Israel," that is, to the Jews, "until the fulness of the Gentiles," the whole body of the Gentile nations, "be come in,"—come into the faith of Christ; "and then," says he, "all Isreal shall be saved; and the receiving them again into covenant with God, shall be as life from the dead," Rom. xi. 15, 25, 26; to them, and to the rest of the world. God himself has promised that the knowledge of the Lord shall fill the earth, as the waters cover the sea. Isa. xi. 9. That from the rising of the sun to the going down of the same, his name shall be great among the Gentiles; and in every place incense shall be offered to his name, and a pure offering. Malachi i. 11. This universal empire of grace is nowhere revealed so clearly, as in the visions of Daniel and St. John. "There was given unto the Son of man," says Daniel, "dominion, and glory, and a kingdom, that all people, nations, and languages, should serve him;" vii. 14. In prophetic vision, he saw "the time come when the saints possessed the kingdom." "And the kingdom and dominion, and the greatness of the kingdom under the whole heaven, shall be given to the people of the saints of the most high God, whose kingdom is an everlasting kingdom, and all dominions shall serve and obey him." Dan. vii. 27. And when the seventh angel sounded, St. John heard "great voices in heaven, saying, the kingdoms of this world are become the kingdoms of our Lord, and of his Christ, and he shall reign for ever and ever." Rev. xi. 15. This happy period is represented as the reign of Christ for a thousand years, when Satan shall be bound, and no more tempt the nations. Oh blessed period! how long wilt thou delay, blessed Jesus! thy kingdom come! Oh hasten it, that we may live no more in this turbulent ocean, but enjoy the blessings of perfect peace.

Perfect peace is mentioned by the prophets as the distinguishing blessing of this period. Then war and all its dismal attendants shall cease; and all the instruments of destruction shall become useless. "Nation shall not lift up sword against nation," says Isaiah, "neither shall they learn war any more. They shall beat their swords into plough-shares, and their spears into pruning-hooks." Isaiah ii. 4. Then peace shall extend itself like a river, chap. lxvi. 12; and the officers and rulers of the world shall then be *peace*, who are now the firebrands of contention, and the thunderbolts of war; Isaiah. lx. 17; then great shall be the peace of Zion's children; chap. liv. 13; and of the increase of this peace there shall be no end. Chap. ix. 6.

Now the grand cause of this blessed peace shall be, that the pacific religion of the Prince of Peace shall not only be professed, but have a powerful efficacy upon the hearts of men to transform them into its own mild and benevolent spirit. Christianized nations, at present, are, alas! as much ravaged with war as perhaps heathen and Mahometan countries: but the reason is, they generally have but the *name* of Christianity, while their prevailing temper is directly opposite to it. Lions and savages will profess themselves the disciples of the inoffensive Lamb of God; and pretend to believe his religion, without imbibing its gentle, pacific genius; but whatever they are who *call* themselves Christians, Christianity *itself* is a humane, benevolent religion. It tends to inspire that universal love, that meekness and forbearance, that regard to justice and equity, which would establish universal harmony in the world; and it tends to subdue those turbulent lusts and passions which are the source of war and fightings. In short, it transforms men into quite other creatures, where it exerts its native influence in full force. Christianity would make a wild Indian savage as meek and harmless as a lamb. Now this will be the case in fact, in that blessed period. The Holy Spirit, by means of the gospel, will transform the savage temper of the world into the very genius of that religion which they will then profess. This glorious change is expressed by the strongest and most beautiful images by Isaiah. The wolf shall dwell inoffensively with the lamb; and the furious leopard shall lie down amicably with the defenceless kid: and the calf, and the young lion, and the fatling together; and they shall be so tame and harmless, that a little child shall lead them. And the cow and the bear shall feed; their young ones shall lie down together, without enmity or injury; and the lion shall eat straw like the ox; and the sucking child, without hurt, shall play on the hole of the venomous asp; and the weaned child shall put his hand with safety on the cockatrice-den. They shall not hurt nor destroy in all my holy mountain, saith the LORD. Isaiah xi. 6–9. What a glorious change is this! and what a happy revolution will it produce in this restless world! Let us look, and long, and pray for this blessed time. Who knows but some of our guilty eyes may see the dawnings of it? The schemes of Providence seem to be now ripening fast to their final result. The prophecies are fulfilling; and who knows but the time of the restitution of all things is just at hand? Many thrones must totter, many kingdoms must fall, which are now the supports of idolatry, imposture, and tyranny, in order to introduce it; and who knows but the present ferment and commotions may work up to this grand revolution? If so, welcome blood and slaughter, and all the terrors of war, though *we* should be involved in the ruin! Welcome, whatever may introduce a season which shall bring so much glory to God and the Redeemer, and so many blessings to mankind!*

I shall conclude with two advices:—

The one is, "humble yourselves under the mighty hand of God, that he may exalt you in due time." 1 Pet. v. 6. You have seen that war is both an evidence and effect of the corruption of our nature, and of the righteous indignation of God against us on this account; and in both these views, it loudly calls upon you to humble yourselves.

The other advice is but a repetition of what I have already recommended to you, namely: "Pray without ceasing." 1 Thess. v. 17. No sign could be more encouraging than to see the praying spirit spreading among us; to see those who have any influence in heaven through their divine Mediator, using their interest in behalf of their country. The efficacy of believing prayer is very great. The encouragements to this duty are

---

* It is but little we can do to promote a national reformation, much less an universal reformation among all nations. The world will sin on still, in spite of all our endeavours; but, if divine grace concur, we may do much to reform the little spot where we dwell. Every man is of some importance in his family, and perhaps in his neighbourhood; and why should we not begin at home? Why should we not labour to reform the place where we live? Why should we not endeavour to become the salt of the earth, to season the huge mass of corruption—the light of the world, to dart some rays of light through the Egyptian darkness that involves our country; and as a city set upon a hill, conspicuous to all around us, for the beauties of holiness? Oh, let us labour to bring about so happy a revolution; let us be ambitious to take the precedence in turning to the Lord, and to be the first fruits of the glorious harvest of righteousness, which we hope for, before the consummation of all things.

many; and I am sure our need of it is peculiarly urgent; therefore, "continue instant in prayer." Rom. xii. 12. To engage you the more, I have the pleasure to inform you, that the synod of New York, and the ministers in Connecticut, have appointed, that on the last Thursday in every month, during these troublesome times, the congregations under their care, should meet together in little societies, and spend a few hours in united prayer to God for our country and nation. And I earnestly recommend it to you, my dear people, to join with your brethren in various parts, upon that day, in so seasonable and important a duty; and who knows what extensive advantage thousands may receive from the prayers of a few? They will, at least, return with blessings into your own bosoms.

SERMON LXIX.

ON THE DEFEAT OF GENERAL BRADDOCK, GOING TO FORT DUQUESNE.

ISAIAH XXII. 12–14.—*And in that day did the Lord God of hosts call to weeping, and to mourning, and to baldness, and to girding with sackcloth: and behold, joy and gladness, slaying oxen, and killing sheep, eating flesh and drinking wine: let us eat and drink; for to-morrow we shall die. And it was revealed in mine ears by the* LORD *of hosts, Surely this iniquity shall not be purged from you till ye die, saith the Lord* GOD *of hosts.**

THE heavy burden of this tragical prophecy falls upon the valley of vision, that is, upon Jerusalem, the metropolis of the Jews. It was called the valley of *vision* because it was enlightened by the visions of the prophets, enjoyed the advantages of revelation, and the privileges of the church of God. But though it was thus graciously distinguished by Heaven, it was not safe from danger. The Assyrians were preparing a powerful army to invade the holy land, and the holy city, because it was degenerated into a land of guilt and a city full of wickedness.

The prophet Isaiah, at the foresight of this, feels all the generous and mournful passions of a patriot, a lover of his country, of liberty, and religion. However others

* Hanover, July 20, 1755.

were sunk into a stupid security all around him, and indulged themselves in mirth and luxury; he is alarmed and mourns for his country. Look away from me, says he, do not put my bursting grief under the restraints of modesty by your presence: I will weep bitterly, labour not to comfort me; for the case requires the full indulgence of sorrow; and it is remediless "because of the spoiling of the daughter of my people." Isa. xxii. 4. Thus was Isaiah affected with the danger of Jerusalem, and his native country.

And, O Virginia! O my country! shall I not lament for thee? Thou art a valley of vision, favoured with the light of revelation from heaven, and the gospel of Jesus: thou hast long been the region of peace and tranquility; the land of ease, plenty, and liberty. But what do I now see? What do I now hear? I see thy brazen skies, thy parched soil, thy withering fields, thy hopeless springs, and thy scanty harvests. Methinks I also hear the sound of the trumpet, and see garments rolled in blood; thy frontiers ravaged by revengeful savages; thy territories invaded by French perfidy and violence. Methinks I see slaughtered families, the hairy scalps clotted with gore; the horrid arts of Indian and popish torture. And, alas! in the midst of all these alarms, I see thy inhabitants generally asleep, and careless of thy fate. I see vice braving the skies; religion neglected and insulted; mirth and folly have still their places of rendezvous. Let our country, let religion, liberty, property, and all be lost: yet still they will have their diversions; luxury spreads her feast, and unmans her effeminate guests. In spite of laws, in spite of proclamations, in spite of the principle of self-preservation, thy officers are generally inactive, thy militia neglected and undisciplined, thy inhabitants unprovided with arms; every thing in a defenceless posture: but few Abranams to intercede for thee; but few to stand in the gap, and make up the breach, to prevent the irruption of vengeance; but few mourning for the sins of the land! "The Lord God of hosts, and every thing around thee, call thee to weeping and mourning, and girding with sackcloth: but instead of this, behold joy and gladness, eating of flesh and drinking of wine; let us eat and drink, for to-morrow we die." And shall I not weep for thee, O my country? Yes; when I forget thee, O Virginia, "let my right hand forget her cunning, and my tongue cleave to the roof of my mouth." Ps. cxxxvii. 5. "My bowels! my bowels! I am pained at the very heart; I cannot hold my peace; because thou hast heard, O my soul, the sound of the trumpet, the alarm of war." Jer. iv. 19. And now to whom shall I speak, and give warning, that they may hear? Behold, their ear is uncircumcised, and they cannot hearken—"I hearkened and heard; but they spoke not aright; no man repented him of his wickedness, saying, What have I done? Every one turneth to his course, as the horse rusheth into the battle. Yea, the stork in the heavens knoweth her appointed times; and the turtle, and the crane, and the swallow, observe the time of their coming; but my people know not the judgment of the Lord," Jer. viii. 6, 7, nor discern the signs of the times. What, then, can I do for thee, O my country? What but weep over thee, pray for thee, and warn thy careless children? To give this seasonable warning is my present design.

There are two things mentioned in this chapter, as glaringly absurd, and highly provoking to God. The one is, that in the military preparations which the Jews made, they had no proper regard to the Supreme Ruler of the world. The other is, that instead of making proper preparations for their own defence, and humbling themselves before God, they were sunk into security, luxury, and wickedness.

They had made some military preparations. Thus far had I studied my discourse, before I was alarmed with the melancholy news that struck my ears last Thursday. Now every heart may meditate terror indeed: now every face may gather blackness; now I may mingle darker horrors in the picture I intended to draw of the state of my country. For what do I now hear? I hear our army is defeated; our general killed; our sole defence demolished;* and what shall we now do? Whence shall we derive our hope? Our militia has hitherto been a mere farce, and most of the inhabitants know little or nothing of the art of war: they are generally unfurnished with arms. What effect the present alarm will have upon them, I cannot yet determine; but I am afraid they are proof against even this, and will still dream on in security. They seem to have this brand upon them, of a people given up to destruction; they cannot realize a danger at the distance of two or three hundred miles, though it be making quick approaches towards them; or, if they be alarmed at length, it will be apt to throw them into an inactive kind of consternation and terror; for it is natural to the presumptuous and secure to fall into this opposite extreme, when the danger they would not fear comes upon them, and this throws them into such hurry and confusion, that they can neither contrive nor prosecute measures for

* What truth may be in the report, is, as yet, unknown; and while it is uncertain, the fate of our country must lie in an anxious uncertainty too This alarm, however, has served to show me into what an anxious consternation the visible approach of danger will cast the presumptuous, and how naturally they fall from the extreme of security to confusion and despondency. If this alarm awaken us to proper activity, I shall account it a happy stratagem of divine Providence. Be this report true or false, it is sufficient to drive us to the throne of grace, with Jehoshaphat's prayer in our mouth: 2 Chron. xx. 12.

their own defence; so that we have little ground to hope for relief from ourselves—as for the neighbouring colonies, they can do no more at best than provide for themselves. Our mother-country is at a great distance, and before we can receive help from thence, our country may be overrun, and fall a helpless prey to our enemies. Our mother-country may also be engaged in war at home; and consequently unable to spare us much assistance so far abroad. To all this, I may add, that we are prodigiously weakened, and our enemies strengthened, by the loss of our fine train of artillery; and the Indians will probably break off their alliance with the English and join the victorious party; and what barbarities we may expect from these treacherous and revengeful savages, I cannot think of without horror. Now what shall we do in these dangerous circumstances? May we not address the throne of grace in the language of Jehoshaphat: "We have no might against this multitude; neither know we what to do; but our eyes are upon thee?" 2 Chron. xx. 12. A guilty, obnoxious people cry to thee in helpless distress, O thou Ruler of heaven and earth! Spare us a little longer, and surround us with thy salvation as with walls and bulwarks. We ought not indeed to content ourselves with lazy prayers; it is our duty also to take all the measures in our power to prevent or escape the impending ruin of our country; but it is certainly our duty to humble ourselves before that God whom we have offended, and to cry mightily to him, if peradventure, he may yet have mercy upon us that we perish not. After this digression, occasioned by so melancholy a report, I shall return to, and prosecute, my intended method.

I was observing, that the Jews had made some preparations for their own defence. They had furnished themselves with weapons out of the armory called the house of the forest. Isaiah xxii. 8. They had broken down the houses of Jerusalem, that with their materials they might fortify the wall, and stop its breaches. Isaiah xxii. 10. They had made ditches to convey the waters of two pools into the city, to furnish them with drink in the siege. Isa. xxii. 9, 11. These preparations they made; and on these they depended, and not on the Lord God of hosts. "Thou didst look in that day to the armour of the house of the forest; but ye have not looked unto the Maker thereof, neither had respect unto him that fashioned it long ago." Isaiah xxii. 8, 11. And hence all their preparations were in vain.

I leave it to be considered, whether we and our country have not been guilty of this piece of practical atheism—whether we have not incurred the curse of the man that trusteth in man, and maketh the arm of flesh his confidence—whether we have not boasted and vapoured of our experienced officers, our veteran soldiers, and our fine train of artillery, and had little or no regard to the Lord of hosts. It is he, my brethren, that manages the affairs of men. This world is a territory of Jehovah's universal empire; and not a sparrow can fall to the ground in it without him. He does what he pleases among the inhabitants of the earth; and they shall all know it, sooner or later—they shall know it to their cost, if they cannot be made sensible of it by gentler measures.

Another sin charged upon the Jews was this, that, instead of making proper preparations for their own defence, and humbling themselves before God, they were sunk in security, luxury, and wickedness. Weeping, mourning, baldness, and girding with sackcloth, were the usual signs and ceremonies of fasting and deep humiliation under the law of Moses, and they are naturally expressive of great distress, sorrow, and lamentation. To such humiliation, repentance, and sorrow, God called them by his prophets, and by the threatening posture of their affairs. But, alas! instead of this, you see what we have been grieved to see in *our* country, nothing but feasting and diversion, luxury, and pleasure. "Behold, joy and gladness, slaying oxen and killing sheep, eating flesh and drinking wine." What audacious conduct is this? what is it but to insult Jehovah, and defy all his threatenings? They acted upon that epicurean maxim, "Let us eat and drink, for to-morrow we shall die;" let us take our pleasure while we may, for there will soon be an end of us! This may be looked upon either as the language of despair—let us be merry now, for we expect shortly to be cut off by our enemies; or as a sneer upon the threatenings of God by his prophet, as if they had said, "We are to die, it seems, to-morrow, according to the denunciation of this precise fellow; let us then enjoy life when we can, regardless of the consequence. Shall this melancholy, timorous creature frighten us out of our pleasures? No, let him say what he will, we will eat, and drink, and be merry."

What effect the present near approach of danger may have upon the inhabitants of our guilty land, I have not yet had time to know; but I am sure, (and it has often sunk my spirits, and alarmed my fears,) this has been the general conduct through our country under all the past threatenings of divine providence; and if this still continue, I shall give thee up, O my beloved land! I must give thee up for lost! Heaven cannot always bear with such daring impiety in us, any more than in the Jews. It was revealed in mine ear by the Lord of hosts, saith the prophet,—this dreadful secret was communicated to me: Surely, this iniquity of despising my threatenings, and refusing to humble yourselves before me, shall not be purged from you until ye die, until ye be cut off by your enemies, saith the LORD of hosts. Isaiah xxii. 14. How much reason we have to fear such a doom, I need not tell you—your own hearts suggest it to you from the present aspect of your affairs.

My design in the prosecution and improvement of this subject is, to point out the causes of the present danger, and the most promising methods to prevent or escape it.

I shall mention but two causes of the present danger— the sins of the land, and our security and inactivity in times past.

I must begin with mentioning the sins of the land, as the first and principal cause of our calamity and danger.

Of this I have often warned you with weeping eyes and an aching heart. Some of you, I hope, have regarded the warning, and forsaken your sins; but to many I have seemed as one that mocketh, or an officious disturber of their security and pleasure. But now, when they are likely to have such dreadful confirmations of this melancholy truth; now, when God seems about to make good the charge against you by the terrors of his judgments, now I hope for a solemn hearing without contempt or ridicule.

The Lord of hosts (I repeat it again) is the supreme Ruler of the kingdoms of the earth, and by an irresistible, though invisible hand, he manages them according to his righteous pleasure. It belongs to him in that character to punish guilty, impenitent nations in this life; I say in this life; for in the world to come, men do not subsist in a civil capacity as societies or nations, but are rewarded or punished as individuals according to their personal works. But in this world there are various connections and relations between them as members of civil society;

and when, in that capacity, they become ripe for temporal punishment, and their iniquities are full, it is the usual method of Providence to chastise them severely, or entirely cut them off.

And where is there a more sinful, obnoxious spot upon our guilty globe than our country? It is the remark of strangers, and of those who have an extensive knowledge of Virginia, that this county is distinguished from the rest by the appearance of religion and good morals. But, ah! what ground have we of complaint and lamentation. And if this is the best part of our country, alas! what shall we say of the rest?

Recollect what you have known of your own, and the conduct of the generality, and take a survey of the practice of the inhabitants; and what a dismal scene opens to your eyes! What numbers of drunkards, swearers, liars, unclean wretches, and such like burden our land! Nay, how few comparatively are they who do not, at least occasionally, fall into one or other of these gross vices? What vanity, luxury, and extravagance, in gaming and other foolish or criminal diversions and pleasures, appear among people of high life and affluent fortunes? And is it not fit they should now feel the want of these mercies which they squandered away? What carelessness and unfaithfulness; what ignorance and laziness; nay, what gross vice and impiety, in sundry of the clergy, whose office it is to teach and reform the world! I must speak out in the present situation of my country, however unwilling I am to touch the sacred character. O Virginia! thy prophets, thy ministers have ruined thee. I speak not of all; some of them, I hope, are an ornament to their character, and a blessing to their country. But can the most generous charity, can even a party spirit, pretend they are all such? And they who are not such, are the lumber, or rather the pests of society. Can religion flourish, when inculcated by such unclean lips? Can the world be reformed by such as so much want reformation themselves? There are some, indeed, who make it the great business of their lives to make men virtuous and good; but alas! we have all been too cold and inactive in this noble work; and we desire to join in the general repentance on this account. How is the house of God forsaken! and what carelessness, vanity, and worldly conversation appear in those that attend! Alas! are these assemblies met to worship the great God, and prepare themselves for their everlasting state? Who would suspect it from their conduct? How is the table of the Lord, the memorial of our dear dying Redeemer, neglected by multitudes, or profaned by daring, profligate sinners? What a general neglect of family-religion prevails through our country? How few are the houses that devoutly call upon God! But, alas! I cannot enumerate particulars. I may say all in a word. "There is but little, very little, practical religion to be seen in our land." Do but form an idea of Christianity from your Bible, and compare with that rule the professors of that religion; and how few can you pronounce real Christians? I speak this in the anguish of my heart; and you may be sure it is extorted from me; for in the whole course of my ministry among you, you have never heard so much of this kind from me before.

Deism and infidelity have also of late made inroads upon us. Men do not like such a holy religion as that which Christ has instituted, and therefore they cavil at it, and go about to patch up another of their own, more favourable to their lusts and pleasures. Perhaps it may be put to trial in the general ruin of our country, whether any religion can support a sinking soul like the religion of Jesus. Then it may appear that "their rock is not as our Rock, our enemies themselves being judges." Deut. xxxii. 31. Then ye that are lovers of pleasure more than lovers of God, ye that make mammon your God, ye that adore the glimmering light of reason instead of the Sun of Righteousness, then "go and cry to the gods ye have chosen; let them deliver you in the time of your tribulation." Judges x. 14.

Now, if the outward conduct of men be generally so bad, alas! what shall we think of their hearts, the secret springs of action within? Oh! what lusts make their dens there! How many cold, hard, disloyal hearts towards God and his Son are to be found in our land! How many impenitent souls, that never have been broken into deep repentance! How many worldly, sensual minds, that grovel in the earth, and have little or no thought of God, of divine things, or of their everlasting state! How many secret neglecters of Christ and salvation through him! Alas! how few hearts long and languish for him! How few are acquainted with the experiences of true, vital Christianity! How few are earnestly striving to enter in at the strait gate, and labouring to be holy in all manner of conversation! How few are mourning for their own sins, and those of the land, and pouring out their prayers night and day in behalf of their country! What practical atheism prevails among us as to the dispensations of Providence! Multitudes do not live in the world as though it were under the Divine government. They seem not "to regard the work of the LORD, nor the operation of his hands," Psalm xxviii. 5, in drought and rains, in war and peace, or in any of the blessings or calamities of life; but they look to secondary causes only and the instruments of divine Providence; and what is this but practically to abjure and renounce

Jehovah from being the ruler of the world he has made? And can he tolerate such rebellion in his subjects? Is it not fit that he should convince them of his supreme government by terrible things in righteousness, and make them know that he is the Lord, and that they are but men? But I am weary of this melancholy history; and I own I am not able to paint it in colours gloomy enough. "We are a sinful nation; a people laden with iniquity, a seed of evil-doers, children that are corrupters." Isaiah i. 4. We are abusers of mercy, and despisers of chastisements; we are transgressors of the law of God, and neglecters of the gospel of Christ; we have all sinned from the highest to the lowest. This is the fruitful source of all our calamities, and the most threatening circumstance that attends us; though there is another very discouraging, and that is,—

Secondly, Our security and inactivity in times past. Our enemies have not come upon us unawares. We had time enough to learn the art of war, and to furnish ourselves with arms, but we would not realize the danger! and now when we begin to be apprehensive of it, the hurry and the consternation will not allow us to make such preparations as we otherwise might. God has also given us space for repentance; and this is certainly an important preparative; but, alas! how has it been neglected! What a thoughtless, impenitent people have we been! and how justly may God give us up to the common fate of the presumptuous and secure: "for when they shall say peace and safety, then sudden destruction shall come upon them as travail upon a woman with child, and they shall not escape." 1 Thess. v. 3.

The rumour of war, and the call of Heaven to repentance, have been the more alarming, as we have been punished with so severe a drought, which alone is no small calamity;

and the next year, which will feel its consequences, will make us sensible of it.

I might mention sundry other causes of our present danger: as the unhappy factions about trifles between the branches of the legislature—the disunited state of the sundry British colonies—our criminal neglect of proper measures to Christianize the Indians, and conciliate them to us in that surest bond—our suffering abandoned traders to intoxicate them with strong drink, and defraud them of their property—our neglecting to keep garrisons on our frontiers, &c. But I must hasten to our second general head—to point out the most promising measure to prevent or escape the danger and ruin of our country.

And my first advice, (and oh! that my voice could sound it to the remotest parts of the country) is this: REPENT! O my countrymen, REPENT! Sin is the cause of our danger; sin is the bane of our land; and this cause cannot be removed but by repentance. " Search and try your ways, and turn unto the Lord." Lam. iii. 40. Recollect your own sins in heart and life; and mourn over them, hate them, forsake them, proclaim eternal war against these enemies of your country and of your souls. As much sin as every one of you have been guilty of, so much has every one of you contributed to the destruction of your country. Therefore, let there be a great mourning among you; let every one of you mourn "apart, and your wives apart." Zech. xii. 12. Down on your knees before your injured Sovereign; confess you have been ungrateful rebels; acknowledge the justice of the punishment, even though he should cut you off. Vow, and resolve, if you have done iniquity, to do it no more. Take a survey also of the sins of your country, and lament over them as your own. And to your repentance, join fasting, as a proper expression of it. I cannot give you a more proper direction than what I shall read to you out of the prophecy of Joel, which was addressed to a people in the like dangerous circumstances; and see what encouragement is given to such humiliation: "Therefore, also, now saith the LORD, turn ye even to me with all your heart, and with fasting, and with weeping, and with mourning. And rend your heart, and not your garments, and turn unto the LORD your God; for he is gracious and merciful, slow to anger, and of great kindness, and repenteth him of the evil. Who knoweth if he will return, and repent, and leave a blessing behind him; even a meat-offering, and a drink-offering unto the LORD your God." Joel ii. 12–14. Join earnest prayer to your repentance and fasting. Cry aloud to God for your country; for your liberty, your property, your religion, your lives, your all—cry to God in secret, in your families, in public; and form yourselves into little societies here and there for prayer. Ye prayerless families, now begin to worship the God that preserves you, lest he "pour out his fury upon you with the heathen, and the families that call not upon his name." Jer. x. 25. In this way the weak and timorous, even women and children, may fight for their country; and from this assistance, which you may give in a peaceful corner, our army may derive their victory; for the "effectual fervent prayer of a righteous man availeth much." James v. 16.

If the present threatening circumstances of our country should take this happy turn; oh! if it should bring the thoughtless inhabitants to repentance and reformation, I should count it the most blessed event mine eyes have ever seen. Let each of us labour to promote so happy an effect.

Secondly, Let me earnestly recommend it to you to furnish yourselves with arms, and to put yourselves in a posture of defence. I hope your officers will not omit their duty; and were any of them present, I should humbly address them, "Gentlemen, I presume you look upon your commissions, not as empty titles of honour, but as peculiar obligations upon you to defend your country. Upon your activity, zeal, and good management, much depends. You may teach your respective companies the art of war; you may require them to furnish themselves with arms: you may and ought to put the laws in execution against the careless and disobedient; you may endeavour to make them sensible of their danger, and the necessity of such preparations. These things, gentlemen, are incumbent upon you; and, I hope, I may take upon me to speak as the mouth of this congregation, that we are willing to observe your orders." But, my brethren, if your officers should be negligent in their part, let your conscience prompt you to do your duty; show that it is a regard to your country, and not a servile fear of the law, that has most influence upon you. Christians should be patriots. What is that religion good for that leaves men cowards upon the appearance of danger? And permit me to say, that I am particularly solicitous that you, my brethren of the dissenters, should act with honour and spirit in this juncture as it becomes loyal subjects, lovers of your country, and courageous Christians. That is a mean, sordid, cowardly soul, that would abandon his country, and shift for his own little self, when there is any probability of defending it. To give the greater weight to what I say, I may take the liberty to tell you I have as little personal interest—as little to lose in this colony as most of you. If I consulted either my safety or my temporal interest, I should soon remove my family to Great Britain or the northern colonies, where I have had very inviting offers. Nature has not formed me for a military life, nor furnished me with any great degree of fortitude and courage; and yet I must declare, that after the most calm and impartial deliberation, I am determined not to leave my country, while there is any prospect of defending it. But, should the case appear desperate, I would advise every man to shift for himself; and I would rather fly to the utmost ends of the earth, than submit to French tyranny and Popish superstition. Certainly he does not deserve a place in any country, who is ready to run from it upon every appearance of danger. Let us then, my brethren, show ourselves men, Britains, and Christians on this trying occasion. What! shall we resign so extensive and flourishing a country—a land of plenty and liberty—shall we tamely resign it to a parcel of perfidious French, and savage Indians? Shall slavery here clank her chain, or tyranny rage with lawless fury? Shall the house of God be turned into a temple of idols? No, sirs; let us make a noble stand for the blessings we enjoy. What though we dissenters have been so unhappy as to lie under some restraints, which we apprehend unkind as well as illegal; let us balance these with the many privileges we enjoy, and they sink into nothing. I also hope, that our rulers will find something else to do, in the present state of our country, than to harass and oppress a number of harmless dissenters, whose only crime it is to follow their conscience and not the direction of their superiors in matters of religion. Nay, I am persuaded that many of them, upon farther acquaintance with us, will be disposed to more moderate measures by their own innate candour and a spirit of liberty. Let us therefore show ourselves worthy of protection and encouragement, by our conduct on this occasion. The event of war is yet uncertain; but let us determine, that if the case should require it, we will courageously leave house and home, and take the field. I pity you, my friends of the softer sex, under the distressing passions which these alarms must excite in you; and indeed, I am not without apprehensions of danger from you. Your soft entreaties and flowing tears may unman the stronger sex, and restrain them from exerting themselves in so good a cause. But, pray let reason, let conscience, let religion, let a regard to yourselves and your children, prevail over your fond and foolish passions; otherwise, you may be accessary to the ruin of your country.

I would also address myself to you, negroes; and I hope you will regard what I say, as you cannot but believe I am your friend. You know I have shown a tender concern for your welfare, ever since I have been in the colony; and you may ask my own negroes whether I treat them kindly or not. Let not any of you think that it is all one whether the French take the country or not, for you will, at worst, be slaves still. You do not know what sort of people the French and Indians are; but I will honestly tell you. They are a cruel, barbarous people; and if you should disobey them, they would torment you, or put you to death in the most shocking manner. It will have weight with such of you as have any concern about religion, to be told, that if you should fall into the hands of the French, you must either give up your religion, or be tied to a stake, and burnt to ashes for it. Then you must pray in Latin, a language that you do not understand one word of; you must not look into your Bible, or try to read; and instead of worshipping God through Jesus Christ, you must worship images and pictures made of stone, wood, or canvas—you must pray to men and women that were once sinners like yourselves; and instead of taking bread and wine in remembrance of Christ, you must believe that the bread is the real body of Christ, a piece of true flesh, and that the wine is changed into the real blood of Christ, by a priest muttering a few words over it—and they would allow you only the use of the bread, but the wine is all the priest's. Now, is not your nature shocked at such a thing as this, under the notion of religion? Do you think such a thing as this would please God, or carry you to heaven? It becomes you, therefore, to do all you can to keep yourselves and our country out of the hands of these fierce and cruel creatures. But to return.

If any of you are frightened and intimidated from venturing your lives for your country, because you are full of fears about your everlasting state, and you would desire to live longer, to make all sure—to such of you I would say, now you find the bad effects of your former negligence—had you given all diligence to make your calling and election sure, you would not have been left in such perplexity in the hour of difficulty. You have no other way now, but diligently to improve the time you have; and if, after trial, you have even trembling hopes of your safe state for eternity, you may courageously venture, and leave the event to God; and your cowardly deserting the cause of your country, and seeking to prolong your lives by that means, will not be a likely way to remove your doubts and fears; you would always be haunted with a consciousness of guilt, and that will cast a gloom over your minds, and obscure the evidences of your hopes. Follow the path of duty wherever it leads; for that will always be found the safest in the issue.

As for such of you as are really unprepared for your latter end, and justly conscious of it; I have sundry things to say to you, and oh! that they may sink deep into your hearts.

First, How may it shock you to think, that you who have lived so long in the world, should now want more time to turn to God, and prepare for eternity? Alas! what have you done with the ten, twenty, thirty, or forty years that God has given you for this purpose? Ah! are they all gone, without doing any of the great work you were sent into the world for? Have they all been wasted upon sin, the flesh, and the world, and sacrificed to the devil? Have you been destroying yourselves all this time? Oh! sirs, have I not told you of this, but in vain? Have I not often warned you of the danger of delays in turning to God? Will you now, at length, believe me? Will you now conclude it is high time for you to regard the things that belong to your peace?

Secondly, If the reason why you desire to preserve your lives longer, be that you may have time to turn to God, and prepare for eternity, then you are carefully improving the time you now have. It is a vain pretence that you want more time for this, if you do not use the time you have. And are you doing so? Are you seeking the Lord in earnest, and endeavouring to repent and turn to him? If not, you only want time to sin longer—to pursue the world and your pleasures longer. And can you expect God will indulge you in such a wicked desire? Thirdly, it is not the want of time, but the want of a heart, that keeps you unconverted. St. Paul was converted in three days, the jailer in a few hours, and St. Peter's hearers under one short sermon; and why may you not hope for the like blessing, if you exert yourselves in earnest? Fourthly, to excite you to this, let me try an argument or two from a new topic. It is you, and such sinners as you, that have brought all these calamities upon your country. Impenitent sinners are the bane of society, and bring down the wrath of God upon it. Therefore, if you would serve your country, repent and be converted.

What a cutting thought may it now be to you, "I am one of the guilty creatures for whom my country is now suffering?" Consider also, if the things you fear should come upon you, how miserable would you be! An angry God above you; a withering, ravaged country, an aceldama, a field of blood around you; a guilty conscience within you; and a burning hell just before you! Then you will borrow the despairing complaint of Saul. "The Philistines make war against me, and God is departed from me." 1 Sam. xxviii. 15. Then you will see the use of religion, and bitterly lament your neglect of it. Therefore now make that your concern.

I shall conclude with two or three remarks.

First, Let us not be too much discouraged. Our country is in danger of famine and the sword; but the case is not desperate. Do not, therefore, give it up as a lost case. Our inhabitants are numerous; some parts of the country have promising crops; our army, we hope, is not cut off; the New England forces are likely to succeed in their expeditions; and we have a gracious, though a provoked God over all: therefore, let us not despond, nor let us think it hard to suffer a little in such a world as this. Let us not think it a mighty matter, that we who have forfeited every blessing, should fall into poverty. We may still have food and raiment somewhere or other; and why should we complain?

It is one character of a good man, that "he is not afraid of evil tidings." Psalm cxii. 7. " Though the fig-tree," says Habakkuk, "shall not blossom, neither shall fruit be in the vines; the labour of the olive shall fail, and the fields shall yield no meat; the flock shall be cut off from the fold, and there shall be no herd in the stalls; yet I will rejoice in the LORD, I will joy in the God of my salvation." Hab. iii. 17, 18. What a noble spirit appears in the forty-sixth Psalm. "We will not be afraid, though the earth be removed, and though the mountains be carried into the midst of the sea; though the waters thereof roar, and be troubled; though the mountains shake with the swelling thereof." "The name of the LORD is a strong tower; the righteous runneth into it, and is safe." Prov. xviii. 10. To have a Friend in heaven, a Friend who is the Lord of armies, what a strong support is this! And what is that religion good for, that will not support a man under trials? It has been a kind of a gracious calamity to our land, that we have not had anything to try our religion, and to distinguish the chaff from the wheat. Now, perhaps the trying time is coming; and "he that endureth to the end shall be saved." Matt. x. 22.

Let me address this in particular to such of you as fear the Lord. You are safe, come what will. Therefore, do not disgrace your religion, by unmanly, cowardly fears; but like David, when he had lost all, and even his wives and his concubines were taken captive,—encourage yourselves in your God. 1 Sam. xxx. 6. But,

Secondly, Be not too presumptuous; "be not highminded, but fear." I am most afraid you should fall into this extreme. We have many reasons to fear; we are a sinful land; we are but poorly provided against war or famine: it is fit we should in our turn experience the fate of other nations, that we may know what sort of a world we live in. We are in danger from foreigners of a gloomy hue—in a state of servility among ourselves. (I speak in this style, that I may give no dangerous intimation to the persons concerned.) It is certain many will be great sufferers by the drought; and many lives will be lost in our various expeditions; our poor brethren in Augusta, and other frontier counties, are slaughtered and scalped. In short, it is certain, be the final issue what it will, that our country will suffer a great deal; therefore, be humble.

Thirdly, Be diligent in prayer for our army, for the unhappy families in our frontiers, &c. "And may the LORD of hosts be with us, and the God of Jacob be our refuge." Psalm xlvi. 7.

SERMON LXX.

GOD THE SOVEREIGN OF ALL KINGDOMS.

DAN. iv. 25.—*The Most High ruleth in the kingdom of men, and giveth it to whomsoever he will.**

THAT this world owes its existence to the creating power of God, and that he established its laws, and put its every wheel in motion, is a truth so evident, that it has extorted the consent of all mankind. But did he then exhaust his omnipotence? And has he been inactive ever since? Did he cast it off his hand, as an orphan-world, deprived of his paternal care, and left to shift for itself? No; as we were at first the creatures of his power, we are still the subjects of his government—he still supports and rules the world which he made. In the material world, events are accomplished according to those laws which he first established in nature; but it is his agency that still continues these laws, and carries them into execution. In the rational world, events are frequently brought to pass by the instrumentality of free agents; but still they are under the direction of the universal cause; and their liberty is not inconsistent with his sovereign dominion, nor does it exempt them from it. Though he makes use of secondary causes, yet he reserves to himself the important character of *the Ruler of the universe*, and is the Supreme Disposer of all events.

* Hanover, March 5, 1755, on a day of fasting and prayer.

This is a truth of infinite moment, and fundamental to all religion; and unless we are met here to-day with a deep impression of this upon our spirits, we are wholly unfit to make a proper improvement of this solemn occasion. It is pertinently observed in that proclamation, in cheerful obedience to which we are now met, that—" In every undertaking it is expedient and necessary to implore the blessing and protection of Almighty God."

But if Almighty God does not govern the world, and order all the affairs of men according to his pleasure, where is the expediency or necessity of imploring his blessing and protection? "A powerful and perfidious enemy is making inroads upon our territories; our religion and our liberty, our property, our lives, and every thing sacred or dear to us, are in danger. We are preparing to make a defence; and our most gracious sovereign has been pleased to send a considerable number of his ships and forces to oppose the unjustifiable attempts of our enemies."

But unless the success of the expedition depend upon the providence of God, to what end do we humble ourselves before him, and implore his help? The thing itself, upon this supposition, would be an incongruity, an empty compliment, a mockery. If he exerts no agency in such cases, but leaves things entirely to their natural course, then we have nothing to fear from his displeasure on the account of sin; and we have nothing to hope from his assistance; and consequently, it is needless and absurd to humble ourselves for the one, or to be importunate with him for the other. I cannot, therefore, inculcate upon you, at present, a more seasonable truth than that contained in my text—" The Most High ruleth in the kingdom of men, and giveth it to whomsoever he will."

Nebuchadnezzer, of whom we read so much in the sacred writings, was the first founder of the rich and powerful Babylonian empire, which was built upon the ruins of that of the Assyrians, the metropolis of which was Nineveh, and sundry other mighty kingdoms. Providence has raised him up to be the scourge of the Jews in particular, the favourite people of God. After his numerous and extensive conquests, while living at ease in grandeur and luxury in his palace, and surveying the glories of Babylon, his magnificent metropolis, his heart was elated—he becomes of great importance in his own sight—he ascribes his successes to himself alone; and arrogates a style that becomes none but the King of heaven: "Is not this great Babylon that *I* have built for the house of the kingdom, by the might of *my* power, and for the honour of *my* majesty?" Dan. iv. 30. While he is thus self-deified, He that is higher than the highest, and who pours contempt upon princes, resents his insolence; and will let him know that he is but a man, by degrading him to a level with the beasts; but he is so gracious as to warn him of it in a dream, that he might escape the doom by a timely repentance; and Daniel gives him a solemn advice, " O king, let my counsel be acceptable to thee, and break off thy sins by righteousness, and thine iniquities by showing mercy to the poor, if it may be a lengthening of thy tranquillity." Dan. iv. 27.

He continued impenitently proud, and did not regard the counsel; and therefore the threatened judgment was inflicted upon him. His case seems to have been this: after divine patience had tried him for a whole year, while he was venting his arrogance in his palace, he was judicially struck, in an instant, with a melancholy madness; and while he was in a raving fury, his domestics turned him out of his palace. There are instances, now-a-day, of persons imagining themselves transformed into other creatures: and Nebuchadnezzar probably fancied himself an ox, and therefore tried to imitate the actions of that animal; he ran wild in the fields with beasts; eat grass like them, and laid abroad under the dews of heaven; until, at length, his hairs grew like eagles' feathers, and his nails, for want of paring, like birds' claws.* At the time appointed, he recovered his reason; made the most humble acknowledgments of the sovereignty of the divine government, and was reinstated in his kingdom.

The text informs us of the design of Heaven in this judgment upon him, and that it should not be removed until it had answered its end. "This is the decree of the Most High—that they shall drive thee from men, and thy dwelling shall be with the beasts of the field, and they shall make thee to eat grass as oxen, and they shall wet thee with the dew of heaven, and seven times," that is, seven years shall pass over thee in this condition, "*until* thou knowest that the Most High ruleth in the kingdom of men, and giveth it to whomsoever he will." Then, and not till then, he was restored to his reason and his kingdom; but he did not enjoy it long, for after a few days, he was cut off by the stroke of death.

I might very properly take occasion from this text to prove the universal agency of Providence in the natural and moral world. But, at present, I must confine myself to the proof and illustration of this important truth—that the Most High is the sole disposer of the fates of kingdoms, and particularly of the events of war.

This is demonstrable from the perfections of God—from the repeated declarations of Scripture—from the common sense of mankind—and from the remarkable coincidence of circumstances in critical times.

First, That the Most high is the sole disposer of the

---

* This seems to be implied, Dan. v. 20, 21.—iv. 16.

fates of kingdoms, and the events of war, is demonstrable from his perfections.

We may infer from his *wisdom,* that he formed the world, and particularly man, for some important design, which he determined to accomplish; but could he expect that this design would be accomplished by free agents, left entirely to themselves, without any direction or control from him? Or would it be consistent with wisdom to form creatures incapable of self-government, and fit subjects for him to rule, and yet exercise no government over them, but leave them entirely to themselves? *Justice* is an awful and amiable attribute. And on whom shall he display it but on rational creatures, who are capable of moral good and evil? Indeed, the display of justice on particular persons may be deferred, as it generally is, to another state; but on societies, as such, it cannot be displayed but in this life; for it is only in this life that they subsist in that capacity; and therefore guilty nations must feel divine judgments in the present state, which supposes that God disposes of them as he pleases. His *goodness,* that favourite perfection, is diffusive and unbounded; but how shall this be displayed in this world, unless he hold the reins of government in his own hands, and distributes his blessings to what kingdom or nation he pleases! If he do not manage their concerns, his *mercy* cannot be shown in delivering them from calamities; nor his *patience,* in bearing with their provocations. His *power* is infinite, and therefore the management of all the worlds he has made, is as easy to him as the concerns of one individual. He *knows all things,* and is *everywhere present;* and can he be an unconcerned spectator of the affairs of his own creatures, and see them run on at random, without interposing? We may as well say in our hearts, with the fool, "There is no God," Psalm liii. 1, as entertain such mean ideas of him, as an idle being, whose happiness consists in inactivity. He will display his perfections in the most God-like manner, and this was his design in the creation of the universe; and since he cannot do this without exercising a perpetual providence over it, we may be assured he will do " according to his will in the army of heaven, and among the inhabitants of the earth." Dan. iv. 35. Indeed, there is something unnatural in the idea of a Creator, who takes no care of his own creatures. Do you who are evil, know how to give good gifts to your children? Are you shocked at the thought of a parent who takes no care of his own children, but leaves them as soon as born, to shift for themselves? And will not the great Father of Nature, who has implanted these parental passions in *your* breasts, will not he look after his own offspring, and manage their affairs. Undoubtedly he will.

Secondly, That God is the supreme Disposer of the fates of kingdoms, and of the events of war, is demonstrable from the repeated declarations of Scripture; and this alone is sufficient proof to those that believe their divine authority.

This great truth, in one form or other, runs through the whole Bible. Sometimes the divine government is asserted to be universal, supreme, and uncontrollable. "Our God is in the heavens; he hath done whatsoever he pleaseth. Psalm cxv. 3. The Lord hath prepared his throne in the heavens; and his kingdom ruleth over all. Ps. ciii. 19. He doth according to his will in the army of heaven, and among the inhabitants of the earth; and none can stay his hand, or say unto him, what doest thou?" Dan. iv. 35. Now his *universal* government, which is so strongly asserted in these passages, implies his *particular* government of the affairs of kingdoms and nations; and the Scriptures declare that the care of Providence extends to the most minute and inconsiderable parts of the creation; and therefore much more does it extend to the affairs of men, and the fates of kingdoms. "He giveth to the beast his food, and to the young ravens that cry: Psalm cxlvii. 9. Behold, the fowls of the air; they sow not; neither do they reap, nor gather into barns; yet your heavenly Father feedeth them." Hence Christ draws the inference now in view, "Are not ye much better—or of more importance—than they?" And therefore must not you be more particularly the objects of your Father's care? "God," says he, "clothes even the grass of the field, which to-day is, and to-morrow is cast into the oven." Matt. vi. 26–30. The value of two sparrows is but one farthing; and yet, says Christ, not one of them can so much as fall to the ground without your Father; that is, without the permission of his providence. Nay, the very hairs of your head, the most trifling things that belong to you, are all numbered—God takes as particular care of them, as if he kept an account of each of them, and not one of them can be lost without his notice. Here again our blessed Saviour makes the same improvement as before, which is directly to my purpose: "Fear ye not, therefore, ye are of more value than many sparrows," Matt. x. 29–31. Does divine Providence take notice of ravens and sparrows, and the grass of the field? and will God not concern himself with the kingdoms of the earth? Does he take care even of the hairs of men's heads? And will he not take care of men themselves? Undoubtedly he will. The Scriptures farther expressly assert, that the promotion and degradation of princes, and the prosperity and destruction of kingdoms, are from God. "Promotion," says the Psalmist, "cometh neither from the east, nor from the west, nor from the south; but God is the judge; he putteth down one, and setteth up another." Ps. lxxv. 6. "He changeth the times and seasons," says

Daniel: "he removeth kings, and setteth up kings." Chap. ii. 21. "The Most High ruleth in the kingdom of men, and giveth it to whomsoever he will." Dan. iv. 32; and sometimes in his wise sovereignty, "Setteth up over it even the basest of men," ver. 17. "When he giveth quietness, who then can make trouble?" Job xxxiv. 29. "Shall there be evil (or affliction) in a city, and the LORD hath not done it?" Amos iii. 6. "Come, behold the works of the LORD, what desolations he hath made in the earth. He maketh wars to cease unto the end of the earth: he breaketh the bow, and cutteth the spear in sunder; he burneth the chariot in the fire." Ps. xlvi. 8, 9. Hence pious warriors have confided for victory in the providence of God, and been sensible that without him, all their military forces were in vain. "Some trust in chariots, and some in horses; but we will remember the name of the Lord our God." And observe the difference: "They are brought down and fallen: but we, (who put our trust in the Lord,) are risen, and stand upright." Ps. xx. 8—xxxiii. 16, 17. Again, we find many instances in the sacred writings of God's overruling the conduct of men, even of the wicked, to accomplish his own great designs, when the persons themselves had nothing in view, but their own interest, or the gratification of their malignant passions; and thus he brings good out of evil.

Who could have had any raised expectations from the sale of Joseph, a poor helpless youth, as a slave into Egypt? His brethren had no other end in it, than to remove out of the way the object of their envy, and their rival in their father's affection. But God had a very important design in it, even the deliverance of the holy family and thousands of others from famishing. And therefore Joseph tells his brethren, "It was not you that sent me hither, but God," Gen. xlv. 8. The crucifixion of Christ was the most wicked action that ever was committed on this guilty globe; and the Jews freely followed their own malignant passions, and were not prompted to it by any influence from God, who cannot tempt to evil. But I need not tell you that this greatest evil is over-ruled for the greatest good of mankind. Though I might easily multiply instances, I can take time only to mention one more, exactly pertinent to my purpose; and this is the haughty and powerful Assyrian monarch, Isaiah x. 5-7. Having pushed his conquests far and wide among other nations, he resolves to turn his victorious arms against the Jews. He was an arbitrary prince in his own empire, and apprehended he was subject to no control. His design in this expedition, was not to chastise the Jews for their sins against Heaven, but to enlarge his own territories, to increase his riches, to display his power, and spread the terror of his name. He proudly thought he acted wholly from himself, and disdained the thought of being a mere agent, commissioned by another. But hear in what a style the King of kings speaks of him and degrades him into a rod, or a mere servant under command. "O Assyrian, the rod of mine anger; and the staff in their hand is mine indignation. I will send him against a hypocritical nation, (namely the Jews;) and against the people of my wrath will I give him a charge to take the spoil, and to take the prey, and to tread them down like the mire of the streets." Thus, says God, I commission him—these are the orders I give him to perform. "Howbeit he meaneth not so, neither doth his heart think so:" he does not so much as know that he has orders from me; much less does he design to obey them, "but it is in his heart to destroy and cut off nations not a few:" this is all his design. And when this haughty Assyrian arrogates to himself the honour of his successes, and vents himself in the most extravagant rant of self-applause, hear how God pours contempt upon him, and speaks of him in the most diminutive language, as a passive axe in his hand to hew rebellious nations; a saw, a rod, a staff of wood. "Shall the axe boast itself against him that heweth therewith? Or shall the saw magnify itself against him that shaketh it? As if the rod should threaten and shake itself against them that lift it up: or as if the staff should lift up itself, as if it were no wood," Isaiah x. 15. What mortifying images are these to represent a powerful and insolent prince? And how strongly may we infer from hence the supreme and absolute dominion of the King of heaven over the kings and empires of our world, and his directing the fate of war? Surely he has the spirits of men wholly under his command, who can make even their sins subservient to his good purposes, and who can accomplish his wise designs by them, even when they have no such thought, but are entirely ignorant of him. Thus he appears worthy of that august character, which he assumes to himself in his word more frequently, perhaps, than any other; I mean, "the Lord of hosts," or the Lord of armies. Thus appears the truth of Solomon's observation, "The king's heart is in the hand of the LORD; he turneth it whithersoever he will," Prov. xxi. 1.

Thirdly, It is the common sense of all mankind, that the affairs of kingdoms, and particularly success in war, depend upon God. Read over the historical parts of the Old Testament, and you will find it the common sense of the Jews, that they should never engage in war, without first consulting God, and imploring his blessing. The instances of this are so many, that it would take up too much time even to mention them. And since Christian kingdoms have been formed, we find the same sense prevailing among them, even in the darkest times. Nay, the very heathens were taught this by their reason, as one of the plainest dictates of the light of nature. They had all of them Gentilial gods for the protection of their nation. They had a Mars and a Minerva; the one the god, and the other the goddess of war. They never engaged in war without anxiously consulting oracles, and offering a profusion of sacrifices and prayers. And after a victory, they were wont to express the grateful sense of their success as from God, by rich offerings, and by consecrating to their deities a part of the spoils they had taken, which they hung up in their temples. Now that which is common to all mankind, in all countries, in all ages, and of every religion, seems to be implanted in their nature by its author; and, consequently, must be true. And since all mankind agree to supplicate divine assistance in their expeditions, and to return him thanks for victory; since they agree in this, however different in sentiments and prejudices, it follows that this is the common sense of the world, and a very important truth, that the fate of war depends upon the divine Superintendent. But I cannot enlarge on this head.

Fourthly, The interposition of Providence is frequently visible in the remarkable coincidence of circumstances to accomplish some important end in critical times.

I am not enthusiastic enough to look upon every event as the effect of an immediate Providence, excluding or controlling the agency of natural causes; but when some important design is in agitation, for the advantage of one nation and the chastisement of another; and every thing, even the most fickle or reluctating causes, seems steadily and uniformly to concur to accomplish it—when the winds and seas, the clouds and rain, conspire to promote it—when the friends of the scheme, perhaps with hesitation and perplexity, are directed to such measures as the event shows to be the most proper to obtain their end—when they are restrained from pursuing measures for which they were very sanguine, which the event shows would have blasted the whole scheme—when the enemies of the design are restrained from such means as would overthrow it, though they seem easy, and such as their own reason might at first sight direct them to—when they are overruled to act contrary to all the rules of prudence and good policy, on which they act in other cases, and so bring confusion and disappointment upon themselves—when an important life is continued or taken away, in a critical juncture, just as is most conducive to the design; I say, when such things as these happen, must we not own that it is the finger of God? Will we affect the philosopher so much as to dispute it? Can we suppose that mere natural causes, that act without design, or that free agents, who act as they please, and who have different views, different prejudices, and contrary interests and inclinations —can we suppose that all these should conspire to promote one design, unless they were under the overruling influence of divine Providence? Must not such a remarkable and even preternatural concurrence of various circumstances convince us of the truth of Solomon's remark, "There are many devices in a man's heart; nevertheless the counsel of the LORD, that shall stand!" Prov. xix. 21. "He disappointeth the devices of the crafty; so that their hands cannot perform their enterprise. He taketh the wise in their own craftiness, and the counsel of the froward is carried headlong." Job v. 12, 13.

Both sacred and profane history may furnish us with many instances of such remarkable interpositions of Providence; but I can, at present, only select a few out of the history of our mother-country, in which we are more particularly concerned, and which may therefore excite our gratitude for the divine goodness to our guilty nation, and break our hearts into penitential sorrows for our unsuitable returns. These may also convince us, that though divine Providence did, in a more visible and miraculous manner, manage the affairs of kingdoms in the earlier ages of the world; yet even in our days, when the age of miracles is ceased, God does really exercise the same government, and dispose the concerns of nations as he pleases.

The first critical time which I would call to your remembrance, is the Spanish invasion in the reign of Queen Elizabeth, 1588. The Spaniards, enriched with the gold of the new world, America, then lately discovered, and their king enraged against England with all the malignity of a papist, and a disappointed expectant of the crown; fitted out a fleet of such a force as the world had never before seen. They proudly called it *the invincible armada;* and, indeed, it seemed to deserve the name. "The seas were overspread with their burden, and the ocean groaned with their weight." England then was but weak by sea, and in no condition to make a defence; so that she seemed on the very brink of popery, and slavery, and ruin. But she had little else to do, but to "stand still, and see the salvation of the LORD." Exodus xiv. 13. Scarce had they displayed their sails to the inviting gales, when He who holds the winds in his treasures, let them loose upon the face of the deep. They were scattered—they were dashed in pieces against one another—they foundered in the mighty waters. And of this mighty fleet, there was hardly one left to carry back the dismal news. And was not this the Lord's doing, and marvellous in our eyes? Psalm cxviii. 23. Did he not make the winds, in their courses, fight for England? In this light it appeared to Queen Elizabeth and her court; and therefore, in commemoration of this remarkable event, medals were struck with this inscription, "AFFLAVIT DEUS, ET DISSIPANTUR:" He blew with his wind, and they were scattered.

This loss was so great a stroke to Spain, that they have not been able to repair it to this day, with all the prodigious treasures of South America. Nevertheless, in the year 1596, they made another attempt upon our mother-country, with a very formidable navy, though not equal to the former. "But (to borrow the words of Rapin, a foreigner, and therefore disinterested,) a violent storm arising in the midst of the voyage, several of the ships were lost, and the rest so dispersed, that the fleet was rendered unserviceable for that year. Thus Elizabeth had the pleasure of hearing that it was disabled from hurting her, before she knew of its sailing." And was not this another remarkable interposition of Heaven in our favour?

The next crisis I shall take notice of is the GUNPOWDER PLOT, on the 5th of November, Old Style, 1605. The infernal power of Popery had formed a scheme at one blow to hurry from the earth our king and the flower of our nobility and great men of the nation, by a mine of gunpowder under the parliament-house. They had carried on the plot with the utmost secresy, and there was no suspicion till the very day before the diabolical scheme was to be carried into execution. It was discovered by the miscarriage of a suspicious letter to Lord Mounteagle, whom they were desirous to save from the general ruin.

The interspace between 1685 and 1688 was a dark period. The British throne, the usual seat of law and liberty, was filled with a prince who was a flaming bigot for popery, and of arbitrary principles of government. The standing laws of the kingdom were laid aside, and the capricious pleasure of the prince was the rule of right and wrong. Charters were extorted from boroughs and corporations. The vilest of men were advanced to places of trust, particularly Jeffries, that monster of cruelty and injustice, to the highest seat of justice. Popish bishops were obtruded upon the church of England, and no fewer than seven Protestant bishops were imprisoned in the tower for no other crime than refusing to read a proclamation intended to introduce popery. The Protestant dissenters, their ministers especially, were perishing in jail, or chased like partridges on the mountains; or if any of them were tolerated, it was not in favour of them, but their worst enemies, the papists.

These, (says an animated writer,*) these were scenes of gloominess and darkness—these were days of horror and despair. How didst thou then, fair liberty, and thou, star-crowned religion, lift thy streaming eyes to heaven! and how didst thou, O my country, faint with thy deadly wounds—how didst thou lie, all pale and ghastly, wallowing in thy blood! Come, glorious deliverer! come, immortal William! for thee is reserved the honour of saving a miserable nation from temporal and spiritual slavery. *Venit, vidit, vicit:* he came, he saw, he delivered. The inconstant winds seemed proud to serve him, and the swelling floods smothered their rage to waft him over. They varied and calmed in a minute when he needed them, and his fleet was carried prosperously through the seas, while that of the enemy was shut up in port. The winds breathed a gentle and favourable gale, until his fleet was secured, and then broke in a violent storm upon that which came against him. They were scattered, and forced into ports: their hopes and the fears of the Protestants were at the same time extinguished; and King William was peaceably fixed upon

* Britain's Remembrancer

the throne, as the guardian of liberty, property, and religion. And can you see nothing of divine Providence in this? Surely you must; unless you regard not the work of the Lord, nor consider the operation of his hands. Psalm xxviii. 5.

When the throne was once cleared of a Popish prince, and a Protestant seated on it, it was a matter of the utmost importance to all posterity to keep it so. This King William had much at heart; and he laboured all his life to get an act of Parliament to exclude all the popish branches of the family, and to settle the succession of the crown in the family of Hanover. the next Protestant branch, in case Queen Anne left no heir, as she did not: but he had so many enemies in both houses of Parliament, that they disconcerted all his measures; and he could not carry his point for sundry years. At last the act passed in both houses; and while the matter was in agitation, he was seized with his last illness; and the last act of his life was giving his assent to that bill, which has been our grand security ever since, against the claims of an abjured pretender.

Thus Providence continued his life till the critical moment; and if he had not lived to establish this law, it is very nnlikely it would ever have been established afterwards; and popery and tyranny would have broken in upon us like a torrent. The same Providence that appeared in the preservation of his life, did also appear in cutting off the life of Queen Anne in a most critical time. It is well known that from the year 1710 to 1714, a number of arbitrary high-flyers, favourites of the Pretender, had wormed themselves into her court, and engrossed the management of affairs; while the brave duke of Marlborough, and the best friends of the nation, were disgraced. If the design can be known from the direct tendency of means, and the characters of the agents, it was plain the scheme was to lay aside the act of succession, and restore the Pretender. And the Jacobite party openly declared, that if the Queen had lived but six weeks longer, their schemes would have been quite ripe for execution. But, at this dangerous crisis, death was sent to cut short the Queen's life, which blasted their design, and the crown descended to the house of Hanover, in the person of King George the First. By this seasonable death, we, who are Protestant dissenters, are delivered from another intolerable imposition. The high-flying party had formed an engine of church-tyranny and persecution against the dissenters; and that was, an act of parliament to tear from them their children, and compel them to be educated in the established church. This act was to take place on the first of August, 1714; but on that very day the Queen died; and the government fell into, and blessed be God, still continues in, the hands of persons more friendly to the liberty of mankind and the sacred rights of conscience; and there may it long continue!

I shall only add, that Providence very remarkably infatuated the rebels in the last rebellion in 1745—turned their counsels into foolishness, and thus delivered the nation. If immediately after the victory they obtained over our forces at Preston-Pans, they had pursued their way to London, they would, very probably, have cut their way to the throne; or at least made the nation a scene of blood. The whole country was struck into a violent panic; our forces were abroad in Flanders; and there was no power to stop the progress of the enemy. But the rebels, instead of pursuing their way to the metropolis, loitered in and about Edinburgh, and wasted their time in a chimerical project of taking the castle of that city:

which both nature and art had rendered impregnable. By this delay, they gave time to the nation to recover from its panic—to the forces to return, and proper preparations to be made to repel them.

And is there nothing of the hand of God in all this? Is it not so evident as to extort an acknowledgment even from the thoughtless and reluctant? Has not God appeared the guardian of that favourite island, Great Britain?

I may now presume, the great truth I had in view is sufficiently evident: namely, that God is the Supreme Disposer of the affairs of nations and the events of war.

If any of you should ask, "In what manner does he do this? Or how is it possible he should do it, when we see no sensible appearances of his controlling the laws of nature, or restraining the liberty of men? Natural causes produce their proper effects; and men fight against men; and perceive they are free to act or not to act, as they please. Where, then, is there any room for the agency of Providence?" I answer, it is the excellency of the Divine government to accomplish its purposes without throwing the world into disturbance and confusion, by great breaches upon its established laws; it accomplishes them, either by continuing the course of nature, or by altering it in so gentle and easy a manner, that it is hardly, if at all, perceivable. And as to men, God carries them on to effect his designs, without offering the least violence to their free and rational nature; and sways their minds so gently, that while they are performing his orders, they often seem to themselves to act from principles wholly within themselves. He manages all events as really as if he had made no use of secondary causes! and yet secondary causes produce their effects, and are, in action, as really as if they were the only agents.* What a surprising, mysterious government; what a perfect administration is this! Yet, I think, we can form some general ideas how the Lord manages the affairs of men, and particularly determines victory in the field of battle as he pleases. The event of war often depends in a great measure upon the winds and waves, clouds and rain. And why may not he, by a secret touch of his hand, order these so as to favour one party, and incommode the other? The fate of war greatly depends on the prudence of counsels, and the courage of the soldiers; and why may we not suppose, that he who formed the souls of men, and knows all their secret springs of action, and how to manage them:—why may we not suppose that he may imperceivably direct the minds of the one party to concert proper measures, and darken and confuse the understandings of the other, to take measures injurious to themselves, and advantageous to the enemy, though they appear right to them, until the event shows them mistaken? He may suggest hints of thoughts, and secretly bias the mind to a certain set of counsels; and yet the influence, though efficacious, may be so gentle, and so consistent with human nature, as hardly to be perceived. Why may he not imperceivably animate the one party with intrepid courage, and damp the other, and strike them with terror? These things and the like may easily be done by "the LORD of hosts, who is wonderful in counsel, and excellent in working." Isaiah xxviii. 29.

This subject is so rich in important inferences, that I am sorry I have not time to mention and enlarge upon them all. I only crave your attention to the following:

---

* " He ceaseless works alone! and yet alone
   Seems not to work; with such perfection framed
   Is this complex, amazing scene of things."—THOMSON'S SEASONS.

First, if God rule in the kingdoms of men, and manage the affairs of the world, then we should live upon earth as in a world governed by divine Providence. Though secondary causes may be used to bless or afflict us; yet let us look upon ourselves as in the hands of God, and all the blessings and afflictions of life as coming from him. Is it God that chastises us with sickness and misfortunes? Can we dare, then, to fly in his face by impatient murmurings and fretful complaints? Rather say, though I might take this ill from my fellow-creatures, yet, if it be *thy* hand, I am dumb, and will not open my mouth, because thou doest it. Psalm xxxix. 9. Are you prosperous and happy? Then it is God that makes you so, however many secondary causes you may observe contributing to it; and must not your devoutest gratitude ascend to him? When you fret at the dispensations of life, remember, you are quarrelling with the divine government. This rebellious temper may show itself about the smallest things. When you find fault with the winds or weather, the heat of summer, or the cold of winter, whom do you find fault with? Is it not with him that is the Disposer of these things? And do you not tremble at such a blasphemous insurrection against him. While a Being of such infinite wisdom, power, and goodness, sits at the helm, it becomes us implicitly to approve all his dispensations, and to be still, and know that he is God. Psalm xlvi. 10.

Secondly, If the affairs of nations are at the disposal of the King of heaven, then how dreadful is the case of a guilty, provoking, impenitent nation! If he be the Supreme Ruler of the kingdoms of the earth, then it belongs to his character to punish the rebellious disobedience to his authority, the contempt of his laws, the abuse of his mercies, and a sullen incorrigibleness under his chastisements. These crimes must turn his heart from a people, and provoke him to punish them. This world, as I observed before, is the only place where societies are punished as such; for in the future world they are dissolved; and every man is dealt with according to his own personal works. And if God be turned against a nation, if he be resolved to punish them, how helpless is their condition! Who can defend them if the Ruler of the universe be their enemy? Now, it is guilt only that can incur his displeasure—it is guilt only that can remove a nation from off its only sure basis—the protection of Heaven. Guilt, therefore, is poison in the veins of a body politic, and will cast it into dreadful convulsions, if not remedied in time by a speedy repentance. And, if this be the case, how may we tremble for our country, and fear the divine displeasure? We have enjoyed a long, uninterrupted peace in this land. We have not been alarmed with the sound of the trumpet, nor seen garments rolled in blood. But what a wretched improvement have we made of this, and many other inestimable blessings? What a torrent of vice, irreligion, and luxury has broken in, and overwhelmed the land? What ignorance of God and divine things; what carelessness about the concerns of religion and a future state? What a neglect of Christ and his precious gospel, has spread, like a subtle poison, among all ranks and characters? How daring are the immoralities of some, their profane oaths, their drunkenness, uncleanness, and many other monstrous vices under which our land groans? What luxury and extravagance in eating and drinking, and especially in diversions and amusements, (if they deserve so soft a name,) may we see among us, especially among persons in high life? How few are the penitent, affectionate, dutiful servants of God among us? How little is the Ruler of the universe regarded by his own creatures in his own world? Creatures supported by his constant bounties, and protected by his guardian care. Alas! my brethren, what shall I say? Most willingly would I draw a veil over the shame of my country; but, alas! it cannot be hid. While such glaring crimes are rampant among us; while such a stupid carelessness about the concerns of eternity prevails among us, it is impossible for the most benevolent charity to avoid the discovery. And may we not fear that the measure of our iniquity is just full? May we not fear that the righteous Judge of the earth will visit us for these things? Under the present happy government, we have enjoyed our liberty, our property, and our religion, and every thing dear to us; but we have abused them all. And may we not fear that these blessings shall be exchanged for the tyranny of a French government, and the superstitions and cruelties of the church of Rome? I hope and pray this may not be our doom; but I think it is the part of stupid presumption, and not of rational courage, to be quite fearless about it. We are, indeed, so happy as to be closely connected with our mother country, and under its protection. But, alas! vice and luxury have spread like a deadly contagion, there, as well as here: and Great Britain is worthy of divine vengeance, as well as we.

Now what shall we do in this case? Shall we put our trust in our military forces? Alas! what can an arm of flesh do for us, if the Lord of hosts desert us? Though our army was never so powerful, how sad would be our case, had we reason to say, like Saul, "The French are upon us, and God is departed from us?" Who can bear the thought? What then remains, but,

Thirdly, That we should humble ourselves before the King of kings, and take all proper means to gain his protection? If God dispose the victory as he pleases, then it is most fit, and absolutely necessary, that we should seek to secure his friendship. If we have such an almighty Ally, we are safe; and if we have provoked his displeasure, and forfeited his friendship, what can we do but prostrate ourselves in the deepest repentance and humiliation before him? for that is the only way to regain his favour. This is the great design of a fast; and from what you have heard, you may see it is not a needless ceremony, but a seasonable and important duty. Indeed, if he did not concern himself in the affairs of men, we need not concern ourselves with him. But since all our successes depend upon his Providence, how fit is it we should mourn over our provocations, and seek his favour? Let us, therefore, follow the advice of Joel, chap. ii. 12–18, and "turn to the Lord with weeping, with mourning, and with fasting." Let us confess our own sins, and the sins of our land, which have brought all our evils upon us. Let us be importunate and incessant in prayer, that God would pour out his Spirit and promote a general reformation; that he would direct our rulers to proper measures, inspire our soldiers with courage, and decide the event of battle in our favour. If the doctrine I have proved be true, then there is a congruity, a fitness in these things; yea, an absolute necessity for them.

To excite you, therefore, to these duties, let your hearts be deeply impressed with the truth I have been inculcating, that our success must come from God, and that without him all the means of our defence are in vain.

Consider the many blesssings you enjoy under the present government. I think it may be truly said that the constitution of the British government is the happiest in all the world. It is a proper mixture of monarchy, aristocracy, and democracy. The people choose their representatives to make laws for them, and the king, as well as the subject, is bound by these laws. No man is disturbed in his liberty, his property, or conscience; nor subjected to the capricious pleasure of the greatest man in the kingdom. I may also safely affirm, that of all the kings in Europe, or perhaps in the world, our gracious sovereign is the most tender of the liberties of his subjects, and zealous for the constitution of his country. Mercy and clemency are his delight; but his gentle nature is pained when he is constrained to exercise even the wholesome severities of justice; and never was a king's government more firmly established in the hearts and affections of his subjects. He is not perpetually making exorbitant claims by a pretended prerogative, like many of his predecessors, especially those of the family of Stewart. He does not assume the province of Heaven to prescribe to conscience, but allows every man the free and unmolested exercise of his religion, who lives inoffensive to the government. And, through the mercy of God, the principles of liberty are more generally embraced than ever in Great Britain. In short, the inhabitants of that favourite island and the colonies dependent upon it, are the happiest of mankind as to all the blessings of government. And shall we not be tenacious of these blessings, which are of such great importance to us, and our posterity, and which were purchased at the expense of their blood, by our brave forefathers.

And now, by way of contrast, let us take a view of the French government, and of our wretched circumstances if we should fall under it. There, every thing is done according to the pleasure of an arbitrary, absolute monarch, who is above law and all control. He may take away the liberty, and even the lives of his subjects, without assigning a reason why. There you must conform to all the superstitions and idolatries of the church of Rome, or lose your life; or, at best, be obliged to flee your country, hungry and famishing, and leave all your estate behind you. Nay, to such a height is persecution carried there now, that they place soldiers to guard the frontiers of the country, and will not allow the Protestants the poor favour of going to beg their bread, or begin the world anew, in a strange country. It is but a little while ago, that a minister was apprehended, condemned, and hanged, all in three hours, and for no other crime but preaching a sermon to a number of Protestants. And even now, such as can make their escape, are flying over in multitudes to Great Britain—that land of liberty. And can you bear the thought, that you and your children should have such an iron yoke as this riveted about your necks? Would you not rather die in defence of your privileges? I am sure you would, if you had the spirit of men or of Christians. Therefore, improve your religion, lest you lose it: make a good use of your liberty, lest you forfeit it; and cry mightily to God for deliverance.

To heighten the terror of a French government, they have on this continent a numerous body of Indian savages in their interest, whom they will hound out upon us; and from them we may expect such bloody barbarities as we cannot bear so much as to think of. If the barbarities should make inroads upon us, as they have begun to do in some of the neighbouring provinces, how miserable are we!

To alarm you the more, reflect upon the growing power of France. She keeps an army of a hundred and forty thousand men on foot, even in time of peace; and is undoubtedly superior to the English by land. She has, also, of late, greatly increased in strength at sea; in which Britain has hitherto maintained the sovereignty. And though in America the French are but few in comparison of the

English, yet they receive very powerful recruits from their mother country.

It is also a most discouraging omen, that though the British colonies are superior in number, yet they are so possessed with a spirit of contention, or so stupidly insensible of danger, that they do not exert themselves with proper vigour for their own defence, or delay it too long to prevent the influence of so active an enemy. If we tamely suffer ourselves to be enslaved, while we are so much superior in power, we well deserve it.

Fourthly, If God govern the world by means of second causes, then it is our duty, according to our characters, to use all proper means to defend our country, and stop the encroachments of our enemies. We have no ground for a lazy confidence in divine Providence; nor should we content ourselves with idle, inactive prayers; but let us rouse ourselves, and be active. Let us cheerfully pay the taxes the government has laid upon us to support this expedition. Let us use our influence to diffuse a military spirit around us. I have no scruple thus openly to declare, that such of you whose circumstances allow of it, may not only lawfully enlist and take up arms, but that your so doing is a Christian duty, and acting an honourable part, worthy of a man, a freeman, a Briton, and a Christian.

SERMON LXXI.

A THANKSGIVING SERMON FOR NATIONAL BLESSINGS.

EZEKIEL xx. 43, 44.—*And there shall ye remember your ways, and all your doings, wherein ye have been defiled; and ye shall loathe yourselves in your own sight, for all your evils that ye have committed. And ye shall know that I am the* LORD, *when I have wrought with you for my name's sake, not according to your wicked ways, nor according to your corrupt doings, O ye house of Israel, saith the Lord* GOD.*

I AM by no means fond of employing your sacred time in harangues upon political or military subjects; and last Sunday I intended to touch upon them once for all, and then confine myself to the more important concerns of religion and eternity; but Providence has surprised us in one week with so many, and such important, turns in our favour, that loyalty, religion, and all the virtues of patriotism and Christianity united, require us to take grateful notice of them. Therefore, I beg an hour of your sacred time for this purpose. I need not tell you, what you already know, that Ticonderoga, Crown Point, and Niagara, are in our possession; nests of savages that had so long ravaged our frontiers; fortifications that had defied our utmost efforts in I know not how many fruitless expeditions, and cost our country and nation so many thousands of money, and so many limbs and lives of our countrymen

* Hanover, Jan. 11, 1759.—Nassau Hall, Aug. 12, 1759.

and fellow-subjects. Before the hour of victory, destined by Heaven, all our attempts were in vain, and issued in inglorious defeats; but when that hour is come, the terror of the Lord falls upon our enemies, and the important acquisitions are made as without hands. The sword of the Lord and of General Amherst gleaming from afar, strike our enemies into a panic; they lose all power of resistance, and the terror of the British name puts them to flight.

After frequent days of fasting and humiliation under the frowns of Heaven upon our country and nation, and still more frequent occasions for them; after the Lord of hosts has called us to weeping and mourning, and all the sad solemnities of repentance and sorrow, for a course of years; behold! through the unmerited, and almost unexpected, mercy of God, we, at length, see one more *day of joy and thanksgiving*. To this agreeable duty, Heaven calls us by the late success of our expeditions; and our government has gratefully obeyed the call; and divine and human authority conspire to render the business of this day our duty. And oh! that we may engage in it with hearts overflowing with gratitude, and all the sacred passions which the occasion requires!

I need not tell you that you have occasion for joy and thanksgiving, when you know, Cape Breton is ours, and Fort Duquesne is abandoned and demolished. Cape Breton, the key of the French settlements in America, the object of our anxious fears, and of fruitless expeditions of immense expense—Cape Breton, whose inexhaustible fishery enriched the treasury of France, and educated so many men for her marine service—Cape Breton, the asylum of the privateers that ruined our trade, and that shut up our entrance by sea into the heart of Canada— Cape Breton, the possession of which puts it in our power to weaken the enemy both in Europe and America, by cutting off their mutual intercourse by navigation : *Cape Breton is ours !* ours with the additional acquisition of the fertile island of St. John—ours, after a short siege, and a very inconsiderable loss*—ours, after a long season of anxious suspense and discouragements; after repeated disappointments and mortifications.

Fort Duquesne, the den of those mongrel savages of French and Indians, who have ravaged our frontiers, captivated and butchered so many of our fellow subjects, and ruined so many poor families—Fort Duquesne, the object of Braddock's ever-tragical and unfortunate expedition,† near which so many brave lives have been repeatedly thrown away in vain—Fort Duquesne, the magazine which furnished our Indian enemies with provisions, arms, and fury, to make their barbarous inroads upon the British settlements, and prevented our growing country from extending its frontiers on the Ohio—Fort Duquesne, is abandoned and demolished; demolished by those hands that built it, without the loss of a man on our side. The terror of the Lord fell upon them, and they fled at the approach of our army, so superior to them in number, and so resolute to pursue the expedition, notwithstanding the severities of approaching winter. What though those, if such there be, who thirsted for their blood, are not gratified? What though our commanders may not have acquired the same military glory, as if they had taken it after all the dreadful formalities of a siege? What though we are not possessed of a fort, arms, and ammunition ready to our hands? These disadvantages are more than balanced by this consideration, so agreeable to every man of humanity and benevolence; that the lives and limbs of men have been spared, many of which, no doubt, must have

---

* Not quite three hundred men.   † Vide the 69th discourse.

been lost in a regular siege; and that only wood, and stone, and iron, and the other materials and furniture of the fort, have felt the violence of our enemies. We have been at a loss to account for the slow motions of our army the last summer; and such domestic politicians are very incompetent judges of an affair so distant from them. But now, methinks, the event makes all plain: they are graciously delayed by the powerful, though invisible and unacknowledged, hand of divine Providence, that the acquisition might be made without the effusion of the precious blood of mankind, and the destruction of human lives and limbs. Many have died by sickness, by rash attempts,* and the unavoidable hardships of a late campaign in that inhospitable wilderness; but how many more, may we reasonably suppose, would have been cut off, had they been obliged to attack the fort? No doubt, some of our friends would never have returned, whom we now have the pleasure of welcoming home with open arms. We did not want the lives of our enemies, but only to drive such troublesome neighbours to a proper distance. This end is fully obtained. And since the French are removed, the Indian savages who have done us the most mischief, will be under a necessity of breaking off their alliance with them, and espouse our interest, or at least become neuters. This is one of the happiest revolutions in our favour that we could wish.

Besides these successes by land in America, in which we are more immediately concerned, success has also attended the arms of Britain on her own element, the ocean; the French trade has sustained irreparable losses

* Such a rash attempt, as far as I can learn, was that of Major Grant and Major Lewis, who marched with seven or eight hundred men, and only small arms, against the fort without orders: which the garrison observing, sallied out, and cut off near three hundred men. The two Majors, men of tried bravery, were taken prisoners and sent to Montreal.

by the capture and destruction of so many of their ships; and their naval force has been prodigiously weakened by the loss of so many men-of-war.

France has also received considerable damage, and Britain equal advantage, by the descents that were made upon her coasts at St. Maloes and Cherbourg. Her numerous army in Germany has melted away, like snow before the sun, and been obliged to abandon Hanover in consternation, after an easy conquest.

In short, notwithstanding some losses and defeats, and particularly that heavy blow at Ticonderoga, which destroyed near two thousand brave men, and rendered a most important expedition abortive, the hand of Providence has been upon our side, the last season, in many illustrious instances; and for these we are called to the delightful work of praise this day.

And certainly we ought also to give praise to God for the unprecedented and almost miraculous successes of our glorious ally, the king of Prussia: a man raised up to be the GREAT INSTRUMENT OF PROVIDENCE, and to astonish the world with the exemplification of that old remark, "that there is no restraint to the LORD, to save by many or few." 1 Sam. xiv. 6. He has stood almost the single champion of the cause of liberty and the Protestant religion, and appeared alone a match for the half of Europe. The Lord is on his side; and what need he fear what man can do unto him? Psalm cxviii. 6. He acknowledges God in all his ways; and those that honour him, he will honour: while those that despise him, shall be lightly esteemed. 1 Sam. ii. 30.

These are the blessings and deliverance we are this day to celebrate. And why has God thus favoured our country and nation? Is it for our sakes, or on account of our merit? No; not for *your sakes* do I do this, saith the

Lord God; be it known unto you: be ashamed and confounded for your own ways, O Britons and Virginians. Ezek. xxxvi. 32. But, according to my text, he hath wrought with us for *his own name's sake*, not according to our wicked ways, nor according to our corrupt doings.

I am not entirely without hopes, that a sinner here and there has been awakened to a serious sense of religion, and turned from his evil ways, by the judgments and chastisements of Heaven upon our country and nation : though as far as my observation or intelligence reaches, the number of such happy converts is but small. The utmost effect of the most alarming dispensations of Providence upon the multitude, has been only a sudden panic and consternation, which has perhaps extorted a transient prayer from them, and put them to a stand for a few moments in their thoughtless, presumptuous career; but it has soon worn off, and produced no lasting and thorough reformation. If you should take a tour through our country, and the British dominions, in general, alas! you will see but little appearance of amendment, since the war commenced: the same infidelity and vice: the same atheistical insensibility of the agency of Providence in the management of human affairs, and particularly in determining the events of war; the same contempt or neglect of the gospel of the Son of God; the same stupid security and unconcernedness about the affairs of the soul; the same langour and indifferency in the worship of God, and the duties of religion; the same appearances of pride, injustice, uncharitableness, contention, and animosity, and all forms of wickedness that can subsist between man and man; the same luxury, intemperance, and extravagant love of pleasure, still prevail among the generality. Their ways are still wicked, and their doings still corrupt.

We must therefore conclude, that the reasons why God

has once more interposed in favour of obnoxious Britons, and their American descendants, are not at all taken from *them*, but from *himself*—from his own great *name*. He hath wrought for us, as he did for his old peculiar people, the Jews, *for his own name's sake*.

But what does this mean?

The *name* of God, in the same writings, very frequently signifies his *nature* and *perfections*. Thus when he proclaimed the *name* of the Lord in the hearing of Moses, (compare Exod. xxxiii. 19, with xxxiv. 6, 7,) the proclamation contained his *nature* and *perfections*, "The LORD, the LORD God, merciful and gracious, long-suffering, and abundant in goodness and truth." Exod. xxxiv. 6. Now, if we understand the *name* of God in this sense, as signifying his nature and perfections, when he is said to deliver a people *for his own name's sake*, the meaning is, that it is not their merit or goodness, but the benevolence and grace of his own nature, that excites him to deliver them. He does good, because it is his nature to do good. His grace is overflowing, and can bear no restraints, where the object is pointed out by divine wisdom. It requires a God of infinite perfections to create a world out of nothing; this is universally granted. But it is often thought of, though equally true, that it also requires a God of infinite perfections, to bear so long with so guilty and provoking a world as ours: it is the patience and long-suffering of a GOD only, that is capable of this. It requires a God of infinite perfections, to deliver a people so ripe for judgment, as Great Britain and her territories. The grace of the most benevolent of mortals, and even of angels, is not equal to this exploit of mercy. This is as far above all created grace, as the production of the universe out of nothing is above all created power. Our God is Godlike and unrivalled in all his works; and in nothing more so than in works of grace and mercy. Oh, "who is a God like unto thee, that pardoneth iniquity, and passeth by the transgression of the remnant of his heritage? He retaineth not his anger for ever, because he delighteth in mercy." Micah vii. 18. Hence it is that guilty Britain and her colonies are this day rejoicing in God their Saviour; and that the arms of a people worthy of destruction have been victorious. Oh, "praise ye the Lord, because he is good;" good in himself, and therefore he doth good; "and his mercy endureth for ever."

But there is another sense in which the *name* of God is often used in Scripture; and that is, to signify his honour and reputation, as the supreme Magistrate of the world. A man's name, in vulgar language, often means his fame or renown. Hence a good or great name signifies a good or great reputation. So it is used when God tells David, "I took thee from following the sheep, to be ruler over my people Israel; and have made thee a *great name*, like *the name* of the great men that are in the earth." In this sense it is used by Isaiah; as to the great God. Isaiah lxiii. 12–14. "That led them by the right hand of Moses with his glorious arm, dividing the water before them, to make himself an everlasting name." Thus God himself uses his own name, Jer. xiii. 11, when he says of the Israelites, that he had caused them to cleave as near to him as a man's girdle to his loins, for this end, "that they might be unto him for a people, and for a NAME, and for a praise, and for a glory." In this sense the name of God is to be understood in the text. And the meaning is, that he wrought this deliverance for his people, for the sake of his own honour and reputation, and to render his fame illustrious in the world. It is, indeed, the applause of his own all-wise mind that he principally regards, and his proceedings being really deserving of the approbation of his creatures, whether they approve them or not. They often ignorantly and presumptuously censure his conduct; but it is enough that he has always the applause of his own all-perfect wisdom, which is the best judge. He does what is right, principally for its own sake; satisfied in his own approbation; and assured that his proceedings will extort the plaudit even of ignorant cavillers, when the reasons of them are fully known, and the grand result appears. Yet, as his conduct is, in itself, always worthy of the applause of his creatures, and as it is both their duty and happiness to approve it, he must take pleasure in seeing them paying him deserved honour, and rendering his name, that is, his fame and reputation, glorious in the world. As the ruler of the universe, he is concerned to do every thing in character, in a manner worthy of himself, and conducive to the honour of his government. And he justly resents it, when the spectators of his proceedings refuse their applause. Hence he is often called a jealous God: he is jealous of his glory, or as mortals speak in modern phrase, he has a high sense of honour; he cannot bear any stain upon it, or any injury to his reputation. He justly demands what he deserves, a good name, from the whole universe; and when this is denied, his honour is touched, and he highly resents it. Therefore, when he is said to bestow any favour, not for the sake of the receivers, but for his own name's sake, the meaning is, that though they have no claim upon him, founded on their own merit, but may be punished in strict justice, yet there are some circumstances that attend the case, which render it more great, more honourable to his character and government, and more conducive to his fame, to forgive them, and bestow unmerited favours upon them, than to punish them according to their demerit. He may have such connections with a people, that it would be liable to misconstruction and censure, it would appear mean and inglorious, if he should cast them off, though they well deserve it.

Of this we have a remarkable instance in the Jewish nation, whom God had chosen as his peculiar people, and established the true religion among them, whom he had, by his own immediate miraculous hand, delivered from Egyptian slavery, conducted through the wilderness, planted in a country particularly allotted for them, espoused their cause, and appeared to all the world as their guardian God. Now when he had, for wise reasons, assumed such relations, and entered into such engagements with them, his honour was peculiarly concerned in their fate; and it would have been a matter of ill-fame for him not to take special care of them. It was this consideration, and not their good conduct, that prevailed with him to own and protect them, as his peculiar people, so long. This appears, in various forms, through all the Old Testament.

This is remarkably evident in the chapter where my text stands. If the honour of God had not been deeply concerned in their preservation, the Israelites would have been early destroyed; for they deserved it even in Egypt, before the divine Hand interposed in their deliverance. In Egypt, in the wilderness, in their own land, in every place, and in every age, their rebellion against their heavenly King arose to such a height, that he represents himself repeatedly as resolving to cut them off. "Then I said, I will pour out my fury upon them, to accomplish my anger against them." Ezek. xx. 8, 13, 21. But lo! his uplifted arm is kindly checked, and the falling blow prevented, by his regard for his own name. Whenever the vindictive denunciation is mentioned, it is immediately added, "But I wrought for my name's sake, that it should not be polluted before the heathen, among whom they were, in whose sight I made myself known unto them." Ezek. xx. 9. There is a particular stress laid upon this circumstance, that he had brought them forth out of Egypt, and made himself known unto them, in the sight of the heathen. Ezek. xx. 14–22. The heathen had seen what peculiar relations he had assumed to this people: the heathen were witnesses how far he had espoused their cause, and what wonders he had wrought in their favour; and they could see how much his honour was engaged to make thorough work, and perfect what he had begun. And should he punish them as soon, and as severely, as their iniquities deserve, and give them up to the power of their enemies, what would the heathen say? What injurious reflections would they cast upon the tutelary God of Israel? How would they blacken his fame, and stain his honour? But out of tenderness for his own honour, he will prevent these reproaches, and still own them as his people, though deserving utter rejection. How cautious he is not to give cavillers any umbrage to blaspheme his name, and injure his reputation, is still more strongly expressed. Deut. xxxii. 26, 27. "I said, I would scatter them into corners, I would make the remembrance of them to cease from among men: were it not that I feared the wrath of the enemy, least their adversaries should behave themselves strangely, and lest they should say, our hand is high, and the LORD hath not done this." It was this fear, speaking after the manner of man, that restrained his hand from punishing them, when they seemed ripe for it. The same sentiment runs through Ezekiel the thirty-sixth, from v. 18–24. "I scattered them among the heathen: and they profaned my holy name:" that is, brought it into disgrace, "when they said to them, these are the people of the LORD, and they are gone forth out of his land." As if they had said, see what a God the God of Israel proves after all. See here, his people are captives and vagabonds in a strange land. He was too weak to protect them, or too fickle to love them long. This blasphemy touched the divine honour, and hurt his fame in the world. Therefore it is immediately added, "I had pity for my holy name:" (it was pity for his own injured name rather than for them, that moved him to deliver them.) "I had pity for mine own holy name, which the house of Israel had profaned among the heathen, whither they went—Thus saith the LORD, I do not this for your sakes, O house of Israel, but for mine own holy name's sake, which ye profaned among the heathen, whither ye went;" (v. 21, 22.) "And I will sanctify my great name, which was profaned among the heathen: and the heathen," who now insult me, "shall know that I am the LORD, for I will gather them out of all countries, and bring them into their own land." It is counted a scandal to me that my people should be the slaves of heathens; but I will wipe off the scandal, by bringing them back to their own land; not because they deserve deliverance, but because my reputation requires it.

This is an argument of great weight in prayers for a people; and as such we find it used by the most prevalent intercessors. Thus Jeremiah prays, "We acknowledge, O Lord, our wickedness, and the iniquity of our fathers: for we have sinned against thee." Thus he acknowledges that they deserved to be utterly rejected. Yet he ventures humbly to plead, "Do not abhor us, for thy name's sake; do not disgrace the throne of thy glory: remember, break not thy covenant with us." Jer. xiv. 20, 21. We have no argument to urge from our own deservings: but, Lord, thine honour is at stake: thou hast condescended to enter into covenant with us; and if thou but seem to break it, it will render thy veracity and faithfulness suspicious, and cast a stain upon thy glory. Therefore, though there be nothing in us to restrain thee from abhorring us; yet have a regard to thine own honour, which is nearly concerned; and do not abhor us, for thy name's sake; do not disgrace thyself.

We find Moses also urging his argument with wonderful skill, and a kind of *almighty* importunity, and always carrying his point in favour of an obnoxious people. When they had fallen into idolatry, and made a golden calf their god, Jehovah says unto Moses, "I have seen this people, and, behold, it is a stiff-necked people. Now, therefore, let me alone," and do not intercede for them. Oh! the astonishing grace and condescension of God! Oh! the astonishing force of believing prayer! God cannot be angry with a guilty, rebellious people, unless Moses give over praying for them." "Let me alone," says he, "that my wrath may wax hot against them, and that I may consume them; and I will make of thee a great nation." And Moses besought the Lord his God, and said, "LORD, why doth thy wrath wax hot against thy people, which thou hast brought forth out of the land of Egypt, with great power, and with a mighty hand?" See how he pleads God's relation to them as *his* people, and what he had done for them, which engaged his honour to continue his protection. He goes on, still touching upon that tender point, the honour of God. "Wherefore," says he, "should the Egyptians speak and say," that is, why shouldst thou give them occasion to reflect, "For mischief did he bring them out, to slay them in the mountains, and to consume them from the face of the earth?" as though they should say, see what all his pretended love for his favourite people is come to at last. He only carried them out into the wilderness, that he might destroy them clandestinely. And is such a God to be trusted? "Therefore," says Moses, "turn from thy fierce wrath, and repent of this evil against thy people;" and so prevent this occasion of reproach. "Remember Abraham, Isaac, and Israel, to whom thou swearest by thine own self, and saidst unto them, I will multiply your seed as the stars of heaven, and all this land will I give unto your seed, and they shall inherit it for ever." Exod. xxxii. 9–14. Thy word, thine oath, is passed, in favour of this people: therefore, thou canst not honourably retract. Moses prevailed, though he had not one argument drawn from their merit to plead; but he engages the divine honour on their side; and this is an argument which even the Almighty could not resist.

Upon the people renewing their rebellion, and God's threatening again, " I will smite them with the pestilence, and disinherit them; and will make of thee a greater nation, and mightier than they;" Numb. xiv. 12–17, Moses tries the force of the old argument again. "Then," says he, "the Egyptians will hear it, for thou broughtest up this people in thy might from among them;" and they will know how far thou hast engaged thyself in their favour; "and the Egyptians will tell it to the inhabitants of this land," that is, the Canaanites; and thus the scandal will spread from country to country; "for they have heard that thou, Lord, art among this people," and hast wrought the most astonishing miracles for them, and ownest them as thy peculiar charge; this matter is public to all the world, and thy dear relation to them cannot be concealed. "Now," says he, "if thou shalt kill all this people, then the nations which have heard the fame of thee, will speak, saying, Because the Lord was not able to bring this people into the land which he sware unto them, therefore he hath slain them in the wilderness." Thus they will take occasion to blaspheme thy power, and they will entertain contemptuous thoughts of the God of Israel. This, you see, is the topic Moses insists upon. He is not content with the divine promise to himself, that God would make him great, and render his posterity more numerous and illustrious than that of Israel; nay, he seems not to have heard it, or at all listened to it, for he takes not the least notice of it in his prayer. He was quite swallowed up in concern for the honour of God, which was at stake; and thus was conformed to God himself, who is peculiarly tender of his honour; and he gave a lively specimen of the prevailing temper of every good man, and set a noble example, to all ages, of the most powerful and acceptable method of prayer. This, indeed, Christ himself also hath particularly taught us; for all the petitions in the prayer he has left for our imitation, are enforced in the conclusion from the divine name only, "For thine is the kingdom, the power, and the glory;" and the very first petition is, "Hallowed be thy name;" or, May thy name be sanctified.

Joshua, the successor of Moses, and the heir of his spirit, urges the same plea in prayer, as the most prevalent with God. Josh. vii. 7, 8, 9. When the Israelites were defeated at Ai, he is nonplussed, and knows not what to say. "O Lord," says he, "what shall I say when Israel turneth their backs before their enemies? For the Canaanites and all the inhabitants of the land shall hear of it, and shall environ us round, and cut off our name from the earth." Thus, like a true patriot, he is deeply concerned for the honour and safety of his nation. But this is not the principal object of his concern: But "what wilt thou do for thy great name?" This is what he is chiefly solicitous about; and this, he knew, was the principal object of solicitude to the divine mind. "If our name be cut off from the earth, what will become of thy name? How can the honour of that be supported, if thou abandon a people whom thou hast in so many ways engaged to preserve?"

I could easily multiply instances of this kind;* but these may suffice to inform you, that the honour of God may be so intimately concerned in the protection of a people, that he may work deliverance for them, even when they deserve to be cut off; and when it would be just and fit to give them up into the hands of their enemies, were it not that he has assumed such relations, and come under such engagements to them.

And now, to apply this to ourselves. Though, no doubt, the reformation of a sinner here and there, and the prayers of the few Lots that are still to be found in the British Sodom, and the interest these righteous persons have with God through Jesus Christ, have been prevailing reasons with the Lord to spare our guilty country and nation, at least a little longer, and to bless our arms with success; yet the most powerful reasons with him has been, the honour of his own great name, or his fame and renown as the Ruler of the world, the Guardian of right, and the Patron of the gospel and true religion.

It has pleased God to choose Great Britain out of the wide world, and to make her the object of his special care for many ages. He has often interposed for her deliverance, when on the very brink of ruin, and never more remarkably than since the reformation from Popery. There he has planted his pure gospel, purged from the corrupt

---

* See Deut. ix. 28; 1 Sam. xii. 22; Jer. xxxiv. 16, 17; Dan. ix. 19; John xii. 27, 28. There is no instance of this sort more remarkable than what we find in Isaiah xxxvi. and xxxvii., where Rabshekah's and his master's blasphemies against the God of Israel, were the occasion of their destruction, and a remarkable deliverance for Israel.

mixtures of Popery; and Great Britain has been the principal bulwark of the Protestant religion, ever since it first spread in Europe. On the other hand, our French and Indian enemies are papists and heathens; and should they prove victorious, they would not only insult us, but our God too. They would spread the scandal among the nations of the world, and the God and the religion of Christians and Protestants would become the scorn of popish and pagan idolaters.

Here I may pertinently introduce an extract of a letter from one of my worthy correspondents in London, a man mighty in prayer, and a zealous friend to his country.[*] Speaking of the easy acquisition the French made of Hanover in Germany, and our various mortifying defeats in America, he says:—"Our fears, at that time, ran high; but did not equal our enemies' boastings. I was informed by one that had been prisoner in France, that the haughtiness of their insulting expressions was not to be conceived. They had made such conquests in America, that they declared our hold there was very feeble; Germany was entirely conquered; the King of Prussia a desperate madman, who was forced to hide and shelter himself in bushes; the conquest of England must inevitably follow, and we must soon be a province of France.

"God beheld their threatenings," says my friend; "and has raised up a Cyrus,[†] and girded him to the war. And oh! what has God wrought by him! It is surprising! It is astonishing!"

Thus also to check the proud insults of our popish and heathen enemies, God has blessed the arms of Britain with success, both on the seas and in America. He seems resolved not to suffer the powers of antichrist to

---

[*] Dennys de Berdt, Esq. [†] The King of Prussia.

triumph any more over the religion of his Son; and in order to do honour to IT, and so to his own name, he preserves from destruction the people who make profession of it, though their sins cry aloud for vengeance, and their own dilatory, languid, and ill-contrived measures, naturally tended to their ruin.

I shall dismiss this subject with three reflections.

The first is, that since God has wrought in us, not for our sake, but for his own name's sake, we ought, in justice and gratitude, to ascribe our victories to him, and not to ourselves. Let us show all due honour to those brave men, who have risked their limbs and lives for our defence, and been the instruments of our deliverance, but let the God of battles stand unrivalled in honour, and be universally acknowledged as the great original Author of all our successes. Particularly, let us suppress a proud, self-righteous spirit, and not once imagine that our victories are the reward of our national goodness; for, alas! we are still a guilty, rebellious, people, that might justly be persecuted and destroyed in anger from under the heaven of the Lord. "Not for your sakes do I this, saith the LORD, be it known unto you: be ashamed and confounded for your own ways." Jehovah has begun to deliver us, to make himself a glorious name: therefore, " Not unto us, O Lord, not unto us, but unto thy name give glory." Psalm cxv. 1. He hath made known his power in our favor, obnoxious criminals as we are, that the heathen might not insult him, and say, " Where is their God ?" He hath let them know, that our God is in the heavens, and hath done whatsoever he pleased. Psalm cxv. 2, 3. Let us, therefore, concur with him in pursuing the same end, and make his praise glorious: otherwise, we are guilty, even upon our Thanksgiving day, of forming a rebellious insurrection against his great design; than which, what can be more insolent and wicked! Therefore, let all the glory and pride, all the vanity and self-confidence of man be abased and confounded at his feet; and let the Lord alone be exalted on this day.

The second reflection is, That, in our intercessions for our country, we should draw our principal argument from the glory of his own name. Here let me give you another extract from the above-mentioned letter of my friend:—" God," says he, " must have the glory; for it is his own arm that must bring salvation. And may we not plead with him *the glory of his name?* For, should our anti-christian enemies prevail, will they not ascribe their successes to their patron saints, and guardian angels; and say, the Protestants' God would not deliver them, when they cried unto him? I must confess," says he, " this plea has lain warm on my heart, at seasons when I have been wrestling with God, for our rebellious, guilty land. And herein, we have Moses, the typical mediator, for our example, and his glorious antitype, into whose hands we commit our cause; and he is head over all things to his church, and has all nature and grace at his disposal."

This, my brethren, is the spirit that prevails in a remnant on the other side of the Atlantic; and no doubt our American deliverances are answers to their prayers. Oh that the same spirit may spread among us; and that we also may learn to pray with the same sacred skill and successful importunity! Prayers enforced with arguments drawn from such insignificant and unworthy creatures as we, will have small efficacy; but arguments derived from his own name, his own honour and glory, will always prevail with God.

The third reflection is, That we should not flatter ourselves, that God is so bound by his honour to protect us, that he can never cast us off, and that we are not in any danger. It has appeared by the event, and nothing else could discover it, that it is not consistent with his honour to give us up a prey to our enemies at *present*. But it may soon be so. Nay, the time may be very near at hand, when the honour of his name, which is now an argument for us, may be an argument against us; that is, when it will no longer consist with the glory of God, but be a matter of ill-fame, for him to own and defend us as his people. Thus the Israelites were preserved, in the midst of enemies, for many ages, because the glory of God's name required it; but, at length, he abandoned them, and cast them out of his favour, for the very same reason, because his glory required it. His glory required, that he should, at length, visit such a wicked people with deserved punishment, that it might appear to all the world that he did not connive at, or patronize their sin. Thus, also, the glory of his name, the only argument now left in our favour, may turn against us, and our country and nation. Do not think that the controversy will thus end, if we persist in our rebellion; no, God will visit our iniquties upon us, as he did upon the Jews, if, like them, we refuse to repent. Perhaps the day of vengeance is at hand. Perhaps the present war may be the dawn of it, notwithstanding the late happy turn of Providence in our favour. A disease may intermit, and yet prove mortal. The sword is still drawn; and the events are very uncertain; and what turn it may yet take, is known only to him who is the supreme Arbiter of war. Therefore, let us this day serve God with fear, and rejoice with trembling. Let us never think ourselves safe, while iniquity abounds so much in our country and nation. .For I can as freely venture the reputation of my judgment upon it now, as when our affairs were in the most discouraging posture, that it will never be well with us, till there be more of the fear and love of God among us; and that we shall never enjoy the happy fruits of peace without interruption, till we secure the divine favour by turning from our evil ways. Without a general reformation, God will, sooner or later, be avenged upon such a nation as this.

But whatever be the issue of the present war, and whatever be the future doom of Britain and her colonies, we have certainly great cause to celebrate our late deliverances and acquisitions, and to keep this day in a proper manner.

But in what manner ought a thanksgiving day to be observed; and how should we celebrate our late acquisitions and deliverances? I answer,

We may lawfully indulge ourselves in all natural and decent expressions of joy. We may keep this day as the Jews did the days of Purim, as a day of gladness and joy, of feasting and sending portions one to another, and gifts to the poor. Esther ix. 19–22, &c. But let us not indulge ourselves in those riotous excesses and extravagances by which days of thanksgiving are profaned by many, under pretence of solemnizing them.

Let us talk over the goodness of God to our king and country: let our hearts and voices concur in his praise: praise him for all our successes, as their original author. And to inflame our gratitude, let us meditate—upon our former disasters and mortifications, under the frowns of Providence; and the distressing circumstances to which we were reduced—upon the happy providence that routed our enemies before us, without the loss of many lives— upon the goodness of God in preserving our friends and relations that went upon the expedition, and restoring them safely to our arms—upon the agreeable prospect of the security of our frontiers, since the nest of savages, that ravaged them, is demolished; and the enlargement of our settlements to the westward—upon the unanimity that now seems to be restored in the ministry at home, and the invaluable blessing of so good a king—upon the prospect of the preservation of the Protestant religion and liberty, even in Germany, where they were in the most imminent danger, by the glorious successes of the King of Prussia, that greatest of men—upon the probability of an honourable peace being restored to the earth, that men may no more kill one another—upon the encouragement we have bravely to venture our lives in defence of our country, if it should again stand in need of our assistance —and especially upon the astonishing goodness and grace of God, who is the author of all these agreeable occurrences, and has once more shown mercy to a people deserving of his wrath. Let such things as these be the delightful materials of your meditations and thanksgivings this day. This duty is so pleasing, that methinks I may expect an universal compliance. Methinks it must be pleasing even to a depraved heart, that is averse to the other duties of religion. HALLELUJAH! "Praise ye the LORD; for it is *good* to sing praises unto our God; for it is *pleasant;* and praise is *comely.*" Psalm cxlvii. 1.

But what if I should tell you, that repentance, that broken-hearted, bitter, mortifying duty, repentance, is a very proper and seasonable duty, even upon this day of rejoicing? My text authorizes me to tell you this; and this is the only particular in it that I have now time to take any further notice of. "There," says the Lord to the Jews, that is, in your own country, when delivered from your enemies, and restored to my favour, and a prosperous state, "*there* shall ye remember your ways, and all your doings, wherein ye have been defiled; and ye shall loathe* yourselves in your own sight, for all your evils that ye have committed."

There is something generous and noble in such a repentance. To repent under the rod; to be sorry for the crime, when about to be executed for it; to humble ourselves and mourn, when feeling the frowns of Heaven; this argues nothing great or generous; this may proceed from an aversion and fear of the punishment, and not of the offence; all this may be merely the effect of self-love, that mean, sneaking passion, which restrains its full power even in infernal spirits; but it is no certain evidence of the least genuine regard to God, or love to holiness. But to be sorry for sin against a *sin-pardoning* God—to repent with a pardon in our hands—to bewail our crimes when we are delivered from the punishment of them—to loathe ourselves for our abominations, when God loves us notwithstanding—to refuse joy, and melt into tears of penitential sorrow upon a day of rejoicing, because we have so basely and ungratefully treated that gracious Being, who has given us cause of joy; to be unable to forgive ourselves such a course of conduct, though God forgives it; nay, to be the more displeased and implacable against ourselves, because we have sinned against a God who is so merciful as to forgive us after all; this is genuine repentance indeed: it shows true greatness of mind, and sincere abhorrence of sin in itself, as base in its own nature: it argues a real concern for the honour of God, and a generous, disinterested love to him and holiness. This is repentance that will stand the test. And oh! that divine grace would this day produce it in the heart of

---

* The original word ܢܩܘܛ is very strong; and signifies *to be quite tired of, or surfeited with a person or thing—to loathe them as being irksome and disgusting —to be grieved—to abominate.* Ezek. xx. 43.

each of us! This would not damp the joy of this day, but render it more refined and elevated. The tears of such a repentance are agreeable bitter-sweets; and to feel a hard, selfish heart broken with it, is a most delightful sensation; as every evangelical penitent knows in some measure by experience. Oh! can we bear the thought of ever sinning more against our gracious guardian, God? If we have any sense of honour or gratitude within us, his goodness will certainly do what all his judgments have failed to do, that is, turns us all from our evil ways, to love and serve him for the future. God grant that it may have this effect, *for his own name's sake!* Amen.

SERMON LXXII.

PRACTICAL ATHEISM, IN DENYING THE AGENCY OF DIVINE PROVIDENCE, EXPOSED.

ZEPHANIAH I. 12.—*And it shall come to pass at that time, that I will search Jerusalem with candles, and punish the men that are settled on their lees; that say in their heart, the* LORD *will not do good, neither will he do evil.**

WHOEVER takes a review of the state of our country, for about two years past, or observes its present posture, must be sensible, that matters have gone very ill with us, and that they still bear a threatening aspect. If our country be entirely under the management of blind chance, according to the uncomfortable doctrines of Atheists and Epicureans, alas! we have reason to be alarmed; for the wheel of fortune has begun to turn against us. If all our affairs be entirely dependent upon natural causes, and wholly subject to the power and pleasure of mortals, it is time for us to tremble; for the arm of flesh has been against us. But if our land be a little province of Jehovah's empire; if all natural causes be actuated, directed, and overruled by his superintending providence; if all our affairs be under his sovereign management, and all our calamities, private and public, be the chastisements of his hand—if, I say, this be the case in fact, as every man believes and wishes, then, it is high time for us to acknow-

* Hanover, April 4, 1756.—Nassau Hall, Nov. 23, 1759.

ledge it, and be deeply sensible of it, and solicitously to inquire how we have incurred the displeasure of our gracious and righteous Governor, that we may amend our conduct, and labour to regain his favour.

And, after a very serious inquiry, I could discover nothing more likely to be the cause of our present calamities from the divine hand, than the general insensibility and practical disbelief of the Providence of God, that prevail among us. This, I apprehend, is the epidemical disease of the age, and is likely to prove fatal, without a timely remedy. Secondary causes are advanced to the throne of God, and the administration of the world is put into their hands, in his stead; feeble, precarious mortals set up for independency, and would manage their affairs themselves, without a proper subordination to that power by whom they live, move, and have their being. If blessings fall to their lot, they ascribe the honour to themselves: or, if they meet with mortifications and calamities, some poor creature must bear the blame; and they will not realize the hand of Providence in such things. I do not mean that the doctrine of divine providence is not an article of our public and professed faith; or that we avow it as our belief, that God has nothing to do with our affairs or the kingdoms of men. But I mean, the temper and conduct of multitudes is equivalent to a professed disbelief of divine providence; or, in the words of my text, "they say," in *their hearts*, "the Lord will not do good, neither will he do evil;" that is, he does not concern himself, one way or other, with human affairs. This they say, in *their hearts;* this is the language of their temper, though with their lips they profess quite the contrary.

This practical Atheism brought the judgments of God upon the Jews, which are so terribly denounced against them by the prophet Zephaniah; and were fully executed, a little time after, in the Babylonish captivity. To that period of national desolation my text refers. "It shall come to pass at that time, that I will search Jerusalem with candles;" I will make the strictest search in every corner and apartment of the city, like persons that search a room with lighted candles. "And I will punish the men that are settled upon their lees;" such men will I find out, wherever they lurk; and no one shall escape. By their being *settled on their lees*, we may understand their riches; for wine grows rich by being kept on the lees. So, by a long scene of peace and prosperity, the inhabitants of Jerusalem were arrived to very great riches: or it may signify a state of security; like wine settled on the lees, they have been undisturbed; they are not moved with the threatenings or judgments of God, which hang over them; and, therefore, they are easy, and sunk in security and luxury. In both these senses, this metaphorical expression may be understood in Jeremiah, " Moab hath been at ease from his youth; and he hath *settled on his lees:*" Jer. xlviii. 11. That is, the kingdom of Moab hath enjoyed a long series of peace and prosperity, and this has advanced them to riches and pleasure; and they are dissolved in ease and luxury. They had not experienced the calamities of war; or, as it is there added, "he hath not been emptied from vessel to vessel, neither hath he gone into captivity;" he hath not been tossed from country to country, but enjoyed a peaceable settlement in his own land for a length of years; or this phrase, "the men that are settled on their lees," may be rendered, with little alteration, "the men that are curdled or corrupted on their lees;"* and then it denotes their corrupt state; they were, as it were, settled and stagnated in their sins: these filthy dregs are mingled and incorporated with their body politic; and they were become a mere mass of corruption; and they must be shaken and tossed with divine judgments, to purge out their filth. Wars and calamities in the moral world are as necessary as storms and tempests in the natural, to keep the sea and air from putrefying; and a constant calm would introduce a general corruption. The mire and dirt must be cast out; which cannot be done without casting the whole body into a violent ferment and commotion.

"I will punish," says Jehovah, "I will punish the men that are settled on their lees." Though I am not fond of a parade of learning in popular discourses, yet it may be worth while to make this criticism, that the word here rendered, "I will *punish*," is in the original Hebrew, the language in which the Old Testament was written, "I will visit."* And this word is very often used to denote the punishments of the Divine hand; and sometimes it is so rendered, "Shall I not *visit* for these things, saith the LORD? Shall not my soul be avenged on such a nation as this?" Jer. v. 9. And this word suggests to us, that sinners are apt to look upon God *as far from them;* they flatter themselves he will let them alone in their sinful security, and that his judgments will always keep at a distance from them; But, says God, I will pay them a *visit:* I will come upon them unexpectedly with the terrors of my displeasure, and let them know, to their surprise, that I am not so far off as they imagine.

This sense is very pertinent in my text, where it is made one part of the character of these devoted Jews, "That they say in their hearts, the LORD will not do good, neither will he do evil." Men are often said in Scripture to say that *in their hearts,* which is their secret thought, or their inward temper; that which is their governing

פקד *

principle, and which directs their practice; though they dare not express it in words, or though it be quite contrary to their outward profession, and the declaration of their lips. To a heart-searching God, the temper of the mind, and the principle of action, is more than equivalent to the strongest declaration in words; and by this he judges of men, and not by the outward appearances and pretensions. To this purpose you read in Ezekiel, "Thus have ye *said*, O house of Israel." But how does this appear? Why, says God, "I knew the things that *come into your mind*, every one of them." Ezek. xi. 5. "You never may have said such a thing in *words*, but it has been in your *thoughts*; it has been in the temper of your hearts; and that is what I regard; that language is very intelligible to me."

Hence, my brethren, you see the charge here brought against the Jews amounts to this, that their temper and practice were such as would not at all agree to the practical belief of a providence. They thought and acted, as if it were their real and professed belief, that the Lord would do neither good nor evil, nor meddle with human affairs. If one should judge of their creed by their practice, he would be apt to conclude it was an article of their faith, that Jehovah had abdicated the throne of the universe, and that the blessings and calamities of life were the mere effects of secondary causes, without the influence, direction, or control of an all-ruling Providence.

This is often represented as the secret sentiment of wicked men, and a special cause of the judgments of God upon guilty nations.

You may see their reasoning dressed in all the pomp of language by Eliphaz, who censoriously charges Job with this atheistic notion. "Thou sayest, how doth God know? Can he judge through the dark cloud? Thick clouds are a covering to him, that he seeth not; and he walketh" at ease, without troubling himself with the affairs of mortals, "in the circuit of heaven." Job xxii. 13, 14. David also represents the preposterous ungodly as querying in this infidel strain—"How doth God know? and is there knowledge in the Most High?" Ps. lxxiii. 11. "They slay the widow and the stranger, and murder the fatherless; yet they say the LORD shall not see; neither shall the God of Jacob regard." Ps. xciv. 6, 7. An arrogant self-sufficiency, and a practical renunciation of divine providence, have brought the judgments of Heaven upon many a powerful nation. Why was Egypt destroyed? It was for her pride in saying, "My river," the river Nile, (on which the land depended for its fruitfulness,) "my river is mine own; and I have made it for myself." Ezek. xxix. 3. When God denounces his judgments against Tyrus, that centre of trade and riches, and mart of nations, it was because she had said in her heart, "I am a God;" I am independent, and owe no subjection to any superior power. But how mortifying is that question, "Wilt thou yet say before him that slayeth thee, I am a God?" alas! you must then lay aside your airs of deity, and own your entire dependence. Ezek. xxviii. 2, 6, 7, 9. Why was Nebuchadnezzar struck with a melancholy madness, and transformed into a brute? It was because he had presumed to speak in this uncreature-like language, "Is not this great Babylon, that *I* have built by the might of *MY* power for the honour of *MY* majesty?" Dan. iv. 30. Observe what stress he lays upon the little, proud monosyllables *I* and *MY*. Daniel, that honest courtier, who had not learned to flatter even kings and monarchs, assigns this as the reason of the destruction of Babylon, and the haughty Belshazzar. "Thou has not humbled thine heart; but thou hast lifted up thine heart against the Lord of heaven; and the God in whose hand thy breath is, and whose are all thy ways:" that is, the God on whom thou art wholly dependent, "hast thou not glorified." Dan. v. 22, 23. But this atheistical insolence appears nowhere with more pride and self-sufficiency, and is nowhere more signally mortified than in the haughty Assyrian monarch, of whom you read in the tenth chapter of Isaiah. Hear the language of his arrogance: "By the strength of *my* hand have I done it; and by *my* wisdom; for I am prudent: and I have removed the bounds of the people, and have robbed their treasures; and I have put down the inhabitants like a valiant man." Isa. x. 13. And was he, indeed, that Godlike, independent, self-sufficient being he took himself to be? Does the God of heaven pronounce him such, and confirm his claim? No. What contempt does he pour upon him! "O, Assyrian," says he, "the rod of mine anger, and the staff in their hand is mine indignation." Ver. 5. He is but a poor passive instrument in my hand, to chastise and punish guilty nations. And "shall the axe boast itself against him that heweth therewith? or shall the saw magnify itself against him that shaketh it? as if the rod should shake itself against them that lift it up; or, as if the staff should lift up itself, as if it were no wood." Isa. x. 15. What mortifying images are these, to represent this haughty conqueror! "Wherefore, it shall come to pass that when the Lord hath performed his whole work of judgment upon Mount Zion, and on Jerusalem," for which he hath raised him up and commissioned him, "then will I punish the fruit of the stout heart of the king of Assyria, and the glory of his high looks." Isa. x. 12.

In short, my brethren, this atheistical affectation of independency, and secret or practical renunciation of divine providence, is the fatal thing that generally overturned the empires, and impoverished, enslaved, and ruined the nations of the earth. This prevailed even among the Jews, the peculiar people of God, and brought his vengeance upon them: even *they* had learned to speak in this atheistical strain, "The LORD hath forsaken the earth, and the LORD seeth not." Ezek. ix. 9.

And, I am afraid, it is for this that Virginia now totters. This is the source of those numerous filthy streams of vice and impiety, which are likely to overwhelm us, and open the flood-gates of divine vengeance. Jehovah, who hears and understands the significant language of the heart and practice, no doubt hears this blasphemy whispered in every corner of our country, "We have nothing to do with Him. The sun, and clouds, and earth conspire to produce food for us; but what hand has *He* in all this? Many parts of our country are languishing under the effects of a severe drought; and the French and Indians are invading our territories, and murdering our fellow-subjects; but what has God to do in all this? We will fight it out with them ourselves, flesh with flesh; and let Him look on as an idle spectator." Horrid language, indeed! and, perhaps, the most audacious sinner among us would not venture to express it with his lips. But, what says the inward temper—what says the practice of our countrymen? This shall be our present inquiry; and for this purpose, I shall,

First, Offer a few arguments to establish the doctrine of a divine providence over the affairs of men, and particularly in national blessings and calamities. I will,

Secondly, Point out some things in the temper and conduct of our countrymen, which argue a secret and practical disbelief of this doctrine. And,

Thirdly, Expose the aggravated wickedness of such a disbelief.

My design, in the whole, is not so much to convince

your understanding, as to impress your hearts with a sense of the divine government over the world. You already speculatively believe it; but the grand defect lies in the efficacy of this belief on your hearts and lives; and this I would willingly supply. It is but a little one, in so narrow a sphere, can do, to reform the country in general, in this particular; and truly this is a painful reflection to him, that, in an agony of zeal, would sometimes wish for a voice to reach every corner of the land, and address all the inhabitants upon this point. But since the extensive benevolence of my soul, in this particular, cannot be gratified, I would at least exert all my little influence among you, my dear people, to banish this atheistic spirit from among you, and prevent your concurring to the destruction of your country, by indulging in it. Therefore attend, while, in the first place, I offer a few arguments, to establish the doctrine of a divine providence over the affairs of men, and particularly in national and public blessings and calamities.

For the proof of this, I am more at a loss what arguments to select out of a great number, than how to invent them. We may argue from the perfections of God, and his relations to us. Can we imagine, that a God of infinite knowledge, power, wisdom, and goodness, would sit idle on the throne of the universe, and be an unconcerned, inactive spectator of his own creatures? Would he make such a world as this, and then cast it off his hand, as an abandoned orphan, and never look after it more? Had he no wise and good designs in the production of this vast and curious frame of things? And will he leave these designs to be accomplished or blasted by chance, or the humours or caprice of mortals? We may argue from the natural dependence of creatures upon the supreme cause, that he did not invest them with the incommunicable attribute of self-sufficiency; but they must depend in acting on Him, on whom they depend for existence. We may argue from our confessed obligations to religion, and the worship of God: if there should be such a thing as religion, there must be a Providence; for it is plain, that if God has nothing to do with us, we have nothing to do with him. Where there is no dependence, there should be no acknowledgment; where there is no beneficence, there should be no gratitude. This is so evident, that Cicero, a heathen, expresses it in the strongest terms. I shall give you a translation of his words. "If," said he, "the gods neither can nor will assist us, nor take any care of us; if they take no notice what we do, and nothing can proceed from them which affects the life of man, why should we pay them worship and honour? why should we pray to them?"*

If I should go about formally to prove this doctrine by particular quotations from Scripture, it would be to insult you, as entirely ignorant of your Bibles. How often do you there find the supreme dominion of Providence over the world asserted in the strongest terms? How often are personal and national blessings and calamities ascribed to divine agency? Rain and fruitful seasons, drought and famine, sickness and health, peace and war, poverty and riches, promotion and abasement, all such events are uniformly represented as at the disposal of the great Lord of the universe. Nay, his Providence is expressly said to

---

* Sin autem Dii neque possunt nos juvare, nec volunt, nec curant omnino; nec quid agamus animadvertunt, nec est quod ab his ad hominum vitam permanere possit: quid est, quod ullos Diis immortalibus cultus, honores, preces adhibeamus? De Nat. Deor. In another place he says, Epicurus sustulit omnem funditus religionem; nec manibus, ut Xerxes; sed rationibus, Deorum immortalium templa et aras evertit. Quid est enim, cur Deos ab hominibus colendos dicas, cum Dii non modo homines non colant, sed omino nihil curent, nihil agant?—

be extended to the hairs of our heads, to young ravens and sparrows, to the lily and grass of the field. And can we then suppose, that he takes no care of men, or of kingdoms and nations? In short, this doctrine is true, or our Bibles are good for nothing; for there is nothing they more frequently and strongly assert.

The testimony of Scripture is so plain, and I have insisted upon it so much, in your hearing, that I shall say no more upon it at present; but I shall produce a class of new and unexpected witnesses to this truth; I mean the heathens, who generally had nothing but the light of Nature for their teacher. Their evidence may be attended with sundry advantages. It will be new to most of you who have not opportunity of perusing their writings: and therefore may make deeper impressions on your minds. It will show you, that the substance of this truth is so evident, that even the light of Nature could discover it, without the special help of Revelation—and it may put you, that call yourselves Christians, to the blush, to find even heathens exceed you in a full persuasion of this truth, and perhaps a practical regard to it.

I shall begin with such heathen witnesses as are recorded in sacred history, sundry of whom have some glimmering light from Revelation, or from their conversation with the Jews.

Let us first hear the extorted confession of that proud, but mortified monarch, Nebuchadnezzar. Daniel iv. 34, &c. "I Nebuchadnezzar lifted up mine eyes unto heaven, and I blessed the Most High, and praised and honoured him that liveth for ever, whose dominion is an everlasting dominion, and his kingdom is from generation to generation. And all the inhabitants of the earth are reputed as nothing: and he doeth according to his will in the army of heaven, and among the inhabitants of the earth; and none can stay his hand, or say unto him, what doest thou? and those that walk in pride, he is able to abase." God complains of that mighty conqueror Cyrus, who was the executioner of his justice upon the powerful Babylonian empire, and many other nations, "I have girded thee, though thou hast not known me." Isaiah xlv. 5. Yet we find even this heathen monarch, at least once, ascribing all his victories to the God of heaven, in his edict for the dismission of the Jews, and the rebuilding of the temple. Ezra i. 2. "Thus saith Cyrus, King of Persia, the Lord God of heaven hath given me all the kingdoms of the earth:" I acknowledge my universal empire is his gift. Hear also Nebuzar-adan upon this head, the general of the King of Babylon. "The Lord thy God (says he to Jeremiah) hath pronounced this evil upon this place: now the Lord hath brought it, and done according as he hath said: because ye have sinned against the Lord, and have not obeyed his voice: therefore this thing has come upon you." You see, my brethren, a heathen could instruct many of our countrymen who are professed Christians, that their sin is the cause of their national calamities. Josephus informs us, that Titus the Roman general, when he took a view of the prodigious strength of Jerusalem, acknowledged that all the force of the Roman army would not have been able to take it, had not the providence of God been upon his side, and against the devoted Jews.

But let us next hear heathens speak their own minds in their own language and writings. Plato, a Greek philosopher, above two thousand years ago, teaches us, "that all things are disposed by him, who takes care of the whole universe for the safety and advantage of the whole; the force and efficacy of whose providence doth diffuse itself through all parts of the universe, according to their nature."* "Shall we not affirm," says he, "with our ancestors, that *mind* and a certain disposing wisdom, does govern?† The Divine mind disposes all things in the best order, and is the cause of all things; and disposes all things in that manner which is best."‡ He also asserts, that it was the doctrine of Ulysses and Socrates as well as his own, "that we cannot so much as move without God." Thus, you see, Plato's evidence is full to the purpose.

The next I shall introduce, is Horace, a Roman poet; and though an epicurean in other things, he very expressly acknowledges a Providence over the kingdoms of the earth and human affairs. "Kings," says he, "have authority over their proper subjects; but Jove (that is the heathen name for Supreme Being) has authority over the kings themselves."§ He asserts, that he alone exercises an equal government over earth and sea, over ghosts and the regions of the dead, over gods and mortals, or, in our style, over men and angels.‖ Nay, he expressly tells the Romans, who then ruled the world, that they had the

---

* Πείθωμεν τὸν νεανίαν τοῖς λόγοις ὡς τῷ τοῦ παντὸς ἐπιμελουμένῳ πρὸς τὴν σωτηρίαν καὶ ἀρετὴν τοῦ ὅλου πάντ' ἐστὶ συντεταγμένα, ὧν καὶ τὸ μέρος εἰς δύναμιν ἕκαστον τὸ προσῆκον πάσχει καὶ ποιεῖ. De Leg. Lib. x. Gale. Part III. p. 471.

† Νοῦν καὶ φρόνησίν τινα θαυμαστὴν συντάττουσαν διακυβερνᾷν. Phileb. Gale ib. p. 469.

‡ Νοῦς ἐστὶν ὁ διακοσμῶν τε καὶ πάντων αἴτιος—τόν γε νοῦν κοσμοῦντα πάντα κοσμεῖν καὶ ἕκαστον τιθέναι ταύτῃ, ὅπῃ ἂν βέλτιστα ἔχῃ. Phaedo, Gale, p. 478.

§ Regum timendorum in proprios greges;
Reges in ipsos imperium est Jovis.—Lib. iii. Car. 1.

‖ Qui terram inertem, qui mare temperat
Ventosum, et umbras, regnaque tristia,
Divosque mortalesque turbas
Imperio regit unus aequo.—Lib. iii. Car. 4.
Dis te minorem quod geris, imperas—
Di multa neglecti dederunt
Hesperiae mala luctuosae.—Ib. Car. 8.

superiority among men, because they behaved themselves inferior to the divine Being; and that the reason of the calamities their country groaned under, was, their neglect of God.

But the principal authority I shall produce is that of Cicero,—one of the greatest men that any age has produced; a great statesman and politician, a Roman senator, and one that sustained the consulship with great honour, which was the highest dignity in that commonwealth. I have been not a little surprised to hear him speak in such strains as these:—"This," says he, "has been the persuasion of our citizens from the beginning, that the gods are the proprietors and rulers of all things; and that those things which are done, are done by their judgment and power; that they are very kind to mankind, and inspect every man's character, what he does, what he commits, with what mind, with what piety, he worships; and that they make a distinction between good and bad men."* He calls "Jove the greatest and best of beings, by whose nod and pleasure, the heaven, the earth, and seas are ruled; which frequently, with violent winds and hurricanes, or with excessive heat, or intolerable cold, has afflicted men, demolished cities, and destroyed the fruits of the earth; and who, on the other hand, gives us all our blessings; the light we enjoy, and the breath we draw."†

* Sit hoc jam à principio persuasum civibus, Dominos esse omnium rerum, ac moderatores Deos, eaque quæ geruntur, eorum geri judicio, ac numine: eosdemque optimè de genere hominum mereri, et qualis quisque sit, quid agat, quid in se admittat, quâ mente, quâ pietate religiones colat, intueri; piorumque et impiorum habere rationem. De Leg.

† Jupiter opt. max. cujus nutu et arbitrio cœlum, terra mariaque reguntur, sæpe ventis vehementioribus, aut immoderatis tempestatibus, aut nimio calore, aut intolerabili frigore hominibus nocuit, urbes delevit, fruges perdidit—at contra commoda quibus utimur; lucemque quâ fruimur, spiritumque quem ducimus, ab eo nobis dari, atque impartiri videmus Orat. pro Rosc.

The Romans, who were at first but a little savage village of banditti and run-aways, had conquered the world, and advanced themselves to universal empire; and this he expressly ascribes to the providence of God, and their own piety. The following passage deserves the attention of even an improved Christian. "Who is there so mad," says he, "that when he takes a view of the heavens, does not perceive that there is a God, and that should think those things which are made with so much wisdom, that human art can hardly attain the knowledge of their order and revolutions, were made by chance: or that having discovered that there is a God, does not also discover, that it is by his providence that this whole empire was founded, increased, and preserved? We may love ourselves," says he to the Roman senate, "as much as we will: but we must own, that we have not conquered the Spaniards by our number, nor the Gauls by our strength, nor the Carthaginians by our policy, nor the Greeks by our learning, nor the natives of this country, Italy: but we have conquered them only by our piety and religion; and by this wisdom only, namely, that we have discovered and acknowledged, that all things are governed by the providence of God; by this wisdom only, have we overcome all nations."* What an humble, creature-like declaration is this! and how may we be surprised to hear

---

* Quis est tam vecors, qui aut, cum suspexerit in cælum, Deos, esse non sentiat, et ea, quæ tantâ mente fiunt, ut, vix quisquam arte ulle ordinem rerum, et, vicissitudinem persequi possit casu fieri putet; aut cum Deos esse intellexerit, non intelligat, eorum numine hoc totum imperium esse natum, et auctum, et retentum? Quàm volumus licet, P. C. ipsi nos amemus: tamen nec numero Hispanos, nec rebore Gallos, nec calliditate Pœnos, nec artibus Græcos, nec denique hoc ipso ejus gentis, ac terræ domestico, nativoque sensu, Italos ipsos ac Latinos, sed pietate ac religione; atque hâc unâ sapientiâ, quod Deorum immortalium numine omnia regi, gubernarique perspeximus, omnes gentes nationesque superavimus. De Harusp.

it from the mouth of a heathen, when we hear so little of this language in a Christian country! The Roman commonwealth was in great danger by the conspiracy of Catiline; and Cicero had been successfully active in detecting and suppressing it; and he promises the Romans that he would put an end to it. "But I do not promise this," says he, "trusting in my own prudence, or in human councils; but in God—and you ought to pray, that he who has made your city so beautiful, so flourishing, and powerful, would defend it, and subdue its enemies by sea and land."* And when the conspiracy was happily suppressed by his vigilance, he gratefully acknowledges a divine Providence in it. "Who† is there," says he, "O Romans, so averse from truth, so presumptuous, so bereft of his senses, as to deny, that all these things which we see, and especially this city, are managed by the power and providence of God! If I should say that it was I that defeated the conspirators, I should take too much upon me, and my arrogance would be insufferable. It was the Supreme God, it was *he*, it was *he* that defeated them, it was his will to preserve our capitol—his will to preserve this city, and these temples—his will that you should be all safe. It was under the conduct of the immortal God, that I formed this

---

* Quæ quidem, ego nec meâ prudentia, neque humanis consiliis fretus. polliceor vobis, Quirites, sed multis et uon dubiis Deorum immortalium significationibus—quos precari, venerari, atque implorare debeatis, ut quam urbem pulcherrimam, florentissimam, potentissimamque esse voluerunt, hanc, omnibus hostium copiis, terra marique superatis—defendant.

† Quis potest esse, Quirites, tam aversus à vero, tam præceps, tam mente captus, qui neget, hæec omnia, quæ videmus, præcipueque hanc urbem, Deorum immortalium nutu atque potestate administrari? Ego si me restitisse dicam, nimium mihi sumam, et non sim ferendus; Ille, ille Jupiter restitit: ille capitolium, ille hæc templa, ille hanc urbem, ille vos omnes salvos esse voluit. Diis ego immortalibus ducibus, hanc mentem, Quirites, voluntatemque suscepi, atque ad hoc tanta indicia perveni.

judgment and determination, and made such a discovery of the plot."

In this manner, my brethren, does one of the greatest men that ever Rome was adorned with, acknowledge the hand of Providence in all his successes; and though vanity was remarkably his foible, he was ashamed to arrogate the glory to himself. When shall our newspapers and political writings be so far reformed, as to speak the language of heathens? Alas! they are stuffed with such empty boasts and bravadoes about our powerful fleet, our brave officers, and so forth, as would have been judged impious and intolerably insolent, in heathen Rome. To acknowledge the divine hand in our victories and defeats, to profess a dependence upon him for success, and acknowledge the utter insufficiency of all our forces without him; this is unpolite and unfashionable; this, to be sure, must be the canting language of an enthusiast, or a Presbyterian; whereas one would think it would be the natural language of every creature. Christians! Protestants! if ye will not learn the doctrine of an all-ruling Providence from your Bibles, learn it, at least, from Plato and Cicero. Can you shut your eyes against the light of nature and of Revelation too, when they mingle their beams, and pour upon you in a flood of day?

Were it necessary to enlarge upon this head, I might add a great many more quotations from sundry of the ancient poets and philosophers;* and I might also show you that this was the belief, not only of the learned men in the heathen world, but of the vulgar or common people in general. This appeared from their anxious con-

* Plato says,—σώζει τὰ τοι αὗτα [scil. ὅσια, he particularly refers to prayer and sacrifice] τοὺς τε ἰδίους οἴκους καὶ τὰ κοινὰ τῶν πόλεων τὰ δ' ἐναντία τῶν κεχαρισμένων, ἀσεβῆ ἃ δὴ καὶ ἀνατρέπει ἅπαντα καὶ ἀπόλλυσιν. Holiness preserves our houses and public communities; but that which is contrary to it, is impious, and subverts and destroys every thing. Euthyphro.

sultations of oracles, their prayers and sacrifices, before they entered into war; and their religious festivals and thank-offerings after victory. And you can hardly meet with one of their authors, but what is full of such accounts. And will not Rome and Greece rise up in judgment against the men of our country, who cast off a practical regard to God in their expeditions, and seem desirous that the arm of flesh alone should fight it out, without the interposition of a superior cause? From this I naturally proceed,

Secondly, To point out some things in the temper and conduct of our countrymen, which argue a secret and practical disbelief of the doctrine of divine Providence. And these, alas! are easily discovered.

"First, Do you think there would be so little prayer among us, if we were generally affected with this truth? If we looked upon the concurrence of Providence of any importance, should we not think it worth while to pray for it, with our most importunate cries? We look to our government to make provision; we try to enlist men; we regard their number, courage, and conduct; their arms and ammunition; but who is there in our land that looks to the Lord? Where are the Abrahams among us, to intercede for our Sodom? Where our Moseses to hold up the hands of prayer, while our forces are engaged? There are, I doubt not, a few persons, and perhaps a few families, here and there, that thus show their friendship for their country; and there are multitudes that seem to join in those forms of prayer for the public, which are used in the places where they respectively attend. But it is most evident, there is but very little of a spirit of prayer in our land. Alas! how many private persons live in the habitual neglect of secret devotion—how many families live and die together, without any appearances of family-religion?

In short, there is but little prayer to be heard in our country on any account; but few that earnestly cry to God for themselves. And how few then, O my neglected country! how few appear as thy advocates at the throne of grace! How few prayers are offered up for *thee!* Now, when men will not so much as earnestly ask the alliance of Providence, is it not plain that they have very slight thoughts of it, and do not seriously believe it? O sirs! it will never be well with our country, until we learn to bow the knees, until poor strangers to the throne of grace begin to frequent it, and until the voice of prayer be heard from every corner of our land. Let others do as they will; but as for us, my brethren, let us become a little congregation of praying souls; and we may do more real service to our country, than an equal number of armed men.

Secondly, Is not the general indulgence of vice, and neglect of religion, a plain evidence of the general disbelief of a divine Providence over our country? That wickedness is almost universally triumphant, and practical religion and the concerns of eternity are generally neglected, is too evident to require a formal proof. Take a journey through our country, mingle in company, enter into families, observe the conduct of men in their retirements; and you will soon meet with the disagreeable conviction. If there be much religion in Virginia, I am sure it is not the religion of our Bibles—it is not the religion of Jesus; it is a religion that consists in swearing, drinking, quarrelling, carousing, luxury, and pleasure—in fraud, covetousness, and the grossest vices and impieties—it is a cold, careless, immoral, prayerless religion; or, at best, it is a religion made up of a few lukewarm, insipid, Sunday formalities of devotion, without life, without spirit, without earnestness. And would it be thus, do you think, if men were deeply sensible that God exercises a providence over the kingdoms of the earth, to punish them for their sins? Would they dare to affront him thus, if they firmly believed that he would resent it in earnest? Or would they be so careless about securing his favour by a conscientious obedience? No; they would be solicitous, above all things, to keep upon good terms with their Supreme Ruler; and they would no more dare to provoke him, than they would set a train of powder under the foundations of their houses, to blow them up. But now they act as if it were their belief, that the Lord has forsaken the earth, and takes no notice of the conduct of the inhabitants; as if they had nothing to hope and nothing to fear from him; and therefore they may do what they please, and shift for themselves as they can.

Thirdly, Is not the general impenitence, notwithstanding the many public calamities under which our country has groaned, a melancholy evidence of this practical atheism? Judgments have crowded thick and heavy upon our land, these twelve months past. Our general has been most ingloriously defeated, and all our high hopes from that expedition mortified. Our northern forces, from which we had still higher expectations, returned, without carrying their designs into execution. The Indian savages, under French instigation, have laid a great part of our country desolate, and murdered many hundreds of our fellow-subjects, in one part or other; and they still continue their depredations and barbarities, and that generally with impunity. To all this I must add, that our promising expedition against the Shawaneese, is coming to nothing; an expedition on which the country has spent about six thousand pounds, and which seemed the best expedient to put an end to the inroads of the savages upon our ravished frontier. We were not without fears of disappointment from various causes: we were apprehensive that they might have heard of the design, and either deserted their towns, or so fortified themselves with the assistance of the French, as to be an over-match for our forces: these were plausible suppositions. But who would ever have suspected that the expedition should fail for want of provisions? that men, leaving a plentiful country, and about to march through a tedious and unknown wilderness, should not take a sufficient supply with them? Who would have thought that men in their senses would have been so stupid and improvident? To me, I must own, it looks like a judicial infatuation. Last summer, our men were killed by one another, in the ever-melancholy engagement on the banks of the Monongahela, and now a provoked God has let us see once more, that he needs not the instrumentality of enemies and arms to blast the expedition of a guilty people. By their own mismanagement, they defeat themselves, and disconcert their own schemes. In truth, my brethren, if there be a divine providence, I think it dreadfully evident that it is against us. All our most promising undertakings issue in disappointments; and nothing prospers that we take in hand. But to return—we have not only suffered by the calamities of war, but a great part of our country is languishing under the effects of a very severe drought, which we, in this neighbourhood, are so happy as to know but little of by experience. Now, if there be a providence, these calamities are inflicted upon us by a divine hand: they are not the random strokes of chance, or the effects of blind fate; but the chastisements or judgments of an angry God. And if he be the inflictor of them, it is certain he inflicts them for the sins of the land. It is sin, it is sin only, that can bring down punishments on the subjects of a just government. But is this generally believed? If it were, would it not strip impenitent sinners of their presumptuous airs, and bring them to the knee, as humble, broken-hearted penitents, at the feet of their injured Sovereign? If every one believed that *his* sins have had a share in bringing down the vengeance of Heaven upon his country, would he not smite upon his breast, and say, alas! what have I done? God be merciful to me a sinner! Would he not immediately attempt a reformation, which is the principal constituent of true repentance? But alas! have these calamities been thus improved by our countrymen? Produce me one instance of conversion, if you can, by all the terrors of war, and by all the alarming apprehensions of famine! Alas! in vain has the blood of our soldiers and fellow-subjects been shed —in vain has nature languished around us, and the earth denied its fruitfulness—in vain has the rod of divine indignation chastised us, if not one soul be brought to repentance by all these means. And if reformation be found impracticable, what must follow but destruction? God may bear long with a guilty people; and, indeed, he has done so with *us :* but he will take them in hand at length: and when he does take them in hand, he will make *thorough* work with them. If chastisement will not amend, vengeance shall destroy. And I am bold to pronounce, that you have no other alternative, but REPENT or PERISH. I will not presume to determine the time, the degree, or the circumstances; but I am bold to renew my declaration, that misery and ruin await our country, if we still continue incorrigibly impenitent. Men and money; arms, ammunition, and fortifications, courage, conduct, and skill, are all necessary for the defence of our land; but there is an unthought-of something as necessary as any, or all these, and that is REFORMATION—a general, public reformation: and without this, all other means will be to no purpose in the issue. I do not now take upon me to prophesy: I only draw a natural consequence from known premises; and infer, what *will be*, from what has *always been*. Thus God has always dealt with the kingdoms of the earth. these have always been the maxims of his providential government. The ruins of Egypt, Babylon, Rome, and many a flourishing city, country, and empire, proclaim this truth. And if we disregard it, it is well if it be not written in the ruins of Virginia ere long. My brethren I must speak to you without reserve: the general impenitence of our inhabitants, under all the providences of God to bring them to repentance, is by far the most discouraging symptom to me; much more so than our divided counsels, our routed armies, and our blasted schemes: indeed, I look upon it as the cause of all these. May I then hope to be heard, at least in the little circle of my own congregation, when, as an advocate for your country, I call you to repentance? O Sirs, you have carried the matter far enough; you have trifled with your God, and delayed your reformation long enough; therefore, from this moment commence humble penitents, and let your country and your souls suffer no more by your wilful wickedness. Whenever you recollect our past calamities, or whenever you meet with the like in time to come, immediately prostrate yourselves before the Lord; plead guilty; guilty; bewail your own sins: and bewail and mourn over the sins of the land. If even all this congregation should be enabled, by divine grace, to take this method, they might, in the sight of God, obtain the glorious character of *deliverers of their country.* Who knows but our Sodom might be spared, for the sake of a few such righteous persons?

Fourthly, Is not the general ingratitude a plain evidence of the general disbelief of a providential government over the world? My brethren, our blessings, in this country, have been distinguishing: the blessings of a good soil, and a healthy and temperate climate—the blessings of liberty, plenty, and a long peace—the blessings of a well-constituted government, and a gentle administration—the invaluable but despised blessings of the gospel of Christ; blessings public and private, personal and relative, spiritual and temporal: in short, it is hard to find a spot upon our globe more rich in blessings, all things considered. But how little gratitude to God for all these blessings? How little is his hand acknowledged in them? Men bless their own good fortune, their industry, or good management, but how few sincerely, and with their whole souls, bless their divine benefactor? Now if his agency were thoroughly believed, would they, could they be so stupidly ungrateful under the reception of so many blessings from him? No; their hearts must glow with love, and their lips must speak his praise.

Fifthly, How little serious and humble acknowledgment of the providence of God in our disappointments and mortifications, is to be found among us! Men murmur and fret in a sort of sullen stupidity; or they cast all the blame upon their fellow-creatures. Those that sneak at home, and know nothing of politics or war, will severely censure the men in power, for imprudent regulations, or negligence —military officers for their bad conduct, or soldiers for their cowardice. But who is it that sees and reveres the hand of an angry God in all this? Alas, the generality seem to think that the world is left to men, to manage as they please; and that God has nothing to do with it. They say in their hearts, "the Lord will not do good, neither will he do evil."

These things may suffice to prove the fact, that this practical atheism is very common and prevalent in our country: and now it is proper I should show the aggravations of it. I therefore proceed,

Thirdly, to expose the horrid wickedness of this atheistical temper and conduct.

And here, had I words gloomy enough to represent the most diabolical dispositions in the infernal regions, they would not be too black for my purpose. I shall throw sundry things together promiscuously upon this head, without any formal order. To deny the agency of Providence, is the most daring rebellion against the King of heaven: it is to abjure his government in his own territories, in his own world, which he has made: it is to draw away his subjects from their allegiance; and to represent him as a mere name; for what is his character as the ruler of the universe but an idle title, if he do not actually exercise a providence over it, but leaves his creatures to themselves, to worry and destroy one another, as they please? If he do not punish the kingdoms of the earth, for their sin; and if the blessings they enjoy, be not the gifts of his hand, it is not worth while to acknowledge his government: for of what benefit is that government that neither rewards nor punishes its subjects? But if God be indeed the author of these things, it must be the most unnatural rebellion, the blackest treason, to deny his agency. To be rejected in his own world by his own creatures—for the great Parent and support of nature to be renounced by the creatures, whom he supports in existence every moment—that all his chastisements, and all his blessings, should not be able to bring his own offspring to acknowledge him: what can be more shocking or provoking? This is also a most ungrateful wickedness. Alas! shall God so richly bless us from year to year; shall he so gently chastise us; and yet be forgotten, disregarded, unacknowledged? It is hard, indeed, if such a country full of blessings cannot bring us so much as dutifully and thankfully to acknowledge him. Alas! shall poor, subordinate, dependent creatures run away with all the glory, and still be made his rivals, or rather, entirely exclude him? What unnatural ingratitude is this? It is likewise intolerable pride and arrogance. Ye poor, precarious beings, that were nothing a little while ago, and that would relapse into nothing this moment, without the support of the divine hand; alas! will *ye* set up for independency and self-sufficiency? Are *you* capable of managing the world, and shifting for yourselves? And is the God, in whom you live, and move, and have your being, become a kind of superfluity to you? Can *you* carry on war, can *you* defend your country, and provide for yourselves without *him*? Will *you* usurp his throne, and set your "heart as the heart of God." Ezek. xxviii. 2. Alas! the province is too high for *you*. "Will *you* say in the hand of him that slayeth you, I am a god?" Ezek. xxviii. 9. What impiety and insolence; what arrogance and blasphemy is this? Will you substitute natural causes for your God, and ascribe all the events you meet with to their independent agency, when they are but the mere instruments of divine Providence? Can Jehovah bear with such a sacrilegious attempt upon the royalties of his crown? Again; this atheistical spirit is the source of all vice and irreligion. If men had an affecting belief, that "verily there is a reward for the righteous, verily there is a God that judgeth in the earth," Ps. lviii. 11; would they neglect him as they do, or would they so audaciously provoke him, and bid him defiance by their sins? No; a conviction of this would bring the sinner to his knee; it would restrain him from every thing that would displease him, and prompt him to every duty. But if the Lord hath forsaken the earth, then every man may consult his pleasure, and do what is good in his own eyes, without control. This, my brethren, as I observed, is the source of that torrent of wickedness, which has overwhelmed our country: mankind say in their hearts, that God will connive at their conduct, or that he takes no notice of it: and hence their presumptuous sin and impenitence. Which leads me to add, that such a spirit prevents the improvement and good effect of all the providences of God towards us and our country. Calamities may make us miserable, fretful, and impatient; but they can never bring us to reformation, and a genuine repentance for our sins against God, unless we are sensible that it is a provoked God that lays them upon us. The bounties of Providence may make us happy, wanton, proud, and self-confident; but they can never fire our hearts with gratitude, nor allure us to obedience, unless we receive them as from his gracious hand. It is the want of this, my brethren, that has rendered all the providence of God so useless to our land: hence it is, they have produced so few, if any, instances, of true conversion. And thus it will be, we shall but abuse mercy, and we never shall learn the art of extracting good out of evil, and profit by our afflictions till we learn this lesson.

And now, sirs, upon the whole, must you not shudder to think what a load of guilt lies upon our country, on account of this spirit of atheism that has spread over it? When the generality of the subjects turn rebels, and promise themselves impunity, is it not time for their Sovereign to come forth against them and make them sensible of his power and authority, to their cost? Is it not time for a neglected, disregarded, forgotten Deity, to take our country in hand, and extort from practical atheists a confession of his government by the pressure of their miseries? Will he always suffer himself to be denied and renounced in his own dominions? I say his *own* dominions; for, assume what airs you will, Virginia is a little province of his universal empire; and all the world shall know it, either by the terrors of his justice, or by our voluntary confession and cheerful subjection. If gentler measures will not do, he may employ French tyranny and Indian barbarity to bring down our haughty spirits, and cause us to own his government, and our dependence and subjection.

Are not some of us guilty of this epidemical, fashionable infidelity? Have you not lived in this world until this moment, without being sensible of that all-ruling Power, by which it is governed? Then you are to be ranked among the destroyers of your country. Alas! such persons are its worst enemies. Prepare, ye infidels, prepare for his judgments to teach you a more creature-like temper. Or if you escape his judgments in this life, prepare for those more dreadful punishments of the world to come, which will oblige the most rebellious spirit in hell to acknowledge that the Lord reigns.

Finally; amid all the tumults of this restless world—amid all the terror of war, and, in short, amid all the events of life of every kind, let us labour to impress our spirits with this truth, that all things are under the management of a wise and good God, who will always do what is best, upon the whole. This will be a source of obedience; this will teach us to turn the greatest miseries into blessings, and to derive good from evil; and this will be a sweet support, and afford us an agreeable calm, amid all the pressures and tossings of this boisterous world, till we arrive at the harbour of eternal rest.

SERMON LXXIII.

THE PRIMITIVE AND PRESENT STATE OF MAN COMPARED.

ROMANS v. 17.—*For if by one man's offence death reigned by one; much more they which receive* [the] *abundance of grace, and of the gift of righteousness, shall reign in life by one, Jesus Christ.**

THE ruin of mankind by the fall of Adam, and the method of redemption by Jesus Christ, are subjects of the utmost importance in the Christian religion: and it is necessary we should have some competent knowledge of them, and be suitably affected with them: otherwise, we cannot be recovered from the ruins of the grand apostacy, nor enjoy the salvation of the gospel. I do not mean, that it is absolutely necessary for any man, much less for plain and illiterate understandings, to know all the niceties of controversy, and to be able to solve all the difficulties and objections, which the ignorance, arrogance, or curiosity of wrangling and presumptuous disputants, have started upon these heads: but the substance and importance of the truths themselves, their principal consequences as to us, and the duties resulting from them; these we ought to understand and feel. This knowledge and sense of these things, is as necessary to our salvation, as a sense of sickness, and a knowledge of the means of cure, is to the recovery of the sick. And, whatever obscurity and perplexity attend these subjects, we have sufficient light

---

* Hanover, December 10, 1758.—Nassau Hall, December 14, 1760.

from our Bibles, from observation and experience, to obtain such a degree of knowledge and sense of them, as is sufficient for this purpose. These subjects, therefore, shall now employ an hour of your sacred time. And may the blessed Spirit of God enable me to discover, and you to receive, the knowledge of his own truths, without adulteration, without corrupt mixtures of human invention, and without partiality and self-flattery! and may He deeply impress our hearts with the knowledge we acquire, and make it a lively principle of practice!

The ruin and recovery of mankind, by the first and second Adam, is the subject of the apostle in the context. His immediate design is to show, the parity in some respects, and the disparity in others, between these two public persons.

We have an instance of this parity and disparity in my text. The instance of parity in this—That as the offence of Adam gave death an universal dominion over all his numerous posterity; so the grace and righteousness of Christ procure and bestow everlasting life to all those who receive these blessings. "As, by one man's offence, death reigned by one, so they, who receive the abundance of grace, and the gift of righteousness, shall reign in life by one, Jesus Christ."

The instance of disparity is this: The superior efficacy of the grace and righteousness of Christ to procure and bestow life, above that of the offence of Adam, to subject mankind to the dominion of death. "If, by one man's offence, death reigned, *how much more* shall they reign in life, who receive the abundance of grace, and of the gift of righteousness from Jesus Christ?" If the offence of Adam was sufficient for the condemnation of all his posterity, *how much more* sufficient is the grace and righteousness of the second Adam, to justify and save *all* that have an interest in him? The expression is very strong and emphatical—THE* ABUNDANCE of grace;" an overflowing, a redundance of grace; not only sufficient, but *more* than sufficient to repair all the ruinous consequences of Adam's fall; sufficient to procure more blessings, than he or his posterity would have enjoyed, even if he had never offended; and to render the *reign*, the *dominion* of life, more glorious and triumphant, than his sin rendered the reign or dominion of death dismal and irresistible. We may gain more by Jesus Christ, than we lost in Adam. He cannot only raise human nature out of its ruins, but repair it in a more glorious form, than that in which it came from the hands of its divine Author at first.

The two great truths which the Apostle has chiefly in view in my text, are these; that by the sin of Adam all mankind are subjected to the power of death; and, that all that accept of the blessings of redemption through Christ, are delivered from the death to which they are exposed by the sin of Adam, and also entitled to a more glorious and happy life, than that, which they lost by Adam's sin: or, in other words, that the blessings of redemption, by Christ, are even more than sufficient to recover us from all the ruinous consequences of the fall of Adam. These, I say, are the truths the apostle has chiefly in view: and these I intend chiefly to illustrate. But I would, by the bye, make some transient remarks on one or two strong and beautiful expressions, which the apostle uses in my text; and which are certainly worthy of notice.

"Death *reigned*"—how dreadfully striking is the re-

* I prefix the particle *the*, to point out the emphasis, answering to the original την, την περισσιαν. The word περισσιαι is to be joined with της δωρεας της δικαιοσυνης. The abundance, the mighty redundance, of the gift of righteousness!

presentation! Death is represented as a mighty all-conquering king, that reigned undethroned, uncontrolled, through a long succession of thousands of years, over all the sons of men, from generation to generation; keeping them in slavery and terror; arresting, imprisoning, stripping them of all their enjoyments, and depriving them even of their lives at pleasure. Death, in this sense, reigns king of kings, as well as of their subjects; the sovereign lord of absolute monarchs, as well as of their slaves; the conqueror of conquerors as well as of their helpless captives. The power of death is *royal*, the power of a *king*—he *reigns*. This wide world is his kingdom—the kingdom of death!—how shocking the idea!—and all mankind are his subjects, his slaves.

"*By one man's offence*, death reigned *by one.*" It was the one offence of one man that gave death his royal dominion. Then death was proclaimed and crowned king of our world, and mankind pronounced his subjects. Oh! the unspeakable mischiefs of that one offence!

But what a glorious contrast strikes our view, in the antithesis, as to those who receive the abundance of grace and the gift of righteousness! "They shall *reign*,"— they shall be made kings, invested with royal power and dignity. They shall reign *in life*—Life shall be the wide-extended territory over which they shall have full dominion: life shall be the furniture of their court, the ornament of their crown, the regalia of their reign. They shall reign in *life*, in opposition to the reign of death; they shall have dominion over that gloomy lord of the sons of Adam. The offspring of the dust, the dying children of Adam the sinner, the feeble mortals that were once the subjects, the slaves of the tyrant death, shall *reign in life,*

"High in salvation and the climes of bliss." *

* Milton.

What a glorious, surprising, miraculous advancement is this! and for this they are indebted, not to themselves, but to the second Adam, the Lord from heaven, who has conquered death for them, and dignified them with life and immortality. "They shall reign in life, *by one, Jesus Christ.*" One Jesus Christ is sufficient to accomplish this illustrious revolution. Oh! what wonders has he wrought! and how worthy is he to receive power, and riches, and wisdom, and strength, and honour, and glory, and blessing. Rev. v. 12.

The emphasis will appear still farther, if we take notice of the comparison implied in the text. If death reigned, *much more* shall they reign. If death reigned by one offence, *much more* shall they reign by the abundance of grace and of the gift of righteousness. If death reigned by one Adam, *much more* shall they reign by one Jesus Christ. He is much more able to quicken, to save, and glorify, than Adam was to kill and destroy. His spiritual children shall reign in life, *much more* absolutely, illustriously, and uncontrollably, than ever death reigned over the sons of Adam. What a glorious exaltation is this! To have the same command over life, as death has had over the enjoyments and lives of mankind—to be as victorious over death, and all its host of sickness and sorrow, as death once was over life and all its pleasures; what a grand and noble representation!*

I now proceed to the illustration of the great truths the apostle has chiefly in view in this verse; and I begin with the first.

That, by the sin of Adam, all mankind are subjected to the power of death.

---

* That St. Paul intended to lay an emphasis on the word *reigning*, appears from his frequent repetition of it in this chapter. Death reigned like a sovereign king, $\iota\beta\alpha\sigma\iota\lambda\epsilon\upsilon\sigma\epsilon\nu$, $\dot{o}$ $\theta\acute{a}\nu\alpha\tau o\varsigma$, from Adam to Moses, (ver. 14.) Sin reigned, $\iota\beta\alpha\sigma\iota\lambda\epsilon\upsilon\sigma\epsilon\nu$, by death. Grace might *reign* through righteousness unto eternal life, (v. 21.)

It is the more necessary to insist upon this, as the doctrine of original sin, as it is commonly called, is not only disputed in our age and country, but too generally denied, and represented as a Calvinistic fiction, supported neither by Scripture nor reason, inferring blasphemous reflections upon the divine perfections, and degrading the dignity of human nature.

We now hear panegyrics upon the powers of man, the dignity of his nature, and I know not what: as though these powers had never been shattered by the first fall. We often hear and read such harangues as these—"Can we suppose that a righteous and good God would inflict punishment upon millions of millions of his own creatures, for an offence committed by another so long before they had a being; an offence in which they had no concurrence, and which they could not possibly have prevented? Is this consistent with the mercy or the justice of God? What horrid ideas must this raise in our minds of our common Father, as an arbitrary, cruel tyrant, that dooms us to bear his displeasure for a crime in which we had no hand? Has not this doctrine a tendency to cool our love, and excite our horror of him, as the enemy of the race of man? And does it not also tend to cherish a mean and sneaking spirit, from an apprehension that we are degraded depraved creatures, instead of that conscious greatness of mind, which proceeds from a sense of the dignity of human nature?"

We are also told, "That as this is not the doctrine of reason, no neither is it that of revelation; that there are but few passages of Scripture that so much as seem to countenance it; and that these will easily admit of another sense: that this, however, cannot be the sense of them, because it is contrary to reason, which a revelation from God can never contradict."

A great deal to this purpose is pleaded; and the representation is so popular and pleasing, as flattering their vanity, that mankind are naturally disposed to embrace it: and those are looked upon as the generous friends of human nature, who entertain such high sentiments of it; whereas those who look upon mankind as a degraded race of creatures, are esteemed rigid, sour, malevolent creatures, that would dishonour the noble workmanship of God, and overwhelm themselves and others with melancholy.

But, let us not be deterred by this, from an impartial examination of the subject. It is likely that in this, as well as in other matters of difference, both parties have gone to extremes; and we are most likely to find the truth in the midway between them. Moderation is a virtue, and also a guide to truth; and may it always actuate and direct our minds!

You may observe, that it is not my present design, nor that of my text, to consider that part of original sin which consists in the corruption of our nature derived from Adam; but only that which consists in the imputation of his guilt to us, or our exposedness to punishment on account of his sin.

Here I would inquire, whether we do suffer punishment on account of Adam's first sin? and how far this punishment may justly extend?

To discover this, I shall compare the primitive and present state of our world, and of mankind in it, as it is represented to us by revelation, reason, experience, and observation.

If the present state of our world be the same with that in which Adam was created, and if all mankind now be placed in the same state and circumstances that he was placed in, while in innocence, then we may conclude, that his posterity do not suffer, or are not punished for his sin; or that the guilt of it is not imputed to them. But if our world is thrown into disorder since his fall, rendered less commodious and more injurious to mankind, and, as it were, branded with the displeasure of God; if mankind, since his fall, groan under a variety of miseries, to which man in his primitive state was not subject; miseries, which cannot justly be inflicted upon a race of innocent creatures, and which are evident indications and effects of divine vengeance; if these miseries are evidently inflicted upon mankind for the sin of their first father, and not their own; if they have lost that holiness which adorned human nature, when first formed, and are morally corrupt and depraved; if this, I say, be the case, then it is evident, we are a fallen race, and lie under the penal effects of Adam's offence.

Now, if we take a view of the primitive state of our world, and of man in it, as it is given us by the ancient Jewish historian and law-giver (Moses) in the beginning of Genesis, we shall find it vastly different from the present state.

In the primitive state, the world was so constituted, as to furnish man with the supports and comforts of life, without hard labour and toil. This is evident from the gracious grants made to the new-made man: "And God said, behold I have given you every herb bearing seed, which is upon the face of all the earth, and every tree, in which is the fruit of a tree yielding seed: to you it shall be for meat." Gen. i. 29. This is also evident, from the curse denounced upon the earth after man's fall. Gen. iii. 17–19. "Unto Adam God said, Because thou hast hearkened unto the voice of thy wife, and hast eaten of the tree of which I commanded thee, saying, Thou shalt not eat of it: cursed is the ground for thy sake; in sorrow shalt thou eat of it all the days of thy life. Thorns also and thistles shall it bring forth to thee—in the sweat of thy face shalt thou eat bread, till thou return unto the ground." This loss of fruitfulness in the earth, or its fruitfulness in thorns and thistles, and things of no use, this toil and sweat to procure even bread, the most common support of life, had no place in the state of innocence, because it is here expressly denounced as the punishment of Adam's sin. But that cannot be threatened or inflicted as a punishment of an offence, which the person endured before his offence. That the state of innocence was a state of ease and spontaneous plenty, we may infer also from the fatherly care of the Creator, in planting a garden in Eden, richly furnished with every tree pleasant to the eye, or good for food, and placing the man there to look after it, not for his toil, but for his pleasure, and to live upon the divine bounty, spontaneously springing out of the earth. Gen. ii. 8, 9.

This is one instance of the dissimilitude between the primitive state of our earth and the present. Instead of this universal fertility of the earth, and the spontaneous plenty of Eden, how great a part of the globe lies waste, in hideous, sandy deserts, in wildernesses of useless or noxious shrubs, in bleak and naked mountains, and horrid abrupt ridges or pyramids of barren rocks? What intemperate seasons, what parching droughts, and drowning rains, what nipping frosts and withering heats, what devastations by earthquakes and inundations, what blastings and mildews, what consumptions by wild beasts, by locusts, caterpillars, and swarms of nameless insects, are the fruits of the earth subject to? And what scanty harvests, what severe famines and dearths proceed from these causes? How many pine away and die by this scarcity? what coarse, insipid, and unwholesome provisions are a great part of mankind obliged to live upon, especially in the eternal winter of Lapland and Greenland, the burning, sandy wastes of Africa, and other barren, inhospitable climates? And is this the paradisaic state of our earth? Did it come out of the hands of its Maker exposed to such disorders, and so scantily furnished with provisions for the sustenance and comfort of its inhabitants? Does it appear like a region designed for the residence of a race of creatures in favour with their Creator? or, rather does it not appear, like the wilds of Siberia, a country into which criminals are transported, and which bears the evident marks of the displeasure of its Maker? Does not its present disordered state pronounce upon all the sons of Adam, the curse once denounced against Adam, "Cursed is the ground for thy sake?" May we not read this curse in every brier and bramble, in every tract of barren land, in every blasted field and scanty harvest? It is evident, the curse affects the ground, not only as to Adam, but also his posterity, through all generations; and, therefore, as it was once inflicted, so it is still continued, on account of his sin, for which they suffer, as well as himself.

Again; is the present state of labour and toil the same with the primitive state of man? It must be owned, that the life of Adam in Paradise was not a life of idleness. for such a life cannot be a happiness, but a burden, to a reasonable creature formed for action. It must also be owned, that a gracious God, according to his usual art, has brought good out of evil, and turned the labour and sweat inflicted at the fall as a curse, into a blessing, as it prevents much sin, which men in a state of idleness would fall into; for none are more liable to temptation, or more ready to employ themselves in doing evil, than the idle. And hence the general prevalence of vice, irreligion, and debauched pleasures among the rich, who can support themselves without labour. But then this happy conversion of the curse into a blessing is altogether owing to the dispensation of grace in Christ, or the new covenant, under which God has been pleased to place our world, after the breach of the first covenant. This degree of labour and toil, as it was originally imposed upon Adam, and is still continued upon his posterity, is a curse, a proper punishment for his sin. This is evident from the form of its first denunciation, "Because thou hast hearkened unto the voice of thy wife, and hast eaten of the tree of which I commanded thee, saying, Thou shalt not eat of it; cursed is the ground for thy sake—in the sweat of thy face shalt thou eat bread;" that is, because thou hast sinned, *therefore*, cursed is the ground for thy sake; and, *therefore*, thou shalt provide thyself bread with sweating labour. This, you see, was the curse of a broken law, the punishment of sin, in its original design, whatever new turn may be given to it by the hand of a Mediator, under a dispensation of grace. And it has eventually, as well as in its own nature, proved a curse to many in all ages.

What labour and fatigue, what hurry and distraction of business run through all ranks of mankind, except a few idle drones, whose indolence is more uneasy than labour itself! What intense application, what anxious contrivance, what painful labour of the head, if not of the hand, exhaust even those who get their livings by more genteel methods—the statesmen, the lawyer, the merchant, &c.! But if we descend to the lower tribes of mankind, the mechanic, the planter, the common soldier, the mariner, the slave—what toils and hardships, what anxious and fatiguing nights and days do they endure, even to furnish a bare substance for themselves and families! And, after all their labour and care, they often suffer want. What days, and months, and years of toiling and sweating, what wearied bones and aching limbs do they endure! And, after all, how poorly do they live! This labour and care hinders their improvement in knowledge, so that they continue stupidly ignorant all their lives, and hardly ever enjoy any of the pleasures becoming a rational nature. This deprives them of the pleasure and ease of leisure; and, what is worse than all, it is the occasion of their neglecting the one thing needful, while they are distracted with many things. How unlike is this to the happy life of Adam in the garden of Eden! Is it not a matter of sense and experience, that the curse of labour and toil denounced upon him, reaches also to his posterity; and, consequently, that they are punished for his sin? Can we suppose that God would doom a number of reasonable, immortal creatures, capable of such high employments, to dig under the earth in mines, or upon its surface in the field—to endure so many toils and hardships, night and day, by land and sea, to procure a poor subsistence for themselves and their dependants; I say, can we suppose this, without supposing that it is inflicted as a penalty for sin? And it is evident, it must be for the sin of our first father, on whom it was denounced. In this instance, you see, there is a visible disparity between the present and original state of our world and human nature; and this disparity is penal; that is, it is inflicted upon Adam and his posterity as the punishment of his sin.

Let us now proceed to another instance, which, for brevity's sake, must be very comprehensive; and that is, man in the state of innocence was not liable to death, or the separation of soul and body. This we may certainly infer from death's being the penalty threatened to his disobedience; but if he had been liable to it while he was innocent, it could not be threatened as a penalty. When it is said, "In the day thou eatest, thou shalt surely die," it is certainly implied, "While thou dost not eat, thou shalt not die, or thou shalt continue to live." So when God pronounces the sentence upon him, after his offence, "Dust thou art, and unto dust shalt thou return," he undoubtedly denounces something new, to which man was not exposed before, and something penal, on account of his sin, Gen. iii. 19; this St. Paul also asserts in express terms. "By man," says he, "by the first man, Adam, came death," 1 Cor. xv. 21; so also, "By one man," namely, Adam, "sin entered into the world, and death by sin, and so death passed upon all men, in that all have sinned," Rom. v. 12. This, therefore, is certain, that death had no place in a state of innocence.

And hence it follows, that the world around was so disposed, as to have no tendency to take away the life of man. Those poisonous animals and vegetables, that now destroy human life, and those beasts of prey, which now sometimes devour man as their food, either had not these noxious qualities, or were under such providential restraints that they could not exert them. Those explosions of lightning above, and earthquakes below; that unwholesome, pestilential air, and all those disorders in the material world, which, in the present state of things, are fatal to mankind, had no place in the paradisaic state of the earth; for if they had existed, and exerted their power, death would have been the natural and unavoidable consequence. We cannot suppose Adam's body was invulnerable, so that the tooth of a lion, the poison of a serpent, or the weight of a mountain could make no impression upon it; nor can we suppose it would have lived, though torn and devoured by beasts of prey, struck with lightning, or buried in an earthquake. Such injuries would undoubtedly have dissolved the frame, and brought on death; and the most probable security against it is, that there would have been no powers in nature to do it such injuries; but these noxious and deadly qualities have been superadded to them since the introduction of sin. Lions, and tigers, and snakes, and other animals that now destroy mankind, and also poisonous plants, did, no doubt, exist before the fall of Adam; but then they either had not these hurtful qualities, or they did not exert them upon man, while innocent. These qualities were weapons of war put into their hands, when they were employed to fight their Maker's quarrel, upon the revolt of mankind. We have more than conjecture, we have Scripture evidence for this, as far as it refers to the brutal creation; for Adam was constituted their lord, and they were not to injure him, but serve him. Thus the Divine charter ran, "God blessed them, (that is, the new-made pair,)—and God said unto them, Replenish the earth, and subdue it; and have dominion over the fish of the sea, over the fowl of the air, and over every thing that moveth upon the earth," Gen. i. 28. To this also the Psalmist refers—" Thou hast made him to have dominion over the works of thy hands; thou hast put all things under his feet; all sheep and oxen, yea, and the beasts of the field;" that is, wild beasts; "the fowl of the air, and the fish of the sea, and whatsoever passeth through the paths of the seas." Ps. viii. 6–8. Thus man was invested with dominion over all the brutal creation, including the most fierce, ungovernable, and poisonous; and this implied an exemption from all, and especially deadly injuries from them. It would have been but a sorry dominion, if a snake or wild beast might lie in ambush for his lord and kill him. We, therefore, conclude, that all the mischiefs that mankind are liable to, from brute creatures, had no place in the world till sin entered into it.

We may also infer, farther, that since man, in his primitive state, was not liable to death, neither was he liable to sickness, pain, and mortal accidents. Death is the consequence and final result of these pains, sicknesses, and accidents; and therefore we cannot suppose them to exist in a state that did not admit of death. Death is often used in Scripture in a large sense, and signifies not only the separation of soul and body, but afflictions, pains, miseries, especially such as are the causes and concomitants of death. In this latitude it may be understood in the first threatening: and, if so, man's exemption from death, in his primitive state, implied an exemption from all the afflictions, pains, and miseries, that are often included in that word.

There is one species of pain, which we may be sure, from express Scripture, human nature would have been free from, had it continued innocent: pains which a tender heart cannot think of without sympathy; pains, which affect the tenderest and fairest, and, I may add, the best part of mankind; which are always agonizing, sometimes mortal; and which attended our entrance into this world; I mean the pains of child-bearing. The command was given early, "Be fruitful and multiply," Gen. i. 28; so that Adam and Eve would have had a numerous posterity, though they had never sinned. But, after the fall, this sentence was passed upon guilty, trembling Eve, "I will greatly multiply thy sorrow and thy conception: in sorrow shalt thou bring forth children." Gen. iii. 16. Here, pain and sorrow are annexed to the whole process of our formation in the womb; sorrow in conception or breeding, and sorrow in bringing forth children. That this would not have been the attendant of the propagation of mankind in a state of innocence, I prove as before. If this had been the attendant of conception and birth in that state, it could not have been inflicted as the punishment of sin: for that cannot be the punishment of sin, which we must suffer though we should not sin.

Now, as this species of pain and sickness could not have afflicted mankind in a state of innocence, may we not, by a parity of reason, conclude, that neither would they have been subject to any other kind of pain or sickness; and that, as Adam was immortal, so he had no seeds or principles of any disease in his constitution, nor was he liable to any hurtful accidents from without?

But if this was the primitive state of human nature, alas! how vastly different from it is the present! And, since the terrible alteration, occasioned by Adam's sin, sensibly affects mankind in every age, as well as himself, how lamentably evident is it, that they share in the penal effects of his sin!

Death has reigned from Adam to Moses, from Moses to Christ, and from Christ to the present generation; death has reigned over persons of every character and every age. And how painful and tormenting are its agonies, and the struggles of dissolving nature! When you view a dying man in his last conflict, with all the shocking symptoms of death strong upon him, can you imagine, that in this way man would have made his passage from world to world, if he did not lie under the imputation of guilt, and the displeasure of his Maker? How terrible is the prospect of death before it comes! How does it embitter the pleasures of life! and how many does the fear of it keep in cruel bondage all their days! What sicknesses, pains, sorrows, and hurtful accidents, are mankind exposed to in every age, before they ripen into death, the grand result of these long-continued calamities! and what distress do the living and the healthy suffer by sympathy, from the sufferings and death of others, especially of dear friends and relatives! What desolations, what distresses and deaths are spread over the face of the earth, by famine, war, pestilence, earthquakes, hurricanes, extremities of heat and cold, and all the nameless disorders to which the natural and moral world is now exposed! How many mischiefs have mankind suffered from savage and poisonous animals, that were made the subjects of man in his primitive state! All these mischiefs, as we have seen, had no place in the state of innocence; but are the penal consequences of the sin of the first man: and it is a matter of daily observation, that they reach to his posterity also. It was his sin that occasioned the rebellion of the brutal creation against their lord; that armed serpents and vipers with deadly stings and poisons, and the lion, the tiger, the bear, and other beasts of prey, with rage, and all the powers of slaughter. These are the executioners of the Divine displeasure, turned loose upon a race of rebels, to avenge the quarrel of their Maker.

These miseries not only affect the adult, but also the young descendants of Adam, before they have done good or evil in their own persons. How many dangerous and deadly accidents are these young immortals exposed to, even while enclosed and guarded by the womb! And with what pain and risk of life do they make their entrance into the world! And how many of them are maimed or perish in the very porch of life! It is often a dubious struggle, whose life must go, the mother's or the child's; and sometimes both perish together. Here I must enlarge a little upon the pains and sorrows of conception and birth, because this is more expressly the penal consequences of the first offence.

During the tedious months of pregnancy, what sick qualms, what nausea and loathing; what unnatural longing; what languor of spirits, and hysterical disorders; what anxious and trembling expectations of the painful hour, and what danger of miscarriages even from trifling accidents, and when the painful hour comes, what exquisite anguish and violent throes—so violent and exquisite, that *the pains of a travailing woman* are become a proverbial expression, to signify the greatest possible misery. How many lose their life in that distressing hour, or receive such injuries as from which they never recover! Thus the manner of our entrance into the world intimates, that we are a race of creatures out of favour with God, and lie under his displeasure from generation to generation. Ye daughters of Eve, while I drop a sympathizing tear over your miseries, I must put you in mind, that you are suffering the bitter effects of the original curse—that you are degenerate creatures yourselves, and the mothers of a guilty and degenerate race. Therefore humble yourselves under the mighty hand of God; and let the sorrows and pains of conception and child-bearing be turned into blessings, by bringing you to a deep sense of your original guilt and depravity. In so tender and urgent a case, I cannot but anticipate the subject of, perhaps, some future discourse, and put you in mind, that though your sex was first in the transgression, and you still feel the effects of the old curse denounced upon your mother Eve; Jesus Christ, the great deliverer, is also the seed of the woman; and in this view, the race of man is indebted to your sex for their deliverance. This seed of the woman, the second Adam, is able and willing to save you in due time, from all the consequences of the curse, if you apply to him by faith. This may be St. Paul's meaning, "The woman being deceived was in the transgression; notwithstanding, she shall be saved in child-bearing, or by child-birth," 1 Tim. ii. 15, by giving birth to the great deliverer, who was made and born of a woman: or, as others understand it, she shall be saved in child-bearing, saved even though she continues to bear children with sorrow and pain, and suffers the fruits of the old curse inflicted upon the sex; that shall not hinder her everlasting salvation, if she continue in faith and charity, and holiness with sobriety.

But to return to the case of infants. If they escape with life into the world, what various calamities are immediately ready to attack the little strangers! How much do they suffer from the unskilfulness, carelessness, or poverty of their parents and nurses! What various nameless diseases and pains, bruises and fatal accidents, are they subject to: the sense of which they express by their crying, the only language they are capable of! What multitudes of them die in their tender years, before they have answered any of the purposes of the present life, only to give their parent a double trouble, first in nursing them, and then in suffering the bereavement of them! It is computed, that at least one half of mankind die under seven years old; and the greater part of this half die before they are moral agents, or capable of personal sin or duty, even in the lowest degree. Whatever therefore they suffer, must be for the sin of another, even Adam their common father, whose offence subjected him and all his posterity to the power of death and the various calamities that precede it. To these early subjects of death, many suppose the apostle refers, when he says, "Death reigned from Adam to Moses, even over them that had not sinned after the similitude of Adam's transgression." Rom. v. 14, over infants, who had not sinned actually in their own persons, as Adam did.

Now is this world, which is so replenished with destructive powers, causes of sickness, sorrow, and death, and which render these miseries inevitable according to the present course of nature: is this world, I say, in that order and harmony, in which it was formed for the residence of upright man? Has it not passed through some dismal alteration, when the earth, the sea, the air, the fire, animals, and vegetables, are full of the principles of sickness, misery, and death, which were once all friendly to human life, and subservient to its preservation or pleasure? Does it not look like a palace turned into a prison, to confine and punish obnoxious rebels? Are these frail, sickly, mortal bodies, such as the pure soul of Adam animated, when it first came out of the hands of its Creator? Does man now retain his original dominion over the brute inhabitants of the earth, the sea, or air? Or have they not rebelled against him, because he has rebelled against his Maker? Is not the curse denounced against Eve entailed upon all her daughters? And is not the sentence passed upon Adam, "Dust thou art, and unto dust thou shalt return," executed upon all his children—executed upon them in such a manner, as shows, it is for *his* sin and not *their own;* and therefore executed upon his infant offspring, before they have contracted personal guilt by actual sin? Are not human bodies now formed so as to be proper recipients of sickness, and various forms of miseries and deaths? And is not all nature around them adapted to answer these dreadful purposes?* What

* I repeat this, because I think great stress ought to be laid upon it. It appears evident to me, that sorrow, pain, sickness, death, and all the miseries to which mankind are now subject, are natural, unavoidable, and necessary, in the present state of the natural and moral world; and that the present state of things is in righteous judgment adapted and disposed to inflict these miseries: and since innocent man was not liable to them, it follows, that the name and disposition of the world is altered, on account of Adam's sin. Nothing is more natural, in the present state of things, than sickness and death to the human body; than the fierceness, poison, and the various destructive qualities, of many animals and vegetables; than storms, earthquakes, unwholesome air, and other causes of misery and death to mankind. These things are natural; I mean to say, agreeable to the established laws of nature, in the present state of the world.

then can be more evident, even from daily experience and observation, than that all mankind do, in fact, suffer for the sin of their first parent, or that the guilt of his sin is imputed to them, and punished upon them? Whether this be consistent with the Divine perfections, and how it comes to pass, we may consider at some other opportunity: we are now only inquiring into the fact; and that it is fact, cannot be denied, without denying a matter of universal sensation and observation.

There are two other instances of dissimilitude between the present and primitive state of man, which I might very properly insist upon; namely, that man was innocent and holy in his original state, and also entitled to everlasting happiness; but that in his present state, both these are forfeited. The time that remains, I shall employ in answering an objection, that the arguments that have been offered may continue firm and unshaken.

It may be objected, that the misery and death of mankind can be no proof of the imputation of Adam's sin to them, because the various tribes of mere animals are exposed to the same. They all return to the dust, as well as man. They are subject to sickness, famine, hurtful accidents, toil, and labour. They bring forth their young with pain and danger. They tyrannize over one another, and many of the greater live upon the small. In short, they share in most of the miseries of human nature,

And if these things had existed with these qualities in the primitive state, diseases, desolations, and death, would have been their natural, necessary, and unavoidable effects. But since the effects did not exist, neither did their causes. Hence it follows, that the whole frame of our world was judicially altered for the worse, in punishment of Adam's sin. And since this world was intended for the habitation of his posterity, as well as his own; and since they suffer the terrible effects of that alteration which it endured as the punishment of his sin; it follows farther, that they share in his punishment, and therefore that the guilt of his sin is somehow laid to their charge.

and suffer some peculiar to themselves. And yet we cannot suppose, that their first ancestor sinned, and that his guilt is imputed to them, and they are punished for it. Why then may we not suppose, that mankind suffer such calamities, without the imputation of the sin of their first ancestor Adam?

To this I answer,

First, That we have no evidence from Scripture or reason, that the brutal creation was formed for immortality, or that they were originally intended to be free from death. But as to man, it has been proved, that in his original state he was not liable to death, nor any of its antecedent or concomitant calamities, but that his gracious Maker intended he should live and be happy for ever, if he continued for ever obedient. Now this consideration shows there is a wide difference between the case of man and that of brutes. In their primitive state, and according to the original destination of their Creator, they appear to have been intended for death, and consequently for the calamities and pains, and sicknesses, that are the causes and attendants of death.* It is probable, they were originally intended to be food for man, and for one another, even in the state of innocence. Hence, St. Peter says, Natural brute beasts, or natural animals without reason, were *made* to be taken

* As immortality appears to be the reward of religion, of which the brutal nature is incapable, because it necessarily supposes the powers of reason in the subject; as we can conceive no valuable end or use which irrational beings could answer in the future state, or world of spirits; and as they could not be immortal here upon earth, because it would be soon overstocked, unless one generation died, to make room for another, it appears highly reasonable to suppose, that brutes in their original state, were intended only to live awhile upon earth, to answer the purposes of their being, and to enjoy the low pleasures suited to their nature; and then to die, and relapse into dust. Certainly, the Creator's freely giving existence, does not oblige him to perpetuate it for ever; or render it unjust for him to take it away.

and destroyed.* Now, if they were *made* for this purpose, their being taken and destroyed is not a punishment for any previous guilt, but only using them according to their original design. But man was not intended for this purpose; he was not made for death at his first creation; and consequently his being subjected to it, must be a punishment that supposes previous sin and guilt. It is no punishment to a brute that it does not enjoy the privileges and immunities of man in his original state: because these were never intended for the brutal nature. But if Adam's posterity are stripped of these privileges and immunities which belonged to their nature in him, and which were ensured both to him and them, if he continued obedient; and if they are stripped of these on account of *his* sin: then it is evident *his* sin is imputed to them, and they are punished for it. This answer will account for the death of mere animals, and the sufferings which death necessarily includes or pre-supposes. But as they are exposed to many sufferings, which death does not necessarily include or pre-suppose, this answer alone is not sufficient; therefore I add,

Secondly, That there is great reason to conclude, that even the brutal tribes of creatures do suffer by the fall of Adam; that they have lost that ease, peace, security, and plenty, in which they would have lived, had he never sinned; and incurred a variety of miseries in consequence of his offence. When they became fierce, savage, and rebellious towards him, they would of course become mischievous and destructive to one another. The poison of the viper and serpent, the carnivorous rage of the lion, the tiger and the bear, which were intended primarily as a punishment to guilty man, would naturally render them injurious to their fellow-brutes. When weeds and plants

* Δοψε ζώα φυσικά. 2. Pet. ii. 12.

received their hurtful qualities, in consequence of Adam's sin, they would, according to the course of nature, be injurious to the beasts that might feed upon them. The barrenness of the earth, the desolations occasioned by intemperate seasons, hurricanes, earthquakes, and other disorders introduced into the material world, by the sin of man, must affect the brutes, as well as man. These must involve them in pain, sickness, death, and various calamities. When their lord was guilty of rebellion against his Master in heaven, his subjects also share in his sufferings: his whole territory is cast into confusion, and all its inhabitants, of every rank, must painfully feel the terrible change. The ground was cursed for his sake; and why may we not suppose the creatures that dwelt upon it were cursed for his sake also? This curse would ultimately affect him, because their sickness and other calamities would disable them from serving him. Indeed it is the conduct of Providence in every age to involve the brutes in the same punishments with mankind. Thus the deluge, the fire and earthquake that destroyed Sodom, the plagues of Egypt, and other public judgments, swept off beasts as well as men, though the sin of men were the cause of these judgments.

That which chiefly confirms me in this belief, is, the authority of St. Paul. "The creature, (says he,) was made subject to vanity, not willingly, but by reason of him who hath subjected it;" that is, the inanimate and brutal creation is reduced into a state of vanity, confusion, and misery, not willingly, not of its own accord, not as the effect of any natural tendency to it, nor as the punishment of its own sin; but it was reduced into this state by a righteous God, who subjected it to vanity, as a just punishment for the sin of man." And as it felt the effects of the

* This passage may admit of another sense, still more expressly to my

first Adam's fall, so it shall share in the glorious deliverance wrought by the second Adam; and it was subjected to vanity with a view to this; for, the apostle adds, "God subjected it in hope* that the creature itself"—even the inanimate and brutal creation also, as well as the children of God, "shall be delivered from the bondage of corruption, into the glorious liberty of the children of God." Their being *delivered* from the bondage of corruption, implies, that they now lie under it. And this phrase, "*the* bondage of corruption," may include all the disorders and miseries they are now groaning under; and since they were not subjected to this willingly, or of their own accord,† or for anything they had done, it follows, they were judicially subjected to it on account of the sin of man. His first sin was an universal mischief to all the inhabitants of the world formed for his residence, both animate and inanimate, rational and irrational: and is the source of all the disorders and miseries that any part of this lower creation groans under. When I view the matter in this light, I am ready to retract the former answer, and to rest in this as sufficient; and perhaps, not only the miseries, but even the death of the animal creation, which in the former answer I accounted for in another way, may be entirely owing to this cause, even the sin of man, their lord and proprietor. "The bondage of corruption," to which

purpose—τον ὑποτάξαντα, the person who subjected the world to vanity, may mean, not the righteous God, but sinning Adam, who by his offence exposed the territory in which he lived to this curse. This is the sense chosen by many expositors; and it appears as reasonable as any. In this sense, the apostle means that the rest of the creatures were subjected by Adam to vanity and misery, as his offence exposed them to it. Rom. viii. 19–21.

* Thus I would translate and connect this passage, and not as it is in our common English translation. Thus Beza renders it; and this the original will naturally bear—διὰ τὸν ὑποτάξαντα ἐπ' ἐλπίδι, ὅτι καὶ αὐτὴ ἡ κτίσις ἐλευθερωθήσεται, &c.

† ἑκοῦσα.

that has exposed them, is a phrase that may, and perhaps *must*, include death, as well as other miseries.

I hope you will excuse me, that I have dwelt so long upon these arguments, and left so little room for a practical improvement. My design has been to give you a rational, solid, deep conviction of this important though mortifying truth. And as some of the topics I have reasoned from are not very common, and may be new to most of you, I thought it necessary to dwell the longer upon them.

Upon a review of the whole, let me exhort you,

To impress your minds deeply with a sense of your degeneracy, that you may cherish humility, and be the more solicitous for deliverance. And,

To improve all the calamities of life, to make you sensible of this.

A HYMN.

(FROM THE REV. DR. DODDRIDGE.)

With flowing eyes and bleeding hearts
  A blasted world survey!
See the wide ruin sin has wrought
  In one unhappy day!

Adam, in God's own image form'd
  From God and bliss estrang'd,
And all the joys of Paradise
  For guilt and horror chang'd!

Ages of labour and of grief
  He mourn'd his glory lost;
At length the goodliest work of Heaven
  Sunk down to common dust.

Oh fatal heritage, bequeath'd
  To all his helpless race!
Thro' various mis'ries, toils and death,
  Thus to the grave we pass.

But, oh my soul, with rapture hear
  The Second Adam's name;
And the celestial gifts he brings,
  To all his seed proclaim.

In holiness and joy complete
  He reigns to endless years,
And each adopted chosen child,
  His glorious image wears.

Praise to his rich, mysterious love
  E'en by our fall we rise;
And gain, for earthly Eden lost,
  A heav'nly Paradise.

SERMON LXXIV.

THE CERTAINTY OF DEATH; A FUNERAL SERMON.

EZEK. xxxiii. 8.—*O wicked man, thou shalt surely die.*—*

MEN love themselves, and therefore delight to hear things favourable to themselves; and a benevolent mind, that feels pain, whenever he occasions pain to the meanest of his fellow-creatures, would delight to dwell upon such pleasing subjects. And as to the happy few, who are really the sincere servants of God, and are holy in heart and life, I may safely gratify this benevolent inclination, and publish the most joyful tidings. I am authorized to "say to the righteous, it shall be well with him." Isaiah iii. 10. "Comfort ye, comfort ye, my people: speak ye comfortably to Jerusalem." Isa. xl. 1, 2. This is the gracious command of God to all his ministers. And oh! how delightful an office to perform it! This only should be the pleasing business of this hour, could I stretch my charity so far as to conclude, that all this promiscuous crowd, without exception, are indeed the dutiful people of God. But was there ever such a pure assembly upon our guilty earth?—upon our earth, where an accursed Ham was found in the little select family of Noah, the best in the whole world—where a Judas mingled among the chosen twelve, the first followers of Jesus—where the tares and the wheat grow together in one field till the harvest;

---

* For Mrs. Burbridge; delivered at Mr. Burbridge's, in James City County, April 22, 1758.

and where we are expressly told, "many are called, but few chosen." Matt. xx. 16. In such a corrupt world, the most generous charity, if under any rational and scriptural limitations, must hesitate at the sight of such a mixed multitude as this—must be jealous over them with a godly jealousy, (2 Cor. xi. 2,) and stand in doubt of them, (Gal. iv. 20,)—must fear, lest there be one, yea, more than one, wicked man among them. That there is too much reason for this suspicion, that even a benevolent mind is constrained to admit it, however unwilling, will appear evident, I presume, to yourselves, before I have finished my discourse. And if there be so much as one wicked man among us, I would, as it were, single him out from the crowd, and discharge this pointed arrow from the quiver of the Almighty against his heart, to give him, not a deadly, but a medicinal wound: "O wicked man, thou shalt surely die." I am obliged, at my peril, to denounce this doom against thee: and I dare not flatter thee with better hopes, unless I would be accessary to thy death, and at once ruin both myself and thee. For observe the context, which contains the instructions of the great Jehovah to his minister Ezekiel, which are equally binding upon all the ministers of his word in every age. "O thou son of man, I have set thee a watchman unto the house of Israel: therefore thou shalt hear the word at my mouth, and warn them from me. When I say unto the wicked, O wicked man, thou shalt surely die; if thou dost not speak to warn the wicked from his way, that wicked man shall die in his iniquity; but his blood will I require at thy hand." This phrase, "I will require his blood at thy hand," signifies, "I will look upon thee as guilty of his murder, and I will punish thee accordingly."* Therefore, if I would not

---

* That this is the import of the phrase, may be learned from Gen. ix. 5, 6, where it is evidently used in this sense: "Surely the blood of your lives

incur the guilt and punishment of murder, soul-murder, the most shocking kind of murder; if I would not destroy you and myself, that you may enjoy the sorry pleasure of flattery, and that I may enjoy the short-lived trifling reward of a little popular applause, I am obliged to tell such of you as are wicked, in the most pungent manner, and as it were by name, "O wicked man, thou shalt surely die:" whoever thou art; however rich, or powerful, or honourable; however bold and presumptuous; however full of flattering hopes; however sure of life in thine own conceit; if thou be wicked, thou shalt *die;* thou shalt *surely* die; or, to use the force of the Hebrew phrase,* *dying thou shalt die;* in death thou shalt die indeed: thou shalt surely die, saith the Lord, and not man: it is the declaration of eternal truth, which cannot fail: it is the sentence of the Lord of hosts, who is able to carry it into execution. That it is *his* sentence, and not man's, you may see by the connection: "The word of the Lord came unto me, saying, When I say unto the wicked, O wicked man, thou shalt surely die." When I say, that is, when I, the Lord of hosts, say this. Let this, therefore, be regarded, not as the rash sentence of censorious mortals, but as the unchangeable constitution and authentic declaration of a wise and righteous God, which must infallibly stand good, whoever oppose; "O wicked man, thou shalt surely die."

But here two interesting questions occur, Who are the wicked? and, what kind of death shall they die?

If we should not first inquire, who the wicked are, I should but speak to the air; for hardly any would apply the character to themselves. It is an odious character;

---

will I require—at the hand of every man's brother will I require the life of man: whoso sheddeth man's blood, by man shall his blood be shed."

* מות תמות. This the Septuagint imitate, θανάτῳ θανατωθήσῃ.

and that alone is the reason why many try to persuade themselves, it is not theirs. But, my brethren, many things that are very disagreeable, are, notwithstanding, true. And it may be our interest to know them, however painful the discovery may be: for now, while we are in a mutable state, we may, through divine grace, change characters; those who are now wicked, and consequently exposed to eternal death, may yet become righteous, the favourites of heaven, and the heirs of eternal life. And the first step towards such a happy change, is, a clear, affecting conviction, that their present character and condition are bad and dangerous. Let us, therefore, submit ourselves to an impartial trial, and endeavour to discover whether the character of the wicked man belong to us or not. I would by no means desire or expect, you should pay me so extravagant a compliment, as to form a judgment of yourselves merely upon my assertion. I refer you to a higher authority, to your own reason and conscience, and especially to the Holy Scriptures. "The Bible, the Bible is the religion of Protestants:"* by the Bible you must be tried at last, by the Supreme Judge: and by that infallible test, I would have you try yourselves now.

The first class of wicked men that I shall take notice of, are profane and gross sinners, who indulge themselves in notorious immoralities. Instead of particularizing them myself, I shall produce to you a list of them, which the apostle has given long ago. "Know ye not, that the unrighteous shall not inherit the kingdom of God?" He seems surprised any should be ignorant of so plain a point as this. "Be not deceived," says he: do not flatter yourselves with better hope; but who are the unrighteous? He tells you particularly; "neither fornicators, nor idola-

* Chillingworth.

ters, nor adulterers, nor effeminate," soft, luxurious creatures, unmanned with sensual pleasures, "nor abusers of themselves with mankind," Sodomites, "nor thieves, nor covetous, nor drunkards, nor revilers, nor extortioners, shall inherit the kingdom of God." 1 Cor. vi. 9, 10. You see the apostle is fixed and peremptory in it, that sinners of this class are universally excluded from the kingdom of heaven—not one of them all shall ever be admitted there, if they continue such. All such shall certainly perish, or else St. Paul was an impostor. To the same purpose he speaks, Gal. v. 19–21; "the works of the flesh are manifest, which are these, adultery, fornication, uncleanness, lasciviousness, idolatry, witchcraft, hatred, variance, emulations, wrath, strife, seditions, heresies, envyings, murders, drunkenness, revellings, and such like: of the which I tell you before," that is, I honestly forewarn you, "as I have also told you in the time past, that they which do such things shall not inherit the kingdom of God." As sin is a monster of so many heads, he does not enumerate them all, but comprehends them in the lump; declaring, that they who practised the vices mentioned, or *such like*, though not exactly the same, shall be excluded from heaven. This was not an occasional declaration, but what he had solemnly repeated at various seasons: "I forewarn you now," says he,." as I have done in times past." He denounces the same doom against these vices in his epistle to the Colossians; "fornication, uncleanness, inordinate affection, evil concupiscence, and covetousness—for which things' sake, the wrath of God cometh on the children of disobedience." Col. iii. 5, 6.

I shall add but one testimony more, "The fearful," the cowardly in the cause of God, "and unbelieving, and the abominable, and murderers, and whoremongers, and sorcerers and idolaters, and all liars, shall have their part in the lake which burneth with fire and brimstone, which is the second death." Rev. xxi. 8. These, you see, are the certain symptoms of the heirs of hell: and if they be admitted into a state of everlasting happiness, while they continue such, it is certain your religion must be false; for the Bible, which is the foundation of your religion, repeatedly declares they shall not be admitted there. It is also observable, that in this black list, you not only find such gross vices as are scandalous in the common estimate of mankind, but also such as are secret, seated in the heart, and generally esteemed but lesser evils. Here you find not only murder, whoredom, idolatry, theft, and such enormous and scandalous sins, but also covetousness, wrath, strife, envyings, unbelief, and such like latent sins, which men generally indulge themselves in, without feeling much guilt upon their consciences, or apprehending themselves in great danger of punishment. These are but foibles and peccadillos—little, trifling sins, in their esteem: but oh! how different an estimate does God form of them! He pronounces them damnable vices, the practice of which will certainly exclude from his favour. And his sentence will stand, whether we will or not.

I should be very sorry so much as to suppose, there are any among you of this abandoned character. But I must propose the matter to your own decision; and at so favourable a tribunal, you will, no doubt, be acquitted, if you be clear. I say, I propose it to yourselves, whether some of you be not drunkards, swearers, liars, whoremongers, extortioners, sabbath-breakers, and the like? Or, if you are free from these grosser forms of vice, do not some of you live in wrath, strife, revelling, and carousing, covetousness, secret uncleanness, and the like? If this be your character, I have another thing to propose to you; and that is, whether it be most likely that you shall be excluded the kingdom of heaven; or that Christ and his apostles, and the other writers of the Holy Scriptures, were deceivers? One or other must be the case; if you be admitted into heaven, then they were certainly deceivers: for they have declared you shall not be admitted. Will you disbelieve their evidence, merely because it is against you? Will you believe nothing but what is in your favour? That would be a strange test of truth indeed.

Thus far you are assisted to judge, who are the wicked; and whether some of you do not belong to this unhappy class. And now I proceed to another class.

Secondly, All those are wicked, who knowingly and wilfully indulge themselves habitually in any one sin, whether it be the omission of a commanded duty, or the practice of something forbidden. Every good man is of the same spirit with David, who could appeal to God himself, "Lord, I have respect to all thy commandments;" Psalm cxix. 6; and with St. Paul, "I delight in the law of God after the inward man." Rom. vii. 22. And consequently, they who have not practical respect to all God's commandments, without exception, and who do not inwardly delight in his law, are of a spirit and character directly contrary to David and Paul; in other words, they are wicked. The wilful and habitual practice of any known sin, and the wilful and habitual neglect of any known duty, are repeatedly mentioned in the Scriptures, as the sure signs of a wicked man. "He that saith, I know him, and keepeth not his commandments, is a liar, and the truth is not in him." 1 John ii. 4. "He that committeth sin," that is, wilfully, knowingly, and habitually, "is of the devil." 1 John iii. 8. "In this the children of God are manifest, and the children of the devil;" verse 10; this is the great difference between them; "whosoever doeth not righteousness, is not of God." Our Lord himself has repeatedly assured us, that all pretensions to love him are vain, unless we keep his commandments. "If a man love me, he will keep my words—he that loveth me not, keepeth not my saying." John xiv. 23, 24. What is it to be a wicked man but to work iniquity? And what is it to work iniquity but to neglect what God has commanded, or practise what he has forbidden? He that does one thing from a regard to God, will endeavour to do every thing from the same principle. And wilful disobedience to him in one instance discovers a disposition which would disobey the divine authority in every instance, if there were the same temptations to it.

Be this, therefore, known to you all, as an undoubted truth, that the wilful habitual indulgence of any known sin, is the inseparable character of a wicked man. You may plead the infirmity of human nature, the strength of temptation, or the innocence of your hearts and intentions, even in the midst of your sins; you may plead that the best have their infirmities, as well as you: and that many around you, are much worse than you—you may plead these, and a thousand such excuses: but plead what you will, all your excuses are in vain; and this still remains an unchangeable truth, that all the habitual practisers of sin are the servants of sin. It matters not whether the sin be secret and clandestine, or public and avowed; whether it be of a greater or smaller size; whether you are stung with remorse for it afterwards or not; whether you intend to forsake it hereafter, or not: such circumstances as these will not alter the case: in spite of such circumstances, if you indulge any one known sin, you bear the infernal brand of wickedness upon you. I grant, that good men sin, and that they are far from perfection of holiness in this life. I grant also, that some of them have fallen, perhaps once in their life, into some gross sin.

But, after all, I must insist, that they do not indulge themselves in the wilful, habitual practice of any known sin, or the wilful, habitual neglect of any known duty. St John expressly tells us, that he that is born of God, neither doth nor can sin, in this sense. 1 John iii. 9. He cannot sin *habitually;* the meaning is, he cannot go on in any one sin as his usual course; but if he fall, it is by surprise; and taking one time with another, he is generally, and for the most part, under the influence of holy principles—these are predominant, or have the mastery within him: and from these he chiefly acts. Again; he cannot sin *wilfully;* that is, with full bent of soul. The prevailing inclination and tendency of his soul is not towards sin: but on the other hand, he really hates it and resists it, even in its most tempting forms; and it is his incessant struggle and honest endeavour to suppress it. He never can abandon himself more to the free, uncontrolled indulgence of the sweetest sin, though it should be only in heart. Both Scripture and Reason renounce those crowds of pretended Christians we have among us, who are under the habitual power of some sin or other, and live in the neglect of some known duty. A servant of Christ, who does not endeavour to do his Master's will, in every known instance, is a contradiction.

And now, are not sundry of you convicted of the character of wicked men, who might not come under the former class of profane sinners? Do not some of you know in your consciences, that there is some little sweet sin (so you esteem it) which you cannot bear to part with? Is there not some duty, which is so disagreeable to you, so contrary to your inclination, to your reputation in the wicked world, or to your temporal interest, that though you are secretly convinced it is your duty, yet you omit it; you put it off; and think God will dis pense with your obedience in so slight a manner? Are not some of you conscious that this is your practice? If so, you must be ranked in the numerous class of wicked men. There, indeed, you have company enough: but company is no security in a combination against Omnipotence.

Thirdly, all those are wicked, who are destitute of those graces and virtues, which constitute the character of positive goodness. Wickedness is a moral *privation*, or the *want* of real goodness. The want of faith, the want of love, repentance, benevolence, and charity, does as really constitute a wicked man, as drunkenness, blasphemy, or any notorious immorality. Certainly I need not particularly mention to you those passages of Scripture, which declare these graces and virtues essential to a good man, and the want of them the grand mark and constituent of a bad one. A good man, that does not love God or mankind; a good man without faith or repentance, is as great a contradiction as a hero without courage, a scholar without learning, a righteous ruler without justice, or a fire without heat. Therefore, if any of you do not believe, that is, if you have not such a realizing persuasion of the truth and importance of the things contained in the word of God, as to impress and govern your heart and life; particularly, if you do not believe in Jesus Christ, which is the grand requirement of the gospel, if you be not deeply sensible of your guilty and helpless condition; and if, as corrupt, helpless sinners, you do not accept Jesus Christ as your only Saviour, and trust in his righteousness alone as the only ground of your acceptance with God; I say, if you have not such a faith as this, you are wicked men; I say, *such a faith as this;* for, as to the faith which is fashionable among us, I mean a mere speculative or historical assent to the truth of the Christian religion, and that Christ is the Messiah; this is but the faith of devils, only with this difference, that devils believe and tremble; whereas, many who have this faith among us, believe and sin without trembling. If you be destitute of the grace of repentance, if you have not a clear conviction and deep sense of your sinfulness in heart and life, by nature and practice; if you be not deeply sorry at heart for your sins, and hate them—hate them all without exception; if you do not hate them, not only on account of the punishment annexed to them, but because of their intrinsic vileness and their contrariety to the Divine purity; if you do not forsake your sins, as well as sorrow for them; and if you do not fly to the mere mercy of God in Jesus Christ for pardon, and place all your dependence upon his righteousness—I say, unless this be your daily experience and practice, you are entirely destitute of true evangelic repentance, and consequently come under the unhappy class of wicked men. If you do not love God with all your hearts, that is, if you have not frequent affectionate thoughts of him; if you do not delight in his service, and in communion with him in divine ordinances; if your love does not produce cheerful, universal obedience, which is the infallible test of love; then you are certainly destitute of the heavenly grace of love; and sure, without this, you will not pretend to the character of good men! A good man, without the love of God, is the grossest absurdity. Finally, if your hearts be not actuated with the generous principle of love and benevolence to mankind; if you do not consult, and endeavour to promote their good as well as your own, and especially the good of their souls by their conversion to God; if you do not habitually observe the rules of justice aud charity in your transactions with them, and do to others what you would reasonably desire them to do to you in like circumstances; if you are dest tute of this temper towards mankind, you are destitute of an essential constituent of a good man, and consequently are wicked. Now if all who are destitute of these qualifications should walk off to the left hand, as they must do another day, would it not thin this crowd? Oh! how few would be left behind! I beseech you to examine yourselves impartially, that you may know your true character.

Fourthly, to sum up the whole, all those are wicked, who still continue in their natural state; who have never been regenerated, or experienced a thorough change of their views and dispositions towards God and divine things. Even our own observation of the natural temper of mankind is sufficient to convince us, though the Scriptures were silent, that they are from their very birth wicked, disinclined to God and holiness, and bent to that which is evil. Alas! you are stupidly ignorant of yourselves, if you do not know, by experience, that this is your case. To this the Scriptures also bear abundant testimony. "That which is born of the flesh, is flesh: and they that are in the flesh, cannot please God." John iii. 6; Rom. viii. 8. "We were by nature children of wrath, even as others;" we and others, that is, all, without exception, are by nature children of wrath, and consequently, by nature wicked: for certainly those who are not wicked, cannot be children of wrath. Eph. ii. 3. Every imagination of the thoughts of man's heart, is only evil continually, from his youth up. Gen. vi. 5; viii. 21. And in their flesh dwells no good thing. Rom. vii. 18. Upon this corruption of human nature, is founded the necessity of that change of temper, which the Scripture calls, and which, therefore, we dare to call, the new birth, or new creation. And since this corruption of human nature is universal, it follows, that all are wicked, who have never experienced this divine change.

This must suffice, at present, in answer to the first question, Who are the wicked? And I hope sundry of you, if you honestly make use of the light you have, have discovered, that whatever flattering hopes you have entertained, you must really place yourselves in the class with wicked men. This is an alarming discovery at any time: but it is much better to receive it now, when the case may be remedied, than in the eternal world, when it will be too late, and your case will be desperate.

And now, O wicked man, whoever thou art, as Ehud said to Eglon, "I have a message from God unto thee," Judges iii. 20, a message not unlike to his; and that is, "Thou shalt surely die." Profane sinner, drunkard, swearer, whoremonger, "thou shalt surely die." You, that knowingly, wilfully, and habitually indulge yourselves in any favourite sin, "you shall surely die." You that are destitute of genuine faith, love, and the other graces and virtues essential to a good man, "you shall surely die." You, that are still the same in temper and disposition, that you were by nature, "you shall surely die." This is the invariable decree of Heaven, that you shall die. You may cast death out of your thoughts: but, for all that, you shall die; you may continue unprepared for it; but you must die. Were you as high and bright as Lucifer, as rich as Crœsus, as powerful as Alexander, you must die. Your wickedness cannot immortalize you. Though you are wicked men now, you shall be dead men ere long: yes, as surely as you now live, you shall die.

But you will perhaps reply, "What is this that you tell us? Is death the lot only of the wicked? Must not all men die, the good as well as the bad? How then can death be threatened as the peculiar doom of the wicked?" The answer to this naturally leads me to

The second question, What kind of death shall the

wicked man die? It is true, natural death is the universal doom of all the sons of men. "How dieth the wise man? as the fool." Eccl. ii. 16. The highest attainments in piety cannot secure an earthly immortality. Peter and Paul are dead, as well as Judas. But though there be no difference in this respect, there is a wide difference in another, and that is, the death of the wicked is quite another thing, or comes under quite a different notion, from the death of the righteous. The death of the wicked, like an officer, from their offended sovereign, strikes off the fetters of flesh, that they may be carried away to the place of execution: but the death of the righteous, like a friendly angel, only opens the doors of their prison, and dismisses them from their bondage in sinful flesh. The righteous, in death, enjoy, more or less, the consolations of an approving conscience, the sweets of the love of God, and the kind supports of an Almighty Saviour's hand. But the wicked die as criminals by the hand of justice; their guilt is unpardoned, and this gives death its sting: they have no almighty Friend in death; but Jesus, who alone can relieve them, is their enemy: they have no reviving sensations of divine love; but guilty reflections and shocking prospects; or, if they entertain hopes of happiness, which most of them probably do, alas! they are but short-lived delusions, which will evanish like a dream in the morning, as soon as the light of eternity flashes upon them. Death dismisses the righteous from all their sins and sorrows, and conveys them into a state of perfect and everlasting holiness and happiness: but the death of the wicked cuts them off from all enjoyments, from all the means and hopes of salvation, and fixes them in an unchangeable, everlasting state of sin and misery: death to them is the gate of hell, the door of their infernal prison, and a sad farewell to all happiness. Then, farewell, a long, an everlasting farewell to the comforts of this life, and all its agreeable prospects: farewell to friends: farewell to hope and peace: farewell to all the means of grace: farewell God, and Christ, and angels, and all the blessedness of heaven. Now, nothing awaits them, but wrath and fiery indignation. Thus, O wicked man, you shall die: and is not this a very different thing from the death of the righteous?

Realize this prospect, sinners, and sure it must startle you. The time is just at hand, when the cold hand of death shall arrest you; when the vital pulse shall cease to beat, and your blood to flow; when your jaws shall fall; the shadow of death hover over your eyes; a ghastly paleness overspread your countenances: and a deadly numbness creep over your frame, and stupefy your active limbs: when the unwilling, lingering soul must be torn from its old campanion of flesh; must bid adieu to all the enjoyments and pursuits of this mortal life, and shoot the gulf of eternity, and launch away: when it must pass into the immediate presence of God, mingle among the strange, unacquainted beings that inhabit the unseen, untried world, and be fixed in an unchangeable state: when your bodies, like that of our deceased friend, must be laid in the cold and gloomy grave, to moulder there, and feed the worms you were wont to tread upon; when you must leave your riches, your honour, your pleasures, which you pursued with so much labour and eagerness, and go as naked out of the world as you came into it; when you are reduced to this extremity, think, O wicked man, think seriously how miserable your condition will be! Then no comfortable reviews of past life! no supporting whispers of conscience within! no God, no Jesus, no Saviour to support you! no encouraging prospects before you! or none but the delusive, evanishing, confounding encouragement of a false and flattering hope! no relief, no gleam of hope from heaven or earth, from God or his creatures! But a guilty life behind you! a corrupt heart, utterly unfit for heaven, and a clamorous, gnawing conscience, within you! an angry God, a frowning Saviour, and a lost heaven above you! a boundless, burning ocean below you! Oh! what a tragical exit, what a melancholy end is this! This is to die indeed: And thus, "O wicked man, thou shalt surely die." Such a death will be the certain doom of persisting, impenitent wickedness. I need make no exception at all, but only that which I have already hinted at, namely, that many a wicked man dies with a self-flattering apprehension, that he is not wicked, and with sanguine hopes of heaven. This is a common case, especially with persons that have not lived under a faithful ministry, to inform them honestly of the nature of religion, and the pre-requisites of salvation. But alas! what a sandy foundation is this! what avails it to enjoy a little delusive relief in the hour of death, when the first entrance into the eternal world will cause the dream to evanish for ever, and leave you to perish without hope, in all the confusion and consternation of a disappointment! with this trifling exception, which is indeed rather an aggravation, than a real mitigation, I denounce from the living God, that thus shall every wicked man among you die, if you still continue such.

But even this, dreadful as it is, is not all: there is, besides this, that dreadful *something*, called the second death, Rev. xxi. 8; ii. 11; xx. 6, 14, which thou, O wicked man, must die. Besides that death, which will put an end to this transitory life, you will have another death to suffer; a death, which will immediately commence when the other is over: a death, which will not be over in a few moments like the other, but the agonies of which will continue—an everlasting death—a state of misery, which will render life worse than death, or being worse than annihilation. Then the soul will be for ever dead to God and holiness—dead to all the means of grace, and all the enjoyments of this life—dead to all happiness and all hope—dead to all the comfortable purposes of existence—dead to every thing that deserves the name of life; in short, dead to every thing but the torturing sensations of pain: to these the soul will be tremblingly alive all over, to eternity: but, alas! to be alive, in this sense, alive only to suffer pain, is worse than death, worse than annihilation. This is the import of that dreadful phrase, "the second death." As life, in the language of Scripture, frequently signifies a state of perfect, everlasting happiness; so death often signifies a state of misery: and the "second death" signifies that second state that follows upon this, which is our first; a state of perfect, everlasting misery! as full of death and misery, as heaven is of life and felicity. Thus, O wicked man, shalt thou surely die: for remember, you have not the character of those who are safe from the "second death." Their character you have in Revelation: "He that overcometh, shall not be hurt of the second death." Rev. ii. 11. It is only the Christian hero, the brave soldier of Jesus Christ, who is enabled by divine grace to conquer his sins within, and all temptations from without: it is he, and he only, that shall escape unhurt by this dreadful king of death. As for others, particularly the "fearful, the unbelieving, whoremongers, and all liars, you are expressly told, they shall have their part in the lake that burneth with fire and brimstone." Here, also, you may see a Scripture definition of the "second death." Rev. xxi. 8; it is to lie in the lake that burneth with fire and brimstone. What a shocking image is this!

And now, when you see the dreadful import of this denunciation, may it not spread terror through this assembly to hear, "Oh, wicked man, thou shalt surely die!" Are your hearts proof against the thunder of his threatening? Are you so fool-hardy, as not to be concerned, whether life or death, eternal life or eternal death, be your doom?

Is there no wicked man in this assembly so much affected, as at least to inquire, "Is there no way to escape? Must I die without relief? Is the sentence past beyond repeal?" No, blessed be God, you are yet alive; and while there is life, there is hope. The gates of eternal despair are not yet shut and barred upon you. Therefore, in the name of God, I assure you, there is hope, there is a possibility of escaping. But in what way? Suppose you sin on, as you have done hitherto, and herd in the crowd of wicked men; suppose you still continue thoughtless about the great concerns of eternity, neglect the Lord Jesus, and attend upon the means of grace in a careless, formal manner—suppose your hearts should never be changed by the almighty power of Divine grace, but still remain hard, impenitent, in love with sin and the world, and destitute of the love of God—suppose you resist the strivings of the Holy Spirit and your own consciences, flatter yourselves with vain hopes of safety, and shut your eyes against the light of conviction—suppose you should abandon yourselves to the pursuit of this world with your usual eagerness, and drown all serious thoughts in the bustle and confusion of secular affairs; I say, suppose you should take this course, is there any hope? No; in this way there is nothing but despair. If you should live as long as Methuselah, and continue in this course, you would still continue wicked, and never become more fit for heaven than you now are; nay, like a body tending to corruption, you would corrupt and putrefy more and more. Consult your reason, consult your Bible, consult anything, except the self-flattering heart of man, and the father of lies; and they will all tell you, that if you persist in this course, you shall surely die. Not one that ever went on in this course has entered into heaven: but in this downward road those crowds persisted, who are now with Judas and Dives, in the place of torment; and, if you tread in their steps, you shall certainly, ere long, be among them.

But if you will attend, I will endeavour to show you what you must do to be saved, and point out to you the way of life and hope. Hear me, O wicked man! who art under the sentence of death; hear me, and I will direct thee how thou mayest procure a repeal of the sentence, and live for ever. Blessed Spirit! we need thy assistance in this attempt. Oh! bear home my feeble words with resistless energy upon the hearts of sinners, that this day they may pass from death to life. Let me again demand your attention to the following directions:

If you would escape death in its most dreadful form, and enter into life, then,

First, Betake yourselves immediately to serious thoughtfulness. No more of your levity and froth; no more of your mirth, and vanity, and dissipation of thought. But now, at last, begin to think; to think seriously and sadly of your sins, of your guilty and wretched condition, of your danger of being for ever miserable, and of the best means of deliverance.

Secondly, Break off from those things that hinder your conversion. No more of your drunkenness, swearing, and other vices. No more mingle in the company of sinners, nor run with them into the same excess of riot. Break off from your over-eager pursuit of the world; and act as if you thought it infinitely worse to be lost for ever, than to be mean and poor in this life.

Thirdly, Diligently use all means that may instruct you in the nature of true religion, and teach you what you should do to be saved: particularly, read the Scriptures, and other good books, and attend upon the most faithful preaching as you have opportunity.

Fourthly, Earnestly pray to God. If you have hitherto had prayerless families, or prayerless closets, let them be so no longer: this evening consecrate them to God by prayer—Pray, particularly, for the Holy Spirit, who alone can thoroughly convert and sanctify you.

Fifthly, Endeavour to receive and submit to the Lord Jesus as your only Saviour. It is through him alone you can be saved: therefore, make use of him as your only mediator, in all your transactions with God.

Finally, Do not delay to follow these directions. Alas! if, with Felix, you put it off to a more convenient season, (Acts xxiv. 25.) there is very little hope. "To-day, if ye will hear his voice, harden not your hearts." (Heb. iii. 15.) "Now is the accepted time: now is the day of salvation." (2 Cor. vi. 2.) Therefore, now, this moment, begin the work. Now dart up a prayer to heaven, "Lord, here is a poor wicked creature, that must die ere long, unless thou have mercy upon me: have mercy upon me, O thou God of mercy." Thus pray, and keep your souls, as it were, always in a praying posture until you are heard.

And now, my dear brethren, what is your resolution upon the whole? Are you resolved to use these means for your deliverance or are you not? If you are, you have great reason to hope for success. But if not, I defy you to find one encouraging word to you in all the Bible. On the other hand, I am commanded, upon my peril, to warn you; and therefore I would once more sound this dreadful alarm in your ears, "O wicked man, thou shalt surely die." And if, when you hear the words of this curse, you bless yourselves in your hearts, and hope better things, God foresaw there would be such self-flattering, presumptuous sinners in the world, and he hath prepared his terrors against them. "If there should be among you a man or a woman, or family or tribe—a root that beareth gall and wormwood, that when he heareth the words of his curse, shall bless himself in his heart, saying, I shall have peace though I walk in the imagination of my heart; the LORD will not spare him; but then the anger of the LORD and his jealousy shall smoke against that man, and all the curses that are written in this book shall lie upon him, and the LORD shall blot out his name from under heaven: and the LORD shall separate him unto evil out of all the tribes of Israel." (Deut. xxix. 19–21.) What a tremendous threatening is this! and you see it stands in full force against those that presumptuously flatter themselves with false hopes of impunity, whether they be men or women, family or tribe: and it will certainly have a dreadful accomplishment upon such of you as disregard this repeated warning, "O wicked man, thou shalt surely die."

I doubt not but there are some of you to whom the character of the wicked does not belong, and therefore are in no danger of dying their death. To you I would speak a few parting words of encouragement. You must die; but oh! death to you will be a harmless, stingless thing—your Father's messenger to fetch you home, that you may be for ever with him. You will have good company in death; Jesus, your faithful and never-failing friend, will then be with you, and support you: and his angels will wait round your dying beds to receive your departing souls, and conduct them to eternal rest. Death will be your birth-day; then you will be born, not a helpless, weeping infant, into a world of sin and sorrow, but a perfect immortal, into a world of consummate happiness and glory. Death will be the last enemy that ever you shall conflict with; after that, you will be conquerors, more than conquerors, for ever. Death to you will be a blessing, and not a curse: so that as to you, I may change the threatening in my text, into a promise, "O good man, thou shalt surely die." Yes, blessed be God, thou shalt die in spite of earth and hell; thou shalt not be doomed to live always in such a sinful wretched world as this; but death, thy friend, will set thee free, and convey thee to the place where Jesus is, and where thy heart is gone before thee. This may, perhaps, seem strange language, that death should become a blessing: but such strange things does Jesus perform for his people. O may we all "die the death of the righteous; and may our last end be like his!" (Numb. xxiii. 10.)

For a more immediate improvement of this funeral occasion, instead of haranguing upon the virtues of the dead, many of which, I doubt not, deserve commendation, my business is with the living, who alone can receive advantage from what I say; and to them I would suggest a few solemn reflections.

First, how uncertain and frail are the nearest ties of relation, and all our domestic and relative happiness! Therefore, how much should we be concerned, to contract immortal friendships, and secure a never-dying happiness!

Secondly, Such bereavements should be made occasions of exercising resignation to the will of God.

Thirdly, Let this instance of mortality put us in mind of our own. Shall others die to warn us that we must die? and shall the warning be in vain?

Fourthly, Let us rejoice that though our friends die, yet the Lord liveth, and blessed be our rock! 2 Sam. xxii. 47. Ps. xviii. 46.

SERMON LXXV.

EVIDENCES OF THE WANT OF LOVE TO GOD.

JOHN v. 42.—*But I know you, that ye have not the love of God in you.**

NOTHING seems to be a more natural duty for a creature—nothing is more essential to religion—nothing more necessary as a principle of obedience, or a qualification for everlasting happiness, than the love of God; and it is universally confessed to be so. Whatever be the object, or whatever be the religion, all acknowledge that the love of God is an essential ingredient in it.

Should we consider only the excellency of the divine Being, and the numerous and endearing obligations of all reasonable creatures to him, we should naturally think, that the love of God must be universal among mankind; and not one heart can be destitute of that sacred, filial passion. But, alas! if we regard the evidence of Scripture or observation we must conclude the contrary. The love of God is a rare thing among his own offspring in our degenerate world. Here in my text, a company of Jews, highly privileged above all nations then upon earth, and making large professions of regard to God, are charged with the want of his love; charged by one that thoroughly knew them and could not be deceived. "I know you, that you have not the love of God in you."

But, blessed be God, his love is not entirely extinct and

* Hanover, April 14, 1756.—New Kent, April 17, 1757.

lost even on our guilty globe. There are some hearts that feel the sacred flame, even among the degenerate sons of Adam.

These two sorts of persons widely differ in their inward temper; and God, who knows their hearts, makes a proper distinction between them. But in this world they are mixed—mixed in families, and in public assemblies; and sometimes the eyes of their fellow mortals can discern but little difference; and they very often mistake their own true character, and rank themselves in that class to which they do not belong. While they continue in this mistake, the one cannot possess the pleasure either of enjoyment or hope; and the other cannot receive those alarms of danger which alone can rouse them out of their ruinous security, nor earnestly use means for the implantation of the sacred principle of divine love in their souls. To remove this mistake is therefore a necessary and benevolent attempt; benevolent not only to the former sort, but even to those who are unwilling to submit to the search, and who shut their eyes against the light of all conviction.

I am afraid many of my hearers, especially in places where I have not frequently officiated, are excited to attend by curiosity, and not by an eager thirst for religious instruction. And while hearing, they are either staring with eager expectation to hear something new and strange, or they are lying in wait to catch at some word or sentiment to furnish them with matter for cavil or ridicule; or they stand upon their guard, lest they should be catched and ensnared inadvertently to a party, or seized with the infection of some false doctrine: and thus all my labours and their attendance are in vain; and immortal souls perish in the midst of the means of salvation. But I tell you, once for all, you need not indulge an eager curiosity; for I have nothing new to communicate to you, unless it be a new thing to you to hear that the love of God is essential to a Christian, and an absolutely necessary pre-requisite to your salvation; and that you cannot be lovers of God, while your temper and conduct have the evident marks of enmity or disaffection to him. Or, if cavil or ridicule be an agreeable entertainment to any of you, you are not likely to be gratified: for the things I have to say are too plain and convictive to be cavilled at by men of sense and candor, and too serious and interesting to be laughed at. Nor need you be cautiously upon your guard; for I assure you, once for all, I have something else to do, than to come here to hang out baits to catch graceless proselytes to a party, or to propagate the infection of some false opinion. I come here to use my poor endeavours to build up such of you as love God, in your most holy faith; and to reconcile such of you to him as are now destitute of his love. This is my professed design: and when you find the drift and tendency of my labours here aim at something opposite to this, pronounce my anathema, and reject me with just abhorrence. This I not only allow, but invite and charge you to do.

The subject now before us is this: Since it is evident that some, under the profession of religion, are destitute of the love of God; and since it is of the utmost importance that we should know our true character in this respect, let us inquire what are those marks whereby we may know whether the love of God dwells in us or not. Let us follow this inquiry with impartiality and self-application; and receive the conviction which may result from it, whether for or against us.

Now it is evident the love of God does not dwell in you, if the native enmity of your hearts against him has not been subdued; if your thoughts and affections do not fix upon him with peculiar endearment, above all other things; if you do not give him and his interests the preference of all things that may come in competition with him; if you do not labour for conformity to him; if you do not love to converse with him in his ordinances; and if you do not make it the great business of your lives to please him by keeping his commandments.

First, The love of God is not in you, if the native enmity of your hearts against him has not been subdued.

This will appear evident to every one that believes the Scripture account of human nature, in its present degenerate state. By nature we are "children of wrath," (Eph. ii. 3:) and certainly the children of wrath cannot be the lovers of God, while such. "That which is born of the flesh is flesh," (John iii. 6,) and the savour of the flesh,* or, as we render it, "the carnal mind is enmity against God." Rom. viii. 7. And hence it is, that "they that are in the flesh cannot please God." Rom. viii. 8. St. Paul gives this character of the Colossians, in their natural state; and there is no reason to confine it to them: that they "were some time alienated, and enemies in their minds by wicked works." Col. i. 21. In short, it is evident from the uniform tenor of the gospel, that it is a dispensation for reconciling enemies and disaffected rebels to God. Hence it is so often expressly called the ministry of *reconciliation:* and ministers are represented as ambassadors for Christ, whose business it is to beseech men, in his stead, to be *reconciled* to God. 2 Cor. v. 18–20. But reconciliation presupposes variance and disaffection to God. From these things, it is evident, that, according to the Scripture account, the present state of nature is a state of disaffection and hostility against God. The authority of Scripture must be sufficient evidence to us, who call ourselves Christians. But this is not all the evidence we have

* φρόνημα τῆς σαρκός.

in this case. This is a sensible matter of fact and experience. For I appeal to all of you that have the least self-acquaintance, whether you are not conscious that your temper, ever since you can remember, and consequently your *natural* temper, has habitually been indisposed and disaffected, or, which is the same, lukewarm and indifferent towards the blessed God—whether you have had the same delight in him and his service, as in many other things—whether your earliest affections fixed upon him, with all the reverence and endearment of a filial heart. You cannot but know, the answer to such inquiries will be against you, and convince you that you are by nature enemies to the God that made you, however much you have flattered yourselves to the contrary.

Now, it is most evident, that since you are by nature enemies to God, your natural enmity to him must be subdued; or, in the language of the New Testament, you must be *reconciled* to him, before you can be lovers of him. And have you ever felt such a change of temper? Such a change of temper could not be wrought in you while you were asleep, or in a state of insensibility. I will not say, that every one who has experienced this, is *assured* that it is a real sufficient change, and that he is now a sincere lover of God; but this I will say, and this is obvious to common sense, that every one who has experienced this, is assured that he has felt a great change, of some kind or other, and that his temper towards God is not the same now as it once was. This, therefore, may be a decisive evidence to you: If divine grace has never changed your temper towards God, but you still continue the same, you may be sure the love of God is not in you. And if this change has been wrought, you have felt it. It was *preceded* by a glaring conviction of your enmity, and the utmost horror and detestation of yourselves upon the account of it. It was *attended* with affecting views of the attractive excellencies of God, and of your obligations to love him; and with those tender and affectionate emotions of the heart towards him, which the passion of love always includes. And it was *followed* with a cheerful universal dedication of yourselves to God and his service. And does conscience (for to that I now address) speak in your favour in this inquiry? Listen to its voice as the voice of God.

Secondly, It is evident, that you have not the love of God in you, if your thoughts and affections do not fix upon him with affectionate endearment above all other things.

This is so obvious to common sense, that I need not take up your time with Scripture quotations: for you would not have the face to profess to a person that you loved him, if, in the mean time, you have told him that he had little or no share in your thoughts and affections. You know by experience, your affectionate thoughts will eagerly pursue the object of your love over wide-extended countries and oceans: and that in proportion to the degree of your love. Now if you love God *sincerely* at all, you love him *supremely;* you love him *above* all persons and things in the universe. To offer *subordinate* love to *supreme* perfection and excellency, what a gross affront! It is essential to the love of God, that it be prevalent, or habitually *uppermost* in your souls. Now if *every* degree of love will engage a proportionable degree of your affectionate thoughts, can you imagine, that you may love God in the *highest* degree, and yet hardly ever have one affectionate thought of him? Can you love him *above all,* and yet think of him with less endearment and frequency than of many other things that you love in an *inferior* degree? Certainly, it is impossible. And is it not as evident to some of you, as almost anything you know of yourselves, that your affectionate thoughts are not frequently fixed upon the blessed God? Nay, are you not conscious, that your thoughts fly off from this object, and pursue a thousand other things with more eagerness and pleasure? Certainly, by a little inquiry, you may easily find out the beaten road of your thoughts and affections, or their favourite object. And why will you not push the inquiry to a determination? Is there any matter of daily sensation and experience more plain to some of you than this, that God is not the object of your highest reverential love, and of your eager desires and hopes? Do you not know in your consciences, that you delight more in a thousand other things: nay, that the thoughts of him, and whatever forces serious thoughts of him upon your minds, are disagreeable to you, and you turn every way to avoid them? Do you not know that you can give your hearts a-loose for days and weeks together, to pursue some favourite creature, without once calling them off, to think seriously and affectionately upon the ever-blessed God? Are not even all the arts of self-flattery unable to keep some of you from discovering a fact at once so notorious, and so melancholy? Well, if this be the case, never pretend that you love God. You may have many commendable qualities—you may have many splendid appearances of virtue— you may have done many actions materially good: but it is evident to a demonstration, that the love of God, the first principle and root of all true religion and virtue, is not in you.

Thirdly, The love of God is not in you, unless you give him and his interests the preference above all other things.

I have told you already, that if you love God at all *in sincerity*, you love him *above all*. And now, I add, as the consequence of this, that if you love him at all, you will give him and his interest the preference before all things that may come in competition with him. You will cleave, with a pious obstinacy, to that which he enjoins upon you, whatever be the consequence: and you will cheerfully resign all your other interests, however dear, when they clash with his. This you will do, not only in speculation, but in practice: that is, you will not only allow him the chief place in your hearts, but you will show that you do allow him the supremacy there, by your habitual practice. I beg you would examine yourselves by this test: for here lies the dangerous delusion of multitudes. Multitudes find it easy to flatter themselves, that they love God above all his creatures, while, in the mean time, they will hardly part with anything for his sake, that their own imaginary interest recommends to them. But this is made the decisive test by Christ himself. " If any man come unto me, and hate not his father, and mother, and wife, and children, and brethren, and sisters, yea, and his own life also, he cannot be my disciple." Luke xiv. 26. By hating these dear relatives, and even life itself, Jesus does not mean positive hatred: for, in a subordinate degree, it is our duty to love them: but he means, that every sincere disciple of his must act *as if* he hated all these, when they come in competition with his infinitely dearer Lord and Saviour; that is, he must part with them all, as we do with things that are hateful to us. This was, in fact, the effect of this love in St. Paul. " What things were gain to me, those," says he, " I counted loss for Christ; yea, doubtless, and I count all things but loss for the excellency of the knowledge of Christ Jesus my Lord: for whom I have *suffered the loss of all things*, and do count them but dung, that I may win Christ." Phil. iii. 7, 8. Now, perhaps, this trial, in all its extent, may never be your lot: though this is not at all unlikely, if a mongrel race of Indian savages and French papists, by whom your country now bleeds in a thousand veins, should carry their schemes into execution; for popery has always been a bloody, persecuting power, and gained its proselytes by the terror of fire and faggot, and the tortures of the inquisition, and not by argument, or any of the methods adapted to the make of a reasonable being. But though this severe trial should never come in your way, yet, from your conduct in lesser trials, you may judge how you would behave in greater. Therefore, inquire, when the pleasures of sin and your duty to God interfere, which do you part with? When the will of God and your own will clash, which do you obey? When the pleasing of God, and the pleasing of men come in competition, which do you choose? When you must give up with your carnal ease or applause among mortals, or violate your duty to God, which has most weight with you? When you must deny yourself, or deny your Saviour, which do you submit to? What is your habitual conduct in such trying circumstances? Do you in such cases give to God and his interests the preference in your practice? If not, your pretended love is reprobated, and appears to be counterfeit. Brethren, it is little matter in this case, what you profess, or speculatively believe: but the grand inquiry is, what is your habitual practice? And if you must be judged by this, is it not evident, that some of you have not the love of God in you?

Fourthly, The love of God is not in you, if you do not labour for conformity to him.

Conformity to him is at once the duty and the peculiar character of every sincere lover of God. "Be ye holy, as I am holy," (Lev. xix. 2.—xxi. 8,) is a duty repeatedly enjoined: and all the heirs of glory are characterized as being "conformed to the image of God's dear Son." Rom. viii. 29. Indeed, love is naturally an assimilating passion. It is excellency, real or apparent, that we love: and it is natural to imitate excellency. We naturally catch the manner and spirit of those we love. Thus if we love God, we shall naturally imitate him; we shall love what he loves, and hate what he hates. We shall imitate his justice, veracity, goodness, and mercy; or, in a word, his holiness. If we love him, nothing will satisfy us till we awake in his likeness. Now, my brethren, does your love stand this test? Are you labouring to copy after so divine a pattern? Have you ever been renewed in knowledge, righteousness, and true holiness, after the image of him that created you? And is it the honest endeavour of your life to be holy in all manner of conversation: holy as God is holy? Can you have the face to pretend you love him, while you do not desire and labour to be like him: and while there is such an indulged contrariety in your temper to his? The pretence is delusive and absurd. Since your conformity to him consists in holiness, let me beg you to inquire again, Do you delight in holiness? Is it the great business of your life to improve in it? and are your deficiencies the burden of your spirits, and matter of daily lamentation and repentance to you? Alas! is it not as evident as almost anything you know concerning yourselves, that this is not your habitual character, and, consequently, that the love of God is not in you?

Fifthly, You have not the love of God in you, if you do not delight to converse with him in his ordinances.

I need not tell you, that friends are fond of interviews, and delight in each other's company. But persons disaffected to one another, are shy, and strange, and keep off. Now God has been so condescending, as to represent his ordinances as so many places of interview for his people, where they may meet with him, or, in the Scripture phrase, *draw near* to him, appear before him, and carry on a spiritual intercourse with him. Hence it is, that they delight in his ordinances: that they love to pray, to hear, to meditate, to commemorate the death of Christ, and to draw near to the throne of grace in all the ways in which it is accessible. These appear to them not only duties, but privileges; exalted and delightful privileges, which sweeten their pilgrimage through this wilderness, and sometimes transform it into a paradise. Now, will your love, my brethren, stand this test? Have you found it·good for you to draw near to God in these institutions? Or are you not indisposed and disaffected to them? Do not some of you generally neglect them? or is not your attendance upon them an insipid, spiritless formality? Have not some of you prayerless closets—prayerless families? And if you attend upon public worship once a week, is it not rather that you may observe an old custom, that you may see and be seen, or that you may transact some temporal business, than that you may converse with God and his ordinances? In short, is it not evident, that devotion is not your delight; and consequently not your daily practice? How then can you pretend, that the love of God dwells in you? What! can you love him, and yet be so shy of him, so alienated from him, and have no pleasure in drawing near to him, and conversing with him? This is contrary to the prevailing temper of every true lover of God. Every true lover of God is of the same spirit with David, who, in his banishment from the house of God, cries out in this affecting strain, "As the hart panteth after the water-brooks, so panteth my soul after thee, O

God. My soul thirsteth for God, for the living God; when shall I come and appear before God?" Ps. xlii. 1, 2. This is certainly your temper, if his love dwell in you.

Sixthly, The love of God is not in you, unless you make it the great business of your lives to please him by keeping his commandments.

It is natural to us to seek to please those we love; and to obey them with pleasure, if they be invested with authority to command us. But those whom we disaffect, we do not study to please: or if we should be overawed and constrained by their authority to obey their commands, it is with reluctance and regret. So, my brethren, if you love God, you will habitually keep his commandments, and that with pleasure and delight. But if you can habitually indulge yourselves in wilful disobedience in any one instance, or if you yield obedience through constraint, it is demonstration against you, that you are destitute of his love. This is as plain as anything in the whole Bible. "If ye love me," says Christ, himself, "keep my commandments." John xiv. 15. "If any man love me, he will keep my words—he that loveth me not, keepeth not my sayings." John v. 23, 24. "Ye are my friends, if ye do whatsoever I command you." John xv. 14. "This is the love of God," says St. John, "that we keep his commandments: and his commandments are not grievous." 1 John v. 3. Keeping his commandments is not grievous, when love is the principle. You see, my brethren, that obedience, cheerful, unconstrained obedience, is the grand test of your love to God. There is more stress laid upon this, in the word of God, than, perhaps, upon any other: and therefore you should regard it the more. Now, recollect, is there not at least some favourite sin, which you wilfully and knowingly indulge yourselves in? And are there not some self-denying mortifying duties, which you dare to omit? And yet you pretend that you love God? You pretend that you love him, though your love is directly opposite to this grand test, which himself has appointed to try it. You may have your excuses and evasions: you may plead the goodness of your hearts, even when your practice is bad—you may plead the strength of temptation, the frailty of your nature, and a thousand other things; but plead what you will, this is an eternal truth, that if you habitually and wilfully live in disobedience to the commandments of God, you are entirely destitute of his love. And does not this flash conviction on some of your minds? Does not conscience tell you just now, that your love does not stand this test?

And now, upon a review of the whole, what do you think of yourselves? Does the love of God dwell in you, or does it not? that is, Do those characters of the want of love belong to you, or do they not? If they do, it is all absurdity and delusion for you to flatter yourselves that you love him; for it is all one as if you should say, "Lord, I love thee, though my native enmity against thee still remains unsubdued. I love thee above all, though my thoughts and affections are scattered among other things, and never fix upon thee. I love thee above all, though I prefer a thousand things to thee and thy interest. I love thee above all, though I have no pleasure in conversing with thee. I love thee above all, though I am not careful to please thee;" that is, I love thee above all, though I have all the marks of an enemy upon me. Can anything be more absurd? Make such a profession of friendship as this to your fellow-creatures and see how they will take it! Will they believe you really love them? No; common sense will teach them better. And will

God, do you think, accept that as supreme love to him, which will not pass current for common friendship among mortals? Is he capable of being imposed upon by such inconsistent pretensions? No; "be not deceived:·God is not mocked." Gal. vi. 7. Draw the peremptory conclusion, without any hesitation, that "the love of God does not dwell in you."

And if this be your case, what do you think of it? What a monstrous soul have you within you, that cannot love God—that cannot love supreme excellence, and all perfect beauty—that cannot love the origin and author of all the excellence and beauty that you see scattered among the works of his hands—that cannot love your divine Parent, the immediate Father of your spirit, and the Author of your mortal frame—that cannot love your prime Benefactor and gracious Redeemer—that cannot love him, "in whom you live, and move, and have your being," Acts xvii. 28, "in whose hand your breath is, and whose are all your ways," Dan. v. 23, and who alone is the proper happiness for your immortal spirit—that can love a parent, a child, a friend, with all their infirmities about them, but cannot love God—that can love the world —that can love sensual and even guilty enjoyments, pleasures, riches, and honours; and yet cannot love God!— that can love every thing that is lovely but God, who is infinitely lovely—that can love wisdom, justice, veracity, goodness, clemency, in creatures, where they are attended with many imperfections; and yet cannot love God, where they all centre and shine in the highest perfection! What a monster of a soul is this! Must it not be a fallen spirit, to be capable of such unnatural horrendous wickedness? Can you be easy, while you have such a soul within you? What a load of guilt must lie upon you! If love be the fulfilling of the whole law, then the want of love must be the breach of the whole law. You break it all at one blow; and your life is but one continued, uniform, uninterrupted series of sinning. The want of love takes away all spirit and life from all your religious services, and diffuses a malignity through all you do. Without the love of God, you may pray, you may receive the sacrament, you may perform the outward part of every duty of religion; you may be just and charitable, and do no man any harm; you may be sober and temperate; but, without the love of God, you cannot do one action that is truly and formally good, and acceptable to God; for how can you imagine he will accept anything you do, when he sees your hearts, and knows that you do it not because you love him, but from some other low, selfish principle? If a man treat you well, and perform for you all the good offices of the sincerest friendship; yet, if you know in the mean time, that he has no real regard for you at all, but acts from some sordid, mercenary views, are you thankful for his services, or do you love him in return? No, you abhor the deceiver, and secretly loathe his services. And will God accept of that as obedience from you, which he knows does not proceed from love to him? No. Hence it is, that as Solomon tells us, the prayer, the sacrifice, and even "the ploughing of the wicked, is sin." Prov. xxi. 4.

Now, I appeal to yourselves, is not this a very dangerous situation? While you are destitute of the love of God, can you flatter yourselves that you are fit for heaven? What! fit for the region of love! fit to converse with a holy God, and live for ever in his presence! Fit to spend an eternity in his service! Can you be fit for these things, while you have no love to him? Certainly not; you must perceive yourselves fit for destruction, and fit for nothing else. You are fallen spirits—*devilized* already.

Disaffection to God is the grand constituent of a devil, the worst ingredient in that infernal composition. And must you not then be doomed to that everlasting fire prepared for the devil and his angels? Are you capable of hoping better things, while the love of God is not in you?

And now, what must you do, when this shocking conviction has forced itself upon you. Must you now give up all hopes? Must you now despair of ever having the love of God kindled in your hearts? Yes; you may, you must give up all hopes, you must despair; if you go on, as you have hitherto done, thoughtless, careless, and presumptuous in sin, and in the neglect of the means which God has appointed to implant and cherish this divine, heaven-born principle in your souls. This is the direct course towards remediless, everlasting despair. But if you now admit the conviction of your miserable condition; if you endeavour immediately to break off from sin, and from every thing that tends to harden you in it; if you turn your minds to serious meditation; if you prostrate yourselves as humble earnest petitioners before God, and continue instant in prayer; if you use every other means of grace ordained for this purpose; I say, if you take this course, there is hope—there is hope! There is as much hope for you, as there once was for any one of that glorious company of saints, now in heaven, while they were as destitute of the love of God as any of you. And will you not take these pains to save your own souls from death? Many have taken more, to save the souls of others: and you have taken a great deal to obtain the transitory, perishing enjoyments of this life. And will you take no pains for your own immortal interests? Oh let me prevail, let even a stranger prevail upon you, to lay out your endeavours upon this grand concern. I must insist upon it, and can take no denial. This is not the peculiarity of a party I am urging upon you. Is it Presbyterianism, or new light, that tells you, you cannot be saved without the love of God? Churchmen and dissenters, Protestants and papists, nay Jews, Mahometans and pagans, agree in this, that the love of God is essential to all true religion: and if you entertain hopes of heaven without it, the common sense of mankind is against you. Therefore, oh, seek to have the love of God shed abroad in your hearts.

As for such of you, and I hope there are sundry such among you, that love God in sincerity, I have not time to speak much to you at present. Go to your Bibles, and there you will find abundant consolation. I shall only refer you to one or two passages, as a specimen. "All things shall work together for good to them that love God." Rom. viii. 28. "Eye hath not seen, nor ear heard, neither have entered into the heart of man, the things which God hath prepared for them that love him." 1 Cor. ii. 9. The love of God in your hearts is a surer earnest of your salvation, than an immediate voice from heaven. Heaven, the element of love, was prepared for such as you: and you need never dread an exclusion.

SERMON LXXVI.

THE OBJECTS, GROUNDS, AND EVIDENCES OF THE HOPE OF THE RIGHTEOUS.

PROV. XIV. 23.—*The wicked is driven away in his wickedness; but the righteous hath hope in his death.**

To creatures that are placed here a few years upon trial for an everlasting state, it is of the greatest importance how they make their departure hence. The gloomy hour of nature's last extremity: it stands in need of some effectual support; and that support can proceed from nothing then present, but only from reviews and prospects; from the review of past life so spent as to answer the end of life; and from the prospect of a happy immortality to follow upon this last struggle.

Now, men will leave the world according to their conduct in it; and be happy or miserable hereafter, according to their improvement of the present state of trial. "The wicked is driven away in his wickedness," says the wisest of men; "but the righteous hath hope in his death."

"The wicked is driven away in his wickedness"—he dies as he lived: he lived in wickedness, and in wickedness he dies. His wickedness sticks fast upon him, when his earthly enjoyments, his friends, and all created comforts leave him for ever. The guilt of his wickedness lies heavy upon him, like a mountain of lead, ready to sink him into the depth of misery. And the principles of

* Henrico, March 6, 1757.

wickedness, which he indulged all his life, still live within him, even in the agonies of death; nay, they now arrive at a dreadful immortality, and produce an eternal hell in his breast. He leaves behind him not only all his earthly comforts, but all the little remains of goodness he seemed to have, while under the restraints of divine grace: and he carries nothing but his wickedness along with him. With this dreadful attendant he must pass to the tribunal of his Judge. To leave his earthly all behind him, and die in the agonies of dissolving nature—this is terrible. But to die *in* his wickedness—this is infinitely the most terrible of all!

He once flattered himself that though he lived in wickedness, he should not die in it. He adopted many resolutions to amend, and forsake his wickedness, toward the close of life, or upon a death-bed. But how is he disappointed? After all his promising purposes and hopes, he died as he lived, in wickedness. This is generally the fate of veterans in sin. They are resolving and re-resolving to reform all their lives; but after all they die the same. They propose to prepare for death and eternity: but they have always some objections against the present time. They have always something else to do to-day; and therefore they put off this work till to-morrow—to-morrow comes, and instead of reforming, they die in their wickedness—to-morrow comes, and they are in hell. Oh! that the loiterers of this generation would take warning from the ruin of thousands of their unhappy ancestors, who have perished by the dread experiment! Brethren! are not some of you in danger of splitting upon the same rock? Are not some of you conscious, that if you should die this moment, you would die in your wickedness? And yet you have but very little fear of dying in this manner: no; you purpose yet to become mighty good, and prepare for death, before you die. So thousands purposed as strongly as you, who are now in hell. The time for repentance was still an *hereafter* to them, till it was irrecoverably past. They were snatched away unexpectedly, by the sudden hand of death, and knew not where they were, till they found themselves in eternity: and thus they had no time for this work: or their thoughts were so much engrossed with their pains, that they had no composure for it: or, they found their sins, by long indulgence, were become invincibly strong, their hearts judicially hardened, and all the influences of divine grace withdrawn: so that the work became impossible. And thus, they died in their sins. And if any of you be so foolhardy as to imitate them in their delays, you may expect to die as they did.

"The wicked is *driven* away in his wickedness"—*driven* away in spite of all his reluctance. Let him cling to life never so fast, yet he must go. All his struggles are vain, and cannot add one moment to his days. Indeed, the wicked have so little taste for heaven, and are so much in love with this world, that if they leave it at all, they must be *driven* out of it—driven out of it, whether they will or not. When they hope for heaven, they do in reality consider it but a shift, or a refuge, when they can no longer live in this their favourite world. They do not at all desire it, in comparison with this world. Here they would live for ever, if they could have their will. But let them grasp never so hard, they must let go their hold. They must be driven away, like chaff before a whirlwind—driven away into the regions of misery—into the regions of misery, I say; for certainly the happiness of heaven was never intended for such as are so disaffected to it; and that prefer this wretched world, with all its cares and sorrows, before heaven itself.

This is the certain doom of the wicked: but who are they? Though the character be so common among us, yet there are few that will own it. It is an odious character: and therefore few will take it to themselves. But there is no room for flattery in the case: and therefore we must inquire, who are the wicked? I answer, all that habitually indulge themselves in the practice of any known wickedness—all that neglect the God that made them, and the Saviour that bought them—all that live in the wilful omission of the known duties of religion and morality—all that have never known by experience what it is to repent and believe; in a word, all that are in their natural state, and have never felt a change of spirit and practice, so great and important, that it may be called, with propriety, a new birth, or a new creation—all such, without exception, are wicked: They are wicked in reality, and in the sight of God, however righteous they may be in their own eyes, or however unblamably some of them may conduct themselves before men.

And are there not some such in this assembly? Is this assembly so glorious and happy a rarity, as not to have one wicked person in it? Alas! I am afraid the most generous charity cannot indulge such a hope. May you make an impartial inquiry into a matter so important! and if you find the character of the wicked is yours, believe it, you must share in the dreadful doom of the wicked, if you continue such.

But I proceed to that part of my text, which I intend to make the principal subject of this discourse—" The righteous hath hope in his death." To have hope in death is to have hope in the most desperate extremity of human nature. Then the spirits flag, and the heart sinks; and all the sanguine hopes of blooming health and prosperity evanish. Then all hopes from things below—

all expectations of happiness from all things under the sun, are cut off. All hopes of escaping the arrest of death, are fled, when the iron grasp of its cold hand is felt. Even in these hopeless circumstances, the righteous man hath hope. The foundation of his hope must be well laid, it must be firm indeed, when it can stand such shocks as these. It is evident the objects of his hope must lie beyond the grave; for on this side of it all is hopeless. His friends and physician despair of him: and he despairs of himself, as to all the prospects of this mortal life. But he does not despair of a happier life in another state: No, he hopes to live and be happy, when the agonies of death are over: and this hope bears him up under them.

This hope I intend to consider as to its objects, its grounds and evidences, and its various degrees and limitations.

First, I am to consider the objects of the righteous man's hope in death. And here I shall only mention his hope of support in death—of the immortality of the soul—of the resurrection of his body—and of perfect happiness in heaven.

In the first place, The righteous man has an humble hope of *support in death*. He has repeatedly intrusted himself into the faithful hands of an almighty Saviour, for life and death, for time and eternity; and he humbly hopes his Saviour will not forsake him now—now, when he most needs his assistance. This was St. Paul's support, under the prospect of his last hour: "I know whom I have believed, and I am persuaded he is able to keep that which I have committed unto him against that day." 2 Tim. i. 12. As if he had said, finding my own weakness, I have committed my all into another hand; and I have committed it to one, whose ability and faithfulness have been tried by thousands, as well as myself; and, therefore, I am confident, he will keep the sacred depositum, and never suffer it to be injured or lost. This was also the support of the Psalmist; "Though I walk," says he, "through the valley of the shadow of death, I will fear no evil; for thou art with me; thy rod and thy staff they comfort me." Psa. xxiii. 4. Yea, it was upon this support St. Paul leaned, when he braved death, in that triumphant language, "Who shall separate us from the love of God? Shall tribulation, or distress, or persecution, or famine, or nakedness, or peril, or sword? Nay; in all these things we are more than conquerors, through him that loved us: for I am persuaded," says he, "that death"—that separates our souls and bodies,—that separates friend from friend,—that separates us from all our earthly comforts, and breaks all our connections with this world, even death itself "shall never separate us from the love of God, which is in Christ Jesus." Rom. viii. 35–39. What a faithful friend, what a powerful guardian is this, who stands by his people, and bears them up in their last extremity, and makes them more than conquerors in the struggle with the all-conquering enemy of mankind! How peculiar a happiness is this, to be able to enjoy the comfort of hope, in the wreck of human nature! How sweet to lean a dying head upon the kind arm of an almighty Saviour! how sweet to intrust a departing soul, as a depositum in his faithful hand! Oh, may you and I enjoy this blessed support in a dying hour! and may we make it our great business in life to secure it! In that gloomy hour, our friends may weep, and wring their hands around our beds; but they can afford us no help—no hope! But Jesus can, as thousands have known by experience. Then he can bear home his promises upon the heart; then he can communicate his love, which is better than life; and by his holy Spirit, bear up and encourage the sinking soul! Blessed Jesus! what friend can compare to thee?—

> " Jesus can make a dying bed
> Feel soft as downy pillows are;
> While on his breast I lean my head,
> And breathe my soul out sweetly there."—WATTS.

But, Secondly, *The immortality of the soul* is an object of the righteous man's hope. He is not like a Bolingbroke, and other infidels, who have made it their interest that there should be no future state, who consider immortality as an object of fear, and therefore try to reason themselves out of the belief of it, and choose to engulf themselves in the abyss of annihilation. That man has indeed a terrible consciousness of his demerit, who dares not trust himself for ever in the hands of a just and gracious God, but wishes to escape out of his hands, though it were by resigning his being. It is not the force of argument that drives our infidels to this. Demonstration and certainty were never so much as pretended for it. And after all the preposterous pains they take to work themselves up to the gloomy hope, that when they die they shall escape punishment by the loss of all the sweets of existence; yet, if I may venture to guess at, and divulge the secret, they are often alarmed with the dreadful *may-be* of a future state. In their solemn and thoughtful moments their hope wavers, and they fear they shall not be more happy than a dog or a stone, when they die. Unhappy creatures! how much are they to be pitied! and were it not for the universal benevolence of that religion which they despise, how justly would they be contemned and abhorred! They are men of pleasure now; they are merry, jovial and gay, and give a loose to all their licentious passions and appetites. But how short, how sordid, how brutal the pleasure! how gloomy, how low, how shocking their highest hope! Their highest hope is to be as much as nothing, in a few years or moments hence, as they were ten thousand years ago. They are men of pleasure, who would lose all their pleasures, if they were angels in heaven: but would lose none of them, if they were swine in the mire. Blessed be God, this gloomy hope is not the hope which the religion of Jesus inspires. No, "he hath brought life and immortality to light through the gospel." 2 Tim. i. 10. He opens to the departing soul the endless prospects of a future state of being: a state, where death shall no more make such havoc and desolations among the works of God: but where every thing is vital and immortal. Hence the righteous man hath hope in his death. He has not made it best for him, that his religion should be false. He is not driven to seek for shelter in the gulf of annihilation; nor to combat with the blessed hopes which reason and revelation unitedly inspire, as his worst enemies. He wishes and hopes to live for ever, that he may for ever enjoy the generous pleasure of serving his God, and doing good to his fellow-creatures. The belief of immortality is not, indeed, peculiar to the righteous: it is the belief of mankind in general, except a few infidels here and there, who are to be regarded as monsters in human nature. But this is not so properly the object of hope, as of fear, to multitudes. They wish it were false, though they cannot believe it is so. They have no joy and peace in believing this; but, like "devils, they believe and tremble." James ii. 19. But, to the righteous man, this is properly an object of hope: the prospect is pleasing to him. If it were a dream, which, blessed be God, it is not, it is a pleasing dream. If it were a delusion, it is a harmless and profitable delusion. It inspires him with noble pleasures, and excites him to glorious deeds, while life lasts: and if it must be entirely given up in death, he will sleep as easy as the most staunch unbeliever upon earth, who lived in the expectation of so terrible a doom. Therefore *maneat mentis gratissimus error!* "Still may the pleasing error cheat the mind!" Thus we might argue even upon the worst supposition that can be made. But we are left in no such uncertainty. This is not a pleasing error, but a pleasing truth; nay, I had almost said, a pleasing demonstration. Such it proves to the righteous man: for oh! how pleasing to the offspring of the dust, to claim immortality as his inalienable inheritance! How transporting to a soul, just ready to take its flight from the quivering lips of the dissolving clay, to look forward, through everlasting ages of felicity, and call them all its own! To sit, and prognosticate, and pause upon, its own futurities—to defy the stroke of death, and smile at the impotent malice of the gaping grave! Oh, what a happiness, what a privilege, is this! And this is what the righteous man in some measure enjoys.

Thirdly, The righteous in death has the hope of the *resurrection of his body.* This glorious hope we owe entirely to Revelation. The ancient philosophers could never discover it by their reason; and when it was discovered by a superior light, they ridiculed it as the hope of worms. But this is a reviving hope to the righteous, in the agonies of death. Those old intimate friends, the soul and body, that must now part, with so much reluctance, shall again meet, and be united in inseparable bonds. The righteous man does not deliver up his body, as the eternal prey of worms, or the irredeemable prisoner of the grave; but his hope looks forward to the glorious dreadful morning of the resurrection; and sees the bonds of death bursting; the prison of the grave flying open; the mouldering dust collected, and formed into a human body once more—a human body, most gloriously improved. This prospect affords a very agreeable support in death, and enables the righteous to say with Job, though I die, "I know that my Redeemer liveth, and that he shall stand at the latter day upon the earth: and though after my skin, worms destroy this body, yet in my flesh shall I see God." Job xix. 25, 26. This corruptible shall put on incorruption, and this mortal shall put on immortality, and death shall be swallowed up in victory. O, death! where is thy sting? O, grave! where is thy victory? 1 Cor. xv. 53–55. This is an illustrious victory indeed; a victory over the conqueror of conquerors, and of all the sons of Adam. And yet, thus victorious shall the frail dying believer be made, over that terror of human nature.

Fourthly, *The perfect and everlasting happiness of heaven* is an object of the righteous man's hope in death. He hopes to drop all his sins, and their attendant train of sorrows, behind him; and to be perfectly holy, and consequently happy, for ever. He hopes to see his God and Saviour, and to spend a happy eternity in society with him, and in his service. He hopes to join the company of angels, and of his fellow-saints of the human race. He hopes to improve in knowledge, in holiness, and in capacities for action and enjoyment, in an endless gradation. He hopes to see the face of his God in righteousness; and to be satisfied, when he awakes, with his image. Ps. xvii. 15. In short, he hopes to be as happy as his nature will possibly admit through an endless duration. Oh, what a glorious hope is this! This has made many a soul welcome death with open arms. This has made them desirous to be with Christ, which is far better. Phil. i. 23. And this has sweetly swallowed up the sensations of bodily pain. Indeed, without this, immortality would be an object of terror, and not of hope: the prospect would be insupportably dreadful. For who can bear the thought of an immortal duration spent in an eternal banishment from God and all happiness, and in the sufferance of the most exquisite pain? But a happy immortality, what can charm us more?

Having thus shown you some of the principal objects of a good man's hope in death, I now proceed.

Secondly, To show you what are the grounds and evidences of such a hope.

It is evident, it is not every kind of hope, that is intended in my text; it is a hope peculiar to the righteous: and it is a hope that shall never be disappointed, or put to shame. This, alas! is not the common popular hope of the world. Job speaks of the hope of the hypocrite: Job viii. 13; xxvii. 8, and one greater than Job tells us, that many will carry their false hopes with them to the very tribunal of their Judge. When he assures them, he never knew them, they hardly think him in earnest: "Strange! dost thou not know us? Have we not eat and drunk in thy presence, and hast thou not taught in our streets?" Luke xiii. 26. St. Paul also tells us, that while some are crying peace and safety, and apprehend no danger, then sudden destruction cometh upon them, as travail upon a woman with child, and they shall not escape. 1 Thess. v. 3. This is likewise evidently confirmed by observation: for how often do we find in fact, that many not only hope for immortality, but for immortal happiness, who give no evidence at all of their title to it, but many of the contrary? Here, then, is a very proper occasion for self-examination. Since there are so many false hopes among mankind, we should solicitously inquire, whether ours will stand the test. To assist us in this inquiry, let us consider what are the peculiar grounds and evidences of the righteous man's hope.

Now it will be universally granted, that God best knows

whom he will admit into heaven, and whom he will exclude—that it is his province to appoint the ground of our hope, and that constitution according to which we may be saved—that none can be saved, but those who have the characters which he has declared essentially necessary to salvation; and that none shall perish, who have those characters. And hence it follows, that the righteous man's hope is entirely regulated by the divine constitution, and the declarations of that holy Word, which alone gives us certain information in this case. This I say is the grand test of a true hope: it expects what God has promised: and it expects it in the way and manner established by him. It is an humble submissive hope: it does not expect happiness, as it were, in spite of him who is the author of it; but it expects happiness just in the manner which he has appointed.

Now what has God appointed to be the ground or foundation of our hope? St. Paul will tell you, "Other foundation can no man lay, than that is laid, which is Jesus Christ." 1 Cor. iii. 11. God himself proclaims, by Isaiah, "Behold, I lay in Zion for a foundation, a stone, a tried stone, a precious corner stone, a sure foundation." Isaiah xxviii. 16. Jesus Christ then is the only sure ground of hope; appointed by God himself. Or, in other words, the free mercy of God, which can be communicated only through Jesus Christ, or, for his sake, is the only sure ground of hope for a sinner. It is upon this, and not upon his own righteousness, that the righteous man dares to build his hope. He is sensible that every other foundation is but a quicksand. He cannot venture to hope on account of his own merit, either in whole, or in part. It is in the mercy, the mere mercy of God, through Jesus Christ, that he trusts. He is gratefully sensible, indeed, that God has wrought many good things in him, and enabled him to perform many good actions: but these are not the ground of his hope, but the evidences of it; I mean, he does not make these any part of his justifying righteousness; but only evidences that he has an interest in the righteousness of Christ, which alone can procure him the blessings he hopes for. Which leads me to add,

That the evidence of this hope is, the righteous man's finding, upon a thorough trial, that the characters which God has declared essentially necessary to salvation, do belong to him. Has God declared, that the regenerate, that believers and penitents, that they who are made holy in heart and life, and none but such, shall be saved? Then is my hope true and sure, when I hope for salvation, because I find these characters belong to me. I know the God of truth will keep his word: and therefore, poor and guilty and unworthy as I am, it is no presumption for me to hope for everlasting happiness from him, if I find myself to be such as he has promised everlasting happiness to.

This, brethren, is the only valid evidence of a good hope. And is this the evidence that encourages you in this important affair? Alas! the world is overrun with delusive hopes, that are so far from being supported by this evidence, that they are supported in direct opposition to it. God has declared, in the plainest and strongest terms, that no drunkard, nor swearer, nor fornicator, nor any similar characters, shall inherit his kingdom: and yet what crowds of drunkards, swearers, fornicators, and the like will maintain their hopes of heaven, in spite of these declarations? He has declared, with the utmost solemnity, that "except a man be born again, he cannot enter into the kingdom of heaven." John iii. 3. And yet what multitudes presume to hope they shall enter there, though they still continue in their natural state, and have no evidences at all of their being born again? God has declared, that "except ye repent, ye shall all perish," Luke xiii. 3, 5, like the infidel Jews; and that "he that believeth not shall be damned." Mark xvi. 16. And yet, how many hope to be saved, though they have never felt the kindly relentings of ingenuous, evangelical repentance, nor the work of faith with power wrought upon their hearts? What can be more plain than that declaration, "Without holiness, no man shall see the Lord?" Heb. xii. 14. And yet multitudes that hate holiness in their hearts, hope to be saved, as well as your precise and sanctified creatures, as they call them. In short, the hopes of many are so far from being supported by the authority of the Scriptures, that they are supported only by the supposition of their being false. If the Scriptures be true, then they and their hopes must perish together: but, if the Scriptures be false, then they have some chance to be saved; though it is but a very dull chance after all: for if they have to do with a lying, deceitful Deity, they have no ground at all of any confidence in him: they must be anxiously uncertain what they should hope, or what they should fear, from his hands. Hence you see, that we should vindicate the truth of God in these declarations, even by way of self-defence: for if the divine veracity fail in one instance, it becomes doubtful in every instance, and we have nothing left to depend upon. If they may be saved, whom God has declared shall perish, then, by a parity of reason, they may perish whom he has characterized as the heirs of salvation: and consequently, there is no certainty that any will be saved at all. Thus, sinners, while establishing their own false hopes, remove all ground of hope, and leave us in the most dreadful suspense.

Brethren! let us regulate our hopes according to his declaration, who has the objects of our hopes entirely at his disposal. When we pretend to improve upon divine constitutions, or, as we think, turn them in our favour, we do in reality but ruin them, and turn them against ourselves. Make that, and that only, the ground and evidence of your hope, which God has made such. Your hope is not almighty, to change the nature of things, or reverse his appointments: but his constitution will stand, and you shall be judged according to it, whether you will or not. Do not make that the ground or evidence of your hope, which he has not so made, or which he has pronounced the characteristic of the heirs of hell. You hope, perhaps, to be saved, though you live in the wilful neglect of some known duty, or in the wilful practice of some known sin. But has God given you any reason for such a hope? You know he has not, but the contrary. You hope he will show mercy to you, because his nature is mercy and love, and he is the compassionate Father of his creatures; or because Christ has died for sinners. But has he given you any assurances, that because he is so merciful—because he is so compassionate a Father—because Christ has died for sinners, therefore he will save you in your present condition? You hope to be saved, because you are as good as the generality, or perhaps better than many around you. But has God made this a sufficient ground of hope? Has he told you, that to be fashionably religious, is to be sufficiently religious; or, that the way of the multitude leads to life? This may be your hope; but is it the authentic declaration of eternal Truth? You know it is not, but quite the contrary. I might add sundry other instances of unscriptural hope; but these may suffice as a specimen. And I shall lay down this as a general rule, which will enable yourselves to make farther discoveries, namely, those hopes are all false, which are opposite to the declarations of God in his word.

Certainly, this needs no proof to such as believe the Divine authority of the Scriptures: and, as for the infidels, it is not the business of this day to deal with them. You who acknowledge the Scriptures as the foundation of your religion, with what force can you entertain hopes unsupported by them, or contrary to them? Hopes, that must be disappointed if God be true; and that cannot be accomplished, unless he prove a liar? Can you venture your eternal all upon such a blasphemous hope as this? But I proceed,

Thirdly, To consider the various degrees and limitations of a good hope in death.

A good hope is always supported by evidence; and, according to the degree of evidence, is the degree of hope. When the evidence is clear and undoubted, then it rises to a joyful assurance: but when the evidence is dark and doubtful, then it wavers, and is weakened by dismal fears and jealousies. Now, I have told you already, that the evidence of a good hope is a person's discovering, by impartial examination, that those characters, which God has pronounced the inseparable characters of those that shall be saved, do belong to him: or, that he has those graces and virtues, which are at once his preparation for heaven, and the evidence of his title to it. Now different believers, and even the same persons at different times, have very different degrees of this evidence. And the reason of this difference is, that sundry causes are necessary to make the evidence clear and satisfactory; and, when any of these are wanting, or do not concur in a proper degree, then the evidence is dark and doubtful. In order to be fully satisfied of the truth and reality of our graces, it is necessary we should arrive to some eminence in them: otherwise, like a jewel in a heap of rubbish, they may be so blended with corruption, that it may be impossible to discern them with certainty. Hence the weak Christian, unless he have unusual supplies of Divine grace, enters the valley of the shadow of death with fear and trembling: whereas he, who has made great attainments in holiness, enters it with courage, or perhaps with transports of joy. It is also necessary to a full assurance of hope, that the Spirit of God bears witness with our Spirit, that we are the sons of God, Rom. viii. 16, or, that he excites our graces to such a lively exercise, as to render them visible by their effects, and distinguishable from all other principles. And therefore, if a sovereign God see fit to withhold his influences from the dying saint, his graces will languish, his past experience will appear confused and doubtful, and consequently his mind will be tossed with anxious fears and jealousies. But if he be pleased to pour out his Spirit upon him, it will be like a ray of heavenly light, to point out his way through the dark shades of death, and open to him the transporting prospects of eternal day, that lies just before him.

Another thing that occasions a difference in this case, is, that an assured hope is the result of frequent self-examination; and, therefore, the Christian that has been diligent in this duty, and all his life been labouring to make all sure against his last hour, generally enjoys the happy fruits of his past diligence, and enters the harbour of rest with a $\pi\lambda\eta\rho o\varphi o\rho i a$, with sails full of the fair gales of hope: but he that has been negligent in his duty, is tossed with billows and tempests of doubts and fears, and is afraid of being shipwrecked in sight of the port.

It is also necessary to the enjoyment of a comfortable hope in death, that the mind be in some measure calm and rational, not clouded with the glooms of melancholy, or thrown into a delirium or insensibility by the violence of the disorder. And, according as this is, or is not the case, a good man may enjoy, or not enjoy, the comforts of hope.

These remarks will help us to discover with what limitations we are to understand my text, "The righteous hath hope in his death." It does not mean that every righteous man has the same degree of hope; or that no righteous man is distressed with fears and doubts in his last moments. But it means, in the

First place, That every righteous man has a substantial reason to hope, whether he clearly see it, or not. His eternal all is really safe; and as all the false hopes of the wicked cannot save *him*, so all his fears cannot destroy *him*, though they may afford him some transient pangs of horror. He is in the possession of a faithful God, who will take care of him; and nothing shall pluck him out of his hands. He sees fit to leave some of his people in their last moments to conflict at once with death and with their more dreadful fears: but even this will issue in their real advantage. And what an agreeable surprise will it be to such trembling souls, to find death has unexpectedly transported them to heaven!

Secondly, When it is said, "the righteous hath hope in his death," it means, that good men, in common, do in fact, enjoy a comfortable hope. There never was one of them that was suffered to fall into absolute despair, in this last extremity. In the greatest agonies of fear and suspicion, the trembling soul has still some glimmering hope to support it; and its gracious Saviour never abandons it entirely. And it is the more common case of the saints, to enjoy more comfort and confidence in death, than they were wont to do in life. Many, that in life were wont to shudder at every danger, and fly at the sound of a shaking leaf, have been emboldened at death to meet the king of terrors, and to welcome his fiercest assault. The soldiers of Jesus Christ have generally left this mortal state in triumph; though this is not an universal rule. And who would not wish and pray for such an exit? that he may do honour to his God and Saviour, and to his religion, with his last breath; that he may discover to the world, that religion can bear him up, when all other supports prove a broken reed; and that his last words may sow the seeds of piety in the hearts of those that surround his dying bed; this every good man should pray and wish for; though it must be left in the hands of a sovereign God to do as he pleases.

Thirdly, When it is said, "the righteous hath hope in his death," it may mean, that the hope which he hath in death shall be accomplished. It is not a flattering, delusive dream, but a glorious reality; and, therefore, deserves the name. His hope shall not make him ashamed, Rom. v. 5, but shall be fulfilled, and even exceeded. However high his expectations, death will convey him to such a state, as will afford him an agreeable surprise; and he will find, that it never entered into his heart to conceive the things that God hath laid up for him, and for all that love him. 1 Cor. ii. 9.

This is the glorious peculiarity of the good man's hope. Many carry their hope with them to death, and will not give it up, till they give up the ghost. But as it is ungrounded, it will end in disappointment and confusion. And oh! into what a terrible consternation will it strike them, to find themselves surrounded with flames, when they expected to land on the blissful coasts of Paradise! To find their Judge and their conscience accusing and condemning, instead of acquitting them!—to find their souls plunged into hell under a strong guard of devils, instead of being conducted to heaven by a glorious convoy of angels!—to feel the pangs and horrors of everlasting despair succeed, in an instant, to the flattering prospect of delusive hope! to fall back to hell from the very gates of heaven! Oh! what a shocking disappointment, what a terrible change is this!

Therefore, now, my brethren, make sure work. Do not venture your souls upon the broken reed of false hope. But "give diligence to make your calling and election sure." 2 Peter i. 10. Now, you may make a profitable discovery of your mistake: if your hope be ungrounded, you have now time and means to obtain a good hope through grace. But then it will be too late: your only chance, if I may so speak, will be lost; and you must for ever stand by the consequences. O, can you bear the thought of taking a leap in the dark into the eternal world; or of owing your courage only to a delusive dream? Why will you not labour to secure so important an interest, beyond all rational possibility of a disappointment? Have you anything else to do, which is of greater, of equal, or comparable importance? Do you think you will approve of this neglect upon a dying bed, or in the eternal world?

Let this subject strengthen the hope of such of you, whose hope will stand the Scripture-test. You must die, 'tis true; your bodies must be the food of worms: but be of good courage: your almighty and immortal Saviour will support you in the hour of your extremity, and confer immortality upon you. He will also quicken your mortal bodies, and re-unite them to your souls, and make your whole persons as happy as your natures will admit. Blessed be God, you are safe from all the fatal consequences of the original apostacy, and your own personal sin. Death, the last enemy, which seems to survive all the rest, shall not triumph over you: but even death itself shall die, and be no more. Oh, happy people! who is like unto you, a people saved by the Lord! Deut. xxxiii. 29.

Let me now conclude with a melancholy contrast: I mean the wretched condition of the wicked in a dying hour. Some of them, indeed, have a hope, a strong hope, which the clearest evidence cannot wrest from them. This may afford them a little delusive support in death; but upon the whole, it is their plague:—it keeps them from spending their last moments in seeking after a well-grounded hope: and as soon as their souls are separated from their bodies, it exposes them to the additional confusion of a dreadful disappointment. Others of them live like beasts; and like beasts they die; that is, as thoughtless, as stupid, about their eternal state, as the brutes that perish. Oh! what a shocking sight is the death-bed of such a stupid sinner! Others, who, with a great deal of pains, made a shift to keep their consciences easy, in the gay hours of health and prosperity, when death and eternity stare them in the face, find this sleeping lion rousing, roaring, and tearing them to pieces. They had a secret consciousness before, that they had no ground for a comfortable hope; but they suppressed the conviction, and would not regard it. But now it revives, and they tremble with a fearful expectation of wrath and fiery indignation. This is especially the usual doom of such as lived under a faithful ministry, and have had a clear light of the gospel, and just notions of divine things forced upon their unwilling minds. It is not so easy for them, as for others, to flatter themselves with false hopes, in the honest, impartial hour of death. Their knowledge is a magazine of arms for their consciences to use to torment them. Oh! in what horrors do some of them die! and how much of hell do they feel upon earth!

Nay, this is sometimes the doom of some infidel profligates, who flattered themselves they could contemn the bugbear of a future state, even in death. They thought they had conquered truth and conscience, but they find themselves mistaken—they find these are unsuppressible, victorious, immortal: and that, though with mountains overwhelmed, they will, one day, burst out like the smothered fires of Ætna; visibly bright and tormenting. Of this the celebrated Dr. Young, whose inimitable pen embellishes whatever it touches, gives us a most melancholy instance, related in the true spirit of tragedy—an instance of a youth of noble birth, fine accomplishments, and large estate, who imbibed the infidel principles of deism, so fashionable in high life, and debauched himself with sensual indulgences; who, by this unkind treatment, broke the heart of an amiable wife, and by his prodigality, squandered away his estate, and thus disinherited his only son—Hear the tragical story from the author's own words:

"The death-bed of a profligate is next in horror to that abyss, to which it leads. It has the most of hell, that is visible on earth; and he that has seen it, has more than faith, he has the evidence of sense to confirm him in his creed. I see it now! for who can forget it? Are there in it no flames or furies? You know not, then, what a seared imagination can figure—what a guilty heart can feel. How dismal is it! The two great enemies of soul and body, sickness and sin, sink and confound his friends, silence and darken the shocking scene. Sickness excludes the light of heaven, and sin excludes the blessed hope. Oh! double darkness! more than Egyptian! acutely to be felt! See! how he lies, a sad, deserted outcast, on a narrow isthmus, between time and eternity, for he is scarcely alive! Lashed and overwhelmed on one side, by the sense of sin! on the other, by the dread of punishment! Beyond the reach of human help, and in despair of divine!

"His dissipated fortune, impoverished babe, and murdered wife, lie heavy on him: The ghost of his murdered time, (for now no more is left) all stained with folly, and gashed with vice, haunts his distracted thought. Conscience, which long has slept, awakes like a giant refreshed with wine; lays waste all his former thoughts and desires: and like a long-deposed, now victorious prince, takes the severest revenges upon his bleeding heart. Its late soft whispers are thunder in his ears: and all means of grace rejected, exploded, ridiculed, are now the bolt that strikes him dead—dead even to the thoughts of death. In deeper distress, despair of life is forgot. He lies a wretched wreck of man on the shore of eternity! and the next breath he draws, blows him off into ruin.—

"The sad evening before the death of that noble youth, I was there. No one was with him, but his physician, and an intimate whom he loved, and whom he had ruined by his infidel principles, and debauched practices. At my coming in, he said;

"You and the physician are come too late. I have neither life nor hope. You would aim at miracles—you would raise the dead.

"Heaven, I said, was merciful———

"Or I should not have been so deeply guilty. What has it not done to bless and to save *me :*—I have been too strong for Omnipotence! I have plucked down ruin.

"I said, the blessed Redeemer———

"Hold! hold! You wound me!—That is the rock on which I split—I denied his name, and his religion.

"Refusing to hear anything from me, or take anything from the physician, he lay silent, as far as sudden darts of pain would permit, till the clock struck. Then, with vehemence :—

"Oh, Time! Time! It is fit thou shouldst thus strike thy murderer to the heart—How, art thou fled for ever? —A month! oh, for a single week! I ask not for years; though an age were too little for the much I have to do!

"On my saying, we could not do too much—that heaven was a blessed place———

"So much the worse. It is lost! it is lost! Heaven is to me the severest part of hell, as the loss of it is my greatest pain.

"Soon after, I proposed prayer.

"Pray, you that can. I never prayed—I cannot pray —nor need I. Is not heaven on my side already? It closes with my conscience. It but executes the sentence I pass upon myself. Its severest strokes but second my own.

"His friend being much touched, even to tears at this, (who could forbear? I could not,) with a most affectionate look he said,

"Keep those tears for thyself. I have undone thee— Dost weep for *me?* that is cruel. What can pain me more?

"Here his friend, too much affected, would have left him.

"No, stay. *Thou* still mayest hope:—therefore, hear me. How madly have I talked? How madly hast thou listened, and believed? But look on my present state, as a full answer to thee and to myself. This body is all weakness and pain: but my soul, as if stung up by torment to greater strength and spirit, is full powerful to reason—full mighty to suffer. And that which thus triumphs within the jaws of mortality, is, doubtless, immortal—And, as for a Deity, nothing less than an Almighty could inflict what I feel.

"I was about to congratulate this passive, involuntary confessor, on asserting the two prime articles of his creed, the existence of a God, and the immortality of the soul, extorted by the rack of nature; when he thus very passionately exclaimed—

"No, no! let me speak on. I have not long to speak —My much-injured friend! My soul, as my body, lies in ruins, in scattered fragments of broken thought. Remorse for the past throws my thoughts on the future. Worse dread of the future strikes it back on the past. I turn, and turn, and find no ray—Didst thou feel half the mountain that is on me, thou wouldst struggle with the martyr for his stake, and bless heaven for the flames:— that is not an everlasting flame: that is not an unquenchable fire.

"How were we struck? Yet soon after, still more. With an eye of distraction, with a face of despair, he cried out:

"My principles have poisoned my friend; my extravagance has beggared my boy; my unkindness has murdered my wife!—And is there another hell?—Oh! thou blasphemed, yet most indulgent Lord God! hell itself is a refuge, if it hides me from thy frown.

"Soon after, his understanding failed. His terrified imagination uttered horrors not to be repeated, or ever forgot. And, ere the sun (which I hope has seen few like him,) arose, the gay, young, noble, ingenuous, accomplished, and most wretched Altamont expired."*

Is not this tragical instance, my brethren, a loud warning to us all, and especially to such of us as may be walking in the steps of this unhappy youth? "Men may live

* See the Centaur not Fabulous.

fools, but fools they cannot die."* Death will make them wise, and show them their true interest, when it is too late to secure it. Ignorance and thoughtlessness, or the principles of infidelity, may make them live like beasts; but these will not enable them to die like beasts—May we live as candidates for immortality! May we now seek a well established hope, that will stand the severest trial! And may we labour to secure the protection of the Lord of life and death, who can be our sure support in the wreck of dissolving nature! May we live the life, that we may die the death of the righteous; and find that dark valley a short passage into the world of bliss and glory! Amen.

LINES

BY THE AUTHOR OF THE FOREGOING SERMON.

Yes! I must bow my head and die!—
  What then can bear my spirit up?
In nature's last extremity,
  Who can afford one ray of hope?

Then all created comforts fail,
  And earth speaks nothing but despair;
And you, my friends, must bid farewell,
  And leave your fellow-traveller.

Yet, Saviour, thy almighty hand,
  Even then, can sure support afford;
Even then that hope shall firmly stand,
  That's now supported by thy word.

Searcher of hearts! O try me now,
  Nor let me build upon the sand;
Oh teach me now myself to know,
  That I may then the trial stand.

* Night Thoughts.

SERMON LXXVII.

THE LOVE OF SOULS, A NECESSARY QUALIFICATION FOR THE MINISTERIAL OFFICE.*

1 THESS. II. 8.—*So, being affectionately desirous of you, we were willing to have imparted unto you, not the gospel of God only, but also our own souls, because ye were dear unto us.*

A COMPLETE ministerial character is a constellation of all those graces and virtues which can adorn human nature; and the want of any one of them leaves a hideous defect in it, that breaks its symmetry and uniformity, and renders it less amiable and less useful. The love of God, and the love of man, and all the various modifications of this sacred passion—ardent devotion and active zeal, charity, compassion, meekness, patience, and humility; the accomplishments of *the man of sense, the scholar,* and the *Christian,* are necessary to finish this character, and make us *able ministers of the New Testament.* Each of these deserves to be illustrated and recommended; but should I attempt to crowd them into one discourse, I should be bewildered and lost in the vast variety of materials. I must, therefore, single out some one particular, some one bright star in this heavenly constellation, to which I would confine your attention on this solemn occasion, and with the sacred splendour of which I would

---

* Preached in Cumberland County, Virginia, July 13, 1758, at the ordination of the Rev. Messrs. Henry Patillo and William Richardson.

adorn both myself and you. Let the subject be BENEVOLENCE, or *the love of souls*. Love is a delightful theme; and those that feel it, take pleasure in thinking and talking about it. Therefore, while this is the subject, we cannot be weary nor inattentive.

The history of mankind cannot furnish us with a more striking instance of benevolence, or the love of souls, than we find in St. Paul, who speaks as like a *father* and an *orator*, as an apostle, in this chapter—a chapter written in such pathetic strains, that I can remember the time, when the reading of it has drawn tears even from heart so hard as mine. " So, being affectionately desirous of you, we were willing to have imparted unto you, not the gospel of God only, but also our own souls, because ye were dear unto us."

The connection seems to be this—"As a nurse cherisheth her children," that is, as a tender mother,* who undertakes to nurse her own children, with fond endearment gives them the breast, and feeds them with her milk, the quintessence of her own blood; "so," saith St. Paul, "being affectionately desirous of you, we were willing to have imparted unto you" the sincere milk of the word, even "the gospel of God," the most precious thing we had to communicate: and not only this, but "our own souls, (or lives also,) because ye were dear unto us."

When he says, "We were willing to have imparted to you our own souls or lives;" he may either mean, that such was his affection for the Thessalonians, and such was the influence his affection had upon his address to them,

---

* The nurse here meant is not the unnatural nurse of modern times, whose mercenary service can never supply a mother's care; but the genuine tender mother; and it should be rendered, "as a nurse cherishes her own [ἑαυτῆς] children."

that he, as it were, breathed out *his soul* in every word. So affectionate, so pathetic, and earnest was his discourse, that it seemed animated with his very soul. Every word came from his heart, and seemed a vehicle to convey his spirit into them. He spoke as if he would have died on the spot, through earnestness to affect them with what he said, that their souls, so dear to him, might be saved. Or, he may mean, that so ardent was his love for them, that he was willing not only to preach to them, but to lay down his life for them: he would willingly endure a natural death, if by that means he might bring them to obtain eternal life. Some of the patriots of antiquity, we are told, loved their country so well, that they generously sacrificed their lives for it. This public spirit, indeed, is almost lost in these dregs of time; but the evidence of ancient history is sufficient to convince us, that such a thing once *was*. And shall not the *love of souls* be as heroic, and work as powerfully? Yes, we find this spirit of sacred patriotism glowing with the utmost ardour in the generous breasts of St. Paul and his brethren. St. Paul breathes out his spirit towards the Philippians: "If," says he, "I be *offered up*,* (as a libation,) upon the sacrifice and service of your faith, I joy and rejoice with you all." St. John also infers this as a matter of obligation, from the consideration of Christ's laying down a life of infinitely greater worth for us. "Hereby," says he, "perceive we the love of God, because he laid down his life for us; and we ought to lay down our lives for the brethren." 1 John iii. 16.

Such, my brethren, ought to be the spirit of every gospel minister: thus dearly should they love the souls of men; and thus ardently desirous should they be to conduct them to Jesus and salvation.

* σπένδομαι, Phil. ii. 17.

My present design is to show *what a happy effect the generous principles of benevolence, or the love of souls, would have upon us in the exercise of the ministerial office.* And this will appear in the following particulars:

First, The prevalence of this disposition will contribute to *ingratiate us* with mankind, *and so promote our usefulness.*

It is not to be expected in the stated course of our ministry, that those should receive advantage by our labours to whom we are unacceptable. If they are disaffected to us, they will also disregard what we say; and while they disregard it, they can receive no benefit from it. The ministry of a contemptible minister will always be contemptible, and consequently useless.

But, on the other hand, when a minister in his congregation appears in a *circle of friends,* whose affections meet in him as their common centre, then his labours are likely to be at once pleasing and profitable to them. When the heart is open to the speaker, his words will gain admission through the same door of entrance. Then there will be no suspicions of imposition, or sinister interested design. Then even hard things will be received, not as the effect of moroseness, but as wholesome severities from faithful friendship. For the confirmation of this, I may appeal to your observations of mankind: you know they will bear many things, and even take them well, from a known friend, which they would warmly resent from others. You know the persuasion, the remonstrance, or admonition of a friend will have great weight, when that of others would be neglected or contemned. In short, you may almost carry any point with mankind, if they are satisfied you love them, and regard their interest; and they also love you: but even real kindnesses from those whom they disaffect, will be received with suspicious caution, and perhaps with indignation.

Now, such is the nature of the ministerial office, that there is much need of this happy prepossession of mankind in our favour, that we may discharge it with comfort and success. We are not only to display the rich grace of the gospel, and the fair prospects of a blessed immortality, but also to denounce the terrors of the Lord, and rouse up again the lightning, and thunder, and tempest of Sinai. We must represent human nature, in its present fallen state, in a very disagreeable and mortifying light; we must overturn the flattering hopes of mankind, and embitter to them the false measures of sin, in which they place so much of their happiness. We must put the cross of Christ on their shoulder, and reconcile them to self-denial, reproach, and various forms of suffering, for the sake of righteousness. We must inculcate upon them a *religion for sinners;* in which self-accusation, remorse, fear, sorrow, and all the painful heart-breakings of repentance are necessary ingredients. We must set ourselves in a strenuous opposition to the favourite lusts of the world, and the ways of the multitude; and this alone will set the world against us as their enemies, and officious disturbers of their peace. We must also exercise the rod of discipline for the correction of offenders; must take upon us the ungrateful office of reprovers, and give the reproof with proper degrees of severity. In short, the faithful discharge of our office will oblige us to use such measures as have been found, by the experience of thousands of years, to be very unpopular and irritating to mankind—measures, which brought upon the prophets, the apostles, and other servants of Christ, the odium of the world, and cost many of them their lives: and if we tread in their steps, we may expect the same treatment in a greater or less degree.

And how shall this unacceptable office be discharged

faithfully, and yet as *inoffensively* and acceptably as may be? I can prescribe no certain expedient for this purpose while the world continues as bad as it is. This is what neither the prophets nor apostles, though inspired from heaven, were ever able to find out. But that which will have the happiest tendency of anything within the reach of humanity is *the prevalence of benevolence*, or the love of souls. It is comparatively easy to a minister, who ardently loves his people to make them sensible he does love them, and is their real friend, even when he is constrained to put on the appearance of severity. Love has a language of its own—a language which mankind can hardly fail to understand; and which flattery and affectation can but seldom mimic with success. Love, like the other passions, has its own look, its own voice, its own air and manner in every thing, strongly expressive of itself. Look at a friend when the sensations of love are tender and vigorous; and you see the generous passion looking upon you through his eyes, speaking to you by his voice, and exprssing itself in every gesture. The most studied and well-managed artifices of flattery and dissimulation have something in them so stiff, so affected, so forced, so unnatural, that the cheat may often be detected, or, at least, suspected. When dissimulation mourns, and puts on the airs of sorrow and compassion, it is but whining and grimace: and when she smiles, it is but fawning and affectation; so hard is it to put on the face of genuine love without being possessed of it; and so easy is it for a *real* friend to *appear* such.

Hence it appears that the most effectual method to convince our hearers we love them, is, to be under the strong influence of that benevolent passion which we profess. The sacred fire of love will blaze out in full evidence, and afford the strongest conviction they can receive that their minister is their *friend* and aims at their best interest, even when he denounces the terrors of the Lord against them, or assumes the unacceptable character of their reprover; and when they are thus happily prepossessed in his favour, they will take almost anything well at his hands. Then, if ever, they will *receive* the truth in love, when they believe it is *spoken* in love. That must be a base, ungenerous sinner indeed, that can look up to the pulpit, and there see an affectionate *friend* in the person of his minister, adorned with smiles of love, or melting into tears of tender pity, and yet resent his faithful freedoms, and hate him as his enemy for telling him the truth. Some ministers are not loved in a suitable degree, by their people. But, not to mention at present the criminal cause of this neglect on the side of the people, I am afraid one common cause is, that *they* do not sufficiently love *them*. Love is naturally productive of love; it scatters its heavenly sparks around, and these kindle the gentle flame where they fall. Oh! that each of us, who sustain the sacred character, may purchase the love of our people with the price of our own love! And may we distribute this to them with so liberal a hand, as always to leave them debtors to us in this precious article? That people should love their minister more than *he* loves *their* souls, is a shocking, unnatural disproportion.

Farther; the prevalence of this sacred passion naturally tends to give our ministrations, and the whole of our behaviour, such an air as will ingratiate us with mankind. Let a minister of Christ ascend the sacred desk, with a heart glowing with the love of souls, and what an amiable, engaging figure does he make, even in the most gloomy and terrible attitude? Then, if he denounces the vengeance of Heaven against impenitent sinners, he passes sentence with tears in his eyes, and the aspect of tender compassion and friendly reluctance. And if he is obliged to put on the stern air of a reprover, he still retains the winning character of the friend of human nature, and the lover of souls. Love gives a smooth, though sharp edge to his address, like a razor set in oil. Love animates his persuasions and exhortations, and gives them additional force. Love breathes through his invitations, and renders them irresistible. Love brightens the evidence of conviction, and sweetly forces it upon unwilling minds: for who would not lay his heart open to a friend? Love mingles smiles with his frowns, and convinces his hearers, that he denounces the morose terrors of the law with all the affectionate benevolence of the gospel; and represents their danger and misery in a tremendous light, merely because he loves them, and is zealous to save them from it. Love would direct him to express *the friend* in conversation, better than all the rules of good-breeding that can be prescribed, and all the affected familiarity and complaisance that the greatest artificer of flattery and dissimulation could use. Love would give a graceful ease, an engaging softness, and a generous open-hearted frankness, to his behaviour. Then, like St. Paul, he would *comfort, and exhort, and charge* his dear people, *as a father doth his children,* (1 Thess. ii. 11:) and would carry all the attractive charms of love with him, wherever he went. This would be an inward principle of conduct; and, therefore, the conduct to which it incites, would be natural, easy, and unsuspicious, and free from stiffness and affectation, which never fails to disgust whenever it is perceived. "Thou God of Love! implant and cherish this noble principle of love in our breasts; and may it actuate us in all our ministrations and adorn and recommend them!"

Secondly, The love of souls will enable and excite us

to exercise the ministry in such a manner as tends to *affect* our hearers, and *make deep impressions* upon their hearts.

Love will move all the springs of sacred oratory, and give a force and spirit to our address, which even a hard heart cannot but feel. When we speak to those we love, we shall speak *in earnest;* and that is the most likely way to speak to the heart. Love will render us sincere, and adorn all our ministrations with the plain, artless garb of sincerity; and the sincerity of the speaker will have no small influence upon the hearers. When love warns of danger, the hearers are alarmed, and apprehend there is danger indeed. When love dissuades, it is the gentle restraint of a friendly hand; and therefore agreeable, or at least tolerable. When love persuades and exhorts, what heart can be obstinate, when it is known it does but persuade to happiness? When men see the *confessed lover of souls* in the pulpit, it is natural for them to say, "Now it is proper I should be attentive, and regard what I hear; for I am convinced the speaker aims at my best interest. His advice I may safely follow, as the voice of benevolence; and even his admonitions and reproofs I should take in good part, as the effects of faithful friendship, that would rather run the risk of my displeasure by plain and honest dealing, than be accessary to my ruin by flattery and excessive complaisance." Thus it is natural for them to reflect; and by these reflections the way is opened into their hearts. Oh! that you and I, my reverend brethren, may make thorough trial for the future of the efficacy of this affectionate preaching! May the arrows we shoot at the hearts of our hearers be pointed with love! Then are they most likely to make a deep *medicinal* wound. The force of love is at once gentle and powerful: it will tenderly affect, when a stern, austere, imperious address never fails to disgust and exasperate; and a languid and indifferent address, the language of a cold unfeeling heart, leaves the hearers as cold and languid as itself.

Thirdly, The ardent love of souls will make a minister of the gospel *diligent* and *laborious* in his office.

How laborious and indefatigable are we in pursuing a point we have so much at heart, and in serving those we love? Therefore, if the love of souls be our *ruling passion*, and their salvation be the object we have in view, with what indefatigable zeal and diligence shall we labour to serve their immortal interests? How gladly shall we spend and be spent for them, though the more abundantly we love, the less we should be loved. 2 Cor. xii. 15. How will this endear our office to us, as an *office of benevolence*, and a *labour of love?* How shall we love and bless the name of our divine Master, who has made it our duty to spend our life in the agreeable work of *serving our friends?* While this benevolent spirit glows in our breasts, we can leave no blanks in the page of life, but all must be filled up, with the offices of friendship. Love, an ever-operating love, will always keep us busy; and that amiable and comprehensive summary of our Master's history, will, in some measure, agree to us, " HE WENT ABOUT DOING GOOD." Acts x. 38. Love will excite us to *preach the word, to be instant in season, out of season.* 2 Tim. iv. 2. Love will give our conversation a right turn; and with a natural unaffected air, drop a word upon every occasion that may edify the *circle of friends*—a circle so wide, that we can never pass over it while in company, with any of the human race. As souls are equal in worth, notwithstanding the various ranks and distinctions among mankind, so the love of souls is an *impartial* passion: like the redeeming love of Christ, it extends to "all kindreds, and tongues, and nations, and languages;" and it will excite us to the most condescending services to the poorest and meanest, as well as the great and honourable. Love will often cast us on the knee, as affectionate intercessors for our *dear friends*, that is, for *all mankind*, and particularly for that part of them which is more immediately entrusted to our ministerial care. Love will inspire our prayers with a kind of *almighty* importunity, and render us unable to bear a refusal in a point that we have so much at heart. Oh! what wonders would love enable us to perform! How many precious hours, now trifled away, would it redeem! What spirit, what life, would it diffuse through our secret devotions and public ministrations! It would adorn our life not only with a shining action here and there, like a single star in the expanse of heaven, but crowd it thick with pious offices of friendship, and generous exploits of benevolence, like the glow of blended splendour from ten thousand stars in the milky way. It would render idleness an intolerable burden, and labour a pleasure; which leads me to observe more particularly, in the

Fourth place, The ardent love of souls will not only make us diligent and laborious in our ministry, but enable us to bear all the hardships and difficulties we may meet with in the discharge of it, with *patience*, and even with *cheerfulness*. Love is strong to suffer, and mighty to conquer, difficulties. The love of fame, the love of riches, the love of honour and pre-eminence, what difficulties has it encountered—what obstructions has it surmounted—what dangers has it dared! How tolerable, yea, how pleasant, has it rendered fatigues and hardships? and how has it rendered dangers and death charming and illustrious! And shall not the nobler passion, *the love of souls*, do vastly more? It *has* already done more. This was the heroic passion that animated St. Paul, and taught him to look upon dangers and death, in their most shocking forms, with a generous contempt. Though he knew that bonds and imprisonments awaited him, yet, "none of these things move me," says he, "neither count I my life dear unto myself, so that I might finish my course with joy, and the ministry which I have received of the Lord Jesus." Acts xx. 24. I point out this *Christian hero* as a specimen; but it would be easy to add many other illustrious names to the list. And would not the sacred fervour of love reconcile even such feeble and cowardly creatures as we, to hardships and dangers, in the service of souls? If we may but save them from everlasting ruin, how insignificant are the greatest difficulties we can suffer in the generous attempt? If we make those happy whom we love, then welcome labour, fatigue, difficulties and dangers; and farewell that ease and indolence, that pleasure or pursuit, that is inconsistent with this main design. Labour is delight,* difficulty inviting, and danger illustrious and alluring, in this benevolent enterprise. Who would not labour with pleasure, and suffer with patience, and even with joy, for the service of souls—souls formed for immortality! souls whom we love even as ourselves! We begrudge a little pains or suffering for those whom we disregard; but love sweetens labour, and lightens every burden.

This I would direct to you, my brethren, who are now to take part with us in this ministry. I doubt not but you are better acquainted with the work you are about to undertake than to need my information, that you are not entering into an office of ease and self-indulgence, but of labour, toil, and difficulty—an office that cannot be faithfully discharged without frequent self-denial, incessant application, and exhausting fatigues. But for your encouragement, remember, all this labour, difficulty, and self-denial, you are to endure in the service of those you

---

* Labor ipse voluptas.

love; and love, you will find, will lighten the burden, and render a life of toil and fatigue more easy and delightful, than indolence and inactivity. Therefore, cherish this generous benevolence, as that which will render you vigorous in doing, and strong in suffering. O that your Divine Master may fire your hearts with much of this truly ministerial spirit!

Fifthly, I observe the prevalence of a spirit of benevolence would happily restrain us from every thing " low, disgraceful, or offensive," in our ministrations, in our conversation and designs.

Let the love of mankind be warm and vigorous in our hearts, and we cannot address them, even upon terrible subjects, in a stern, unrelenting manner—a manner that looks more like a *scold*, than a Christian orator; and that tends rather to exasperate, than reform. But we shall denounce the most terrible things, in a soft language, and with as mild and gentle an aspect as faithfulness will allow, or compassion inspire.

Let love be the spring of your conduct, and it will render it courteous without affectation, insinuating without artifice, engaging without flattery, and honest without a huffish bluntness. This will guard us against all airs of insolence and affected superiority in conversation, and a distant, imperious behaviour, that seems to forbid access, and never fails to excite disgust. When a man appears of vast importance to *himself*, and assumes state, he will, for that very reason, appear very insignificant and contemptible to others. But if we tenderly love those with whom we converse, it will render our conversation affable, sociable, and condescending, and modest. And this will be found the best expedient to engage the esteem of mankind, and procure that respect which pride with all its artifices seeks in vain: for that maxim, repeated more than once by our blessed Lord, who knew mankind so well, will hold good in this case, "He that exalteth himself shall be abased: and he that humbleth himself shall be exalted." Luke xiv. 11.—xviii. 14.

The ardent love of souls will render us meek and patient under kind treatment, and keep down those sallies of passion, which are at once so unmanly and unministerial. This will sweeten our temper, and purge out those sour humours, that render men peevish, sullen, and ready to blaze out into anger at every provocation. This lamb-like spirit will conform us to the Lamb of God, "who, when he was reviled, reviled not again, and when he suffered, he threatened not," 1 Pet. ii. 23, nor burst out into a flame of passion.

If love be predominant in the heart, it will happily disable us from aiming at sordid ends, and from taking sordid measures to obtain those ends. Then we shall not labour for the applause of mankind, but for their salvation. We shall not seek their silver and gold, but their souls: and we shall be able to say with St. Paul, "We seek not *yours*, but *you*." 2 Cor. xii. 14. Though we may not only be willing to receive, but justly insist upon, a competent support, from those in whose service we spend our lives; yet if the love of their souls, and not of their money, be uppermost in our hearts, it will inspire us with such moderation, contentment, and noble negligence, as to earthly things, and with such apparent zeal and earnestness for their salvation, that if they have the least degree of candour, they cannot but be convinced that it is the latter, and not the former, which we have most at heart, and chiefly labour to promote. This principle will restrain us from all the artifices of avarice, and from ever wearing a "cloak of covetousness." 1 Thess. ii. 5. It would enable us so to behave, as may afford mankind sufficient matter of conviction, that we need not be *hired* to do them good offices, and endeavour to save their souls; but that we do it *freely*, were it possible for us to make the attempt successfully, without devoting all that time and strength to it, which others lay out in providing for themselves and their families.

Thus I have shown you, in a few instances, by way of specimen, what a happy influence the love of souls would have upon the ministerial character, and consequently upon those among whom we exercise our office. And I hope you will forgive me, my reverend fathers and brethren, if I have, as it were, forgotten there are any present but you, and that I have talked over the matter with you among ourselves. Indeed, my thoughts were so engrossed with that peculiar share which we have in the subject, that it seemed unnatural to me to take notice of its reference to mankind in general, and how much the love of souls is the duty of hearers as well as ministers.

But now, my brethren of the laity, I must turn my address to you: and the first improvement I would have you make of what you have heard, is, to learn from it in what light you should look upon your ministers. Look upon us as "the friends, the lovers of your souls." If you can discover that we are not worthy of that character in some suitable degree, then it is your right as men, as Christians, and I may add, as Presbyterians, to reject us, and not own us as your ministers. But, while you cannot but acknowledge us in that sacred character, you are bound to esteem us as your friends—the real friends of your best interests.

And while you look upon us in this light, will you not practically treat us as such? Will you not regard the instructions, the exhortations and warnings, which you hear from your *friends*, who feel themselves deeply interested in your happiness? "Now we live, if ye stand fast in the Lord:" (1 Thess. iii. 8,) but, O! it *kills* us to see you destroy yourselves. Will you not bear with our severity, since it is the warmest benevolence to you, that constrains us to use it? When we would engage you to a life of holiness, why do you fly off, as if you were afraid of being overreached, and caught in some snare? We are *your friends* that persuade you; and why will you apprehend any injury from us? When we would dissuade you from the pursuit of guilty pleasures, why are you so stiff, and tenacious of them? Do you think we love you so little, that we could begrudge you any real happiness, or would be officious to impair it? No, indeed, my dear brethren, such a design is so far from our hearts, that to promote your happiness in time and eternity, is the great end of all our labours. When we would put the cross of Christ on your shoulders, and compel you to carry it; when we inculcate upon you a life of self-denial, mortification, and repentance, believe me, it is because we love you, and are fully persuaded this course will turn out best for you in the issue. Do we denounce the curses of the law against you? do we severely reprove, and loudly alarm you? why, what possible motive can we have to this, but love, honest, disinterested love? We love you, and therefore cannot bear the thought that you should perish for want of faithful warning. Were self-love our principle, we are not so dull, but we could learn the art of flattery, and prophesy smooth things, as well as others. But we are afraid for ourselves, as we are afraid for you, lest it should be said to us, when the wall, which we have daubed with untempered mortar, is fallen, "Where is the daubing, wherewith ye have daubed it?" (Ezek. xiii. 12.) And will you not regard the warning of a friendly voice? Will you not fear, when love itself points out your danger, and dare conceal it no longer?

Let me also propose it to you, since your ministers love you, ought you not to love them in return? Does not love deserve love? Ought you not to *esteem them highly in love,* if not for their own, yet " for their works' sake?" 1 Thess. v. 13. And ought you not to give them proper expressions of your love, by improving their affectionate endeavours for your own benefit? Do but permit them to be the instruments of making you happy, and you gratify them in the main point. For this purpose, while they *speak* the truth in love, do you *receive* it in love; and cheerfully submit to their admonitions and reproofs, which, however often they meet with angry resentments, are the most substantial evidences of a faithful disinterested friendship which they can possibly give you. Here also I may add, and I hope without offence, since in this place I can have no personal concern in it myself, that you should express your love to your ministers by cheerfully and generously contributing to their support. While they love you so tenderly, while they spend their time, their strength, and all their abilities in your service, can you be so sneaking, so ungenerous, so ungrateful as to leave them and their families to suffer want, and incur the contempt entailed upon poverty? Sure you cannot be guilty of such a conduct?

Finally, let me exhort you to love your own souls. Certainly your ministers should not be singular in this. If they are so strongly obliged to love the souls of others, surely you must be obliged to love your own. It may seem strange that I should exhort creatures to love themselves, whose guilt and misery are so much owing to the *excess* of that principle. But alas! the soul is hardly any part of that *self,* which they so immoderately love: no, that precious immortal part is disregarded, as if it were but a trifling excrescence, like their nails or their hair, incapable of pleasure or pain. But, oh! *love their souls;* make sure of *their* happiness, whatever becomes of you in other respects; for what would it profit you, if you should gain the whole world, and lose your own souls? Matt. xvi. 26.

Let me now resume the consideration of my subject, as it refers to us of the sacred character. Methinks we may claim a peculiar property in this day; as we are peculiarly concerned in the business of it. We often preach to *others;* but let us for once preach to *ourselves*; and let *the love of souls* be the generous, and delightful subject. The subject may recommend itself; and what has been said, strongly enforces it. But, alas! I feel there is one heart among us, that stands in need of farther excitements. Therefore, though I doubt not but I might address myself to all my fathers and brethren, without offence, I must indulge myself in soliloquy and preach to one that *needs it most*. I mean *myself.*

My glorious and condescending Lord, who has endowed mankind with a wise variety of capacities, and assigned to each of them his proper work, agreeably to the various exigencies of the world they inhabit, has appointed me the most pleasing work, the work of love and benevolence. He only requires me to act *the friend of human nature,* and show myself *a lover of souls*—souls whom He loves, and whom he redeemed with the blood of his heart—souls whom his Father loves; and for whom he gave up his own Son unto death—souls, whom my fellow-servants of a superior order, the blessed angels love; and to whom they concur with me in ministering—souls, precious in themselves, and of more value than the whole material universe

—souls that must be happy or miserable, in the highest degree, through an immortal duration—souls united to me by the endearing ties of our common humanity—souls for whom I must give an account to the great Shepherd and Bishop of souls—souls whom none hate but the malignant ghosts of hell, and those fallen spirits in flesh, who are under their influence upon earth. And oh! can I help loving these dear souls? Why does not my heart always glow with affection and zeal for them? Oh! why am I such a languid friend, when the love of my Master and and his Father is so ardent? when the ministers of heaven are flaming fires of love, though they do not share in the same nature? and when the object of my love is so precious and valuable? The owners of those souls often do not love them; and they are likely to be lost for ever by the neglect. Oh! shall not I love them? shall not love invigorate my hand, to pluck them out of the burning? Yes, I will, I must love them. But ah; to love them more! Glow, my zeal! kindle my affections! speak, my tongue! flow, my blood! be exerted, all my powers! be my life, if necessary, a sacrifice to save souls from death! Let labour be a pleasure; let difficulties appear glorious and inviting, in this service. O thou God of Love! kindle a flame of love in this cold heart of mine; and then I shall perform my work with alacrity and success.

But I must drop my soliloquy and return to you my venerable friends; and I shall take up no more of your time, than just to glance at a collateral inference from my subject; and that is, if we should love our hearers, and even all mankind, then certainly we should *love one another*. If when we see one another in judicatures, or at any other place, we see our *friends*, how pleasing and delightful will it render all our interviews? If mutual confidence and union of hearts subsist among us, with what ease, harmony and pleasure shall we manage all our affairs? If we *love one another with a pure heart fervently*, with what life and ardour will it inspire our intercessions for each other, when we are far apart, in our respective closets? How will it teach us to bear one another's burdens, to sympathize with each other, to compromise differences, to forgive infirmities, and *agree to differ*, that is, differ peaceably, if in anything we should differ in sentiment. How sweet is friendship, how reviving the conversation, and even the very sight of a friend! Blessed be God, this pleasure we have enjoyed in our little presbytery; and I must add, in all the ecclesiastical judicatures to which I have ever belonged. This has rendered absence on such occasions so painful a self-denial to me, that nothing but incapacity could constrain me to submit to it. The conviction of duty, and the impulse of friendship, pushed me on the same way, and were irresistible.

I am so happy as to be able to furnish you with a new argument for brotherly love and harmony among us, in a presbyterial capacity; and that is, the union between the synods of New York and Philadelphia, to which we belong—a union of which I was witness; and which appeared to me not a merely external artificial bond, which would soon break to pieces, but an union of hearts. And I must say, that however warm have been my desires, and however sanguine my hopes of peace, yet I never expected to see so truly pacific a spirit prevail in both bodies, and such a generous forgiveness and oblivion of past mutual offences. May the same spirit of peace circulate far and wide among ministers and people; and may it reach to this colony, where we so peculiarly need that additional strength which results from a state of union. This is not only my wish and prayer, but my hope: and as the union of synods leaves the people in the possession of their right to choose their own ministers, as much as while we were in a divided state: as all objections from the Protest, which was long looked upon as an insuperable obstacle, are effectually removed, by both synods agreeing in the general principles of protestation, and by the synod of Philadelphia declaring, "That they never judicially adopted the protestation entered Anno Domini seventeen hundred and forty-one, nor do account it a synodical act;" and as the synod of New York have done proper honour to what they account the late *work of God*, in which I shall always esteem it both my duty and my right peaceably to concur with them; I say, as the union has been formed upon such fair and honourable terms, I hope it will be acceptable to the people in general, and that instead of endeavouring to re-kindle the flames of contention, they will honestly endeavour to improve the advantages of a state of peace and union; and then the God of peace will be with them. *Amen.*

THE MANNER OF ORDINATION, &c.

I now proceed to prepare the way more immediately for the solemnity of this day: and for the sake of the hearers in general, it may be proper for me to show, in a few words, the *design* and *propriety* of ordination by the imposition of hands, and *who* are the persons invested with the power of ordination.

It is agreeable to the common practice of mankind, to signify the conveyance of important offices by some solemn *rite;* and God wisely condescends to deal with men in their own manner, and to cast his transactions with them into the model of their transactions with one another. Thus,

THE MANNER OF ORDINATION. 521

in particular, he has appointed that the investiture of persons with the sacred office should be performed with the significant ceremony of *laying on of hands*. This is evident from St. Paul's exhortation to Timothy, "Neglect not the gift that was given thee by prophecy, with *the laying on of the hands* of the presbytery." 1 Timothy iv. 14. He intimates in his second Epistle, that he had a peculiar share in that solemnity, or *presided* at the occasion; for, says he, "I put thee in remembrance, that thou stir up the gift of God, which is in thee, by the putting on of *my* hands." 2 Tim. i. 6. Thus Paul himself, and his colleague Barnabas, were set apart to their mission to the heathen world; for St. Luke informs us, that while the prophets and teachers of the church of Antioch were ministering to the Lord, and fasting, "the Holy Ghost said, separate me Barnabas and Saul, for the work whereunto I have called them. And when they had *fasted, and prayed, and laid their hands upon them,* they sent them away." Acts xiii. 2, 3. To this also St. Paul refers, when he enjoins Timothy to "*lay hands* suddenly on no man;" 1 Tim. v. 22; that is, to invest no man with the sacred office, till he had taken sufficient time to be satisfied of his qualifications. This solemn rite was used for the like purpose under the law of Moses; and from thence it was transferred to the Christian church. Thus, when Joshua was nominated his successor, the Lord commands Moses, "Take thee Joshua, the son of Nun, a man in whom is the Spirit, and *lay thine hand upon him,* and give him a charge. And Moses did as the LORD had commanded him." Num. xxvii. 18–23. Deut. xxxiv. 9. This ceremony was also used upon other solemn occasions both under the Old and New Testament, as in the authoritative benedictions of the inspired patriarchs and prophets; Gen. xlviii. 14, 15, &c. Mark x. 16; in miraculously healing the sick;

Mark vi. 5, and xvi. 18, and in conveying the extraordinary gifts of the Holy Ghost, on which account the imposition of hands generally attended baptism, in the apostolic age. Acts viii. 15–17, and xix. 5, 6. Heb. vi. 2.

It must be granted, that in the ordinary ages of the church, when miraculous powers have ceased, this rite cannot answer *all* the same purposes, in the same extent, as in the age of miracles and inspiration. There is no such virtue in the hand of a bishop or presbytery, as to *infuse* ministerial qualifications, or the gifts of the Spirit: and all pretensions to such a power, are arrogant, enthusiastical and ridiculous. Yet, there are sufficient reasons for the *continued* use of this rite in the church in all ages. It may still answer some important ends, for the sake of which it should be used, though it may not now answer *all* the ends it once did. It may now serve, as well as in the apostolic age, as a solemn significant sign of a man's consecration to the sacred office. It may now serve as well as then, as a significant ceremony in solemn ministerial benedictions, or in the presbytery's prayer to God for his blessing upon the person so peculiarly devoted to his service; after the example of Christ, the patriarchs and prophets. And it may also be used now, as well as ever, as a significant sign and seal of the *ordinary* gifts and graces of the Spirit, which are the privilege of the church, and particularly of its ministers in all ages. Of this it may still be a proper sign, as baptism is still a sign of *regeneration* and the *remission* of sins; and, therefore, still administered, though it be not now followed with such *miraculous* effects as in the apostolic age. When the *main* ends of an ordinance can be *substantially* answered, there is always good reason for its continuance, whatever *circumstantial* variations it may be subjected to.

Upon such principles as these the generality of Christians, in all ages have practised ordination by the *imposition of hands* as a divine institution still in force. And upon these principles we now intend to proceed in investing these our brethren with the sacred office.

But here a question lies in our way, which has been much agitated in the world, to *whom* does the power of ordination belong? To a *presbytery*, that is, to a collective body of ministers of the *same rank* and order? or to a *bishop*, that is, to a minister of a *superior order*, above the rest of the clergy? To this my time will allow me to give but a short answer.

First, it may be easily proved, by an induction of particulars, that 'επίσκοπος and πρεσβύτερος, bishop or presbyter, in the New Testament, signify the *same office*, and are applied to the *common* ministers of the gospel *promiscuously;* and consequently, that there is no such office by divine appointment, as that of a bishop in the modern sense of the word, that is, a *diocesan* bishop, of an order *superior* to the rest of the clergy. Now, if there should be no such office, certainly the power of ordination cannot belong to it; for it cannot belong to a nonentity, or an usurped authority. I bind myself to make out this, when called to it; but now I must pass it over thus superficially.

Secondly, I remark, that ordination is an *act of presbytery* appears from sundry scripture instances. The apostles were all upon an *equality*, or formed a *presbytery;* and they concurred in this act. Thus Paul and Barnabas jointly ordained elders in every city. Acts xiv. 23. Timothy, as I observed before, was ordained by the laying on of the hands of the *presbytery*, 1 Tim. iv. 14, in which it seems St. Paul presided. 2 Tim. i. 6. And we have seen that Paul and Barnabas were ordained by the prophets and teachers, or as they may be called, the *presbytery* of Antioch. I add,

Thirdly, That ordination is, I think, universally acknowledged to be an *act of government;* and consequently to belong to those who are invested with the government of the church: but the power of church-government is committed to the ministers of the gospel *in general:* therefore, so is the power of ordination. That the power of church-government is committed to ministers *in common*, is evident from more passages of the New Testament than I can take time to quote. St. Paul speaks of it as belonging to elders, or presbyters, " to *rule* well," as well as to "labour in word and doctrine." 1 Tim. v. 17. "Them that have the *rule* over you," is his periphrasis for the ministers of the churches to whom he writes. Heb. xiii. 7, 17, 24. He mentions it as a necessary qualification of a minister, that, "he *rule* his own house" well; "for," says he, "if a man know not how to *rule* his own house, how shall he take care of the church of God?" 1 Tim. iii. 4, 5. This implies, that it belongs to the province of every minister, to *rule* the church of God, as the master of a house does his family. So also, when *submission* and *obedience* are required, on the part of the people, it implies a power to *rule*, on the part of the elders or presbyters. Of this many instances might be given. See 1 Cor. xvi. 16; Heb. xiii. 17; 1 Thess. v. 12, 13. Now, since it is evident, that ordination is an *act of government*, and that the power of government belongs to the ministers *in general*, it follows, that the power of ordination also belongs to ministers *in general*, and should not be appropriated to a *superior* order of bishops. Therefore, without encroachment or usurpation, we proceed, in the name of the Lord Jesus, to exercise this power.

And now, my dear brethren, the solemn business of the

day comes very near you. You are just entering into the most solemn engagement, that human nature is capable of: you have already had some trial of your work; and though no doubt the trial has discovered to you so much of your weakness and insufficiency as may keep you always humble and dependent upon divine grace; yet, I hope, you have found it a delightful work—the *work of love*—the *office of friendship*; and therefore pleasing. I hope you have already found, that you serve a good master; and that you never desire to change for another: no, you are fixed for life, and even for eternity. The churches also have had trial of your ministerial qualifications; and we have reason to hope, they are so well satisfied, that it is their general and earnest desire, you should be invested with full authority to exercise all the branches of the sacred office. And this presbytery, from the repeated trials they have had of your piety, learning, and other qualifications, judge you fit to take part with them in the ministry. You are therefore desired, and solemnly charged, in the presence of God, to give an honest answer to the following questions:

Do you heartily believe the divine authority of the Christian religion, as taught in the Holy Scriptures of the Old and New Testament? And do you promise, that in the strength of God, you will resolutely profess it, and adhere to it, though it should cost you all that is dear to you in the world, and even life itself?

Do you receive the Westminster Confession of Faith, as the confession of *your faith:* that is, do you believe it contains an excellent summary of the pure doctrines of Christianity as taught in the Scriptures, and as purged from the corruptions of popery, and other errors that have crept into the church? And do you purpose to explain the Scriptures agreeably to the *substance* of it?

Do you receive the directory for worship and government composed by the Westminster Assembly, as agreeable to the word of God, and promise to conform to the *substance* of it?

Can you honestly declare, that as far as you can discover, after frequent examination, you have reason to hope, that the religion you now undertake to teach, has had a sanctifying efficacy upon yourselves, and made you habitually holy in heart and life?

Can you honestly declare, that as far as you know yourselves, after strict examination, you do not undertake the holy ministry from any low, interested and mercenary views; but with a sincere, prevailing aim at the glory of God and the salvation of men?

Do you solemnly promise, depending upon divine grace, for assistance, that you will faithfully and zealously endeavour to discharge all the duties of the sacred office with which you are now about to be invested; particularly, that you will be diligent in prayer, reading, study, preaching, ministering the sacraments, exercising ecclesiastical discipline, and edifying conversation?

Do you promise that you will endeavour to form your conduct, and that of your families, as far as your influence can extend, that they may be imitable examples to all around you of that holy religion which you profess and preach?

Do you profess your willingness, in meekness of spirit, to submit in the Lord to the discipline and government of the church of Christ, and the admonitions of your brethren?

Finally; Do you resolve and promise, that you will continue in the faithful discharge of your office, so long as you have life, strength and opportunity, to whatever discouragements and suffering it may expose you?

As you have thus made a good confession before many

witnesses, and given us ground to hope that God has really called you to this office, we proceed, in the name and by the authority of the Lord Jesus, solemnly to set you apart to it, by prayer and the imposition of hands, which himself has appointed for this purpose.

[Here Mr. Patillo, and Mr. Richardson kneeled down, and the presbytery put their hands upon them; and he that presided offered up a solemn prayer over them, agreeably to the materials recommended in the Westminster Directory upon this head.]

And now, our dear brethren and fellow-servants in the gospel, as Moses laid his hands on Joshua, and gave him a charge, so we, in this solemn posture, "charge you before God and the Lord Jesus Christ, who shall judge the quick and the dead, at his appearing, and his kingdom, preach the word; be instant in season, out of season; reprove, rebuke, exhort, with all long-suffering and doctrine, 2 Tim. iv. 1, 2; that you may save yourselves, and those that hear you." 1 Tim. iv. 16. We solemnly charge you, to "take heed to yourselves, and to all the flock over which the Holy Ghost has made you overseers, to feed the church of God, which he hath purchased with his own blood." Acts xx. 28. Remember the consequences of this day's transaction will follow you through all eternity. Therefore, make it the business of your lives to perform your obligations. The oath of God is upon you, and ye are witnesses against yourselves, that ye have chosen the Lord for your master, to serve him. "And now, brethren, we commend you to God, and to the word of his grace, which is able to build you up, and to give you an inheritance among all them which are sanctified." Acts xx. 32. But I would not encroach; and therefore leave this charge to be finished by another.*

* The Rev. Mr. John Todd, A. M.

And as a token of our receiving you into ministerial communion, as members of this presbytery, we give you the the right hand of fellowship.

[Here each member of the presbytery gave Messrs. Patillo and Richardson his right hand.]

And with our hand we give you our heart. We welcome you as new labourers into our Lord's vineyard; and we wish, we hope, and pray you may long be employed there with great pleasure and success. We cannot help pouring out a torrent of fatherly wishes and prayers for you. May the great God make you able ministers of the New Testament. May you shine as illustrious luminaries in the church—" holding forth the word of life." Phil. ii. 16. And may you be made the happy instruments of "turning many from darkness to light." Acts xxvi. 18. " Oh! may your whole lives be one uninterrupted course of pleasing labour to yourselves, and extensive usefulness to the world. And when you die, may you fall with the dignity of ministers of Jesus. May this be your rejoicing in your last agonies, and in the nearest view of the supreme tribunal, even the testimony of your consciences, that in simplicity and godly sincerity, not by fleshly wisdom, but by the grace of God, you have had your conversation in the world. 2 Cor. i. 12. And when Christ, who is your life, shall appear, then may you also appear with him in glory. Col. iii. 4. O thou supreme Lord of the world, and King of the church, thus let these thy servants live, and thus let them die. *Amen.*

SERMON LXXVIII.

THE OFFICE OF A BISHOP A GOOD WORK.

1 TIM. III. 1.—*This is a true saying, if a man desire the office of a bishop, he desireth a good work.**

IT is agreeable to the common sense and common practice of mankind, that persons should be invested with important offices by some solemn and significant ceremony: and it is an instance of the wisdom and condescension of the great God, that he deals with men in their own manner, and models his transactions with them, into the form of their transactions with one another. Thus, in particular, he has appointed, that the investiture of persons with the sacred and important office of the gospel ministry, should be performed by the laying on of the hands of the presbytery, attended with solemn fasting and prayer. To this St. Paul refers, when he exhorts Timothy not to neglect the gift that was in him, which was given him by prophecy, with the laying on of the hands of the presbytery; 1 Tim. iv. 14, at which solemnity, it seems, St. Paul presided; for, in the second epistle, he gives the same exhortation to the same person, in terms that imply thus much: "I put thee in remembrance *once more*, that thou stir up the gift of God, which is in thee, by the put-

* Hanover, Virginia, June 5, 1757.—At the ordination of the Rev. Mr. John Martin, to the ministry of the gospel.

Certus est hic sermo, si quis episcopatum desiderat, præclarum opus desiderat.—BEZA.

Fidelis est sermo, quod si quis concupiscit presbyterium; opus bonum concupiscit.—TREM. ex. SYR.

ting on of MY hands." 2 Tim. i. 6. Thus Paul himself and Barnabas were set apart for their mission to the Gentile world. Acts xiii. 2, 3. While the prophets and teachers of the church of Antioch were ministering to the Lord, and fasting " the Holy Ghost said, Separate me Barnabas and Saul, for the work whereunto I have called them. And when they had *fasted and prayed*, and *laid their hands upon them*, they sent them away." This is probably included in " the doctrine of laying on of hands," which the apostle enumerates among " the first principles of the doctrine of Christ," Heb. vi. 1, 2, and to this he refers, when he enjoins Timothy, 1 Tim. v. 22. " Lay hands suddenly on no man." This solemn rite was used for the like purpose under the law of Moses, and from thence was transferred to the gospel church. Thus, when Joshua was nominated his successor, the Lord commands Moses, " Take thee Joshua the son of Nun, a man in whom is the Spirit, and *lay thine hands upon him;* and set him before Eleazar the priest, and before all the congregation; and give him a charge in their sight. And Moses did as the LORD commanded him; and he took Joshua and set him before Eleazar the priest, and before all the congregation; and he *laid his hands upon him*, and gave him a charge, as the LORD commanded." Numbers xxvii. 18–23; Deut. xxxiv. 9. This solemn rite was used also upon other occasions both under the Old and New Testament: as in the authoritative benedictions of the patriarchs and prophets, under the immediate inspiration of the Holy Spirit: Gen. xlviii. 14, 15, &c.; Mark. x. 16; in miraculously healing the sick: Mark xvi. 18, and vi. 5; and especially in communicating the gifts of the Holy Spirit, not only to the persons invested with the ministerial office, but to the primitive Christians in general. Acts viii. 15–17, and xix. 5, 6; Heb. vi. 2. And hence the imposition of hands generally attended, or soon followed upon, baptism, in the apostolic age.

This is the best precedent I can recollect for annexing a solemn charge to the imposition of hands. Indeed, a charge given in so solemn a posture, is so weighty and affecting, that methinks it is impossible not to feel it at the time; or for those that have once felt it, ever to forget it afterwards.

It is evident, that in the ordinary ages of the church, when miracles are become needless for the confirmation of our religion, the imposition of hands in investing persons with the ministerial office, cannot answer all the same purposes, in the same extent, as in the apostolic age of miracles and inspirations. The hands of a bishop or a presbytery cannot now confer the Holy Ghost, or any of his miraculous gifts; and the high and extravagant pretensions of this kind, that have been made, have cherished superstition and enthusiasm in some, and exposed the institution itself to the ridicule and contempt of others. But though the institution cannot now answer all the same purposes, in the same extent, as in the apostolic age, yet there is no reason to lay it entirely aside, or to esteem it an idle insignificant ceremony. It may still answer some ends, common to the ordinary and extraordinary ages of the church. And there may be sundry purposes even now, so analogous to the miraculous purposes of the primitive institution, that it may be very proper still to retain it, on account of this analogy. It may now serve, as well as in miraculous ages, as a solemn ceremony and significant sign of a man's consecration to the sacred office. It may now serve, as well as in miraculous ages, as a solemn rite in ministerial benedictions, or in the presbytery's earnest prayer to God for his blessing upon the person so peculiarly devoted to his service; after the example of Christ, the patriarchs and prophets. And it may also be used now, as properly as ever, as a significant sign and seal of the ordinary gifts and graces of the Holy Ghost, which are the privilege of the church of Christ, and particularly of its ministers in all ages. Of this it may still be a sign; as baptism is still a sign of regeneration and the forgiveness of sins: and therefore still observed, though it be not now followed with such miraculous effects, as in the apostolic age. When the ends of an ordinance can be *substantially* answered, there is always a good reason for its continuance, to whatever circumstantial variations it may be subject.

Upon such principles as these the generality of Christians in all ages have looked upon ordination by the laying on of hands, as a divine institution still in force. This is the solemnity, that has occasioned our present meeting; and, I hope, that in so large an assembly, there are not a few, who have been and still are, wafting up their earnest prayers to God, that his efficacious blessing may attend a solemnity so important in itself, and so unusual in this colony.*

My text will furnish materials for a discourse adapted to this occasion. "This is a true saying, if a man desire the office of a bishop, he desireth a good work." To explain and improve the sundry parts of which shall be my present business.

"*The office of bishop.*"—What is meant by this office, or what rank a *bishop* should bear in the Christian church, is a debate that has been managed with great learning and plausibility: and alas! with much uncharitableness and fury, on both sides, for a long time. I am not able to add anything new to the argumentative part of the controversy: and I am sure I am not disposed to add anything to the heat and fury of it. But the present occasion renders it necessary for me to declare my sentiments upon this point, with the reasons of them: in order to show you

* This was the first Presbyterian ordination in Virginia.

the principles on which the validity of Presbyterian ordination, to be solemnized at the close of this hour, is founded.

We may easily know what the office of a bishop is, in a certain church, for which I have the sincerest benevolence and veneration, though I cannot think and practice in some little things as she does. In that church, we know, a bishop is an officer of a distinct and superior order among the clergy; as distinct from the rest of the clergy, as a colonel from a captain, or a justice of the peace from a constable; and superior to them in his revenues, in his civil rank, and in ecclesiastical authority. As to his revenues, they generally amount to two or three thousand pounds sterling per annum, while many of the inferior clergy have hardly the fiftieth part of that income. As to his civil rank, he is a peer of the realm, and a member of the House of Lords. His ecclesiastical authority extends to many things, which the common clergy are supposed incapable of; such as, the over-sight of the clergy in his diocess, (which many perhaps include some hundreds of them) as *they* oversee the laity—the power of ordaining priests and deacons, and degrading them; of confirming catechumens; of holding spiritual courts, &c. At the head of this hierarchy is an archbishop, who oversees these overseers, and has pretty much the same power over the bishops as *they* have over the common clergy. The bishops are supposed to be so much engaged in these more honourable duties of their function, that they are very seldom employed in the lower and more laborious duties of the pastoral office, such as preaching the word, and administering the sacraments. This is a brief view of the office of bishop, in that church from which we have the misfortune to dissent; and the church of Rome has pretty much the same notion of it; which certainly cannot add to its popularity among Protestants.

But the inquiry now before us, is not, what is meant by an English bishop; but what is meant by an apostolic New Testament bishop? Whether it be indeed a distinct superior order of ministers; or whether it be a name common, and equally applicable, to ministers in general, without distinction?—whether certain acts of authority are peculiar to a bishop, according to the apostolic constitution? or whether they equally belong to all ministers of the gospel? You see this inquiry will lead you to your Bibles: and I hope, you are all so far protestants, as to join with the great Chillingworth in saying "The Bible! the Bible! is the religion of protestants."

It is a strong presumption, in my view, that Jesus Christ never intended to establish a superior order among his ministers; but, on the other hand, that they should all stand upon equal ground: in that he checks the proud contention of his disciples for superiority in the following strong terms; " Ye know, that the princes of the Gentiles exercise dominion over them; and they that are great, exercise authority upon them: but it shall not be so among you;" Matt. xx. 25, 26, that is, in civil courts, there are officers of various orders, and various ranks of nobility: but among you, the officers of my kingdom, it shall not be so : but you shall be all of one order.

But that which appears decisive in this point is, that the term *bishop*, in the New Testament, does not, in one instance, signify a superior order of ministers; but is indisputably applied to all the ministers of the gospel in general.

The officers of the apostolic church were of two kinds, ordinary and extraordinary: and both are enumerated by the apostle. The ascended Redeemer gave some apostles; and some prophets; and some evangelists; and some pastors and teachers. Eph. iv. 11. The *apostolate* was an extraordinary office, and ceased with the twelve who were invested with it by Christ himself. To this office belonged the administration of the word and sacraments, and the exercise of discipline. But besides these ordinary duties of the ministerial office, there were some grand peculiarities that belonged to the apostles. They were the immediate witnesses of Christ's resurrection; and therefore it was an essential qualification for their office, that they had seen him after his resurrection; which St. Paul intimates in that query, "Have I not seen Jesus Christ our Lord?" 1 Cor. ix. 1. They were also endowed with the gift of tongues, and other miraculous powers of the Spirit, which they were enabled to communicate to others. Thus they were qualified to be the first founders of the church, and propagators of the gospel among all nations. But it needs no proof, that they had no successors in these extraordinary parts of their office; and consequently, the superiority of the apostles cannot be urged as an argument for the superiority of bishops over the rest of the clergy, in ordinary ages: nor can it be pretended, without intolerable arrogance, that bishops, without one of the distinguishing qualifications of the apostles, are their successors in office.

The next rank of officers, namely *prophets*, were persons inspired with the knowledge of things future. And it is not pretended, that theirs was an office of perpetual standing in the church.

As for the *evangelists*, they were itinerant ministers, or commissaries under the apostles, who travelled among the churches, and made such regulations as were wanting. This seems to have been the only peculiarity of their office: and in other respects it does not appear, that they were superior to the common ministers of the gospel. Therefore it is not to my purpose to inquire, whether their office should be still continued in the church or not.

The ordinary ministers of the gospel, are those whom the apostle here calls *pastors* and *teachers*. They are denominated from their office. Because the churches under their care, are often represented as flocks, which they were to feed, guide, and guard; therefore they are called *pastors* or *shepherds*. Because it was their office to teach the great doctrines and precepts of the gospel; therefore they are called teachers. Because the term [πρεσβύτεροι] *elders*, which properly signifies elders in age; did at length become a respectable term for honourable officers, like the Roman word, *Senator;* or rather because those were generally ordained to the ministry, who had been of longest standing in the churches, and were properly [πρεσβύτεροι] *elders*, in Christianity, if not in age, in opposition to the [νεόφυτοι] *novices*, who were but lately introduced into the church, and were but *juniors* in Christianity; therefore the ministers of the gospel are often called [πρεσβύτεροι] *elders*. And because it was their office to *oversee*, to *visit*, and *to take care of* their churches, as a shepherd does his flock: therefore they were called [επίσκοποι] *bishops*, or overseers. Wherever the word *bishop* occurs in our translation of the New Testament, it is always [επίσκοπος] in the original: and the proper signification of this word, is an *overseer*, or *inspector*. So it is sometimes translated, particularly in the Acts. " Take heed to the flock, over which the Holy Ghost hath made you *overseers*." Chap. xx. 28. The original word is επισκόπους, the same which is elsewhere translated *bishops*. So also, " Feed the flock of God which is among you, taking the *oversight* thereof, not through constraint, but willingly." 1 Pet. v. 2. Here again the original word is ἐπισκοποῦντες which, indeed, properly signifies *taking the over-sight;* but might be rendered *discharging the office of a bishop*, with as much propriety as ἐπισκόπους, is any where rendered *bishop*. You see, then, that the title of *bishop*, according to its original signification, which is, an *overseer*, does not denote a superior order of clergy; but is applicable equally to all the ministers of the gospel in general, whose common duty it is to take the *over-sight* of their flocks.

And as the original sense of the word will admit of this application; so we find, in fact, that it is applied promiscuously to all ministers without distinction; and that the very same persons, who in some places are called *presbyters* or *elders*, are in other places called *bishops:* and consequently a *presbyter* and a *bishop*, in the sense of the New Testament, signify the very same person. Of this I shall give you a few instances. A remarkable one of this kind, you have in the passage just quoted for another purpose. St. Paul being on his way to Jerusalem, was desirous of an interview with the ministers of the Ephesian church: and therefore we are told " From Miletus he sent to Ephesus, and called the *elders* of the church." Observe the persons he sent for were the *elders* or *presbyters*, Acts xx. 17, (compared with verse 28), of the church: and these were the persons that came: for it is added, when *they* (the *presbyters*) were come to him, he said unto *them,* " Ye know after what manner I have been with you at all seasons." And thus he goes on in a very affecting discourse to them; and then, addressing himself to the very same persons a little before called *elders* or *presbyters*, he exhorts them to take heed to all the flock, over which the Holy Ghost had made them *overseers*. Here, as I observed before, the original word rendered *overseers,* is the same with that which is translated *bishops*, in other places, in the New Testament. And it is undeniably evident, that the very same persons who are called [πρεσβυτέρους] *presbyters* or *elders* in the seventeenth verse, are called [επισκόπους] *bishops*, in the twenty-eighth; and consequently a scripture-*bishop*, and a *presbyter* or *elder*, are the same thing, or denote the same office.*

A like instance we have in the Epistle to Titus. "For this cause," says St. Paul, "left I thee in Crete, that thou shouldst set in order the things that are wanting, and ordain *elders* or *presbyters*† in every city." Chap. i. 5–7. He then proceeds to describe the qualifications of those, whom Titus should ordain elders or presbyters. "If any man be blameless, the husband of one wife," &c. And still speaking of the same point, he immediately adds, "For a *bishop* must be blameless." Here it is evident, that by *bishop* he means the same person, and the same office, as by *elder* or *presbyter* just before. In this sense, his argument is conclusive, and the transition natural; and stands thus: "Ordain only such to the office of a presbyter or bishop, who are blameless; for a bishop or presbyter must be blameless." But if we suppose, that by these two titles he means to offices of a distinct order, the argument is languid, and the transition impertinent; for it would stand thus: "Ordain no man a presbyter unless he be blameless, for this reason, because a bishop, an officer of a distinct and superior order must be blameless." This would be as weak and impertinent, as if I should say, no

---

* This is the remark of Jerome, Chrysostom, Theodoret, Oecumenius, and Theophylact. And Dr. Whitby, though a strenuous advocate for modern episcopacy, pleads strongly in support of the remark, against Dr. Hammond, who, indeed, asserts the same thing, though very preposterously; insisting that here, bishops are called presbyters, but not presbyters bishops. Vid Whitby in loc.

† πρεσβτέρους.

man shall be made a deacon, to look after the poor, unless he be a scholar, because a minister of the gospel must be a scholar. We therefore conclude, that an apostolic bishop signified no more than a presbyter, or an ordinary minister of the gospel.

We may also draw the same conclusions from a passage in Peter: "The elders," or presbyters, "who are among you, I exhort," says he, "who also am an elder," or co-presbyter: 1 Pet. v. 1, 2, $\sigma v\mu\pi\rho\epsilon\sigma\beta\acute{v}\tau\epsilon\rho o\varsigma$. "Feed the flock of God which is among you, taking the oversight thereof, not through constraint, but willingly." I had occasion to tell you before, that the original word here used ($\epsilon\pi\iota\sigma\kappa o\pi o\tilde{v}\nu\tau\epsilon\varsigma$) might be rendered *discharging the office of a bishop*, with as much propriety as any word in the New Testament is rendered *bishop*. And as the apostle expressly calls those, to whom he directs his exhortation, *presbyters*, it unavoidably follows, that the *discharging the office of a* Scripture-*bishop*, belongs to *presbyters*, or to the ministers of the gospel in common, and consequently that both these terms denote one and the same office.

From these instances, I think it evident, that according to the truly primitive and apostolic plan, all the ministers of the gospel are of the same order, and that there should be no superiority among them but what may be among persons of the same order. Were it necessary, and did my time allow, I might confirm this opinion by the testimonies of some of the fathers, particularly of those who lived nearest to the apostolic age. Though it must be owned, that the distinction between bishops and presbyters was early introduced into the church; and the gradation still went on, till at length the bishop of Rome usurped the character of universal bishop, and exalted himself above all that is called God, or is worshipped. 2 Thes. ii. 4. Indeed, the Episcopal scheme gives room, and consequently lays a temptation to ambitious men, to climb until they come to the top of the hierarchy. But when all ministers are upon a level, and their office is not attended with secular honours and riches, they have not such room, or temptation to ambition; and the highest character they can aspire to, is that of humble laborious servants of Christ and the souls of men.

Having discovered, that the office of a bishop in my text, signifies the same with that of an ordinary minister of the gospel,* it may be proper briefly to mention the principal powers and duties of this office.

To the office of a gospel minister, then, it belongs to preach the word; to administer the sacraments; to concur in the ordination of persons duly qualified to this office; and to rule the church of God. The two first particulars are hardly disputed; but upon the two last, it may be necessary to offer a few observations.

It has been urged by the patrons of diocesan episcopacy, that the ordination of ministers, and the government of the church, are acts of authority, peculiar to the superior order of bishops. But if, as has been proved, there be no such superior order, according to the original constitution of the New Testament, it follows, that ministers must be ordained, and the church governed by presbyters: or there can be no ordination or church government at all.

That ordination is the act of a presbytery, appears from sundry passages of Scripture. The apostles were all upon an equality; and they concurred in this act. Thus Paul and Barnabas jointly ordained elders in every

---

* That the ancient church understood the text in this sense appears from the Syriac version, in which επισκοπη *the office of a bishop,* is rendered *presbyterium.* So Tremellius translates it:—Si quis concupiscit *presbyterium,* opus bonum concupiscit.

city, with fasting and prayer. Acts xiv. 23. Timothy, as I observed before, was ordained by the laying on of the hands of the presbytery, 1 Tim. iv. 14, in which St. Paul presided. 2 Tim. i. 6. And Paul and Barnabas were ordained to their mission among the Gentiles, by the prophets and teachers, or, as they may be called, the *presbytery* of Antioch. Acts xiii. 2, 3.

Ordination is universally acknowledged to belong to them that have the government of the church of Christ committed to them. But this we find, is committed to the ministers of the gospel in general: therefore, so is ordination. St. Paul speaks of it as the province of elders or presbyters to rule or preside* well, no less than to labour in the word and doctrine.† When he is writing to a particular church, "*them that have the rule over you,*" or your guides,‡ a frequent phrase for its ministers. He mentions it as a necessary qualification of ministers in common, "that they rule" or preside; 1 Cor. xvi. 16; "over their houses well: for," says he, "if a man know not how to rule his own house, how shall he take care of the church of God?" This implies, that it belongs to the province of every minister, to rule and take care of the church of God, as the master of a house does of his family. So also, wherever *submission* and *obedience* is required on the part of the people, it implies a power to *rule* on the part of the elders or presbyters. Thus, it is said, "*submit* yourselves—to every one that helpeth with us, and laboureth;" or, as it may be more properly rendered, to every fellow-worker [with us] and labourer;§ that is, according to the use of the word elsewhere,‖ every

---

* προεστῶτες πρεσβύτεροι, 1 Tim. v. 17.
† ἡγουμένοι, Heb. xiii. 7, 17, 24. ‡ προιστάμενον, 1 Tim. iii. 4, 5.
§ παντὶ τῷ συνεργοῦντι καὶ κοπιῶντι.
‖ 1 Tim. v. 17.—οἱ κοπιῶντες λόγῳ καὶ διδασκαλίᾳ. St. Paul calls Timothy, who was undoubtedly a minister, συνεργὸς μοῦ, my fellow-worker.

"labourer in word and doctrine." "*Obey* them that *have the rule* over you, and *submit* yourselves: for they watch for your souls, as they that must give account." Heb. xiii. 17. "We beseech you, brethren, to know them which labour among you, and are *over* you in the Lord, and admonish you, and to esteem them very highly in love for their work's sake." 1 Thess. v. 12, 13. You see, from these instances, that to labour in the word and doctrine, and to *rule* the church of God, are duties that belong to one and the same office, namely, that of presbyters, or ordinary ministers of the gospel: and therefore, all the acts of church government, and particularly that of ordination, belong equally to them all in general.

Here I would observe, that by the power of church-government, I do not mean, nor does the New Testament design, a power to *lord* it over God's heritage—a power to dictate and prescribe, in matters of faith and practice, what Jesus Christ, the great head of the church, has not prescribed in his word—a power over the persons or estates of the laity; or to govern the church with the secular arm. Such a power has been usurped by ambitious ecclesiastics, and many countries still groan under the tyranny. But this is not the power with which Christ has invested his ministers. They only have power to admit new members into the church, upon finding them properly qualified—power to instruct, advise, comfort, and admonish their charge, according to their circumstances—a power of using proper measures with offending members to bring them to repentance—to exclude them from the peculiar privileges of the church, if they continue obstinately impenitent; and to re-admit them upon their repentance. These are the principal acts of the governing power of ministers of the gospel. And what is this, but a power essential to all societies, in which there is any order

THE OFFICE OF A BISHOP A GOOD WORK. 543

or decorum? A power of ruling, without oppressing; of executing Christ's laws, not of imposing laws of their own; in short, a power of doing good!

I now proceed to the other parts of my text; in considering which, I shall have the happiness of being more practical.

"If any man *desire* the office of a bishop." The word here rendered *desire*,* is very strong and emphatical; and signifies to *catch at*—to *reach after*—to be *carried away with eager desires*. And this naturally leads me to say something of those inward struggles and perplexities— those eager desires and agonies of zeal, which honest souls generally feel before they enter into the ministry; and by which it pleases God to qualify them for it. I have now nothing to do with those unhappy creatures, who desire and catch at the sacred office as a post of honour, profit, or ease; or, as the last shift for a livelihood, when other expedients have failed. Such deserve to be exposed in severer terms than I am disposed to use; and I cannot but tremble to think what account they will be able to give to the great Bishop of souls, and Judge of the universe.

But, as to those honest souls, who engage in it with proper motives and views, they are generally determined to it after many hard conflicts and reluctations. Some of them had the advantage of an early education, with a view to some other office. But when it pleases God to rouse them out of their security, and bring them under the strong but agreeable constraints of the love of Christ— when their eyes are opened to see the dangerous situation of a slumbering world around them; and their hearts are fired with a generous zeal for the honour of God and

---

* ὀρέγεται. Hederic, et Patric, reddunt ὀρέγω per *porrigo, extendo*; ὀρέγομαι per *porrigor, extendor, porrectis manibus capto*.

Jesus Christ, and the salvation of their perishing fellow-sinners; then they begin to cast about, and inquire, in what way they are most likely to promote these important interests: and as the ministry of the gospel appears to them the most promising expedient for this purpose, they devote their whole life, and all their accomplishments, to this humble and despised office, and give up all their other prospects, whatever tempting scenes of riches, grandeur, or ease, might lie open before them.

Others have been put to learning in their childhood by their parents, and by them have been intended for the church, in order to get a living; when neither party had a view to the sacred office from just and honourable motives, but considered it in the same light with other trades. Thus many commence ministers of the gospel, from the very same principles that others commence lawyers, physicians, or merchants. But, when it pleases God to awaken the careless youth to a serious sense of religion, and qualify him in reality for that office, which he presumptuously aimed at from sordid motives, or in complaisance to his parents; then, though the office he chooses be the same, yet the principles and reasons of his choice are very different: now they are sublime, disinterested, and divine. Others have spent their early days equally thoughtless of God, of a liberal education, and of the ministerial office. But when they are brought out of darkness into light, and fired with the love of God, and a benevolent zeal for the salvation of men, then they begin to languish and pine away with generous anxieties, how they may best promote the glory of God, and be of service to the immortal interests of mankind, in the world. And while they are thus perplexed, the agitations of their own thoughts, or perhaps the conversation of a friend, turns their minds to the sacred office. "Oh that I might have the honour of employing my life, and all that I am and have, in recommending that dear Redeemer, who, I hope, has died for me, and had pity on this once perishing soul of mine. Oh! that it might be my happiness to contribute something towards promoting his cause in the world, and saving souls from death. Oh! if it should be but *one* soul, I should count it a sufficient reward for all the labours of my whole life." These are the noble motives that operate upon such a person to desire the office of a bishop. But alas! a thousand discouragements rise in his way. His being so far advanced in life, his want of an early education, the difficulty of acquiring a competency of learning in his circumstances: these appear as insuperable obstructions in his way; and oblige him frequently to give up all hopes of accomplishing his desire. But when he has relinquished the desperate project, his uneasiness returns; his panting desires revive; and he can obtain no rest, till he is at length constrained to make the attempt, in the name of God, and leave the issue to him. He hopes he shall either have his zealous desires gratified, in building up the church of God; or, at least, that he shall be approved in his generous, though unsuccessful endeavour, and hear it said to him, as it was to David, "Thou didst well, that it was in thine heart." 1 Kings viii. 18.

But though this group of discouragements may be peculiar to such as devote themselves to the service of the church after that early part of life which is most favourable to a liberal education, is unhappily lost; yet, there are other discouragements, which all meet with, more or less, who enter into this office with proper views. They are deeply sensible of the difficulty of a faithful discharge of this office—of its solemn and tremendous consequences, both with regard to themselves, and their hearers, which made even the chief of the apostles to cry out, "and who is sufficient for these things?" 2 Cor. ii. 16—of the various opposition they may expect from the world, who love darkness rather than light, because their deeds are evil, John iii. 19, and especially of their want of proper abilities to discharge, with honour and success, an office. so difficult and so important. These discouragements, which strike them back, and the impulses of a generous zeal, which push them on, often throw them into a ferment, and agitate them with various passions; so that they can enjoy no ease in the thoughts either of prosecuting or declining the design. Now they give it up in discouragement: but immediately they are seized with agonies of zeal, and resolve, in a dependance upon divine strength, to break through all discouragements, and make the attempt, at all adventures. Again, their fears arise, and strike them off from the design. Again, their zeal revives, and impels them to pursue it. They can find no heart for any other pursuit. Or, if they fly to some other business, like Jonah to Tarshish, to avoid the mission, Providence appears against them, and raises some furious storm, that oversets all their schemes: till, at length, they are constrained to yield, and surrender themselves to God, to be used by him according to his pleasure. If they had resolved with Jeremiah, "I will not make mention of him, nor speak in his name," they find like him, that the word of God is in their heart, as a burning fire shut up in their bones, and they are weary with forbearing, and they cannot stay. Jer. xx. 9.

We find many of the great and good men of antiquity in such a struggle, when God was about to send them upon a mission for him. Moses forms a great many excuses—from his own meanness: "Who am I, that I should go unto Pharaoh, and that I should bring forth the children of Israel out of Egypt?" Ex. iii. 11—from the incredulity of those to whom he was sent: "Behold, they will not believe me, nor hearken unto my voice:" Ex. iv. 1—from his want of qualifications for the mission: "O my Lord, I am not eloquent: I am slow of speech, and of a slow tongue," v. 10. And when all these excuses are removed, he prays to be excused at any rate; "O my Lord, send, I pray thee, by the hand of him whom thou wilt send," v. 13. As, if he had said, "employ any one in this mission, rather than me." We repeatedly perceive the same reluctance in Jeremiah, "Ah! Lord God," says he, "I cannot speak, for I am a child." Jer. i. 6. And elsewhere, in a passage that has rather a harsh sound, according to our translation,* Jer. xx. 7; but should be rendered thus: "Thou hast *persuaded* me, O Lord, and I *was persuaded;* that is, to undertake the prophetical office: "Thou art stronger than I, and hast prevailed;" prevailed over all my reluctance. "I said, I will not make mention of him, nor speak any more in his name. But his word was in my heart as a burning fire shut up in my bones, and I was weary with forbearing, and I could not stay." So Ezekiel tells us, that when he went to discharge his office, "he went in bitterness, and in the heat of his spirit; but the hand of the LORD was strong upon him," and he could not resist the almighty impulse. Ezek. iii. 14.

Thus, you see, with what reluctance those generally engage in the sacred office, who are justly sensible of its importance and difficulty, and of their own weakness. Men, whose choice is directed by their parents, or proceeds from the love of popular applause—from avarice, or some other low, selfish principle, may rush thoughtlessly into it; and in the presumptuous pride of self-confidence, imagine themselves equal to the undertaking. But those honest souls, who know what they are going about, and what they themselves are, if they *reach* after this sacred

* Our translators render it " Thou hast deceived me, and I was deceived."

office, it is with a trembling hand. They do indeed desire it, most ardently desire it; but it is when they are under the sweet constraints of the love of Christ, and the souls of men. This bears them away like a torrent, through all difficulties; and they would willingly hazard their lives in the attempt. But notwithstanding this ardour, their hearts frequently fail, and recoil; and, at such times, nothing but necessity could push them on.

Through such struggles as these, my brethren in the gospel, have you entered into that office, which you are now painfully discharging. Your desire after it was indeed ardent and inextinguishable: but oh! what strong reluctance, what hard conflicts have you felt when you compared your own furniture with the work you had to do? And these discouragements have appeared to you perhaps, in so affecting a light, even since you have been invested with your office, that you would most willingly have resigned it. But "necessity is laid upon you; yea, wo unto you, if you preach not the gospel." 1 Cor. ix. 16. Therefore, in an humble dependence upon divine assistance, you resolve to continue in it, whatever discouragements arise from a sense of your own imperfections, or from the unsuccessfulness of your labours in the world. And at times you feel, that God is with you, as a mighty terrible one; and causes his pleasure to prosper in your hands; and renders your hardest labours your highest delights: and then, oh then, you would not exchange your pulpit for a throne, nor envy ministers of state, if you may be but ministers of the glorious gospel. Then "you magnify your office:" Rom. xi. 13, and count it a very great grace, that you, who are so little among the saints, should be employed to preach the unsearchable riches of Christ. You find, indeed, that the office of a bishop is a *good work*—good, pleasant, benevolent, divine.

But still it is a *work*. So the apostle calls it in my text, "The office of a bishop a good *work*." "It is the name of a *work*, not of a dignity,"* says St. Augustine. If a man desire the office of a bishop from right principles, he desireth—not a secular dignity—not a good benefice—not a post of honour or profit—not an easy idle life—but he desireth a *work ;* a *good* work indeed it is: but still it is a *work*.

It may properly be called a *work*, if we consider the duties of the office, which require the utmost assiduity, and some of which are peculiarly painful and laborious. It is the minister's concern, in common with other Christians, to work out his own salvation; to struggle with temptation; to be always in arms to bear down the insurrections of sin in his heart; and to discharge all the ordinary duties of the Christian life, towards God, his neighbour, and himself. This work is as necessary, as important, as difficult to him, as to his hearers. And I appeal to such of you as have ever engaged in it, whether this alone be not extremely difficult and laborious. It is, indeed, noble and delightful; but still it is laborious. But besides this, there is a great, an arduous and laborious work *peculiar* to the office of a bishop, or minister of the gospel, which not only is sufficient to exhaust all his time and abilties, but which requires daily supplies of strength from above to enable him to perform it. To employ his hours at home, not in idleness, or worldly pursuits, but in study and devotion, that his head and heart may be furnished for the discharge of his office—to preach the word, instant in season and out of season, with that vigorous exertion, and those agonies of zeal, which exhaust the spirits, and throw the whole frame into such a ferment as hardly any other labour can produce—to visit the sick, and to teach his

* Nomen operis, non dignitatis.

people in general, from house to house, in the more social and familiar forms of private instruction—to do all this, not as a thing by-the-by, or a matter of form, but with zeal, fidelity, prudence, and incessant application, as the main business of life; deeply solicitous about the important, consequences—to do this with fortitude and perseverance, in spite of all the discouragements of unsuccessfulness and the various forms of opposition that may arise from earth and hell—to abide steady and unshaken under the strong gales of popular applause, and the storms of persecution— to bless, when reviled; to forbear, when persecuted; to entreat, when defamed; to be abased as the filth of the world, and the off-scouring of all things; (1 Cor. iv. 12, 13,) to give no offence in anything, that the ministry be not blamed; but in all things to approve himself as the minister of God: (2 Cor. vi. 3, 4,)—to preach Christianity out of the pulpit, by his example as well as in it, by his discourses; and to make his life a constant sermon. This, this, my brethren, is the work of a bishop, or a minister of the gospel. "And who is sufficient for these things?" Is not this a work that would require the strength of an angel?* And yet this work must be done—done habitually, honestly, conscientiously, by us frail mortals, that sustain this office; or else we shall be condemned as slothful and wicked servants. This thought must for ever sink our spirits, were it not that Christ is our strength and life. Yes, my dear fellow-labourers, such weaklings as we may spring up, and lay hold of his strength; and we can do all things through Christ strengthening us. (Phil. iv. 13.) Thus you have experienced in hours of dejection; and unless the Lord had been your help, your souls, ere now, had dwelt in silence. (Psalm xciv. 17.) Hence, by-the-by, you may see the reason why the Lord hath appointed, that

* Onus humeris angelorum formidandum.

they who preach the gospel should live by it: it is because, that time, those abilities, and those labours, which others lay out in providing for themselves and their dependants, must be laid out by them in serving others, by a faithful discharge of their office. If they thus devote themselves to the duties of their function, it is but just and reasonable that those for whom they labour, should provide for their subsistence while they are serving them. But if those who style themselves ministers, do not suffer their office to restrain them from secular pursuits; if it only employ an hour or two once a week, upon a day in which it is unlawful even for the laity to mind their worldly affairs; in short, if, notwithstanding their office, they have the same opportunities with other people, to provide themselves a living, I see no reason why they should be supported at the public charge—supported at the public charge, to serve themselves! They are a kind of supernumerary placemen, or pensioners and drones in society. "The labourer is worthy of his hire;" (Luke x. 7; 1 Tim. v. 18,) but the loiterer deserves none. But this I mention by-the-by.

You see, my brother,[*] what it is you are now to engage in. You have desired the office of a bishop; and after many struggles and disappointments, the object of your desire appears now within your reach. But remember, it is not a post of honour, profit, or ease, that you are about to be advanced to; but it is *a work*. You are now entering upon a life of painful labour, fatigue, and mortification. Now you have nothing to do but to *work* for your Lord and Master: to *work*, not merely for an hour or two once a week, but every day, in every week, and through your whole life. If you enter into your closet, it must be to pray. If you enter your study, it

[*] Here the address was particularly directed to Mr. Martin.

must be to think what you shall say to recommend your Master, not yourself; and to save the souls that hear you. If you enter into the pulpit, it must be not to "preach yourself, but Christ Jesus the Lord;" (2 Cor. iv. 5,) not to set yourself off as a fine speaker, a great scholar, or a profound reasoner, but to preach Christ crucified, and the humble, unpopular doctrines of Jesus of Galilee; and to beseech men, in his stead, to be reconciled to God; to warn every man, and teach every man, that you may present every man perfect in Christ Jesus. (Col. i. 28.) If you go into the world, and mingle in conversation, it must be to drop a word for Christ; and let mankind see, that you live, as well as talk, like a Christian. If you travel about from place to place, among necessitous vacancies, it must be to diffuse the vital savour of your Master's name, and not your own. If you settle, and undertake a particular charge, it must be to watch for souls, as one that must give account; (Heb. xiii.17,) and industriously to plant and water that spot which is laid out for you in the Lord's vineyard. Here, my friend, here is your work; and while you survey it, I doubt not but you are ready to renew the exclamation, "Who is sufficient for these things?" (2 Cor. ii. 16.) This work will leave no blanks in your time, but is sufficient to employ it well. It will leave none of your powers idle, but requires the utmost exertion of them every one. It is the work of your Sundays, and of your week days—the work of your retirement, and your social hours—the work of soul and body—of the head and heart—the work of life and death: a laborious, anxious, uninterrupted work. But, blessed be God! it is, after all, a *good* work.

It is a *good* work, whether you consider—for whom—with whom—or for what you work.

The ministers of the gospel work *for* God, who is carrying on the grand scheme of salvation in our world. His immediate service is the peculiar business of their lives. Their office calls them to minister at his altar, while others are called even in duty to mind the labours and pursuits of this world. Of them it may be said, in a peculiar degree, what holds true of Christians in common in a lower sense, They neither live to themselves, nor die to themselves: but whether they live, they live unto the Lord; or whether they die, they die unto the Lord: so that, living and dying, they are the Lord's. Rom. xiv. 7, 8. Now, who would not work for the God that made them, that gives them all their blessings, and that alone can make them happy through an immortal duration? Who would not work for so good, so excellent, so munificent a master? Oh! how good a work is this!

Ministers also work for Jesus Christ. It was he that originally gave them their commission; it was he that assigned them their work; it is he that is interested in their success. It is *his* work they are engaged in; the great work of saving sinners, in which he himself worked for three-and-thirty painful, laborious years; and to promote which, he suffered all the agonies of crucifixion. And blessed Jesus! who would not work for thee! for thee, who didst work and suffer so much for us! Oh! while we feel the constraints of thy love, who can forbear crying out with Isaiah, "Here am I; send me!" Isa. vi. 8. Send me to the ends of the earth; send me among savage barbarians; send me through fire and water; send me where thou wilt, if it be for thee, here, Lord, I go: I would undertake the hardest work, if it be for thee: for oh! what work can be so good, so grateful, so pleasant!

Again, the ministers of the gospel work for the souls

of men. To do good to mankind is the great purpose of their office. It is their business to serve the best interests of others, to endeavour to make men wise and good, and consequently happy, in time and eternity: to make them useful members of civil and religious society in this world; and prepared heirs of the inheritance of the saints in light: in short, to refine and advance human nature to the highest possible degree of moral excellence, glory and happiness. Is not this the most generous beneficent office in all the world? And how good, how pleasing, and how delightful must it be, in this view, to a benevolent soul! It is an office the most friendly to civil government, and the happiness of the world in general. And if ecclesiastics have often proved firebrands in society, and disturbers of the peace of mankind, it has not been owing to the nature, design, and tendency of their office, but to their being carried headlong by their own avarice or ambition, or some other sordid lust, to abuse it to purposes directly contrary to those for which it was intended and adapted. Every minister of the gospel ought to have a benevolent, generous, patriotic spirit, and be the friend of human nature, from noble and disinterested views: otherwise, his temper and his office appear a shocking contrariety to each other. But when they agree, he is a public blessing to the world, and an immortal blessing to the souls of men. Thus, you see, this office is a *good work*, if we consider *for whom* the work is done.

Let us next consider *with whom* the ministers of the gospel work; and we shall see how *good* their employment is. They are *workers together with God*, 2 Cor. vi. 1, engaged in carrying on the same gracious design which lay so near *his* heart from eternity; for the execution of which, he sent his Son into the world; has appointed various means of grace, under the various dispensations of religion, during the space of near six thousand years; and manages all the events of time, by his all-ruling providence.

They are also *co-workers with Jesus Christ :* promoting the same cause, for which he became man; for which he lived the life of a servant, and died the death of a malefactor and a slave. Jesus, their Lord and Master, condescended to be their predecessor in office, and to become the preacher of his own gospel. They are engaged, though in an humbler sphere, in that work, which he is now carrying on, since his return to his native heaven. And whenever the pleasure of the Lord prospers in their hands, he actually works with them, and is the author of all their successes. He sends his Spirit to convince the world, by their means, of sin, of righteousness, and of judgment, John xvi. 8, and to make his gospel powerful for the salvation of those that hear it. Oh! were it not for his concurrence, all the little religion which is in the world would immediately expire; and the united efforts of all the ministers upon earth, would not be able to preserve one spark of it alive.

They may also be called *fellow-workers with the Holy Spirit*, whose great office it is to sanctify depraved creatures, and prepare them for the refined happiness of heaven. While they are speaking to the ear, He speaks to the heart, and causes men to *feel*, as well as to hear, the gospel of salvation.

They also act *in concert with angels :* for what are these glorious creatures but "ministering spirits, sent forth to minister for them who shall be heirs of salvation?" Heb. i. 14. An angel once condescended to call a minister of the gospel his *fellow-servant*. "I am thy *fellow-servant*," says the angel to John, (the fellow-servant) "of thy *brethren* that have the testimony of Jesus," Rev. xix. 10.

And when these servants of an humbler order have finished their painful ministration on earth, they shall join their fellow-servants of a higher class in the court of heaven, and perhaps, share in the much more exalted forms of angelic ministration. This seems implied in that text where the angel of the Lord protests to Joshua the high-priest, saying, "Thus saith the LORD of hosts; if thou wilt walk in my ways, and if thou wilt keep my charge, then thou shalt also judge my house, and shalt also keep my courts, and I will give thee places to walk among these that stand by." Zech. iii. 5–7. And who are they *that stand by?* You are told, "*The angel of the* LORD *stood by.*" Among these, therefore, Joshua had places given him to walk, as the companion and fellow-servant of angels.

Ministers also are engaged in that work, in which the apostles went before them. In this good cause, they travelled over sea and land, they laboured, they spent their lives, and at last gloriously departed. Yes, my fellow-labourers, they felt the generous toils, and braved the heroic dangers of your office, long before you. In this good cause, thousands of martyrs have shed their blood—thousands of *ministers*, in various ages, and in various countries, have spent their strength, their life, their all.

In short, *all the good men* that ever have been, that now are, or ever shall be upon earth, concur in the same good work with you, according to their respective characters. To make men wise, holy, and happy, is their united effort—the object they have in view in their prayers, in their instructions, in their conversation, and in all their endeavours.

All good beings, in the whole compass of the vast universe, befriend your design; and none are against it but fallen spirits on the earth and in hell. And must not this be a good work in which such a glorious company concur? and oh! who would not work in such company? with God, with Christ, with the Holy Spirit, with angels, with apostles, with martyrs, with all good men upon the face of the earth? Who would be so shocking a singularity as not to join with this assembly in the work. Or who can question its goodness, since such an assembly join in it?

The office of a bishop will farther appear a *good* work, if it be considered *for what* it is that ministers work. They do not indeed work for a reward upon the footing of personal merit; but they hope for it on the plan of the gospel, through Jesus Christ. In this view, like Moses, they have "a respect to the recompense of the reward." Heb. xi. 26. God will not forget their honest, though feeble, and frequently unsuccessful labours in his own work. "They that turn many to righteousness shall shine as the stars for ever and ever." Dan. xii. 3. If a cup of cold water, given to the meanest disciple of Christ, shall not be unrewarded, what rich rewards must be prepared for those who employ their time, their abilities, their life, their all, in the most important, benevolent, and laborious services for his church which he has purchased with his own blood? Crowns of distinguished brightness, and thrones of superior dignity are reserved for them: and in proportion to their labours here will be their glory and felicity in the world to come. In serving their divine Master and the souls of men, they are serving themselves; and in promoting the interests of others, they most effectually promote their own. Thus, their duty and interest—the interest of mankind and their own are wisely and graciously united, and mutually promote each other. And thus it appears, their laborious and painful work is *good*—good in *itself*, good for *the world*, and good for *themselves*.

To sum up the whole—whatever contempt the ministerial office has lain under; how much soever it has been disgraced, and rendered useless, and even injurious, by the unworthy conduct of such as have thrust themselves into it, from base and mercenary views; yet, it is in itself, and in its natural tendency, the most noble, benevolent, and useful office in the world. To be the minister of Jesus Christ, the King of kings, and Lord of lords, is a greater honour than to be prime minister to the most illustrious monarch upon earth. To save souls from death, is a more heroic exploit, than to rescue enslaved nations from oppression and ruin. To make a multitude of wretched, perishing souls rich with the unsearchable treasures of Christ, is a more generous charity, than to clothe the naked, or feed the hungry. To refine depraved spirits, and improve into a fitness for the exalted employments and enjoyments of heaven, is a higher pitch of patriotism, than to civilize and polish barbarous nations, by introducing the arts and sciences, and a good form of government among them. To negotiate a peace between God and man, and prevent the terrible consequences of the unnatural, unequal war, that has so long been waged between them, is a more benevolent and important service than to negotiate a peace between contending nations—to stop the current of human blood, and heal the deadly wounds of war. Let those, therefore, who are called to this blessed work, join with St. Paul, though in an humbler order, and thank the Lord Jesus Christ, who hath enabled them, for "that He counted them faithful, putting them into the ministry." 1 Tim. i. 12. Let them "magnify their office," not by assuming airs of superiority, or by making ostentatious claims to powers that they have nothing to do with, but by rejoicing more in it, than in crowns and thrones—by supporting it with dignity, that is, acting up to their high character; and by so exercising it, as to render it an extensive blessing to the world. This will be the best expedient to keep themselves and their office above contempt, and to gain the approbation of God and man.

But when we reflect upon the dignity, the importance, the difficulty, and the grand consequences of this office, it may render us who sustain it, peculiarly sensible of our constant need of supplies of Divine grace, to enable us to discharge it. Alas! we know nothing of ourselves, if we imagine we are equal to it. St. Paul, with all his apostolic furniture, humbly acknowledges, "We are not sufficient of ourselves to think anything as of ourselves: but our sufficiency is of God; who also hath made us able ministers of the New Testament." 2 Cor. iii. 5, 6. "Who is Paul," says he, "and who is Apollos, but ministers by whom ye believed, even as the Lord gave to every man?" Observe, their success was just as the *Lord gave* to every man. "Neither is he that planteth anything, neither he that watereth; but God that giveth the increase:" He is all in all. 1 Cor. iii. 5–7. If I laboured more abundantly than others, says he, it was not I, but the grace of God which was with me. 1 Cor. xv. 10. Thus, my brethren, it becomes us to be always dependent upon Divine grace. It becomes us to be often on the knee at the throne of mercy, petitioning for help and success: and if we are, in any measure, blessed with either, we should arrogate nothing to ourselves, but ascribe all the glory to him, who condescends to distribute gifts to men, and to crown these gifts with his Divine blessing.

Hence, also, my brethren of the laity, you may see how much ministers need the assistance of your prayers.

Even the great St. Paul did not disdain to ask the prayers of common Christians, but repeats his request over and over. And I, from much more urgent necessity, as the mouth of these my brethren, beg this charity of you for myself and them. Surely, you cannot deny it, especially as yourselves will reap the advantage in the issue: for whatever ministerial abilities God may bestow upon us, in answer to your prayers, they are to be employed for your service: and it is our being so poorly qualified to serve you, that extorts this request from us, and is the cause of many a weeping, melancholy hour to us.

You must, also, hence see, that it is your concern to concur with ministers of the gospel in promoting the benevolent and important ends of their office. Endeavour so to attend upon their ministrations, as that you yourselves may be saved by them. And endeavour by your conversation and example, and all methods in your power, to make them useful to others. Oh! let us all, ministers and people, form a noble confederacy against the kingdom of darkness, and make a vigorous attack upon it, with our united forces. Let us all enlist volunteers—as good soldiers, under Jesus; and in our post, whether high or low, do all we can to promote his kingdom. Amen.

A HYMN.

BY THE AUTHOR OF THE SERMON FOREGOING.

(*Varied from Dr. Doddridge.*)

With grateful hearts come let us sing,
The gifts of our ascended King;
Though long since gone from earth below,
Through every age his bounties flow.

The Saviour, when to heav'n he rose
In splendid triumph o'er his foes
His gifts on rebel men bestowed,
And wide his royal bounties flow'd.

Hence sprang th' *apostles'* honoured name,
More glorious than the hero's fame '
Evangelists and *prophets* hence
Derive the blessings they dispense.

In humbler forms, to bless our eyes,
Pastors from hence and *teachers* rise;
Who, though with feebler rays they shine,
Still gild a long-extended line.

From Christ their various gifts derive,
And fed by Christ their graces live;
While, guarded by his mighty hand,
'Midst all the rage of hell they stand.

Thus *teachers, teachers* shall succeed
When we lie silent with the dead!
And unborn churches, by their care,
Shall rise and flourish large and fair.

Pastors and people join and sing,
This constant, inexhausted spring,
Whence through all ages richly flow
The streams that cheer the church below.

SERMON LXXIX.

A CHRISTMAS-DAY SERMON.*

LUKE II. 13, 14.—*And suddenly there was with the angel a multitude of the heavenly host,† praising God, and saying, Glory to God in the highest, and on earth, peace, good-will towards men.*

THIS is the day which the church of Rome, and some other churches that deserve to be placed in better company have agreed to celebrate in memory of the Prince of Peace, the Saviour of men, the incarnate God, Immanuel. And I doubt not, but many convert superstition into rational and scriptural devotion, and religiously employ themselves in a manner acceptable to God, though they want the sanction of divine authority for appropriating this day to a sacred use. But, alas! it is generally a season of sinning, sensuality, luxury, and various forms of extravagance; as though men were not celebrating the birth of the holy Jesus, but of Venus, or Bacchus, whose most sacred rites were mysteries of iniquity and debauchery. The birth of Jesus was solemnized by armies of angels; they had their music and their songs on this occasion. But how different from those generally used among mortals! "Glory to God in the highest, on earth, peace, good will to men!" This was their song. But is the music and dancing, the feasting and rioting, the idle

---

* New Kent, Dec. 25, 1758.—Nassau Hall, Dec. 25, 1760.
† στρατιας ουρανιου, the soldiery of heaven.

songs and extravagant mirth of mortals at this season, a proper echo or response to this angelic song? I leave you to your own reflections upon this subject, after I have given the hint; and I am sure, if they be natural and pertinent, and have a proper influence upon you, they will restrain you from running into the fashionable excesses of riot on this occasion.

To remember and religiously improve the incarnation of our divine Redeemer, to join the concert of angels, and dwell in ecstatic meditation upon their song; this is lawful, this is a seasonable duty every day; and consequently upon this day. And as Jesus improved the feast of dedication,* though not of divine institution, as a proper opportunity to exercise his ministry, when crowds of the Jews were gathered from all parts; so I would improve this day for your instruction, since it is the custom of our country to spend it religiously, or idly, or wickedly, as different persons are differently disposed.

But as the seed of superstition which have some times grown up to a prodigious height, have been frequently sown and cherished by very inconsiderable incidents, I think it proper to inform you, that I may guard against this danger, that I do not set apart this day for public worship, as though it had any peculiar sanctity, or we were under any obligations to keep it religiously. I know no human authority, that has power to make one day more holy than another, or that can bind the conscience in such cases. And as for divine authority, to which alone the sanctifying of days and things belongs, it has thought it sufficient to

* John x. 22. This festival was instituted by Judas Macabæus in memory of the restoration of the temple and the altar, after they had been profaned by their heathen enemies; the original account of which we have, 1 Mac. iv. 56, &c.; where what is called τὰ ἐγκαίνια by the evangelist, is called τὸν ἐγκαινίσμον (v. 56) and ἅι ἡμέραι ἐγκαινισμοῦ.—See also Joseph. Antiq. I. xii. c. 11.

consecrate one day in seven to a religious use, for the commemoration both of the birth of this world, and the resurrection of its great Author, or of the works of creation and redemption. This I would religiously observe; and inculcate the religious observance of it upon all. But as to other days, consecrated by the mistaken piety or superstition of men, and conveyed down to us as holy, through the corrupt medium of human tradition, I think myself free to observe them or not, according to conveniency, and the prospect of usefulness; like other common days, on which I may lawfully carry on public worship or not, as circumstances require. And since I have so fair an opportunity, and it seems necessary in order to prevent my conduct from being a confirmation of present superstition, or a temptation to future, I shall, once for all, declare my sentiments more fully upon this head.

But I must premise, that it is far from my design, to widen the differences subsisting among Christians, to embitter their hearts against each other, or to awaken dormant controversies concerning the extra-essentials of religion. And if this use should be made of what I shall say, it will be an unnatural perversion of my design. I would make every candid concession in favour of those who observe days of human institution, that can consist with truth and my own liberty. I grant, that so many plausible things may be offered for the practice as may have the appearance of solid argument, even to honest inquirers after truth. I grant, that I doubt not but many are offering up acceptable devotion to God on this day; devotion proceeding from honest, believing hearts, and therefore acceptable to him on any day—acceptable to him, notwithstanding their little mistake in this affair. I grant, we should, in this case, imitate the generous candour and forbearance of St. Paul, in a similar case. The converts to Christianity from among the Jews, long retained the prejudices of their education, and thought they were still obliged, even under the gospel dispensation, to observe the rites and ceremonies of the law of Moses, to which they had been accustomed, and particularly those days which were appointed by God to be religiously kept under the Jewish dispensation. The Gentile converts, on the other hand, who were free from these early prejudices of education and custom, and had imbibed more just notions of Christian liberty, looked upon these Jewish holy-days as common days, and no longer to be observed. This occasioned a warm dispute between these two classes of converts, and St. Paul interposes, not so properly to determine which party was right, (that was comparatively a small matter,) as to bring both parties to exercise moderation and forbearance towards each other, and to put a charitable construction upon their different practices in these little articles; and particularly to believe concerning each other, that though their practices were different, yet the principle from which they acted was the same, namely, a sincere desire to glorify and please God, and a conscientious regard to what they apprehended was his will. "Him that is weak in the faith, receive ye, but not to doubtful disputations—one man esteemeth one day above another; another esteemeth every day alike. He that regardeth the day, regardeth it unto the Lord; and he that regardeth not the day, to the Lord he doth not regard it," Rom. xiv. 1, 5, 6; that is, it is a conscientious regard to the Lord, that is the principle upon which both parties act, though they act differently in this matter. Therefore, says the apostle, "Why dost thou judge thy brother?" why dost thou severely censure him for practicing differently in this little affair?—"hast thou faith?" says he, hast thou a full persuasion of what is right in these punctilios and ceremonials? Then, "have it to thyself before God;" verse 22. Keep it to thyself as a rule for thy own practice, but do not impose it upon others, nor disturb the church of Christ about it. It becomes us, my brethren, to imitate this catholicism and charity of the apostle, in these little differences; and God forbid I should tempt any of you to forsake so noble an example. But then the example of the same apostle will authorize us modestly to propose our own sentiments and the reasons of our practice, and to warn people from laying a great stress upon ceremonials and superstitious observances. This he does particularly to the Galatians, who not only kept the Jewish holy-days, but placed a great part of their religion in the observance of them. "Ye observe days, and months, and times, and years;" therefore, says he, "I am afraid of you, lest I have bestowed upon you labour in vain." Gal. iv. 10, 11. The commandments of God have often been made void by the traditions of men; and human inventions more religiously observed than divine institutions; and when this was the case, St. Paul was warm in opposing even ceremonial mistakes.

Having premised this, which I look upon as much more important than the decision of the question, I proceed to show you the reasons why I would not religiously observe days of human appointment, in commemoration of Christ and the saints. What I have to say shall be particularly pointed at what is called Christmas-day: but may be easily applied to all other holy-days instituted by men.

The first reason I shall offer is, that I would take my religion just as I find it in my Bible without any imaginary improvements or supplements of human invention. All the ordinances which God has been pleased to appoint, and particularly that one day in seven, which he has set apart for his more immediate service, and the commemoration of the works of creation and redemption, I would honestly endeavour to observe in the most sacred manner. But when ignorant presuming mortals take upon them to refine upon Divine institutions, to make that a part of religion, which God has left indifferent, and consecrate more days than he has thought necessary; in short, when they would mingle something of their own with the pure religion of the Bible: then I must be excused from obedience, and beg leave to content myself with the old, plain, simple religion of the Bible. Now that there is not the least appearance in all the Bible of the Divine appointment of Christmas, to celebrate the birth of Christ, is granted by all parties; and the Divine authority is not so much as pretended for it. Therefore, a Bible-Christian is not at all bound to observe it.

Secondly, the Christian church, for at least three hundred years, did not observe any day in commemoration of the birth of Christ. For this we have the testimony of the primitive fathers themselves. Thus Clemens Alexandrinus, who lived about the year one hundred and ninety-four, "We are commanded to worship and honour him, who, we are persuaded, is the Word, and our Saviour and Ruler, and through him, the Father; *not upon* certain particular or *select days*, as some others do, but constantly practising this all our life, and in every proper way." Chrysostom, who lived in the fourth century, has these words, "It is not yet ten years, since this day, that is, Christmas, was plainly known to us;" and he observes, the custom was brought to Constantinople from Rome. Now since this day was not religiously observed in the church in the first and purest ages, but was introduced as superstitions increased, and Christianity began to degenerate very fast into popery; ought not we to imitate the purity of these primitive times, and retain none of the superstitious observances of more corrupt ages?

Thirdly, if a day should be religiously observed in memory of the birth of Christ, it ought to be that day on which he was born. But that day, and even the month and the year, are altogether uncertain. The Scriptures do not determine this point of chronology. And perhaps they are silent on purpose, to prevent all temptation to the superstitious observance of it; just as the body of Moses was secretly buried, and his grave concealed, to guard the Israelites from the danger of idolizing it. Chronologers are also divided upon the point: and even the ancients are not agreed.* The learned generally suppose that Christ was born two or three years before the vulgar reckoning. And as to the month, some suppose it was in September, and some in June. And they imagine it was very unlikely, that he was born in the cold wintry months of December, because we read, that at the time of his birth, shepherds were out in the field, watching their flocks by night; which is not probable at that season of the year. The Christian epocha, or reckoning time from the birth of Christ, was not introduced till about the year five hundred; and it was not generally used till the reign of

---

* Clemens Alexandrinus mentions the different opinions about it in his time, especially among the heretics; for as to the catholics, they pretended to determine nothing about it in his day. "There are some," says he, "who very curiously determine not only the year, but also the day of our Saviour's birth, which they say is the 28th year of Augustus, and the 25th of the month Pachon. The followers of Basilides celebrate also the day of his baptism, and say, that is the 15th year of Tiberius, and the 15th of the month Tabi. But others say, it is the 11th of the same month. Some of them also say, that he was born on the 24th or 25th of Pharmouthi." But none of these computations fix it on the 25th of December.

Charles the Great, about the year eight hundred, or a little above nine hundred years ago. And this must occasion a great uncertainty, both as to the year, month, and day. But why do I dwell so long upon this? It must be universally confessed, that the day of his birth is quite uncertain: nay, it is certain that it is not that which has been kept in commemoration of it. To convince you of this, I need only put you in mind of the late parliamentary correction of our computation of time by introducing the new-style; by which Christmas is eleven days sooner than it was wont to be. And yet this chronological blunder still continues in the public prayers of some, who give thanks to God, that Christ was born *as upon this day.* And while this prayer was offered up in England and Virginia on the twenty-fifth of December old-style, other countries that followed the new-style, were solemnly declaring in their thanksgivings to God, that Christ was born eleven days sooner; that is, on the fourteenth of December. I therefore conclude, that neither this day or any other was ever intended to be observed for this purpose.

Finally, superstition is a very growing evil; and therefore the first beginnings of it ought to be prevented. Many things that were at first introduced with a pious design, have grown up gradually into the most enormous superstition and idolatry in after ages. The ancient Christians, for example, had such a veneration for the pious martyrs, that they preserved a lock of hair, or some little memorial of them; and this laid the foundation for the expensive sale and stupid idolizing of the relics of the saints in popish countries. They also celebrated their memory, by observing the days of their martyrdom. But as the number of the martyrs and saints real or imaginary, increased, the saints' days also multiplied to an extravagant degree, and hardly left any days in the year for any other purpose. And as they had more saints than days in the year, they dedicated the first of November for them all, under the title of *All-saints-day.* But if the saints must be thus honoured, then certainly much more ought Jesus Christ. This seemed a natural inference: and accordingly, these superstitious devotees appointed one day to celebrate his birth, another his baptism, another his death, another the day of Pentecost, and an endless list that I have not time now to mention. The apostles also must be put into the Kalendar: and thus almost all the days in the year were consecrated by superstition, and hardly any left for the ordinary labours of life. Thus the people are taught to be idle the greatest part of their time, and so indisposed to labour on the few days that are still allowed them for that purpose. This has almost ruined some popish countries, particularly the Pope's dominions in the fine country of Italy, once the richest and best improved in the world. Mr. Addison, Bishop Burnet, and other travellers, inform us, that every thing bears the appearance of poverty, notwithstanding all the advantages of soil and climate: and that this is chiefly owing to the superstition of the people, who spend the most of their time as holy-days. And if you look over the Kalendar of the church of England, you will find that the *festivals* in one year, amount to thirty-one. The *fasts* to no less than ninety-five, to which add the fifty-two Sundays in every year, and the whole will make one hundred and seventy-eight: so that only one hundred and eighty-seven days will be left in the whole year, for the common purposes of life. And whether the poor could procure a subsistence for themselves and their families by the labour of so few days, and whether it be not a yoke that neither we nor our fathers are able to bear, I leave you to judge. It is true, that but very few of these feasts and fasts are now observed, even by the members of the established church. But then they are still in their Kalendar and Canons, and binding upon them by the authority of the church; and as far as they do not comply with them, so far they are *dissenters :* and in this, and in many other respects, they are *generally dissenters*, though they do not share with us in the infamy of the name. Now, since the beginnings of superstitious inventions in the worship of God are so dangerous in their issue, and may grow up into such enormous extravagance, we ought to shun the danger, by adhering to the simplicity of the Bible-religion, and not presume to make more days or things holy, than the all-wise God has been pleased to sanctify. He will be satisfied with the religious observance of his own institutions; and why should not we? It is certainly enough, that we be as religious as he requires us. And all our will-worship is liable to that confounding rejection, "Who hath required this at your hands?" Isaiah i. 12.

I now proceed to what is more delightful and profitable, the sublime anthem of the angels: "Glory to God in the highest! on earth, peace! good will to men!"

What a happy night was this to the poor shepherds, though exposed to the damps and darkness of midnight, and keeping their painful watches in the open field!* An illustrious angel, clothed in light which kindled midnight into noon, came upon them, or suddenly hovered over them in the air, and the glory of the Lord, that is, a bright

---

* —" In midnight shades, on frosty ground,
They could attend the pleasing sound.
Nor could they feel December cold, nor think the darkness long."—
DR. WATTS.

A CHRISTMAS-DAY SERMON.

refulgent light, the usual emblem of his presence shone round about them. No wonder the poor shepherds were struck with horror, and overwhelmed at the sight of so glorious a phenomenon. But when God strikes his people with terror, it is often an introduction to some signal blessing. And they are sometimes made sore afraid, like the shepherds, even with the displays of his glories. The first appearance even of the great deliverer, may seem like that of a great destroyer. But he will at length make himself known as he is, and allay the fears of his people. So the gentle angel cheers and supports the trembling shepherds, "Fear not," says he, you need not tremble, but rejoice at my appearance; "for *behold*," observe and wonder, "*I bring you*," from heaven, by order from its Sovereign, "*good tidings of great joy*,"* the best that was ever published in mortal ears, not only to you, not only to a few private persons or families, not only to the Jewish nation; but good tidings of great joy, "*which shall be to all people*," to Gentiles as well as Jews, to all nations, tribes, and languages—to all the various ranks of men—to kings and subjects—to rich and poor; to free and bond: therefore let it circulate through the world, and resound from shore to shore. And what is this news that is introduced with so sublime and transporting a preface? It is this: "For unto you is born this day in the city of David, a Saviour, which is Christ the Lord." Unto *you* mortals —unto you miserable sinners, is born a *Saviour*—a Saviour from sin and ruin: a Saviour of no mean or common character, but *Christ*, the promised Messiah, anointed with the Holy Spirit; and invested with the high office of Mediator; Christ the *Lord*, the Lord and ruler of heaven

---

* The original has a force in it, which I cannot convey into a translation: but one that understands Greek, is struck with it at first sight—εὐαγγελίζομαι 'ὑμῖν χαρὰν μεγάλην. Luke ii. 10.

and earth, and universal nature. He is *born*—no longer represented by dark types and prophecies, but actually entered in the world—born *this day*—the long expected day is at length arrived; the prophecies are accomplished, and the fulness of time is come:—born *in the city of David*, in Bethlehem, and therefore of the seed and lineage of David, according to the prophecies: though he be a person of such eminence, *Christ the Lord* is now a feeble infant, just born. The Son born, and the Child given, he is the mighty God, the everlasting Father, the Prince of Peace." Isaiah ix. 6.

The condescension of the angel, and the joyful tidings he brought, no doubt recovered the shepherds from their consternation, and emboldened them to lift up their faces. And how was their joy heightened, that they were chosen and appointed by Heaven, to be the first visitants to this new-born Prince? "This shall be a sign to you," said the angel, by which you may know this divine Infant from others. What shall be the sign? shall it be, that they will find him in a palace, surrounded with all the grandeur and majesty of courts, and attended by the emperors, kings and nobles of the earth; lying in a bed of down, and dressed in silks, and gold, and jewels? This might be expected, if we consider the dignity of his person. It would be infinite condescension for him to be born even in such circumstances as these. But these are not the characteristics of the incarnate God: no, says the angel, This shall be a sign to you, "*ye shall find the babe, wrapped in swaddling clothes, lying in a manger.*" LYING IN A MANGER. Luke ii. 12. Astonishing! who could expect the new-born Son of God to be there?—there, lying in straw, surrounded only with oxen and horses, and waited upon only by a feeble, solitary mother, far from home, among unkind, regardless strangers, who would not allow her room in the inn, even in her painful hour. Perhaps her poverty disabled her from bearing her expenses in the ordinary way; and therefore she must take up her lodging in a stable. In such circumstances of abasement did the Lord of glory enter our world. In these circumstances he was "*seen of angels*," 1 Tim. iii. 16; who were wont to behold him in another form, in all the glories of the heavenly world. And how strange a sight must this be! How bright a display of his love to the guilty sons of men!

The angel, that was the willing messenger of these glad tidings, did not descend from heaven alone. He appears to have been the hierarch, or commandant of an army of angels, that attended him on this grand occasion. For suddenly there was with him a *multitude* of the heavenly host, or, as it might be rendered, of the *militia* or *soldiery of heaven.*[*] The angels are not a confused irregular body, or unconnected independent individuals; but a well-disposed system of beings, with proper subordinations; all marshalled into ranks under proper commanders. Hence they are called "thrones, and dominions, and principalities, and powers;" Col. i. 16; and we read of angels and archangels; 1 Thess. iv. 16; of Michael and his angels; Rev. xii. 7. They are called in the military style, the Lord's *hosts;* Psalm ciii. 21, cxlviii. 2; and the *army* of heaven; Dan. iv. 35. Rev. xix. 14; to signify the order established among them, and also their strength and unanimity to execute the commands of their sovereign, to repel the dragon and his angels, and defend the feeble heirs of salvation, on whom they condescend to wait. Order and subordination is still retained even among the fallen angels in the kingdom of darkness. Hence we read of the prince of the devils; Matt. ix. 34; the dragon and his angels;

[*] πλῆθος ςρατιᾶς οὐρανίου.

Rev. xii. 7; legions of devils; Mark v. 9; which was a division of the Roman army, something like that of a regiment among us.

Now a regiment of the heavenly militia descended with their officer, to solemnize and publish the birth of their Lord, when he took upon him our nature. And no sooner had their commander delivered his message, than they immediately join with one voice, filling all the air with their heavenly music; "praising God, and saying, glory to God in the highest! on earth, peace! good-will to men!" The language is abrupt, like that of a full heart: the sentences short, unconnected, and rapid; expressive of the ecstasy of their minds.

"Glory to God in the highest!" This deservedly leads the song. It is of more importance in itself, in the estimate of angels, and of all competent judges, than even the salvation of men. And the first and chief cause of joy and praise from the birth of a Saviour is, that he shall bring glory to God. Through him, as a proper medium, the divine perfections shall shine forth with new, augmented splendour. Through him, sinners shall be saved in a way that will advance the honour of the divine perfections and government: or if any of them perish, their punishment will more illustriously display the glory of their offended Sovereign. The *wisdom, grace, and mercy* of God, are glorified in the contrivance of this scheme of redemption, and making millions of miserable creatures happy for ever. His *power* is glorified, in carrying this scheme into execution, in spite of all opposition. His *justice* is glorified, in the atonement and satisfaction made for the sins of men by an incarnate Deity, and in the righteous and aggravated punishment executed upon those that obstinately reject this divine Saviour, and who therefore perish without the least umbrage of excuse. Oh!

what wonders does Jehovah perform, in prosecution of this method of salvation! What wonders of pardoning mercy and sanctifying grace! What miracles of glory and blessedness does he form out of the dust, and the polluted fragments of human nature! What monuments of his own glorious perfections does he erect, through all the extensive regions of heaven! From these wonderful works of his, the glory of his own name breaks forth upon the worlds of angels and men, in one bright unclouded day, which shall never be obscured in night, but grow more and more illustrious through the endless ages of eternity! Of this, the choir of angels were sensible at the birth of Christ; and therefore they shout aloud in ascriptions of glory to God. It was especially on this account they rejoiced in this great event. And all believers rejoice in it principally on this account too. "Glory to God," is the first note in the song of angels: and "hallowed be thy name;" that is, let thy name be sanctified, or glorified, is the first petition in the prayer of men. The glory of God should always be nearest our hearts: to this every thing should give way; and we should rejoice in other things, and even in our own salvation, as they tend to promote this. Such is the temper of every good man: his heart is enlarged, and extended beyond the narrow limits of self: he has a generous tender regard for the glory of the great God; and rejoices in the way of salvation through Christ, not merely as it makes him happy, but especially as it advances and displays the divine honour. This is his temper, at least in some hours of refined, exalted devotion. Self is, as it were, swallowed up in God. And brethren, is this your temper?

"Glory to God *in the highest!*"—In the *highest;* that is, in the *highest strains.* Let the songs of men and angels be raised to a higher key, on this great occasion. The usual strains of praise are low and languid, to celebrate the birth of this illustrious prince. This is a more glorious event than ever has yet happened in heaven or earth; and therefore demands a new song, more exalted and divine than has ever yet employed even the voices of angels. At the birth of nature, the sons of God, the angels, sang together, and shouted for joy: but when the Author and Lord of nature is born, let them raise a loftier and a more ecstatic anthem of praise.

Or, "Glory to God *in the highest*," may signify, let glory be given to God in the *highest heaven* by all the choirs of *angels*. This celestial squadron call upon their fellow-angels, whom they left behind them in their native heaven, to echo to their song, and fill those blessed regions with the melody of new ascriptions of praise, as if they had said—though men receive the benefit, let all the angels of heaven join in the song of gratitude. Though men be silent, and refuse to celebrate the birth of their Saviour and Lord; though earth does not echo with his praise, though more intimately concerned; let the heavenly inhabitants sound aloud their ascriptions of glory, and supply the guilty defect of ungrateful mortals.

Or finally, "Glory to God *in the highest*," may mean, glory to God who *dwells* in the *highest heavens :* glory to the high and lofty one, that inhabiteth eternity, and dwelleth in the high and holy place; Isaiah lvii. 15, and yet condescends to regard man that is a worm, Job xxv. 6, and sends his Son to assume his humble nature, to lie in a manger, and die upon a cross for him. Glory to God for this astonishing condescension and grace!

The next article of this angelic song is, "Peace on earth!" Peace to rebel man with his offended Sovereign; peace with angels; peace with conscience; peace between man and man; universal peace on earth, that region of discord and war.

Peace *with God to rebel man*. The illustrious Prince now born comes to make up the difference, and reconcile the world to their offended Sovereign. He is the great Peace-maker, who shall subdue the enmity of the carnal mind, and reduce the revolted sons of Adam to a willing subjection to their rightful Lord. He will bring thousands of disloyal hearts to love God above all, which were wont to love almost every thing more than Him. He will reconcile them to the laws of his government, and the practice of universal obedience and holiness. He will set on foot a treaty of *peace* in the *ministry* of the gospel, and send out his ambassadors, to beseech the rebels in his stead, to be reconciled to God. He will also reconcile God to man, by answering all the demands of his law and justice, paying the debts of insolvent sinners, and making amends for all their offences. He will appear as an all-prevailing advocate with his Father, in favour of a rebel world, and turn his heart to them again. So that this revolted province of his dominions shall again become the object of his love, and he will look down and smile upon the obnoxious sons of men. Oh happy peace! Oh blessed peace-maker! that puts an end to so fatal and unnatural a war, and brings the Creator and his creatures, the offended Sovereign and his rebellious subjects into mutual friendship again, after the grand breach, that seemed likely never to be made up, and indeed never could be made up but by so great and powerful a Mediator; a Mediator of infinite dignity, merit and authority, able to remove all obstructions in the way of both parties.

The Peace proclaimed on this grand occasion may also imply, *Peace with angels*; peace between the inhabitants of heaven and earth. The angelic armies, the militia of heaven, are always upon the side of their Sovereign; always at war with his enemies, and ready to fight his battles. And upon the apostacy of our world they were ready to take up arms against the rebels. But now, when their Sovereign proclaims peace, they lay down their arms, they acquiesce in the peace, and receive the penitent, returning rebels with open arms. These benevolent beings rejoice in the restoration of their fellow-creature man to the divine favour, and shout forth their songs of praise upon the publication of the news.

Again; this proclamation of peace may include *peace with conscience.* When man commenced an enemy to his Maker, he became an enemy to himself: his own conscience took up arms against him, and is perpetually fighting the cause of its Lord. But now the guilt of past sin may be washed away from the conscience with the pacific blood of Jesus, and all its clamors silenced by his all-satisfying righteousness. And now the peace will be preserved, and the contracting of new guilt prevented, by the sanctifying influence of the grace of this new-born Prince. His grace shall change disloyal hearts, and reform rebellious lives; and those shall enjoy the approbation of their conscience, who were wont to sweat and agonize under its tormenting accusations. Thus, self-tormenting sinners shall be reconciled to themselves; and peace in their own breasts shall be a perennial source of happiness: a happiness

"Which nothing earthly gives, nor can destroy,
The soul's calm sunshine, and the heartfelt joy."—POPE.

Farther; peace on earth includes peace between man and man. Now the Prince of peace is born; and upon his appearance let animosity and discord, contentions and wars cease; and let universal harmony and benevolence prevail through the world. Let the bonds of love unite all the sons of Adam together in the closest friendship. It was love that constrained him to put on the nature of man, and to change his throne in heaven for a manger: love is the ruling passion of his soul: love is the doctrine he shall preach: love is the disposition he shall inspire; and love is the first principle of his religion. Therefore, let all the world be melted and moulded into love. Let the wolf and the lion put on the nature of the lamb; and let nothing hurt or destroy through all the earth. Let nation no more lift up sword against nation: let them beat their swords into ploughshares, and their spears into pruning-hooks; and let them learn war no more. For of him it is foretold, that in his days abundance of peace shall flourish, so long as the moon endureth. Psa. lxxii. 7. This, my brethren, has already been accomplished in part: for peace and benevolence is the genius of Christianity; and wherever it has prevailed, it has introduced peace and harmony in families, in neighbourhoods, and among nations: nor can the present disturbed state of things, the animosities, quarrels and wars, that are in the world, disprove what I say: for these prevail only so far as the Christian spirit does not prevail. Just as much as there *is* of these among men, just so much of Christianity is *wanting;* just so far the genuine tendency of the birth of Jesus fails of its efficacy. However, we rejoice in the hope, that our world shall yet see better times, and experience the full effects of this illustrious birth: when the kingdom of the Prince of peace shall become universal, and diffuse peace among all nations. Oh! when shall that glorious revolution commence!

The next article in the song of angels is, "Good-will towards men." That is, the good-will and grace of God is now illustriously displayed towards men, sinful and unworthy as they are. And may they dutifully receive it, and enjoy all the happy effects of it!

Thus the angels *declared, foretold,* and *wished.* They *declared* that even then glory would redound to God, peace be established on earth, and the good-will and favour of God enjoyed by guilty men. And they *foretold* that thus it would be more and more to the end of time, and even through all eternity. And they also *wished* these glorious effects might follow, as agreeable to the high regard they had for the divine honour, and their generous benevolence to their unworthy fellow-creatures, men.

This suggests a question, and also an answer to it. The question is, since the angels were not redeemed by Jesus Christ, and do not share in the benefits of redemption, as man does, why did they thus rejoice and sing at his birth? This we can account for from their regard to the glory of God, and their good-will to men.

Their happiness consists in the knowledge and love of God: and the more he displays his perfections in his works, the more they know of him, and consequently the more they love him. Now the redemption of sinners through Jesus Christ gives the most upright and amiable view of the divine perfections: and on this account the inhabitants of heaven rejoice in it. They know more of God from this great event, than from all his other works of creation and providence. Hence St. Peter represents them as bending and looking with eager eyes, to pry into this mystery,* St. Paul also intimates, that the founding of a church in our guilty world, and particularly the gathering of the poor outcast Gentiles into it, was a secret even to the angels, till revealed by the event; and that the revelation of it discovered to them more of the wisdom

---

* εἰς ἃ ἐπιθυμοῦσιν ἄγγελοι παρακύψαι. 1 Pet. i. 12.

>   See how they bend! see how they look!
>   Long had they read the eternal book,
>   And studied dark decrees in vain:
>   The cross of Calvary makes them plain.—WATTS' LYR.

of God, than they ever knew before. "This," says he, "was a mystery, which from the beginning of the world was hid in God;" but it is now revealed, " to the intent that unto principalities and powers,"—to the various ranks of angels, " might be known by the church the *manifold wisdom* of God." Eph. iii. 8, 10. This cleared up many of the dark events of Providence, which they could not before account for: and enabled them to see farther into the designs of divine wisdom. Methinks when Abel, or the first saint from our world, arrived in heaven, the glorious natives of that country were struck with agreeable surprise, and wondered how he came there. They were ready to give up the whole race for lost, like their kindred angels that fell; and could contrive no possible method for their recovery. And how then are these earth-born strangers admitted into heaven? And when they found, by the proceedings of divine Providence, that God had gracious designs towards our world, and that these designs were to be accomplished by his Son, must they not be agreeably perplexed and bewildered to find out the manner in which he would accomplish them? In what way could he satisfy divine justice, who was himself the judge? How could he die for sin, who was all-immortal? These and the like difficulties must perplex the inquiries even of angels. But now all is made plain; now the grand secret is disclosed. The Son of God must become the son of man, must obey the law, and die upon the cross; and thus he was to accomplish the great design, and restore guilty man to the favour of God.* Angels must rejoice at this discovery, as advancing the glory of God, and increasing their own happiness.

* "Now they are struck with deep amaze,
Each with his wings conceals his face:
Now clap their sounding plumes and cry
The wisdom of a Deity!"—WATTS.

Again: the angels are benevolent beings, and therefore rejoice at the birth of Christ, as tending to the salvation of poor sinners of the race of man. The Lord of angels tells us, "there is joy in the presence of the angels of God over one sinner that repenteth." Luke xv. 10. And how much more must they rejoice to see the grand scheme disclosed, by which numerous colonies were to be transplanted from our guilty world to people the heavenly regions, and perhaps fill the vacant seats of the fallen angels?

I may add, it is not unlikely that the angels may receive some great advantages, to us unknown, by the mediation of Christ; though they do not need a mediator in the same sense that we do. But I have not time to enlarge upon this.

You now see the reasons of the joy of angels on this occasion: and it is no wonder they sung, "Glory to God in the highest, for peace proclaimed on earth, and goodwill towards men."

But how ought we to improve this subject more immediately for our own advantage? This is our great concern; for we are personally interested in it, which the angels were not; at least, not in the same degree. Hence then,

We may learn how we ought to celebrate the birth of Christ—celebrate it like angels, not with balls and assemblies—not with revelling and carousing, and all the extravagances that are usual at this season; as if you were celebrating the birth of Venus or Bacchus, or some patron of iniquity; not with the sound of bells, muskets and cannons, and the other demonstrations of joy, upon occasions of a civil nature. Some of these are not innocent upon any occasion, and have a direct tendency to make men still more thoughtless, and giddy, and to prevent the blessed effects of this illustrious birth. Others of them, though lawful upon seasons of public national joy, for temporal blessings or deliverances, yet are impious and profane, when practised in honour of the incarnation of the holy Jesus. You will all grant, no doubt, that religious joy ought to be expressed in a religious manner; that the usual mirth, festivity, and gayety of a birth-night, in honour of our earthly sovereign, are not proper expressions of joy for the birth of a spiritual Saviour—a Saviour from this vain world—from sin and hell. Therefore, I say, celebrate it as the angels did; giving glory to God in the highest, in your songs of praise; giving him glory by dwelling upon the wonders of redemption, in delightful meditation; by giving him your thoughts and affections; and by a life of devotion and universal obedience. Celebrate the birth of this great Prince of peace, by accepting that peace which angels proclaimed. Give a welcome reception to this glorious stranger. Do not turn him out of doors, as the Bethlemites did; but entertain him in your hearts. Let every faculty of your souls open to receive him. "Lift up your heads, O ye gates: and be ye lift up, ye everlasting doors, and the king of glory shall come in." (Psalm xxiv. 7.) O let every heart cry, "Come in, thou blessed of the LORD: wherefore standest thou without?" (Gen. xxiv. 31.) He came to procure and restore peace between God and man; therefore I, his poor ambassador, "pray you in his stead, be ye reconciled to God." (2 Cor. v. 20.) No longer continue in arms, rejecting his authority, trampling upon his laws, and refusing the offers of his grace: otherwise this peace will not extend to you; but war, eternal war, will continue between you and the Lord God omnipotent. But if the boldest rebel among you this day submit to his government, you shall enjoy the blessed peace, which angels proclaimed at his entrance into the world, and which he left as a legacy to his friends, when he was about to leave it. (John xiv. 27.) Make peace also with your own conscience; and scorn to live at variance with yourselves. How ill do you take it, when others condemn you? and can you be easy, while perpetually condemning yourselves? Let conscience have full liberty to exercise its authority upon you, as Jehovah's deputy, and dare not to disobey its orders. Live in peace also with one another. Silence; ye noisy brawlers: the Prince of Peace is born. Peace! be still! ye contentious, angry passions: the Prince of peace is born. Away slander, backbiting, quarreling, envy, malice, revenge—away to your native hell: for know ye not, that the Prince of peace has entered into this world, and forbid you to appear upon it? Thus, brethren, celebrate the birth of the Saviour, and that not only upon this day, but every day through all your lives: and thus you may have a *merry Christmas* all the year round.

To conclude. What encouragement may this angelic proclamation afford to trembling, desponding penitents? Fear not; for behold I bring you good tidings of great joy; for to you is born a Saviour, Christ the Lord. O! do not your hearts spring within you at the news? I have somewhere heard of a crowd of criminals under condemnation, confined in one dungeon: and upon a messenger's arriving from their king, and proclaiming a pardon, they all rushed out so eagerly to receive the pardon, and see the publisher of the joyful news, that they trod and crushed one another to death. And shall there be no such pressing and crowding to Jesus Christ in this assembly to-day? Shall there be no such eagerness among us to receive a pardon from his hands? Alas! will any of you turn this greatest blessing of heaven into a curse? Was it your destroyer that was born, when the angels sung the birth of a Saviour? Indeed, if you continue to neglect him, you will find him such to you; and it would have been better for you, that neither you nor HE had ever been born. Even the birth of the Prince of peace proclaims eternal war against *you*. I therefore now pray you in his stead to be reconciled to him. *Amen.*

A HYMN.

The Nativity of Christ. By Dr. WATTS.

"SHEPHERDS, rejoice, lift up your eyes,
  And send your fears away;
News from the regions of the skies,
  Salvation's born to-day.

Jesus, the God, whom angels fear,
  Comes down to dwell with you;
To-day he makes his entrance here,
  But not as monarchs do.

No gold, nor purple swaddling bands,
  Nor royal shining things:
A manger for his cradle stands,
  And holds the King of kings."—

Thus Gabriel sang, and straight around
  The heavenly armies throng;
They tune their harps to lofty sound
  And thus conclude the song:

"Glory to God that reigns above,
  Let peace surround the earth;
Mortals shall know their Maker's love,
  At their Redeemer's birth."

Lord! and shall angels have their songs,
  And men no tunes to raise?
O! may we lose these useless tongues,
  When they forget to praise!

Glory to God that reigns above,
  That pitied us forlorn;
We join to sing our Maker's love,
  For there's a Saviour born.

SERMON LXXX.

CHRISTIANS SOLEMNLY REMINDED OF THEIR OBLIGATIONS.

JOSHUA XXIV. 22.—*And Joshua said unto the people, Ye are witnesses against yourselves, that ye have chosen you the* LORD *to serve him. And they said, we are witnesses.*

SHOULD we view the conduct of mankind towards God, we should be tempted to think they are under no obligations to him, but entirely at their own disposal, and at liberty to act as they please. Who would imagine that he is their God, when they are so careless about his worship; their master, when they are so negligent in his service; their father, when they are so regardless of their duty to him; or their ruler, when they follow their own wills without consulting his pleasure? And much less should we imagine they have voluntarily taken upon them the most sacred and solemn obligations to him.

But is this really the case? Are they indeed quite lawless and unobliged? Have they a right to use the proud language of Pharaoh, "Who is the Lord, that we should obey his voice?" No; let them act as they will, let them think what they please, they are under the strongest possible obligations to the great God: nay, they have generally assumed voluntary obligations upon themselves. This is our case in particular; especially since the solemn transaction of the last Lord's day: a transaction which I would now help you to review, that you may the better improve it in future life. In this view, I may accommodate to you the words of my text, "Ye are witnesses against yourselves, that ye have chosen the Lord to serve him." And you cannot but confess with the Israelites, that you are witnesses.

Joshua, the brave general of the people of Israel, had not only settled them in the promised land, but had used all his influence, during his life, to engage them to the Lord. And when by the course of nature, he must take his farewell of them, and could use his personal influence with them no longer, he is solicitous to leave them so fast bound to the Lord, that he might die with the pleasing hope, that they would continue in his service from generation to generation. For this end he calls them together, and makes his last speech to them, which I think, is a pattern of persuasive oratory, not equalled by any of the ancient Greeks and Romans. After drawing them on to choose the Lord for their God, and bind themselves to his service, over and over, by their own personal act, and of their own free choice, he takes them at their word, and holds them fast. And to render the obligation more solemn, and strike them with greater horror at the violation of it, he addresses them as witnesses against themselves, that they had chosen the Lord to serve him.

Accommodating the words to our circumstances, I intend,

I. To show, that we are under obligations to serve the Lord from our own choice, or voluntary engagements.

II. To inquire, *how* and *when*, or in what respects, and at what periods of time, we are witnesses against ourselves, that we have thus chosen the Lord to serve him.

I. I am to show, that we are under obligations to serve

the Lord from our own choice, or voluntary engagements.

Here I would premise, that though *voluntary* obligations, taken upon ourselves by our *own* act, have something of a *peculiar* force in them, yet they are not the *only* obligations we are under to serve the Lord. We are bound to be his servants, whether we *will* or *not*. His character as our *Creator*, our *preserver*, and *benefactor*, and as a being of *supreme excellency*, give him the most firm and indisputable right to our obedience. And our relations to him as his *creatures*, his *beneficiaries*, and *dependents*, lay a foundation for obligations, which are not *suspended* upon our *consent*. Our consent is not a matter of *favour*, but of indispensable *obligation*. We are *born* his *servants*, and must *continue* so, as long as we *exist*. We can no more *dissolve* our obligations to him, than we can *destroy* that being which we received from him. If *children* do naturally owe duty to their *parents*, who *begat* them and who *provide* for them; if *subjects* owe obedience to their *sovereign*, in return for his *protection;* certainly we are by *nature* under the strongest ties of duty to our *heavenly* Father and *supreme* King. The case is not here as among *equals*, who are under no obligations to one another, *till* they enter into them by *voluntary* contract. But here, the obligation is founded in *nature*, and therefore *prior* to, and *independent* upon, all acts of our *own*. It is *naturally* our duty to serve the Lord, whether we *consent* or *not:* and our not consenting is so far from keeping us *free* from obligations to him, that our not consenting is *itself* an act of rebellion, and a breach of obligations.

Consider this, ye licentious sinners, who think, that if you have not been *baptized*, or though you may have been baptized in infancy, yet if you do not *personally renew* your obligations at the Lord's table, you are not bound to serve God, and make religion your business. Do your obligations, then, depend upon so *precarious* a foundation, as your own *consent?* Is there any merit in your enmity to God and his service, which makes you unwilling to choose it? Will this *excuse* your conduct, when it is its principal *aggravation?* Will your strong *love* to sin, which is the reason that you will not renounce it, *excuse* your continuance in it? Will you argue thus, and yet pretend to be a *man,* that is, a *reasonable* creature?— must your creation, your preservation, and all the mercies God has bestowed upon you, pass for nothing? Is it nothing at all, that he formed you by his power, when you had no being? that he has followed you with blessings, every moment, for a length of years? nay, that he has bought you with the blood of his Son? Do these things lay no obligation upon you? Are you at liberty to treat such a Being just as you please? Be it known to you, that you *are,* that you always *have been,* that you always *will be,* bound to be his servants; and you can never get free from the obligation in heaven, earth, or hell, or any part of the universe. You may refuse to comply with it, you may rebel, may incur his displeasure, and ruin yourselves by your obstinacy; but you can never break the tie, while you have a spark of being. Let this fasten conviction on such of you, as refuse your consent to the covenant of grace, and will not assume voluntary engagements to the service of God. It is not a proposal left to your discretion; but it is enjoined upon you by the highest authoaity, under the severest penalties: and if you refuse, you must perish for ever for your inexcusable rebellion. Are you blessing yourselves, that last Sunday, while others entered into such solemn engagements, you kept yourselves free? Alas! your freedom is but slavery to sin and Satan. You do but struggle to keep out of those hands that would save you. Your refusal is so far from setting you at liberty to neglect God with impunity, that it is itself an aggravated wickedness, and will bring upon you the heaviest vengeance from his hands. And (which perhaps you do not think of) you are not free after all. You are bound, firmly bound by an eternal obligation, though you should always exclude yourselves from baptism, and the sacred table. You may refuse to comply with it, but you cannot throw it off, do what you will.

But though we are all under obligations to God, independent upon, and prior to our own consent; yet there are a class of obligations, which we have personally, and by our own act, taken upon ourselves: and in the breach of these we are guilty of more direct and aggravated perjury. These are of different kinds, and assumed upon different occasions. There is probably none of us, but what has voluntarily entered into them at one time or other: particularly in sickness, under apprehensions of danger, under a fresh sense of some remarkable mercy, under horror of conscience, and especially in baptism and the Lord's Supper. In these two ordinances, we do in a more solemn and public manner, engage ourselves to the service of God. And as the one is frequently dispensed among us, and it is high time for us to know its design; and as we attended upon the other so very lately, I intend at present to consider particularly the engagements we have entered into on these occasions. And I shall first begin with the sacrament of

BAPTISM. We have generally been baptized, either in infancy, upon the dedication of our parents, or in adult years, upon our making a profession of the Christian faith, and dedicating ourselves to God by our own personal act. And in what time or manner soever we were baptized, we do actually and personally, or virtually and by our representatives, choose the Lord to serve him.

Baptism may be considered in various views; and in whatever view we consider it, we shall find it lays us under solemn obligations to this.

We may consider it as a badge of Christianity, and a mark of our being the disciples, the followers, and servants of Jesus Christ. Hence it was, that in the apostolic times, as soon as persons embraced Christianity, and professed faith in Christ, they were baptized in his name. They hereupon were considered as the professed servants of Christ, and solemnly bound by their own voluntary promise, to serve him and live according to his religion. Baptism, in this respect, may be illustrated by a soldier, taking upon him the livery of his commander, whereby he may be distinguished from others; or by the ancient practice of putting a mark upon servants, in token of their belonging to such a master.

Baptism may also be considered, in a view something like this, as an initiation into the church of Christ, or as the door of entrance into that sacred society, which enjoys the means and the hopes of salvation. Hence also in the apostolic age, those who professed a desire to commence members of the Christian church, were baptized; and upon this, they were entitled to all the privileges of the church, while they behaved in character; and obliged themselves to live as becomes the members of so holy a society. Now they were looked upon as called and gathered out of the wide world, the usurped kingdom of Satan, and introduced into the Church of Christ, as his children and servants; and they were solemnly obliged to live in character. The view of the ordinance may be illustrated by a soldier enlisting himself under his general, and so making himself one of his army, whereby he engages to submit to military discipline, and to fight faithfully under his commander. Or, it is like a person's becoming a member of the court or corporation by taking the oaths, and other tests necessary to his admission.

Now, my brethren, if you consider baptism in these views, you cannot but see that such of you as have been the subjects of it, have chosen the Lord to serve him. The case is the same, in this respect, whether you have been baptized in infancy or in adult years: for if you were baptized in infancy, your parents had a right to devote you to God, and transact for you, and you are obliged to stand to their engagements in your behalf. This you acknowledge in civil affairs. The land you receive as an inheritance from them you claim a right to; and you own yourselves bound by contracts made in your name, during your minority. Or if you have been baptized in adult age, as sundry of your negroes have been, when you were capable of acting for yourselves, you have in your own persons, and by your own act, taken these obligations upon you. Here then see the ties you are under. You have taken upon you the mark and badge of the followers, the disciples and servants of Christ: you wear his livery. And are you not bound to behave according to these relations? Are you at liberty to behave as others, who make no profession of his name? If you, after all, turn rebels, and act as his enemies, or if you are friends only in show, are you not guilty of perjury—perjury in the highest degree?

You have also been admitted into that select society, which Christ has called out of the world, and owns as his peculiar people. You professedly belong to a holy nation. You have enrolled your names in the sacred register of the citizens of Zion. And does not this oblige you to be holy, in all manner of conversation? Are you at liberty to violate the laws of God, which are the constitution of this society? Is it no criminal defect in you to be destitute of that holiness of heart and life, which is essential to a true member of this holy community? Does not conviction unavoidably flash upon some of your minds from this topic? Have you always conducted yourselves, as persons that have been thus early consecrated to God, and separated from the world that lieth in wickedness? Do you, my young friends, carry these daily obligations into practice? or are not sundry of you breaking them, and practically renouncing your baptism every day? And you, poor negroes, who have been baptized at full age, how do you live? Do you live, since you became the professed followers of Christ, as you did before, or as those do who will not take him for their Lord? May one know that you are Christians, and have been baptized, by your holy conversation? or are not some of you found in the ways of sin, with Christ's mark upon you? Have you not broken the solemn promises before God, and this assembly? If so, when you are baptized, you did not do what was pleasing to God, but were guilty of lying to him; and your case is now a great deal worse than when you were professed heathens. Alas! my brethren, if we take a view of the lives of the generality of our countrymen, who would conclude that Virginia is a baptized country? Are these drunken, swearing, cheating, lying, careless, prayerless creatures, are these baptized disciples of the holy Jesus? They are bound, indeed, to be so; and to live accordingly: but oh, what a load of perjury burdens our land on this account! Truly, sirs, it may strike us with horror to think, how this holy ordinance of Jesus Christ is abused among us. It is become a mere ceremony to give a name to the child, or bring it into the fashion. There is no divine ordinance but what is grossly profaned among us; but none, methinks, so much as this. And when the matter will be brought to an account, how terrible will it be to multitudes!

Again; baptism is a sign of regeneration, or of our dying to sin, and entering into a new state of existence, with new principles and views, to walk in newness of life. I say it is a sign, an outward sign of this; though not the thing itself. The papists have made the sign and the thing signified, to be one and the same in the Lord's Supper, supposing that the outward elements of bread and wine are transubstantiated into the real body and blood of Christ. And some of us have fallen into the like error with respect to the sacrament of baptism; supposing that to be baptized, and to be really born again, are one and the same thing. However, it must be granted, it is an outward sensible sign, of inward invisible grace. So the apostle repeatedly represents it. Rom. vi. 4. "We are buried with him by baptism into death;" that is, it is a sign of our dying to sin, which bears a kind of resemblance to Christ's dying a natural death—"that like as Christ was raised up from the dead by the glory of the Father, even so we also should walk in newness of life," that is, live a life of holiness, entirely new, and different from our former course. Baptism is also called the circumcision of Christ made without hands, in which we put off the body of the sins of the flesh, (Col. ii. 11,) and "are purged from our old sins." 2 Peter i. 9. Here then, ye that have been baptized, and had the sign, inquire whether you have had the thing signified? whether you have been so thoroughly renewed, in the spirit of your mind, and so have entered upon a new course of life that you may be justly said to be born again, to be quickened with a new life, and to be new creatures? Have you any evidence of such a change? If not, your baptism was a solemn lie, in the presence of an omniscient God. Happy we, had we as many among us born of the Spirit, as have been born of water: as many new hearts and new lives, as baptized persons! then our country would indeed bear the appearance of a Christian country. But alas! how different is the case in fact! How many that have been washed with baptismal water, wallow in the pollutions of sin? how many cherish the old man with his affections and lusts, instead of walking in newness of life? However, you see what manner of persons you are bound to be by your baptismal obligations: and if you are not such, you are most grossly perjured. Nay, such of you as have been baptized upon your own account, have *expressly* professed, before you were admitted, and *virtually* in the act of baptism, that upon the best inquiries you could make, you had reason to hope, that you were really born again, and heartily determined to lead a new life of holiness and virtue. And if you had no reason for this hope, you are again convicted of a solemn lie to an omniscient God, who knows your hearts, and cannot be cheated by your vain pretensions.

Another view of baptism, somewhat like this, the apostle gives us, (1 Pet. iii. 21.) "Baptism," says he, "doth save us, not the putting away of the filth of the flesh, but the *answer* of a good conscience towards God." That external baptism with water, which may wash away the filth of the flesh, is so insufficient to salvation, and so vain a thing, that it hardly deserves the name: and inward purity of heart and a good life are of so much importance to that complete baptism, which is saving, that that deserves to be called baptism by way of eminence. The word here rendered the *answer* of a good conscience [ἐπερώτημα] properly signifies a *restipulation*, or an *answer* made to *terms proposed* for acceptance; and seems to refer to the proposal of the articles of the Christian covenant, which was made to those that offered themselves to baptism. And hence we learn, that they particularly engaged to be holy, or to maintain a good conscience towards God. To this you have also engaged yourselves in this ordinance: and have you endeavoured to live accordingly? Do you honestly labour to keep a clear conscience, and to purge yourselves from all filthiness of the flesh and spirit? If not, you are again convicted of a perfidious breach of vows.

But that view, in which I would particularly consider baptism at present, is, as it is a sign and seal of the covenant of grace, and of our dedication to the Father, Son, and Holy Spirit.

By the covenant of grace, I mean the gospel scheme of salvation for sinners through the mediation of Jesus Christ. The blessings proposed on God's part are pardon of sin, sanctifying grace, and eternal salvation; or, in the short and comprehensive form often used in the sacred writings, that he will be our God; that is, that the Father will be our Father, the Son our Saviour, and the Holy Ghost our Sanctifier. On our part, we are required to renounce the devil, the world, and the flesh,—the trinity of the wicked, to devote ourselves to God, and to take the Father, Son, and Holy Spirit to be our God. This implies repentance, faith, love, and a determinate efficacious purpose to walk in universal obedience for the time to come.

Now baptism is a token of this: we are baptized in the name of the Father, of the Son, and of the Holy Ghost, as a sign and seal of our consent to this contract; or, that we are devoted to the sacred Trinity, and take each person in the Godhead, under that relation which they respectively sustain in the economy of man's redemption. This is a primary and principal design of baptism; and all of us, who have been baptized, have thus professedly entered into the bonds of God's covenant.

Hence it follows, with regard to you, negroes, that have been baptized in adult years, that you have publicly professed, that you did truly repent of all your sins, that you did believe in Jesus Christ with all your hearts, with the Æthiopian eunuch; and that you did devote yourselves entirely and for ever to God, and engage in a course of universal and persevering obedience. And were you sincere in this transaction? You have publicly declared it both in words and by a significant action; and if you were not really what you professed to be, you solemnly and publicly declared a lie both to God and man; and does not such a load of guilt lie heavy upon you? Oh! must you not shudder to reflect how treacherously, how villainously, how hypocritically you have acted under the cloak of religion? Alas! will such a baptism as this save you? No; you will sink into hell with the livery of Christ upon you, and it would be more tolerable for you in the day of judgment, if you had still continued wild heathens in the deserts of Africa.

Again; since you have thus, of your own choice, entered into such engagements, are you not bound to live according to them? If, after all, you live unholy, and refuse to walk according to the gospel, you break covenant with God, you undo your baptism; and, as it were, renew your covenant with the devil. And have not some of you been guilty of this very thing? Alas! do you not tremble at the thought? You have cut yourselves off from all the blessings of the covenant of grace, and brought upon you all the opposite curses. You have renounced the Father, Son, and Spirit; and chosen the devil, the world, and the flesh, in their stead. The water of baptism has been, as it were, a deadly poison to you. It has been like the bitter water of jealousy that caused the curse, under the law, which made the belly to swell, and the thigh to rot. Numb. v. 21. It has been a pollution rather than a purification; you have "been washed to fouler stains." And is it not time now for you to begin that repentance in reality, which you should have had, and which you professed, when you were baptized?

Let this be a warning to such of you as have no reason to think you truly believe and repent, not to rush to baptism in that condition. Sundry of you are very eager to apply to a minister to be baptized, while you hardly know why you desire it, or are only desirous to be in the fashion; or, at best, have only a confused notion, that it may do you good, as is necessary though you know not for what. And I am afraid some of you do not scruple to lie to God and man, in order to be admitted; professing faith and repentance, and a desire to be the servant of God, when in reality you know nothing about it. Well; remember, that though man cannot know your hearts, yet God does, and will call you to an account for this deceitful dealing. Alas! poor things, why should you heap more sin upon your sinking souls, by pretending to become Christians, when you are not? First, labour to be Christians indeed; let that be your principal concern; and then come and be baptized, aud welcome. You will say, perhaps, "other negroes are baptized; and why not I?" But, consider, some other negroes have been in great trouble about their souls; their hearts have been broken for sin; they have accepted of Christ as their only Saviour; and are Christians indeed: and when you are such, it will be time enough for you to be baptized. Others of them, I fear, are but hypocrites, and have been admitted upon a false profession; and are you desirous to become such? Will you follow so dangerous an example, and add the guilt of hypocrisy to your other sins?

Finally; is it not proper, that you should often renew this covenant which you entered into, in baptism? For this purpose, among others, the *Lord's Supper* was instituted; and you are bound to partake of it for that end. I must confess, I do not understand that Christianity which is so common among us, that persons who think themselves qualified for baptism, should absent themselves from the Lord's Supper—that they should be so forward to enter into covenant with God in the one, and so backward to renew it in the other. The qualifications for both ordinances, in adults, are substantially the same. Faith, repentance, and a willingness to be devoted to God, are necessary to baptism: and these things only are necessary and sufficient for the Lord's Supper. Our obligations to the latter are as strong and endearing as to the former, if there be any force in the last dying injunctions of Jesus Christ. This was the practice in the apostolic church, that persons were first baptized upon their profession of faith in Christ, and then, upon the same ground, they were immediately, and of course, entitled to the Lord's Supper, and partook of it. But how different is the practice in modern times? Persons who justly think themselves unqualified for the Lord's table, and either through carelessness, or some little tenderness of conscience, absent themselves from it, do, notwithstanding, make no scruple to claim a right to baptism for themselves and their children. But this is a gross absurdity: for if they are prepared for the one, they are for the other also. By baptism we are introduced into the Christian society; and the Lord's Supper is a privilege of that society, to be enjoyed when we are initiated into it. Now, whoever is fit to be admitted into a society, is also fit to enjoy the privileges of that body into which he is admitted; for his fitness for admission is nothing else but his fitness to enjoy the privileges of that body. How unaccountable and inconsistent, therefore, is the conduct of multitudes among us! They think they would be no Christians if they should continue unbaptized; but as for the Lord's Supper, it is a kind of a work of supererogation, or a superfluity in their religion; and they flatter themselves they may be very good Christians without that. And thus they live, half-excommunicated by their own act. I would not have you, negroes, or others, who have been baptized in riper years, to come to that ordinance while unprepared; nor would I have you baptized while unprepared: the case is substantially the same. But this you must know, that if after you have been baptized, you do not communicate at the Lord's table, you are but almost Christians in the sight of the church; you act a very inconsistent part; and you live in a constant course of sin, neglecting a known duty, enjoined upon all the followers of Christ.

As for such of you as have been baptized in your infancy, I have a few things to say to you, founded upon the view I have given you of baptism as a solemn entrance into covenant with God.

The first thing is, that you are obliged by your baptismal engagements, to live devoted to God, from your first capacity of action. You were given up by those who had the disposal of you to the Father, the Son, and the Holy Ghost. And the obligation is binding upon you, as soon as you are capable of acting for yourselves. And if you refuse to perform it, you are guilty of perjury, and renounce your baptism. You do virtually say, "I retract and disavow the covenant made in my name with the Father,

Son, and Spirit; and I will not stand to it." By your baptismal obligations, you were bound to walk every day as in covenant with God; that is, to believe, to repent, and yield universal obedience, every day of your life; and consequently every day that you spend in unbelief, in impenitence, or in any instance of wilful disobedience, is filled up with perjury. And what a shocking scene does this open! not only one, ten, or a hundred instances of perjury, but a whole life, which is nothing else but one continued series of perjury! Every day, every year since you have been capable of acting for yourselves, filled up with the grossest perjury!

I would recommend this particularly to the consideration of the young people that hear me. Some of you, I hope, feel this early obligation; and make it your great business to perform it. But, alas! how many thoughtless, gay, vain, and profligate young creatures are to be found among us? Is this not the general character of the youth of our country; and have these been baptized? have these been so early devoted to God? Alas! who would imagine it from their conduct? Can such claim the blessings of the covenant of grace, when they are renouncing it every day? Can such a load of perjury lie easy upon their consciences? My young friends, be it known unto you, that you are the Lord's: you are devoted things—consecrated vessels; you have enlisted under Jesus Christ; you have bound yourselves servants to God. Therefore with the authority of a minister of God, I am sent in quest of you this day. I apprehend you as his property; I arrest you as deserters, and require your immediate return to your duty. He is willing to receive you again upon your repentance; but if you still continue renegades from his service, he will at length outlaw you. The season of grace will be over, and he will commission his judgments to destroy you. Therefore, my dear youth, let me persuade you to think of your conduct. The guilt of perjury in some slight, civil affair, has struck some with such horror, that it has cast them into melancholy and despair. And can you without uneasiness, reflect upon your life as a series of the most direct, audacious perjury against God? Believe me, you are not your own; therefore, return to your rightful owner; and bitterly repent of your base, ungrateful desertion of his good service. This point would not require persuasion, were you not extremely degenerate. Do you indeed need to be persuaded to choose so good a master, the Lord of heaven and earth? so complete a portion as the supreme and all-sufficient Good? so agreeable and advantageous a service, as that of religion, which is rewarded with an eternity of the most perfect happiness? Is the sordid drudgery of sin and Satan so pleasant, or so advantageous in its consequences, that it should be hard to dissuade you from it? And (which is still more strange and discouraging) shall I fail in carrying such a point with any of you? Alas! are you so surprisingly and obstinately wicked? My children and youth, "for whom I travail in birth again till Christ be formed in you," Gal. iv. 19; do not put me off with a refusal this day. Remember how early you have been given up to God; remember, that when you are sinning with the greatest gayety, when you are dissolving in pleasure, when you are carousing in mirth and extravagant diversions, every act is a breach of the vows of God, which are upon you; for still you are under obligations to God, and you can never get free from them, unless you can annihilate your very beings.

Here let me hint, by the by, at the duty of parents. The early dedication of your children to God, furnishes you with a very proper motive to make them sensible of their duty. And were it duly improved for this purpose, the good effects of baptism, and its subserviency to early piety, would be more frequent and visible. Take your little creatures up in your arms, and with all the powerful oratory which the fond heart of a father and the warm heart of a Christian can make you master of, put them in mind of their early baptism; explain to them the nature of that ordinance; and labour to make them sensible of the obligations that lie upon them in consequence of it. Warn them of the danger of breaking covenant with God, and living a life of perjury. That good man, Mr. Philip Henry, drew up for his children, the following short form of the baptismal covenant, which excellently represents its nature and obligations.

"I take God the Father to be my choicest good and highest end; I take God the Son to be my Prince and Saviour; I take God the Holy Ghost to be my sanctifier, teacher, guide, and comforter; I take the word of God to be my rule in all my actions: and the people of God to be my people in all conditions: I do likewise devote and dedicate to the Lord, my whole self, all I am, and all I can do; and this I do deliberately, sincerely, freely, and for ever."

This he taught his children, and they repeated it every Sunday evening: the good old gentleman adding, "So say, and so do, and you are made for ever." He laboured to bring them to understand, and consent to, this covenant. And when they grew up, he made them all write it over severally with their own hands, and very solemnly set their names to it; and he kept it by him, telling them, that it should be produced as a witness against them, in case they should afterwards depart from God.

Thus, my brethren, do you endeavour to make your children sensible of their early obligations, and bring them to consent to this covenant, and you have reason to hope, that abused and profaned ordinance will be of great service to them.

This naturally leads me to the other thing, I would recommend to such of you, as have been baptized in infancy; and that is, when you are come to years of discretion, you should in your own persons solemnly and explicitly renew your covenant with God. You stand no more upon the footing of your parents' representativeship; but it is expected, that you either confirm or renounce the contract they made for you. It is expected, you should now make a choice for yourselves: God expects it, and his church expects it. Therefore, choose ye this day whom ye will serve. Had the case been difficult, you have had time enough to deliberate; but it is as plain as whether you shall choose life or death. Can you bear to live longer in a state of atheism, without any God at all: I mean without any freely chosen by your own act? Come then, this day choose that God, to whom you were devoted. From a determinate purpose, that you will be his for the future. Acknowledge freely the obligations that were so early laid upon you. Enter into an explicit covenant with God, and frequently renew it, in your hours of secret prayer; and solemnly set your seal to it at the Lord's table.

As baptism is appointed for your first entrance into covenant with God, the Lord's Supper is appointed for renewing it in your own persons. It is expected, that all who are willing to stand to the covenant made for them in their infancy, do express it in this way, and voluntarily take the obligation upon themselves. And therefore, such of you as are arrived to years, and yet live in the neglect of the Lord's Supper, do virtually renounce your baptismal covenant, by refusing to renew and confirm it by your own act. Now, we see how you choose to act when left to choose for yourselves; we see, that you want to be off the bargain; you are not willing to be devoted to the sacred Trinity; but would alienate yourselves from the service. It is really astonishing how inconsistently persons act in this respect: they will retain the Christian name, and yet will not renew the Christian covenant in the ordinance instituted for that purpose. They claim the privilege of baptism for their children; and yet refuse to seal the covenant of grace themselves at the Lord's table. How common a practice is this, all over our country? But what authority have they thus to pick and choose what divine ordinances to observe, and what to neglect? or what right have they to the privileges of the covenant of grace for themselves or their children, who refuse to renew their personal consent to that covenant? It is the grossest absurdity.

This I would apply particularly to children and youth. I would not have you by any means to rush unprepared to the Lord's Supper: but this I must tell you, that so long as you are unprepared for it, so long you are guilty of violating your covenant with God. So long as you wilfully neglect opportunities of renewing your obligations, so long you refuse to be the Lord's and retract your baptismal covenant. You practically disavow the Christian religion, by refusing one instituted sign and seal of the Christian profession; and you so far declare yourselves heathens and infidels. Therefore, my young friends, prepare, prepare to renew your covenant at the Lord's table: and lament, that you have omitted it so long. I would remind you again, that I would not have you unprepared communicants: alas! we have too many already. But I would have you repent, believe, and heartily consent to the gospel, and then come and seal your contract.

From the view I have given you of the nature and design of baptism, you cannot but see the justice of the remark I have already made, that this ordinance is most grossly profaned in our land. It is prostituted to those sinners, who openly violate the fundamental laws of the Christian society; and therefore have no right to any of its special privileges. It is profaned by the irreverence of parents and sureties, who rush to it, as though it were but an old custom. It is profaned by them in that they do not endeavour to make their children sensible of their obligations in consequence of it, and to educate them in the fear of God. It is profaned, insulted, and grossly abused by thousands, who forget the guide of their youth, and forsake the covenant of their God; who break through all its obligations and live impenitent in sin. It is profaned by those inconsistent half Christians among us, who refuse to renew their baptismal covenant at the Lord's table. In short, it is the occasion of national guilt: our country is overrun with this worst kind of perjury: and in this sense I may say, "Because of swearing the land mourneth." Jer. xxiii. 10. And oh! shall not the reflection produce a public, national repentance? Shall we not grieve, that we have sworn falsely to God himself, and dealt treacherously with him?

I now proceed to those obligations which are peculiar to the Lord's Supper; and my address shall be more immediately directed to you that partook in that ordinance the last Lord's day. But my time is so far elapsed, and what I have to say on this head, will so naturally coincide with the former, that I shall be but short upon it.

You have, my fellow-communicants, made a good confession before many witnesses. You have openly, before heaven and earth, avouched the Lord to be your God, and devoted yourselves to him as his people. You may use the language of the Psalmist with peculiar propriety,

"Thy vows are upon me, O God!" Psalm lvi. 12. And now what remains, but that you endeavour to carry your engagements into execution, if you would avoid the dreadful guilt of perjury; if you would inherit the blessings of the covenant into which you have entered; if you would enjoy peace of conscience, and the joyful hopes of heaven; if you would stop the mouths of the enemies of religion, and bring it into reputation; if those are the objects of your desire, then remember and perform your vows. Alas! can you bear the thought of returning again to folly, and undoing all that you have done? How melancholy is the prospect, that probably before the next sacrament some of you will expose yourselves to the rod of church-discipline by your misconduct? To avoid this, take the following directions; "Be not high-minded, but fear." Rom. xi. 20. "Let him that thinketh he standeth, take heed lest he fall." 1 Cor. x. 12. Always be upon your watch, and retain a deep sense of your weakness, and exposedness to temptation; be sensible of your dependence upon God; look and pray to him for strength; and trust not in yourselves, or you are gone. Endeavour to maintain a lively sense of religion upon your spirits; and for this purpose, make it a matter of conscience to attend upon all the means of grace, and let no opportunity, whether public or private, pass by without improvement. Alas! the negligence and laziness of Christians in hearing the word, in reading, prayer, and meditation, is the occasion of their cooling in religion; and then they are perpetually liable to stumble and fall. Take a proper care of your temporal affairs; and make not religion an excuse for idleness. But oh! mind the one thing needful above all; and let not this insinuating world get uppermost in your hearts.

My brethren, I should call this a happy spot, if all of

you, who were communicants last Lord's day, should behave as Christians for the future, and at last all meet at a table of nobler entertainment in heaven. But alas! if there was a Judas in the select society of the twelve apostles, how many Judases must we suppose are to be found among the sixteen times twelve communicants in this congregation? May not the thought awaken our suspicion, and set us upon inquiring, "Lord, is it I?" Matt. xxvi. 22. However, I would make your engagements as binding as possible; and therefore I must tell you, that, however you behave, "you are witnesses against yourselves, that you have chosen the Lord to serve him:"— Which leads me,

Secondly, To inquire *how and when*, or in what respects, and at what periods of time, we are witnesses against ourselves that we have chosen the Lord to serve him.

Joshua, in appealing to the Israelites as witnesses against themselves, in this case, might mean, that as every one was conscious of his own transaction, he himself was a witness against himself, if he should prove treacherous in his engagements; or, that as they had observed the transactions of each other, they would each of them be witnesses against one another; and that both in the present and future world. In both of these senses, I intend to consider the subject.

First, You yourselves are witnesses against *yourselves*, that you have chosen the Lord to be your God. You know and confess that you have been dedicated to God in baptism; and some of you know, it was your own act and deed, when capable of choosing for yourselves. You also know in your own consciences, you were last Sunday, and at other times, at the table of the Lord; and there you renewed your covenant with God afresh; and with the memorials of a crucified Saviour in your hands, made the most solemn vows, that you would serve the Lord for the future. Are not your consciences witness to these transactions? You may try to suppress the evidence by violence or bribery; but I am apt to think, you will find it difficult, with all your art, to keep them entirely silent. When they catch you in an act of sin, or in the neglect of duty, they will whisper within, "Remember, man, thou wast baptized; remember, thou hast been at the table of the Lord. Thou hast had such transactions with God, as promised better things. And is this the result? Is it thus thou performest thy obligations? Is this the baptized Christian? Is this the communicant?" And hereupon, your consciences will bring you in guilty of perjury, and forebode the judgments of God coming upon you. Thus you are not likely to enjoy even the sordid pleasure of sin, without molestation. You have a witness within that remonstrates against your conduct. You will be self-condemned, condemned by yourselves, when you are both judge and party; and who can then acquit you? Methinks, whenever you see a child presented to baptism, it may strike you with a sense of guilt; "Thus," you may say, "in this manner was I devoted to God; but how treacherously have I revolted from him!" Methinks, the remembrance of the table of the Lord may perpetually haunt you while you are walking in the ways of sin. But though you may be able to manage your consciences, so that they may not afford you much uneasiness, while in this world, yet they will speak—they will speak plain and bold—they will speak home to your hearts, in that dread, eternal world, to which you are hastening. There, these suppressed evidences will have fair play. Then no charge will be brought against you by your Judge, but your consciences will re-echo, "Guilty! guilty!" And thus, you *will consume away* an eternity in accusing and condemning yourselves. Oh! impenitent sinners, how will you long for a lethe—a river of oblivion, when shut up in the belly of hell, that you might drink, and forget that ever you had a drop of baptismal water upon you, or that ever you sat in the posture of a communicant at the sacred table? But, alas! conscience will keep the painful remembrance fresh in your mind for ever. Conscience will then upbraid, "you that are now the prey of devils, and the fuel of infernal flames, were once devoted to God. You that are now the companions of damned ghosts, were once among the saints, and wore the badge of the disciples of Christ. But you were insincere and treacherous in all this; and now your privileges are become your curses. You sunk into hell, as it were, with the water of baptism upon your flesh, with the sacred bread and wine, the emblems of a crucified Saviour, in your hands, and with the mark of Christians upon you." Oh! what scope for tormenting self-reflections is here! Oh! how cutting will these reviews be! reviews of transactions passed millions of millions of ages ago. This, sirs, will be the consequence, if you fall from your sacramental engagements; you will be your own accusers, and your own tormentors. Therefore, now beware of so dreadful a doom.

Secondly, You are witnesses against *one another*, that you have chosen the Lord to serve him. You have seen the transactions that have passed between God and you in this house; you have seen some baptized themselves; some presenting their children to baptism, and so renewing their own covenant with God; some sealing their religious engagements at the Lord's table. These things we can witness against one another, neighbour against neighbour, parents against children, children against parents, brothers against brothers, friend against friend, husband against wife, and wife against husband. If we see or hear of any of you falling into immoralities, or neglecting the duties of religion and virtue, we can witness, that you promised better things. If any of you who have enjoyed the privilege of baptism among us for your children, still live in the neglect of family religion, here is a numerous crowd of witnesses, to testify that you are perjured; for we heard you solemnly promise it. One would think, the very sight of one another, should make you ashamed, and afraid to offend. You would not willingly be known and marked for a perfidious, dishonest villain in civil affairs; and will you be guilty of perfidy towards God and his church, without shame or remorse? My brethren, you are too far and too publicly engaged to be religious, to be capable now of deserting with honour and integrity. Therefore, let those who were witnesses of your vows, be also the witnesses of your performance of them. Now "Pay your vows to the Lord in the presence of all his people." Ps. xxii. 25. Whenever you see this place, methinks you may cry out with Jacob, "O how dreadful is this place! this is no other than the house of God, and this is the gate of heaven." Gen. xxviii. 17. Let the sight of your minister, and every one that has been witness to your transactions with God strike you with the remembrance of your duty, and excite you to perform it: and thus be silent, but powerful monitors to each other, and derive advantage even from the sight of one another.

But our intercourse with one another in this world will soon be over, and we must be parted, and pass solitary through the valley of the shadow of death, friendless and companionless. And can we then be witnessess against each other beyond the present state? Yes, my brethren, we must all meet in the region of spirits: we must all stand at the judgment-seat of Christ: and there especially we shall be witnesses against each other. To realize this awful interview, let us suppose (what I am afraid will be the case in fact,) that some of you who have been baptized in infancy, will then be found on the left hand of the Judge, and be accused of violating the covenant of your God: suppose the witnesses are called to prove the charge, (for, as the process will be intended, not for the information of the omniscient Judge, but to convince the world, who can judge only by apparent evidence of the justice of the doom, this supposition may be matter of fact,) your father, mother, or sureties, (as many of my hearers were baptized in the church of England, I mention sureties on purpose for their conviction,) will stand forth, and witness, "Lord, though this be our child, yet we must bear testimony against him, that we did devote him to thee in baptism; and he who now stands among the trembling criminals on thy left hand, was once introduced into thy church, and had thy holy name called upon him." Then those that were spectators of the transaction, will stand forth and declare, "Lord, all this is true; we ourselves saw him solemnly devoted to thy service." Then the minister will declare, "Lord, with this hand I baptized him in thy name; and I once had some hopes he would have made an useful member of thy church; but now I see he is a condemned, lost outcast."

Or suppose some of you negroes, who have been baptized upon your profession of faith for yourselves, accused of having once engaged yourselves to the service of God, and afterwards forsaking it; and witnesses are called to prove the fact; this whole congregation may rise up and declare with one mouth, "Lord, we heard him with our own ears profess, that he renounced all his sins, and gave up himself to thee to be thy servant for ever." And your minister must also witness, "Lord, he declared to me in private, that he did really repent of all his sins, that he did believe in thee with all his heart, and that he was heartily willing and desirous to be thy servant for ever. This, Lord, I had from his own mouth. Had he not made this profession, I would not have admitted him to thine ordinance. But as I could not judge of the sincerity of his heart, but by his declaration, I was obliged to admit him: and he renewed the same declaration publicly in the presence of thy people: and we, who could only judge by outward profession, hoped he was sincere. But how sadly are we disappointed."

Or, suppose some of you who entered into a covenant with God last Lord's day, should then be found workers of iniquity, what a crowd of witnesses will rise up against you to prove that you have voluntarily promised better things? One can witness, "Lord, I saw him at thy table!" Another, "Lord, he sat next to me on the same seat!" And your poor minister, "Lord, he received the elements from my hands: Lord, I conversed with him privately; and he told me, that as far as he knew his own heart, he was sincerely penitent for his sins, heartily willing to be thy servant for ever, and resolved to live a life of holiness for the time to come. This he professed to me, and as I could only judge of outward profession, I was obliged to receive him among the number of thy people." In short, sinners, you cannot possibly escape: judgment will pass against you, and that with the clearest evidence. God the Father will condemn you; Jesus, the only advocate for sinners, will condemn you: your nearest relations and friends will condemn you; the whole universe will condemn you; you will condemn one another: nay, you will condemn yourselves; your own consciences will cry out, "O Lord, thou hast judged righteously; for all these charges are true: I can neither deny nor excuse them!" Evidences will then crowd in against you from every quarter. The three that bear record in heaven, the Father, the Word, and the Holy Ghost, will witness against you. The elect angels, that are performing their ministry invisibly in the assemblies of the saints, will witness to the transactions that they saw you engaged in. And may not the sundry ministers that have laboured among you, shake off the dust of their feet, as a witness against you. Matt. x. 14. May they not shake their garments and say, "Your blood be upon your own heads; we are clean?" Acts xviii. 6. Nay, the heavens shall reveal your iniquity, and the earth shall rise up against you. Job. xx. 27. The rust of your "gold and silver, for which you exchanged your souls, shall be a witness against you, and shall eat your flesh as it were fire. James v. 3. The stone shall cry out of the wall, and the beam out of the timber shall answer it. Hab. ii. 11. And (if I may use the bold figure of Joshua, in the conclusion of his last address) behold these pews, these pillars, and this pulpit, shall be a witness against you: for they have heard all the words of the Lord; therefore these shall be a witness against you, if you forsake the Lord your God. My brethren, I hope I can say, I discharge those duties of my office, which belong to the present state, with some degree of cheerfulness among you. But there is an office, which some of you, I am afraid, will oblige me to perform at the tribunal of the supreme Judge, the very prospect of which may make me shudder: and that is, to be a swift witness against you. All this praying, and hearing, and baptizing, and communicating, will not be forgotten, as soon as performed: no, the matter will have a re-hearing in the other world. And oh! endeavour, my dear people, endeavour so to improve my labours among you, that I may give in my testimony with joy. Let me read the apostle's advice in this case, Heb. xiii. 17: "Obey them that have the rule over you, and submit yourselves: for they watch for your souls, as they that must give account: that they may do it with joy, and not with grief; for that is unprofitable for you."

SERMON LXXXI.

THE GUILT AND DOOM OF IMPENITENT HEARERS.*

MATTHEW XIII. 14.—*By hearing ye shall hear, and shall not understand: and seeing ye shall see, and shall not perceive.*

THIS is a tremendous threatening of long standing, first denounced by Jehovah himself in the days of Isaiah, and frequently cited by Christ and his apostles in the New Testament, as being still in force, and capable of application to various periods of the world. It is a threatening from God, not that he would recall the commission of his ministers, or remove them, but that he would give them a commission in wrath, and continue their ministry, as a judgment upon their hearers. It is a threatening not of the loss of the means of salvation, but of their being continued as the occasions of more aggravated guilt and punishment: a threatening to those that have abused the means of grace; not that they shall attend upon them no more, but that they shall attend upon them, but receive no advantage from them: a threatening that they shall hear, that is, that their life and rational powers, the ministry of the word of God, and all things necessary for hearing, shall be continued to them; but by all their hearing they shall not understand; they shall not receive instructions that will be of any real service to them: they shall not understand any thing to a saving purpose. Their knowledge may be increased, and their heads filled with bright

* Hanover, Nov. 12, 1758.

notions and speculations; but all their improvements will be of no solid or lasting advantage to them ; so that their hearing is equivalent to not hearing, and their understanding to entire ignorance.—" Seeing ye shall see, and not perceive;" you shall have your eyes open, or the usual exercise of your rational powers; and the sacred light of instruction shall shine around you; but even in the midst of light, and with your eyes open, you shall perceive nothing to purpose : the good you see, you will not choose: and the evil and danger you see, you will not shun, but run into it, willingly and obstinately. And certainly such seeing as this does not deserve the name.

The connection in which Christ introduces these words, is this: As he had clothed his discourse in the eastern dress of parables or allegories, his disciples, apprehending that this was not the plainest method of instruction, and that the multitude did not understand him, put this question to him, " Why speakest thou to them in parables ?" " He answered and said unto them, because unto you it is given to know the mysteries of the kingdom of heaven, but unto them it is not given." This informs us, there is a dreadful distinction made, even in this world, between the hearers of the gospel, though they mingle in the same assembly, hear the same preacher, and seem to stand upon the same footing. Thus the disciples of Christ and the unbelieving crowd were upon a par; but, says Christ, to you it is given to know the mysteries of the kingdom of heaven, or the glorious doctrines of the gospel; and therefore you will easily perceive them through the veil of parables, which will be an agreeable medium of instruction to you. But to the unbelieving crowd, it is not given to know these mysteries; though they attend upon my ministry, it is not intended that they should be made wiser or better by it; and therefore, I involve my instructions in the obscurity of parables, on purpose that they may not understand them. Alas! my dear brethren, what if such a distinction should be made between us, who meet together for the worship of God from week to week in this place!

The reason of this distinction will show the justice of it; and that is assigned in the next verse: "For whosoever hath, to him shall be given, and he shall have more abundance: but whosoever hath not, from him shall be taken away, even that he hath:" the meaning is, whosoever improves the privileges he hath, shall have these privileges continued to him with a blessed addition—whosoever makes a good use of the means of grace, he shall have grace given him to make a still better use of them. Whosoever has opened his mind to receive the light from past instructions, shall have farther light and farther instructions: to him it is given to know the mysteries of the kingdom of heaven; and they shall be conveyed to him in such forms of instruction as he will be able to understand. "But whosoever hath not," whosoever makes no more improvement of his privileges, than if he had none given him to improve, from him shall be taken away those neglected privileges. He that has obstinately shut his eyes against the light of instruction in times past, shall be punished with the loss of that light for the future—though the light still continue to shine round him, yet he shall be left in his own chosen darkness, and divine grace will never more open his mind. He is given up as unteachable, though he may still sit in Christ's school. It is no longer the design of the gospel to show him the way to eternal life, though he may still enjoy the ministry of it: and God in his providence may order things so, as to *occasion*, though not properly to *cause*, his continuance in ignorance and infidelity.

Here, by-the-by, I would make a remark to vindicate this dreadful instance of the execution of divine justice, which is more liable to the cavils of human pride and ignorance than perhaps any other. The remark is, that God may justly inflict *privative* as well as *positive* punishment upon obstinate sinners; or, in plainer terms, he may with undoubted justice punish them by *taking away* the blessings they have abused, or *rendering* those blessings *useless* to them, as well as by inflicting positive misery upon them. This is a confessed rule of justice; and it holds good as to spirituals as well as temporals. May not God as justly take away his common grace, and deny future assistance, to an obstinate sinner, who has abused it, as deprive him of health or life? Why may he not as justly leave him destitute of the sanctified use of the means of grace he has neglected and unimproved in this world, as of the happiness of heaven, in the world to come? This is certainly a righteous punishment: and there is also a propriety and congruity in it: it is proper and congruous that the lovers of darkness should not have the light obtruded upon them; that the despisers of instruction, should receive no benefit from it; that those who improve not what they have, should have no more, but should lose even what they have. Thus their own choice is made their curse, and their sin their punishment. But to return.

"Therefore," says Jesus, "I speak to them in parables;" *therefore*, that is, acting upon the maxim I have just laid down, that those who abuse the light they have, shall have no more, I speak to them on purpose in this mystical form, that they may still remain in darkness, while I am communicating instruction to my teachable disciples: "because they seeing, see not; and hearing they hear not, neither do they understand;" because, though they have the exercise of their senses and intellectual powers, and have enjoyed my instructions so frequently, they still obstinately persist in ignorance and infidelity; and in that, let them continue: it is no longer the design of my ministry to teach to convert them.

"And in them," says he, "is fulfilled the prophecy of Isaiah, which saith, by hearing, ye shall hear, and shall not understand; and seeing, ye shall see, and shall not perceive." And then follow the reasons of this tremendous judgment: "For this people's heart is waxed gross, and their ears are dull of hearing, and their eyes they have closed; lest at any time they should see with their eyes, and hear with their ears, and should understand with their heart, and should be converted, and I should heal them:" they seem afraid of their own conversion, and therefore do all they can to prevent the efficacy of the means of grace upon them. Such must be given up as desperate; and though they may still live among the means of grace, it is no longer the design of them to be of any service to them.

You see, as I observed at first, this is a denunciation of long standing—about two thousand five hundred years old. It was accomplished in Isaiah's time, when God looked out for a messenger to send to the Jews, not to convert them, but to leave them inexcusable in their impenitence, and so aggravate their guilt and punishment. "Whom shall I send?" says Jehovah; "and who will go for us? Isaiah vi. 8. As if he had said, I do not intend to deprive this obstinate people of the ministry of my servants, but am about to send them another: and where shall I find one that will accept so thankless and fruitless an office? Isaiah offers his service as a volunteer: "Here am I, says he, send me." And then his commission is made out in these terrible terms, expressive rather of the office of an executioner than of a messenger of peace: "Go, and tell this people, hear ye indeed, but understand not; and see ye indeed, but perceive not. Make the heart of this people fat, and make their ears heavy, and shut their eyes, lest they see with their eyes, and hear with their ears, and understand with their heart, and convert, and be healed." About seven hundred years after, we find this denunciation applied to the Jews by Jesus himself in my text. It was applied to the same people some time after by the evangelist, John, chap. xii. 39, 40: " Therefore they could not believe," says he, "because that Esaias said again, he hath blinded their eyes and hardened their heart; that they should not see with their eyes, nor understand with their heart, and be converted, and I should heal them." Some years after, it was applied by St. Paul to the unbelieving Jews in Rome; upon his preaching the gospel to them, " Some believed the things that were spoken, and some believed not:" and with respect to the latter he says, "Well spake the Holy Ghost by Isaiah the prophet unto our fathers, saying, go unto this people, and say, hearing ye shall hear, and shall not understand; and seeing ye shall see, and not perceive." Acts xxviii. 24–27.

Thus we can trace the accomplishment of this old denunciation in various periods. And is it antiquated and without force in our age? May it not reach to Virginia and Hanover, as well as to Judea and Jerusalem? Yes, my brethren, if the sin of the Jews be found among us, that is, the abuse of the means of instruction, then the curse of the Jews lies in full force against us. The ministry of the word may be continued among us, but many that attend upon it, may not receive any advantage from it; nay, their advantage may not be so much as attended by its continuance among them, but rather the aggravation of their sin and ruin. A dreadful thought! which I would willingly avoid, but some late occurrences have forced it upon my mind: and since I cannot exclude it, I will endeavour to make the best use of it for your warning.

After some weeks of anxious perplexity, unknown before: and after using all the means in my power to discover my duty with all the impartiality I was capable of, I came at length to a determination to send a final absolute refusal to the repeated application of the trustees of the college of New Jersey. Had interest been my motive, I should undoubtedly have preferred two hundred a year, before a scanty hundred. Had honour been my motive, I should have chose to have sat in the president's chair in Nassau Hall,* rather than continued a despised and calumniated new-light parson in Virginia. Or had ease been my motive, I should have preferred a college life, before that of a hurried, fatigued itinerant. But you that have known me for so many years, I dare affirm, do not need this new evidence to convince you that these are not the governing motives of my behaviour: and for those who are determined at all adventures not to think well of a Presbyterian, the most conspicuous disinterestedness and integrity of conduct will not be free from their malignant censures and constructions; and it is likely to be an article of their creed, living and dying, that I am not an honest man, but a designing, artful impostor.

And now, my dear people, as far as I know or expect, we shall live and die together: and if I may judge of *you* by what I feel *myself*, the shock we have received, will unite us the closer together for the future. The warm opposition you made to my removal, was indeed somewhat surprising to me: for I did not imagine I appeared of so

---

* Mr. Davies, it appears, had received an invitation to the college at Princeton, in *New Jersey;* but at that time refused accepting it.—Vide the the following sermon.

much importance to any society upon earth, as I found I did to you: and though no man can well be offended with so generous an error as the excess of love, yet I must tell my dear friends, that I hope religion in this place is supported by a stronger pillar than such a feeble mortal as I: otherwise, it is a very sorry religion indeed. The eternal God, the rock of ages, is the foundation that supports it: and we should always remember, even in the ardour of friendship, that he is a jealous God; jealous of his honour, and warmly resents it, when any of his poor servants are made the idols of his people, and draw off their regard from him. And I am afraid, some of you are in danger of this idolatry. I have indeed been shocked at the high character I have heard of myself on this occasion. What am I at best, but an unworthy minister of Christ, by whom some of you have believed? I have planted and watered the word among you: but God alone gave the increase. "So then neither is he that planteth anything, neither he that watereth; but God that giveth the increase." 1 Cor. iii. 6, 7. He is all in all; and let none of his creatures be complimented as his rival, lest he degrade the idol, and render it despicable in the eyes of all. "Cease ye from man, whose breath is in his nostrils; for wherein is he to be accounted of?" Isa. ii. 22. But to return,

It is likely I shall live and die with you, my dear people. And I cannot but hope, some of you will flourish in the courts of the Lord, and bring forth the fruits of holiness, even under the cultivations of so unskilful a hand as mine—that you will understand the mysteries of the kingdom of heaven, though you should have no better teacher than I: for blessed are your eyes for they see; and blessed are your ears for they hear. Matt. xiii. 16. Having presided in the worship of God among you, in the church upon earth, I shall, if the fault does not lie on my side, join your glorious concert in heaven, and bear some humble part in the more exalted worship of the church triumphant in glory. Well, my brethren, let us help one another by our mutual prayers, and all the assistance we can give each other: let us go on unanimously like fellow-pilgrims, through the wilderness, like fellow-candidates for the same glory, and fellow-heirs of the inheritance of the saints in light. The wilderness does not extend very far before us. May you not ken Immanuel's land, even from where you now stand? A few weary steps more, and our pilgrimage will end in everlasting rest. Our fellow-pilgrims are dropping off one after another every year; and some of them have got the start of us within a few weeks past. Well, we shall soon overtake them; and in a little time the hindmost in the procession will get safe through the wilderness. All hail! to this class of my hearers. But my present discourse is intended for persons of a different character; and therefore you must not expect to hear anything more addressed to you to-day.

As to those, to whom my labours for above ten years have been of no real service for their conversion to God; I must own I have very discouraging thoughts of them. It is most likely, either that God will let them alone, and suffer them to run on into the burning; or that he will make use of some other hand to pluck them out. All the means that I can use with them have been so often tried in vain, that there is but little reason to hope, they will ever have any efficacy upon them. Yet I must not entirely despair even of these: I have some little hope, sinners, that the happy time is coming, when some word spoke by that feeble breath, which has hitherto only reached your ears, will be enforced with almighty power upon our hearts, and bring you to the knee as broken-hearted penitents before God. I cannot part with the little hope I have, that we shall yet see a day of the Son of Man in this place; and then the old gospel, even from the lips of your usual minister, will be quite a new thing— then the hardiest sinner among you will not be able to resist it with so much ease as he does now; but will be constrained to yield to its power, and be made a willing captive to the obedience of faith. Who could live without some little hope of this kind? For can any of you bear the thought, that not only veteran sinners should persist in their obstinacy, and perish, but that a new set of immortals, I mean the crowds of youth and children among us, should grow up, and never see a day of divine power and grace? Alas! if this should be the case, they will only grow up in guilt, and ripen for punishment; and the little religion that is to be found among us, will die away with its present subjects. Let us therefore not only wish and pray for such a visitation from on high, but also let us humbly hope for it. We indeed do not deserve it: but oh! God is merciful and gracious; and whenever he has bestowed this favour, it has always been upon the undeserving. If such a happy period should come, before my eyes are shut in death, I should have my hands full of business once more—business of the most agreeable and benevolent kind—directing broken-hearted, trembling, desponding sinners to the all-sufficient Saviour, Jesus Christ; after whom but very few are now inquiring, as if he were antiquated, or become a superfluity.

But whatever hopes I entertain of this nature, I cannot but fear that my ministry will continue useless to some of you. I am afraid some of you will still have your usual opportunities of attending upon it, without receiving any real benefit from it: or, "that hearing, you shall hear, and not understand: and seeing, you shall see, and not perceive." I know no better method to guard you against this danger, than to warn you of it in time; and this is my principal design at present. For this purpose,

I shall mention the presages and symptoms of the approach of this tremendous judgment—the judgment of having the ministry of the gospel continued, not as the mean of salvation but as the occasion of more aggravated sin and punishment.

Now the presages and symptoms of the approach of such a judgment, are such as these—The abuse or neglect of the ministry of the gospel in time past—Incorrigible obstinacy under chastisements—Growing insensibility, or hardness of heart—Repeated violences to the motions of the Holy Spirit, and convictions of conscience, or obstinate sinning against knowledge—The withdrawing of divine influences—And, as the consequence of all, a general decay of religion. In the first place,

One constant presage of this judgment is, the abuse or neglect of the ministry of the gospel in time past.

This is implied, as you have seen, in the maxim on which divine justice proceeds in the infliction of this judgment, namely, that "from him that hath not,"—who improves not what he hath, " shall be taken away, even that which he hath." Mark iv. 25. This was the character of the Jews, against whom this judgment was denounced: they had long enjoyed the ministry of the prophets, of Christ and his apostles; but had hardened themselves against the good effects of it, and continued unreformed and impenitent. In short, all the judgments of God of every sort are inflicted upon mankind only for their sin; and consequently this judgment in particular proceeds from this cause. But then it must be remembered, that this particular judgment is not inflicted for every sin: for who then can escape? but for one particular kind of sin, the neglect or non-improvement of the means of grace, and particularly the ministry of the gospel. It is because men have heard so often without advantage, that they are condemned to hear without understanding. It is because they have had the use of their eyes, and the light of divine instruction shining around them, a long time, without their becoming wiser or better, that they are doomed to see and not perceive. This in particular, and not their sins in general, is the cause of this tremendous curse.

And is there no such thing as this to be found among us? Have not some of you been favoured with the means of grace for a length of years, yet you are still unconverted, ignorant, and impenitent? Do not your consciences tell you that you still persist in the neglect of those duties, of which you have been convinced, and to which you have been persuaded a thousand times? And do you not still indulge some favourite sin, though you have been warned, reproved, dissuaded, and reasoned with for years together? What repeated, lively representations have you had of divine things? And yet are you not still unaffected with them? All that you have heard of the evil and danger of sin, has not turned you from it, nor struck you with a just abhorrence of it. All that you have heard of the reasonableness, obligation, happiness and blessed consequences of a life of religion, has not turned you to it; but you act as if you were afraid you should be converted, and God should hear you. The very means which have broken the hearts of others into ingenuous repentance, you have had as well as they; and yet your hearts are hard and insensible; nay, are they not growing harder and harder every day? The discoveries of Jesus Christ made in the gospel have attracted the love of thousands to him: and the very same discoveries have been exhibited to you, and yet you remain thoughtless of him and disaffected to him.

To be a little more particular: you have had sufficient means to convince you of the duty of family religion; of the evil of drunkenness, lying, Sabbath-breaking, covetousness, pride, carnal security, indifferency in religion; of the depravity of your nature; and the absolute necessity of the righteousness of Christ for your justification, and of the influence of the Holy Spirit for your sanctification, and yet these means have had no suitable effect upon you. And have you not then reason to fear that this judgment hangs over your heads, "that hearing, you shall hear, and not understand; and seeing, you shall see, and not perceive?" Perhaps the judgment, near as it is, may be averted, if you take warning: and now begin with all your might to improve the means of grace. But, oh! if you delay, and trifle on, the curse may light upon you and never be removed: and then you are as certainly and irrecoverably undone, as if the gates of eternal despair were now shut upon you.

Secondly, incorrigible obstinacy under the chastisements of the divine hand, is another dreadful presage of the approach of this judgment.

The various afflictions, public, domestic, and personal, with which our heavenly Father chastises the sons of men, are excellent means of repentance and reformation: and they have often effect upon those, with whom all other means had been used in vain. But when even these wholesome severities, which, one would think, would awaken the most secure to some sensibility, are obstinately disregarded, and men sin on still, even under the angry hand of God, lifted up to smite them, it argues an incorrigible hardness of heart; and they incur the same curse with those that misimprove the ministry of the gospel. The affliction may be removed; but it may be removed in judgment; as a father gives over correcting an incorrigible child, and leaves him to himself. But, oh! how much better to lie under the rod, than to be given up as desperate, and for that reason dismissed from the discipline of our heavenly Father!

I need not tell you, my brethren, that we have of late years been under the chastisements of heaven of various kinds. You all know, we live in a country ravaged by a savage war; the seasons of the year have been unfavourable to the fruits of the earth: and contagious and deadly diseases have raged with unusual violence in our neighbourhood, and made painful breaches in some of our families. But who has been awakened, who has been reformed, who has been converted to God, by all these chastisements? If you know any, they are certainly very few. If this then be a prognostic of the impending judgment threatened in my text, is there not reason to fear that it is ready to fall upon some of us? God may say of such, Let them alone; why should they be stricken any more. Isaiah i. 5. Or he may continue afflictions as the executioners of his vengeance, while he denies his sanctifying blessing to them, and no more afflicts by way of fatherly chastisement for our amendment.

Growing insensibility or hardness of heart, is, thirdly, a most threatening presage of the near approach of this awful judgment.

This indeed is the very beginning of the judgment, and the first perceivable effect of it; and as the sinner improves in hardness of heart, this curse falls heavier and heavier upon him, and is the cause of this horrid improvement. Hence you find in Scripture, a hard heart, a stiff neck, a reprobate mind, a seared conscience, a soul past feeling, are mentioned as the dreadful characteristics of a soul judicially given up of God.

And is every heart among us free from this alarming

symptom? Can every one among us say, "I am as easily and deeply affected with eternal things, and the ministry of the gospel has as much effect upon me now, as it had five or ten years ago?" Alas! must not some of you say, on the other hand, "Once I remember I was deeply concerned about my everlasting state; some years ago I was alarmed with a sense of my sin and danger, and earnestly used my utmost endeavours to obtain an interest in the Saviour; but now it is all over; now lie I secure and unconcerned, except that now and then I am involuntarily seized with pangs of despairing horror, which wear off, without any good effect. But though I am now so easy and careless, I cannot pretend that my state is really more safe now, than it was when I was so anxiously concerned about it." May not this be the language of some of you? If so, I must honestly tell you, you are near unto cursing. Your hearts are waxen fat, and your ears dull of hearing: and therefore you have great reason to fear the dreadful God, whose grace and patience you have so long ungratefully abused, is about to pronounce the sentence upon you, "Hearing ye shall hear, and not understand; and seeing ye shall see, and not perceive:" you shall enjoy the means of grace, as usual, but you shall receive no advantage from them. Must not your hearts meditate terror, while this heavy curse hangs over you? And will you not fly from it, and use all means possible to escape?

Fourthly, Repeated violences to the Spirit of God, and your own consciences, or an obstinate continuance in sin against knowledge, is an alarming symptom of the approach of this judgment.

Though a distinction may be made in some instances between those restraints and good tendencies which proceed from the Spirit of God, and those which proceed from your own consciences, it is not to my present purpose to make the distinction. They both tend to restrain you from sin, and excite you to a religious life; and therefore their tendency is the same. And I doubt not but the Spirit of God and your own consciences have repeatedly striven even with the most hardened sinner among you; and it has often cost you violent struggling to make effectual resistance. Have you not had some thoughtful, pensive, solemn, intervals, notwithstanding all your preposterous endeavours to live a life of dissipation, and to continue in your thoughtless career? Have you not had strong convictions of your guilt and danger, and the necessity of a new heart and a new life, and dismal misgivings and forebodings of heart, as to the consequences of your present conduct? Have you not, in these solemn moments formed many good resolutions and vows, and determined you would live no longer as you have done! Have you not found yourselves, as it were, weary and surfeited with a course of sin, and your desires going out after Christ? Has not some sermon, or passage of Scripture, or alarming providence, roused you for a while out of your security, and had a strange, irresistible force upon your hearts? Well, in such seasons as these, the Holy Spirit, and your own consciences were striving with you; and had you cherished these sacred motions, you might ere now have been sincere converts and heirs of heaven. But alas! have you not rebelled and grieved the Holy Spirit, and done violence to your own consciences? Have you not talked, or laughed, or trifled, or laboured away these thoughtful hours, and done your utmost to recover your stupid security again? Alas! in so doing, you trod in the very steps of those desperate sinners, who have been abandoned of God, and sealed up under his irrevocable curse. Many indeed, who have done this, have at length been subdued by the power of God, and happily constrained to forego all their resistance; but oh! this has not been the blessed end of all, who have thus fought against God; no, many of them have been given up, and allowed to gain a victory ruinous to themselves. Therefore, as you have reason to hope, you have also reason to fear; and you have undoubtedly good reason to give over your resistance, and submit to God and conscience, lest he abandon you to yourselves. And then, though you may still enjoy the gospel and its ordinances, they will be of no service to you; nay, this will not be the end God has in view in continuing these privileges; his design is the benefit of others, who mingle with you in the same assembly, and enjoy these means in common with you. *They* may be converted, and healed by them: But as for *you*, "hearing ye shall hear, and not understand; and seeing ye shall see, and not perceive;" and this will be your condemnation, that light is come into the world, and you have loved darkness rather than light. John iii. 19.

Under this head I must add, that every instance of wilful sinning against knowledge is the most dangerous and provoking manner of sinning. The language of such a practice is, "Lord, I know this is displeasing to thee; and yet I will do it." What insufferable insolence is this in a worm of the earth! How provoking must it be to the supreme majesty! and what ravages must it make in the conscience! The wretch that can venture upon this, may venture upon anything. Surely such a course of wilful sinning against knowledge, must expose the daring sinner to the heaviest judgment of heaven. And according to the course of nature, it tends to harden him in impenitence; for the only way in which a sinner may be wrought upon for his conversion, is by letting him know his duty: but when he puts this knowledge at defiance, and obstinately does his pleasure in spite of it, what service can instruction do to him? what benefit can he receive from the ministry of the gospel? It is time such a one should be left "to hear, and not understand; and to see, and not perceive." Indeed, this is in a great measure his character already. He runs into ruin with his eyes open, and wittingly rejects the means of his salvation.

Fifthly, the withdrawing of Divine influence, is a dismal symptom of this judgment.

Whatever proud and self-conceited notions men entertain of their sufficiency for the purposes of religion, it is a certain truth, confirmed both by the testimony of Scripture, and the experience of near six thousand years, that the blessed Spirit of God is the sole author of all that little religion that has been among men in every age: and when he withdraws then religion withers, like the fruits of the earth without sun and rain. It is also evident, both from Scripture, and the history of the church, that there are certain seasons, in which the Spirit is plentifully poured out; and then multitudes of sinners, that had sat under the gospel unmoved from year to year, are converted; and religion wears another aspect, in a country, or a congregation, according to the extent of the showers of Divine influences. Then the case of sinners is hopeful; and it is a blessing to be born in such a day of the Son of man; for God works effectually *within ;* and there are many peculiar helps and advantages for conversion *without ;* then ministers preach, and Christians pray, converse, and do every thing in another manner—a manner peculiarly adapted to strike conviction, to lead the convinced to Christ, and to bring down blessings upon the world. But when the abuse of so great a blessing provokes a jealous God to withdraw his influences, then the affairs of religion put on another face: offences happen; a spirit of contention begins to rise; sinners grow insolent; the gospel loses its force upon the consciences of men; ministers grow languid and faint-hearted, and though their compositions may be even more judicious and masterly, than when they had more effect, yet the spirit, the life, the energy, the *unknown something* that gave them their irresistible efficacy, is wanting.' But few sinners are awakened; and the impressions of such are superficial, and they seem to halt, and make but slow progress, in returning to God; and as to the crowd of sinners, they go on careless, unawakened and unreformed under the preaching of the gospel, and harden themselves more against it. It is comparatively an easy thing for them to keep down their conscience, to resist the Spirit, and to sin away the week, though they have heard the gospel on Sunday. Now, in such a season, the case of sinners is very discouraging: there is but a very dull chance, if I may so speak, for their conversion. They may "hear indeed, but they do not understand: they may see indeed, but not perceive." And from the brief description I have given you of such a season, have you not reason to fear, that it is your lot to live in such a time—a time when the blessed Spirit, that has long been striving with Hanover, has, in a great measure left it. And if he has left it, you may be sure he has left it in displeasure, and in judgment: he has left it because he has been ill-treated, and could bear it no longer. And he is gone! Then *the glory is departed!* 1 Sam. iv. 22. You may still have your favourite minister; you may still have sermons, and all the ordinances of the gospel: but alas! "hearing you shall hear, and not understand; and seeing you shall see, and not perceive:" and the very means that ripen others for heaven, will only cause you to rot and putrefy, till you drop, as it were by your own weight into hell.

When the Spirit is withdrawn, it is not only a sign that the judgment threatened in my text is near, but that it is actually executed: for the absence of the Spirit is the great reason why sinners attend upon the ministry of the gospel without any real advantage. The curse is actually fallen: but oh! I hope it may be removed, at least, from some of you: and now is the time for you to make the trial.

Lastly, A general decay of religion is a symptom, and indeed a part of this judgment.

This is the consequence of the foregoing particulars: and when this is the case, it is evident the judgment has fallen upon some, and is likely to fall upon many. When a people enjoy the ministry of the gospel, and yet religion does not gain ground, but declines, then it is evident, some "hearing, hear not, and seeing, see not."

And I leave you to judge, whether this alarming symptom be not upon us. Religion is evidently declining amongst us in some instances: and how little ground does it gain in others?

To conclude: Let such of you as have reason to apprehend, that you are "near unto cursing," (Heb. vi. 8,) pay a proper regard to this consideration, that if it be possible to escape it, now is the most likely time you will ever see: and the longer you delay, the greater will be your danger. Therefore now endeavour with all your might, to hear to purpose, when you do hear; and see to advantage when you do see. "Behold, now is the accepted time: behold now is the day of salvation." 2 Cor. vi. 2.

SERMON LXXXII.

THE APOSTOLIC VALEDICTION CONSIDERED AND APPLIED.

2 Cor. xiii. 11.—*Finally, brethren, farewell. Be perfect, be of good comfort, be of one mind, live in peace: and the God of love and peace shall be with you.**

FAREWELL, especially a final *farewell* among brethren is a very melancholy word, the language of bereaved love. And little did I once think I should ever have occasion to pronounce this doleful sound in the ears of my dear congregation in HANOVER, with whom I fully expected to live and die. Both my first settlement here and my final removal were altogether unexpected. A few weeks be-

---

* This discourse is entitled, "A Farewell Sermon, addressed to the Presbyterian Congregation in Hanover, Virginia, July 1, 1759, on the Author's removal to the College in New Jersey.

The *Rev. David Bostwick*, M. A., of New York, in a preface to Mr. Davies' sermon on the "Death of his Majesty King George the Second," favours us with the following information: "The unusual lustre with which he shone could not long be confined to that remote corner of the world, (Hanover, in Virginia,) but soon attracted the notice and pleasing admiration of men of genius, learning, or piety, far and near; and therefore on a vacancy at the College of New Jersey, occasioned by the decease of two former presidents, (*a*) in a close and awful succession, he was elected to that important office in the year 1759.

"Distressing as it was, both to him and his people, united in the strongest bonds of mutual affection, to think of a separation; yet, a conviction of absolute duty, resulting from the importance of the station, from various concurring providences; and lastly, from the unanimous advice of his reverend brethren convened in synod, determined him to accept the proposal."

(*a*) The Rev. Mr. Aaron Burr, 1757, and the Rev. Mr. Jonathan Edwards, who succeeded him, and died the winter following.

fore I made my first visit to HANOVER I had no more thoughts of it as my pastoral charge, than of the remotest corner of the world; but was preparing to settle in ease near my native place,* till the more urgent necessity and importunity of the people here, constrained me to alter my resolution. It is known to no mortal but myself with what reluctance, fear, and trembling, I accepted your call. The rawness and inexperience of my youth, and the formidable opposition then made both by church and state, when a dissenter was stared at with horror, as a shocking and portentous phenomenon, were no small discouragements in my way. For some years I durst hardly venture to appear but in the pulpit, or in my study; lest, by a promiscuous conversation with the world at large, I should injure the cause of religion, by some instance of unguarded conduct. In short, my self-diffidence rose so high, that I often thought I had done a great exploit, when I had done no harm to this important interest, which I had a sincere desire, though but little ability, to promote. But having obtained help of God, I continue to this day. And I am not ashamed publicly to own these early discouragements, that if I have done the least good to any of you, God may have all the glory, who has bestowed so unmerited an honour upon the unworthiest of his servants, and made use of such clay to open the eyes of the blind; and that I may remove the despondency, into which some of you have sunk, of ever finding your present loss repaired in my successor.

But when, after many an anxious conflict, I accepted your call, I fully expected I was settled among you for life. I did not foresee, nor seek for, nor even desire an occasion to remove, notwithstanding the various difficulties attending my situation: and whatever advantageous offers

* *St. George's* in the territories of Pennsylvania.

have been made to me on either side the *Atlantic*, have not had the force of temptations. It was in my heart to live and die with you: and such of you as best know my circumstances, and how little I shall carry from Virginia after eleven years' labour in it, must be convinced in your own conscience, and can assure others, that worldly interest was not the reason of my attachment. I hope I understand my office better than to make a money-business of it, or a trade to acquire an estate. Or if this had been my design, I would have chosen some other place than HANOVER to carry on the trade. This, such of you as have been most generous to me, and to whom I shall be always grateful, have often professed yourselves sensible of, with more friendly anxiety than I could have expected or desired.

To satisfy you of the reason of my present removal, I will give you a brief impartial account of the whole affair.

The college of NEW JERSEY, though an infant institution, is of the utmost importance to the interests of religion and learning in several extensive and populous colonies. From it both church and state expect to be supplied with persons properly qualified for public stations; and it has already been very useful to both in this respect. Before the irreparable breach made in it, by the death of that excellent man, President BURR, its members were increased to near a hundred; and there was no small prospects of considerable additions every year. But alas! President BURR, its father, is no more. Upon his removal, the trustees made choice of the Rev. Mr. EDWARDS to succeed him, the profoundest reasoner, and the greatest divine, in my opinion, that AMERICA ever produced. His advancement to the place, gave the public sanguine expectations of the future fame and prosperity of the college. But alas! how short is human foresight! how uncertain and blind are the highest expectations of mortals! He was seated in the president's chair but a few days, when he was taken sick and died, and left a bereaved society to lament the loss, and pine away under it. An earthquake spread a tremour through a great part of our solid continent on that melancholy day in which he died;* but how much more did NASSAU HALL tremble, when this pillar fell! Some of the trustees, to my great surprise, had some thoughts of me, upon the first vacancy that happened. But knowing the difficulty of my removal, and being very unwilling to bereave my congregation, they made an attempt, upon President EDWARD's death to furnish the college with another; and therefore chose the Rev. Mr. LOCKWOOD, a gentleman of a worthy character in New England. But being disappointed as to him, they elected me on the 16th of last August, and were at the trouble and expense of sending two messengers to solicit the affair with me and the presbytery. I can honestly say, never did anything cast me into such anxious perplexities. Never did I feel myself so much in need of divine direction, and so destitute of it. My difficulty was not to find out my own inclination which was, pre-engaged to Hanover, but the path of duty; and the fear of mistaking it, in so important a turn of life, kept me uneasy night and day. I submitted the matter to the presbytery, and gave them an honest representation of it, as far as it was known to me. As I was at an entire loss in my own mind to discover my duty, I could not, upon the authority of my own judgment, approve or reject their decision; but I cheerfully acquiesced in it, and sent it, with my own negative answer to the board of trustees, and expected never to hear any more about it. But the trustees, to my still greater surprise, made a second application, requesting I

* March 22, 1758.

would act as vice-president during the winter, till the synod should sit, when the judgment of the presbytery might be referred to that higher judicature. After making all the inquiries in my power to discover what was my duty in so perplexing a case, I thought I had certainly found out the will of God, and returned an absolute refusal in the strongest terms: transferring all my interest at the board to another gentleman,* whom I looked upon as incomparably better qualified for the place, and of whose election I then had considerable hopes. Upon this I was as much settled in Hanover in my own mind as ever; and, as many of you may remember, publicly congratulated you upon the pleasing prospect. But how was I surprised and struck into a consternation, to receive a third application in more importunate terms than ever! This again unsettled my mind, and renewed my perplexities; though I was encouraged to hope, that when I had so sincerely committed my way unto the Lord, he would direct my path, and order things so, as that the result should discover my duty. This third application, as I informed the trustees in my answer, constrained me only to admit a *mere possibility* of its being my duty to comply; but my mind was still almost established in the contrary persuasion. It constrained me only to lay myself open to conviction, and no longer shut up the avenues of light; and therefore I came to this conclusion—To mention at large, all my difficulties and objections—to insist that my first election should be null, because my electors were not then apprised of my objections—and to leave it to the trustees, after hearing all that could be said against it, whether to re-elect me at their next meeting. But even this was not all: I farther insisted, that in case they should re-elect me, it should be referred to the synod of New York and Philadelphia,

* Dr. Samuel Finley.

whether I should accept the place. This is a brief view of my proceedings in the affair: and for fuller intelligence I must refer you to my friends, the elders of this congregation, to whom I have communicated all the letters I have received or written, that they may be able to satisfy you. And I can assure you in their presence, that all of them that heard my answer, expressed their acquiescence in it. The result of the affair, when left upon this footing, has been, that I was re-chosen at the board of trustees by a much greater majority than at first; and that the synod, consisting of an unusual number of ministers from various parts, after hearing at large what could be said upon both sides, not only consented to my acceptance of the proposal, but even dissolved my pastoral relation to my dear charge, and ordered my removal by an almost unanimous vote. This has brought the tedious, anxious affair to a final issue, and disarms all my resistance, so that I can struggle no longer. It was one of my vows, on the solemn day of my ordination, that I would be subject to my brethren in the Lord, in all things lawful. It is therefore very impertinent to object, that " I might stay after all, if I would." It is true, it is in my power to refuse to comply with my duty, even when it appears: it is in my power to violate my solemn vows, and incur the guilt of perjury by disobedience to my brethren, in that judicature to which I belong: that is, it is in my power, as a free agent, to sin. But this is a preposterous power, which I hope God will enable me never willingly to exercise. Oh that his grace may always happily disable me from disobeying the call of duty.

I am sorry to take up so much of your sacred time in a narrative in which I have so much personal concern, but it is wholly owing to my solicitude to satisfy you as to the reasons of my conduct. For though my dear connections with Virginia are now broken, and my personal interest can receive no advantage or injury from your friendship or resentment, yet, since we must part, I would by all means part in peace, and prevent all unkind and suspicious thoughts of one whom you once tenderly loved, and who will always tenderly love you, wherever he goes, and whatever you think of him. To stop the clamorous mouths of the censorious world, is what I do not at all intend; because I know it is impossible. They will put what construction they please, even upon the most unsuspicious and disinterested actions; and nothing but the approbative sentence of the universal Judge from the supreme tribunal, is likely to silence their calumnies. They will make it an article of their creed, living and dying, that secular advantage is the object I have all along had in view, and in pursuit of which I am now about to remove. But among those whom I had once the pleasure of calling *my people,* I hope I shall find none of this censorious and malignant turn. I have always found you candid, and ready to err upon the generous extreme of charity as to your once loved minister; and such I hope to find you at parting.

——*At parting!*—Alas! and must we part?—My heart fails at the thought. The most endeared friendship I have for you; the affectionate gratitude I feel for you as my benefactors; the anxieties that rush upon my heart, lest when you are, as it were, disbanded, and left as sheep without a shepherd, you should wander, and the little religion that has been among you should die away; my tender sympathy with you under your sorrows and discouragements; the diffidence and horror that seize me at the thought of entering into a sphere of action so arduous and untried, as that to which I am removing; these and a thousand other things render this a very painful and melancholy parting to me. Yet, part we must; therefore,

"Finally, my brethren, farewell. Be perfect; be of good comfort; be of one mind; live in peace; and the God of love and peace shall be with you." This is *St. Paul's* valedictory salutation and advice to the church of *Corinth;* and I would briefly illustrate the several parts of it, as pertinent to your present circumstances.

First of all, *Be perfect:* that is, labour after perfection in holiness; cherish every grace and virtue to maturity. Fill up the defects still remaining in your church: restore every disjointed member to its proper place; and correct whatever is amiss.*

This advice may refer to the exercise of discipline in the church; as much as to say, "If any offending member has been excluded your communion, and now appears penitent, or if any one has been unjustly laid under censure, restore him in the spirit of meekness to his former standing in the church, and confirm your love towards him." In this view, I would particularly recommend this apostolic advice to the elders of this congregation, whenever an occasion occurs of carrying it into practice.

Or the advice may refer to individuals; and then it is an exhortation to every particular church-member to improve in personal religion; as if he should say, "After all the means of sanctification you have enjoyed, you may still find yourselves deficient in every grace and virtue: therefore aspire and labour after higher attainments. You may still find many things amiss in you; therefore endeavour to reform and rectify them. You may perhaps find yourselves upon the decline in religion; therefore labour to recover what you have lost, and restore what is

---

* This is the full import of the word καταρτίζεθε, here rendered, "Be perfect." So *Chrysostom;* τελειοι γινεθε, και αναπληροῦτε τα λειπόμενα. Others, "Be restored, repaired, or completed:" for καταρτίζειν, properly signifies *luxatum membrum in locum reponere;* to set a dislocated limb.

decaying. Strengthen the things that remain, which are ready to die, that your works may be found perfect before God." Rev. iii. 2.

Far be it from me, my brethren, to think that now, when you are deprived of your minister, you may lawfully make a stand in your Christian progress, or allow yourselves to slide down the slippery, descending road of apostacy. You are still obliged to grow in grace, and in the knowledge of our Lord and Saviour JESUS CHRIST. And you will still enjoy sufficient means for that purpose, notwithstanding your present bereavement. The throne of grace is still accessible: your closets are still open for you; and you may enjoy the sweet privilege of secret devotion. Bibles and an unusual variety of excellent books are still within your reach: and these alone are sufficient to "make you wise unto salvation," when you have no opportunity of attending upon the public ministry. You may also receive advantage from your occasional attendance upon public worship in the established church: and I hope you will always retain those catholic principles I have endeavoured to inculcate upon you, and willingly receive all the spiritual good you can, wherever it may be obtained. I also hope and pray, with *Moses*, that "the LORD, the GOD of the spirits of all flesh, may set a man over this congregation; a man in whom is the Spirit, who may go out and come in before you; that the congregation of the LORD be not as sheep which have no shepherd." Numb. xxvii. 16–18. If you continue your earnest endeavours, and "pray to the Lord of the harvest," methinks I can assure you, upon the truth of the divine promises, that he will not suffer this spot of his vineyard to run waste, but will send a labourer into it, and leave you no reason to be sorry at the exchange.

The apostle's second farewell advice is, "*Be of good*

comfort:" that is, take courage and rejoice in the LORD. Be not swallowed up in excessive sorrows: do no despond, whatever gloomy and frowning appearances things may wear as to yourselves, your church, or your country: but maintain a cheerful confidence in GOD, in the most discouraging circumstances. His fatherly love, his great and precious promises, the faithful care of his providence, the sweet experience which you and his people in all ages have had of his goodness, the privileges and blessings, temporal and spiritual, which he still leaves in your possession, even when he strips you of others; these and a thousand other considerations may support and comfort you: and it is your duty, as well as your privilege, to derive from them that encouragement, they are adapted to afford. It affects me with the tenderest sympathy, my brethren, to see any of you drooping, and sunk into despondency, at the prospect of my departure. But "be of good comfort, and strengthen yourselves in the Lord your God." If you are the children of his grace, "though your father and your mother forsake you, the LORD will take you up." Psalm xxvii. 10; and he "will never, never, never* leave you, nor forsake you. The Lord, the great Bishop of souls, will be your Shepherd; and then you shall not want."

Or this advice may be rendered, "*Be ye exhorted,*"† that is, be persuasible, and regard the exhortations I have given you. This is a very proper advice for me to give you, when I have but a day longer to stay in HANOVER. Remember, my dear friends, the many exhortations you have heard, in the course of eleven years,

---

* The emphasis of the unusual run of negatives in the original will not only bear, but seems to require this translation: Οὐ μή σε ἀνῶ οὐδ' οὐ μή σε ἐγκαταλίπω. To this purpose Dr. Doddridge renders it, Heb xiii. 5.

† παρακαλεῖσθε.

from my mouth, as well as from my brethren, who have occasionally officiated among you. Oh "remember how you have received and heard; and hold fast, and repent." Rev. iii. 3. Among you I have spent the prime of my life; among you I have laboured and toiled in the delightful work of serving your souls; and God is witness, that "I have declared to you the whole counsel of God," as far as I knew it, "and kept nothing back." And will you not regard the word of exhortation, so often repeated, and so long continued? Alas! have I preached, and you heard, for eleven years in vain? Eleven such years is a long and important space in the life of a minister of the gospel, and of his dying hearers, who must soon give an account to the supreme Judge of their improvement of so precious a season. Therefore, oh recollect and seriously regard the many solemn exhortations you have heard.

The apostle's third valedictory advice is, "*Be of one mind.*" This does not so properly refer to unity of sentiment in every little article and disputable punctilio, which is not to be expected in this state of imperfection, in which even good men, who always agree in the essentials of religion, may differ in a thousand circumstantials: I say, this does not so properly refer to unity of sentiment in this respect, as to *unity of affection** *and design*, as much as to say, "However you may differ in lesser matters, be *one in heart*, one in affection, and *attend to the same great concern*, the salvation of your souls, and the advancement of practical holiness: mind this above all, and set your affections upon it. This is that point in which you should and may agree, even when you cannot think alike in smaller things."

* φρονειν is a word that I think is never applied to the intellect, but always to the affections: and φρονειτε τὸ αὐτό, may be rendered, *mind the same thing: set your affections upon the same thing.* So Col. iii. 2. Τὰ ἄνω φρονειτε, is rendered, "set your affections on things above,"

This I would particularly inculcate upon you, my dear brethren, of whom I am now taking my leave. You may differ among yourselves about a thousand less things in religion and civil life, but oh! do not *differ in heart*. Still love one another: forbear and forgive one another. Give, as well as take the liberty of thinking for yourselves: and do not make a perfect uniformity of opinion in every thing the test of Christianity, nor the ground of your charity. Would you regard the last advice of a dying man, a dying friend, a dying minister? Well, from this day I am dead to you: and one principle article of my last advice to you is, "Love one another. Have fervent charity among yourselves; that charity that suffereth long, and is kind; that envieth not; that is not easily provoked; that thinketh no evil; that beareth all things, believeth all things, hopeth all things, endureth all things." 1 Cor. xiii. 4, 5, 8. This, my brethren, is the Christian temper; the very mind that was in Christ Jesus. And by this shall all men know that ye are his disciples, if ye love one another. John xiii. 35. It is an old tradition, that the beloved disciple *John*, when he was so enfeebled with age that he could not preach, thought it worth his while to be carried into the congregation every Lord's day, just to repeat this benevolent exhortation, "Little children, love one another." And this I would most affectionately inculcate upon you with my last breath. This will contribute to your mutual happiness, to your growth in religion, to the prosperity of your congregation, and to the comfort of your future minister. And may the God of love stamp this part of his amiable image upon your hearts!

If we give the word another turn, *mind the same thing*, I may take occasion to inculcate upon you the one thing needful, the choice of which I have so often recommended to you; even the care of your souls, and the concerns of eternity. Oh make this your main study: pursue this with all your might: be unanimous in this, whatever other differences subsist among you; agree at least not to ruin yourselves for ever by a course of sin: agree at least to walk to heaven in the same road of practical holiness. However variously and freely you think, oh be of one mind in this! Akin to this, is

The apostle's fourth and last valedictory advice, *Live in peace*: be of a pacific temper and practice towards all men, especially those that are members of the same church with you.

Offences, my brethren, will happen among you, which will render it difficult even for the lovers of peace to maintain it, and enjoy their favourite blessing. And a thousand trifles will happen every day, which will be made an occasion of contention by proud and turbulent spirits, that delight in noise and animosities. Angry contests and ill-will may rise from very trivial causes, and spread among you, like a conflagration. Some small difference in opinion, a little matter of property, a supposed neglect or contempt, the whisper of tattlers and busy bodies, and a thousand other trifles, may strike the spark, which may burst out into a destructive blaze. Therefore be upon your guard against every thing that may break the peace of the society to which you belong. Be patient and forbearing; not blustering and quick of resentment. Be meek and humble, not insolent, imperious and over-bearing. Be pliable, self-diffident, and submissive; not obstinate, head-strong, and self-willed. Be yielding to others, and do not usurp the province of universal dictators. Be at peace with God, and love the common Father of mankind; and if you love him that begat, you will naturally love them that are begotten of him. 1 John v. 1. This is the way to cultivate and preserve peace, and restore it when lost. And if you go on in this way, you may hope you will continue a flourishing society, and that *the God of love and peace will be with you;* which is the motive the apostle urges to enforce his exhortation.

But this is not the whole extent of your duty. You are to cultivate peace not only among yourselves in your own congregation, but to follow peace with *all men.* If it be possible, as much as lieth in you, live peaceably with *all men.* Rom. xii. 18. Maintain peace with your brethren around you of the established church; and never let differences in religion break up good neighbourhood, or interrupt the good offices in civil life. Indeed, if men will quarrel with you because you think for yourselves in matters in which every man must give an account of himself to God; because you will not follow the multitude to do evil, but resolve to save your souls, though you should be singular in the attempt; because you will not be of their mind in every punctilio, nor take your religion upon trust for them: I say, if men will quarrel with you on such accounts as these, you cannot help it: the breach of peace is chargeable upon them; and you are not obliged to give up truth, religion and liberty, to gratify their humour. Be tenacious of truth and liberty, and contend earnestly for the faith, Jude, 3, but still in the spirit of meekness, for the wrath of man worketh not the righteousness of God. James i. 20. Were I never to speak a word more, I could venture to affirm, that it is the cause of liberty and the gospel, and not a carnal faction, or a schismatical body, that you, my dissenting brethren, have been promoting: and this is the true grace of God in which you stand. 1 Peter v. 12. The longer I live, the more I am confirmed, that the simple method of worship I have practised, free from the ceremonies of human invention, and those doctrines of grace so mortifying to the pride of man, and so unfashionable in our age and country, which I have taught you, are agreeable to the pure gospel of Christ, pleasing to God, and conducive to your salvation. I am so far from advising you to give up this cause for the sake of peace, that, on the other hand, it is my solemn charge to you, in the name of God, zealously to maintain and promote it. But this you may do without breaking the peace of church or state: this you may do, and yet maintain a peaceable temper and conduct towards those that differ from you.

Thus "mind the same thing, and live in peace," and be assured, upon the authority of an inspired apostle that *"the God of love and peace will be with you,"* and distinguished you with his gracious presence. There is a peculiar propriety and fitness in this; that the God of love should be with those who love one another; that the God of peace should be with those that delight in peace, and maintain it; that is, that he should dwell with those that are like him. What can be more becoming? what can be more in character? Such do you endeavour to be, my brethren, and the God of love and peace will be with you, though your once-loved minister can be with you no longer. He will dwell among you; and his gracious presence will more than supply the absence of all his creatures. If he be with you, he will cause his church among you to flourish, and adorn every individual in it with the beauties of holiness. If the God of love and peace be with you, he will cause love and peace to prevail among you, and render you a society of friends and brethren, walking unanimously to the same heavenly country, like affectionate fellow-pilgrims. If he be with you, his gospel will not be that languid, feeble, inefficacious thing that it has been for some time; but even occasional opportunities of worship will be more serviceable to you, than stated have been; and even your silent Sabbaths, will be more delightful seasons, than those you have spent in his house, without his gracious presence. God grant you may enjoy this blessing in time, till you are advanced into his more immediate presence in a happy eternity!

Thus have I endeavoured to illustrate the apostle's general farewell advice. The remaining part of my design is, to take my leave of the several classes and ranks among you in a particular manner, and to give you a few parting advices adapted to your respective characters.

FAREWELL, ye saints of the living God, ye "few names even in HANOVER, that have not defiled your garments." Ye shall *fare well* indeed. That God, whose the earth is, and the fullness thereof; that God, who makes angels happy, and whose goodness extends from the highest archangels down to the sparrows, the young ravens, and the lily and grass of the field; that God is your God, and has undertaken your welfare. That God will be your God for ever; and he will be your guide even until death. Psa. xlviii. 14. He will guide you by his counsel through the intricacies of life, and then receive you into glory. Psa. lxxiii. 24. Survey the sacred treasury of the divine promises laid up for you in the Bible, and stand lost in delightful wonder at your own riches. Behold the immense inheritance which the blood of Christ has purchased for you, and the grace of God bestowed upon you by an unalienable title. "All things are yours: whether Paul or Apollos, or Cephas:" all the ministers of Christ, and all their various gifts, are for your service; and if you are deprived of one of them, God will provide you another, or in some way make up the loss. "All things are yours, whether the world, or life, or death, or things present or things to come: all are yours; and ye are Christ's, and Christ is God's;" 1 Cor. iii. 21, 22, 23. It doth not yet appear what you shall be. I have known you broken-hearted penitents; honest, laborious, weeping seekers of Jesus, and conscientious, though imperfect observers of his will: I have known you poor mortal creatures, sometimes trembling, sometimes rejoicing, sometimes nobly indifferent at the prospect of death. But I hope yet to know you under a higher character; glorious IMMORTALS, perfect in holiness, vigorous and bright, and full of devotion, "as the rapt seraphs adore and burn;" and qualified to bear a part in a more sublime and divine worship of the heavenly temple. There I hope to find some humble seat among you, and spend a blessed eternity in the divine intimacy of immortal friendship, without interuption or the fear of parting. Therefore adieu; but not for ever. Adieu for a few years, or months, or days, till death collects us to our common home, in our Father's house above. You have been the joy of my life, under all the discouragements and fatigues of my ministry; and to your prayers I owe the comfort and success I have had among you. You have great interest in the court of heaven, through the all-prevailing intercession of that advocate, Jesus Christ the righteous; therefore I beg you would always afford me the charity of your prayers, wherever I go, till the weeping voice of prayer be changed into rapturous strains of praise. If I have been so happy as to improve you in divine knowledge, and help you in your pilgrimage through this wilderness, I esteem it one of the most delightful actions of my life, and one of the greatest blessings of God to the unworthiest of his servants; and to him alone I would have you and myself ascribe all the glory. "Neither is he that planteth any thing; neither he that watereth; but God, that giveth the increase;" 1 Cor. iii. 7; he is all in all.

If there be among you any of my spiritual children; any that have received their first deep and effectual impressions of religion from my ministry, though it should be the meanest among you, I most heartily bid you farewell. It was worth my while to come into existence, and pass through the hard and dubious conflict of life, if my Maker has been pleased to use my feeble, unskillful hand to save some soul from death. This is a more noble and benevolent exploit than to save a kingdom from the heaviest temporal slavery; for what is an earthly kingdom to an immortal spirit? I take my leave of you with all the fond endearments of a fatherly heart; for what is my hope, or joy, or crown of rejoicing? Are not even ye in the presence of our Lord Jesus Christ at his coming? Yes, ye are my glory, and my joy. "Therefore, my brethren, dearly beloved, and longed for, my joy and crown, so stand fast in the Lord, my dearly beloved." Phil. iv. 1. Endeavour to make daily proficiency in every branch of true goodness, and beware of apostacy. Having begun in the spirit, beware that you do not end in the flesh. Remember, it is only he that endureth to the end, that shall be saved; but if any man draw back, God's soul shall have no pleasure in him. Heb. x. 38.

Shall I say FAREWELL, impenitent sinners? Alas! you cannot *fare well*, however heartily I wish it. "There is no peace, saith the LORD, unto the wicked." Isa. xlviii. 22; and whoever speaks peace to you, in your present condition, does but heal your hurt slightly, and flatter you to your ruin; for who can bless whom God hath not blessed? Your consciences bear witness, "that you have had precept upon precept, and line upon line," during my ministry among you—That I have not shunned to declare to you all the counsel of God, Acts xx. 27; and have kept back nothing that was likely to be profitable to you. Acts xx. 20.

I have warned you, in season and out of season—I have reproved, rebuked, and exhorted you, with all long-suffering and doctrine. 2 Tim. iv. 2. I have preached to you as a dying man to dying men, and—now the time of my departure is at hand—I must take my farewell of you. Receive, all of you, my brethren, the word of exhortation, from the lips of him, whose voice has so often sounded an alarm in your ears; though I fear, as to many of you, without the desired effect. My voice, it is probable, will never more be heard by you. This will be the last time. Oh recollect the many invitations I have given you on the one hand, and threatenings on the other. Heaven forbid that any of them should arise in judgment against you another day! Behold, now is the accepted time; behold, now is the day of salvation. 2. Cor. vi. 2. To-day, if ye will hear his voice, harden not your hearts. I beseech you, once more, and I may say, once for all, in Christ's stead, be ye reconciled to God. 2 Cor. v. 20. Do not cause me to appear, as a swift witness against you another day—the day of universal retribution—Flee, flee, all of you, from the wrath to come—lay hold on the hope that is set before you. I have finished my message among you. Oh forget it not. Lay it seriously to heart. If the word you have heard from my lips, prove not a savour of life unto life, it will, it must be a savour of death unto death. Farewell—" finally, brethren, farewell; be perfect, be of good comfort, be of one mind, live in peace: and the God of love and peace shall be with you,"—which may God grant for Christ's sake. *Amen.*

POEMS.

RETAINED AS SPECIMENS OF THE AUTHOR'S POETRY.*

ON THE BIRTH OF JOHN ROGERS DAVIES,

THE AUTHOR'S THIRD SON.

Thou little wondrous miniature of man,
Form'd by unerring Wisdom's perfect plan,
Thou little stranger from eternal night,
Emerging into life's immortal light;
Thou heir of worlds unknown, thou candidate
For an important everlasting state,
Where this young embryo shall its powers expand
Enlarging, rip'ning still, and never stand.
This glimm'ring spark of being, just now struck
From nothing by the all-creating Rock,
To immortality shall flame and burn,
When suns and stars to native darkness turn;
Thou shalt the ruins of the worlds survive,
And through the rounds of endless ages live.
Now thou art born into an anxious state
Of dubious trial for thy future fate:
Now thou art listed in the war of life,
The prize immense, and O! severe the strife.

Another birth awaits thee, when the hour
Arrives that lands thee on th' eternal shore;
(And O! 'tis near, with winged haste 'twill come,
Thy cradle rocks towards the neighb'ring tomb;)
Then shall immortals say, "A son is born,"
While thee as dead mistaken mortals mourn;
From glory then to glory thou shalt rise,
Or sink from deep to deeper miseries;
Ascend perfection's everlasting scale,
Or still descend from gulf to gulf in hell.

---

* We learn from the Rev. Thomas Gibbons D. D., of London, the first Editor of Mr. Davies sermons, that the latter very frequently annexed to his sermons hymns of his own composition. It is greatly to be regretted that they were not published by Dr. Gibbons in connection with the sermons.

[EDITOR OF THE BOARD OF PUBLICATION.]

Thou embryo-angel, or thou infant fiend,
A being now begun, but ne'er to end,
What boding fears a Father's heart torment,
Trembling and anxious for the grand event,
Lest thy young soul so late by Heav'n bestow'd
Forget her Father, and forget her God !
Lest, while imprison'd in this house of clay,
To tyrant lusts she fall a helpless prey !
And lest, descending still from bad to worse,
Her immortality should prove her curse !

Maker of souls ! avert so dire a doom,
Or snatch her back to native nothing's gloom.

ON THE WORDS OF OUR LORD,

"LOVEST THOU ME?"—JOHN XXI. 17.

My God, the wretch that does not love thy name,
To life and being forfeits all his claim ;
And may he sink to nothing, whence he came !
Or let the yawn of the dire mouth of hell
Receive him, with his fellow-fiends to dwell.

O, if my heart does not to thee aspire,
If aught with equal fervour I desire,
I'm self-condemn'd, and doomed myself to fire ;
Let not my guilty breath profane thine air,
Nor groaning earth the monstrous burden bear ;
Let clouds with vengeance big, burst o'er my head,
And volleys of red thunder strike me dead ;
The sun convert his gentle rays to flames,
And blast the miscreant with his vengeful beams :
The whole creation rise in arms for Thee,
To vindicate the rights of thy divinity.

Vile wretch, that dares refuse to love a God,
Who form'd me man out of my native clod:
Whose breath the faculty of love inspir'd,
And with the heav'nly spark my bosom fir'd :
Whose uncreated beauties charm the sight
Of gazing angels in the realms of light.

Thy glories, faintly copied, round me shine,
Great God! and beam thro' all these works of thine,
Proclaiming Thee their Origin divine:
Thy grace diffus'd around in thousand rills,
A thousand worlds with endless rapture fills:
Thou, too, when man to dreadful ruin fell,
Helpless, unpitied on the brink of hell,
When frowning justice did the prey demand,
And none could rescue from its vengeful hand,
Thou, touch'd with pity, didst avert his doom,
And gave thy Son a victim in his room!
Nail'd to the cross the bleeding Saviour hangs,
And courts my love with groans and dying pangs
O! I must love—nor can the pains or blood
Of an incarnate God be withstood!

Yet ah! in some dark hour I scarcely know
Whether I love my gracious God, or no;
Gloomy suspicions, painful jealousies,
And anxious doubts in all their horrors rise:
I hear the whisp'ring of misgiving fear,
Thy love is feign'd, thine ardour insincere."—
Too true, too true, my trembling soul replies,
Else whence so often could these langours rise?
Ah! these unruly passions would not rove
Thus wildly, were they fir'd with sacred love,
Nor would the fervours of devotion die
So often, and by pow'rs lethargic lie.

And yet, my God, in some bright moment too,
Methinks I feel the flame divinely glow:
To thee my passions with such ardour move,
That if I love thee not, I know not what I love.
If I'm deceiv'd in this with empty show,
Then my existence is uncertain too;
An universal skeptic I commence
Amidst the glare of brightest evidence,
In spite of reason, and in spite of sense!
O! if I love Thee not, as fears suggest,
Why am I in thine absence thus distress'd:
Whence this strange tumult, this uneasy pain,
Till thy sweet smiles compose my soul again?

Whence these wild pantings of intense desire?
Or why should breathing dust so high aspire?
I see my busy fellow-worms pursue
Created good, and nothing nobler view;

They lavish life away estrang'd from thee,
In undisturb'd, serene stupidity.
And why like them can't I contented play ?
And eat, and drink, and sleep my hours away ?
Whence this immense ambition in my mind,
To scorn all joys but those of heav'nly kind ?
Why should a worm, an animated clod,
Disdain all bliss beneath a boundless God ?
O what but the attractive force of love
Thus rais'd my spirit to the worlds above ?

Say, great Omniscient ! for thou know'st my heart
Can nature charm me, if thy smiles depart ?
Can riches, pleasures, honours, empires, crowns,
Or friends delight me, if I feel thy frowns ?
No ; all creation dwindles to a toy,
And heav'n itself is stripp'd of every joy ;
The radiant sun is darken'd to my eyes,
And every blooming beauty round me dies.

Thou great Invisible ! thou dear Unknown !
Why thus to thee should my affections run,
Thus through the objects of my senses break,
And charms unseen, and hidden glories seek !
Deep in recesses of approachless light
Thou sitt'st beyond my feeble sight:
Yet drawn by some strange mystic influence,
I love thee more than all that strikes my sense,
Than all my ears have heard, or eyes have seen,
Or all my fancy's liveliest pow'rs can feign ?

O ! if thy love does not my heart inflame,
Why does my soul rejoice at Jesus' name ?
His name is music to my ravish'd ears,
Sweeter than that which charms the heav'nly spheres,
A cheering cordial to my fainting breast ;
My hope, my joy, my triumph, and my rest.

I spring from earth, and heav'n is my abode,
When I can speak those charming words, "My God."
My God ! celestial rapture's in the sound ;
Be thou but mine, and all the sun rolls round,
Without one secret murmur, I resign ;
I have enough ; may I but call thee *mine*.

O! if I love thee not, why do I choose,
Why love a mansion in thine earthly house?
The sacred morning shines with heav'nly rays,
More bright, more charming than ten thousand days,
Which bids me visit that delightful place.
There would I dwell, and pass my life away,
Till death conveys me to a brighter day.

In all the institutions of thy grace
For thee I look, and long to see thy face:
When at thy throne I bow the suppliant knee,
Is prayer a thoughtless, cold formality?
Or can my prayers content me without thee?
No; these are but the channels of thy grace:
Transparent glasses where I see thy face;
I thirst for living waters all in vain,
Should'st thou thy gracious influence restrain:
The radiant mirrors show me nothing fair,
Unless I see my God reflected there.

Then peace, my restless and suspicious heart;
And ye, dire boding jealousies, depart:
I love my God, or else I nothing love,
And the pure flame ere long shall blaze above.
And in its native element aspire,
Without one mist to damp, or cloud t' obscure the fire.

CPSIA information can be obtained
at www.ICGtesting.com
Printed in the USA
LVHW111735170422
716440LV00004B/248